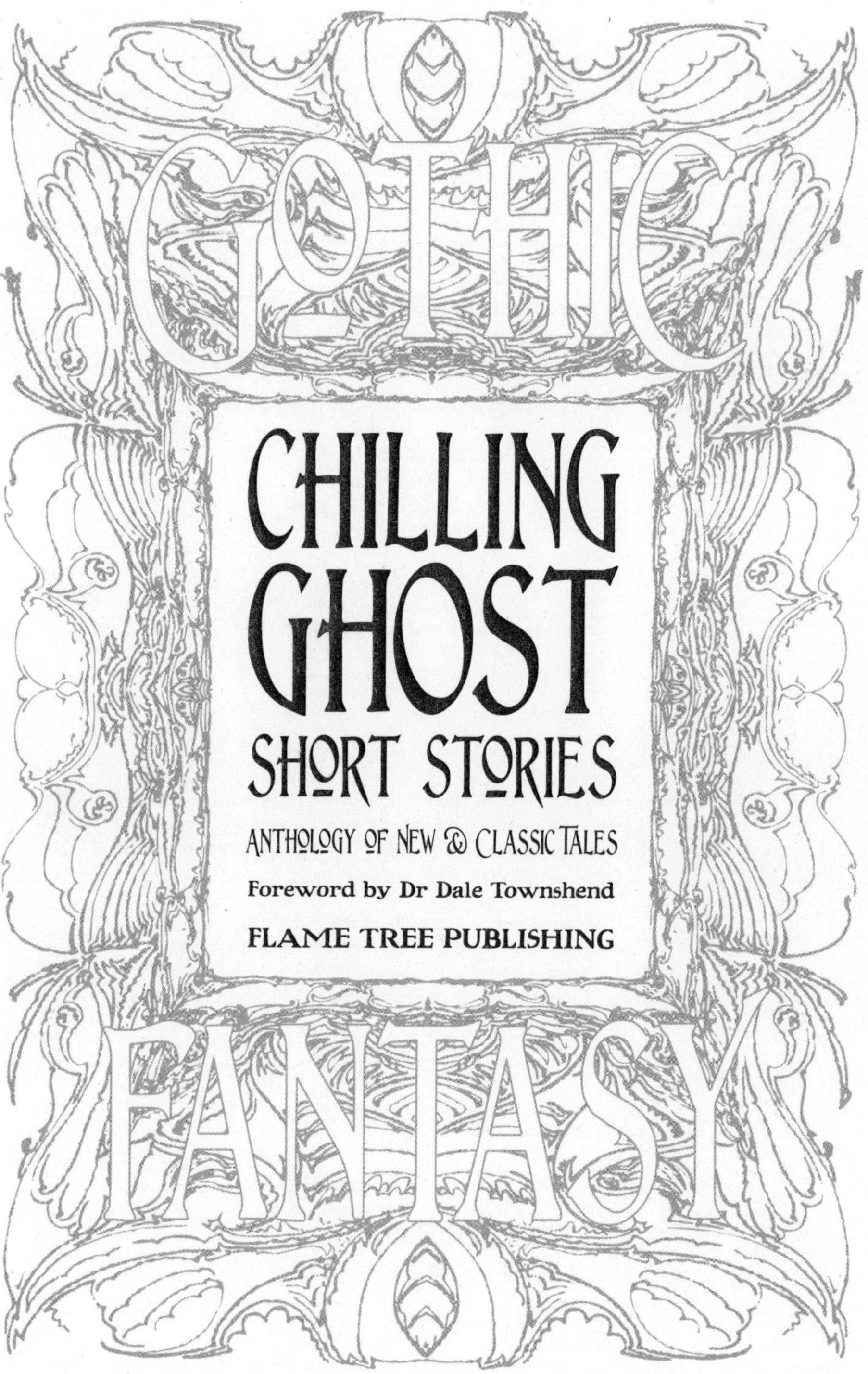

CHILLING GHOST SHORT STORIES

ANTHOLOGY OF NEW & CLASSIC TALES

Foreword by Dr Dale Townshend

FLAME TREE PUBLISHING

This is a FLAME TREE Book

With special thanks to Amanda Crook, Kaiti Porter

FLAME TREE PUBLISHING
6 Melbray Mews, Fulham,
London SW6 3NS, United Kingdom
www.flametreepublishing.com

First published 2015

17 19 18
3 5 7 9 10 8 6 4

ISBN: 978-1-78361-375-5

The cover image is created by Flame Tree Studio
based on artwork by Slava Gerj and Gabor Ruszkai.

A copy of the CIP data for this book is available from the British Library.

Printed and bound in Turkey

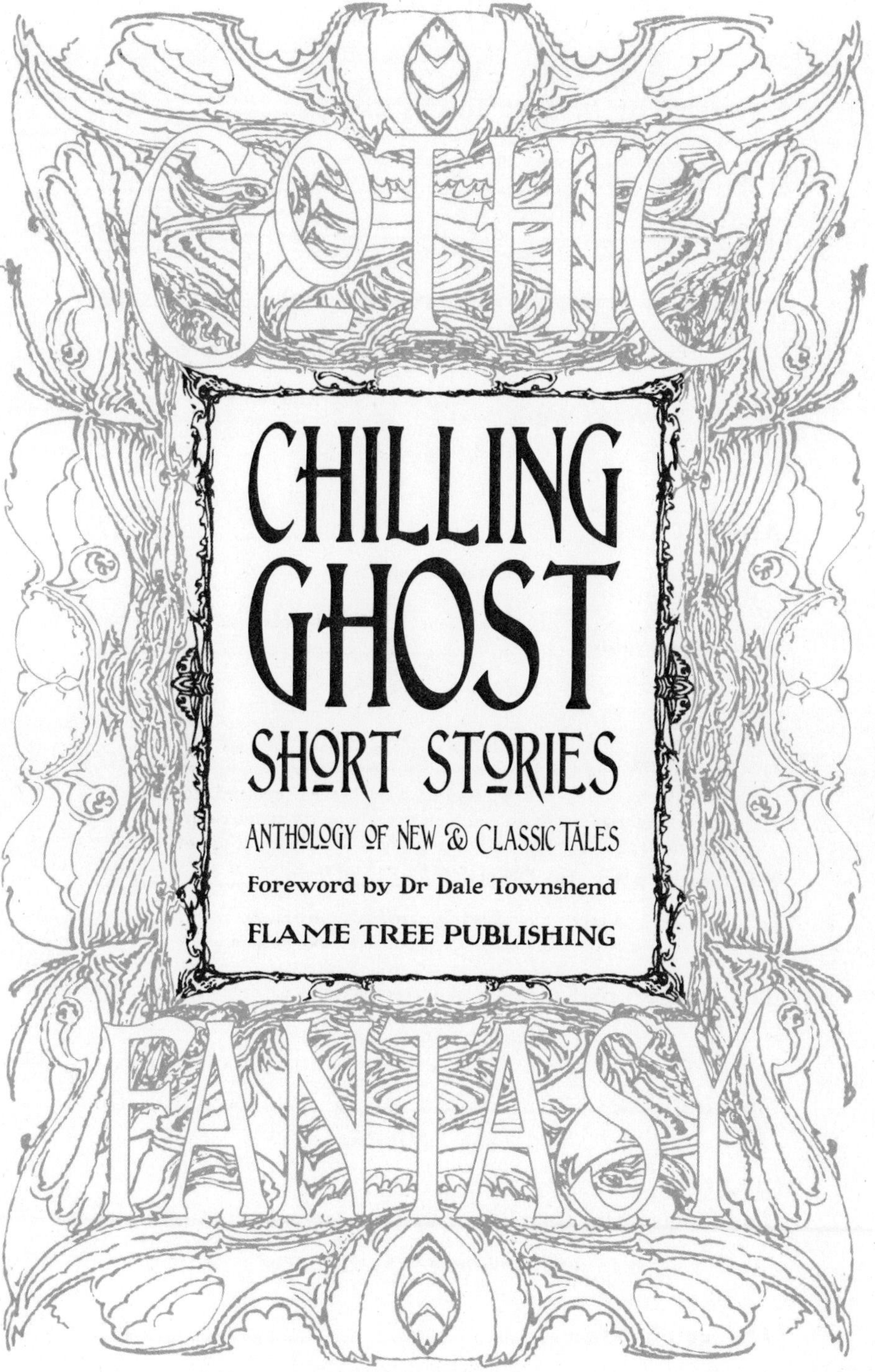

CHILLING GHOST SHORT STORIES

ANTHOLOGY OF NEW & CLASSIC TALES

Foreword by Dr Dale Townshend

FLAME TREE PUBLISHING

Contents

Foreword: Chilling Ghost Stories

WHILE THE SPECTRE may have entered mainstream popular fiction with the publication of Horace Walpole's *The Castle of Otranto* on Christmas Eve in 1764, it was really only in the nineteenth century that the ghost story came most fully into its own. In Gothic fictions of the late eighteenth and earlier nineteenth centuries, tales of spirits, ghosts and hauntings had often occupied only a smaller inset narrative in a much longer piece, such as the notorious ghost of the Bleeding Nun in Matthew Gregory Lewis's Gothic romance, *The Monk* (1796), or 'Wandering Willie's Tale', the frequently anthologized ghostly episode from Walter Scott's historical novel, *Redgauntlet* (1824). Implicit in these aesthetic choices was the assumption that tales of ghosts, spectres and sprites could most effectively be handled in shorter literary forms, such as ballads, fragments and tales, since the frisson, that distinctive narrative tension or 'chill' upon which the ghost story so depends, could not always be effectively sustained across longer works.

To this opportunity, writers of shorter fiction in the nineteenth century eagerly responded, inviting into their tales the spectral beings that had been uniformly exorcised and expelled, explained away and parodied in such texts as Ann Radcliffe's *The Mysteries of Udolpho* (1794) and Jane Austen's *Northanger Abbey* (1817). Between the years 1830 and 1890, the ghost story in Britain and America became one of the most popular literary modes; its appeal was exploited in the middle of the century by writers as diverse as Charles Dickens, Edgar Allan Poe, Elizabeth Gaskell, Wilkie Collins, Joseph Thomas Sheridan Le Fanu and Margaret Oliphant. Closely linked with the rise of the professional female writer in the Victorian period, ghost stories were central to the work of Mary Elizabeth Braddon, Mrs Henry Wood, Vernon Lee, Amelia Edwards and Charlotte Riddell. Unlike the ghosts of earlier Gothic writing, which had often been decidedly wooden, theatrical affairs, the spectres of the Victorian and Edwardian ghost story assume a certain 'realistic' air: no longer located in the far-flung regions of medieval Europe, these are the ghosts that haunt the contemporary British present, the spirits that return to vex and plague the everyday realms of modern domestic existence. Dickens's 'The Signal-Man' (1866), for example, tells the story of a haunting that occurs in the prosaic, seemingly unromantic realms of the modern railway industry. Similarly, in a story such as W.W. Jacobs's 'The Monkey's Paw' (1902), the occultic and near-ghostly happenings occur not in the haunted castles and abbeys of the eighteenth-century Gothic tradition, but rather in the suburban home of an ordinary bourgeois family.

Much the same applies to the chilling turns of Joseph Thomas Sheridan Le Fanu's 'An Authentic Narrative of a Haunted House' (1862), set as it is in a middle-class suburban home in a British seaside town. And yet, as the nineteenth-century American poet Emily Dickinson famously put it, 'One need not be a chamber to be haunted, / One need not be a house; / The brain has corridors surpassing / Material place.' Indeed, with increasing frequency as the century wears on, the ghost enters the dark recesses of the human mind, assuming particularly psychological significance in the work of M.R. James, Walter de la Mare, Rudyard Kipling, Edith Wharton, Algernon Blackwood, Elizabeth Bowen and others. It is striking in this regard to note that a ghost story such as Henry James's 'The Altar of the Dead' (1895) contains no 'actual' spectre so much as the ghosts of the dead that haunt the mind of the mournful protagonist, George Stransom, rendering him, too, somewhat spectral in the process. Ever more ambiguous in both their provenance and their demands, these spirits on the limits of consciousness come to occupy the shadowy place between dream and wakefulness, rationalism and superstition; in some instances, they are the projections of a guilty psyche, in others, the figure of justice and revenge. Though the subject of light-hearted parody in Oscar Wilde's 'The Canterville Ghost' (1887), as well as in stories by Rudyard Kipling, H.G. Wells and Jerome K. Jerome from the 1880s onwards, the ghost returns in the fractured, anxious psyches of early twentieth-century modernism, in the works of Virginia Woolf and May Sinclair. As Freud somewhat categorically declared in his essay on 'The Uncanny' in 1919, "All supposedly educated people have ceased to believe officially that the dead can become visible as spirits."

As much as it had challenged the spirit of human optimism, the Great War had shattered a belief in ghosts. For the ghost story, however, the notion of belief has never been at stake. Prior to the rise of the Gothic, so-called 'apparition narratives' of the early eighteenth century employed tales of supernatural activity so as to drive home certain religious truths: to believe in ghosts was also to embrace Christian conceptualisations of the afterlife, a defiant clinging to a form of religious faith in the face of materialist and rationalist philosophy. From Horace Walpole onwards, though, the ghost becomes merely an object of popular entrainment, stripped of all the theological significance that it once had. The form of the ghost story continues to survive and, indeed, thrive on the basis of the horrors and terrors, the characteristic thrills and chills of the Gothic mode, that lie at its heart. In what, though, do its curious pleasures consist? Perhaps the one characteristic that is common to all of the stories in this collection is a sense of obscurity, ambivalence and indecision. While the ghost story may often contain within itself means of validating and verifying the supernatural events that it relates, the reader is always left in a state of ambiguity at the tale's end. Herein, perhaps, lies the secret of the form's charm and appeal: the sheer pleasure of mystery and uncertainty in a world that is increasingly dominated by reason, rationality and science.

Dale Townshend, 2015

Publisher's Note

THIS COLLECTION of *Gothic Fantasy* stories is part of a new anthology series, which includes sumptuous hardcover editions on Horror, Ghosts and Science Fiction. Each one carries a potent mix of classic tales and new fiction, forming a path from the origins of the gothic in the early 1800s, with the dystopian horror of Mary Shelley's 'The Mortal Immortal' to the chill of M.R. James's classic ghost stories, and the fine stories of the many modern writers featured in our new series. We have tried to mix some renowned classic stories (Edgar Allan Poe's 'The Black Cat'), with the less familiar (E.M. Forster's 'The Machine Stops'), and a healthy dose of previously unpublished modern stories from the best of those writing today.

Our 2015 call for new submissions was met by a tidal wave of entries, so the final selection was made to provide a wide and challenging range of tales for the discerning reader. Our editorial board of six members read each entry carefully, and it was difficult to turn down so many good stories, but inevitably those which made the final cut were deemed to be the best for our purpose, and we're delighted to be able to publish them here.

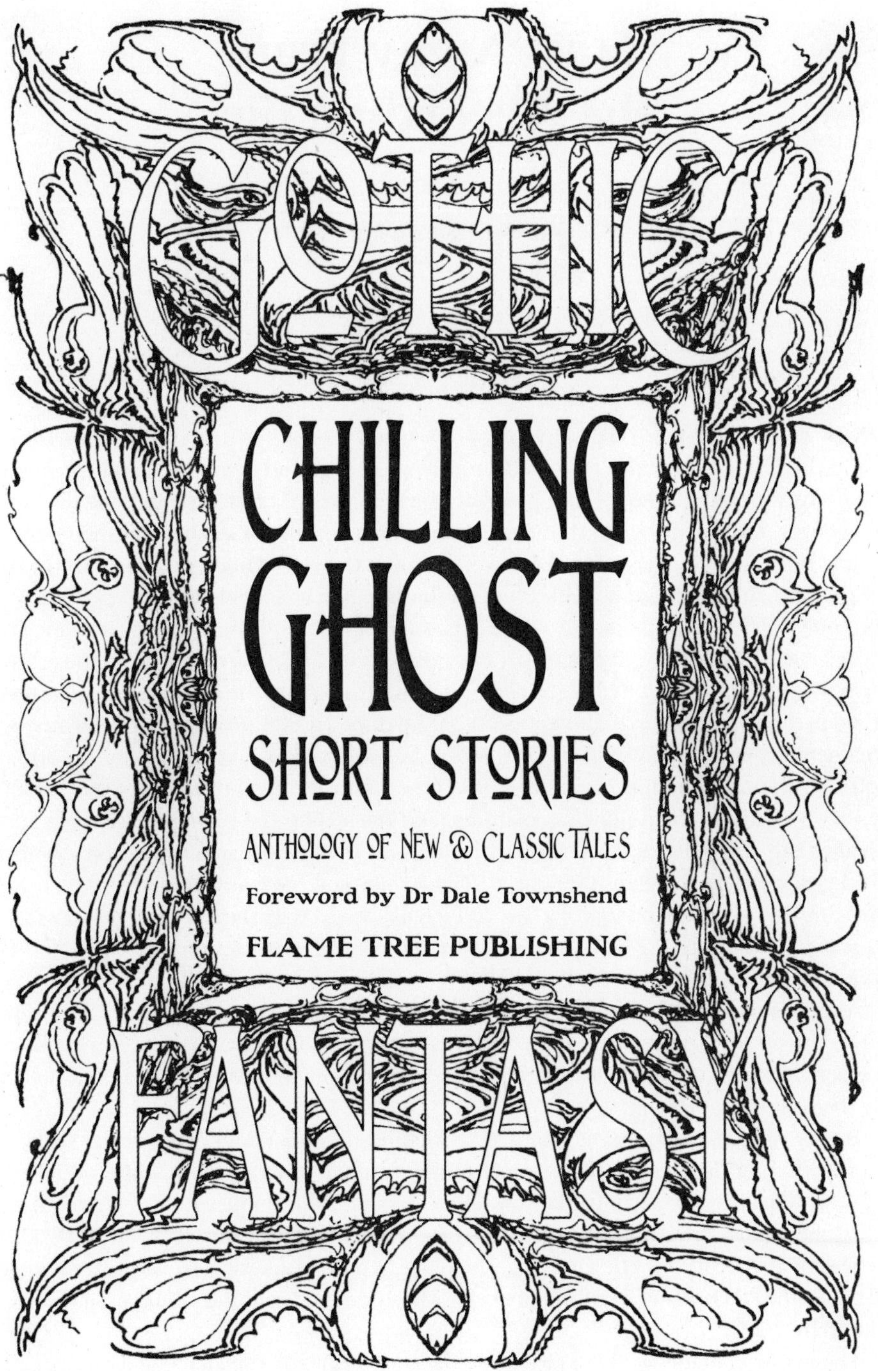
GOTHIC
CHILLING GHOST
SHORT STORIES
ANTHOLOGY OF NEW & CLASSIC TALES
Foreword by Dr Dale Townshend
FLAME TREE PUBLISHING
FANTASY

Stay Away from the Accordion Girl

Jonathan Balog

ONCE THERE WAS A YOUNG MAN who carried his pack across the country. He took work where he could find it, usually manual labor of one kind or another, and left when he felt it was time to move on. Since he'd left home at the age of fifteen he'd dug ditches for the county, washed dishes in restaurants, manned a cotton gin all through the night, and picked more strawberries than there were stars in the sky. When he worked in town his employers usually set him up with a bed. In the summer, when help was in high demand in the countryside, he slept outside with his pack for a pillow and God's green earth for a bed.

One year he was traveling through the valley and he came across a farm house with a *Help Wanted* sign nailed to a fence post out front. He walked through the gate and up the stone pathway to the porch and knocked on the door. He was greeted by the farmer, a tall weather-beaten old man with a warm smile, and welcomed inside. As they sat drinking coffee at the kitchen table, the farmer told him he was in need of a hand for the coming season. He needed help plowing, planting, and harvesting the corn and soybeans in the coming Fall, as well as a hand with the hundred other jobs that needed doing with the chickens, goats, and sheep they raised. The farmer and his wife could offer him a room plus three meals a day, on top of a five dollar daily wage. After the harvest he was welcome to stay for the winter or leave as he saw fit. The young man accepted the job, and they shook on it.

After they'd spent an hour or so getting to know each other, the young man excused himself to explore the grounds. He walked under the twin apple trees on the front lawn, past the barn, and up and down the unplowed fields with which he'd be intimately connected for the next eight months.

By the time he got back the sun had set behind the mountains. The farmer's wife had prepared a glorious dinner for the three of them, and that night he ate better than he had all year. When they were finished, wanting to stay on their good side, he offered to wash the dishes himself. He thanked them both for their hospitality, gave a yawn, and said that he was ready to turn in. The farmer nodded, and said it would be wise to get a full night's sleep, as they'd be rising early the next day. He stood, and told the young man he'd show him to his room.

The young man followed the farmer up the stairs and into a small room with a cot and a bedside table. He thanked the farmer yet again, but told him that while he wouldn't mind stashing his pack in the room, he was used to sleeping outside.

For a moment the warmth went out of the farmer's eyes.

"That wouldn't be a good idea. I'll have to insist that you stay indoors."

"Why?"

"Jackals have been known to prowl the land at night. Earlier this year we had to rewire the chicken coop after they'd broken in and slaughtered every last one. My wife went out to feed the chickens the next morning, and the whole place was a mess. Just feathers and guts and splintered wood everywhere. God, it was awful."

The young man nodded and agreed to the bed. As soon as his head hit the pillow, he was enveloped in the fatigue of the day.

* * *

Virginia

Dexter almost spilled his coffee playing with the GPS on his dashboard. It had been operating perfectly since the start of the trip, but ten minutes after they left the interstate it seemed like they'd traveled into a satellite black hole.

"Could you please not do that?" Rob asked.

"Just give me a sec."

"OK, something like six thousand people die every year due to distracted driving. Would it kill you to just pull over?"

Dexter bit his tongue. The whole point of the trip was to give themselves a breather. They'd both been taking comfort in the hope that their constant arguments were rooted more in the stress of day-to-day living than in anything inherently wrong in their relationship. If they had a fight this soon, they may as well turn around and admit defeat.

"Do me a favor and get those directions out of the glove box."

Rob found the print-out and scanned the first page.

"It looks like we're gonna be on this road for an hour. After you cross the county line, take the second exit. Then there's gonna be a bunch of quick turns, and we should be there."

For the entire stretch of highway they saw nothing but forest. There was no one behind them, and they passed a car going the opposite direction every few minutes. Dexter wondered briefly how many trees had been cut down to build this passageway just so a few city people could get back to nature every year.

By the time they reached Black Willow Farm it was almost noon. He steered the Toyota down the mile of unpaved driveway, lined neatly with the trees of the farm's namesake.

* * *

He awoke just after midnight. Perhaps he'd heard a noise, or perhaps it was just the disorientation that comes with sleeping in a new place. Either way, he figured it would be a while before he could drift off again, so he decided to step outside for a smoke.

He padded across the kitchen floor in his bare feet, and tried to turn the knob without making any noise. The night air was cool but still with the mountains blocking the breeze. The only noise was the distant rustling of animals and crickets.

He sat on the porch steps and rolled a cigarette, watching his own private night-time wilderness. Living in town had its pleasures, but there was something majestic about being alone for miles in every direction at night. There was a sense that everything was yours, that you could do whatever you wanted, to say nothing of the infinite mysteries hidden in the dark.

A faint hum drifted over the air. He cocked an ear, trying to discern what kind of animal it could be, and realized it wasn't an animal at all, but music. Someone was playing a slow country ballad. Most people would have wondered who could possibly be out and about at this hour, and so far from the nearest town, but over the last ten years he'd had plenty of encounters with his fellow travelers on the back-roads of life, and one thing they had in common was that they kept their own hours. They were just as likely to travel under moonlight as any other time.

It was coming from the direction of the road. He pitched his cigarette and walked across the lawn, the cool grass feeling good on his callused feet. He passed the gate and approached the oak trees that declared the property line, and peered around the corner at the path that had led him there earlier that day. There was a certain number of vagabond archetypes he'd expected to see. What he saw was none of them.

There was a girl on the road. She might have been about ten years old, but it was hard to tell since she was walking away. She was wearing a long white dress, and had no shoes. She was carrying an accordion and playing it as she walked. It was a sad, pretty song he'd never heard before.

At the time he didn't fully understand why he kept quiet. If the farmer was right about the jackals, it wasn't safe for a kid to be walking around by herself at night. Someone should warn her. Besides, he was an innately curious guy. He wanted to know the girl's story, where she came from, who she was traveling with, why on earth she was playing music in the middle of nowhere.

He watched her walk away, the song resonating in his mind, strumming his veins. She looked so vulnerable, a little lost piece of white cloth floating down the path, where any number of beasts could leap out and devour her at any moment. He didn't make a sound.

Later, the song played on in his dreams.

* * *

Rob was busy typing away on his MacBook as his coffee cooled beside it on the wooden porch table. Dexter sat nearby and sipped his own mug in silence. Ideally he'd have preferred that they'd left work behind completely for the week, but he knew Rob was always happiest when he was making headway on a project. Besides, they'd gotten what they'd paid for. The coolness from the early morning dew would soon be off-set by Spring sunshine. As far as the eye could see, flowers and trees were in glorious resurrection. Most importantly, they were the only guests. It was the furthest possible thing from DC.

"So," Rob said. "I think I'm gonna use the old man's story in the book."

"Oh," said Dexter. Generally he was willing to give Rob the privacy he needed to write, but was always happy when he volunteered to discuss a work in progress. He took it as a gesture indicating that Rob wanted to share an intimate part of his life, and as such, he always gave him his full attention. Even when Rob threw out an idea that seemed completely off the wall, he responded with skepticism laced with encouragement. "Do you think that'll work?"

"What do you mean?"

"I mean, I thought the idea was for it to be a book of folklore for kids. If you put in something modern, isn't that going to off-set all the traditional stuff?"

"No, that's what so great about it!" Rob said. "So many of these stories were born out of a collective fear of the unknown. But where's the unknown today? We've shone the flashlight everywhere and scared away all the shadow monsters. But this place..."

He gestured to the backyard wilderness.

"This is a place where these stories can still percolate. There's no Wi-fi. Your GPS doesn't work. It's a blind spot in the Great Digital Eye. I mean, if *I* were a monster, this is where I'd hide."

Dexter nodded. He didn't share Rob's love of ghost stories (or kids, for that matter), but it was that passion with which Rob undertook everything he did that made him love him so much.

"Think about it. How fucking cool would it be if I'd discovered a brand new folktale and was the first to write it down? It would demonstrate how they're still relevant." Rob finally took a sip from his own mug. "Besides, it's a great story."

"Yeah, and it's also more than a little graphic. Aren't you worried about traumatizing the kids?"

"They'll thank me when they're older."

* * *

The next morning, he had a hearty breakfast with the farmer and his wife, and the two men went to work in the field. It was still early enough in the Spring for them to work with their heads uncovered, and they operated the plow without breaking a sweat. Neither mentioned it, but both of them were savoring the atmosphere, knowing full well that the oppressive July heat would be there soon enough.

They ate their lunch in silence. When they finished, the farmer packed his pipe and the young man took the opportunity to roll a cigarette. As the farmer ticked off a list of all he hoped to have finished by sundown, the young man remembered what he'd seen the previous night. He shared the story.

"What do you think? Ever seen her before?"

The farmer nodded. "She lives in the hills with her family."

"What are they doing up there?"

"I have no idea. Now listen, and I'm very serious here: don't talk to her. Don't even let her know you're around. If you see her coming, I want you to walk away. Understood?"

"Why?" he said. "What's wrong with her?"

The farmer bought a moment of thought with his pipe. "If she thinks she has a friend here, she'll be back. Like I said, I don't know what they could possibly be doing out here. There's no work around for miles. Maybe they're trapping their own food. I don't know. I'm just hoping they'll be moving on soon. Now are you absolutely sure she didn't see you last night?"

"Yeah. I'm positive."

"Good," the farmer said, and put away his pipe. "Let's get back to work."

He didn't mention it again that day, but for the next few hours he kept wondering why the farmer had dodged his questions. If the farmer thought they were dangerous, why couldn't he give a reason?

* * *

"OK, this doesn't seem weird to you?"

"Of course it does!" Rob replied. "That's what's so great about it. We're actually witnessing the formation of a local legend."

He was coasting on a wave of euphoria, and Dexter hated to throw him off, but the whole thing felt wrong.

"Babe, come on. We meet this lonely old guy. You tell him you're writing a book of ghost stories. He tells you a story about a demon girl with an accordion, and that night we just happen to actually see a little girl with an accordion wandering around? Don't you think that's a bit of a coincidence?"

"First of all, he's not lonely. He and his family have lived here forever. Second, there's no way he could have known we'd be out there."

Rob had a point. He had never had sex outside before, and when Dexter had suggested they head out to the woods after midnight, he'd thought it would be a memorable way to kick off their first vacation together. Unfortunately the surprise appearance of the girl had killed the mood. As he'd irritably pulled his jeans back on while his boyfriend stared from behind the foliage, it occurred to Dexter that this was probably how new parents felt.

"I'm not saying he staged the whole thing,' he argued. 'I'm saying he knew about the girl and made up the story, thinking he might be able to get his place mentioned in your book. The girl probably lives somewhere around here."

"Yeah, because kids are always walking around the middle of nowhere by themselves at one in the morning."

Dexter leaned back on the bed and watched Rob peel off his T-shirt. He sat at the foot of the bed to take off his shoes. In some ways Rob was one of the most intelligent people he'd ever met, and sometimes he just put him at a loss for words.

"So what? You're saying you really believe him?"

"No, I just..." Rob paused for a moment to strip down to his boxer briefs, then sat back down on the bed, not quite facing him but not quite turned away. "Probably all these campfire stories were based on something that actually happened, something with a perfectly rational explanation. The people who made up the stories were trying to entertain each other, but I think on some level they were trying to make sense out of a world they didn't entirely understand, and the stories were manifestations of their subconscious fears."

"OK," he said. "So what's the old guy afraid of?"

"I don't know. Maybe we'll find out."

Rob leaned over and kissed him. It wasn't an obligatory kiss, but a sincere one of genuine affection and gratitude.

"Thanks again for taking us out here, Dex. It's seriously appreciated."

Rob allowed himself to be enveloped in his arms, savoring the moment while it lasted.

Outside, the lonely night whispered its secrets.

* * *

A week later, he heard the song again.

He'd settled into life on the farm quickly. Every morning they rose at dawn. The farmer worked him to death, but he was a kind-hearted man. Like all people who spend a lot of time alone with their thoughts, his mind was a reservoir of anecdotes and opinions, and their conversations out in the field always made the day go by fast. He was usually exhausted after dinner, and would borrow one of the old couple's books until he fell asleep.

But on the seventh night, he couldn't sleep. Something had changed in the air that made it impossible for him to move into a comfortable position. As he lay in bed reading, the grandfather clock in the living room chiming at quarter to midnight, he heard the accordion riding the breeze through his open window.

He got out of bed and stood with his elbows on the windowsill. It was the same song as before, and she seemed to be keeping tune with the stars, as if the night sky itself was an instrument and she was playing the music of the universe. He couldn't remember the last time he'd heard or seen something so beautiful.

The memory of his conversation with the farmer was in the back of his mind, but it didn't matter. He had to see her again. Not even bothering to pull on his shirt, he crept down the stairs and out the kitchen door. The song was still being played loud and clear when he made his way to the end of the path, the sound coming right from the other side. He peeked between the trees.

She had just passed by. She was about half as far away as the last time he'd seen her. Before the distance and the crescent moon had given him only a blurry outline, but now, close and under a half-moon, he could see her wavy light brown hair and the blue stitched patterns that held her dress together. She walked slowly yet deliberately, a parade of one.

His throat itched to call for her attention. He wanted to ask for her story, almost as much as he wanted to ask himself why he was so captivated by her mystery. Yet the old man's warning, his solemn tone, held him back.

An owl screeched. It was a sound he'd grown accustomed to throughout his years of wandering, and normally he might not have even noticed. But he'd been so lost in the moment that the noise stabbed at his nerves and drew out a startled gasp. Enough to catch the girl's attention. The music stopped. She turned her head.

He ducked back behind the trees, silently cursing himself. He waited a moment, listening for the sound of approaching feet. When none came he dared to peer through the brush. She was still there. She hadn't moved any closer, but she was facing his direction. Her face was smooth and unblemished, more the look of an upper class city kid than a traveler, and she wore a blank expression. No fear, no anticipation, no indication of any reaction to his presence at all. He wondered if she could see him through the branches. He was pretty sure that his body was camouflaged by the foliage, but for a long moment it felt like their eyes were locked.

For reasons that he couldn't articulate, the look made him uncomfortable. He backed away from the trees and retreated to the house. As he reached the door, he heard the song resume, and carry on down the road.

* * *

Dexter had to walk all over the grounds before he found the old man. He was at the far end of the driveway, trimming the rosebushes around the sign that welcomed any and all travelers to Black Willow Farms.

"Hey."

"Oh hello, Mr Rice!" the old man said, glancing over at Dexter before snipping off a branch, working the pruners with his Mickey Mouse gloves. "Everything all right with the room?"

"Yeah, it's been great. Thanks."

"Well, we really appreciate you and your friend staying here now. It's still early in the season. Be a while before it starts to pick up."

"Sure," he said. "Listen, that story you told us the first night we were here, about the girl and the drifter?"

"Yeah."

"Where did you hear that? Do you remember who first told it to you?"

"Hmmm..." The old man paused for a moment, then snipped off the end of a leafy branch. "Probably my grandmother."

"Your grandmother?"

"Yep. She was full of stories like that. Whenever she babysat me and my sister, we'd sit by the fireplace and listen to her for hours. For some reason, that particular one always stood out in my mind."

Dexter nodded. His questions began to feel heavier in his gut, and they tasted stale as he let them out of his mouth.

"I guess she wrote it herself?"

"Oh, no. Supposed to be a local legend."

"Right," he replied. "Have you ever seen the girl?"

"Me? Lord, no," the old man said, working with his back to him. "Couple guests have seen her, though."

He's playing you for a spot in the book. Don't let on that you know.

"You don't say."

"Yep. Said they did, anyway. Course they might have just been messing with me."

Now lay it on him casually.

"We saw her the other night."

The old man stopped what he was doing and looked at him. Dexter stood with his hands in his pockets, not moving a muscle for fear that he'd spoil his composure.

"Really." His voice was flat.

"Yeah. We went out for a walk in the woods the second night and heard her accordion. We checked it out and saw her walking down the road. She had on a white dress, just like you said."

"She didn't see you, did she?"

Dexter was blindsided by this reaction. He'd been expecting one of two responses. If the old man truly had no ulterior motives, he would have simply humored the story until they changed subjects. If he was putting on an act and trying to worm his way into literary history, he would have reacted with a theatrical, overdramatic display of alarm and warning.

What he was doing instead was trying as hard as he could not to look worried. If he was acting, this was one of the best performances Dexter had ever seen.

"No, she didn't see us."

"OK, good."

"Actually, Rob saw her again last night. He went for a walk, and when he came back he said he'd seen her again. He said she was walking down the road, playing the prettiest song he'd ever heard."

"Did she see him?"

The subtle hint of urgency in the old man's tone was arresting. For a moment his mask of nonchalance slipped, and he suddenly looked much older. Older and afraid.

"No. Rob says she never even knew he was there."

"Well, that's good," the old man said.

As Dexter walked back down the driveway, their conversation wore on his mind like an awkward first date. He had no idea what the old man's game was, but he sure as hell wasn't going to play into it.

He wouldn't give him the pleasure of relating Rob's description of how innocent the girl's eyes had looked, how badly he wanted to know her story.

* * *

The following morning when he came down to the breakfast table, the farmer and his wife were nowhere to be found. He looked around the first floor and called out their names. No reply. He brewed the coffee himself, and after he finished his first cup and they still hadn't appeared, he went looking for them outside.

He found them by the goat pen. The farmer was leaning on a post. His wife was standing by, a hand over her mouth. He could tell something was wrong by their slumped shoulders and deflated posture. When he got close enough he saw what it was.

The goats had been slaughtered. All of them. Their partially eaten carcasses were strewn about the pen like something between a battlefield and an abattoir. The side of the hut built to give them shelter during storms and keep them safe from wolves at night was splashed with burgundy, and clumps of fur floated in little puddles of blood. Entrails hung from the fence like garlands. The head of one lay sideways on the roof.

Whatever had massacred the animals had not only been strong enough to rip the door of the hut off its hinges, but completely pulverize it in the process. It lay across the ground in a hundred splintered pieces. A few were sticking out of the dead hides.

"I told you to stay away from her."

He said nothing. At first he choked on the realization that somehow this had happened because of him, that in a way he couldn't yet comprehend, his contact with the girl had brought this about. Then he was about to reproach the farmer for being so cryptic in his warnings. But the farmer beat him to it.

"I'm sorry," he said. "I should have explained everything from the beginning."

"Oh, what could you have told him?" his wife cut in. "We don't even understand it ourselves."

"Yes, but we have a pretty good idea how it works." The farmer finally met the eyes of the young man. "Let's go inside."

They walked back into the kitchen. The farmer poured out what was left of the coffee and joined them at the table. He ran a rough hand through his thinning hair.

"Like my wife said, we don't know what she is."

"Have you ever seen her?"

"No," he said. "Neither of us have. But we've heard stories. In town. They say there's a girl who walks the roads at night playing her accordion. They say she uses it to lure people in."

"Lure them in for what?"

For a moment, neither of them said anything. Finally the farmer's wife answered.

"Listen," she said. "She's eaten now, so she's probably not going to bother us for a while. So we can consider ourselves lucky. But you need to stay inside at night. And if you ever, ever hear that song again, you need to drop what you're doing and run as fast as you can and don't look back. Understood?"

He studied her, then glanced back at the farmer.

"It wasn't jackals that got into your chicken coop, was it?"

The farmer placed his coffee cup in the sink, and put his hands on the back of his chair. "We got off lucky," he said. "Remember that."

Later that morning they built a pyre to burn the carcasses. It made him feel sick to touch them, thinking of the sheer bewildered terror that must have charged through their brains during their final moments on earth. When he removed the head from the top of the hut and carried it to the piling, he held it at arm's length with its face turned away. He didn't want to think about the last thing those eyes had seen.

When the goats were nothing more than a pile of ashes, they went about the rest of the day's chores. Both made attempts at conversation, but there was a coldness underscoring each attempt. Everything they said was a reminder of what they weren't saying.

* * *

"All right, game over. I don't give a fuck if we get a refund or not. We're leaving."

Dexter was pacing around their bedroom while Rob crouched down just outside the open door on the porch. He was looking at the sheep's head that had been waiting for them that morning. Its dirty white wool was splotched with pink and red, and a stump of bone protruded from the hole where the neck had been severed. A pale tongue lolled out of its open mouth. Rob never mentioned it, but he was surprised at how bored and indifferent the eyes looked. He would have expected them to be wide open with the preserved shock of their final moments.

"Come on, let's pack up. This place sucks anyway. We could've gone to Virginia Beach and gotten a room at off-season rates."

"Just chill out for a second, all right?"

"No, I'm *not* gonna chill out. They've been fucking with us since we got here. I'm gonna go to the front desk right now."

He brushed past Rob on the porch, side-stepping to avoid the head.

When Dexter reached the lobby, no one was there. The door was locked, and there was a hand-written sign hanging from inside the window.

We had to run into town. Be back by noon. Please help yourselves to anything in the kitchen.

He slammed the door with the underside of his fist, and walked back towards their room. When he got there he found Rob still sitting on the porch.

"They're not here. Of course."

"Listen Dex," Rob said, putting on his conciliatory air. "We don't know for a fact that it was them."

Dexter was mustering all of the self-control he had to keep from losing his temper.

"Who else could it possibly be?"

"I don't know. But you have a serious problem with this. You get a first impression of someone, and then there's no changing your mind."

"Rob," he began, hanging caution on his words like lead weights. "Please tell me you don't think it was the little girl."

"No," Rob said, "I just..."

"Just what?"

He avoided Rob's eyes as he selected his words.

"Look, we're in a different world out here. We're making all these assumptions about them. Maybe they're making assumptions about us. Maybe that's what the story's really about. The distrust between locals and outsiders."

"Rob, this isn't a story!" This time he didn't bother keeping the exasperation out of his tone. "You're so obsessed with these urban legends, or..." Dexter reminded himself that they were pretty far from the urban world. "...whatever they are, that you're ready to let yourself fall into one!"

Rob stood and took his hands. It was the sincerity in his gaze, the conviction that he'd thought his decision through with both his head and heart, that won Dexter over. It was the adhesive that had held together the longest relationship he'd had since college. If he denied it now, their castle was built on clouds.

"One more night. That's all I'm asking. If you still want to leave tomorrow, we can go."

When the old man and his family came home, they didn't bother talking to them. Rob nudged the head into a garbage bag and dumped it in a can out front. When the sun went down, they got in the car and drove to a Greek restaurant twenty miles away that the family had told them about on the first night. Over time, the dinner conversation turned to the book. They talked about how great it would be when Rob was able to quit teaching and write full time. Rob talked about the incredible work the illustrator had already done, how the images were going to give kids nightmares for years.

They got back to Black Willow Farm just after eleven. Dexter fished two Ambien out of his toiletry bag, popped one, and handed the other to Rob. He didn't notice Rob palming it and tossing it into the wastebasket.

"I love you," he said, head on the pillow, as the motions of his inner world began to slow and blur.

That was the last time he ever saw Rob alive.

* * *

After dinner he went to his room, but left the light on.

Too many things felt wrong. The farmer and his wife were hiding something. Why else would they keep avoiding his questions? Why were they saying so little about something so important?

He'd seen plenty of strange things in his life, but he didn't believe in ghosts. Of all the stories he'd heard around campfires from one side of the country to the next, the one thing they all had in common was that there was nothing underneath them but the fears of the storyteller. The girl was real – he'd seen her with his own eyes – and she belonged to some sort of strange gypsy family who lived in the hills. Nothing more.

However, that didn't mean these people weren't dangerous, and what they'd done to the goats, together with the old couple's cryptic behavior, had brought him to the conclusion that staying at the farm was no longer wise. He decided then that he would leave in the morning. If he left early enough he could be in the next town before dusk. He'd explain everything to the couple before he left. Maybe they'd even understand. They'd been kind to him, and he hated walking out on a job, but he couldn't help it if he didn't feel safe.

It was just as he was finalizing this decision that he heard the noise. It stabbed at his nerves in the way that can only be done by a noise in the middle of the night, when you know perfectly well that there's no logical reason for you to hear any noise at all. The initial shock was soothed into a steady flow of dread, coasting on the notes that blended into melody.

The melody carried by an accordion.

It was coming from the first floor, the same sad, slow, pretty tune he'd heard on the road. Somehow she'd gotten into the house. Even more bewilderingly, it didn't seem to have woken up anyone else.

He dug into his bag and pulled out a pocket knife. He'd bought it from an old soldier years ago and carried it every day since. The blade was big enough that flashing it usually put an end to heated arguments, and on the few times that it hadn't, he'd managed to make his point without leaving any permanent damage. He wasn't afraid of a little girl, but there was no telling if she was alone.

He walked down the stairs into the kitchen. The song was coming from the living room. Staying close to the wall he crept up to the doorway and looked inside.

She was sitting in a chair with her back to him. Her wavy brown hair looked wilder than he'd remembered. She was wearing the same white dress, and it was untied at the back, showing a crooked triangle of porcelain-pale skin. Her fingers worked the buttons and keys of the accordion like a virtuoso.

His eyes scanned the room. No one else was there.

The music filled the room like a mist, clouding his judgement and blurring his fear. The absurdity of it all was far from his mind as he walked across the floor. He spoke a soft greeting. She didn't move.

He laid a hand on a small shoulder.

When she turned and rose, the face he saw was both young and as old as time itself. Her hands rested on his shoulders, which should have been impossible due to their height difference, but there they were. Her hair had taken on a life of its own, the tangled locks hanging in the air like the snakes of Medusa. Her head lolled back ever so subtly.

And that's when he saw her teeth.

He couldn't move. The second her lips parted she gave a screech which resonated in his skull, making him feel like his brain was being stabbed by needles from every direction, piercing the nerves that enabled movement. She leered at him with insane, ravenous eyes that might have seen empires rise and fall.

He reached an epiphany in his final moments that, given more time, he might have realized the farmer and his wife had known all along:

The accordion had plowed the fields.

His fear had sown the seeds.

And now it was harvest time.

The Man Who Went Too Far

E.F. Benson

THE LITTLE VILLAGE OF ST. FAITH'S nestles in a hollow of wooded hill up on the north bank of the river Fawn in the county of Hampshire, huddling close round its grey Norman church as if for spiritual protection against the fays and fairies, the trolls and "little people," who might be supposed still to linger in the vast empty spaces of the New Forest, and to come after dusk and do their doubtful businesses. Once outside the hamlet you may walk in any direction (so long as you avoid the high road which leads to Brockenhurst) for the length of a summer afternoon without seeing sign of human habitation, or possibly even catching sight of another human being. Shaggy wild ponies may stop their feeding for a moment as you pass, the white scuts of rabbits will vanish into their burrows, a brown viper perhaps will glide from your path into a clump of heather, and unseen birds will chuckle in the bushes, but it may easily happen that for a long day you will see nothing human. But you will not feel in the least lonely; in summer, at any rate, the sunlight will be gay with butterflies, and the air thick with all those woodland sounds which like instruments in an orchestra combine to play the great symphony of the yearly festival of June. Winds whisper in the birches, and sigh among the firs; bees are busy with their redolent labour among the heather, a myriad birds chirp in the green temples of the forest trees, and the voice of the river prattling over stony places, bubbling into pools, chuckling and gulping round corners, gives you the sense that many presences and companions are near at hand.

Yet, oddly enough, though one would have thought that these benign and cheerful influences of wholesome air and spaciousness of forest were very healthful comrades for a man, in so far as nature can really influence this wonderful human genus which has in these centuries learned to defy her most violent storms in its well-established houses, to bridle her torrents and make them light its streets, to tunnel her mountains and plough her seas, the inhabitants of St. Faith's will not willingly venture into the forest after dark. For in spite of the silence and loneliness of the hooded night it seems that a man is not sure in what company he may suddenly find himself, and though it is difficult to get from these villagers any very clear story of occult appearances, the feeling is widespread. One story indeed I have heard with some definiteness, the tale of a monstrous goat that has been seen to skip with hellish glee about the woods and shady places, and this perhaps is connected with the story which I have here attempted to piece together. It too is well-known to them; for all remember the young artist who died here not long ago, a young man, or so he struck the beholder, of great personal beauty, with something about him that made men's faces to smile and brighten when they looked on him. His ghost they will tell you "walks" constantly by the stream and through the woods which he loved so, and in especial it haunts a certain house, the last of the village, where he lived, and its garden in which he was done to death. For my part I am inclined to think that the terror of the Forest dates chiefly from that day. So, such as the story is, I have set it forth in connected form. It is based partly on the accounts of the villagers, but mainly on that of Darcy, a friend of mine and a friend of the man with whom these events were chiefly concerned.

* * *

The day had been one of untarnished midsummer splendour, and as the sun drew near to its setting, the glory of the evening grew every moment more crystalline, more miraculous. Westward from St. Faith's the beechwood which stretched for some miles toward the heathery upland beyond already cast its veil of clear shadow over the red roofs of the village, but the spire of the grey church, over-topping all, still pointed a flaming orange finger into the sky. The river Fawn, which runs below, lay in sheets of sky-reflected blue, and wound its dreamy devious course round the edge of this wood, where a rough two-planked bridge crossed from the bottom of the garden of the last house in the village, and communicated by means of a little wicker gate with the wood itself. Then once out of the shadow of the wood the stream lay in flaming pools of the molten crimson of the sunset, and lost itself in the haze of woodland distances.

This house at the end of the village stood outside the shadow, and the lawn which sloped down to the river was still flecked with sunlight. Garden-beds of dazzling colour lined its gravel walks, and down the middle of it ran a brick pergola, half-hidden in clusters of rambler-rose and purple with starry clematis. At the bottom end of it, between two of its pillars, was slung a hammock containing a shirt-sleeved figure.

The house itself lay somewhat remote from the rest of the village, and a footpath leading across two fields, now tall and fragrant with hay, was its only communication with the high road. It was low-built, only two storeys in height, and like the garden, its walls were a mass of flowering roses. A narrow stone terrace ran along the garden front, over which was stretched an awning, and on the terrace a young silent-footed man-servant was busied with the laying of the table for dinner. He was neat-handed and quick with his job, and having finished it he went back into the house, and reappeared again with a large rough bath-towel on his arm. With this he went to the hammock in the pergola.

"Nearly eight, sir," he said.

"Has Mr Darcy come yet?" asked a voice from the hammock.

"No, sir."

"If I'm not back when he comes, tell him that I'm just having a bathe before dinner."

The servant went back to the house, and after a moment or two Frank Halton struggled to a sitting posture, and slipped out on to the grass. He was of medium height and rather slender in build, but the supple ease and grace of his movements gave the impression of great physical strength: even his descent from the hammock was not an awkward performance. His face and hands were of very dark complexion, either from constant exposure to wind and sun, or, as his black hair and dark eyes tended to show, from some strain of southern blood. His head was small, his face of an exquisite beauty of modelling, while the smoothness of its contour would have led you to believe that he was a beardless lad still in his teens. But something, some look which living and experience alone can give, seemed to contradict that, and finding yourself completely puzzled as to his age, you would next moment probably cease to think about that, and only look at this glorious specimen of young manhood with wondering satisfaction.

He was dressed as became the season and the heat, and wore only a shirt open at the neck, and a pair of flannel trousers. His head, covered very thickly with a somewhat rebellious crop of short curly hair, was bare as he strolled across the lawn to the bathing-place that lay below. Then for a moment there was silence, then the sound of splashed and divided waters, and presently after, a great shout of ecstatic joy, as he swam up-stream with the foamed water standing in a frill round his neck. Then after some five minutes of limb-stretching struggle with the flood, he turned over on his back, and with arms thrown wide, floated down-stream, ripple-cradled and inert. His eyes were shut, and between half-parted lips he talked gently to himself.

"I am one with it," he said to himself, "the river and I, I and the river. The coolness and splash of it is I, and the water-herbs that wave in it are I also. And my strength and my limbs are not mine but the river's. It is all one, all one, dear Fawn."

* * *

A quarter of an hour later he appeared again at the bottom of the lawn, dressed as before, his wet hair already drying into its crisp short curls again. There he paused a moment, looking back at the stream with the smile with which men look on the face of a friend, then turned towards the house. Simultaneously his servant came to the door leading on to the terrace, followed by a man who appeared to be some half-way through the fourth decade of his years. Frank and he saw each other across the bushes and garden-beds, and each quickening his step, they met suddenly face to face round an angle of the garden walk, in the fragrance of syringa.

"My dear Darcy," cried Frank, "I am charmed to see you."

But the other stared at him in amazement.

"Frank!" he exclaimed.

"Yes, that is my name," he said laughing, "what is the matter?"

Darcy took his hand.

"What have you done to yourself?" he asked. "You are a boy again."

"Ah, I have a lot to tell you," said Frank. "Lots that you will hardly believe, but I shall convince you –"

He broke off suddenly, and held up his hand.

"Hush, there is my nightingale," he said.

The smile of recognition and welcome with which he had greeted his friend faded from his face, and a look of rapt wonder took its place, as of a lover listening to the voice of his beloved. His mouth parted slightly, showing the white line of teeth, and his eyes looked out and out till they seemed to Darcy to be focused on things beyond the vision of man. Then something perhaps startled the bird, for the song ceased.

"Yes, lots to tell you," he said. "Really I am delighted to see you. But you look rather white and pulled down; no wonder after that fever. And there is to be no nonsense about this visit. It is June now, you stop here till you are fit to begin work again. Two months at least."

"Ah, I can't trespass quite to that extent."

Frank took his arm and walked him down the grass.

"Trespass? Who talks of trespass? I shall tell you quite openly when I am tired of you, but you know when we had the studio together, we used not to bore each other. However, it is ill talking of going away on the moment of your arrival. Just a stroll to the river, and then it will be dinner-time."

Darcy took out his cigarette case, and offered it to the other.

Frank laughed.

"No, not for me. Dear me, I suppose I used to smoke once. How very odd!"

"Given it up?"

"I don't know. I suppose I must have. Anyhow I don't do it now. I would as soon think of eating meat."

"Another victim on the smoking altar of vegetarianism?"

"Victim?" asked Frank. "Do I strike you as such?"

He paused on the margin of the stream and whistled softly. Next moment a moor-hen made its splashing flight across the river, and ran up the bank. Frank took it very gently in his hands and stroked its head, as the creature lay against his shirt.

"And is the house among the reeds still secure?" he half-crooned to it. "And is the missus quite well, and are the neighbours flourishing? There, dear, home with you," and he flung it into the air.

"That bird's very tame," said Darcy, slightly bewildered.

"It is rather," said Frank, following its flight.

* * *

During dinner Frank chiefly occupied himself in bringing himself up-to-date in the movements and achievements of this old friend whom he had not seen for six years. Those six years, it now appeared, had been full of incident and success for Darcy; he had made a name for himself as a portrait painter which bade fair to outlast the vogue of a couple of seasons, and his leisure time had been brief. Then some four months previously he had been through a severe attack of typhoid, the result of which as concerns this story was that he had come down to this sequestered place to recruit.

"Yes, you've got on," said Frank at the end. "I always knew you would. A.R.A. with more in prospect. Money? You roll in it, I suppose, and, O Darcy, how much happiness have you had all these years? That is the only imperishable possession. And how much have you learned? Oh, I don't mean in Art. Even I could have done well in that."

Darcy laughed.

"Done well? My dear fellow, all I have learned in these six years you knew, so to speak, in your cradle. Your old pictures fetch huge prices. Do you never paint now?"

Frank shook his head.

"No, I'm too busy," he said.

"Doing what? Please tell me. That is what everyone is for ever asking me."

"Doing? I suppose you would say I do nothing."

Darcy glanced up at the brilliant young face opposite him.

"It seems to suit you, that way of being busy," he said. "Now, it's your turn. Do you read? Do you study? I remember you saying that it would do us all – all us artists, I mean – a great deal of good if we would study any one human face carefully for a year, without recording a line. Have you been doing that?"

Frank shook his head again.

"I mean exactly what I say," he said, "I have been *doing* nothing. And I have never been so occupied. Look at me; have I not done something to myself to begin with?"

"You are two years younger than I," said Darcy, "at least you used to be. You therefore are thirty-five. But had I never seen you before I should say you were just twenty. But was it worth while to spend six years of greatly-occupied life in order to look twenty? Seems rather like a woman of fashion."

Frank laughed boisterously.

"First time I've ever been compared to that particular bird of prey," he said. "No, that has not been my occupation – in fact I am only very rarely conscious that one effect of my occupation has been that. Of course, it must have been if one comes to think of it. It is not very important. Quite true my body has become young. But that is very little; I have become young."

Darcy pushed back his chair and sat sideways to the table looking at the other.

"Has that been your occupation then?" he asked.

"Yes, that anyhow is one aspect of it. Think what youth means! It is the capacity for growth, mind, body, spirit, all grow, all get stronger, all have a fuller, firmer life every day. That is something, considering that every day that passes after the ordinary man reaches the full-blown flower of his strength, weakens his hold on life. A man reaches his prime, and remains, we say, in his prime, for ten years, or perhaps twenty. But after his primest prime is reached, he slowly, insensibly weakens. These are the signs of age in you, in your body, in your art probably, in your mind. You are less electric than you were. But I, when I reach my prime – I am nearing it – ah, you shall see."

The stars had begun to appear in the blue velvet of the sky, and to the east the horizon seen above the black silhouette of the village was growing dove-coloured with the approach of moon-rise. White moths hovered dimly over the garden-beds, and the footsteps of night tip-toed through the bushes. Suddenly Frank rose.

"Ah, it is the supreme moment," he said softly. "Now more than at any other time the current of life, the eternal imperishable current runs so close to me that I am almost enveloped in it. Be silent a minute."

He advanced to the edge of the terrace and looked out standing stretched with arms outspread. Darcy heard him draw a long breath into his lungs, and after many seconds expel it again. Six or eight times he did this, then turned back into the lamplight.

"It will sound to you quite mad, I expect," he said, "but if you want to hear the soberest truth I have ever spoken and shall ever speak, I will tell you about myself. But come into the garden if it is not too damp for you. I have never told anyone yet, but I shall like to tell you. It is long, in fact, since I have even tried to classify what I have learned."

They wandered into the fragrant dimness of the pergola, and sat down. Then Frank began:

"Years ago, do you remember," he said, "we used often to talk about the decay of joy in the world. Many impulses, we settled, had contributed to this decay, some of which were good in themselves, others that were quite completely bad. Among the good things, I put what we may call certain Christian virtues, renunciation, resignation, sympathy with suffering, and the desire to relieve sufferers. But out of those things spring very bad ones, useless renunciations, asceticism for its own sake, mortification of the flesh with nothing to follow, no corresponding gain that is, and that awful and terrible disease which devastated England some centuries ago, and from which by heredity of spirit we suffer now, Puritanism. That was a dreadful plague, the brutes held and taught that joy and laughter and merriment were evil: it was a doctrine the most profane and wicked. Why, what is the commonest crime one sees? A sullen face. That is the truth of the matter.

"Now all my life I have believed that we are intended to be happy, that joy is of all gifts the most divine. And when I left London, abandoned my career, such as it was, I did so because I intended to devote my life to the cultivation of joy, and, by continuous and unsparing effort, to be happy. Among people, and in constant intercourse with others, I did not find it possible; there were too many distractions in towns and work-rooms, and also too much suffering. So I took one step backwards or forwards, as you may choose to put it, and went straight to Nature, to trees, birds, animals, to all those things which quite clearly pursue one aim only, which blindly follow the great native instinct to be happy without any care at all for morality, or human law or divine law. I wanted, you understand, to get all joy first-hand and unadulterated, and I think it scarcely exists among men; it is obsolete."

Darcy turned in his chair.

"Ah, but what makes birds and animals happy?" he asked. "Food, food and mating."

Frank laughed gently in the stillness.

"Do not think I became a sensualist," he said. "I did not make that mistake. For the sensualist carries his miseries pick-a-back, and round his feet is wound the shroud that shall soon enwrap him. I may be mad, it is true, but I am not so stupid anyhow as to have tried that. No, what is it that makes puppies play with their own tails, that sends cats on their prowling ecstatic errands at night?"

He paused a moment.

"So I went to Nature," he said. "I sat down here in this New Forest, sat down fair and square, and looked. That was my first difficulty, to sit here quiet without being bored, to wait without being impatient, to be receptive and very alert, though for a long time nothing particular happened. The change in fact was slow in those early stages."

"Nothing happened?" asked Darcy rather impatiently, with the sturdy revolt against any new idea which to the English mind is synonymous with nonsense. "Why, what in the world *should* happen?"

Now Frank as he had known him was the most generous but most quick-tempered of mortal men; in other words his anger would flare to a prodigious beacon, under almost no provocation, only to be quenched again under a gust of no less impulsive kindliness. Thus the moment Darcy had spoken, an apology for his hasty question was half-way up his tongue. But there was no need for it to have travelled even so far, for Frank laughed again with kindly, genuine mirth.

"Oh, how I should have resented that a few years ago," he said. "Thank goodness that resentment is one of the things I have got rid of. I certainly wish that you should believe my story – in fact, you are going to – but that you at this moment should imply that you do not, does not concern me."

"Ah, your solitary sojournings have made you inhuman," said Darcy, still very English.

"No, human," said Frank. "Rather more human, at least rather less of an ape."

"Well, that was my first quest," he continued, after a moment, "the deliberate and unswerving pursuit of joy, and my method, the eager contemplation of Nature. As far as motive went, I daresay it was purely selfish, but as far as effect goes, it seems to me about the best thing one can do for one's fellow-creatures, for happiness is more infectious than small-pox. So, as I said, I sat down and waited; I looked at happy things, zealously avoided the sight of anything unhappy, and by degrees a little trickle of the happiness of this blissful world began to filter into me. The trickle grew more abundant, and now, my dear fellow, if I could for a moment divert from me into you one half of the torrent of joy that pours through me day and night, you would throw the world, art, everything aside, and just live, exist. When a man's body dies, it passes into trees and flowers. Well, that is what I have been trying to do with my soul before death."

The servant had brought into the pergola a table with syphons and spirits, and had set a lamp upon it. As Frank spoke he leaned forward towards the other, and Darcy for all his matter-of-fact commonsense could have sworn that his companion's face shone, was luminous in itself. His dark brown eyes glowed from within, the unconscious smile of a child irradiated and transformed his face. Darcy felt suddenly excited, exhilarated.

"Go on," he said. "Go on. I can feel you are somehow telling me sober truth. I daresay you are mad; but I don't see that matters."

Frank laughed again.

"Mad?" he said. "Yes, certainly, if you wish. But I prefer to call it sane. However, nothing matters less than what anybody chooses to call things. God never labels his gifts; He just puts them into our hands; just as he put animals in the garden of Eden, for Adam to name if he felt disposed."

"So by the continual observance and study of things that were happy," continued he, "I got happiness, I got joy. But seeking it, as I did, from Nature, I got much more which I did not seek, but stumbled upon originally by accident. It is difficult to explain, but I will try.

"About three years ago I was sitting one morning in a place I will show you tomorrow. It is down by the river brink, very green, dappled with shade and sun, and the river passes there through some little clumps of reeds. Well, as I sat there, doing nothing, but just looking and listening, I heard the sound quite distinctly of some flute-like instrument playing a strange unending melody. I thought at first it was some musical yokel on the highway and did not pay much attention. But before long the strangeness and indescribable beauty of the tune struck me. It never repeated itself, but it never came to an end, phrase after phrase ran its sweet course, it worked gradually and inevitably up to a climax, and having attained it, it went on; another climax was reached and another and another. Then with a sudden gasp of wonder I localised where it came from. It came from the reeds and from the sky and from the trees. It was everywhere, it was the sound of life. It was, my dear Darcy, as the Greeks would have said, it was Pan playing on his pipes, the voice of Nature. It was the life-melody, the world-melody."

Darcy was far too interested to interrupt, though there was a question he would have liked to ask, and Frank went on:

"Well, for the moment I was terrified, terrified with the impotent horror of nightmare, and I stopped my ears and just ran from the place and got back to the house panting, trembling, literally in a panic. Unknowingly, for at that time I only pursued joy, I had begun, since I drew my joy from Nature, to get in touch with Nature. Nature, force, God, call it what you will, had drawn across my face a little gossamer web of essential life. I saw that when I emerged from my terror, and I went very humbly back to where I had heard the Pan-pipes. But it was nearly six months before I heard them again."

"Why was that?" asked Darcy.

"Surely because I had revolted, rebelled, and worst of all been frightened. For I believe that just as there is nothing in the world which so injures one's body as fear, so there is nothing that so much shuts up the soul. I was afraid, you see, of the one thing in the world which has real existence. No wonder its manifestation was withdrawn."

"And after six months?"

"After six months one blessed morning I heard the piping again. I wasn't afraid that time. And since then it has grown louder, it has become more constant. I now hear it often, and I can put myself into such an attitude towards Nature that the pipes will almost certainly sound. And never yet have they played the same tune, it is always something new, something fuller, richer, more complete than before."

"What do you mean by 'such an attitude towards Nature'?" asked Darcy.

"I can't explain that; but by translating it into a bodily attitude it is this."

Frank sat up for a moment quite straight in his chair, then slowly sunk back with arms outspread and head drooped.

"That," he said, "an effortless attitude, but open, resting, receptive. It is just that which you must do with your soul."

Then he sat up again.

"One word more," he said, "and I will bore you no further. Nor unless you ask me questions shall I talk about it again. You will find me, in fact, quite sane in my mode of life. Birds and beasts you will see behaving somewhat intimately to me, like that moor-hen, but that is all. I will walk with you, ride with you, play golf with you, and talk with you on any subject you like. But I wanted you on the threshold to know what has happened to me. And one thing more will happen."

He paused again, and a slight look of fear crossed his eyes.

"There will be a final revelation," he said, "a complete and blinding stroke which will throw open to me, once and for all, the full knowledge, the full realisation and comprehension that I am one, just as you are, with life. In reality there is no 'me,' no 'you,' no 'it'. Everything is part of the one and only thing which is life. I know that that is so, but the realisation of it is not yet mine. But it will be, and on that day, so I take it, I shall see Pan. It may mean death, the death of my body, that is, but I don't care. It may mean immortal, eternal life lived here and now and for ever. Then having gained that, ah, my dear Darcy, I shall preach such a gospel of joy, showing myself as the living proof of the truth, that Puritanism, the dismal religion of sour faces, shall vanish like a breath of smoke, and be dispersed and disappear in the sunlit air. But first the full knowledge must be mine."

Darcy watched his face narrowly.

"You are afraid of that moment," he said.

Frank smiled at him.

"Quite true; you are quick to have seen that. But when it comes I hope I shall not be afraid."

For some little time there was silence; then Darcy rose.

"You have bewitched me, you extraordinary boy," he said. "You have been telling me a fairy-story, and I find myself saying, 'Promise me it is true.'"

"I promise you that," said the other.

"And I know I shan't sleep," added Darcy.

Frank looked at him with a sort of mild wonder as if he scarcely understood.

"Well, what does that matter?" he said.

"I assure you it does. I am wretched unless I sleep."

"Of course I can make you sleep if I want," said Frank in a rather bored voice.

"Well, do."

"Very good: go to bed. I'll come upstairs in ten minutes."

Frank busied himself for a little after the other had gone, moving the table back under the awning of the veranda and quenching the lamp. Then he went with his quick silent tread upstairs and into Darcy's room. The latter was already in bed, but very wide-eyed and wakeful, and Frank with an amused smile of indulgence, as for a fretful child, sat down on the edge of the bed.

"Look at me," he said, and Darcy looked.

"The birds are sleeping in the brake," said Frank softly, "and the winds are asleep. The sea sleeps, and the tides are but the heaving of its breast. The stars swing slow, rocked in the great cradle of the Heavens, and –"

He stopped suddenly, gently blew out Darcy's candle, and left him sleeping.

Morning brought to Darcy a flood of hard commonsense, as clear and crisp as the sunshine that filled his room. Slowly as he woke he gathered together the broken threads of the memories of the evening which had ended, so he told himself, in a trick of common hypnotism. That accounted for it all; the whole strange talk he had had was under a spell of suggestion from the extraordinary vivid boy who had once been a man; all his own excitement, his acceptance of the incredible had been merely the effect of a stronger, more potent will imposed on his own. How strong that will was, he guessed from his own instantaneous obedience to Frank's suggestion of sleep. And armed with impenetrable commonsense he came down to breakfast. Frank had already begun, and was consuming a large plateful of porridge and milk with the most prosaic and healthy appetite.

"Slept well?" he asked.

"Yes, of course. Where did you learn hypnotism?"

"By the side of the river."

"You talked an amazing quantity of nonsense last night," remarked Darcy, in a voice prickly with reason.

"Rather. I felt quite giddy. Look, I remembered to order a dreadful daily paper for you. You can read about money markets or politics or cricket matches."

Darcy looked at him closely. In the morning light Frank looked even fresher, younger, more vital than he had done the night before, and the sight of him somehow dinted Darcy's armour of commonsense.

"You are the most extraordinary fellow I ever saw," he said. "I want to ask you some more questions."

"Ask away," said Frank.

* * *

For the next day or two Darcy plied his friend with many questions, objections and criticisms on the theory of life and gradually got out of him a coherent and complete account of his experience. In brief then, Frank believed that "by lying naked," as he put it, to the force which controls the passage of the stars, the breaking of a wave, the budding of a tree, the love of a youth and maiden, he had succeeded in a way hitherto undreamed of in possessing himself of the essential principle of life. Day by day, so he thought, he was getting nearer to, and in closer union with the great power itself which caused all life to be, the spirit of nature, of force, or the spirit of God. For himself, he confessed to what others would call paganism; it was sufficient for him that there existed a principle of life. He did not worship it, he did not pray to it, he did not praise it. Some of it existed in all human beings, just as it existed in trees and animals; to realise and make living to himself the fact that it was all one, was his sole aim and object.

Here perhaps Darcy would put in a word of warning. "Take care," he said. "To see Pan meant death, did it not?"

Frank's eyebrows would rise at this.

"What does that matter?" he said. "True, the Greeks were always right, and they said so, but there is another possibility. For the nearer I get to it, the more living, the more vital and young I become."

"What then do you expect the final revelation will do for you?"

"I have told you," said he. "It will make me immortal."

But it was not so much from speech and argument that Darcy grew to grasp his friend's conception, as from the ordinary conduct of his life. They were passing, for instance, one morning down the village street, when an old woman, very bent and decrepit, but with an extraordinary cheerfulness of face, hobbled out from her cottage. Frank instantly stopped when he saw her.

"You old darling! How goes it all?" he said.

But she did not answer, her dim old eyes were riveted on his face; she seemed to drink in like a thirsty creature the beautiful radiance which shone there. Suddenly she put her two withered old hands on his shoulders.

"You're just the sunshine itself," she said, and he kissed her and passed on.

But scarcely a hundred yards further a strange contradiction of such tenderness occurred. A child running along the path towards them fell on its face, and set up a dismal cry of fright and pain. A look of horror came into Frank's eyes, and, putting his fingers in his ears, he fled at full speed down the street, and did not pause till he was out of hearing. Darcy, having ascertained that the child was not really hurt, followed him in bewilderment.

"Are you without pity then?" he asked.

Frank shook his head impatiently.

"Can't you see?" he asked. "Can't you understand that that sort of thing, pain, anger, anything unlovely throws me back, retards the coming of the great hour! Perhaps when it comes I shall be able to piece that side of life on to the other, on to the true religion of joy. At present I can't."

"But the old woman. Was she not ugly?"

Frank's radiance gradually returned.

"Ah, no. She was like me. She longed for joy, and knew it when she saw it, the old darling."

Another question suggested itself.

"Then what about Christianity?" asked Darcy.

"I can't accept it. I can't believe in any creed of which the central doctrine is that God who is Joy should have had to suffer. Perhaps it was so; in some inscrutable way I believe it may have been so, but I don't understand how it was possible. So I leave it alone; my affair is joy."

They had come to the weir above the village, and the thunder of riotous cool water was heavy in the air. Trees dipped into the translucent stream with slender trailing branches, and the meadow where they stood was starred with midsummer blossomings. Larks shot up carolling into the crystal dome of blue, and a thousand voices of June sang round them. Frank, bare-headed as was his wont, with his coat slung over his arm and his shirt sleeves rolled up above the elbow, stood there like some beautiful wild animal with eyes half-shut and mouth half-open, drinking in the scented warmth of the air. Then suddenly he flung himself face downwards on the grass at the edge of the stream, burying his face in the daisies and cowslips, and lay stretched there in wide-armed ecstasy, with his long fingers pressing and stroking the dewy herbs of the field. Never before had Darcy seen him thus fully possessed by his idea; his caressing fingers, his half-buried face pressed close to the grass, even the clothed lines of his figure were instinct with a vitality that somehow was different from that of other men. And some faint glow from it reached Darcy, some thrill, some vibration from that charged recumbent body passed to him, and for a moment he understood as he had not understood before, despite his persistent questions and the candid answers they received, how real, and how realised by Frank, his idea was.

Then suddenly the muscles in Frank's neck became stiff and alert, and he half-raised his head, whispering, "The Pan-pipes, the Pan-pipes. Close, oh, so close."

Very slowly, as if a sudden movement might interrupt the melody, he raised himself and leaned on the elbow of his bent arm. His eyes opened wider, the lower lids drooped as if he focused his eyes on something very far away, and the smile on his face broadened and quivered like sunlight on still water, till the exultance of its happiness was scarcely human. So he remained motionless and rapt for some minutes, then the look of listening died from his face, and he bowed his head satisfied.

"Ah, that was good," he said. "How is it possible you did not hear? Oh, you poor fellow! Did you really hear nothing?"

A week of this outdoor and stimulating life did wonders in restoring to Darcy the vigour and health which his weeks of fever had filched from him, and as his normal activity and higher pressure of vitality returned, he seemed to himself to fall even more under the spell which the miracle of Frank's youth cast over him. Twenty times a day he found himself saying to himself suddenly at the end of some ten minutes' silent resistance to the absurdity of Frank's idea: "But it isn't possible; it can't be possible," and from the fact of his having to assure himself so frequently of this, he knew that he was struggling and arguing with a conclusion which already had taken root in his mind. For in any case a visible living miracle confronted him, since it was equally impossible that this youth, this boy, trembling on the verge of manhood, was thirty-five. Yet such was the fact.

July was ushered in by a couple of days of blustering and fretful rain, and Darcy, unwilling to risk a chill, kept to the house. But to Frank this weeping change of weather seemed to have no bearing on the behaviour of man, and he spent his days exactly as he did under the suns of June, lying in his hammock, stretched on the dripping grass, or making huge rambling excursions into the forest, the birds hopping from tree to tree after him, to return in the evening, drenched and soaked, but with the same unquenchable flame of joy burning within him.

"Catch cold?" he would ask, "I've forgotten how to do it, I think. I suppose it makes one's body more sensible always to sleep out-of-doors. People who live indoors always remind me of something peeled and skinless."

"Do you mean to say you slept out-of-doors last night in that deluge?" asked Darcy. "And where, may I ask?"

Frank thought a moment.

"I slept in the hammock till nearly dawn," he said. "For I remember the light blinked in the east when I awoke. Then I went – where did I go? – oh, yes, to the meadow where the Pan-pipes sounded so close a week ago. You were with me, do you remember? But I always have a rug if it is wet."

And he went whistling upstairs.

Somehow that little touch, his obvious effort to recall where he had slept, brought strangely home to Darcy the wonderful romance of which he was the still half-incredulous beholder. Sleep till close on dawn in a hammock, then the tramp – or probably scamper – underneath the windy and weeping heavens to the remote and lonely meadow by the weir! The picture of other such nights rose before him; Frank sleeping perhaps by the bathing-place under the filtered twilight of the stars, or the white blaze of moon-shine, a stir and awakening at some dead hour, perhaps a space of silent wide-eyed thought, and then a wandering through the hushed woods to some other dormitory, alone with his happiness, alone with the joy and the life that suffused and enveloped him, without other thought or desire or aim except the hourly and never-ceasing communion with the joy of nature.

They were in the middle of dinner that night, talking on indifferent subjects, when Darcy suddenly broke off in the middle of a sentence.

"I've got it," he said. "At last I've got it."

"Congratulate you," said Frank. "But what?"

"The radical unsoundness of your idea. It is this: All nature from highest to lowest is full, crammed full of suffering; every living organism in nature preys on another, yet in your aim to get close to, to be one with nature, you leave suffering altogether out; you run away from it, you refuse to recognise it. And you are waiting, you say, for the final revelation."

Frank's brow clouded slightly.

"Well?" he asked, rather wearily.

"Cannot you guess then when the final revelation will be? In joy you are supreme, I grant you that; I did not know a man could be so master of it. You have learned perhaps practically all that nature can teach. And if, as you think, the final revelation is coming to you, it will be the revelation of horror, suffering, death, pain in all its hideous forms. Suffering does exist: you hate it and fear it."

Frank held up his hand.

"Stop; let me think," he said.

There was silence for a long minute.

"That never struck me," he said at length. "It is possible that what you suggest is true. Does the sight of Pan mean that, do you think? Is it that nature, take it altogether, suffers horribly, suffers to a hideous inconceivable extent? Shall I be shown all the suffering?"

He got up and came round to where Darcy sat.

"If it is so, so be it," he said. "Because, my dear fellow, I am near, so splendidly near to the final revelation. Today the pipes have sounded almost without pause. I have even heard the rustle in the bushes, I believe, of Pan's coming. I have seen, yes, I saw today, the bushes pushed aside as if by a hand, and piece of a face, not human, peered through. But I was not frightened, at least I did not run away this time."

He took a turn up to the window and back again.

"Yes, there is suffering all through," he said, "and I have left it all out of my search. Perhaps, as you say, the revelation will be that. And in that case, it will be good-bye. I have gone on one line. I shall have gone too far along one road, without having explored the other. But I can't go back now. I wouldn't if I could; not a step would I retrace! In any case, whatever the revelation is, it will be God. I'm sure of that."

The rainy weather soon passed, and with the return of the sun Darcy again joined Frank in long rambling days. It grew extraordinarily hotter, and with the fresh bursting of life, after the rain, Frank's vitality seemed to blaze higher and higher. Then, as is the habit of the English weather, one evening clouds began to bank themselves up in the west, the sun went down in a glare of coppery thunder-rack, and the whole earth broiling under an unspeakable oppression and sultriness paused and panted for the storm. After sunset the remote fires of lightning began to wink and flicker on the horizon, but when bed-time came the storm seemed to have moved no nearer, though a very low unceasing noise of thunder was audible. Weary and oppressed by the stress of the day, Darcy fell at once into a heavy uncomforting sleep.

He woke suddenly into full consciousness, with the din of some appalling explosion of thunder in his ears, and sat up in bed with racing heart. Then for a moment, as he recovered himself from the panic-land which lies between sleeping and waking, there was silence, except for the steady hissing of rain on the shrubs outside his window. But suddenly that silence was shattered and shredded into fragments by a scream from somewhere close at hand outside in the black garden, a scream of supreme and despairing terror. Again, and once again it shrilled up, and then a babble of awful words was interjected. A quivering sobbing voice that he knew, said:

"My God, oh, my God; oh, Christ!"

And then followed a little mocking, bleating laugh. Then was silence again; only the rain hissed on the shrubs.

All this was but the affair of a moment, and without pause either to put on clothes or light a candle, Darcy was already fumbling at his door-handle. Even as he opened it he met a terror-stricken face outside, that of the man-servant who carried a light.

"Did you hear?" he asked.

The man's face was bleached to a dull shining whiteness.

"Yes, sir," he said. "It was the master's voice."

* * *

Together they hurried down the stairs, and through the dining-room where an orderly table for breakfast had already been laid, and out on to the terrace. The rain for the moment had been utterly stayed, as if the tap of the heavens had been turned off, and under the lowering black sky, not quite dark, since the moon rode somewhere serene behind the conglomerated thunder-clouds, Darcy stumbled into the garden, followed by the servant with the candle. The monstrous leaping shadow of himself was cast before him on the lawn; lost and wandering odours of rose and lily and damp earth were thick about him, but more pungent was some sharp and acrid smell that suddenly reminded him of a certain châlet in which he had once taken refuge in the Alps. In the blackness of the hazy light from the sky, and the vague tossing of the candle behind him, he saw that the hammock in which Frank so often lay was tenanted. A gleam of white shirt was there, as if a man sitting up in it, but across that there was an obscure dark shadow, and as he approached the acrid odour grew more intense.

He was now only some few yards away, when suddenly the black shadow seemed to jump into the air, then came down with tappings of hard hoofs on the brick path that ran down the pergola, and with frolicsome skippings galloped off into the bushes. When that was gone Darcy could see quite clearly that a shirted figure sat up in the hammock. For one moment, from sheer terror of the unseen, he hung on his step, and the servant joining him they walked together to the hammock.

It was Frank. He was in shirt and trousers only, and he sat up with braced arms. For one half-second he stared at them, his face a mask of horrible contorted terror. His upper lip was drawn back so that the gums of the teeth appeared, and his eyes were focused not on the two who approached him but on something quite close to him; his nostrils were widely expanded, as if he panted for breath, and terror incarnate and repulsion and deathly anguish ruled dreadful lines on his smooth cheeks and forehead. Then even as they looked the body sank backwards, and the ropes of the hammock wheezed and strained.

Darcy lifted him out and carried him indoors. Once he thought there was a faint convulsive stir of the limbs that lay with so dead a weight in his arms, but when they got inside, there was no trace of life. But the look of supreme terror and agony of fear had gone from his face, a boy tired with play but still smiling in his sleep was the burden he laid on the floor. His eyes had closed, and the beautiful mouth lay in smiling curves, even as when a few mornings ago, in the meadow by the weir, it had quivered to the music of the unheard melody of Pan's pipes. Then they looked further.

Frank had come back from his bathe before dinner that night in his usual costume of shirt and trousers only. He had not dressed, and during dinner, so Darcy remembered, he had rolled up the sleeves of his shirt to above the elbow. Later, as they sat and talked after dinner on the close sultriness of the evening, he had unbuttoned the front of his shirt to let what little breath of wind there was play on his skin. The sleeves were rolled up now, the front of the shirt was unbuttoned, and on his arms and on the brown skin of his chest were strange discolourations which grew momently more clear and defined, till they saw that the marks were pointed prints, as if caused by the hoofs of some monstrous goat that had leaped and stamped upon him.

Audio Tour

Trevor Boelter

"C'MON, KIDDO, this is supposed to be fun," said Jack's father, as they watched the spraying surf coat a couple of middle-aged nuns a few steps down. "Think of it this way, later in life, when you are going through your bucket list, you can scratch this one off."

Jack liked his Dad. He was a man who was always up for an adventure. The family called him "Captain Vacation," because he always had a list of activities and sightseeing tours wherever they visited.

This spring break trip was brought to you by San Francisco, which was a pretty awesome town in Jack's eyes, even when forced to spend time with his unhip parents and kid sister.

"Bucket list, huh?"

Jack knew what it meant, he just didn't think that he should have to add this to his vocabulary when he was only a year into puberty – and man, that had been a bitch to deal with. The hormones raged, like when he watched those tattooed girls careening down the steep hills of San Francisco on skateboards.

"You mean Alcatraz isn't on your bucket list?" his father asked, smiling at him.

His mom and Kat, the little brat, were in the bathroom, as the wee one puked her brains out due to ferry-sickness.

"Dad! I don't have a bucket list. I'm fourteen!"

His father shook his head. "You're right. But it moves fast, buddy. Hell, I remember being your age and seeing *Return of the Jedi* five times!"

That's what Jack liked about his father. Although he was very unhip, he could sometimes be cool, but only *sometimes*.

Jack's buddy, Devin, had parents who were nearing sixty – Jesus H. Ramirez – that's like living with grandparents. But then again, Devin's dad did have the best music collection in town.

Parents just aren't what they used to be – stodgy and out of touch. Now they were way in touch, so much that it got pretty annoying… at times.

Jack already had to change his Facebook account twice to keep the unsuspecting snoops out of his life. Not that he had anything of merit to hide. But that could change at any moment. What if some girl wanted him to sneak out in the middle of the night? It wouldn't help if she posted it on his wall and had his mom comment that doorbell ditching and tee-peeing people's yards was illegal.

Oh, brother – another family trip with the Carlsons. Good times.

His mom and Kat made their way back. Kat's face was no longer matching her purple shirt, but had the white glowing shock of one of those soldiers in *Saving Private Ryan*.

Jack smiled as he thought about Kat running up the beach in Normandy, dodging bullets, bodies and bombs all dressed in purple. She'd be like a big purple target.

"What's so funny, Jack?" his mom asked.

"Just thinking about a movie," he replied, hiding that grin and remembering to keep his mouth shut, as a girl around the age of sixteen sauntered by, taking snapshots with her iPhone.

The ferry had come upon the dock at Alcatraz, and the procession of the cattle commenced. And all to see where they held the bad guys, except for Clint Eastwood, who was still pretty badass for being a living mummy.

Kat's color returned as soon as she jumped off the boat and, of course, started mooning over some lavender wildflowers that were growing along the side of the bluffs.

Jack followed his family up the steps into the entrance of the ancient prison, which to his dismay, looked less majestic than *The Rock* had promised.

"This place is haunted, you know?" his father said, nudging Jack in the ribs.

"Kickass!" Jack replied, to which his mom made the obligatory, "Jack Carlson! Watch your mouth."

Inside the Rock now, they waited in line as the park rangers took the tickets, all dressed in yellow rain slickers. The sky was certainly dark, and the wind had kicked up a nice early April breeze, which oozed into the cracks and loose windows of the Alcatraz main hall.

Moving slowly along, Jack stared at the greenish and white paint that peeled in rippled sheets. Everything looked dead. This was a giant tomb, and this gave Jack the strange feeling that he was walking over a bone yard.

"Dad? Did they execute people here?" Jack asked.

"Oh, sure. Probably stuck them in the gas chamber or hanged them."

"There were no executions in Alcatraz. That happens up the way in San Quentin," said a nosy ranger, who clipped another ticket and took the four in his father's hand.

"Which is better, the group tour or the audio tour?" Jack's father asked.

The ranger murmured without looking up, "Audio tour. Hands down."

That was a good thing, because the guided tour's line was packed, while the audio tour kiosk had a fraction of the ferry audience.

A lady ranger, of about thirty or five hundred, Jack couldn't be sure, handed out little contraptions with these awful fuzzy headphones.

"Bring 'em back when you're finished," she chirped in a repetitive fashion. "Check them now, so you don't get a dud."

Jack put the headphones over his ears, which helped lessen the biting cold that nipped at the tips. Jack hit the *Play* button:

"Welcome to Alcatraz! This guided tour is brought to you by our good friends at Keely Electronics – where all your iPhone, Android and stereo needs can be found at the best prices."

Jack gave the lady ranger a thumbs up. Looking to his parents, he hit *Stop*.

"I guess we just follow along with the recording," Jack said, thinking to himself, that he would finally get a few blessed minutes alone.

His father was busy molding the headphones to his abnormally large head. "Don't cause any trouble, because they'll throw you in the hole."

"Thanks, Dad." Jack put the headphones back over his ears and hit *Play*.

Immediately, there were the sounds of shouting men, slamming cell doors, guards yelling for a headcount. In true hi-def stereo sound – Alcatraz was coming alive.

"As we guide you through this tour of Alcatraz, we require that there is no flash photography, smoking or talking loudly. Please make sure not to disturb our other guests as we bring you 'Alcatraz: The Guided Tour.'"

The narrator was some actor he had never heard of, but Jack saw his father feign a look of surprise and nudge his mother. He must be somebody, indeed.

They walked together as a group, making sure to dodge the guided tour that was already a few feet ahead.

Those with the headphones sniffed around in different cells, stopping occasionally to listen to the directions of the narrator, and then continued on.

They moved along Broadway – the main cellblock, that folks like Al Capone, The Bird Man, and other gangsters and dangerous criminals once called home.

In between the narration, the crystal clear recreation of past events played in a near perfect auditory hallucination.

This was definitely up Jack's alley, and he was glad that he could now check this off on his bucket list.

Jack walked into a cell, imagining what it must have been like to spend all his time in a cubbyhole no bigger than his mother's closet.

Some of the cells that were closed were made up to look like the real deal, with painted oil pictures of the San Francisco Bay and of the great city that lay beside it, along with a very uncomfortable-looking bed and a dreadful toilet.

The narrator instructed Jack to walk down the hall and take a right at the corner. Jack followed along, hanging back a little bit further, enjoying his space for a while longer.

"Psst! Hey, Kid!"

Jack spun around. The voice had come from one of the cells. "Yeah, you, Kid! Come here! I've got something to –."

Jack took off his headphones. The voice had sounded so real, so three-dimensional that he thought someone had called to him. Without the headphones, there was only the sound of shuffling feet and the droning tour guide.

Placing the headphones back over his ears, the narration continued "...He's been looking for the right person to help out, and I think that might be you. Do me a favor, open this door here."

Jack stood in front of a closed cell door. This was definitely part of the scripted tour, as Jack saw an older guy nearby opening the door of another cell and going in. Jack pulled the cell door open. It was heavy and rusted, but after putting his weight behind it, the door rolled open.

"That's perfect! Don't do it too much to set off the guards. This will give me a chance to find him. You look like a good kid, I can tell. You're smart like him. He likes smart kids."

The narrator picked up again, discussing the hole and why a prisoner would be forced to live in that environment. Jack was perplexed. "Stupid audio tour," he said, "Probably on random shuffle."

Jack picked up his speed – Alcatraz wasn't enormous and around the corner, he could see his father walking hand in hand with Kat.

His dad turned around, caught a glimpse of Jack and nodded his head. Jack flashed a peace sign.

"How you doing, Kid?"

This was a different voice coming from a nearby bench, or so it seemed. This voice was not the high-pitched squeak of the first, but deeper, gravelly, confident.

"I've been looking for the right guy for the job and my buddy, Buck, says you might be the one. So listen up, I don't have a lot of time, and neither do you. This tour only lasts another twenty minutes. So what's required is quick action, fast reflexes and a good mind. You got that?"

Jack walked along, and he saw his father try to talk Kat into touring the inside of the hole. That's where he'll tell her later on, when she is being bad, she'll go if she doesn't shape up. Jack laughed, thinking about his sister spending the night in solitary confinement on Alcatraz.

"This is no time for laughing, bucko! I asked you a question. Do you have what it takes?"

Jack stopped. That voice seemed to be coming from everywhere; this 3-D technology was simply amazing.

"Answer the goddamn question. You're wasting my time. Are you ready?"

Jack, out of reflex and shock that his audio tour was swearing at him, said, "Yes!"

The old guy, who had been lingering nearby Jack, shot him a glance. Jack waved.

"Okay. That's what I need to hear. From now on, I'll do the talking. There will be a couple of moments where I'll need you to pipe up, but we'll get to that. The first thing you have to do is get the hell out of this cellblock. I don't want to spend any more time in here than I have to."

Jack stopped again – this audio tour was certainly getting strange.

"See that doorway down there that says *Exit*? I want you to go out there. Don't worry about the alarm. It's on the frizz."

Jack looked at the tour ahead of him; they continued to mill about, held captive by their own narrators. Jack wondered what kind of tricks they had been instructed to undertake. Or maybe Jack received a special, different tour by mistake. In any case, Jack grinned. This was going to be fun.

He turned away from the group and moved toward the exit.

"Pick up the pace, son. We've got eighteen minutes before Mommy and Daddy raise the alarm. We don't need that. Now hop to it."

Just as the voice said, the alarm was shut off. He passed safely and quietly through the door, which opened to a long, dank hallway.

"This is where you'll have to seriously kick those sneakers into high gear. Head over to that enclave and wait."

Jack ran over to the little dip in the hall, which had steps that went down.

"Good, now wait – don't even breathe."

There was the sound of another door opening around the bend. Two people talked quietly to one another as a metal clunk of a door opened and closed.

"Perfect, kiddo. We're moving double time now, down the hall, the last door on the left."

Jack did just as he was told, as his feet echoed on the hard concrete floor. He opened the door and let it close with a clunk behind him. Jack was now out of the Alcatraz facility and standing before a long stairway leading down. Down the stairs, Jack could see two yellow-coated rangers moving at a medium pace and turn a corner.

"Don't worry about them. Layoffs have been threatened by the state, and it looks like Alcatraz may be shut down for good. Which is why today is as important as ever. We've got less than fifteen minutes to get this done and get you back."

Jack spoke out loud, "What exactly are we doing?"

"It'll all make sense. And I'll do the talking. Now Jack, do you see that dip in the wall up ahead?"

Reality crashed down upon Jack. This wasn't a game; this wasn't some strange audio tour with an interactive chapter. Jack looked around for hidden cameras – and though there were security cameras they remained fixed to their mounts at the corner of the room. Would that old dude from *The Rock* come jumping out of a cell? Jack could bet that his Dad would love that.

But there was nothing out of the ordinary – except for the voice booming in his ears.

Jack pulled off his headphones. A lone seagull cawed and swooped above him and headed off into the rocks nearby.

From the headphones, Jack could hear the voice, "Jack! Jack! Please… put the earmuffs on! Jack, please!"

"I don't want to," Jack said, now frightened by the gravity of the world bearing down upon him. His parents would be looking for him – Lord knows, they'd call every ranger on the island to start looking for him. He didn't want to deal with this.

"Jack Carlson! Jack Andrew Carlson, put these goddamn earmuffs on!"

Yep, this was real – it wasn't a dream, and Jack felt like throwing up.

"If you don't put the earmuffs on, I'll tell everyone you beat off to that yearbook picture of…"

Jack threw the headphones back on. "Don't!"

"Got your attention, didn't I? Look, Jack, I can read your mind like a book. It's my special skill nowadays. I know this is strange, but it'll make sense if you follow my lead. Trust me on this. I'm not going to hurt you – hell, I couldn't if I tried. I've been on this rock way too long, and I need to get off of it. You're my only hope, buster."

"And what if I don't?" Jack asked, very near to the point of tossing the headphones and device as far as he could.

"I'll make you a deal. Sometime in the future when you need help, I'll provide it. I can't tell you what it will be, but I'll do everything in my power. You do me the favor, and I'll do you one back. You have a long life ahead, you'll need some help now and again."

"Are you sure I won't get in trouble?"

"Not if you do exactly as I say. We have twelve minutes left, but you have to listen to me. *And I mean, to the letter!* You got that?"

Jack nodded and asked the voice for a name. The voice was quiet for a moment, and Jack wondered if he'd scared it off. But then it came back. "It's Frank. You ready?"

"Sure."

Following the voice, Jack leapt over the dip of the wall and headed into the wilderness of the island.

Frank was very specific about where Jack should step, about which rock to hold onto, and before long Jack found himself climbing down through a crevice in the ground. He could hear the swirling, crashing opera of water below.

Though Jack was frightened, Frank kept him calm by anticipating every emotion along with every step.

"Don't step there, it's too wet. Kick it with your shoe. Wipe off that moss. Now hold onto that stone. No, not that one, you numbskull – that one! Yeah. That's the ticket, hang on now. Just relax. You're climbing a prehistoric ladder, that's all."

Frank's encouraging words propelled Jack along the path. Frank also kept a log on the time until high tide: "Nine minutes, seven minutes, and five minutes to high tide."

Jack looked below; he was climbing a downward slope into the belly of an underwater cavern. The water rushed in a quick, frothy push. Although the volume seemed low, the amount of water was growing.

Jack could see the rolling pebbles and rocks that had been crushed and smoothed over millions of years.

"Okay, one more step, and I want you to leap off. You'll get a little wet, but that won't hurt anyone."

Jack jumped as he was told and landed with a thud. He wobbled and fell on his ass, sending a copious amount of brilliant white water over his bottom half.

Frank laughed. "That'll wake you up. Okay, up and Adam. We've got three minutes left."

Jack crawled to his feet, soaked, his toes already growing numb. But now he was getting excited, "Frank, are you leading me to buried treasure?"

"That depends on what you believe is treasure. For me, it's the most valuable thing in the world. Now up ahead, you see that rock, move it. Yeah, it's big and heavy, but you can do it."

Jack found the BBQ-sized boulder and yanked on the ridged and sharp surface. It was perched on other rocks and it had some give. Jack pushed with all his might, and the boulder rolled off, slapping down into the gravel floor, spraying off a fine mist of water as the tide rolled in.

"Good, now see that one and that one, get those out of here. Keep going."

Jack threw rock after rock, until he could see something wedged beneath; it was white, it shined.

"Oh, God," Jack said.

"You found it! You found it!"

Underneath the rocks were the bones of a human skeleton. There were scraps of blue cloth that hung around the edges of the carcass.

"Prison blues don't fade, you know."

Frank laughed – he was thrilled. His voice grew quick and ecstatic.

"Okay, this is pretty simple, you're going to grab these bones and toss them into the water."

Jack removed another rock and was horrified to see the leering grin of a broken skull. Seaweed stuck to the crown, a crater the size of a fist caved in the side.

"The current may have snatched me, but the rocks gave me the knock-out punch. Sucked me in here, and I've been stuck on the rock ever since. Can't say for sure what happened to the other guys. But after all our planning, years of preparation and a flawless escape, I get brained the second we leave the shore. This island, I tell you, it doesn't like you to leave of your own accord."

Jack was compelled to pick up the skull. Was this really the body of the voice he was hearing?

"Time's up, Jack. High tide is coming in. Scatter these bones into the water – the tide will spread them out. Once that happens, I'm free. But do me a favor. I want to see the City. Take a couple of my teeth."

Jack gagged, "Ewww, gross, Frank!" Jack dropped the skull and began chucking the skeleton bones into the water.

The water reached his knees and climbed higher with each new wave.

"Seriously! Pull a couple of teeth out of my skull and put them in your pocket."

Jack grimaced but complied. He took hold of the two front teeth and pulled. They snapped off like a number ticket at the local deli. Jack put the teeth in his pocket, as the water reached his crotch. "Cold!" Jack yelled.

"Okay, here we go again. You'll have to be extra careful, because you're wet, but we can do this…"

Jack was right. His parents noted him gone longer than five minutes, and soon every ranger on the island was in pursuit.

Following Frank's orders, Jack made it safely back up to the prison. When Jack jumped back over the dip in the wall and found his parents and a serious throng of rangers, he was completely soaked, covered in mud. His hands and arms were scratched, his jacket torn, and a tired look of bliss was plastered to his face.

Jack thought up his own excuse, that he followed the audio tour the wrong way. Got stuck outside, tried to climb around, slipped down a hill and this was the result.

And in a way, it was true.

Jack tried to slip the earphones on one last time to hear Frank's final instructions, but the chirpy ranger snatched the audio deck from his hand and absconded with it. Jack started to protest, but realized he was safer without it. He kept quiet, as his inner Frank told him to keep his trap shut.

After the scare was over and the Carlson family was back on the ferry boat, his father said, "And you missed the best part. They showed exactly how Frank Morris escaped."

Jack was quiet for a moment, then put his arm around his father and said, "He didn't escape, Dad. He just got misplaced."

His father found it funny, but it was horribly depressing for Jack.

Later that night, after a long hot shower and some Chinatown chop suey, Jack fired up his iPod, inserted his ear buds and hit *Play*.

Instead of music, Frank's voice came through the ear buds – but the voice was lighter, bubblier.

"Thanks a bundle, Jack! Remember, I owe you! But you've got one more thing to do. Take one of my teeth and toss it out the window. The other one you're going to keep. Yeah, I know it's gross, but it'll come in handy someday."

Jack got out of his bed, making sure not to wake Kat in her purple pajamas, and opened the small hotel window a crack. He fished into his backpack and found one of the teeth, which felt electric. He threw it out the window, where it clattered briefly on the sill and then slipped out into the San Francisco night.

Frank's voice seemed quieter now, free, as he spoke through the iPod: "Here's the deal. I'll always come to help you if I can. If you get into a jam and need someone to talk you out of it, I will. I won't help you do anything illegal, and I can't go against fate. But if I can, I'll help. Deal?"

Jack held the remaining tooth in his palm. "Deal," he said.

And when Jack dropped the tooth in his backpack, the music resumed and Frank was gone.

Ten years later, when Jack worked a summer as a volunteer fireman, he found himself in a situation during a very bad wildfire. He was with a group of ten other guys, and they were surrounded on all sides by flames that were closing in.

The newspapers would later report that Jack was very specific with the men; they had to follow his directions to the very letter. If they didn't, they would perish.

One of the survivors was later quoted about the rescue led by Jack:

"...And all the while he organized us and led us through hell's mouth, that cocky sumbitch was listening to rock-n-roll music on his headphones *the entire time*."

The Messenger

by Robert W. Chambers

Little gray messenger,
Robed like painted Death,
Your robe is dust.
Whom do you seek
Among lilies and closed buds
At dusk?
Among lilies and closed buds
At dusk,
Whom do you seek,
Little gray messenger,
Robed in the awful panoply
Of painted Death?

*

All-wise,
Hast thou seen all there is to see with thy two eyes?
Dost thou know all there is to know, and so,
Omniscient,
Darest thou still to say thy brother lies?

I

"THE BULLET ENTERED HERE," said Max Fortin, and he placed his middle finger over a smooth hole exactly in the center of the forehead.

I sat down upon a mound of dry seaweed and unslung my fowling piece.

The little chemist cautiously felt the edges of the shot-hole, first with his middle finger, and then with his thumb.

"Let me see the skull again," said I.

Max Fortin picked it up from the sod.

"It's like all the others," he repeated, wiping his glasses on his handkerchief. "I thought you might care to see one of the skulls, so I brought this over from the gravel pit. The men from Bannalec are digging yet. They ought to stop."

"How many skulls are there altogether?" I inquired.

"They found thirty-eight skulls; there are thirty-nine noted in the list. They lie piled up in the gravel pit on the edge of Le Bihan's wheat field. The men are at work yet. Le Bihan is going to stop them."

"Let's go over," said I; and I picked up my gun and started across the cliffs, Portin on one side, Môme on the other.

"Who has the list?" I asked, lighting my pipe. "You say there is a list?"

"The list was found rolled up in a brass cylinder," said the chemist. He added: "You should not smoke here. You know that if a single spark drifted into the wheat –"

"Ah, but I have a cover to my pipe," said I, smiling.

Fortin watched me as I closed the pepper-box arrangement over the glowing bowl of the pipe. Then he continued:

"The list was made out on thick yellow paper; the brass tube has preserved it. It is as fresh today as it was in 1760. You shall see it."

"Is that the date?"

"The list is dated 'April, 1760.' The Brigadier Durand has it. It is not written in French."

"Not written in French!" I exclaimed.

"No," replied Fortin solemnly, "it is written in Breton."

"But," I protested, "the Breton language was never written or printed in 1760."

"Except by priests," said the chemist.

"I have heard of but one priest who ever wrote the Breton language," I began.

Fortin stole a glance at my face.

"You mean – the Black Priest?" he asked.

I nodded.

Fortin opened his mouth to speak again, hesitated, and finally shut his teeth obstinately over the wheat stem that he was chewing.

"And the Black Priest?" I suggested encouragingly. But I knew it was useless; for it is easier to move the stars from their courses than to make an obstinate Breton talk. We walked on for a minute or two in silence.

"Where is the Brigadier Durand?" I asked, motioning Môme to come out of the wheat, which he was trampling as though it were heather. As I spoke we came in sight of the farther edge of the wheat field and the dark, wet mass of cliffs beyond.

"Durand is down there – you can see him; he stands just behind the mayor of St. Gildas."

"I see," said I; and we struck straight down, following a sun-baked cattle path across the heather.

When we reached the edge of the wheat field, Le Bihan, the mayor of St. Gildas, called to me, and I tucked my gun under my arm and skirted the wheat to where he stood.

"Thirty-eight skulls," he said in his thin, high-pitched voice; "there is but one more, and I am opposed to further search. I suppose Fortin told you?"

I shook hands with him, and returned the salute of the Brigadier Durand.

"I am opposed to further search," repeated Le Bihan, nervously picking at the mass of silver buttons which covered the front of his velvet and broadcloth jacket like a breastplate of scale armor.

Durand pursed up his lips, twisted his tremendous mustache, and hooked his thumbs in his saber belt.

"As for me," he said, "I am in favor of further search."

"Further search for what – for the thirty-ninth skull?" I asked.

Le Bihan nodded. Durand frowned at the sunlit sea, rocking like a bowl of molten gold from the cliffs to the horizon. I followed his eyes. On the dark glistening cliffs, silhouetted against the glare of the sea, sat a cormorant, black, motionless, its horrible head raised toward heaven.

"Where is that list, Durand?" I asked.

The gendarme rummaged in his despatch pouch and produced a brass cylinder about a foot long. Very gravely he unscrewed the head and dumped out a scroll of thick yellow paper closely covered with writing on both sides. At a nod from Le Bihan he handed me the scroll. But I could make nothing of the coarse writing, now faded to a dull brown.

"Come, come, Le Bihan," I said impatiently, "translate it, won't you? You and Max Fortin make a lot of mystery out of nothing, it seems."

Le Bihan went to the edge of the pit where the three Bannalec men were digging, gave an order or two in Breton, and turned to me.

As I came to the edge of the pit the Bannalec men were removing a square piece of sailcloth from what appeared to be a pile of cobblestones.

"Look!" said Le Bihan shrilly. I looked. The pile below was a heap of skulls. After a moment I clambered down the gravel sides of the pit and walked over to the men of Bannalec. They saluted me gravely, leaning on their picks and shovels, and wiping their sweating faces with sunburned hands.

"How many?" said I in Breton.

"Thirty-eight," they replied.

I glanced around. Beyond the heap of skulls lay two piles of human bones. Beside these was a mound of broken, rusted bits of iron and steel. Looking closer, I saw that this mound was composed of rusty bayonets, saber blades, scythe blades, with here and there a tarnished buckle attached to a bit of leather hard as iron.

I picked up a couple of buttons and a belt plate. The buttons bore the royal arms of England; the belt plate was emblazoned with the English arms and also with the number "27."

"I have heard my grandfather speak of the terrible English regiment, the 27th Foot, which landed and stormed the fort up there," said one of the Bannalec men.

"Oh!" said I; "then these are the bones of English soldiers?"

"Yes," said the men of Bannalec.

Le Bihan was calling to me from the edge of the pit above, and I handed the belt plate and buttons to the men and climbed the side of the excavation.

"Well," said I, trying to prevent Môme from leaping up and licking my face as I emerged from the pit, "I suppose you know what these bones are. What are you going to do with them?"

"There was a man," said Le Bihan angrily, "an Englishman, who passed here in a dog-cart on his way to Quimper about an hour ago, and what do you suppose he wished to do?"

"Buy the relics?" I asked, smiling.

"Exactly – the pig!" piped the mayor of St. Gildas. "Jean Marie Tregunc, who found the bones, was standing there where Max Fortin stands, and do you know what he answered? He spat upon the ground, and said: 'Pig of an Englishman, do you take me for a desecrator of graves?'"

I knew Tregunc, a sober, blue-eyed Breton, who lived from one year's end to the other without being able to afford a single bit of meat for a meal.

"How much did the Englishman offer Tregunc?" I asked.

"Two hundred francs for the skulls alone."

I thought of the relic hunters and the relic buyers on the battlefields of our civil war.

"Seventeen hundred and sixty is long ago," I said.

"Respect for the dead can never die," said Fortin.

"And the English soldiers came here to kill your fathers and burn your homes," I continued.

"They were murderers and thieves, but – they are dead," said Tregunc, coming up from the beach below, his long sea rake balanced on his dripping jersey.

"How much do you earn every year, Jean Marie?" I asked, turning to shake hands with him.

"Two hundred and twenty francs, monsieur."

"Forty-five dollars a year," I said. "Bah! you are worth more, Jean. Will you take care of my garden for me? My wife wished me to ask you. I think it would be worth one hundred francs a month to you and to me. Come on, Le Bihan – come along, Fortin – and you, Durand. I want somebody to translate that list into French for me."

Tregunc stood gazing at me, his blue eyes dilated.

"You may begin at once," I said, smiling, "if the salary suits you?"

"It suits," said Tregunc, fumbling for his pipe in a silly way that annoyed Le Bihan.

"Then go and begin your work," cried the mayor impatiently; and Tregunc started across the moors toward St. Gildas, taking off his velvet-ribboned cap to me and gripping his sea rake very hard.

"You offer him more than my salary," said the mayor, after a moment's contemplation of his silver buttons.

"Pooh!" said I, "what do you do for your salary except play dominoes with Max Portin at the Groix Inn?"

Le Bihan turned red, but Durand rattled his saber and winked at Max Fortin, and I slipped my arm through the arm of the sulky magistrate, laughing.

"There's a shady spot under the cliff," I said; "come on, Le Bihan, and read me what is in the scroll."

In a few moments we reached the shadow of the cliff, and I threw myself upon the turf, chin on hand, to listen.

The gendarme, Durand, also sat down, twisting his mustache into needlelike points. Fortin leaned against the cliff, polishing his glasses and examining us with vague, near-sighted eyes; and Le Bihan, the mayor, planted himself in our midst, rolling up the scroll and tucking it under his arm.

"First of all," he began in a shrill voice, "I am going to light my pipe, and while lighting it I shall tell you what I have heard about the attack on the fort yonder. My father told me; his father told him."

He jerked his head in the direction of the ruined fort, a small, square stone structure on the sea cliff, now nothing but crumbling walls. Then he slowly produced a tobacco pouch, a bit of flint and tinder, and a long-stemmed pipe fitted with a microscopical bowl of baked clay. To fill such a pipe requires ten minutes' close attention. To smoke it to a finish takes but four puffs. It is very Breton, this Breton pipe. It is the crystallization of everything Breton.

"Go on," said I, lighting a cigarette.

"The fort," said the mayor, "was built by Louis XIV, and was dismantled twice by the English. Louis XV restored it in 1730. In 1760 it was carried by assault by the English. They came across from the island of Groix – three shiploads, and they stormed the fort and sacked St. Julien yonder, and they started to burn St. Gildas – you can see the marks of their bullets on my house yet; but the men of Bannalec and the men of Lorient fell upon them with pike and scythe and blunderbuss, and those who did not run away lie there below in the gravel pit now – thirty-eight of them."

"And the thirty-ninth skull?" I asked, finishing my cigarette.

The mayor had succeeded in filling his pipe, and now he began to put his tobacco pouch away.

"The thirty-ninth skull," he mumbled, holding the pipe stem between his defective teeth – "the thirty-ninth skull is no business of mine. I have told the Bannalec men to cease digging."

"But what is – whose is the missing skull?" I persisted curiously.

The mayor was busy trying to strike a spark to his tinder. Presently he set it aglow, applied it to his pipe, took the prescribed four puffs, knocked the ashes out of the bowl, and gravely replaced the pipe in his pocket.

"The missing skull?" he asked.

"Yes," said I, impatiently.

The mayor slowly unrolled the scroll and began to read, translating from the Breton into French. And this is what he read:

"*On the Cliffs of St. Gildas, April 13, 1760.*

"On this day, by order of the Count of Soisic, general in chief of the Breton forces now lying in Kerselec Forest, the bodies of thirty-eight English soldiers of the 27th, 50th, and 72nd regiments of Foot were buried in this spot, together with their arms and equipments."

The mayor paused and glanced at me reflectively.

"Go on, Le Bihan," I said.

"With them," continued the mayor, turning the scroll and reading on the other side, "was buried the body of that vile traitor who betrayed the fort to the English. The manner of his death was as follows: By order of the most noble Count of Soisic, the traitor was first branded upon the forehead with the brand of an arrowhead. The iron burned through the flesh and was pressed heavily so that the brand should even burn into the bone of the skull. The traitor was then led out and bidden to kneel. He admitted having guided the English from the island of Groix. Although a priest and a Frenchman, he had violated his priestly office to aid him in discovering the password to the fort. This password he extorted during confession from a young Breton girl who was in the habit of rowing across from the island of Groix to visit her husband in the fort. When the fort fell, this young girl, crazed by the death of her husband, sought the Count of Soisic and told how the priest had forced her to confess to him all she knew about the fort. The priest was arrested at St. Gildas as he was about to cross the river to Lorient. When arrested he cursed the girl, Marie Trevec –"

"What!" I exclaimed, "Marie Trevec!"

"Marie Trevec," repeated Le Bihan; "the priest cursed Marie Trevec, and all her family and descendants. He was shot as he knelt, having a mask of leather over his face, because the Bretons who composed the squad of execution refused to fire at a priest unless his face was concealed. The priest was l'Abbé Sorgue, commonly known as the Black Priest on account of his dark face and swarthy eyebrows. He was buried with a stake through his heart."

Le Bihan paused, hesitated, looked at me, and handed the manuscript back to Durand. The gendarme took it and slipped it into the brass cylinder.

"So," said I, "the thirty-ninth skull is the skull of the Black Priest."

"Yes," said Fortin. "I hope they won't find it."

"I have forbidden them to proceed," said the mayor querulously. "You heard me, Max Fortin."

I rose and picked up my gun. Môme came and pushed his head into my hand.

"That's a fine dog," observed Durand, also rising.

"Why don't you wish to find his skull?" I asked Le Bihan. "It would be curious to see whether the arrow brand really burned into the bone."

"There is something in that scroll that I didn't read to you," said the mayor grimly. "Do you wish to know what it is?"

"Of course," I replied in surprise.

"Give me the scroll again, Durand," he said; then he read from the bottom: "I, l'Abbé Sorgue, forced to write the above by my executioners, have written it in my own blood; and with it I leave my curse. My curse on St. Gildas, on Marie Trevec, and on her descendants. I will come back to St. Gildas when my remains are disturbed. Woe to that Englishman whom my branded skull shall touch!"

"What rot!" I said. "Do you believe it was really written in his own blood?"

"I am going to test it," said Fortin, "at the request of Monsieur le Maire. I am not anxious for the job, however."

"See," said Le Bihan, holding out the scroll to me, "it is signed, 'L'Abbé Sorgue.'"

I glanced curiously over the paper.

"It must be the Black Priest," I said. "He was the only man who wrote in the Breton language. This is a wonderfully interesting discovery, for now, at last, the mystery of the Black Priest's disappearance is cleared up. You will, of course, send this scroll to Paris, Le Bihan?"

"No," said the mayor obstinately, "it shall be buried in the pit below where the rest of the Black Priest lies."

I looked at him and recognized that argument would be useless. But still I said, "It will be a loss to history, Monsieur Le Bihan."

"All the worse for history, then," said the enlightened Mayor of St. Gildas.

We had sauntered back to the gravel pit while speaking. The men of Bannalec were carrying the bones of the English soldiers toward the St. Gildas cemetery, on the cliffs to the east, where already a knot of white-coiffed women stood in attitudes of prayer; and I saw the somber robe of a priest among the crosses of the little graveyard.

"They were thieves and assassins; they are dead now," muttered Max Fortin.

"Respect the dead," repeated the Mayor of St. Gildas, looking after the Bannalec men.

"It was written in that scroll that Marie Trevec, of Groix Island, was cursed by the priest – she and her descendants," I said, touching Le Bihan on the arm. "There was a Marie Trevec who married an Yves Trevec of St. Gildas –"

"It is the same," said Le Bihan, looking at me obliquely.

"Oh!" said I; "then they were ancestors of my wife."

"Do you fear the curse?" asked Le Bihan.

"What?" I laughed.

"There was the case of the Purple Emperor," said Max Fortin timidly.

Startled for a moment, I faced him, then shrugged my shoulders and kicked at a smooth bit of rock which lay near the edge of the pit, almost embedded in gravel.

"Do you suppose the Purple-Emperor drank himself crazy because he was descended from Marie Trevec?" I asked contemptuously.

"Of course not," said Max Fortin hastily.

"Of course not," piped the mayor. "I only – Hello! what's that you're kicking?"

"What?" said I, glancing down, at the same time involuntarily giving another kick. The smooth bit of rock dislodged itself and rolled out of the loosened gravel at my feet.

"The thirty-ninth skull!" I exclaimed. "By jingo, it's the noddle of the Black Priest! See! there is the arrowhead branded on the front!"

The mayor stepped back. Max Fortin also retreated. There was a pause, during which I looked at them, and they looked anywhere but at me.

"I don't like it," said the mayor at last, in a husky, high voice. "I don't like it! The scroll says he will come back to St. Gildas when his remains are disturbed. I – I don't like it, Monsieur Darrel –"

"Bosh!" said I; "the poor wicked devil is where he can't get out. For Heaven's sake, Le Bihan, what is this stuff you are talking in the year of grace 1896?"

The mayor gave me a look.

"And he says 'Englishman.' You are an Englishman, Monsieur Darrel," he announced.

"You know better. You know I'm an American."

"It's all the same," said the Mayor of St. Gildas, obstinately.

"No, it isn't!" I answered, much exasperated, and deliberately pushed the skull till it rolled into the bottom of the gravel pit below.

"Cover it up," said I; "bury the scroll with it too, if you insist, but I think you ought to send it to Paris. Don't look so gloomy, Fortin, unless you believe in werewolves and ghosts. Hey! what the – what the devil's the matter with you, anyway? What are you staring at, Le Bihan?"

"Come, come," muttered the mayor in a low, tremulous voice, "it's time we got out of this. Did you see? Did you see, Fortin?"

"I saw," whispered Max Fortin, pallid with fright.

The two men were almost running across the sunny pasture now, and I hastened after them, demanding to know what was the matter.

"Matter!" chattered the mayor, gasping with exasperation and terror. "The skull is rolling uphill again," and he burst into a terrified gallop, Max Fortin followed close behind.

I watched them stampeding across the pasture, then turned toward the gravel pit, mystified, incredulous. The skull was lying on the edge of the pit, exactly where it had been before I pushed it over the edge. For a second I stared at it; a singular chilly feeling crept up my spinal column, and I turned and walked away, sweat starting from the root of every hair on my head. Before I had gone twenty paces the absurdity of the whole thing struck me. I halted, hot with shame and annoyance, and retraced my steps.

There lay the skull.

"I rolled a stone down instead of the skull," I muttered to myself. Then with the butt of my gun I pushed the skull over the edge of the pit and watched it roll to the bottom; and as it struck the bottom of the pit, Môme, my dog, suddenly whipped his tail between his legs, whimpered, and made off across the moor.

"Môme!" I shouted, angry and astonished; but the dog only fled the faster, and I ceased calling from sheer surprise.

"What the mischief is the matter with that dog!" I thought. He had never before played me such a trick.

Mechanically I glanced into the pit, but I could not see the skull. I looked down. The skull lay at my feet again, touching them.

"Good heavens!" I stammered, and struck at it blindly with my gunstock. The ghastly thing flew into the air, whirling over and over, and rolled again down the sides of the pit to the bottom. Breathlessly I stared at it, then, confused and scarcely comprehending, I stepped back from the pit, still facing it, one, ten, twenty paces, my eyes almost starting from my head, as though I expected to see the thing roll up from the bottom of the pit under my very gaze. At last I turned my back to the pit and strode out across the gorse-covered moorland toward my home. As I reached the road that winds from St. Gildas to St. Julien I gave one hasty glance at the pit over my shoulder. The sun shone hot on the sod about the excavation. There was something white and bare and round on the turf at the edge of the pit. It might have been a stone; there were plenty of them lying about.

II

WHEN I ENTERED my garden I saw Môme sprawling on the stone doorstep. He eyed me sideways and flopped his tail.

"Are you not mortified, you idiot dog?" I said, looking about the upper windows for Lys.

Môme rolled over on his back and raised one deprecating forepaw, as though to ward off calamity.

"Don't act as though I was in the habit of beating you to death," I said, disgusted. I had never in my life raised whip to the brute. "But you are a fool dog," I continued. "No, you needn't come to be babied and wept over; Lys can do that, if she insists, but I am ashamed of you, and you can go to the devil."

Môme slunk off into the house, and I followed, mounting directly to my wife's boudoir. It was empty.

"Where has she gone?" I said, looking hard at Môme, who had followed me. "Oh! I see you don't know. Don't pretend you do. Come off that lounge! Do you think Lys wants tan-colored hairs all over her lounge?"

I rang the bell for Catherine and 'Fine, but they didn't know where "madame" had gone; so I went into my room, bathed, exchanged my somewhat grimy shooting clothes for a suit of warm, soft knickerbockers, and, after lingering some extra moments over my toilet – for I was particular, now that I had married Lys – I went down to the garden and took a chair out under the fig-trees.

"Where can she be?" I wondered. Môme came sneaking out to be comforted, and I forgave him for Lys's sake, whereupon he frisked.

"You bounding cur," said I, "now what on earth started you off across the moor? If you do it again I'll push you along with a charge of dust shot."

As yet I had scarcely dared think about the ghastly hallucination of which I had been a victim, but now I faced it squarely, flushing a little with mortification at the thought of my hasty retreat from the gravel pit.

"To think," I said aloud, "that those old woman's tales of Max Fortin and Le Bihan should have actually made me see what didn't exist at all! I lost my nerve like a schoolboy in a dark bedroom." For I knew now that I had mistaken a round stone for a skull each time, and had pushed a couple of big pebbles into the pit instead of the skull itself.

"By jingo!" said I, "I'm nervous; my liver must be in a devil of a condition if I see such things when I'm awake! Lys will know what to give me."

I felt mortified and irritated and sulky, and thought disgustedly of Le Bihan and Max Fortin.

But after a while I ceased speculating, dismissed the mayor, the chemist, and the skull from my mind, and smoked pensively, watching the sun low dipping in the western ocean. As the twilight fell for a moment over ocean and moorland, a wistful, restless happiness filled my heart, the happiness that all men know – all men who have loved.

Slowly the purple mist crept out over the sea; the cliffs darkened; the forest was shrouded.

Suddenly the sky above burned with the afterglow, and the world was alight again.

Cloud after cloud caught the rose dye; the cliffs were tinted with it; moor and pasture, heather and forest burned and pulsated with the gentle flush. I saw the gulls turning and tossing above the sand bar, their snowy wings tipped with pink; I saw the sea swallows sheering the surface of the still river, stained to its placid depths with warm reflections of the clouds. The twitter of drowsy hedge birds broke out in the stillness; a salmon rolled its shining side above tidewater.

The interminable monotone of the ocean intensified the silence. I sat motionless, holding my breath as one who listens to the first low rumor of an organ. All at once the pure whistle of a nightingale cut the silence, and the first moonbeam silvered the wastes of mist-hung waters.

I raised my head.

Lys stood before me in the garden.

When we had kissed each other, we linked arms and moved up and down the gravel walks, watching the moonbeams sparkle on the sand bar as the tide ebbed and ebbed. The broad beds of white pinks about us were atremble with hovering white moths; the October roses hung all abloom, perfuming the salt wind.

"Sweetheart," I said, "where is Yvonne? Has she promised to spend Christmas with us?"

"Yes, Dick; she drove me down from Plougat this afternoon. She sent her love to you. I am not jealous. What did you shoot?"

"A hare and four partridges. They are in the gun room. I told Catherine not to touch them until you had seen them."

Now I suppose I knew that Lys could not be particularly enthusiastic over game or guns; but she pretended she was, and always scornfully denied that it was for my sake and not for the pure love of sport. So she dragged me off to inspect the rather meager game bag, and she paid me pretty compliments, and gave a little cry of delight and pity as I lifted the enormous hare out of the sack by his ears.

"He'll eat no more of our lettuce," I said attempting to justify the assassination.

"Unhappy little bunny – and what a beauty! O Dick, you are a splendid shot, are you not?"

I evaded the question and hauled out a partridge.

"Poor little dead things," said Lys in a whisper; "it seems a pity – doesn't it, Dick? But then you are so clever –"

"We'll have them broiled," I said guardedly, "tell Catherine."

Catherine came in to take away the game, and presently 'Fine Lelocard, Lys's maid, announced dinner, and Lys tripped away to her boudoir.

I stood an instant contemplating her blissfully, thinking, "My boy, you're the happiest fellow in the world – you're in love with your wife."

I walked into the dining-room, beamed at the plates, walked out again; met Tregunc in the hallway, beamed on him; glanced into the kitchen, beamed at Catherine, and went upstairs, still beaming.

Before I could knock at Lys's door it opened, and Lys came hastily out. When she saw me she gave a little cry of relief, and nestled close to my breast.

"There is something peering in at my window," she said.

"What!" I cried angrily.

"A man, I think, disguised as a priest, and he has a mask on. He must have climbed up by the bay tree."

I was down the stairs and out of doors in no time. The moonlit garden was absolutely deserted. Tregunc came up, and together we searched the hedge and shrubbery around the house and out to the road.

"Jean Marie," said I at length, "loose my bulldog – he knows you – and take your supper on the porch where you can watch. My wife says the fellow is disguised as a priest, and wears a mask."

Tregunc showed his white teeth in a smile. "He will not care to venture in here again, I think, Monsieur Darrel."

I went back and found Lys seated quietly at the table.

"The soup is ready, dear," she said. "Don't worry; it was only some foolish lout from Bannalec. No one in St. Gildas or St. Julien would do such a thing."

I was too much exasperated to reply at first, but Lys treated it as a stupid joke, and after a while I began to look at it in that light.

Lys told me about Yvonne, and reminded me of my promise to have Herbert Stuart down to meet her.

"You wicked diplomat!" I protested. "Herbert is in Paris, and hard at work for the Salon."

"Don't you think he might spare a week to flirt with the prettiest girl in Finistère?" inquired Lys innocently.

"Prettiest girl! Not much!" I said.

"Who is, then?" urged Lys.

I laughed a trifle sheepishly.

"I suppose you mean me, Dick," said Lys, coloring up.

"Now I bore you, don't I?"

"Bore me? Ah, no, Dick."

After coffee and cigarettes were served I spoke about Tregunc, and Lys approved.

"Poor Jean! He will be glad, won't he? What a dear fellow you are!"

"Nonsense," said I; "we need a gardener; you said so yourself, Lys."

But Lys leaned over and kissed me, and then bent down and hugged Môme – who whistled through his nose in sentimental appreciation.

"I am a very happy woman," said Lys.

"Môme was a very bad dog today," I observed.

"Poor Môme!" said Lys, smiling.

When dinner was over and Môme lay snoring before the blaze – for the October nights are often chilly in Finistère – Lys curled up in the chimney corner with her embroidery, and gave me a swift glance from under her dropping lashes.

"You look like a schoolgirl, Lys," I said teasingly. "I don't believe you are sixteen yet."

She pushed back her heavy burnished hair thoughtfully. Her wrist was as white as surf foam.

"Have we been married four years? I don't believe it," I said.

She gave me another swift glance and touched the embroidery on her knee, smiling faintly.

"I see," said I, also smiling at the embroidered garment. "Do you think it will fit?"

"Fit?" repeated Lys. Then she laughed.

"And," I persisted, "are you perfectly sure that you – er – we shall need it?"

"Perfectly," said Lys. A delicate color touched her cheeks and neck. She held up the little garment, all fluffy with misty lace and wrought with quaint embroidery.

"It is very gorgeous," said I; "don't use your eyes too much, dearest. May I smoke a pipe?"

"Of course," she said selecting a skein of pale blue silk.

For a while I sat and smoked in silence, watching her slender fingers among the tinted silks and thread of gold.

Presently she spoke: "What did you say your crest is, Dick?"

"My crest? Oh, something or other rampant on a something or other –"

"Dick!"

"Dearest?"

"Don't be flippant."

"But I really forget. It's an ordinary crest; everybody in New York has them. No family should be without 'em."

"You are disagreeable, Dick. Send Josephine upstairs for my album."

"Are you going to put that crest on the – the – whatever it is?"

"I am; and my own crest, too."

I thought of the Purple Emperor and wondered a little.

"You didn't know I had one, did you?" she smiled.

"What is it?" I replied evasively.

"You shall see. Ring for Josephine."

I rang, and, when 'Fine appeared, Lys gave her some orders in a low voice, and Josephine trotted away, bobbing her white-coiffed head with a "Bien, Madame!"

After a few minutes she returned, bearing a tattered, musty volume, from which the gold and blue had mostly disappeared.

I took the book in my hands and examined the ancient emblazoned covers.

"Lilies!" I exclaimed.

"Fleur-de-lis," said my wife demurely.

"Oh!" said I, astonished, and opened the book.

"You have never before seen this book?" asked Lys, with a touch of malice in her eyes.

"You know I haven't. Hello! What's this? Oho! So there should be a de before Trevec? Lys de Trevec? Then why in the world did the Purple Emperor –"

"Dick!" cried Lys.

"All right," said I. "Shall I read about the Sieur de Trevec who rode to Saladin's tent alone to seek for medicine for St. Louise? Or shall I read about – what is it? Oh, here it is, all down in black and white – about the Marquis de Trevec who drowned himself before Alva's eyes rather than surrender the banner of the fleur-de-lis to Spain? It's all written here. But, dear, how about that soldier named Trevec who was killed in the old fort on the cliff yonder?"

"He dropped the de, and the Trevecs since then have been Republicans," said Lys – "all except me."

"That's quite right," said I; "it is time that we Republicans should agree upon some feudal system. My dear, I drink to the king!" and I raised my wine glass and looked at Lys.

"To the king," said Lys, flushing. She smoothed out the tiny garment on her knees; she touched the glass with her lips; her eyes were very sweet. I drained the glass to the king.

After a silence I said: "I will tell the king stories. His majesty shall be amused."

"His majesty," repeated Lys softly.

"Or hers," I laughed. "Who knows?"

"Who knows?" murmured Lys; with a gentle sigh.

"I know some stories about Jack the Giant-Killer," I announced. "Do you, Lys?"

"I? No, not about a giant-killer, but I know all about the werewolf, and Jeanne-la-Flamme, and the Man in Purple Tatters, and – O dear me, I know lots more."

"You are very wise," said I. "I shall teach his majesty English."

"And I Breton," cried Lys jealously.

"I shall bring playthings to the king," said I – "big green lizards from the gorse, little gray mullets to swim in glass globes, baby rabbits from the forest of Kerselec –"

"And I," said Lys, "will bring the first primrose, the first branch of aubépine, the first jonquil, to the king – my king."

"Our king," said I; and there was peace in Finistère.

I lay back, idly turning the leaves of the curious old volume.

"I am looking," said I, "for the crest."

"The crest, dear? It is a priest's head with an arrow-shaped mark on the forehead, on a field –"

I sat up and stared at my wife.

"Dick, whatever is the matter?" she smiled. "The story is there in that book. Do you care to read it? No? Shall I tell it to you? Well, then: It happened in the third crusade. There was a monk whom men called the Black Priest. He turned apostate, and sold himself to the enemies of Christ. A Sieur de Trevec burst into the Saracen camp, at the head of only one hundred lances, and carried the Black Priest away out of the very midst of their army."

"So that is how you come by the crest," I said quietly; but I thought of the branded skull in the gravel pit, and wondered.

"Yes," said Lys. "The Sieur de Trevec cut the Black Priest's head off, but first he branded him with an arrow mark on the forehead. The book says it was a pious action, and the Sieur de Trevec got great merit by it. But I think it was cruel, the branding," she sighed.

"Did you ever hear of any other Black Priest?"

"Yes. There was one in the last century, here in St. Gildas. He cast a white shadow in the sun. He wrote in the Breton language. Chronicles, too, I believe. I never saw them. His name was the same as that of the old chronicler, and of the other priest, Jacques Sorgue. Some said he was a lineal descendant of the traitor. Of course the first Black Priest was bad enough for anything. But if he did have a child, it need not have been the ancestor of the last Jacques Sorgue. They say he was so good he was not allowed to die, but was caught up to heaven one day," added Lys, with believing eyes.

I smiled.

"But he disappeared," persisted Lys.

"I'm afraid his journey was in another direction," I said jestingly, and thoughtlessly told her the story of the morning. I had utterly forgotten the masked man at her window, but before I finished I remembered him fast enough, and realized what I had done as I saw her face whiten.

"Lys," I urged tenderly, "that was only some clumsy clown's trick. You said so yourself. You are not superstitious, my dear?"

Her eyes were on mine. She slowly drew the little gold cross from her bosom and kissed it. But her lips trembled as they pressed the symbol of faith.

III

ABOUT NINE O'CLOCK the next morning I walked into the Groix Inn and sat down at the long discolored oaken table, nodding good-day to Marianne Bruyere, who in turn bobbed her white coiffe at me.

"My clever Bannalec maid," said I, "what is good for a stirrup-cup at the Groix Inn?"

"Schist?" she inquired in Breton.

"With a dash of red wine, then," I replied.

She brought the delicious Quimperlé cider, and I poured a little Bordeaux into it. Marianne watched me with laughing black eyes.

"What makes your cheeks so red, Marianne?" I asked. "Has Jean Marie been here?"

"We are to be married, Monsieur Darrel," she laughed.

"Ah! Since when has Jean Marie Tregunc lost his head?"

"His head? Oh, Monsieur Darrel – his heart, you mean!"

"So I do," said I. "Jean Marie is a practical fellow."

"It is all due to your kindness –" began the girl, but I raised my hand and held up the glass.

"It's due to himself. To your happiness, Marianne"; and I took a hearty draught of the schist. "Now," said I, "tell me where I can find Le Bihan and Max Fortin."

"Monsieur Le Bihan and Monsieur Fortin are above in the broad room. I believe they are examining the Red Admiral's effects."

"To send them to Paris? Oh, I know. May I go up, Marianne?"

"And God go with you," smiled the girl.

When I knocked at the door of the broad room above little Max Fortin opened it. Dust covered his spectacles and nose; his hat, with the tiny velvet ribbons fluttering, was all awry.

"Come in, Monsieur Darrel," he said; "the mayor and I are packing up the effects of the Purple Emperor and of the poor Red Admiral."

"The collections?" I asked, entering the room. "You must be very careful in packing those butterfly cases; the slightest jar might break wings and antennas, you know."

Le Bihan shook hands with me and pointed to the great pile of boxes.

"They're all cork lined," he said, "but Fortin and I are putting felt around each box. The Entomological Society of Paris pays the freight."

The combined collection of the Red Admiral and the Purple Emperor made a magnificent display.

I lifted and inspected case after case set with gorgeous butterflies and moths, each specimen carefully labeled with the name in Latin. There were cases filled with crimson tiger moths all aflame with color; cases devoted to the common yellow butterflies; symphonies in orange and pale yellow; cases of soft gray and dun-colored sphinx moths; and cases of grayish nettle-bed butterflies of the numerous family of *Vanessa*.

All alone in a great case by itself was pinned the purple emperor, the *Apatura Iris*, that fatal specimen that had given the Purple Emperor his name and quietus.

I remembered the butterfly, and stood looking at it with bent eyebrows.

Le Bihan glanced up from the floor where he was nailing down the lid of a box full of cases.

"It is settled, then," said he, "that madame, your wife, gives the Purple Emperor's entire Collection to the city of Paris?"

I nodded.

"Without accepting anything for it?"

"It is a gift," I said.

"Including the purple emperor there in the case? That butterfly is worth a great deal of money," persisted Le Bihan.

"You don't suppose that we would wish to sell that specimen, do you?" I answered a trifle sharply.

"If I were you I should destroy it," said the mayor in his high-pitched voice.

"That would be nonsense," said I, "like your burying the brass cylinder and scroll yesterday."

"It was not nonsense," said Le Bihan doggedly, "and I should prefer not to discuss the subject of the scroll."

I looked at Max Portin, who immediately avoided my eyes.

"You are a pair of superstitious old women," said I, digging my hands into my pockets; "you swallow every nursery tale that is invented."

"What of it?" said Le Bihan sulkily; "there's more truth than lies in most of 'em."

"Oh!" I sneered, "does the Mayor of St. Gildas and St. Julien believe in the **loup-garou**?"

"No, not in the **loup-garou**."

"In what, then – Jeanne-la-Flamme?"

"That," said Le Bihan with conviction, "is history."

"The devil it is!" said I; "and perhaps, Monsieur the mayor, your faith in giants is unimpaired?"

"There were giants – everybody knows it," growled Max Fortin.

"And you a chemist!" I observed scornfully.

"Listen, Monsieur Darrel," squeaked Le Bihan; "you know yourself that the Purple Emperor was a scientific man. Now suppose I should tell you that he always refused to include in his collection a Death's Messenger?"

"A what?" I exclaimed.

"You know what I mean – that moth that flies by night; some call it the Death's Head, but in St. Gildas we call it 'Death's Messenger.'"

"Oh!" said I, "you mean that big sphinx moth that is commonly known as the 'death's-head moth.' Why the mischief should the people here call it death's messenger?"

"For hundreds of years it has been known as death's messenger in St. Gildas," said Max Fortin. "Even Froissart speaks of it in his commentaries on Jacques Sorgue's *Chronicles*. The book is in your library."

"Sorgue? And who was Jacques Sorgue? I never read his book."

"Jacques Sorgue was the son of some unfrocked priest – I forget. It was during the crusades."

"Good Heavens!" I burst out, "I've been hearing of nothing but crusades and priests and death and sorcery ever since I kicked that skull into the gravel pit, and I am tired of it, I tell you frankly. One would think we lived in the dark ages. Do you know what year of our Lord it is, Le Bihan?"

"Eighteen hundred and ninety-six," replied the mayor.

"And yet you two hulking men are afraid of a death's-head moth."

"I don't care to have one fly into the window," said Max Fortin; "it means evil to the house and the people in it."

"God alone knows why he marked one of his creatures with a yellow death's head on the back," observed Le Bihan piously, "but I take it that he meant it as a warning; and I propose to profit by it," he added triumphantly.

"See here, Le Bihan," I said; "by a stretch of imagination one can make out a skull on the thorax of a certain big sphinx moth. What of it?"

"It is a bad thing to touch," said the mayor wagging his head.

"It squeaks when handled," added Max Fortin.

"Some creatures squeak all the time," I observed, looking hard at Le Bihan.

"Pigs," added the mayor.

"Yes, and asses," I replied. "Listen, Le Bihan: do you mean to tell me that you saw that skull roll uphill yesterday?"

The mayor shut his mouth tightly and picked up his hammer.

"Don't be obstinate," I said; "I asked you a question."

"And I refuse to answer," snapped Le Bihan. "Fortin saw what I saw; let him talk about it."

I looked searchingly at the little chemist.

"I don't say that I saw it actually roll up out of the pit, all by itself," said Fortin with a shiver, "but – but then, how did it come up out of the pit, if it didn't roll up all by itself?"

"It didn't come up at all; that was a yellow cobblestone that you mistook for the skull again," I replied. "You were nervous, Max."

"A – a very curious cobblestone, Monsieur Darrel," said Fortin.

"I also was a victim to the same hallucination," I continued, "and I regret to say that I took the trouble to roll two innocent cobblestones into the gravel pit, imagining each time that it was the skull I was rolling."

"It was," observed Le Bihan with a morose shrug.

"It just shows," said I, ignoring the mayor's remark, "how easy it is to fix up a train of coincidences so that the result seems to savor of the supernatural. Now, last night my wife imagined that she saw a priest in a mask peer in at her window –"

Fortin and Le Bihan scrambled hastily from their knees, dropping hammer and nails.

"W-h-a-t – what's that?" demanded the mayor.

I repeated what I had said. Max Fortin turned livid.

"My God!" muttered Le Bihan, "the Black Priest is in St. Gildas!"

"D-don't you – you know the old prophecy?" stammered Fortin; "Froissart quotes it from Jacques Sorgue:

"'When the Black Priest rises from the dead,
St. Gildas folk shall shriek in bed;
When the Black Priest rises from his grave,
May the good God St. Gildas save!'"

"Aristide Le Bihan," I said angrily, "and you, Max Fortin, I've got enough of this nonsense! Some foolish lout from Bannalec has been in St. Gildas playing tricks to frighten old fools like you. If you have nothing better to talk about than nursery legends I'll wait until you come to your senses. Good-morning." And I walked out, more disturbed than I cared to acknowledge to myself.

The day had become misty and overcast. Heavy, wet clouds hung in the east. I heard the surf thundering against the cliffs, and the gray gulls squealed as they tossed and turned high in the sky. The tide was creeping across the river sands, higher, higher, and I saw the seaweed floating on the beach, and the lançons springing from the foam, silvery threadlike flashes in the gloom. Curlew were flying up the river in twos and threes; the timid sea swallows skimmed across the moors toward some quiet, lonely pool, safe from the coming tempest. In every hedge field birds were gathering, huddling together, twittering restlessly.

When I reached the cliffs I sat down, resting my chin on my clenched hands. Already a vast curtain of rain, sweeping across the ocean miles away, hid the island of Groix. To the east, behind the white semaphore on the hills, black clouds crowded up over the horizon. After a little the thunder boomed, dull, distant, and slender skeins of lightning unraveled across the crest of the coming storm. Under the cliff at my feet the surf rushed foaming over the shore, and the lançons jumped and skipped and quivered until they seemed to be but the reflections of the meshed lightning.

I turned to the east. It was raining over Groix, it was raining at Sainte Barbe, it was raining now at the semaphore. High in the storm whirl a few gulls pitched; a nearer cloud trailed veils of rain in its wake; the sky was spattered with lightning; the thunder boomed.

As I rose to go, a cold raindrop fell upon the back of my hand, and another, and yet another on my face. I gave a last glance at the sea, where the waves were bursting into strange white shapes that seemed to fling out menacing arms toward me. Then something moved on the cliff, something black as the black rock it clutched – a filthy cormorant, craning its hideous head at the sky.

Slowly I plodded homeward across the somber moorland, where the gorse stems glimmered with a dull metallic green, and the heather, no longer violet and purple, hung drenched and dun-colored among the dreary rocks. The wet turf creaked under my heavy boots, the black-thorn scraped and grated against knee and elbow. Over all lay a strange light, pallid, ghastly, where the sea spray whirled across the landscape and drove into my face until it grew numb with the cold. In broad bands, rank after rank, billow on billow, the rain burst out across the endless moors, and yet there was no wind to drive it at such a pace.

Lys stood at the door as I turned into the garden, motioning me to hasten; and then for the first time I became conscious that I was soaked to the skin.

"However in the world did you come to stay out when such a storm threatened?" she said. "Oh, you are dripping! Go quickly and change; I have laid your warm underwear on the bed, Dick."

I kissed my wife, and went upstairs to change my dripping clothes for something more comfortable.

When I returned to the morning room there was a driftwood fire on the hearth, and Lys sat in the chimney corner embroidering.

"Catherine tells me that the fishing fleet from Lorient is out. Do you think they are in danger, dear?" asked Lys, raising her blue eyes to mine as I entered.

"There is no wind, and there will be no sea," said I, looking out of the window. Far across the moor I could see the black cliffs looming in the mist.

"How it rains!" murmured Lys; "come to the fire, Dick."

I threw myself on the fur rug, my hands in my pockets, my head on Lys's knees.

"Tell me a story," I said. "I feel like a boy of ten."

Lys raised a finger to her scarlet lips. I always waited for her to do that.

"Will you be very still, then?" she said.

"Still as death."

"Death," echoed a voice, very softly.

"Did you speak, Lys?" I asked, turning so that I could see her face.

"No; did you, Dick?"

"Who said 'death'?" I asked, startled.

"Death," echoed a voice, softly.

I sprang up and looked about. Lys rose too, her needles and embroidery falling to the floor. She seemed about to faint, leaning heavily on me, and I led her to the window and opened it a little way to give her air. As I did so the chain lightning split the zenith, the thunder crashed, and a sheet of rain swept into the room, driving with it something that fluttered – something that flapped, and squeaked, and beat upon the rug with soft, moist wings.

We bent over it together, Lys clinging to me, and we saw that it was a death's-head moth drenched with rain.

The dark day passed slowly as we sat beside the fire, hand in hand, her head against my breast, speaking of sorrow and mystery and death. For Lys believed that there were things on earth that none might understand, things that must be nameless forever and ever, until God rolls up the scroll of life and all is ended. We spoke of hope and fear and faith, and the mystery of the saints; we spoke of the beginning and the end, of the shadow of sin, of omens, and of love. The moth still lay on the floor quivering its somber wings in the warmth of the fire, the skull and ribs clearly etched upon its neck and body.

"If it is a messenger of death to this house," I said, "why should we fear, Lys?"

"Death should be welcome to those who love God," murmured Lys, and she drew the cross from her breast and kissed it.

"The moth might die if I threw it out into the storm," I said after a silence.

"Let it remain," sighed Lys.

Late that night my wife lay sleeping, and I sat beside her bed and read in the Chronicle of Jacques Sorgue. I shaded the candle, but Lys grew restless, and finally I took the book down into the morning room, where the ashes of the fire rustled and whitened on the hearth.

The death's-head moth lay on the rug before the fire where I had left it. At first I thought it was dead, but when I looked closer I saw a lambent fire in its amber eyes. The straight white shadow it cast across the floor wavered as the candle flickered.

The pages of the Chronicle of Jacques Sorgue were damp and sticky; the illuminated gold and blue initials left flakes of azure and gilt where my hand brushed them.

"It is not paper at all; it is thin parchment," I said to myself; and I held the discolored page close to the candle flame and read, translating laboriously:

"I, Jacques Sorgue, saw all these things. And I saw the Black Mass celebrated in the chapel of St. Gildas-on-the-Cliff. And it was said by the Abbé Sorgue, my kinsman: for which deadly sin the apostate priest was seized by the most noble Marquis of Plougastel and by him condemned to be burned with hot irons, until his seared soul quit its body and fly to its master the devil. But when the Black Priest lay in the crypt of Plougastel, his master Satan came at night and set him free, and carried him across land and sea to Mahmoud, which is Soldan or Saladin. And I, Jacques Sorgue, traveling afterward by sea, beheld with my own eyes my kinsman, the Black Priest of St. Gildas, borne along in the air upon a vast black wing, which was the wing of his master Satan. And this was seen also by two men of the crew."

I turned the page. The wings of the moth on the floor began to quiver. I read on and on, my eyes blurring under the shifting candle flame. I read of battles and of saints, and I learned how the Great Soldan made his pact with Satan, and then I came to the Sieur de Trevec, and read how he seized the Black Priest in the midst of Saladin's tents and carried him away and cut off his head first branding him on the forehead. "And before he suffered," said the Chronicle, "he cursed the Sieur de Trevec and his descendants, and he said he would surely return to St. Gildas. 'For the violence you do to me, I will do violence to you. For the evil I suffer at your hands, I will work evil on you and your descendants. Woe to your children, Sieur de Trevec!'" There was a whirr, a beating of strong wings, and my candle flashed up as in a sudden breeze. A humming filled the room; the great moth darted hither and thither, beating, buzzing, on ceiling and wall. I flung down my book and stepped forward. Now it lay fluttering upon the window sill, and for a moment I had it under my hand, but the thing squeaked and I shrank back. Then suddenly it darted across the candle flame; the light flared and went out, and at the same moment a shadow moved in the darkness outside. I raised my eyes to the window. A masked face was peering in at me.

Quick as thought I whipped out my revolver and fired every cartridge, but the face advanced beyond the window, the glass melting away before it like mist, and through the smoke of my revolver I saw something creep swiftly into the room. Then I tried to cry out, but the thing was at my throat, and I fell backward among the ashes of the hearth.

* * *

When my eyes unclosed I was lying on the hearth, my head among the cold ashes. Slowly I got on my knees, rose painfully, and groped my way to a chair. On the floor lay my revolver, shining in the pale light of early morning. My mind clearing by degrees, I looked, shuddering, at the window. The glass was unbroken. I stooped stiffly, picked up my revolver and opened the cylinder. Every cartridge had been fired. Mechanically I closed the cylinder and placed the revolver in my pocket. The book, the Chronicles of Jacques Sorgue, lay on the table beside me, and as I started to close it I glanced at the page. It was all splashed with rain, and the lettering had run, so that the page was merely a confused blur of gold and red and black. As I stumbled toward the door I cast a fearful glance over my shoulder. The death's-head moth crawled shivering on the rug.

IV

THE SUN was about three hours high. I must have slept, for I was aroused by the sudden gallop of horses under our window. People were shouting and calling in the road. I sprang up and opened the sash. Le Bihan was there, an image of helplessness, and Max Fortin stood beside him polishing his glasses. Some gendarmes had just arrived from Quimperlé, and I could hear them around the corner of the house, stamping, and rattling their sabers and carbines, as they led their horses into my stable.

Lys sat up, murmuring half-sleepy, half-anxious questions.

"I don't know," I answered. "I am going out to see what it means."

"It is like the day they came to arrest you," Lys said, giving me a troubled look. But I kissed her and laughed at her until she smiled too. Then I flung on coat and cap and hurried down the stairs.

The first person I saw standing in the road was the Brigadier Durand.

"Hello!" said I, "have you come to arrest me again? What the devil is all this fuss about, anyway?"

"We were telegraphed for an hour ago," said Durand briskly, "and for a sufficient reason, I think. Look there, Monsieur Darrel!"

He pointed to the ground almost under my feet.

"Good heavens!" I cried, "where did that puddle of blood come from?"

"That's what I want to know, Monsieur Darrel. Max Fortin found it at daybreak. See, it's splashed all over the grass, too. A trail of it leads into your garden, across the flower beds to your very window, the one that opens from the morning room. There is another trail leading from this spot across the road to the cliffs, then to the gravel pit, and thence across the moor to the forest of Kerselec. We are going to mount in a minute and search the bosquets. Will you join us? Bon Dieu! but the fellow bled like an ox. Max Fortin says it's human blood, or I should not have believed it."

The little chemist of Quimperlé came up at that moment, rubbing his glasses with a colored handkerchief.

"Yes, it is human blood," he said, "but one thing puzzles me: the corpuscles are yellow. I never saw any human blood before with yellow corpuscles. But your English Doctor Thompson asserts that he has –"

"Well, it's human blood, anyway – isn't it?" insisted Durand, impatiently.

"Ye-es," admitted Max Fortin.

"Then it's my business to trail it," said the big gendarme, and he called his men and gave the order to mount.

"Did you hear anything last night?" asked Durand of me.

"I heard the rain. I wonder the rain did not wash away these traces."

"They must have come after the rain ceased. See this thick splash, how it lies over and weighs down the wet grass blades. Pah!"

It was a heavy, evil-looking clot, and I stepped back from it, my throat closing in disgust.

"My theory," said the brigadier, "is this: Some of those Biribi fishermen, probably the Icelanders, got an extra glass of cognac into their hides and quarreled on the road. Some of them were slashed, and staggered to your house. But there is only one trail, and yet – and yet, how could all that blood come from only one person? Well, the wounded man, let us say, staggered first to your house and then back here, and he wandered off, drunk and dying, God knows where. That's my theory."

"A very good one," said I calmly. "And you are going to trail him?"

"Yes."

"When?"

"At once. Will you come?"

"Not now. I'll gallop over by-and-by. You are going to the edge of the Kerselec forest?"

"Yes; you will hear us calling. Are you coming, Max Fortin? And you, Le Bihan? Good; take the dog-cart."

The big gendarme tramped around the corner to the stable and presently returned mounted on a strong gray horse, his saber shone on his saddle; his pale yellow and white facings were spotless. The little crowd of white-coiffed women with their children fell back as Durand touched spurs and clattered away followed by his two troopers. Soon after Le Bihan and Max Fortin also departed in the mayor's dingy dog-cart.

"Are you coming?" piped Le Bihan shrilly.

"In a quarter of an hour," I replied, and went back to the house.

When I opened the door of the morning room the death's-head moth was beating its strong wings against the window. For a second I hesitated, then walked over and opened the sash. The creature fluttered out, whirred over the flower beds a moment, then darted across the moorland toward the sea. I called the servants together and questioned them. Josephine, Catherine, Jean Marie Tregunc, not one of them had heard the slightest disturbance during the night. Then I told Jean Marie to saddle my horse, and while I was speaking Lys came down.

"Dearest," I began, going to her.

"You must tell me everything you know, Dick," she interrupted, looking me earnestly in the face.

"But there is nothing to tell – only a drunken brawl, and someone wounded."

"And you are going to ride – where, Dick?"

"Well, over to the edge of Kerselec forest. Durand and the mayor, and Max Fortin, have gone on, following a – a trail."

"What trail?"

"Some blood."

"Where did they find it?"

"Out in the road there." Lys crossed herself.

"Does it come near our house?"

"Yes."

"How near?"

"It comes up to the morning room window," said I, giving in.

Her hand on my arm grew heavy. "I dreamed last night –"

"So did I –" but I thought of the empty cartridges in my revolver, and stopped.

"I dreamed that you were in great danger, and I could not move hand or foot to save you; but you had your revolver, and I called out to you to fire –"

"I did fire!" I cried excitedly.

"You – you fired?"

I took her in my arms. "My darling," I said "something strange has happened – something that I cannot understand as yet. But, of course, there is an explanation. Last night I thought I fired at the Black Priest."

"Ah!" gasped Lys.

"Is that what you dreamed?"

"Yes, yes, that was it! I begged you to fire –"

"And I did."

Her heart was beating against my breast. I held her close in silence.

"Dick," she said at length, "perhaps you killed the – the thing."

"If it was human I did not miss," I answered grimly. "And it was human," I went on, pulling myself together, ashamed of having so nearly gone to pieces. "Of course it was human! The whole affair is plain enough. Not a drunken brawl, as Durand thinks; it was a drunken lout's practical joke, for which he has suffered. I suppose I must have filled him pretty full of bullets, and he has crawled away to die in Kerselec forest. It's a terrible affair; I'm sorry I fired so hastily; but that idiot Le Bihan and Max Fortin have been working on my nerves till I am as hysterical as a schoolgirl," I ended angrily.

"You fired – but the window glass was not shattered," said Lys in a low voice.

"Well, the window was open, then. And as for the – the rest – I've got nervous indigestion, and a doctor will settle the Black Priest for me, Lys."

I glanced out of the window at Tregunc waiting with my horse at the gate.

"Dearest, I think I had better go to join Durand and the others."

"I will go, too."

"Oh, no!"

"Yes, Dick."

"Don't, Lys."

"I shall suffer every moment you are away."

"The ride is too fatiguing, and we can't tell what unpleasant sight you may come upon. Lys, you don't really think there is anything supernatural in this affair?"

"Dick," she answered gently, "I am a Bretonne." With both arms around my neck, my wife said, "Death is the gift of God. I do not fear it when we are together. But alone – oh, my husband, I should fear a God who could take you away from me!"

We kissed each other soberly, simply, like two children. Then Lys hurried away to change her gown, and I paced up and down the garden waiting for her.

She came, drawing on her slender gauntlets. I swung her into the saddle, gave a hasty order to Jean Marie, and mounted.

Now, to quail under thoughts of terror on a morning like this, with Lys in the saddle beside me, no matter what had happened or might happen was impossible. Moreover, Môme came sneaking after us. I asked Tregunc to catch him, for I was afraid he might be brained by our horses' hoofs if he followed, but the wily puppy dodged and bolted after Lys, who was trotting along the highroad. "Never mind," I thought; "if he's hit he'll live, for he has no brains to lose."

Lys was waiting for me in the road beside the Shrine of Our Lady of St. Gildas when I joined her. She crossed herself, I doffed my cap, then we shook out our bridles and galloped toward the forest of Kerselec.

We said very little as we rode. I always loved to watch Lys in the saddle. Her exquisite figure and lovely face were the incarnation of youth and grace; her curling hair glistened like threaded gold.

Out of the corner of my eye I saw the spoiled puppy Môme come bounding cheerfully alongside, oblivious of our horses' heels. Our road swung close to the cliffs. A filthy cormorant rose from the black rocks and flapped heavily across our path. Lys's horse reared, but she pulled him down, and pointed at the bird with her riding crop.

"I see," said I; "it seems to be going our way. Curious to see a cormorant in a forest, isn't it?"

"It is a bad sign," said Lys. "You know the Morbihan proverb: 'When the cormorant turns from the sea, Death laughs in the forest, and wise woodsmen build boats.'"

"I wish," said I sincerely, "that there were fewer proverbs in Brittany."

We were in sight of the forest now; across the gorse I could see the sparkle of gendarmes' trappings, and the glitter of Le Bihan's silver-buttoned jacket. The hedge was low and we took it without difficulty, and trotted across the moor to where Le Bihan and Durand stood gesticulating.

They bowed ceremoniously to Lys as we rode up.

"The trail is horrible – it is a river," said the mayor in his squeaky voice. "Monsieur Darrel, I think perhaps madame would scarcely care to come any nearer."

Lys drew bridle and looked at me.

"It is horrible!" said Durand, walking up beside me; "it looks as though a bleeding regiment had passed this way. The trail winds and winds about here in the thickets; we lose it at times, but we always find it again. I can't understand how one man – no, nor twenty – could bleed like that!"

A halloo, answered by another, sounded from the depths of the forest.

"It's my men; they are following the trail," muttered the brigadier. "God alone knows what is at the end!"

"Shall we gallop back, Lys?" I asked.

"No; let us ride along the western edge of the woods and dismount. The sun is so hot now, and I should like to rest for a moment," she said.

"The western forest is clear of anything disagreeable," said Durand.

"Very well," I answered; "call me, Le Bihan, if you find anything."

Lys wheeled her mare, and I followed across the springy heather, Môme trotting cheerfully in the rear.

We entered the sunny woods about a quarter of a kilometer from where we left Durand. I took Lys from her horse, flung both bridles over a limb, and, giving my wife my arm, aided her to a flat mossy rock which overhung a shallow brook gurgling among the beech trees. Lys sat down and drew off her gauntlets. Môme pushed his head into her lap, received an undeserved caress, and came doubtfully toward me. I was weak enough to condone his offense, but I made him lie down at my feet, greatly to his disgust.

I rested my head on Lys's knees, looking up at the sky through the crossed branches of the trees.

"I suppose I have killed him," I said. "It shocks me terribly, Lys."

"You could not have known, dear. He may have been a robber, and – if – not – did – have you ever fired your revolver since that day four years ago when the Red Admiral's son tried to kill you? But I know you have not."

"No," said I, wondering. "It's a fact, I have not. Why?"

"And don't you remember that I asked you to let me load it for you the day when Yves went off, swearing to kill you and his father?"

"Yes, I do remember. Well?"

"Well, I – I took the cartridges first to St. Gildas chapel and dipped them in holy water. You must not laugh, Dick," said Lys gently, laying her cool hands on my lips.

"Laugh, my darling!"

Overhead the October sky was pale amethyst, and the sunlight burned like orange flame through the yellow leaves of beech and oak. Gnats and midges danced and wavered overhead; a spider dropped from a twig halfway to the ground and hung suspended on the end of his gossamer thread.

"Are you sleepy, dear?" asked Lys, bending over me.

"I am – a little; I scarcely slept two hours last night," I answered.

"You may sleep, if you wish," said Lys, and touched my eyes caressingly.

"Is my head heavy on your knees?"

"No, Dick."

I was already in a half doze; still I heard the brook babbling under the beeches and the humming of forest flies overhead. Presently even these were stilled.

The next thing I knew I was sitting bolt upright, my ears ringing with a scream, and I saw Lys cowering beside me, covering her white face with both hands.

As I sprang to my feet she cried again and clung to my knees. I saw my dog rush growling into a thicket, then I heard him whimper, and he came backing out, whining, ears flat, tail down. I stooped and disengaged Lys's hand.

"Don't go, Dick!" she cried. "O God, it's the Black Priest!"

In a moment I had leaped across the brook and pushed my way into the thicket. It was empty. I stared about me; I scanned every tree trunk, every bush. Suddenly I saw him. He was seated on a fallen log, his head resting in his hands, his rusty black robe gathered around him. For a moment my hair stirred under my cap; sweat started on forehead and cheek bone; then I recovered my reason, and understood that the man was human and was probably wounded to death. Ay, to death; for there at my feet, lay the wet trail of blood, over leaves and stones, down into the little hollow, across to the figure in black resting silently under the trees.

I saw that he could not escape even if he had the strength, for before him, almost at his very feet, lay a deep, shining swamp.

As I stepped forward my foot broke a twig. At the sound the figure started a little, then its head fell forward again. Its face was masked. Walking up to the man, I bade him tell where he was wounded. Durand and the others broke through the thicket at the same moment and hurried to my side.

"Who are you who hide a masked face in a priest's robe?" said the gendarme loudly.

There was no answer.

"See – see the stiff blood all over his robe," muttered Le Bihan to Fortin.

"He will not speak," said I.

"He may be too badly wounded," whispered Le Bihan.

"I saw him raise his head," I said, "my wife saw him creep up here."

Durand stepped forward and touched the figure.

"Speak!" he said.

"Speak!" quavered Fortin.

Durand waited a moment, then with a sudden upward movement he stripped off the mask and threw back the man's head. We were looking into the eye sockets of a skull. Durand stood rigid; the mayor shrieked. The skeleton burst out from its rotting robes and collapsed on the ground before us. From between the staring ribs and the grinning teeth spurted a torrent of black blood, showering the shrinking grasses; then the thing shuddered, and fell over into the black ooze of the bog. Little bubbles of iridescent air appeared from the mud; the bones were slowly engulfed, and, as the last fragments sank out of sight, up from the depths and along the bank crept a creature, shiny, shivering, quivering its wings.

It was a death's-head moth.

* * *

I wish I had time to tell you how Lys outgrew superstitions – for she never knew the truth about the affair, and she never will know, since she has promised not to read this book. I wish I might tell you about the king and his coronation, and how the coronation robe fitted. I wish that I were able to write how Yvonne and Herbert Stuart rode to a boar hunt in Quimperle, and how the hounds raced the quarry right through the town, overturning three gendarmes, the notary, and an old woman. But I am becoming garrulous and Lys is calling me to come and hear the king say that he is sleepy. And his highness shall not be kept waiting.

The King's Cradle Song

Seal with a seal of gold
The scroll of a life unrolled;
Swathe him deep in his purple stole;
Ashes of diamonds, crystalled coal,
Drops of gold in each scented fold.

Crimson wings of the Little Death,
Stir his hair with your silken breath;
Flaming wings of sins to be,
Splendid pinions of prophecy,
Smother his eyes with hues and dyes,
While the white moon spins and the winds arise,
And the stars drip through the skies.

Wave, O wings of the Little Death!
Seal his sight and stifle his breath,
Cover his breast with the gemmed shroud pressed;
From north to north, from west to west,
Wave, O wings of the Little Death!
Till the white moon reels in the cracking skies,
And the ghosts of God arise.

Ghost Farm

by Zach Chapman

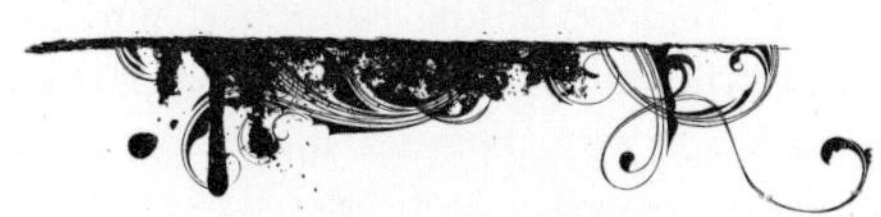

OUTSIDE THE MANOR, rain pelted the rural landscape, turning the fields to marsh and the roads to muck. An impossibly broad figure stood alone, toiling away with a spade, digging shallow, unmarked graves. A dozen luxury vehicles seemed out of place, parked neatly next to the gravedigger and slanted manor.

Inside the manor, a potential client spoke with a fake British accent. "I never drink anything bottled this century," he said, waving his chubby hand, dismissing the complementary wine.

The waiter nodded and continued down the table, pouring the dark wine for any client who wanted. Altogether there were thirteen. Most were over forty; all were white. They complained loudly over their empty dinner plates. The steak had been too bloody, far too rare. And there was a sweet stench to the manor, like rotten candy.

It was almost midnight.

When the hour finally struck, a chime filled the dining hall and a tall man wearing a well-tailored suit appeared at the head of the table. "Good evening, ladies and gentlemen. I trust the meal was rather filling. My name is Irving. I will be your representative and tour guide tonight. You have already read and signed the release so you'll know that before you can see any of our products you'll be strip-searched for cellphones, electronic devices, and anything that may be used as a recording device."

A few clients who had not read the fine print grumbled at that.

"We have streamlined the process. Your comfort is one of our greatest concerns. Though after any purchases…" He smiled wickedly. At the side of the room, a curtain raised, revealing two doors. "Strip-searches shall be quick. Once this is over, we go downstairs to the Sub-Villa."

After every client momentarily shed their timeless formal attire behind closed doors, Irving led them down a cracked spiral staircase. The smell of wet stone, and many years, betrayed the age of the place. It was much older than the slanted manor that was built around it. Centuries old. More than that. Timeless. And dark.

Irving brought the clients to a halt. "Once you step off this staircase and into the antechamber, you shall be in a very elite, very small group, even if you don't purchase any of our products. Fewer than eleven hundred souls have passed through these hallways." He paused for impeccable dramatic effect. "Ladies and gentlemen, are you ready?"

The group flowed out of the spiral staircase, nearly tripping over themselves in excitement, and crowded the hallway.

"The Sub-Villa has been in business for many years. As you should know, our products are world famous. Though, of course, our business does not take credit. Tonight you will see all products we have to offer at the moment, hear some testimonies and glimpse the casting process." Irving ushered the clients forward through the cramped hallway. "Without further ado, let us meet the first product."

Black rock walls and sconces and echoes flanked the clients. Irving led the party to a windowed panel, nothing but shadows on the other side. When he flipped a panel on the sidewall, a light on the other side of the panel flickered on. Through warped glass, rows of pews faced them. Sitting on a pew was a bearded man, gray and withered. To his left lay a rope with three thick bloody knots tied at one end. On a second inspection, one could see wet visible protrusions from under his robe, welts the size of a child's fist.

"The Sub-Villa has named him The Apostate. He has been with us for twenty years. He is our most budget-friendly product."

"How much?" A client asked.

Irving's thin mustache twitched. "Please hold all questions regarding pricing for your after tour appraising consultation. Now... before we apprehended him, The Apostate was charged with abusing an altar-boy. He has been repenting for quite some time now; still, this product is not advised for households with small children."

"How are the products chosen?" a woman in her early forties asked.

"We have a large database where subjects are monitored. There are many determining factors. We ensure that we have a large variety of products at any given time."

"Mr Irving, what physical object will the product haunt?"

"That is a good question. In The Apostate's rare case, the client will have the option to choose –" Irving pointed through the window "– between that crucifix he wears, and that gruesome rope. More details will be revealed on the casting process later this evening. Let us continue onto more of the products."

Just as the holding cell became black, another one down the hallway lit up. The woman from earlier touched the glass, running her fingers over the ancient warps.

"If you could, avoid touching the glass. Your psychic resonance may disrupt our processes. Also, unwanted products may taint you. The Sub-Villa does not condone any trauma or psychic phenomena brought on without the purchase of our products. If you witness any, please see one of our certified exorcists for a diagnosis and plan. Let me be clearer: haunts without purchase is theft of service."

Inside the next cell stood a mumbling woman. Irving hefted a lever up and down until the glass shook and slowly disappeared into the ceiling as he cranked. At the soft noises of Irving's assertions, the woman looked up; swollen holes gaped under her eyebrows. Many of the clients gasped. Irving stepped forward into the cell. "If you want to touch, now is a good opportunity. Please dip your hands in our psychic disinfectant agent. It's a variant of Vatican holy water, brewed with something special." He motioned to a bowl at the side of the cell. "This will insure there is no residual bleeding. You may touch her arms, cheek, hair, but please don't be too invasive."

Upon hearing Irving's voice, the woman wailed but made no motion to move. Her mouth was absent of teeth and tongue. Several clients quickly washed their hands in the disinfectant and began running their hands on her cold skin.

A redheaded woman was too terrified to proceed. Two others also refused to touch the blind woman.

"Cold feet?" Irving did his best to hide a grin.

He continued his pitch. "This one is modeled after the classic Hag. A beautiful gothic legend. Many accounts of similar past products have stated the entity floats above their beds, howling. Witnesses report a dread so deep it causes paralysis or a terror that causes involuntary screaming. Extreme cases may cause shortness of breath or an inability to scream. In recent years we've put a warning on these products; avoid buying if household members suffer from asthma or have any chronic disorders that disrupt normal breathing."

The more excited clients spoke giddily.

"Ahh, feel how cold she is, Martha."

"How creepy."

"Darling, isn't she wonderful? She reminds me of grandmother."

"Oh, I like her! That moan she makes is terrifying."

"It looks like she's weeping blood."

"Her skin is so cold. It feels real."

Irving smiled. "I assure you. She's real… There are many more products for you to see tonight. Now you've had a chance to touch her, please rinse your hands in the holy water provided at the exit. That *is* mandatory."

Reluctant fingers wriggled away from The Hag's skin. Irving motioned the crowd out of the cell as he spoke. "As I said before, some products we have are similar to popular ones sold in the past. However, this does not mean each product isn't unique. Every entity is an individual – different from its predecessors."

"So we are not getting a generic hag?"

"Sir, none of our products are *generic*." Irving said as he lowered the glass panel shut behind the last exiting client. Irving led the way to the next cell. Inside stood a man who must have been seven feet tall. Long stringy hair fell past his broad, slumped shoulders. At some point, he'd freed himself from a straitjacket. Broken buckles and ripped seams dangled off him.

"The Patient. When he was fourteen he murdered his family with a cordless circular saw after tying them to their beds in their sleep. Before the Sub-Villa obtained The Patient, he terrorized and killed four families. He's heavily sedated to keep him in a safe, manageable state. When obtaining this one, he broke a Villa employee's neck and vivisected him. We suggest this product goes to a home whose occupant is intimately familiar with the paranormal, preferably one who has a strong connection with his or her spirit guide."

The Patient slowly walked toward the glass, staring intently through it. A vein in The Patient's forehead pulsed and he bared his teeth. A shudder ran through the clients.

At first, his screams were incomprehensible. His face swelled red. Spit flecked the glass divider but on the other side his thunderous voice was little more than a murmur. "I'll break down this glass wall and stab you with the shards. Do you hear me?"

"Even with the sedation drugs, he is rather excitable." Irving pulled out a handkerchief and dabbed his forehead. It appeared to be a practiced motion.

Suddenly The Patient pounded on the glass. The *boom* echoed off the stone floor and ceiling. He thrust his fists against the glass again, the metal buckles making sharp pangs as they slapped against the barrier.

A client's laughter roared back. "Oh, I like this one. He has audacity. He'd make a great fright to put in my brother's house."

Boom. Boom. Boom. Irving looked uneasy as the glass wavered. Hairline cracks manifested at the edges. Irving's tenor voice was even. "If you would all step back from The Patient."

The Patient's fists smashed through the glass, sending shards and droplets of blood across the hall. Clients shrieked, scattering away in all directions. Irving put himself between the clients and The Patient, snatching a device from inside his breast pocket. His long finger pulled the trigger of an electrical stun gun as The Patient closed in on him. Two electrode darts shot from the gun and found purchase in The Patient's hulking chest.

Click. Click. Click.

His attacker dropped immediately, convulsing. His head cracked against the floor and his eyes rolled up into his skull. White foam frothed from his mouth then slowly turned brown as it mixed with blood.

Irving raised thin eyebrows as a quiet applause passed through the clients. "I apologize. It appears something unprofessional always tends to happen. Is anyone hurt? No? Good. Any questions about this beast?"

A client clearly trying to hide a large erection asked, "Can we kill him?"

"I'm sorry?"

"I mean if we purchase this product. Are we allowed to physically kill them before the casting process? They have to die anyways before that. Can we be the ones that do that?"

"Hmm. You'll have to work that out during your after-tour appraising consultation. It is doable but it'll surely be more expensive."

None of the other clients had any questions. Mostly, they stared at The Patient's twitching body, watching as dark liquid filled the cracks in the stone floor. Irving ushered them forward and the gorgeous redhead client asked, "What about him?"

"Our staff is already on it. Let's round the corner. We'll come back to visit the rest of the products on this row after this mess has been seen to."

Irving showed the potential clients a variety of inspired products: Mr Voodoo, The Addict, The Bride, Chaeronea of Lyon, The Doctor, The Twins I and II (a unique set of products), Yotsuya the Samurai, Banshee, The Infected, Jaw, The Father, Klepto, The Paraplegic and The Aborigine. Each product was met with the appropriate awes, gasps and questions. Unfortunately, there was a lull of clichéd products down the final corridor, all with similar origins and product warnings: Cutter, The Slaver, Slicer, Ripper, The Tongueless and The Butcher.

Just as the clients grew restless, Irving led them away from the cells to a room full of wooden racks.

"This is the Totem Incubation Room."

The odor of mold choked the atmosphere of the small room and mixed with a more sinister scent. The smell of earthen shadows. Of things that have died, but still live. Hundreds of totems lined the shelving: on the one closest to Irving sat jewelry, a framed black and white photograph, a thick leather book, a sharpened spoon, china figurines, a metal rook chess piece, several crucifixes, a scepter, a rusted cordless circular saw and a globe.

Some in the group chatted lightheartedly over which products they planned to buy, a few others grumbled complaints. Their tones edged on bitterness when one client discovered another wanted the same haunt. "I wonder how *that* will be determined during our after-tour appraising consultation," the disgruntled client spat at the other as their argument escalated.

Irving cut the two off. "Gentlemen and ladies, mind these items. This is where alternative totems are stored. Touching one during this process can be quite detrimental to your psychic health."

The group quieted down and listened to Irving talk around the details of how exactly souls were bound to the totems. To his left hung five robes with embroidered runes, dimly glowing.

To his right was a vat of dark liquid. Irving explained that the vat contained liquid morphic resonance amplifiers and that the robes helped the caster (sometimes he, himself) channel the soul into the correct medium – the chosen totem – by matching certain vibrational frequencies.

As Irving neared the end of his explanation, an elderly client reached for a golden locket dangling off a splintered shelf. As his fingers wrapped around it, the lights flickered. Irving's eyes darted to the man's grasp on the totem. Like a bullwhip, Irving snatched the totem out of the client's fingers.

He chanted loudly as the whole room began to rumble; totems rattled on their racks. A few fell to the floor. Smoke boiled from the tight fist Irving had made around the locket. A client shrieked. Irving dipped his hand in the vat, pulled it out and slammed it down on the closest surface available. Flexing his fist several times, he sighed and wrapped his handkerchief around his trembling hand.

"That was dangerous. Everyone in here was at risk." He shook his head. "Tonight has been quite adventurous. Very well, I believe this to be the climax of our evening. The tour is adjourned." He led them out of the Totem Incubation Room. "Now. There are two paths to choose from. Path one: You are ready to make your purchases and be counseled through your appraising consultation."

He peered around, making eye contact with each individual potential client. "Path two: Maybe the thought of owning a ghost no longer seems as glamorous as you had once thought. Maybe you just took the tour and never had any intention of buying. Maybe the tour has disgusted you. Or maybe you just aren't ready for the purchase."

He continued as a mammoth-sized man stepped out of the shadows. "Option one, form a line and follow Brute out of the antechamber. Pardon his saturated state. He'd been digging graves to accommodate the new sales. Option two, please follow me. I'll lead you to the exit."

Four clients, led by the redheaded woman, fell in behind Irving. Irving cocked an eyebrow at her. "Are you certain? No product struck your fancy?"

"Very certain," she said, determination in her voice.

"Right, then. No swaying you." He marched the four down the gloomy corridor until they reached a 1930s-style elevator. He motioned the clients ahead of him, through the folding lattice doors and said, "Ladies and gentlemen, careful on your step. This old elevator bounces and sways."

He helped each into the elevator and took a step back into the hallway as the lattice doors slammed shut. Steel cables cried under the weight of the occupants.

"What's the meaning of this?" the redhead demanded. "Are you going to show us out or not? How are we to get to our cars?"

"Brute will have to deal with your cars, I'm afraid. One of you asked earlier how we obtain our products. Now you'll see first hand."

He cranked a lever to the side of the elevator. Instead of going up, the elevator shook, then descended slowly. Shouts filled the chamber. *Yes,* Irving thought. *What great specimens. One day they'll make great haunts.*

"You can't do this!"

"Stop this elevator right now!"

Irving turned, walking back toward where the real money was and whistled a tune. The shouts stalked him as he strolled, so he whistled harder. *Now,* he thought, *time to make some sales.*

Mrs Zant and the Ghost

Wilkie Collins

I

THE COURSE OF THIS NARRATIVE describes the return of a disembodied spirit to earth, and leads the reader on new and strange ground.

Not in the obscurity of midnight, but in the searching light of day, did the supernatural influence assert itself. Neither revealed by a vision, nor announced by a voice, it reached mortal knowledge through the sense which is least easily self-deceived: the sense that feels.

The record of this event will of necessity produce conflicting impressions. It will raise, in some minds, the doubt which reason asserts; it will invigorate, in other minds, the hope which faith justifies; and it will leave the terrible question of the destinies of man, where centuries of vain investigation have left it – in the dark.

Having only undertaken in the present narrative to lead the way along a succession of events, the writer declines to follow modern examples by thrusting himself and his opinions on the public view. He returns to the shadow from which he has emerged, and leaves the opposing forces of incredulity and belief to fight the old battle over again, on the old ground.

II

THE EVENTS happened soon after the first thirty years of the present century had come to an end.

On a fine morning, early in the month of April, a gentleman of middle age (named Rayburn) took his little daughter Lucy out for a walk in the woodland pleasure-ground of Western London, called Kensington Gardens.

The few friends whom he possessed reported of Mr Rayburn (not unkindly) that he was a reserved and solitary man. He might have been more accurately described as a widower devoted to his only surviving child. Although he was not more than forty years of age, the one pleasure which made life enjoyable to Lucy's father was offered by Lucy herself.

Playing with her ball, the child ran on to the southern limit of the Gardens, at that part of it which still remains nearest to the old Palace of Kensington. Observing close at hand one of those spacious covered seats, called in England "alcoves", Mr Rayburn was reminded that he had the morning's newspaper in his pocket, and that he might do well to rest and read. At that early hour the place was a solitude.

"Go on playing, my dear," he said; "but take care to keep where I can see you."

Lucy tossed up her ball; and Lucy's father opened his newspaper. He had not been reading for more than ten minutes, when he felt a familiar little hand laid on his knee.

"Tired of playing?" he inquired – with his eyes still on the newspaper.

"I'm frightened, papa."

He looked up directly. The child's pale face startled him. He took her on his knee and kissed her.

"You oughtn't to be frightened, Lucy, when I am with you," he said, gently. "What is it?" He looked out of the alcove as he spoke, and saw a little dog among the trees. "Is it the dog?" he asked.

Lucy answered:

"It's not the dog – it's the lady."

The lady was not visible from the alcove.

"Has she said anything to you?" Mr Rayburn inquired.

"No."

"What has she done to frighten you?"

The child put her arms round her father's neck.

"Whisper, papa," she said; "I'm afraid of her hearing us. I think she's mad."

"Why do you think so, Lucy?"

"She came near to me. I thought she was going to say something. She seemed to be ill."

"Well? And what then?"

"She looked at me."

There, Lucy found herself at a loss how to express what she had to say next – and took refuge in silence.

"Nothing very wonderful, so far," her father suggested.

"Yes, papa – but she didn't seem to see me when she looked."

"Well, and what happened then?"

"The lady was frightened – and that frightened me. I think," the child repeated positively, "she's mad."

It occurred to Mr Rayburn that the lady might be blind. He rose at once to set the doubt at rest.

"Wait here," he said, "and I'll come back to you."

But Lucy clung to him with both hands; Lucy declared that she was afraid to be by herself. They left the alcove together.

The new point of view at once revealed the stranger, leaning against the trunk of a tree. She was dressed in the deep mourning of a widow. The pallor of her face, the glassy stare in her eyes, more than accounted for the child's terror – it excused the alarming conclusion at which she had arrived.

"Go nearer to her," Lucy whispered.

They advanced a few steps. It was now easy to see that the lady was young, and wasted by illness – but (arriving at a doubtful conclusion perhaps under the present circumstances) apparently possessed of rare personal attractions in happier days. As the father and daughter advanced a little, she discovered them. After some hesitation, she left the tree; approached with an evident intention of speaking; and suddenly paused. A change to astonishment and fear animated her vacant eyes. If it had not been plain before, it was now beyond all doubt that she was not a poor blind creature, deserted and helpless. At the same time, the expression of her face was not easy to understand. She could hardly have looked more amazed and bewildered, if the two strangers who were observing her had suddenly vanished from the place in which they stood.

Mr Rayburn spoke to her with the utmost kindness of voice and manner.

"I am afraid you are not well," he said. "Is there anything that I can do –"

The next words were suspended on his lips. It was impossible to realize such a state of things; but the strange impression that she had already produced on him was now confirmed. If he could believe his senses, her face did certainly tell him that he was invisible and inaudible to the woman whom he had just addressed! She moved slowly away with a heavy sigh, like a person disappointed and distressed. Following her with his eyes, he saw the dog once more – a little smooth-coated terrier of the ordinary English breed. The dog showed none of the restless activity of his race. With his head down and his tail depressed, he crouched like a creature paralyzed by fear. His mistress roused him by a call. He followed her listlessly as she turned away.

After walking a few paces only, she suddenly stood still.

Mr Rayburn heard her talking to herself.

"Did I feel it again?" she said, as if perplexed by some doubt that awed or grieved her. After a while her arms rose slowly, and opened with a gentle caressing action – an embrace strangely offered to the empty air! "No," she said to herself, sadly, after waiting a moment. "More perhaps when tomorrow comes – no more today." She looked up at the clear blue sky. "The beautiful sunlight! the merciful sunlight!" she murmured. "I should have died if it had happened in the dark."

Once more she called to the dog; and once more she walked slowly away.

"Is she going home, papa?' the child asked.

"We will try and find out," the father answered.

He was by this time convinced that the poor creature was in no condition to be permitted to go out without someone to take care of her. From motives of humanity, he was resolved on making the attempt to communicate with her friends.

III

THE LADY left the Gardens by the nearest gate; stopping to lower her veil before she turned into the busy thoroughfare which leads to Kensington. Advancing a little way along the High Street, she entered a house of respectable appearance, with a card in one of the windows which announced that apartments were to let.

Mr Rayburn waited a minute – then knocked at the door, and asked if he could see the mistress of the house. The servant showed him into a room on the ground floor, neatly but scantily furnished. One little white object varied the grim brown monotony of the empty table. It was a visiting-card.

With a child's unceremonious curiosity Lucy pounced on the card, and spelled the name, letter by letter: "Z, A, N, T," she repeated. "What does that mean?"

Her father looked at the card, as he took it away from her, and put it back on the table. The name was printed, and the address was added in pencil: "Mr John Zant, Purley's Hotel."

The mistress made her appearance. Mr Rayburn heartily wished himself out of the house again, the moment he saw her. The ways in which it is possible to cultivate the social virtues are more numerous and more varied than is generally supposed. This lady's way had apparently accustomed her to meet her fellow-creatures on the hard ground of justice without mercy. Something in her eyes, when she looked at Lucy, said: "I wonder whether that child gets punished when she deserves it?"

"Do you wish to see the rooms which I have to let?" she began.

Mr Rayburn at once stated the object of his visit – as clearly, as civilly, and as concisely as a man could do it. He was conscious (he added) that he had been guilty perhaps of an act of intrusion.

The manner of the mistress of the house showed that she entirely agreed with him. He suggested, however, that his motive might excuse him. The mistress's manner changed, and asserted a difference of opinion.

"I only know the lady whom you mention," she said, "as a person of the highest respectability, in delicate health. She has taken my first-floor apartments, with excellent references; and she gives remarkably little trouble. I have no claim to interfere with her proceedings, and no reason to doubt that she is capable of taking care of herself."

Mr Rayburn unwisely attempted to say a word in his own defence.

"Allow me to remind you –" he began.

"Of what, sir?"

"Of what I observed, when I happened to see the lady in Kensington Gardens."

"I am not responsible for what you observed in Kensington Gardens. If your time is of any value, pray don't let me detain you."

Dismissed in those terms, Mr Rayburn took Lucy's hand and withdrew. He had just reached the door, when it was opened from the outer side. The Lady of Kensington Gardens stood before him. In the position which he and his daughter now occupied, their backs were toward the window. Would she remember having seen them for a moment in the Gardens?

"Excuse me for intruding on you," she said to the landlady. "Your servant tells me my brother-in-law called while I was out. He sometimes leaves a message on his card."

She looked for the message, and appeared to be disappointed: there was no writing on the card.

Mr Rayburn lingered a little in the doorway on the chance of hearing something more. The landlady's vigilant eyes discovered him.

"Do you know this gentleman?" she said maliciously to her lodger.

"Not that I remember."

Replying in those words, the lady looked at Mr Rayburn for the first time; and suddenly drew back from him.

"Yes," she said, correcting herself; "I think we met –"

Her embarrassment overpowered her; she could say no more.

Mr Rayburn compassionately finished the sentence for her.

"We met accidentally in Kensington Gardens," he said.

She seemed to be incapable of appreciating the kindness of his motive. After hesitating a little she addressed a proposal to him, which seemed to show distrust of the landlady.

"Will you let me speak to you upstairs in my own rooms?" she asked.

Without waiting for a reply, she led the way to the stairs. Mr Rayburn and Lucy followed. They were just beginning the ascent to the first floor, when the spiteful landlady left the lower room, and called to her lodger over their heads: "Take care what you say to this man, Mrs Zant! He thinks you're mad."

Mrs Zant turned round on the landing, and looked at him. Not a word fell from her lips. She suffered, she feared, in silence. Something in the sad submission of her face touched the springs of innocent pity in Lucy's heart. The child burst out crying.

That artless expression of sympathy drew Mrs Zant down the few stairs which separated her from Lucy.

"May I kiss your dear little girl?" she said to Mr Rayburn. The landlady, standing on the mat below, expressed her opinion of the value of caresses, as compared with a sounder method of treating young persons in tears: "If that child was mine," she remarked, "I would give her something to cry for."

In the meantime, Mrs Zant led the way to her rooms.

The first words she spoke showed that the landlady had succeeded but too well in prejudicing her against Mr Rayburn.

"Will you let me ask your child," she said to him, "why you think me mad?"

He met this strange request with a firm answer.

"You don't know yet what I really do think. Will you give me a minute's attention?"

"No," she said positively. "The child pities me, I want to speak to the child. What did you see me do in the Gardens, my dear, that surprised you?" Lucy turned uneasily to her father; Mrs Zant persisted. "I first saw you by yourself, and then I saw you with your father," she went on. "When I came nearer to you, did I look very oddly – as if I didn't see you at all?"

Lucy hesitated again; and Mr Rayburn interfered.

"You are confusing my little girl," he said. "Allow me to answer your questions – or excuse me if I leave you."

There was something in his look, or in his tone, that mastered her. She put her hand to her head.

"I don't think I'm fit for it," she answered vacantly. "My courage has been sorely tried already. If I can get a little rest and sleep, you may find me a different person. I am left a great deal by myself; and I have reasons for trying to compose my mind. Can I see you tomorrow? Or write to you? Where do you live?"

Mr Rayburn laid his card on the table in silence. She had strongly excited his interest. He honestly desired to be of some service to this forlorn creature – abandoned so cruelly, as it seemed, to her own guidance. But he had no authority to exercise, no sort of claim to direct her actions, even if she consented to accept his advice. As a last resource he ventured on an allusion to the relative of whom she had spoken downstairs.

"When do you expect to see your brother-in-law again?" he said.

"I don't know," she answered. "I should like to see him – he is so kind to me."

She turned aside to take leave of Lucy.

"Good-by, my little friend. If you live to grow up, I hope you will never be such a miserable woman as I am." She suddenly looked round at Mr Rayburn. "Have you got a wife at home?" she asked.

"My wife is dead."

"And you have a child to comfort you! Please leave me; you harden my heart. Oh, sir, don't you understand? You make me envy you!"

Mr Rayburn was silent when he and his daughter were out in the street again. Lucy, as became a dutiful child, was silent, too. But there are limits to human endurance – and Lucy's capacity for self-control gave way at last.

"Are you thinking of the lady, papa?" she said.

He only answered by nodding his head. His daughter had interrupted him at that critical moment in a man's reflections, when he is on the point of making up his mind. Before they were at home again Mr Rayburn had arrived at a decision. Mrs Zant's brother-in-law was evidently ignorant of any serious necessity for his interference – or he would have made arrangements for immediately repeating his visit. In this state of things, if any evil happened to Mrs Zant, silence on Mr Rayburn's part might be indirectly to blame for a serious misfortune. Arriving at that conclusion, he decided upon running the risk of being rudely received, for the second time, by another stranger.

Leaving Lucy under the care of her governess, he went at once to the address that had been written on the visiting-card left at the lodging-house, and sent in his name. A courteous message was returned. Mr John Zant was at home, and would be happy to see him.

IV

MR RAYBURN was shown into one of the private sitting-rooms of the hôtel.

He observed that the customary position of the furniture in a room had been, in some respects, altered. An armchair, a side-table, and a footstool had all been removed to one of the windows, and had been placed as close as possible to the light. On the table lay a large open roll of morocco leather, containing rows of elegant little instruments in steel and ivory. Waiting by the table, stood Mr John Zant. He said "Good-morning" in a bass voice, so profound and so melodious that those two commonplace words assumed a new importance, coming from his lips. His personal appearance was in harmony with his magnificent voice – he was a tall, finely-made man of dark complexion; with big brilliant black eyes, and a noble curling beard, which hid the whole lower part of his face. Having bowed with a happy mingling of dignity and politeness, the conventional side of this gentleman's character suddenly vanished; and a crazy side, to all appearance, took its place. He dropped on his knees in front of the footstool. Had he forgotten to say his prayers that morning, and was he in such a hurry to remedy the fault that he had no time to spare for consulting appearances? The doubt had hardly suggested itself, before it was set at rest in a most unexpected manner. Mr Zant looked at his visitor with a bland smile, and said:

"Please let me see your feet."

For the moment, Mr Rayburn lost his presence of mind. He looked at the instruments on the side-table.

"Are you a corn-cutter?" was all he could say.

"Excuse me, sir," returned the polite operator, "the term you use is quite obsolete in our profession." He rose from his knees, and added modestly: "I am a Chiropodist."

"I beg your pardon."

"Don't mention it! You are not, I imagine, in want of my professional services. To what motive may I attribute the honour of your visit?"

By this time Mr Rayburn had recovered himself.

"I have come here," he answered, "under circumstances which require apology as well as explanation."

Mr Zant's highly polished manner betrayed signs of alarm; his suspicions pointed to a formidable conclusion – a conclusion that shook him to the innermost recesses of the pocket in which he kept his money.

"The numerous demands on me –" he began.

Mr Rayburn smiled.

"Make your mind easy," he replied. "I don't want money. My object is to speak with you on the subject of a lady who is a relation of yours."

"My sister-in-law!" Mr Zant exclaimed. "Pray take a seat."

Doubting if he had chosen a convenient time for his visit, Mr Rayburn hesitated.

"Am I likely to be in the way of persons who wish to consult you?" he asked.

"Certainly not. My morning hours of attendance on my clients are from eleven to one." The clock on the mantelpiece struck the quarter-past one as he spoke. "I hope you don't bring me bad news?" he said, very earnestly. "When I called on Mrs Zant this morning, I heard that she had gone out for a walk. Is it indiscreet to ask how you became acquainted with her?"

Mr Rayburn at once mentioned what he had seen and heard in Kensington Gardens; not forgetting to add a few words, which described his interview afterward with Mrs Zant.

The lady's brother-in-law listened with an interest and sympathy, which offered the strongest possible contrast to the unprovoked rudeness of the mistress of the lodging-house. He declared that he could only do justice to his sense of obligation by following Mr Rayburn's example, and expressing himself as frankly as if he had been speaking to an old friend.

"The sad story of my sister-in-law's life," he said, "will, I think, explain certain things which must have naturally perplexed you. My brother was introduced to her at the house of an Australian gentleman, on a visit to England. She was then employed as governess to his daughters. So sincere was the regard felt for her by the family that the parents had, at the entreaty of their children, asked her to accompany them when they returned to the Colony. The governess thankfully accepted the proposal."

"Had she no relations in England?" Mr Rayburn asked.

"She was literally alone in the world, sir. When I tell you that she had been brought up in the Foundling Hospital, you will understand what I mean. Oh, there is no romance in my sister-in-law's story! She never has known, or will know, who her parents were or why they deserted her. The happiest moment in her life was the moment when she and my brother first met. It was an instance, on both sides, of love at first sight. Though not a rich man, my brother had earned a sufficient income in mercantile pursuits. His character spoke for itself. In a word, he altered all the poor girl's prospects, as we then hoped and believed, for the better. Her employers deferred their return to Australia, so that she might be married from their house. After a happy life of a few weeks only –"

His voice failed him; he paused, and turned his face from the light.

"Pardon me," he said; "I am not able, even yet, to speak composedly of my brother's death. Let me only say that the poor young wife was a widow, before the happy days of the honeymoon were over. That dreadful calamity struck her down. Before my brother had been committed to the grave, her life was in danger from brain-fever."

Those words placed in a new light Mr Rayburn's first fear that her intellect might be deranged. Looking at him attentively, Mr Zant seemed to understand what was passing in the mind of his guest.

"No!" he said. "If the opinions of the medical men are to be trusted, the result of the illness is injury to her physical strength – not injury to her mind. I have observed in her, no doubt, a certain waywardness of temper since her illness; but that is a trifle. As an example of what I mean, I may tell you that I invited her, on her recovery, to pay me a visit. My house is not in London – the air doesn't agree with me – my place of residence is at St. Sallins-on-Sea. I am not myself a married man; but my excellent housekeeper would have received Mrs Zant with the utmost kindness. She was resolved – obstinately resolved, poor thing – to remain in London. It is needless to say that, in her melancholy position, I am attentive to her slightest wishes. I took a lodging for her; and, at her special request, I chose a house which was near Kensington Gardens."

"Is there any association with the Gardens which led Mrs Zant to make that request?"

"Some association, I believe, with the memory of her husband. By the way, I wish to be sure of finding her at home, when I call tomorrow. Did you say (in the course of your interesting statement) that she intended – as you supposed – to return to Kensington Gardens tomorrow? Or has my memory deceived me?"

"Your memory is perfectly accurate."

"Thank you. I confess I am not only distressed by what you have told me of Mrs Zant – I am at a loss to know how to act for the best. My only idea, at present, is to try change of air and scene. What do you think yourself?"

"I think you are right."

Mr Zant still hesitated.

"It would not be easy for me, just now," he said, "to leave my patients and take her abroad."

The obvious reply to this occurred to Mr Rayburn. A man of larger worldly experience might have felt certain suspicions, and might have remained silent. Mr Rayburn spoke.

"Why not renew your invitation and take her to your house at the seaside?" he said.

In the perplexed state of Mr Zant's mind, this plain course of action had apparently failed to present itself. His gloomy face brightened directly.

"The very thing!" he said. "I will certainly take your advice. If the air of St. Sallins does nothing else, it will improve her health and help her to recover her good looks. Did she strike you as having been (in happier days) a pretty woman?"

This was a strangely familiar question to ask – almost an indelicate question, under the circumstances. A certain furtive expression in Mr Zant's fine dark eyes seemed to imply that it had been put with a purpose. Was it possible that he suspected Mr Rayburn's interest in his sister-in-law to be inspired by any motive which was not perfectly unselfish and perfectly pure? To arrive at such a conclusion as this might be to judge hastily and cruelly of a man who was perhaps only guilty of a want of delicacy of feeling. Mr Rayburn honestly did his best to assume the charitable point of view. At the same time, it is not to be denied that his words, when he answered, were carefully guarded, and that he rose to take his leave.

Mr John Zant hospitably protested.

"Why are you in such a hurry? Must you really go? I shall have the honour of returning your visit tomorrow, when I have made arrangements to profit by that excellent suggestion of yours. Good-by. God bless you."

He held out his hand: a hand with a smooth surface and a tawny colour, that fervently squeezed the fingers of a departing friend. "Is that man a scoundrel?" was Mr Rayburn's first thought, after he had left the hotel. His moral sense set all hesitation at rest – and answered: "You're a fool if you doubt it."

V

DISTURBED by presentiments, Mr Rayburn returned to his house on foot, by way of trying what exercise would do toward composing his mind.

The experiment failed. He went upstairs and played with Lucy; he drank an extra glass of wine at dinner; he took the child and her governess to a circus in the evening; he ate a little supper, fortified by another glass of wine, before he went to bed – and still those vague forebodings of evil persisted in torturing him. Looking back through his past life, he asked himself if any woman (his late wife of course excepted!) had ever taken the predominant place in his thoughts which Mrs Zant had assumed – without any discernible reason to account for it? If he had ventured to answer his own question, the reply would have been: Never!

All the next day he waited at home, in expectation of Mr John Zant's promised visit, and waited in vain.

Toward evening the parlour-maid appeared at the family tea-table, and presented to her master an unusually large envelope sealed with black wax, and addressed in a strange handwriting. The absence of stamp and postmark showed that it had been left at the house by a messenger.

"Who brought this?" Mr Rayburn asked.

"A lady, sir – in deep mourning."

"Did she leave any message?"

"No, sir."

Having drawn the inevitable conclusion, Mr Rayburn shut himself up in his library. He was afraid of Lucy's curiosity and Lucy's questions, if he read Mrs Zant's letter in his daughter's presence.

Looking at the open envelope after he had taken out the leaves of writing which it contained, he noticed these lines traced inside the cover:

"My one excuse for troubling you, when I might have consulted my brother-in-law, will be found in the pages which I inclose. To speak plainly, you have been led to fear that I am not in my right senses. For this very reason, I now appeal to you. Your dreadful doubt of me, sir, is my doubt too. Read what I have written about myself – and then tell me, I entreat you, which I am: A person who has been the object of a supernatural revelation? or an unfortunate creature who is only fit for imprisonment in a mad-house?"

Mr Rayburn opened the manuscript. With steady attention, which soon quickened to breathless interest, he read what follows:

VI

The Lady's Manuscript

YESTERDAY MORNING the sun shone in a clear blue sky – after a succession of cloudy days, counting from the first of the month.

The radiant light had its animating effect on my poor spirits. I had passed the night more peacefully than usual; undisturbed by the dream, so cruelly familiar to me, that my lost husband is still living – the dream from which I always wake in tears. Never, since the dark days of my sorrow, have I been so little troubled by the self-tormenting fancies and fears which beset miserable women, as when I left the house, and turned my steps toward Kensington Gardens – for the first time since my husband's death.

Attended by my only companion, the little dog who had been his favourite as well as mine, I went to the quiet corner of the Gardens which is nearest to Kensington.

On that soft grass, under the shade of those grand trees, we had loitered together in the days of our betrothal. It was his favourite walk; and he had taken me to see it in the early days of our acquaintance. There, he had first asked me to be his wife. There, we had felt the rapture of our first kiss. It was surely natural that I should wish to see once more a place sacred to such memories as these? I am only twenty-three years old; I have no child to comfort me, no companion of my own age, nothing to love but the dumb creature who is so faithfully fond of me.

I went to the tree under which we stood, when my dear one's eyes told his love before he could utter it in words. The sun of that vanished day shone on me again; it was the same noontide hour; the same solitude was around me. I had feared the first effect of the dreadful contrast between past and present. No! I was quiet and resigned. My thoughts, rising higher than earth, dwelt on the better life beyond the grave. Some tears came into my eyes. But I was not unhappy. My memory of all that happened may be trusted, even in trifles which relate only to myself – I was not unhappy.

* * *

The first object that I saw, when my eyes were clear again, was the dog. He crouched a few paces away from me, trembling pitiably, but uttering no cry. What had caused the fear that overpowered him?

I was soon to know.

I called to the dog; he remained immovable – conscious of some mysterious coming thing that held him spellbound. I tried to go to the poor creature, and fondle and comfort him.

At the first step forward that I took, something stopped me.

It was not to be seen, and not to be heard. It stopped me.

The still figure of the dog disappeared from my view: the lonely scene round me disappeared – excepting the light from heaven, the tree that sheltered me, and the grass in front of me. A sense of unutterable expectation kept my eyes riveted on the grass. Suddenly, I saw its myriad blades rise erect and shivering. The fear came to me of something passing over them with the invisible swiftness of the wind. The shivering advanced. It was all round me. It crept into the leaves of the tree over my head; they shuddered, without a sound to tell of their agitation; their pleasant natural rustling was struck dumb. The song of the birds had ceased. The cries of the water-fowl on the pond were heard no more. There was a dreadful silence.

But the lovely sunshine poured down on me, as brightly as ever.

In that dazzling light, in that fearful silence, I felt an Invisible Presence near me. It touched me gently.

At the touch, my heart throbbed with an overwhelming joy. Exquisite pleasure thrilled through every nerve in my body. I knew him! From the unseen world – himself unseen – he had returned to me. Oh, I knew him!

And yet, my helpless mortality longed for a sign that might give me assurance of the truth. The yearning in me shaped itself into words. I tried to utter the words. I would have said, if I could have spoken: "Oh, my angel, give me a token that it is You!" But I was like a person struck dumb – I could only think it.

The Invisible Presence read my thought. I felt my lips touched, as my husband's lips used to touch them when he kissed me. And that was my answer. A thought came to me again. I would have said, if I could have spoken: "Are you here to take me to the better world?"

I waited. Nothing that I could feel touched me.

I was conscious of thinking once more. I would have said, if I could have spoken: "Are you here to protect me?"

I felt myself held in a gentle embrace, as my husband's arms used to hold me when he pressed me to his breast. And that was my answer.

The touch that was like the touch of his lips, lingered and was lost; the clasp that was like the clasp of his arms, pressed me and fell away. The garden-scene resumed its natural aspect. I saw a human creature near, a lovely little girl looking at me.

At that moment, when I was my own lonely self again, the sight of the child soothed and attracted me. I advanced, intending to speak to her. To my horror I suddenly ceased to see her. She disappeared as if I had been stricken blind.

And yet I could see the landscape round me; I could see the heaven above me. A time passed – only a few minutes, as I thought – and the child became visible to me again; walking hand-in-hand with her father. I approached them; I was close enough to see that they were looking at me with pity and surprise. My impulse was to ask if they saw anything strange in my face or my manner. Before I could speak, the horrible wonder happened again. They vanished from my view.

Was the Invisible Presence still near? Was it passing between me and my fellow-mortals; forbidding communication, in that place and at that time?

It must have been so. When I turned away in my ignorance, with a heavy heart, the dreadful blankness which had twice shut out from me the beings of my own race, was not between me and my dog. The poor little creature filled me with pity; I called him to me. He moved at the sound of my voice, and followed me languidly; not quite awakened yet from the trance of terror that had possessed him.

Before I had retired by more than a few steps, I thought I was conscious of the Presence again. I held out my longing arms to it. I waited in the hope of a touch to tell me that I might return. Perhaps I was answered by indirect means? I only know that a resolution to return to the same place, at the same hour, came to me, and quieted my mind.

The morning of the next day was dull and cloudy; but the rain held off. I set forth again to the Gardens.

My dog ran on before me into the street – and stopped: waiting to see in which direction I might lead the way. When I turned toward the Gardens, he dropped behind me. In a little while I looked back. He was following me no longer; he stood irresolute. I called to him. He advanced a few steps – hesitated – and ran back to the house.

I went on by myself. Shall I confess my superstition? I thought the dog's desertion of me a bad omen.

Arrived at the tree, I placed myself under it. The minutes followed each other uneventfully. The cloudy sky darkened. The dull surface of the grass showed no shuddering consciousness of an unearthly creature passing over it.

I still waited, with an obstinacy which was fast becoming the obstinacy of despair. How long an interval elapsed, while I kept watch on the ground before me, I am not able to say. I only know that a change came.

Under the dull grey light I saw the grass move – but not as it had moved, on the day before. It shrivelled as if a flame had scorched it. No flame appeared. The brown underlying earth showed itself winding onward in a thin strip – which might have been a footpath traced in fire. It frightened me. I longed for the protection of the Invisible Presence. I prayed for a warning of it, if danger was near.

A touch answered me. It was as if a hand unseen had taken my hand – had raised it, little by little – had left it, pointing to the thin brown path that wound toward me under the shrivelled blades of grass.

I looked to the far end of the path.

The unseen hand closed on my hand with a warning pressure: the revelation of the coming danger was near me – I waited for it. I saw it.

The figure of a man appeared, advancing toward me along the thin brown path. I looked in his face as he came nearer. It showed me dimly the face of my husband's brother – John Zant.

The consciousness of myself as a living creature left me. I knew nothing; I felt nothing. I was dead.

When the torture of revival made me open my eyes, I found myself on the grass. Gentle hands raised my head, at the moment when I recovered my senses. Who had brought me to life again? Who was taking care of me?

I looked upward, and saw – bending over me – John Zant.

VII

THERE, THE MANUSCRIPT ENDED.

Some lines had been added on the last page; but they had been so carefully erased as to be illegible. These words of explanation appeared below the cancelled sentences:

"I had begun to write the little that remains to be told, when it struck me that I might, unintentionally, be exercising an unfair influence on your opinion. Let me only remind you that I believe absolutely in the supernatural revelation which I have endeavoured to describe. Remember this – and decide for me what I dare not decide for myself."

There was no serious obstacle in the way of compliance with this request.

Judged from the point of view of the materialist, Mrs Zant might no doubt be the victim of illusions (produced by a diseased state of the nervous system), which have been known to exist – as in the celebrated case of the book-seller, Nicolai, of Berlin – without being accompanied by derangement of the intellectual powers. But Mr Rayburn was not asked to solve any such intricate problem as this. He had been merely instructed to read the manuscript, and to say what impression it had left on him of the mental condition of the writer; whose doubt of herself had been, in all probability, first suggested by remembrance of the illness from which she had suffered – brain-fever.

Under these circumstances, there could be little difficulty in forming an opinion. The memory which had recalled, and the judgment which had arranged, the succession of events related in the narrative, revealed a mind in full possession of its resources.

Having satisfied himself so far, Mr Rayburn abstained from considering the more serious question suggested by what he had read.

At any time his habits of life and his ways of thinking would have rendered him unfit to weigh the arguments, which assert or deny supernatural revelation among the creatures of earth. But his mind was now so disturbed by the startling record of experience which he had just read, that he was only conscious of feeling certain impressions – without possessing the capacity to reflect on them. That his anxiety on Mrs Zant's account had been increased, and that his doubts of Mr John Zant had been encouraged, were the only practical results of the confidence placed in him of which he was thus far aware. In the ordinary exigencies of life a man of hesitating disposition, his interest in Mrs Zant's welfare, and his desire to discover what had passed between her brother-in-law and herself, after their meeting in the Gardens, urged him into instant action. In half an hour more, he had arrived at her lodgings. He was at once admitted.

VIII

MRS ZANT WAS ALONE, in an imperfectly lighted room.

"I hope you will excuse the bad light," she said; "my head has been burning as if the fever had come back again. Oh, don't go away! After what I have suffered, you don't know how dreadful it is to be alone."

The tone of her voice told him that she had been crying. He at once tried the best means of setting the poor lady at ease, by telling her of the conclusion at which he had arrived, after reading her manuscript. The happy result showed itself instantly: her face brightened, her manner changed; she was eager to hear more.

"Have I produced any other impression on you?" she asked.

He understood the allusion. Expressing sincere respect for her own convictions, he told her honestly that he was not prepared to enter on the obscure and terrible question of supernatural interposition. Grateful for the tone in which he had answered her, she wisely and delicately changed the subject.

"I must speak to you of my brother-in-law," she said. "He has told me of your visit; and I am anxious to know what you think of him. Do you like Mr John Zant?"

Mr Rayburn hesitated.

The careworn look appeared again in her face. "If you had felt as kindly toward him as he feels toward you," she said, "I might have gone to St. Sallins with a lighter heart."

Mr Rayburn thought of the supernatural appearances, described at the close of her narrative. "You believe in that terrible warning," he remonstrated; "and yet, you go to your brother-in-law's house!"

"I believe," she answered, "in the spirit of the man who loved me in the days of his earthly bondage. I am under his protection. What have I to do but to cast away my fears, and to wait in faith and hope? It might have helped my resolution if a friend had been near to encourage me." She paused and smiled sadly. "I must remember," she resumed, "that your way of understanding my position is not my way. I ought to have told you that Mr John Zant feels needless anxiety about my health. He declares that he will not lose sight of me until his mind is at ease. It is useless to attempt to alter his opinion. He says my nerves are shattered – and who that sees me can doubt it? He tells me that my only chance of getting better is to try change of air and perfect repose – how can I contradict him? He reminds me that I have no relation but himself, and no house open to me but his own – and God knows he is right!"

She said those last words in accents of melancholy resignation, which grieved the good man whose one merciful purpose was to serve and console her. He spoke impulsively with the freedom of an old friend

"I want to know more of you and Mr John Zant than I know now," he said. "My motive is a better one than mere curiosity. Do you believe that I feel a sincere interest in you?"

"With my whole heart."

That reply encouraged him to proceed with what he had to say. "When you recovered from your fainting-fit," he began, "Mr John Zant asked questions, of course?"

"He asked what could possibly have happened, in such a quiet place as Kensington Gardens, to make me faint."

"And how did you answer?"

"Answer? I couldn't even look at him!"

"You said nothing?"

"Nothing. I don't know what he thought of me; he might have been surprised, or he might have been offended."

"Is he easily offended?" Mr Rayburn asked.

"Not in my experience of him."

"Do you mean your experience of him before your illness?"

"Yes. Since my recovery, his engagements with country patients have kept him away from London. I have not seen him since he took these lodgings for me. But he is always considerate. He has written more than once to beg that I will not think him neglectful, and to tell me (what I knew already through my poor husband) that he has no money of his own, and must live by his profession."

"In your husband's lifetime, were the two brothers on good terms?"

"Always. The one complaint I ever heard my husband make of John Zant was that he didn't come to see us often enough, after our marriage. Is there some wickedness in him which we have never suspected? It may be – but how can it be? I have every reason to be grateful to the man against whom I have been supernaturally warned! His conduct to me has been always perfect. I can't tell you what I owe to his influence in quieting my mind, when a dreadful doubt arose about my husband's death."

"Do you mean doubt if he died a natural death?"

"Oh, no! no! He was dying of rapid consumption – but his sudden death took the doctors by surprise. One of them thought that he might have taken an overdose of his sleeping drops, by mistake. The other disputed this conclusion, or there might have been an inquest in the house. Oh, don't speak of it any more! Let us talk of something else. Tell me when I shall see you again."

"I hardly know. When do you and your brother-in-law leave London?"

"Tomorrow." She looked at Mr Rayburn with a piteous entreaty in her eyes; she said, timidly: "Do you ever go to the seaside, and take your dear little girl with you?"

The request, at which she had only dared to hint, touched on the idea which was at that moment in Mr Rayburn's mind.

Interpreted by his strong prejudice against John Zant, what she had said of her brother-in-law filled him with forebodings of peril to herself; all the more powerful in their influence, for this reason – that he shrank from distinctly realizing them. If another person had been present at the interview, and had said to him afterward: "That man's reluctance to visit his sister-in-law, while her husband was living, is associated with a secret sense of guilt which her innocence cannot even imagine: he, and he alone, knows the cause of her husband's sudden death: his feigned anxiety about her health is adopted as the safest means of enticing her into his house – if those formidable conclusions had been urged on Mr Rayburn, he would have felt it his duty to reject them, as unjustifiable aspersions on an absent man. And yet, when he took leave that evening of Mrs Zant, he had pledged himself to give Lucy a holiday at the seaside: and he had said, without blushing, that the child really deserved it, as a reward for general good conduct and attention to her lessons!

IX

THREE DAYS LATER, the father and daughter arrived toward evening at St. Sallins-on-Sea. They found Mrs Zant at the station.

The poor woman's joy, on seeing them, expressed itself like the joy of a child. "Oh, I am so glad! so glad!" was all she could say when they met. Lucy was half-smothered with kisses, and was made supremely happy by a present of the finest doll she had ever possessed. Mrs Zant accompanied her friends to the rooms which had been secured at the hotel. She was able to speak confidentially to Mr Rayburn, while Lucy was in the balcony hugging her doll, and looking at the sea.

The one event that had happened during Mrs Zant's short residence at St. Sallins was the departure of her brother-in-law that morning, for London. He had been called away to operate on the feet of a wealthy patient who knew the value of his time: his housekeeper expected that he would return to dinner.

As to his conduct toward Mrs Zant, he was not only as attentive as ever – he was almost oppressively affectionate in his language and manner. There was no service that a man could render which he had not eagerly offered to her. He declared that he already perceived an improvement in her health; he congratulated her on having decided to stay in his house; and (as a proof, perhaps, of his sincerity) he had repeatedly pressed her hand. "Have you any idea what all this means?" she said, simply.

Mr Rayburn kept his idea to himself. He professed ignorance; and asked next what sort of person the housekeeper was.

Mrs Zant shook her head ominously.

"Such a strange creature," she said, "and in the habit of taking such liberties that I begin to be afraid she is a little crazy."

"Is she an old woman?"

"No – only middle-aged. This morning, after her master had left the house, she actually asked me what I thought of my brother-in-law! I told her, as coldly as possible, that I thought he was very kind. She was quite insensible to the tone in which I had spoken; she went on from bad to worse. "Do you call him the sort of man who would take the fancy of a young woman?" was her next question. She actually looked at me (I might have been wrong; and I hope I was) as if the "young woman" she had in her mind was myself! I said: "I don't think of such things, and I don't talk about them." Still, she was not in the least discouraged; she made a personal remark next: "Excuse me – but you do look wretchedly pale." I thought she seemed to enjoy the defect in my complexion; I really believe it raised me in her estimation. "We shall get on better in time," she said; "I am beginning to like you." She walked out humming a tune. Don't you agree with me? Don't you think she's crazy?"

"I can hardly give an opinion until I have seen her. Does she look as if she might have been a pretty woman at one time of her life?"

"Not the sort of pretty woman whom I admire!"

Mr Rayburn smiled. "I was thinking," he resumed, "that this person's odd conduct may perhaps be accounted for. She is probably jealous of any young lady who is invited to her master's house – and (till she noticed your complexion) she began by being jealous of you."

Innocently at a loss to understand how she could become an object of the housekeeper's jealousy, Mrs Zant looked at Mr Rayburn in astonishment. Before she could give expression to her feeling of surprise, there was an interruption – a welcome interruption. A waiter entered the room, and announced a visitor; described as "a gentleman".

Mrs Zant at once rose to retire.

"Who is the gentleman?" Mr Rayburn asked – detaining Mrs Zant as he spoke.

A voice which they both recognized answered gayly, from the outer side of the door: "A friend from London."

X

"WELCOME TO ST. SALLINS!" cried Mr John Zant. "I knew that you were expected, my dear sir, and I took my chance at finding you at the hotel." He turned to his sister-in-law, and kissed her hand with an elaborate gallantry worthy of Sir Charles Grandison himself. "When I reached home, my dear, and heard that you had gone out, I guessed that your object was to receive our excellent friend. You have not felt lonely while I have been away? That's right! that's right!" he looked toward the balcony, and discovered Lucy at the open window, staring at the magnificent stranger. "Your little daughter, Mr Rayburn? Dear child! Come and kiss me."

Lucy answered in one positive word: "No."

Mr John Zant was not easily discouraged.

"Show me your doll, darling," he said. "Sit on my knee."

Lucy answered in two positive words – "I won't."

Her father approached the window to administer the necessary reproof. Mr John Zant interfered in the cause of mercy with his best grace. He held up his hands in cordial entreaty. "Dear Mr Rayburn! The fairies are sometimes shy; and this little fairy doesn't take to strangers at first sight. Dear child! All in good time. And what stay do you make at St. Sallins? May we hope that our poor attractions will tempt you to prolong your visit?"

He put his flattering little question with an ease of manner which was rather too plainly assumed; and he looked at Mr Rayburn with a watchfulness which appeared to attach undue importance to the reply. When he said: "What stay do you make at St. Sallins?" did he really mean: "How soon do you leave us?" Inclining to adopt this conclusion, Mr Rayburn answered cautiously that his stay at the seaside would depend on circumstances. Mr John Zant looked at his sister-in-law, sitting silent in a corner with Lucy on her lap. "Exert your attractions," he said; "make the circumstances agreeable to our good friend. Will you dine with us today, my dear sir, and bring your little fairy with you?"

Lucy was far from receiving this complimentary allusion in the spirit in which it had been offered. "I'm not a fairy," she declared. "I'm a child."

"And a naughty child," her father added, with all the severity that he could assume.

"I can't help it, papa; the man with the big beard puts me out."

The man with the big beard was amused – amiably, paternally amused – by Lucy's plain speaking. He repeated his invitation to dinner; and he did his best to look disappointed when Mr Rayburn made the necessary excuses.

"Another day," he said (without, however, fixing the day). "I think you will find my house comfortable. My housekeeper may perhaps be eccentric – but in all essentials a woman in a thousand. Do you feel the change from London already? Our air at St. Sallins is really worthy of its reputation. Invalids who come here are cured as if by magic. What do you think of Mrs Zant? How does she look?"

Mr Rayburn was evidently expected to say that she looked better. He said it. Mr John Zant seemed to have anticipated a stronger expression of opinion.

"Surprisingly better!" he pronounced. "Infinitely better! We ought both to be grateful. Pray believe that we are grateful."

"If you mean grateful to me," Mr Rayburn remarked, "I don't quite understand –"

"You don't quite understand? Is it possible that you have forgotten our conversation when I first had the honour of receiving you? Look at Mrs Zant again."

Mr Rayburn looked; and Mrs Zant's brother-in-law explained himself.

"You notice the return of her colour, the healthy brightness of her eyes. (No, my dear, I am not paying you idle compliments; I am stating plain facts.) For that happy result, Mr Rayburn, we are indebted to you."

"Surely not?"

"Surely yes! It was at your valuable suggestion that I thought of inviting my sister-in-law to visit me at St. Sallins. Ah, you remember it now. Forgive me if I look at my watch; the dinner hour is on my mind. Not, as your dear little daughter there seems to think, because I am greedy, but because I am always punctual, in justice to the cook. Shall we see you tomorrow? Call early, and you will find us at home."

He gave Mrs Zant his arm, and bowed and smiled, and kissed his hand to Lucy, and left the room. Recalling their interview at the hotel in London, Mr Rayburn now understood John Zant's object (on that occasion) in assuming the character of a helpless man in need of a sensible suggestion. If Mrs Zant's residence under his roof became associated with evil consequences, he could declare that she would never have entered the house but for Mr Rayburn's advice.

With the next day came the hateful necessity of returning this man's visit.

Mr Rayburn was placed between two alternatives. In Mrs Zant's interests he must remain, no matter at what sacrifice of his own inclinations, on good terms with her brother-in-law – or he must return to London, and leave the poor woman to her fate. His choice, it is needless to say, was never a matter of doubt. He called at the house, and did his innocent best – without in the least deceiving Mr John Zant – to make himself agreeable during the short duration of his visit. Descending the stairs on his way out, accompanied by Mrs Zant, he was surprised to see a middle-aged woman in the hall, who looked as if she was waiting there expressly to attract notice.

"The housekeeper," Mrs Zant whispered. "She is impudent enough to try to make acquaintance with you."

This was exactly what the housekeeper was waiting in the hall to do.

"I hope you like our watering-place, sir," she began. "If I can be of service to you, pray command me. Any friend of this lady's has a claim on me – and you are an old friend, no doubt. I am only the housekeeper; but I presume to take a sincere interest in Mrs Zant; and I am indeed glad to see you here. We none of us know – do we? – how soon we may want a friend. No offence, I hope? Thank you, sir. Good-morning."

There was nothing in the woman's eyes which indicated an unsettled mind; nothing in the appearance of her lips which suggested habits of intoxication. That her strange outburst of familiarity proceeded from some strong motive seemed to be more than probable. Putting together what Mrs Zant had already told him, and what he had himself observed, Mr Rayburn suspected that the motive might be found in the housekeeper's jealousy of her master.

XI

REFLECTING IN THE SOLITUDE of his own room, Mr Rayburn felt that the one prudent course to take would be to persuade Mrs Zant to leave St. Sallins. He tried to prepare her for this strong proceeding, when she came the next day to take Lucy out for a walk.

"If you still regret having forced yourself to accept your brother-in-law's invitation," was all he ventured to say, "don't forget that you are perfect mistress of your own actions. You have only to come to me at the hotel, and I will take you back to London by the next train."

She positively refused to entertain the idea.

"I should be a thankless creature, indeed," she said, "if I accepted your proposal. Do you think I am ungrateful enough to involve you in a personal quarrel with John Zant? No! If I find myself forced to leave the house, I will go away alone."

There was no moving her from this resolution. When she and Lucy had gone out together, Mr Rayburn remained at the hotel, with a mind ill at ease. A man of readier mental resources might have felt at a loss how to act for the best, in the emergency that now confronted him. While he was still as far as ever from arriving at a decision, some person knocked at the door.

Had Mrs Zant returned? He looked up as the door was opened, and saw to his astonishment – Mr John Zant's housekeeper.

"Don't let me alarm you, sir," the woman said. "Mrs Zant has been taken a little faint, at the door of our house. My master is attending to her."

"Where is the child?" Mr Rayburn asked.

"I was bringing her back to you, sir, when we met a lady and her little girl at the door of the hotel. They were on their way to the beach – and Miss Lucy begged hard to be allowed to go with them. The lady said the two children were playfellows, and she was sure you would not object."

"The lady is quite right. Mrs Zant's illness is not serious, I hope?"

"I think not, sir. But I should like to say something in her interests. May I? Thank you." She advanced a step nearer to him, and spoke her next words in a whisper. "Take Mrs Zant away from this place, and lose no time in doing it."

Mr Rayburn was on his guard. He merely asked: "Why?"

The housekeeper answered in a curiously indirect manner – partly in jest, as it seemed, and partly in earnest.

"When a man has lost his wife," she said, "there's some difference of opinion in Parliament, as I hear, whether he does right or wrong, if he marries his wife's sister. Wait a bit! I'm coming to the point. My master is one who has a long head on his shoulders; he sees consequences which escape the notice of people like me. In his way of thinking, if one man may marry his wife's sister, and no harm done, where's the objection if another man pays a compliment to the family, and marries his brother's widow? My master, if you please, is that other man. Take the widow away before she marries him."

This was beyond endurance.

"You insult Mrs Zant," Mr Rayburn answered, "if you suppose that such a thing is possible!"

"Oh! I insult her, do I? Listen to me. One of three things will happen. She will be entrapped into consenting to it – or frightened into consenting to it – or drugged into consenting to it –"

Mr Rayburn was too indignant to let her go on.

"You are talking nonsense," he said. "There can be no marriage; the law forbids it."

"Are you one of the people who see no further than their noses?" she asked insolently. "Won't the law take his money? Is he obliged to mention that he is related to her by marriage, when he buys the licence?" She paused; her humour changed; she stamped furiously on the floor. The true motive that animated her showed itself in her next words, and warned Mr Rayburn to grant a more favourable hearing than he had accorded to her yet. "If you won't stop it," she burst out, "I will! If he marries anybody, he is bound to marry *me*. Will you take her away? I ask you, for the last time – will you take her away?"

The tone in which she made that final appeal to him had its effect.

"I will go back with you to John Zant's house," he said, "and judge for myself."

She laid her hand on his arm:

"I must go first – or you may not be let in. Follow me in five minutes; and don't knock at the street door."

On the point of leaving him, she abruptly returned.

"We have forgotten something," she said. "Suppose my master refuses to see you. His temper might get the better of him; he might make it so unpleasant for you that you would be obliged to go."

"My temper might get the better of me," Mr Rayburn replied; "and – if I thought it was in Mrs Zant's interests – I might refuse to leave the house unless she accompanied me."

"That will never do, sir."

"Why not?"

"Because I should be the person to suffer."

"In what way?"

"In this way. If you picked a quarrel with my master, I should be blamed for it because I showed you upstairs. Besides, think of the lady. You might frighten her out of her senses, if it came to a struggle between you two men."

The language was exaggerated; but there was a force in this last objection which Mr Rayburn was obliged to acknowledge.

"And, after all," the housekeeper continued, "he has more right over her than you have. He is related to her, and you are only her friend."

Mr Rayburn declined to let himself be influenced by this consideration, "Mr John Zant is only related to her by marriage," he said. "If she prefers trusting in me – come what may of it, I will be worthy of her confidence."

The housekeeper shook her head.

"That only means another quarrel," she answered. "The wise way, with a man like my master, is the peaceable way. We must manage to deceive him."

"I don't like deceit."

"In that case, sir, I'll wish you good-by. We will leave Mrs Zant to do the best she can for herself."

Mr Rayburn was unreasonable. He positively refused to adopt this alternative.

"Will you hear what I have got to say?" the housekeeper asked.

"There can be no harm in that," he admitted. "Go on."

She took him at his word.

"When you called at our house," she began, "did you notice the doors in the passage, on the first floor? Very well. One of them is the door of the drawing-room, and the other is the door of the library. Do you remember the drawing-room, sir?"

"I thought it a large well-lighted room," Mr Rayburn answered. "And I noticed a doorway in the wall, with a handsome curtain hanging over it."

"That's enough for our purpose," the housekeeper resumed. "On the other side of the curtain, if you had looked in, you would have found the library. Suppose my master is as polite as usual, and begs to be excused for not receiving you, because it is an inconvenient time. And suppose you are polite on your side and take yourself off by the drawing-room door. You will find me waiting downstairs, on the first landing. Do you see it now?"

"I can't say I do."

"You surprise me, sir. What is to prevent us from getting back softly into the library, by the door in the passage? And why shouldn't we use that second way into the library as a means of discovering what may be going on in the drawing-room? Safe behind the curtain, you will see him if he behaves uncivilly to Mrs Zant, or you will hear her if she calls for help. In either case, you may be as rough and ready with my master as you find needful; it will be he who has frightened her, and not you. And who can blame the poor housekeeper because Mr Rayburn did his duty, and protected a helpless woman? There is my plan, sir. Is it worth trying?"

He answered, sharply enough: "I don't like it."

The housekeeper opened the door again, and wished him good-by.

If Mr Rayburn had felt no more than an ordinary interest in Mrs Zant, he would have let the woman go. As it was, he stopped her; and, after some further protest (which proved to be useless), he ended in giving way.

"You promise to follow my directions?" she stipulated.

He gave the promise. She smiled, nodded, and left him. True to his instructions, Mr Rayburn reckoned five minutes by his watch, before he followed her.

XII

THE HOUSEKEEPER was waiting for him, with the street-door ajar.

"They are both in the drawing-room," she whispered, leading the way upstairs. "Step softly, and take him by surprise."

A table of oblong shape stood midway between the drawing-room walls. At the end of it which was nearest to the window, Mrs Zant was pacing to and fro across the breadth of the room. At the opposite end of the table, John Zant was seated. Taken completely by surprise, he showed himself in his true character. He started to his feet, and protested with an oath against the intrusion which had been committed on him.

Heedless of his action and his language, Mr Rayburn could look at nothing, could think of nothing, but Mrs Zant. She was still walking slowly to and fro, unconscious of the words of sympathy which he addressed to her, insensible even as it seemed to the presence of other persons in the room.

John Zant's voice broke the silence. His temper was under control again: he had his reasons for still remaining on friendly terms with Mr Rayburn.

"I am sorry I forgot myself just now," he said.

Mr Rayburn's interest was concentrated on Mrs Zant; he took no notice of the apology.

"When did this happen?" he asked.

"About a quarter of an hour ago. I was fortunately at home. Without speaking to me, without noticing me, she walked upstairs like a person in a dream."

Mr Rayburn suddenly pointed to Mrs Zant.

"Look at her!" he said. "There's a change!"

All restlessness in her movements had come to an end. She was standing at the further end of the table, which was nearest to the window, in the full flow of sunlight pouring at that moment over her face. Her eyes looked out straight before her – void of all expression. Her lips were a little parted: her head drooped slightly toward her shoulder, in an attitude which suggested listening for something or waiting for something. In the warm brilliant light, she stood before the two men, a living creature self-isolated in a stillness like the stillness of death.

John Zant was ready with the expression of his opinion.

"A nervous seizure," he said. "Something resembling catalepsy, as you see."

"Have you sent for a doctor?"

"A doctor is not wanted."

"I beg your pardon. It seems to me that medical help is absolutely necessary."

"Be so good as to remember," Mr John Zant answered, "that the decision rests with me, as the lady's relative. I am sensible of the honour which your visit confers on me. But the time has been unhappily chosen. Forgive me if I suggest that you will do well to retire."

Mr Rayburn had not forgotten the housekeeper's advice, or the promise which she had exacted from him. But the expression in John Zant's face was a serious trial to his self-control. He hesitated, and looked back at Mrs Zant.

If he provoked a quarrel by remaining in the room, the one alternative would be the removal of her by force. Fear of the consequences to herself, if she was suddenly and roughly roused from her trance, was the one consideration which reconciled him to submission. He withdrew.

The housekeeper was waiting for him below, on the first landing. When the door of the drawing-room had been closed again, she signed to him to follow her, and returned up the stairs. After another struggle with himself, he obeyed. They entered the library from the corridor – and placed themselves behind the closed curtain which hung over the doorway. It was easy so to arrange the edge of the drapery as to observe, without exciting suspicion, whatever was going on in the next room.

Mrs Zant's brother-in-law was approaching her at the time when Mr Rayburn saw him again.

In the instant afterward, she moved – before he had completely passed over the space between them. Her still figure began to tremble. She lifted her drooping head. For a moment there was a shrinking in her – as if she had been touched by something. She seemed to recognize the touch: she was still again.

John Zant watched the change. It suggested to him that she was beginning to recover her senses. He tried the experiment of speaking to her.

"My love, my sweet angel, come to the heart that adores you!"

He advanced again; he passed into the flood of sunlight pouring over her.

"Rouse yourself!" he said.

She still remained in the same position; apparently at his mercy, neither hearing him nor seeing him.

"Rouse yourself!" he repeated. "My darling, come to me!"

At the instant when he attempted to embrace her – at the instant when Mr Rayburn rushed into the room – John Zant's arms, suddenly turning rigid, remained outstretched. With a shriek of horror, he struggled to draw them back – struggled, in the empty brightness of the sunshine, as if some invisible grip had seized him.

"What has got me?" the wretch screamed. "Who is holding my hands? Oh, the cold of it! the cold of it!"

His features became convulsed; his eyes turned upward until only the white eyeballs were visible. He fell prostrate with a crash that shook the room.

The housekeeper ran in. She knelt by her master's body. With one hand she loosened his cravat. With the other she pointed to the end of the table.

Mrs Zant still kept her place; but there was another change. Little by little, her eyes recovered their natural living expression – then slowly closed. She tottered backward from the table, and lifted her hands wildly, as if to grasp at something which might support her. Mr Rayburn hurried to her before she fell – lifted her in his arms – and carried her out of the room.

One of the servants met them in the hall. He sent her for a carriage. In a quarter of an hour more, Mrs Zant was safe under his care at the hotel.

XIII

THAT NIGHT A NOTE, written by the housekeeper, was delivered to Mrs Zant.

"The doctors give little hope. The paralytic stroke is spreading upward to his face. If death spares him, he will live a helpless man. I shall take care of him to the last. As for you – forget him."

Mrs Zant gave the note to Mr Rayburn.

"Read it, and destroy it," she said. "It is written in ignorance of the terrible truth."

He obeyed – and looked at her in silence, waiting to hear more. She hid her face. The few words she had addressed to him, after a struggle with herself, fell slowly and reluctantly from her lips.

She said: "No mortal hand held the hands of John Zant. The guardian spirit was with me. The promised protection was with me. I know it. I wish to know no more."

Having spoken, she rose to retire. He opened the door for her, seeing that she needed rest in her own room.

Left by himself, he began to consider the prospect that was before him in the future. How was he to regard the woman who had just left him? As a poor creature weakened by disease, the victim of her own nervous delusion? or as the chosen object of a supernatural revelation – unparalleled by any similar revelation that he had heard of, or had found recorded in books? His first discovery of the place that she really held in his estimation dawned on his mind, when he felt himself recoiling from the conclusion which presented her to his pity, and yielding to the nobler conviction which felt with her faith, and raised her to a place apart among other women.

XIV

THEY LEFT St. Sallins the next day.

Arrived at the end of the journey, Lucy held fast by Mrs Zant's hand. Tears were rising in the child's eyes.

"Are we to bid her good-by?" she said sadly to her father.

He seemed to be unwilling to trust himself to speak; he only said:

"My dear, ask her yourself."

But the result justified him. Lucy was happy again.

The Return of Gunnar Kettilson

Vonnie Winslow Crist

CELIA SAT STRAIGHT-BACKED on an oak bench in her moonlit kitchen with the long-handled ax stretched across her lap. She listened for the shambling footsteps of her husband, Gunnar Kettilson, comforted in small measure by the presence of her great aunt beside her on the bench.

"Do you think he will come?" Celia whispered as she rubbed the wooden ax handle with her thumb and wondered if there'd be maggots.

"We should light the welcome candle," said Rona.

The white-haired woman set the butcher knife she'd been holding in her right hand on the floor, stood, propped the fire poker from her left hand against the bench, and walked to the fireplace. She withdrew a blazing splinter of wood from the fire.

"This night, one night, by full moon's light,
We call you, Gunnar Kettilson.
Come home, cruel draugr.
Come home, bitter revenant," chanted Rona as she lit a solitary white candle balanced in a silver candlestick, and placed it on the windowsill.

The elderly woman extinguished the splinter, returned to the bench, and patted Celia's forearm before picking the butcher knife back up. "We should know before long if we sealed him in the grave or if he'll return."

"What more could we have done?"

Celia's aunt answered her with a tilt of her head and a flutter of her heavily-veined hands.

As they sat in silence listening to the seawind in the trees, Celia recalled the somber funeral procession that carried Gunnar up the hill to the cemetery. She'd followed closely behind the casket beside Rona and Gunnar's father, Lars. The whole village had marched after them. The whole village *had* to attend, because Lars owned the fish factory, cannery, and most of the fishing ships where the villagers worked. And Lars retaliated against anyone he suspected of not showing sufficient respect to the Kettilson family.

"Lift your chin up, woman," Lars had growled as they'd followed the casket. "Be proud you were married to a Kettilson." Then, he'd grabbed her upper arm, squeezed it hard, glared at her with his cold blue eyes. "And unless you're carrying his child, I'll have you out on the street within a year. And if you carry a babe…" He'd scowled, and added, "He'll be mine at birth. You were never in love with my son, only interested in the Kettilson money."

Celia had opened her mouth to argue, but before she could utter a word in her defense, Aunt Rona had stared the hulking patriarch of the Kettilson family in his pale, mean eyes, and hissed, "Shame on you, Lars. She's lost a husband, and he's not yet beneath the ground. The spirits of the dead remember such slander."

Lars had pressed his thin lips together so tightly that they'd turned white, but he hadn't argued with Rona – for Rona was Fae-Blessed. The old woman was known for her rune-reading, healing herbs, and blessing spells. And Lars would naturally suspect she knew darker magics, too.

Celia watched the welcome candle's flame flicker. She wondered if Gunnar saw its light from the graveyard. Poor Gunnar. Celia's eyes filled when she thought about her husband. His mother was dead before he was three. It was whispered in the dark corners of the village that Dalla Kettilson had been beaten to death by her husband in front of their son. Though the official story given by Lars was that Dalla had slipped on a rain-slick stone and tumbled over a cliff to the sea rocks below. And no one dared challenge Lars, lest the same fate befall them.

Gunnar had grown up in a household without a mother's love where the least infraction resulted in tongue-lashings and belt-beatings from Lars. She believed that's where her husband's temper had been honed. Kind to her when they first met, sweet to her while he courted her, Gunnar grew angrier after their wedding. His death at the cannery had almost been a blessing, for Celia had fully expected to die at his hand.

Though he'd tried to control his temper, Gunnar had flown into a blind rage twice during their brief marriage. The first time, he'd accused Celia of flirting after he'd seen her talking to the butcher on the street in front of his shop. In his anger, he'd flung her down the stairs. Luckily, she'd only broken her arm.

The second time had occurred after Lars told his son that Celia had worn a revealing dress to the fish market. Gunnar had slammed her against the wall, and then, hit the wall beside her head with his fist five or six times. She'd shown him the dress she'd been wearing, and he'd realized his father was manipulating him again.

After both violent fits, he'd knelt before Celia crying, and begged her forgiveness. And, though she knew it would probably be the end of her, Celia had forgiven Gunnar.

Leave him, friends had whispered. But leaving Gunnar meant leaving the village and Aunt Rona. And Celia was sure that no matter how far away she fled, there was no escaping the revenge of Lars Kettilson.

Celia wiped her eyes with the back of her hand. Perhaps the saddest thing about the marriage was that Celia really did love Gunnar, and she knew that Gunnar loved her, too. He was just so damaged from his childhood, and every day at work, Lars poured even more nasty, ugly thoughts into his son's ears. And then there was the babe. Only she and Gunnar knew about her pregnancy, and he'd seemed so happy. Maybe a baby would have made a difference in…

"Listen," said Aunt Rona as she leaned forward. "Someone is coming."

"Do you think it's him?"

"Who else? The villagers are locked tight in their homes tonight with no candles burning. This is the first full moon since the first new moon after Gunnar's death. This is the night he can return." The Fae-Blessed woman who was her great-aunt brushed a tear from Celia's cheek with her leathery fingertips. "We are alone, my dear. No one will even look out their windows until dawn."

"Lars keeps his candles burning. I can see the Kettilson Keep lit bright as day through the window."

Aunt Rona snorted. "He's a fool. Always was."

"Perhaps Gunnar won't return." Celia bit her lip. "We did everything we could to keep him beneath the ground. We placed a pair of open scissors on his chest; we hid twigs from an alder tree in his clothes; we even tied his big toes together to make it impossible for him to walk..."

"Yes, we did what we could." Her great-aunt patted Celia's forearm again. "Still, the undead have their ways of figuring out how to return."

"But he should be confused. We had nine men from the village lift and lower Gunnar's coffin three times. And each time they turned the coffin around. How can he find his way?"

Aunt Rona shrugged. "We didn't wall up the door he exited by the last time, so he can still enter this house."

"The door couldn't be walled up. Gunnar's father forbade it."

"And you, my dear, were too kindhearted to drive straight pins through his eyes. Both things might have helped." Her aunt lifted her hands up, let them drop to her lap. "But a determined draugr will always find a way to rise from the grave."

"But I did nothing to harm him. I only loved him. Why should he hurt me?"

"The undead return to finish the unfinished. The undead return for vengeance. The undead return for their own reasons."

A loose shutter slammed against the side of the house, and the broom they'd used to block the back porch clattered down the steps.

"Did you hear that?" gasped Celia.

"It is Gunnar," responded her aunt as she tossed a handful of salt into the air in front of them.

Both women tightened their grips on their weapons as the dragging, thumping sound of footsteps on the back porch grew louder, then stopped. The door handle jiggled.

"Do you think he'll be death black or corpse pale?" queried Celia in a quavering whisper.

"*Hel-blár* or *nár fõir*? It matters not. Our actions must be the same," answered the Fae-Blessed old woman.

The two women stood and faced the draugr as the kitchen door swung open.

"Celia," the white-faced corpse slurred. "Celia."

And as Celia had feared, there were maggots. Wads of squirming white fly-children oozed from the wounds on Gunnar's once handsome face where the canning machines had sliced into him. His longish blond hair was caked with dried blood and dirt. His feet were bare, and frayed red twine was still attached to the two big toes.

"Celia," the draugr who'd been Gunnar said again as he lifted something in his pallid hand.

"Lars," gasped Celia as she saw what dangled from her late husband's left fist by its thick white hair.

The moonlight bounced off Lars Kettilson's exposed teeth. It appeared that the draugr had ripped his father's head from its body. Blood dripped from the ragged bit of neck attached to the head and from the sides of its mouth. Lars's blue eyes were wide open and glassy. His face had a surprised expression on it.

"It would seem Lars Kettilson should have extinguished his lights," noted Rona.

Though she couldn't tear her eyes away from the grisly trophy in the draugr's left hand to look at her aunt's face, the tone of the old woman's voice indicated she was happy with the way things had turned out for Lars. Slowly, Celia's gaze drifted over to what the Draugr Gunnar clasped in his right hand. She gulped down a scream. It was a heart, not unlike the sheep hearts she'd seen in the village butcher shop. But Celia knew this heart didn't belong to a sheep.

The draugr nodded at them, turned around, shuffled through the kitchen door onto the porch. He paused, turned, and beckoned the women to follow him with the hand that held his father's heart.

"Do as he asks," urged Rona as she stepped beyond the ring of salt at their feet.

Celia followed her aunt's example, though she still gripped the ax tightly. "What does Gunnar want?"

"We shall find out," answered Rona the Fae-Blessed. "We shall find out, indeed."

The women followed the draugr to their backyard fire-pit where earlier they'd stacked wood soaked in oil in readiness for the ritual to send a soul back to the realm of the dead after zombification.

The Draugr Gunnar surveyed the readied bonfire and grunted. He tossed his father's head and heart onto the wood, and then, knelt beside the fire-pit. He turned his mangled, maggoty face up to gaze at his wife and slurred, "Celia, save me."

"I can't," she responded. Her eyes burned. Her throat constricted. The ax in her hands felt heavy and awkward. "I can't."

"But I can," said Rona as she grabbed the ax handle, lifted the woodsman's tool, swung it horizontally, and lopped off the draugr's head.

The head bounced, then rolled to a stop three or four meters away. The draugr's body toppled over, spilling a stream of black blood and maggots at their feet.

"Gunnar," Celia screamed, then reached for his body. But the sight of the wriggling maggots kept her from touching him.

"Bring a lit splinter from the fireplace," ordered her aunt.

Celia's feet seemed frozen to the ground.

"Now," shouted Rona.

She ran into the house, pulled a piece of kindling that burned brightly from the fireplace, and hurried back to her aunt. While she was gone, Rona had used her knife to carve out Gunnar's heart. She tossed it onto the ready-to-be-lit bonfire beside Gunnar's head and Lars's head and heart as Celia handed her the kindling.

"Gunnar Kettilson, rest now beneath the sod.
Your wife is safe and will bear you a child..."

Celia gasped at the words. She'd told no one but Gunnar of her belief that she was pregnant.

Her uncannily wise aunt smiled at her, nodded, and then, continued the chant:

"Your last deed was a necessary act.
Depart in peace, and do not look back."

In a harsher tone, Rona the Fae-Blessed continued:

"Lars Kettilson, rot beneath the grass.
You showed kindness to none,
and none will mourn as you pass.
Go to your new world,
cursed and despised.
May you suffer and burn
till the stars leave the skies."

Celia's aunt drew a sign in the air with her forefinger, tossed the flaming kindling onto the well-laid, well-oiled bonfire. It flared into a roaring inferno.

"Help me," she instructed Celia.

The women loaded Gunnar's decapitated body onto a sledge and dragged it back to the cemetery. They pushed the headless corpse into its open grave. Rona withdrew a small vial of water from a nearby holy well and sprinkled it on Gunnar's remains.

"*Blessed Mother,*

purify this good man's flesh.

Let him sleep in peace

till the final awakening," Celia and Rona sang as they pushed soil on top of Gunnar's body. When the corpse was covered, they returned to their house. And though the sledge was easier to drag without the weight of Gunnar's body, Celia's feet felt leaden as she neared the bonfire.

"When all that is left are embers, we'll shovel them into buckets, place the buckets on the sledge, and drag the ashes and embers to the sea," explained her aunt. "There, we'll toss them into the waves."

"*To be scrubbed and scattered.*

To be pounded and purified," chanted Celia.

"Yes, my dear. And then, we'll find Lars's body. Have a quick service and burial. No open coffin. No questions."

"Won't people want to know what happened?"

"People will know what happened, though none will ever speak of it save on icy winter nights when sea winds wails, cold trees tap at the window, and children huddle around the hearth begging for stories of ghosts and trolls and draugar."

"It doesn't seem fair. Gunnar could have been a good man."

"Gunnar was a good man," Rona assured her. "He crawled from his grave to see to it that you and his child would be provided for. And I dare say that his spirit will hover close to you all the days of your life."

Celia watched the fire consume the wood, oil, and flesh of the Kettilson men. She shook her head. "I think you're overly romantic, Auntie."

"Perhaps Celia, Mistress of Kettilson Keep."

"What?"

"You're the grieving daughter-in-law of Lars, widow of Gunnar, and soon-to-be mother of Gunnar's child. You'd better get used to the title."

"I didn't consider..."

"No, but I think Gunnar did," replied Rona the Fae-Blessed as she nodded at Gunnar's ghost standing guard, even now, beside his beloved Celia.

Flaming Fuses

Donna Cuttress

THE ISLAND STOOD PROUD of the fast-flowing river. It was a neglected place; no one built a prison on it, or a billionaire's home. The government had never used it for chemical testing and jets did not pretend to blow it up. It was a piece of land that no one wanted, like a mole on perfect skin. There were huts on it, dilapidated, barely standing against the rough weather that battered them, but nothing else that was visible.

Craig and Shaun were going to fix them. They sat on the bonnet of their van, passing a pair of secondhand binoculars between them, examining the buildings from the river bank. The river was wide, the tides ran swiftly and would carry a person out to the open sea within minutes.

Craig rolled a cigarette. His fingers, numb from the cold, pressed the tobacco. The air made Shaun's sinuses tingle, his eyes watered.

"How long have those huts been up?"

Craig lit his cigarette, hands cupped around his lighter's flame.

"They were built about a hundred years ago. Someone stayed there when this was a main shipping line. They had to light a torch at night or in fog, warn the passing ships and boats it was there."

He exhaled the cigarette smoke.

"How long is this job again?"

Craig fumbled with the piece of paper he pulled from his jacket pocket.

"Three days. We have to make the main hut waterproof and update the electrics, for the university."

Shaun had another look at the island, the cold metal frames of the binoculars burning the tender flesh around his eyes.

"Okay, I just hope I can stand being stranded on an island with you! I might jump in and try to swim to shore after a day."

Craig threw the stump of his cigarette into the wind.

"Tide would kill you, mate, or the cold!"

Shaun had another look at the island. He thought he saw someone on the island. A fast black shadow, spearing through the mist that was delicately beginning to cloud their view. He rested the binoculars down on the bonnet.

"And no one's been there for years?"

Craig jumped off the bonnet and stretched his arms upward.

"No one's lived on it for years. Would you?"

Shaun looked again; the island was almost obliterated by the mist.

"Definitely not. I'd rather die than live there."

* * *

The tug boat pulled alongside the jetty, struggling against the approaching tide. Tools and supplies had already been delivered, in crates and boxes waiting to be opened. Craig and Shaun threw their bags onto the shore and jumped onto the jetty. The tug began to pull away before they even had a chance to turn and wave to the skipper.

Shaun stared at the desolate scene in front of him. The place was scattered with dead bird bones and guano. Rotted wood from the huts was strewn on the path, everywhere was wet, dampened through mists and sea spray. Spiked grasses poked through cracked concrete paving slabs, thick tendrils bent against the winds that buffeted the place every day. Wires hung down from the only habitable place, clattering against the windows that faced the head of the island. The beacon was still there, just; its iron skeleton was rusted, its belly long empty of wood or coal.

"It's worse than the pictures, Craig."

Craig grabbed his bag and headed toward the main hut.

"Let's get settled first while this fog clears."

A fog bank was approaching, cutting off the shore. Shadows of houses that they knew were there, slowly began to disappear. A greyness settled between them, dulling all sound and sight. Shaun suddenly felt fearful, terrified of not being visible.

"Now I know how those prisoners felt on Alcatraz."

Craig was trying various keys in the corroded lock that secured the door of their new temporary home. A yellow light that slowly blinked at either end of the island, stumps of concrete with an electric lamp cemented into them, was the only sign that the island was even there. Small pin-pricks of warning.

In the damp cabin, the small grime-covered window panes rattled. Shaun scraped the dirt with his fingernail and peeked through the scratch marks.

"I'm glad you can't see through these windows. Fancy waking up to see a great big ship heading toward you. Terrifying! It took courage to stay here. Imagine the advert for the job. '*Seeking man who likes ships, the sound of the sea and one's own company.*'"

Craig lit the small gas ring cooker they had brought and tried to turn the rusted tap on. A pipe banged somewhere in the room and brown water flew out of the spout. Shaun jumped, the noise was so sudden.

"Fresh water? Out here?"

The water carried on running until it became clear. Craig tasted it with his fingers.

"Must be from a rainwater tank, probably more dangerous than the water. It'll be made of lead, like the pipes."

Craig filled a kettle from their own supply of fresh water and placed it on their stove. The blue light illuminated the room as the dull fog outside darkened everywhere else.

"There was only one man. He was posted on here when he was fourteen. Died here. He never left. Think he's even buried on the island."

He pulled clothes from his bag as Shaun waited for him to continue. Craig lit his cigarette from the gas ring and unrolled a sleeping bag.

"Cal Duffield, he was called."

He threw a crumpled up journal onto the table. It was a cobbled-together photocopied book, all rips and staples that Craig had lifted from a library. A thin history for a small place.

"Some late night reading for you."

He put on another jumper, the hut was freezing. Shaun settled tentatively on an old cot, Craig lay on the floor, looking at their job list, muttering, "Fix windows, check roof tiles and pipes. Secure the island for a new telecommunications mast."

Until that was connected, communication was by a two-way radio. Shaun, who always complained about being too contactable, felt cut off. Adrift. He lay back on the creaking cot, his back beginning to ache, listening to the water flow around them. The tide washed against the shore only a few feet away. He felt drowsy, swallowed up, resting in the belly of a sea monster.

Shaun heard a scraping noise, swift and angry. He thought he could smell fireworks, then realized it was sulfur, and a match burst into flame in his eyeline. Its soft blue glow illuminated a face. A face so close it breathed on him. Its rheumy eyes with their pale irises studied him. Blackened teeth chattered, releasing a peaty odor from its throat. It sneered at him. A dark knitted hat, pushed back from the lined forehead, showed scarred, flaked skin. He stared at Shaun, almost sucking the breath from him. Shaking fingers with red knuckles and blackened nails held a burning match that quickly faded. Shaun was mute. This nightmare was too close. His heart boomed in his chest, pressure growing in his esophagus.

Who is this man? Where was Craig?

Thankfully, the match extinguished. He could hear the river again and the engine of a passing boat. He made himself move, a smothering pressure now lifted.

"Craig! You awake?"

The wait felt endless.

"Yeah. I am now."

His voice was muffled under the sleeping bag. Craig sat up and reached for his torch resting on the floor. He shone it toward Shaun who was shaking, barely breathing.

"There was a man in here. An old man. Watching me while I slept. He struck a match right by my face!"

Craig flashed the light around the room, searching. He shuffled out of his sleeping bag, shoved his bare feet into his boots and ran to check the door and window. Both were secure.

"You've had a nightmare, mate! It's not surprising."

Shaun got up, put on his boots and coat, his hands trembling with fear and cold. He almost pulled the old door off its hinges.

"I need some air."

He stumbled across the muddied pathway, stopping at the small jetty. The nightmare had been vivid; Shaun felt as though he were still in it. Then he saw the first body. He thought it was just rubbish at first. Trash thrown overboard by a reckless crew. Shaun looked closer. It was a body, drifting face down, its billowing jacket looked like a collapsing lung. Then there was another, a woman, her long hair swishing on the surface, her dress dulled, bare arms blotched and scabbed, flesh exposed by nibbling fish. There was another, a sailor's grimacing terror caught in his last drowning moments, gripping a useless life vest. He saw body after body floating in the small bay. Shaun covered his eyes, rubbed them with the freezing heel of his hands. Terrified, he looked up. There were no bodies, no death, just the river and the dilapidated jetty. The sound of a choking boat engine wheezed as it passed in the fog.

Craig waited. It wasn't like Shaun to get so spooked. He sat on his sleeping bag, and shone the torch around the room. The light caught something underneath Shaun's cot. A burned down, blackened match.

* * *

The piercing cry of the whistling kettle woke Shaun up from a brief snatch of sleep. Every time he closed his eyes he saw that face and the bodies…

"The fog's beginning to close in. We'll have to be careful, things can get slippy."

Craig passed him a hot cup of coffee, and they both sat drinking in silence.

"Some nightmare!" Shaun laughed. "Felt real, though."

Craig smiled, deciding not to tell him about the match. They had a lot of work to do and had to be finished by the time the boat came to collect them. They dressed, ate a couple of chocolate bars and gathered their tools. The day passed quickly, measuring, smashing and dismantling. Craig stopped by some overgrowth.

"I don't remember seeing this on the plans."

It was a rounded patch of thickened planks that grass had encroached on. Shaun stood at its edge.

"Careful, it could rotted," Craig said, stepping back.

They both stopped as the dull engine noise of a passing ship echoed around them. The fog had dulled their view again, a distant foghorn sounded intermittently.

"What do you think it is?" Craig tapped the wood with his steel-toed boot.

"If we were on land I would say it was a manhole cover of some sort, or a well. Maybe that's where the fresh water comes from."

"We're in the middle of a salt water river, *idiot*, that leads out to the sea! I don't think it's a well… Could be a tunnel? Maybe Old Cal got sick of waiting for the tug to collect him. He dug his way to shore."

Neither wanted to admit that in this silent place, this rotted wood unnerved them. They decided to investigate it later.

That evening they sat in the hut listening to their radio and the sounding foghorns. Craig was squinting at the list of jobs under the nightlight, slowly crossing them off as he read them. Shaun looked out of the window at the dulling autumn light.

"How come the ships don't hit the island? There's no beacon lit anymore."

"Radar. They all have it, and seafaring maps, I suppose."

He looked out of the window with Shaun. A small fishing boat sailed past. They watched as the cabin lights appeared, then drifted away leaving nothing but the echo of the engine.

"They should have just built a lighthouse."

Shaun began to write in the condensation on the window, illegible in the light.

They struggled into their sleeping bags, and began to doze off as the dimmed light and radio voices lulled them to sleep.

CRACK!

"What's that?" Craig sat up, heart pounding, disorientated, hearing only the gentle music of something classical playing.

CRACK!

Where's Shaun? Shaun?

He sat himself up and reached out to the light at his side. He fumbled with a box of matches and tried to light the shortened wick in the lamp. The flame burned dull and blue.

CRACK!

He felt the floor shift and tried to get up. The ground was giving way, he could feel it. He was outside, standing by the wooden cover! How was he here?

The timbers moved as though breathing beneath him. He saw fingers, ripped skin, and blackened nails scratching through the cracked slats. Craig stumbled backward. He was going to fall through the rotted wood! Where was Shaun? He could hear a faint voices.

"Help?"

"Help us, please."

Craig lost his footing; he fell face downward as the timbers gave way under his weight. He smashed through trying to grab anything to save himself, letting the torch fall from his grasp. Craig fell into a darkness that stank of rotting flesh and had to be hell.

"Wake up, Craig!"

He opened his eyes and looked around him. It was the hut, there was a radio playing, the lamp was electric, not oil, and he was alive. He sat up and checked the floor beneath him. Shaun was staring at him.

"Nightmare?"

Craig nodded.

He stumbled over to the window to open it, but the frame did not move. Craig breathed against the glass, he had seen something.

"What is it, Craig?"

Shaun felt an uneasy panic. Craig was the level-headed one, and now he was acting just as crazy as him. He could hear him fumbling with a box, then that noise. *A match being struck*. The purple light illuminated the window. Craig's shaking hand sending beams of light on the glass.

"*Cal Duffield Island Master 1850–1913*."

Shaun covered his mouth to stop himself almost laughing. The light shone through the words, highlighting the elaborate cursive script, not Shaun's usual handwriting.

"I… I don't remember writing that."

They both stared at each other, feeling engulfed by this abandoned island. A slow tide of terror sweeping along the shore, drowning them. The match burnt out, leaving the grey dawn.

"One more day and we're done here. The boat will be back for us. Let's just finish the job and if we both stay awake we'll be safe."

Throughout the day their movements slowed. Their arms ached and they both began to cough, chests heavy, lungs wet. Craig knew there was something under the timbers. The island's malaise emanated from there. He stood on their edge and reached out for a large stone that had settled by the path. He wanted to release what haunted this island. An island that nobody wanted except Cal Duffield.

He lifted the stone above his head. Shaun gripped the handle of a hammer, waiting.

"Do it, Craig!"

He threw the rock with such force that overhead seagulls screamed as the wood caved in, splintering and crashing downward.

"We could have walked over this and fallen through!"

Shaun leaned over, trying to see how deep the hole went.

"There's something there!" he shouted and fell to his knees to reach in. Craig wanted to stop him, but he felt exhausted. He wanted to let the cold winds roll him into the river and the sea beyond. Shaun grabbed a long wooden pole that was leaning against the wall of the pit. He snatched it in case the rest of the timber crumbled. It was about ten feet long with a large rusted hook at the end.

"It's like those hooks they used to drag struggling kids out of the swimming baths with."

He passed it to Craig. He shielded his eyes from the twilight sun as he looked at it.

"Maybe he used it to drag fallen cargo ashore?"

They smiled at each other. Craig moved first.

"There might be treasure down there!"

He reached the pole into the pit.

"It's hooked *something*! No wonder Duffield never left."

They laughed, and it felt like a release. Something had dissipated, a virus in the fog, pressure building from the isolation.

Craig dragged the pole upward. Through the blackness the hooked object appeared. It was a skull with a large jagged hole smashed through the cranium. The hook entered through the mouth, poking out through an eye socket.

Everything stopped, the river, the clouds. Both men screamed, swore and fell backward. Craig dropped the pole.

"A skull! Did you see it, Shaun? A skull!"

They both sat on the grass, breathing heavily. This was not the treasure they had hoped. Craig stood up, easing his feet to the very edge of the pit, staring into the darkness. He had to see what was at the bottom. He took the matches from his pocket, and slid the cardboard box casing. He looked at the box. It was old, probably been here since Cal Duffield. His hand shook as he looked at the faded green box.

"Bryant and May… Flaming Fuses… the old name for matches."

He struck it, the sound louder than before. Shaun covered his ears, he felt as though the sandpaper was in his brain. Craig dropped the match into the pit. The small blue light briefly illuminated the cave that Duffield created. It was a grave of four, perhaps five bodies. Twelve feet deep. Bones and rags in differing stages of decay. He struck another match and dropped it. Shaun watched him.

"I saw them on the first night, ghosts floating in the water. I thought I was imagining it…"

* * *

Craig poured hot water into the cups and quickly mixed it with huge spoonfuls of coffee. They had to stay awake, the nightmares were too real, but in those silent early hours they soon dozed off. Eyes flickering shut.

That noise. A match being struck. They both woke. Shaun spilled cold coffee onto the floor as his mug slipped away from him. The hut was in darkness apart from the dim glow of an oil lamp.

Craig whispered,

"You awake, Shaun, you seeing this?"

"Yes!"

The door opened, an aggressive hand grabbed the handle of the lamp, straying light fell on his face. The same that had woke Shaun. The man was dragging something heavy and wet. It banged against the door jamb with a squelching thud.

"Let's get you inside, man overboard," and he laughed as he dragged the bloated body through the door. He knelt beside it, rifling through what looked like a uniform. He ripped a silver chain from its neck, pulling at the charm it held, then examined the dead man's pockets, sorting through seaweed and copper coins which he quickly took. He cracked open the man's mouth, looking for gold teeth, then let the head drop in disgust when there were none.

Craig and Shaun watched as the man looked out of the window to check the beacon, flames sputtered in the buffering winds. The man grabbed a box of matches from the table and put them in his pocket, opened the door, and taking hold of the long pole from the wall outside, dragged the dead hooked sailor outside.

"What a big fish you are!"

The door closed. Shaun and Craig edged toward the door, opening it slightly, needing to see what he did. In the light of the beacon, they watched Cal Duffield, Master of the Island, open the trapdoor to the pit and kick the body of the dead sailor into it. He let the lid slam shut, and threw the long hook to the ground. Duffield, heaving his heavily booted feet through the muddy pathway, threw two logs onto the beacon from a dumped hessian sack.

He headed back to the hut, swaying in the torchlight, whistling a slow tune through his rotten teeth. Shaun and Craig hid behind the door, not breathing, watching this miserable ghost at its worst. He examined the silver charm from the drowned sailor, then cleaned it on the sleeve of his oilskin. From underneath the cot Shaun had slept on, he pulled out a tin box from a hole in the boards. Duffield pulled the matchbox from his pocket, slid it open and took out a key. The box burst with trinkets, charms and lockets. In two separated compartments were coins and gold teeth; it was laden with drowned memories. He tossed in the charm, locked the box and shoved it back into its resting place.

The ghost stumbled outside, banging the door after it. Craig felt inside his pocket. It was the box of matches he had been using ever since he had arrived. Shaun watched him slide the box open. Inside was a small rusted key, among several unspent matches. He reached underneath the cot. The boards were loose, slipping apart quickly. Craig reached his hand into the gap and grabbed hold of the tin box. He placed it on the cot and opened it; tarnished treasure spilled out.

Craig felt the cold hook grab him around the neck, the blunt rusted point slowly piercing the flesh of his throat. He felt his windpipe close as any oxygen he had was pushed from his body.

"Another big fish! How did you get here? Ferry's not due for days."

He yanked Craig backward away from the bed. The box tipped and the stolen treasures shone in the lamplight. Duffield smacked Craig's head against the door jamb, trying to knock him out.

"How did you get here? Answer me!"

Dizzy, Craig tried to grab the hook from his throat, but his arms flailed around him, searching for purchase on anything as he was dragged along the wet paving slabs. He could not shout, as he felt his breath fade. His fingers ripped at the grasses, trailing in the muddy path, his feet kicked out behind him.

Shaun! Where is Shaun? his thoughts raced, as he began blacking out.

Call Duffield kicked open the trapdoor. Craig could smell the stench of the decaying bodies inside, left to rot in an unconsecrated grave.

"You can go in with all the other flotsam and jetsam!"

Duffield dragged Craig's body to the pit.

"*Cal Duffield!*"

Shaun was screaming, stood next to the burning beacon of the island, struggling to hold a pitcher of water above his head. He screamed the name again. Duffield dropped the hook, leaving Craig gasping for air.

"You cannot do that! You cannot extinguish the beacon!"

Shaun emptied the pitcher over the flames, and kicked its contents into the river. The embers hissed and cracked against the freezing salt water. The old man screamed as he searched his pockets for matches, his flaming fuses to relight the beacon, panicking and gibbering to himself as the wind blew around him. His straggly grey hair stuck wet to his mouth, masking his panic-stricken voice. Duffield stopped, as Craig stumbled next to him, shaking the old box of matches.

"Looking for these?"

Craig threw the box into the pit of bloated bodies, those unfortunates who had washed ashore drowned in accidents, suicides and shipwrecks. Cal Duffield tried to catch them, falling into the pit, screaming about the beacon.

The bones and rotted flesh became animated, grabbing at the man who had tossed them away like rubbish. Wet bony hands reached for his face and throat, gouging his eyes and ripping his hair. Craig dropped the door over them and the screams stopped instantly. The past was contained.

Dawn began to rise. The fog had lifted, leaving only a dull mist. A faint outline of the opposing bank was now visible. Craig and Shaun sat on the small jetty and waited for the tug. Neither dared mention the treasure, the hut or the pit. Cal Duffield could suffer forever. The ghosts of the drowned had waited, and their business was settled for now.

The House, the Garden, and Occupants

by Amanda C. Davis

THIS IS ANNE, with shreds of her gown wisping away like the edges of clouds, at the elbow of the grand staircase where the iron-framed window overlooks a patch of garden entombed in briars. She casts a glow onto the wall that reflects faintly but bestows her no shadow. She is riveted to the window; her face is watery, difficult to make out, but her posture reveals her inner workings. A clock chimes midnight. Slowly, she lowers her head. Slowly, she turns from the window. She takes a single step upstairs before she dissipates like fog under the sun.

The first time she took this path she followed it to her bedroom, to a letter-opener strewn on her writing desk, to her bath, to her grave. Now she exists only in a narrow series of moments. She only completed this path once.

Anne comes with the first stroke of midnight and leaves with the last; she knows nothing but midnight, and the word that falls from her ghostly lips, unheard, and those things have composed the full of her existence for over one hundred years.

* * *

This is the column of light that flares in the garden, as tall as a tree and bright as an angel, just after the last chime of midnight. It burns bright for a single blink of an eye before it collapses to the earth, leaving the night empty and dead. A pool of light lingers at its base. The garden shifts. Its shadows follow no rules.

The column of light, in its youngest years, answered to Boy, and then to Groom, and a host of careless and vicious names in between, but the only name it will answer to now is the last one it knew, the one that Anne called it. If the light speaks, it has never been heard; if it knows anything at all, it is the single moment of flaring and falling, too quick to grasp. Its existence is an eternal cycle of light and dark. It moves so fast that life from its perspective might be a single blur of light. But it will never tell.

* * *

This is the roil of malice that dwells in the crack above the lintel of the front door, a seething coil tight as a Gordian knot, black as blindness, in a place no light can reach.

* * *

This is Jacob Winterbeam, twenty-five, who has sunk the savings of his brief life into an estate that has by disrepair or disrepute been spared the indignity of subdivisions and commercial zoning. He rolls his suitcase behind him and props it at the base of the grand staircase and puts his hands on his hips and wonders just what he has gotten himself into. He wears a brown suit jacket over his blue jeans; he affected a style of fashion when he was a teaching assistant and hasn't been able to shake it. He is as unchangeable as Anne, in some ways.

Jacob knows a former classmate who he thinks might look at him in a new light if he can restore the house and gardens the way he thinks he can – the way he said he could. He imagines her perched at the base of the grand staircase with a steaming mug between both hands, knees up, head tilted toward him, laughing. It isn't such a far-fetched dream. She'd sat with him in a similar way at school. If he'd only said something then…

But soon, soon he'll really have something to talk about. To promise her.

Jacob stows his bags in the kitchen – the only really livable room left – and takes a long, slow walk around his new property. The gardens first. They are expansive, and labyrinthine with overgrowth. He notices strange square indentations in the moss where stables or sheds have been mown down and grown over. There are boggy parts and places made impassable with wild briars. Jacob has plans for the landscape (he wants to keep the wildflowers, to let it retain the lush blowsy look that charmed him so much) but his real effort will go toward restoring the house.

The foundation is solid. The walls will hold. The only heat is by fireplace and if there was ever air conditioning, it was an arcane system of cold wet cloths over strategically open windows, maintained by knowledge long-lost. It's spring, so Jacob expects not to scald or freeze. The downstairs is superficially a shambles, but Jacob has seen good paneling behind the mothy wallpaper and tapped on solid stone behind crumbling doorframes. The house persists.

The roof is a tragedy of misuse, a leaking, rotted thatch, and the condition of the rooms below it makes him weep. The ground floor has been thrashed about but the upper floors have been gutted, drenched, burnt, and infested. Their ecological structure is vast: molds and fungi, pale grass sprouting in the corners from wayward seeds, insects and arachnids, mice in the walls, birds in the rafters.

Still! The foundation is solid. Jacob sees in triple: what the house is, what the house was, what the house will be.

He calls the former classmate and tells her that he's moved in. He's ready to begin. She's very excited for him. He spills his hopes and dreams and hangs up before telling her the one thing he's wanted to say to her for five years. The one thing he can only tell her when he's made something of himself. When he's completed the house.

* * *

This is Jacob meeting Anne for the first time.

He has a plastic mug of water in his hand and is trudging upstairs in his boxers and a t-shirt from high school. (The first room on the left is livable! It's such a triumph that he has moved out of the kitchen.) Anne blinks into the moment like smoke from an extinguished fire. Jacob stops where he is.

Anne stares out the window. She lowers her head. Turns. Puts her wisp of a foot on the first stair after the landing and dissolves into the dark of night.

Jacob sits down so he doesn't fall. He is clutching the plastic mug harder than he has ever clutched anything in his life. His stomach is wrong, his heart an enraged prisoner of his ribs. He thinks – clarity returning, but not reason – "But I paid in cash!" He is indignant. The house is his! Fully his! What is this colorless thing doing in *his* house?

He sits on the staircase until it occurs to him that she might return. He goes back downstairs and gets his keys and wallet and spends the night in a hotel in his boxers and high-school t-shirt, reliving midnight repeatedly through incessant, shivery dreams.

* * *

This is the former classmate that Jacob is trying to impress. Her name is Kamren.

She's wearing a plaid jacket nipped in at the waist and a quirky knit cap over her long, straight hair, angling her chin toward the restored part of the roof. "This place is incredible."

Jacob's chest swells. "Wait 'til you see the garden. It's still this huge mess but I cut through the growth so you can walk around – this place was really vast once, it's been chipped away a little, but look how much is still intact. I found some stone paths and cleaned them up. Come look!"

She has her head tilted toward him as he talks; Kamren is deaf in one ear, so she reads lips and approaches conversations from charmingly particular angles. She follows him around to the footprint of the vanished stable. The column of light rears near here, nightly – but Jacob doesn't know that yet. "I can't believe it," she says, over and over. "Are you going to live here when you're done?"

"I might," he says, "I might. Actually –"

He is so desperately excited, the day is so bright and Kamren has come such a long way that he does what he promised not to do, and tells her about Anne.

Her grin falters, her eyes crinkle, and he can tell she's not sure whether he's joking or not, so he shrugs and says, "That's what I saw, anyway. Funny old houses."

"Old houses," she agrees. "How's it on the inside? What are you doing with the flooring?"

He tells her about the flooring.

The other thing he wants to tell her eats at his lungs until he can barely breathe.

* * *

This is not the second time Jacob has seen Anne. It's the fortieth. It *is* the first time he has dared stand where she stands, and see what she sees.

Tonight, he is at the landing long minutes before midnight, fully-dressed, chilled through, terrified at his own boldness. If he's right (he's sure he's right) the spirit whose name he doesn't know will appear directly on top of him. He doesn't know where to look – she'll be on him, within him! – so he looks where she looks. Out the window.

He resolutely resists checking his watch. She's coming, but counting it down would make him crazy.

The wild growth of the estate is shaping into something that will pass for gardens someday. He's wired much of the house for electricity but the garden is still a well of dark. Untrimmed trees and bowers hide the sky. Tense with anticipation as he is, he can still enjoy the pride seeping through him as he takes in what he's accomplished so far.

She appears in – around – through him. Jacob staggers and falls. He crashes an arm against the marble stair and his single roared curse echoes on the paneled walls. Anne holds her position; stares; droops; turns; and puts her foot through Jacob's chest before whisking out of the single brief scene that she forever plays. This time Jacob whispers his curse. He'd thought he was used to being around her, but the chill of her heel through his heart hurt like a punch. He turns his eyes to the window.

From the corner of the garden, almost out of sight, a column of light explodes like a beacon and immediately extinguishes. In its moment, it is white as the glare of the sun on snow.

Jacob leaps to his feet, but the column of light is gone, and does not return.

He sits again, working things out. Of course the column of light in the garden was a passing car. Of course it was a dog-walker with a flashlight or a couple of trespassing kids. Of course it was a wet stone reflecting the full moon. Of course.

Of course it was natural. Except deep in the blinding depths, Jacob is sure he saw that the column of light had a face.

* * *

This is the creak of the unspooling roil of malice, flexing its coils like a waking snake, feeling for the crack in its lintel, feeling for the walls, feeling, feeling.

Listening.

* * *

This is the corner of the garden where Jacob saw the column of light, and this time, he's ready; he has a hat and a baseball bat and a flashlight and a folding chair and he is going to sit here until midnight passes and he's convinced himself that this expensive, unhelpful, *needy* house has only one ghost in it.

Instead, he sees the column of light again.

It is a burst, a brilliant flicker. It is an explosion. It is a ray of heaven. It comes just after midnight and lives until Jacob blinks. It is a mayfly of an apparition.

For the first time, Jacob is infuriated by the brevity of his hauntings. How is he supposed to truly understand what he is seeing if it lives in bursts of moments like this? "*Who are you?*" he screams at the darkness, and immediately regrets it; he's out in the country, but he still has neighbors. In a different voice, he says, "Who are you and what do you want?"

The column of light doesn't answer; it's long gone. Anne has never answered him either.

Jacob employs technology the following night. His video cameras capture nothing. But he sees the column of light a second time, and now he's sure: it has a face, and it's looking at the house.

He sleeps in the restored room where Anne died, fitfully, waking himself often with guesses and revelations and the dull chilly suspicion that even now, after midnight has ended and the visions gone, he is not alone.

* * *

This is what Jacob learns at the historical society, after enduring an hour of unbearable chit-chat and paying his five-dollar membership fee and learning to work a microfiche: her name is Anne, and she slit her wrists with a letter opener in the bath.

He's delighted to have found her, but puzzled that she appears not at the moment of suicide, but on the staircase landing, at what could surely be any random moment of her life.

She must have ascended thousands of times, pausing often. What gave that moment the gravity that caused her to stick fast to it, long after her death? Could it possibly be nothing more than a glitch in her personal record, an inexplicable, inconsequential pebble in the stream of time? Jacob doesn't think so, but he's at a loss to guess otherwise.

He finds nothing else in the microfiche, but he was never good at research.

Jacob makes plans while scraping the chipped paint from the dining-room wall. He's a planner; how could he have brought the house this far, on this budget, without a plan? He knows cameras and recording devices won't help him. He knows there are two hauntings, but only one still seems human, and he only knows one name. He knows Anne stands at the window and he has watched her enough times, closely enough, to know that while she stares, before her head droops, her watery lips speak a silent word.

Kamren reads lips.

Jacob has his plan.

* * *

This is creepy, Kamren types into her cell phone, leaning against the wrought-iron railing around the landing of the grand staircase. *You're freaking me out.* She's a fan of horror movies and Halloween, so she loves it. She knows she's being pranked but has to admit that so far, it's a fun one.

Stay in position, Jacob texts back. *You only have a second. Don't miss it. Are you in position?*

Sure, she lies brightly, and moves back to the spot where he put her, which is not as comfortable.

In the garden, Jacob paces, certain his timing will be wrong, convinced that this will be the one night Anne doesn't come, imagining a vast tree of fate branching into millions of possible failures. He's not sure whether he'll have another chance at this. Even if the ghostly cycle repeats tomorrow night, Kamren won't be here, and he realizes – with a dull shock – he's almost less interested in exorcising his home than in Kamren watching him do it.

It's that kind of misplaced focus that's going to ruin things, he tells himself, and starts pacing again.

In the crack over the lintel, the roil of malice throbs.

It is no longer a person (or perhaps never was). It is not even the echo of a long-ago vile act. The roil is a reduction: pure intent. Its long invisible feelers sense interruption of itself – somewhere, something thwarts it. The roil dribbles from the crack above the lintel. Threads like the tips of grapevines twine through the house and garden.

The intent turns itself into action.

Kamren startles as Jacob's text vanishes from her phone. The screen is black. She whacks it on the heel of her palm, tries to flick it on and off. Nothing. She's impressed at how far he's going just to get a rise out of her. But through the window she sees the silhouette of Jacob waving his arms. He points to his hand. His phone is dark too? What's the point of that? Overkill, she thinks.

She turns from the window just in time to see Anne approach.

Kamren freezes. Anne stares out the window – toward Jacob, Kamren thinks, toward the other-thing-Jacob-says-he-saw – and her lips move. Kamren, who has been lip-reading since elementary school, sees it as clearly as she hears the chime of the clock under the stairs.

One word. Anne lowers her head. She has nothing more to say. She turns her back on the window.

It's no prank. It's such a powerful word. Kamren is electrified by purpose. The moment is at hand. Jacob told her to text the moment Anne spoke, but the phone is still black, and Jacob is so far away!

Kamren does something she will later dream about: she launches herself through Anne to grapple at the window.

Anne is made of cold and longing and regret and time, infinite time. Kamren tries hard to ignore all that. She grabs the window crank. Jacob's within shouting distance. Perhaps she can shout –

The roil of malice strikes like a viper. The handle comes off in Kamren's hand. The window won't open. Anne is turning, turning, time dilates like a flower, and Kamren knows the moment is almost gone, and that to let Anne endure one more moment of midnight would be a hellish cruelty.

She puts her elbow through the window and draws it back salted in glass. She stoops to the opening.

"*Beloved!*" she screams through the gap. "*She said Beloved!*"

"Beloved," says Jacob. He turns just quickly enough to see the column flare tree-tall. "Anne said 'Beloved!'"

Like a fountain, the column of light gushes up. Not like a fountain, not like itself, it stays.

What happens next isn't a groan or a scream, it's both, only inaudible, a wind of unspoken word, a tornado composed solely of Anne's name. Jacob, suddenly terrified, staggers. The column of light tears from the spot where it has sprung every night for over a century and streams across the garden toward the house. It is absurd and terrible. Jacob's throat clenches. He's not sure why.

On the landing, Anne's foot stops on the first step toward the upstairs. Kamren turns from the window. She has seen the column of light making its charge toward them and thinks she will die of horror or joy. "Anne," she says, "Beloved is coming!"

Anne turns. She has never turned before.

"Beloved," she says, and this time, even Jacob could have heard her.

Anne's dim glow sends out sparks until she is a blue flame, a torch against the cold stone wall. She passes Kamren without giving her a second glance – why would she? – and hurtles downstairs like Mercury. Her feet might or might not touch the marble.

The column of light and the bright blue remnants of Anne meet in the open door, under the lintel where the roil of malice lives, and collide.

This is the last moment.

Light floods the house and garden. Light fills the cracks where light has never been. The roil of malice shrivels like hairs put to flame. It has no power against this union. The three – Anne and column and roil – implode to a dot so bright it could burn steel. The clock chimes midnight. All three vanish.

Jacob stands in the garden holding his dead cell phone, baffled and exhausted, feeling as if he has seen God. His mind tells him a hundred stories about what might have happened a hundred years ago, all inventions, because how could he ever know? They are overlaid by a hundred more stories wondering what might have happened if Anne and her Beloved had heard each other call their names all those years ago.

But it's over. The air is clean. He's certain. At last, Anne and her Beloved have left midnight. At last, they will be together come morning.

And tomorrow, Jacob will tell Kamren what he has wanted to tell her since the day he first saw her brush her hair from her shoulder and smile his way. He knows just what word he will use. Suddenly, he's not at all afraid of what she might say in return.

* * *

This is the house, Jacob and Kamren tell each other later; it's messy, it's perfect, and it's complete.

The Signal-Man

by Charles Dickens

"HALLOA! BELOW THERE!"

When he heard a voice thus calling to him, he was standing at the door of his box, with a flag in his hand, furled round its short pole. One would have thought, considering the nature of the ground, that he could not have doubted from what quarter the voice came; but instead of looking up to where I stood on the top of the steep cutting nearly over his head, he turned himself about, and looked down the Line. There was something remarkable in his manner of doing so, though I could not have said for my life what. But I know it was remarkable enough to attract my notice, even though his figure was foreshortened and shadowed, down in the deep trench, and mine was high above him, so steeped in the glow of an angry sunset, that I had shaded my eyes with my hand before I saw him at all.

"Halloa! Below!"

From looking down the Line, he turned himself about again, and, raising his eyes, saw my figure high above him.

"Is there any path by which I can come down and speak to you?"

He looked up at me without replying, and I looked down at him without pressing him too soon with a repetition of my idle question. Just then there came a vague vibration in the earth and air, quickly changing into a violent pulsation, and an oncoming rush that caused me to start back, as though it had force to draw me down. When such vapour as rose to my height from this rapid train had passed me, and was skimming away over the landscape, I looked down again, and saw him re-furling the flag he had shown while the train went by.

I repeated my inquiry. After a pause, during which he seemed to regard me with fixed attention, he motioned with his rolled-up flag towards a point on my level, some two or three hundred yards distant. I called down to him, "All right!" and made for that point. There, by dint of looking closely about me, I found a rough zigzag descending path notched out, which I followed.

The cutting was extremely deep, and unusually precipitate. It was made through a clammy stone, that became oozier and wetter as I went down. For these reasons, I found the way long enough to give me time to recall a singular air of reluctance or compulsion with which he had pointed out the path.

When I came down low enough upon the zigzag descent to see him again, I saw that he was standing between the rails on the way by which the train had lately passed, in an attitude as if he were waiting for me to appear. He had his left hand at his chin, and that left elbow rested on his right hand, crossed over his breast. His attitude was one of such expectation and watchfulness that I stopped a moment, wondering at it.

I resumed my downward way, and stepping out upon the level of the railroad, and drawing nearer to him, saw that he was a dark sallow man, with a dark beard and rather heavy eyebrows. His post was in as solitary and dismal a place as ever I saw. On either side, a dripping-wet wall of jagged stone, excluding all view but a strip of sky; the perspective one way only a crooked prolongation of this great dungeon; the shorter perspective in the other direction terminating in a gloomy red light, and the gloomier entrance to a black tunnel, in whose massive architecture there was a barbarous, depressing, and forbidding air. So little sunlight ever found its way to this spot, that it had an earthy, deadly smell; and so much cold wind rushed through it, that it struck chill to me, as if I had left the natural world.

Before he stirred, I was near enough to him to have touched him. Not even then removing his eyes from mine, he stepped back one step, and lifted his hand.

This was a lonesome post to occupy (I said), and it had riveted my attention when I looked down from up yonder. A visitor was a rarity, I should suppose; not an unwelcome rarity, I hoped? In me, he merely saw a man who had been shut up within narrow limits all his life, and who, being at last set free, had a newly-awakened interest in these great works. To such purpose I spoke to him; but I am far from sure of the terms I used; for, besides that I am not happy in opening any conversation, there was something in the man that daunted me.

He directed a most curious look towards the red light near the tunnel's mouth, and looked all about it, as if something were missing from it, and then looked at me.

That light was part of his charge? Was it not?

He answered in a low voice – "Don't you know it is?"

The monstrous thought came into my mind, as I perused the fixed eyes and the saturnine face, that this was a spirit, not a man. I have speculated since, whether there may have been infection in his mind.

In my turn, I stepped back. But in making the action, I detected in his eyes some latent fear of me. This put the monstrous thought to flight.

"You look at me," I said, forcing a smile, "as if you had a dread of me."

"I was doubtful," he returned, "whether I had seen you before."

"Where?"

He pointed to the red light he had looked at.

"There?" I said.

Intently watchful of me, he replied (but without sound), "Yes."

"My good fellow, what should I do there? However, be that as it may, I never was there, you may swear."

"I think I may," he rejoined. "Yes; I am sure I may."

His manner cleared, like my own. He replied to my remarks with readiness, and in well-chosen words. Had he much to do there? Yes; that was to say, he had enough responsibility to bear; but exactness and watchfulness were what was required of him, and of actual work – manual labour – he had next to none. To change that signal, to trim those lights, and to turn this iron handle now and then, was all he had to do under that head. Regarding those many long and lonely hours of which I seemed to make so much, he could only say that the routine of his life had shaped itself into that form, and he had grown used to it. He had taught himself a language down here – if only to know it by sight, and to have formed his own crude ideas of its pronunciation, could be called learning it. He had also worked at fractions and decimals, and tried a little algebra; but he was, and had been as a boy, a poor hand at figures. Was it necessary for him when on duty always to remain in that channel of damp air, and could he never rise into the sunshine from between those high stone walls? Why, that depended upon times and circumstances. Under some conditions there would be less upon the Line than under others, and the same held good as to certain hours of the day and night. In bright weather, he did choose occasions for getting a little above these lower shadows; but, being at all times liable to be called by his electric bell, and at such times listening for it with redoubled anxiety, the relief was less than I would suppose.

He took me into his box, where there was a fire, a desk for an official book in which he had to make certain entries, a telegraphic instrument with its dial, face, and needles, and the little bell of which he had spoken. On my trusting that he would excuse the remark that he had been well educated, and (I hoped I might say without offence) perhaps educated above that station, he observed that instances of slight incongruity in such wise would rarely be found wanting among large bodies of men; that he had heard it was so in workhouses, in the police force, even in that last desperate resource, the army; and that he knew it was so, more or less, in any great railway staff. He had been, when young (if I could believe it, sitting in that hut – he scarcely could), a student of natural philosophy, and had attended lectures; but he had run wild, misused his opportunities, gone down, and never risen again. He had no complaint to offer about that. He had made his bed, and he lay upon it. It was far too late to make another.

All that I have here condensed he said in a quiet manner, with his grave dark regards divided between me and the fire. He threw in the word "Sir" from time to time, and especially when he referred to his youth – as though to request me to understand that he claimed to be nothing but what I found him. He was several times interrupted by the little bell, and had to read off messages, and send replies. Once he had to stand without the door, and display a flag as a train passed, and make some verbal communication to the driver. In the discharge of his duties, I observed him to be remarkably exact and vigilant, breaking off his discourse at a syllable, and remaining silent until what he had to do was done.

In a word, I should have set this man down as one of the safest of men to be employed in that capacity, but for the circumstance that while he was speaking to me he twice broke off with a fallen colour, turned his face towards the little bell when it did not ring, opened the door of the hut (which was kept shut to exclude the unhealthy damp), and looked out towards the red light near the mouth of the tunnel. On both of those occasions, he came back to the fire with the inexplicable air upon him which I had remarked, without being able to define, when we were so far asunder.

Said I, when I rose to leave him, "You almost make me think that I have met with a contented man."

(I am afraid I must acknowledge that I said it to lead him on.)

"I believe I used to be so," he rejoined, in the low voice in which he had first spoken; "but I am troubled, sir, I am troubled."

He would have recalled the words if he could. He had said them, however, and I took them up quickly.

"With what? What is your trouble?"

"It is very difficult to impart, sir. It is very, very difficult to speak of. If ever you make me another visit, I will try to tell you."

"But I expressly intend to make you another visit. Say, when shall it be?"

"I go off early in the morning, and I shall be on again at ten tomorrow night, sir."

"I will come at eleven."

He thanked me, and went out at the door with me. "I'll show my white light, sir," he said, in his peculiar low voice, "till you have found the way up. When you have found it, don't call out! And when you are at the top, don't call out!"

His manner seemed to make the place strike colder to me, but I said no more than, "Very well."

"And when you come down tomorrow night, don't call out! Let me ask you a parting question. What made you cry, 'Halloa! Below there!' tonight?"

"Heaven knows," said I. "I cried something to that effect –"

"Not to that effect, sir. Those were the very words. I know them well."

"Admit those were the very words. I said them, no doubt, because I saw you below."

"For no other reason?"

"What other reason could I possibly have?"

"You had no feeling that they were conveyed to you in any supernatural way?"

"No."

He wished me good-night, and held up his light. I walked by the side of the down Line of rails (with a very disagreeable sensation of a train coming behind me) until I found the path. It was easier to mount than to descend, and I got back to my inn without any adventure.

Punctual to my appointment, I placed my foot on the first notch of the zigzag next night, as the distant clocks were striking eleven. He was waiting for me at the bottom, with his white light on. "I have not called out," I said, when we came close together; "may I speak now?" "By all means, sir." "Good-night, then, and here's my hand." "Good-night, sir, and here's mine." With that we walked side by side to his box, entered it, closed the door, and sat down by the fire.

"I have made up my mind, sir," he began, bending forward as soon as we were seated, and speaking in a tone but a little above a whisper, "that you shall not have to ask me twice what troubles me. I took you for someone else yesterday evening. That troubles me."

"That mistake?"

"No. That someone else."

"Who is it?"

"I don't know."

"Like me?"

"I don't know. I never saw the face. The left arm is across the face, and the right arm is waved – violently waved. This way."

I followed his action with my eyes, and it was the action of an arm gesticulating, with the utmost passion and vehemence, "For God's sake, clear the way!"

"One moonlight night," said the man, "I was sitting here, when I heard a voice cry, 'Halloa! Below there!' I started up, looked from that door, and saw this Someone else standing by the red light near the tunnel, waving as I just now showed you. The voice seemed hoarse with shouting, and it cried, 'Look out! Look out!' And then again, 'Halloa! Below there! Look out!' I caught up my lamp, turned it on red, and ran towards the figure, calling, 'What's wrong? What has happened? Where?' It stood just outside the blackness of the tunnel. I advanced so close upon it that I wondered at its keeping the sleeve across its eyes. I ran right up at it, and had my hand stretched out to pull the sleeve away, when it was gone."

"Into the tunnel?" said I.

"No. I ran on into the tunnel, five hundred yards. I stopped, and held my lamp above my head, and saw the figures of the measured distance, and saw the wet stains stealing down the walls and trickling through the arch. I ran out again faster than I had run in (for I had a mortal abhorrence of the place upon me), and I looked all round the red light with my own red light, and I went up the iron ladder to the gallery atop of it, and I came down again, and ran back here. I telegraphed both ways, 'An alarm has been given. Is anything wrong?' The answer came back, both ways, 'All well.'"

Resisting the slow touch of a frozen finger tracing out my spine, I showed him how that this figure must be a deception of his sense of sight; and how that figures, originating in disease of the delicate nerves that minister to the functions of the eye, were known to have often troubled patients, some of whom had become conscious of the nature of their affliction, and had even proved it by experiments upon themselves. "As to an imaginary cry," said I, "do but listen for a moment to the wind in this unnatural valley while we speak so low, and to the wild harp it makes of the telegraph wires."

That was all very well, he returned, after we had sat listening for a while, and he ought to know something of the wind and the wires – he who so often passed long winter nights there, alone and watching. But he would beg to remark that he had not finished.

I asked his pardon, and he slowly added these words, touching my arm –

"Within six hours after the Appearance, the memorable accident on this Line happened, and within ten hours the dead and wounded were brought along through the tunnel over the spot where the figure had stood."

A disagreeable shudder crept over me, but I did my best against it. It was not to be denied, I rejoined, that this was a remarkable coincidence, calculated deeply to impress his mind. But it was unquestionable that remarkable coincidences did continually occur, and they must be taken into account in dealing with such a subject. Though to be sure I must admit, I added (for I thought I saw that he was going to bring the objection to bear upon me), men of common sense did not allow much for coincidences in making the ordinary calculations of life.

He again begged to remark that he had not finished.

I again begged his pardon for being betrayed into interruptions.

"This," he said, again laying his hand upon my arm, and glancing over his shoulder with hollow eyes, "was just a year ago. Six or seven months passed, and I had recovered from the surprise and shock, when one morning, as the day was breaking, I, standing at the door, looked towards the red light, and saw the spectre again." He stopped, with a fixed look at me.

"Did it cry out?"

"No. It was silent."

"Did it wave its arm?"

"No. It leaned against the shaft of the light, with both hands before the face. Like this."

Once more I followed his action with my eyes. It was an action of mourning. I have seen such an attitude in stone figures on tombs.

"Did you go up to it?"

"I came in and sat down, partly to collect my thoughts, partly because it had turned me faint. When I went to the door again, daylight was above me, and the ghost was gone."

"But nothing followed? Nothing came of this?"

He touched me on the arm with his forefinger twice or thrice giving a ghastly nod each time:

"That very day, as a train came out of the tunnel, I noticed, at a carriage window on my side, what looked like a confusion of hands and heads, and something waved. I saw it just in time to signal the driver, Stop! He shut off, and put his brake on, but the train drifted past here a hundred and fifty yards or more. I ran after it, and, as I went along, heard terrible screams and cries. A beautiful young lady had died instantaneously in one of the compartments, and was brought in here, and laid down on this floor between us."

Involuntarily I pushed my chair back, as I looked from the boards at which he pointed to himself.

"True, sir. True. Precisely as it happened, so I tell it you."

I could think of nothing to say, to any purpose, and my mouth was very dry. The wind and the wires took up the story with a long lamenting wail.

He resumed. "Now, sir, mark this, and judge how my mind is troubled. The spectre came back a week ago. Ever since, it has been there, now and again, by fits and starts."

"At the light?"

"At the Danger-light."

"What does it seem to do?"

He repeated, if possible with increased passion and vehemence, that former gesticulation of, "For God's sake, clear the way!"

Then he went on. "I have no peace or rest for it. It calls to me, for many minutes together, in an agonised manner, 'Below there! Look out! Look out!' It stands waving to me. It rings my little bell –"

I caught at that. "Did it ring your bell yesterday evening when I was here, and you went to the door?"

"Twice."

"Why, see," said I, "how your imagination misleads you. My eyes were on the bell, and my ears were open to the bell, and if I am a living man, it did not ring at those times. No, nor at any other time, except when it was rung in the natural course of physical things by the station communicating with you."

He shook his head. "I have never made a mistake as to that yet, sir. I have never confused the spectre's ring with the man's. The ghost's ring is a strange vibration in the bell that it derives from nothing else, and I have not asserted that the bell stirs to the eye. I don't wonder that you failed to hear it. But I heard it."

"And did the spectre seem to be there, when you looked out?"

"It was there."

"Both times?"

He repeated firmly: "Both times."

"Will you come to the door with me, and look for it now?"

He bit his under lip as though he were somewhat unwilling, but arose. I opened the door, and stood on the step, while he stood in the doorway. There was the Danger-light. There was the dismal mouth of the tunnel. There were the high, wet stone walls of the cutting. There were the stars above them.

"Do you see it?" I asked him, taking particular note of his face. His eyes were prominent and strained, but not very much more so, perhaps, than my own had been when I had directed them earnestly towards the same spot.

"No," he answered. "It is not there."

"Agreed," said I.

We went in again, shut the door, and resumed our seats. I was thinking how best to improve this advantage, if it might be called one, when he took up the conversation in such a matter-of-course way, so assuming that there could be no serious question of fact between us, that I felt myself placed in the weakest of positions.

"By this time you will fully understand, sir," he said, "that what troubles me so dreadfully is the question, What does the spectre mean?"

I was not sure, I told him, that I did fully understand.

"What is its warning against?" he said, ruminating, with his eyes on the fire, and only by times turning them on me. "What is the danger? Where is the danger? There is danger overhanging somewhere on the Line. Some dreadful calamity will happen. It is not to be doubted this third time, after what has gone before. But surely this is a cruel haunting of me. What can I do?"

He pulled out his handkerchief, and wiped the drops from his heated forehead.

"If I telegraph Danger, on either side of me, or on both, I can give no reason for it," he went on, wiping the palms of his hands. "I should get into trouble, and do no good. They would think I was mad. This is the way it would work – Message: 'Danger! Take care!' Answer: 'What Danger? Where?' Message: 'Don't know. But, for God's sake, take care!' They would displace me. What else could they do?"

His pain of mind was most pitiable to see. It was the mental torture of a conscientious man, oppressed beyond endurance by an unintelligible responsibility involving life.

"When it first stood under the Danger-light," he went on, putting his dark hair back from his head, and drawing his hands outward across and across his temples in an extremity of feverish distress, "why not tell me where that accident was to happen – if it must happen? Why not tell me how it could be averted – if it could have been averted? When on its second coming it hid its face, why not tell me, instead, 'She is going to die. Let them keep her at home'? If it came, on those two occasions, only to show me that its warnings were true, and so to prepare me for the third, why not warn me plainly now? And I, Lord help me! A mere poor signal-man on this solitary station! Why not go to somebody with credit to be believed, and power to act?"

When I saw him in this state, I saw that for the poor man's sake, as well as for the public safety, what I had to do for the time was to compose his mind. Therefore, setting aside all question of reality or unreality between us, I represented to him that whoever thoroughly discharged his duty must do well, and that at least it was his comfort that he understood his duty, though he did not understand these confounding Appearances. In this effort I succeeded far better than in the attempt to reason him out of his conviction. He became calm; the occupations incidental to his post as the night advanced began to make larger demands on his attention: and I left him at two in the morning. I had offered to stay through the night, but he would not hear of it.

That I more than once looked back at the red light as I ascended the pathway, that I did not like the red light, and that I should have slept but poorly if my bed had been under it, I see no reason to conceal. Nor did I like the two sequences of the accident and the dead girl. I see no reason to conceal that either.

But what ran most in my thoughts was the consideration how ought I to act, having become the recipient of this disclosure? I had proved the man to be intelligent, vigilant, painstaking, and exact; but how long might he remain so, in his state of mind? Though in a subordinate position, still he held a most important trust, and would I (for instance) like to stake my own life on the chances of his continuing to execute it with precision?

Unable to overcome a feeling that there would be something treacherous in my communicating what he had told me to his superiors in the Company, without first being plain with himself and proposing a middle course to him, I ultimately resolved to offer to accompany him (otherwise keeping his secret for the present) to the wisest medical practitioner we could hear of in those parts, and to take his opinion. A change in his time of duty would come round next night, he had apprised me, and he would be off an hour or two after sunrise, and on again soon after sunset. I had appointed to return accordingly.

Next evening was a lovely evening, and I walked out early to enjoy it. The sun was not yet quite down when I traversed the field-path near the top of the deep cutting. I would extend my walk for an hour, I said to myself, half an hour on and half an hour back, and it would then be time to go to my signal-man's box.

Before pursuing my stroll, I stepped to the brink, and mechanically looked down, from the point from which I had first seen him. I cannot describe the thrill that seized upon me, when, close at the mouth of the tunnel, I saw the appearance of a man, with his left sleeve across his eyes, passionately waving his right arm.

The nameless horror that oppressed me passed in a moment, for in a moment I saw that this appearance of a man was a man indeed, and that there was a little group of other men, standing at a short distance, to whom he seemed to be rehearsing the gesture he made. The Danger-light was not yet lighted. Against its shaft, a little low hut, entirely new to me, had been made of some wooden supports and tarpaulin. It looked no bigger than a bed.

With an irresistible sense that something was wrong – with a flashing self-reproachful fear that fatal mischief had come of my leaving the man there, and causing no one to be sent to overlook or correct what he did – I descended the notched path with all the speed I could make.

"What is the matter?" I asked the men.

"Signal-man killed this morning, sir."

"Not the man belonging to that box?"

"Yes, sir."

"Not the man I know?"

"You will recognise him, sir, if you knew him," said the man who spoke for the others, solemnly uncovering his own head, and raising an end of the tarpaulin, "for his face is quite composed."

"O, how did this happen, how did this happen?" I asked, turning from one to another as the hut closed in again.

"He was cut down by an engine, sir. No man in England knew his work better. But somehow he was not clear of the outer rail. It was just at broad day. He had struck the light, and had the lamp in his hand. As the engine came out of the tunnel, his back was towards her, and she cut him down. That man drove her, and was showing how it happened. Show the gentleman, Tom."

The man, who wore a rough dark dress, stepped back to his former place at the mouth of the tunnel.

"Coming round the curve in the tunnel, sir," he said, "I saw him at the end, like as if I saw him down a perspective-glass. There was no time to check speed, and I knew him to be very careful. As he didn't seem to take heed of the whistle, I shut it off when we were running down upon him, and called to him as loud as I could call."

"What did you say?"

"I said, 'Below there! Look out! Look out! For God's sake, clear the way!'"

I started.

"Ah! it was a dreadful time, sir. I never left off calling to him. I put this arm before my eyes not to see, and I waved this arm to the last; but it was no use."

Without prolonging the narrative to dwell on any one of its curious circumstances more than on any other, I may, in closing it, point out the coincidence that the warning of the Engine-Driver included, not only the words which the unfortunate Signal-man had repeated to me as haunting him, but also the words which I myself – not he – had attached, and that only in my own mind, to the gesticulation he had imitated.

Victorians

James Dorr

THE FIRST THING I REMEMBERED of my early childhood was the fog. I must have been only five years old when I left the house that I had been born in – beyond that my mind was still pretty much blank – and I would not have returned even now, more than thirty years later, except that I had finally married. Her name was Amelia and I had met her in Chicago, but now I traveled home alone. I had determined to open the house first and, only after it had been restored to a livable condition, to send for my bride.

I crested a hill and, just as the road hooked down toward the river and to the town I would find across it, I caught my first glimpse of the house my father had been born in too – the house he had died in and that my mother had fled from just after, never to come back. That, at least, was what they had told me after I had been taken away, to another state, to be raised by a cousin on my mother's side.

The fog, a persistent feature of autumn during those first years of my life, had always been thickest nearest the river. Above it, however, under a pale late afternoon sun, I could just make out the eight-sided top of the great central tower – the Queen Anne tower that dominated so many Victorian homes of its age – as well as the tips of three of the highest pinnacled chimneys. Memory came back in driblets and pieces. I knew that when I approached the next day to take possession, I would recognize below them the sharply peaked hip roof, broken at angles by the main gables that clutched the tower within the ell they formed at their crossing. The tower itself, with its latticed, oval, stained-glass windows, would soar a full story over even the tallest of these, a clear rise of nearly seventy feet from its base to the scale-shingled dome that crowned it.

Memories continued to come back unbidden. I followed the road down a series of switchbacks until the top of the double lane iron bridge I knew I would find loomed out from an ever increasing fog. By now I had lost sight of my parents' home altogether, but in my mind I could hear the voice of a young attorney reading a will.

The will specified that the house would be mine, but only after I had gotten married.

The young attorney, a Stephen Larabie – really no more than a clerk at the time – explained to me what my older cousin protested seemed an unusual provision. "Your father," the lawyer said, "fully expects you not to marry until you've tasted somewhat of the world, just as he did. But at the same time you must eventually take on the obligations of manhood, as well as its pleasures, and settle down. The house, that you will not obtain until you do so, is intended to be a reminder."

My cousin who, in that I was a minor, had been court appointed to speak for my interests, had laughed at that. "You mean young Joseph" – he gestured toward me – "is being told that he has permission to sow his wild oats when he gets a bit older, but, until he's grown out of such urges, to stay out of town. In other words, not to keep out of trouble, but just out of scandal."

The lawyer cleared his throat. "Something like that, yes. I doubt you knew Joseph's father well – as you do know, he was always reclusive and rarely visited even immediate family members after his own marriage – but he, like his house, was quite Victorian in his nature."

"You mean that he was a hypocrite, don't you?" my cousin asked.

I remember now that the lawyer had glanced in my direction to see if I had understood anything of what he and my cousin were saying, but I had already begun to play with his pens and inkwell.

"Some people claimed that of him, yes. At least that he might at times have followed a double standard." He cleared his throat a second time. "In any event," he said as he stood up, having come to the end of his papers and seemingly anxious to usher us out, "the will specifies that this firm will keep the house in trust until Joseph is ready."

And now I was ready, by my father's will. The firm, now owned by Stephen Larabie, had apparently kept an eye on my own various comings and goings as well as the house. And so, three days after Amelia and I had returned from our honeymoon, I received the telegram that had brought me back to this place, at best still scarcely half-recollected, that yet had so overshadowed my first years.

So ran my thoughts now as I reached the bridge and, turning my lights on low, carefully picked my way across it. Fortunately, the fog seemed less thick on the river's town side and, even though it was starting to get dark, I found the hotel I had made reservations at with surprisingly little trouble. Since I was tired from a full day's drive, I checked into my room and showered and changed first, then decided to have a couple of drinks and something to eat in the small restaurant I had earlier spotted just off the lobby.

When I sat down, the hostess smiled at me, and somehow I found that I couldn't help thinking how much the opposite, and yet, in terms of the abstract of beauty, how much the same she was as Amelia. Where, for example, my own wife was blonde and her figure slender, the restaurant hostess was every bit as buxom and dark. Where Amelia was quiet, the hostess appeared, as other customers came to be seated, almost too vivacious. And afterward, when she winked at me while I took out my card to pay the bill, I learned that even her name was much like my wife's, and yet unlike it, as well.

Her name was Anise.

When I returned to my room later on, I placed my wife's picture on the dresser and went to sleep quickly. The first thing next morning, I looked up Attorney Larabie's office.

As soon as I strode in through the door, I was struck by how quickly my mind recalled the tiniest details of my visit, some thirty years past, down to and including the stain on the wood floor where I had dropped one of the young lawyer's pens. The man who confronted me now, however, must have been fifty-five or sixty.

"Mr Parrish?" he said, extending his hand. "Mr Joseph Parrish?"

I nodded and accepted his handshake.

"Are you Stephen Larabie? I got your telegram..."

"Yes," he said, before I could add more. Still gripping my hand, he pulled me over to a table and sat me down, then produced a thick sheaf of papers. "Couple of things I'll need you to sign first," he continued. "That'll most likely take up the whole morning so, unless you have some objection, I thought we might have a quick lunch after that and then take a look at the house together."

I nodded, wondering somewhat distractedly if lunch would be at the hotel restaurant and, if so, if the hostess, Anise, would be on duty for that meal as well. I shook the thought away and soon enough became lost in contracts and deeds instead. Lunch, in fact, turned out to be a quick affair at a hamburger place just outside of town, on the way to the bridge. And then, as river fog started to thin, giving some hope of a clear if not wholly sun-filled afternoon, we found ourselves on the steep and winding road up the cliff on the other side.

Larabie turned to me while I was driving. "How much do you remember of your father?" he asked. "Or, for that matter, of your mother?"

"Very little," I had to confess. I searched my memory and nothing came, yet I had the feeling that if I just waited – waited until I was inside the house that they had lived in...

"You do know, at least, that your father was murdered?"

Larabie paused, reacting, perhaps, to what I imagined was my blank expression. I had no such memory.

"That's what the police said in any event," he finally continued after some seconds. I *did* remember that when, with my cousin, I had been in his office before, the younger Larabie had struck me as being every bit as taciturn about giving out excessive information.

"Did they catch the man who did it?" I asked. Again, attempt to recall as I might, I had no memory – at least not yet – and hence no real feeling one way or the other. But I was beginning to have a foreboding.

"Figured it was probably a drifter," Larabie answered, his voice sounding thoughtful. "A lot of people were moving from town to town those days – mostly farmers who'd been foreclosed on. Big farms forcing out smaller holdings. And you've got to realize that this was a small town. People generally disliked sharing local troubles with outsiders. So the police just poked around a little outside the house – set up a few roadblocks – but they never did catch him."

"M-my mother wasn't murdered too, was she?" It had suddenly occurred to me what he might have been trying to hint at and, while I didn't really remember her any more than I did my father, the thought of my mother's death by violence somehow *was* shocking.

"Oh no," he said quickly. "In fact it was her who phoned the police. Figured she must have been out when it happened and had you with her, but came home just after. Sort of a lucky reversal for her, though, that that's the way it worked out." He hesitated for a moment.

"What do you mean?"

"It was your father who usually went out while she and you were the ones left behind." He hesitated again, then frowned. "I may as well tell you, your father was somewhat of a ladies' man. Good looking man even in his late thirties, just like you, and everyone knew it – except maybe her. Used to be a whorehouse where the hotel is now and some said he spent more time in that than he did in his own house."

"Really?" I asked. I was about to ask him more when we reached the crest of the hill we were climbing. The road widened and, just at that moment, a ray of sun burst through the clouds overhead. The house could now be seen suddenly rising, dominating the next ridge over, in all its flamboyant, old-fashioned splendor.

As we approached, it loomed higher and higher, the light glinting off the gingerbread scroll work that framed the huge front third-story gable. I pulled up into its curving driveway, got out of the car and let my eyes wander – below the trim of the gable, in shadow, the arch of a balcony pointed yet higher to the great tower, half impaled by the slant to its right, and the cast-iron finialed crest of the main hip roof behind it. And yet above that, thrust to the sky, the three major chimneys – the tallest one crowned with a wired, glass-balled spire that was meant to catch lightning, my new memory prompted – added their own bursting streaks of color. An almost blood-colored patterned-brick red, when the sun struck full on it, that, in the jumbled gray and white of friezes and rails of the building below them, was matched alone by the stained-glass red of the tower's downward spiraling ovals.

I walked, as if in a dream, to the house – apparently long-repressed memories came back of the tower windows lighting a second and third-story staircase before it curved backward up into the attic. Others of diamond-panes in the front parlor. I scarcely noticed Larabie's presence until we stood on the broad front veranda.

"You'll notice we kept the property up for you, Mr Parrish," the lawyer said. "Painted it most recently only last summer, in fact." He pulled a notebook out of his pocket, along with a large, old-fashioned iron key. "You'll notice we nailed up the lower-floor windows with furring strips – this far from town why take any chances? – but, once we're inside, the smaller fireplaces you'll see sealed off were boarded up in your grandfather's time. After they put in the central gas heating."

I nodded dumbly. Yes. I remembered. One of the lesser, back left chimneys went down to the basement. I watched as he twisted the key in the door, only half noticing that it opened with hardly a squeak. I smelled the fresh oil – they had, apparently, kept up the inside as well as the outside – not just of hinges, but of the darkly polished woodwork that surrounded us as we stepped into the shallow, box-like reception hall.

"Just a moment now, Mr Parrish." Larabie spoke in almost a whisper. He handed me the first of the keys, then produced a second. He twisted it in a smaller lock across from the entrance we had just come through, then pushed back the double sliding doors that opened the wall to the huge, oak paneled, main staircase hall.

"Your mother went with this house, Mr Parrish," Larabie said as he stood aside to let me look. To try to remember. Second only in size to the large formal dining room, the hall, with its stairs angling up to the right and around the back wall, was the dominant feature of the first floor. "Your mother was frail, white-skinned and slender, with pale blonde hair," the attorney continued. "There were times when she would descend, the white of her clothes standing out as well from the dark wood around her, and look the perfect Victorian lady. Times when I'd come here on legal business..."

I nodded. I saw. I remembered my mother on that staircase, saw in her now, in retrospect, the thin, almost sickly Romantic ideal that would have held sway not so much in her time here, but generations before when the house had been first constructed. I longed now to climb the stairs – now I remembered how she would pause at the corner landing, letting me dash to her so we could go to the main hall together. But first I had to know something more.

I turned to Larabie.

"You told me just before we came to the top of the cliff that my father was murdered. But not my mother..."

"No, Mr Parrish. She was the one who called the police – I think I may have said that already – but, when they arrived here, they came through the sliding doors, just as we did, and the only person they found in the hall was you. You told them your mother had gone away. That was all you would tell them. But when they asked you about your father, you pointed, silently, to the rear archway that leads to the kitchen."

More memory came back – the memory of blood. Of *wanting* to forget what I…

"Under the circumstances," I heard the attorney continue, as if at a distance, "no one blamed your mother. For leaving you that way. She must have been so horribly frightened – and she did keep her wits about her long enough to make sure help came. She had always been such a frail woman…"

Incongruously, I thought of my wife then – fragile and pale. The bride I would send for who, people might say, would fit comfortably in with this house as well. Then – stark contrast – of yet another detail I suddenly found I remembered. My father had been murdered in the kitchen, had almost staggered out past the pantry, past the back stairs and into the service hall when he had fallen.

An axe in his back.

I must have begun to look Victorian-pale myself. I felt the attorney's hand on my shoulder. Now I remembered the men in uniform, blood being cleaned up in the kitchen later by neighbors, my own panic at missing my mother. My wondering when I would see her come down the main staircase again.

"Mr Parrish?" Larabie's voice was very low. "Mr Parrish – perhaps you'd like to come out for some fresh air?"

I shook my head slowly. "No," I answered. "Everything does look in order, however, so why don't *you* wait outside if you'd like to. I just want to do a little exploring on my own, to get an idea of how much work it'll take before Amelia – before Mrs Parrish and I can move in."

Larabie nodded. "Upstairs, you'll find we pretty much left everything alone. May be dusty, though. Didn't even put drop cloths down much above the second floor."

"I think you've done an excellent job with what I've seen so far," I assured him. I took a deep breath, then looked at my wristwatch and glanced toward the front door. "I shouldn't be any more than an hour…"

I waited, gazing up at the main staircase until I heard the outside door close, then turned to the back hallway and the kitchen. On my left, I passed the downstairs parlor first and then the dining room, noting the bay window in the latter – the first-story bulge that jutted out onto the side veranda, forming the base of the four-story tower. Once in the kitchen, I took a deep breath. I saw, at least in my mind's eye, the stains. I thought for some reason of the ink I had spilled myself on Larabie's floor as I imagined my mother calling me, saw her standing over the sink, the door that led to the yard and the woodshed behind the house still yawning open, her hands red with blood.

My mother's hands. *Why?*

I watched as she washed them, then followed a trail of water stains this time – pale, clear drops diluting a deeper red – back toward my father. It circled, minced, avoided expanding pools of crimson as it reached the telephone in the hallway, then returned to the door by the pantry that led to the back stairs. The stairs my mother would never use because, as she used to say, "It isn't proper."

The stairs that rose toward the outside wall, then curved and spiraled up through the tower until they angled back into the attic.

A child's "secret passage."

I followed the trail.

I heard my mother's voice. "Joseph," she said, as we climbed the spiral, "you must forget everything that you've seen. It's only a game, like the games your father played down in the village. Games I might have been told about, but had never believed until he came home, more drunk than usual, early this morning." We reached the top, where the stairs straightened out again for their final climb up to the attic, and the sun suddenly shone through the windows, filling the tower with spotlights of blood red. "While he was sleeping," my mother continued, "I thought of a game too."

My mother had always used the front staircase. The back stairs were dusty. And one had to stoop to get from the attic into the tunnel beneath the front gable. But this was different – this was a game.

I straightened up, bumped my head, realized I stood in the attic myself now.

I had trouble breathing the stuffy air. I leaned against a rough brick column – the front parlor chimney, my memory told me – and felt the flange where it thrust through the roof brush against my shoulder. I blinked my eyes, hard, to clear my vision and, when I opened them up again, I saw what still looked like a pool of blood.

Again a memory – a recognition. I was already within the front gable. The red that I saw was the light of the sun, spilling out from a second low arch where the gable roof met the tower's final top level. I heard my mother's voice warning me to be sure to brush my pants carefully before, once the game we would play was ended, I went back downstairs. I saw my mother kneeling next to me as we crawled through the final tunnel.

We came to a child's hidden pirate castle. A room of oval stained-glass windows that served as portholes, of worn out sheets and ropes carefully hung from the open beams of the dome roof above as a ship's sails and banners.

I helped my mother build a tower within the great tower's uppermost room, helped her make a stair-like heap of the boxes and trunks I'd dragged in for years from the main attic proper as pirate treasure.

"Now you must help me with one thing more," she said when we were finished. She climbed to the top and began to pull on the ropes that hung toward her. "Hold my legs. That's right. And now I want you to promise me that everything that has happened today will be our secret. Do you promise, Joseph?"

"Yes, Mother," I said. The memory was clear now.

"I want you to think of this as a game. Like playing pirates. Do you understand?"

"Yes, Mother," I said again.

"Good. Now your mother must walk the plank – just like in a game. As soon as you feel me move my feet, I want you to push me off these boxes and knock them over, just as if you were a real pirate captain pushing me off the plank. I want you to go downstairs after you've done that, without looking back. Some men will come later and all you must tell them is that your mother went away. Do you promise, Joseph?"

I had promised.

I blinked again. I stood alone in the tower now. Raising my eyes to the dome above me, I gazed at my mother, her flesh long since shrunken into a parchment against her body, still hanging in the red light of the windows just as I had left her.

And somehow, for no reason whatsoever, I thought of Amelia who so resembled her, walking down the front, formal staircase. Amelia, my bride, also somewhat reclusive, who I was sure, as soon as the house was cleaned and ready, would come to love it and make it her own.

And then, without willing to, I thought as well of the restaurant hostess. I could not help it. Of dark, round-curved Anise who lived in town and would be waiting.

The New Catacomb

Arthur Conan Doyle

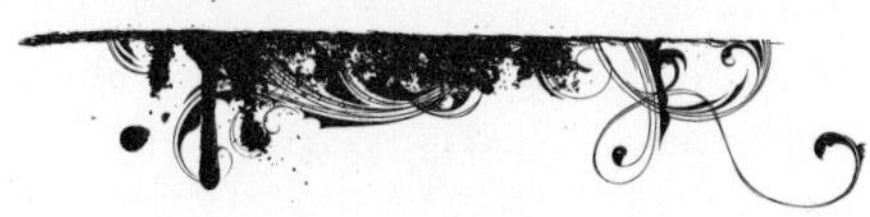

"LOOK HERE, BURGER," said Kennedy, "I do wish that you would confide in me."

The two famous students of Roman remains sat together in Kennedy's comfortable room overlooking the Corso. The night was cold, and they had both pulled up their chairs to the unsatisfactory Italian stove which threw out a zone of stuffiness rather than of warmth. Outside under the bright winter stars lay the modern Rome, the long, double chain of the electric lamps, the brilliantly lighted cafés, the rushing carriages, and the dense throng upon the footpaths. But inside, in the sumptuous chamber of the rich young English archaeologist, there was only old Rome to be seen. Cracked and timeworn friezes hung upon the walls, grey old busts of senators and soldiers with their fighting heads and their hard, cruel faces peered out from the corners. On the centre table, amidst a litter of inscriptions, fragments, and ornaments, there stood the famous reconstruction by Kennedy of the Baths of Caracalla, which excited such interest and admiration when it was exhibited in Berlin. Amphorae hung from the ceiling, and a litter of curiosities strewed the rich red Turkey carpet. And of them all there was not one which was not of the most unimpeachable authenticity, and of the utmost rarity and value; for Kennedy, though little more than thirty, had a European reputation in this particular branch of research, and was, moreover, provided with that long purse which either proves to be a fatal handicap to the student's energies, or, if his mind is still true to its purpose, gives him an enormous advantage in the race for fame. Kennedy had often been seduced by whim and pleasure from his studies, but his mind was an incisive one, capable of long and concentrated efforts which ended in sharp reactions of sensuous languor. His handsome face, with its high, white forehead, its aggressive nose, and its somewhat loose and sensual mouth, was a fair index of the compromise between strength and weakness in his nature.

Of a very different type was his companion, Julius Burger. He came of a curious blend, a German father and an Italian mother, with the robust qualities of the North mingling strangely with the softer graces of the South. Blue Teutonic eyes lightened his sun-browned face, and above them rose a square, massive forehead, with a fringe of close yellow curls lying round it. His strong, firm jaw was clean-shaven, and his companion had frequently remarked how much it suggested those old Roman busts which peered out from the shadows in the corners of his chamber. Under its bluff German strength there lay always a suggestion of Italian subtlety, but the smile was so honest, and the eyes so frank, that one understood that this was only an indication of his ancestry, with no actual bearing upon his character. In age and in reputation, he was on the same level as his English companion, but his life and his work had both been far more arduous. Twelve years before, he had come as a poor student to Rome, and had lived ever since upon some small endowment for research which had been awarded to him by the University of Bonn. Painfully, slowly, and doggedly, with extraordinary tenacity and single-mindedness, he had climbed from rung to rung of the ladder of fame, until now he was a member of the Berlin Academy, and there was every reason to believe that he would shortly be promoted to the Chair of the greatest of German Universities. But the singleness of purpose which had brought him to the same high level as the rich and brilliant Englishman, had caused him in everything outside their work to stand infinitely below him. He had never found a pause in his studies in which to cultivate the social graces. It was only when he spoke of his own subject that his face was filled with life and soul. At other times he was silent and embarrassed, too conscious of his own limitations in larger subjects, and impatient of that small talk which is the conventional refuge of those who have no thoughts to express.

And yet for some years there had been an acquaintanceship which appeared to be slowly ripening into a friendship between these two very different rivals. The base and origin of this lay in the fact that in their own studies each was the only one of the younger men who had knowledge and enthusiasm enough to properly appreciate the other. Their common interests and pursuits had brought them together, and each had been attracted by the other's knowledge. And then gradually something had been added to this. Kennedy had been amused by the frankness and simplicity of his rival, while Burger in turn had been fascinated by the brilliancy and vivacity which had made Kennedy such a favourite in Roman society. I say "had," because just at the moment the young Englishman was somewhat under a cloud. A love-affair, the details of which had never quite come out, had indicated a heartlessness and callousness upon his part which shocked many of his friends. But in the bachelor circles of students and artists in which he preferred to move there is no very rigid code of honour in such matters, and though a head might be shaken or a pair of shoulders shrugged over the flight of two and the return of one, the general sentiment was probably one of curiosity and perhaps of envy rather than of reprobation.

"Look here, Burger," said Kennedy, looking hard at the placid face of his companion, "I do wish that you would confide in me."

As he spoke he waved his hand in the direction of a rug which lay upon the floor. On the rug stood a long, shallow fruit-basket of the light wicker-work which is used in the Campagna, and this was heaped with a litter of objects, inscribed tiles, broken inscriptions, cracked mosaics, torn papyri, rusty metal ornaments, which to the uninitiated might have seemed to have come straight from a dustman's bin, but which a specialist would have speedily recognised as unique of their kind. The pile of odds and ends in the flat wicker-work basket supplied exactly one of those missing links of social development which are of such interest to the student. It was the German who had brought them in, and the Englishman's eyes were hungry as he looked at them.

"I won't interfere with your treasure-trove, but I should very much like to hear about it," he continued, while Burger very deliberately lit a cigar. "It is evidently a discovery of the first importance. These inscriptions will make a sensation throughout Europe."

"For every one here there are a million there!" said the German. "There are so many that a dozen savants might spend a lifetime over them, and build up a reputation as solid as the Castle of St. Angelo."

Kennedy sat thinking with his fine forehead wrinkled and his fingers playing with his long, fair moustache.

"You have given yourself away, Burger!" said he at last. "Your words can only apply to one thing. You have discovered a new catacomb."

"I had no doubt that you had already come to that conclusion from an examination of these objects."

"Well, they certainly appeared to indicate it, but your last remarks make it certain. There is no place except a catacomb which could contain so vast a store of relics as you describe."

"Quite so. There is no mystery about that. I *have* discovered a new catacomb."

"Where?"

"Ah, that is my secret, my dear Kennedy. Suffice it that it is so situated that there is not one chance in a million of anyone else coming upon it. Its date is different from that of any known catacomb, and it has been reserved for the burial of the highest Christians, so that the remains and the relics are quite different from anything which has ever been seen before. If I was not aware of your knowledge and of your energy, my friend, I would not hesitate, under the pledge of secrecy, to tell you everything about it. But as it is I think that I must certainly prepare my own report of the matter before I expose myself to such formidable competition."

Kennedy loved his subject with a love which was almost a mania – a love which held him true to it, amidst all the distractions which come to a wealthy and dissipated young man. He had ambition, but his ambition was secondary to his mere abstract joy and interest in everything which concerned the old life and history of the city. He yearned to see this new underworld which his companion had discovered.

"Look here, Burger," said he, earnestly, "I assure you that you can trust me most implicitly in the matter. Nothing would induce me to put pen to paper about anything which I see until I have your express permission. I quite understand your feeling and I think it is most natural, but you have really nothing whatever to fear from me. On the other hand, if you don't tell me I shall make a systematic search, and I shall most certainly discover it. In that case, of course, I should make what use I liked of it, since I should be under no obligation to you."

Burger smiled thoughtfully over his cigar.

"I have noticed, friend Kennedy," said he, "that when I want information over any point you are not always so ready to supply it."

"When did you ever ask me anything that I did not tell you? You remember, for example, my giving you the material for your paper about the temple of the Vestals."

"Ah, well, that was not a matter of much importance. If I were to question you upon some intimate thing would you give me an answer, I wonder! This new catacomb is a very intimate thing to me, and I should certainly expect some sign of confidence in return."

"What you are driving at I cannot imagine," said the Englishman, "but if you mean that you will answer my question about the catacomb if I answer any question which you may put to me I can assure you that I will certainly do so."

"Well, then," said Burger, leaning luxuriously back in his settee, and puffing a blue tree of cigar-smoke into the air, "tell me all about your relations with Miss Mary Saunderson."

Kennedy sprang up in his chair and glared angrily at his impassive companion.

"What the devil do you mean?" he cried. "What sort of a question is this? You may mean it as a joke, but you never made a worse one."

"No, I don't mean it as a joke," said Burger, simply. "I am really rather interested in the details of the matter. I don't know much about the world and women and social life and that sort of thing, and such an incident has the fascination of the unknown for me. I know you, and I knew her by sight – I had even spoken to her once or twice. I should very much like to hear from your own lips exactly what it was which occurred between you."

"I won't tell you a word."

"That's all right. It was only my whim to see if you would give up a secret as easily as you expected me to give up my secret of the new catacomb. You wouldn't, and I didn't expect you to. But why should you expect otherwise of me? There's Saint John's clock striking ten. It is quite time that I was going home."

"No; wait a bit, Burger," said Kennedy; "this is really a ridiculous caprice of yours to wish to know about an old love-affair which has burned out months ago. You know we look upon a man who kisses and tells as the greatest coward and villain possible."

"Certainly," said the German, gathering up his basket of curiosities, "when he tells anything about a girl which is previously unknown he must be so. But in this case, as you must be aware, it was a public matter which was the common talk of Rome, so that you are not really doing Miss Mary Saunderson any injury by discussing her case with me. But still, I respect your scruples; and so good night!"

"Wait a bit, Burger," said Kennedy, laying his hand upon the other's arm; "I am very keen upon this catacomb business, and I can't let it drop quite so easily. Would you mind asking me something else in return – something not quite so eccentric this time?"

"No, no; you have refused, and there is an end of it," said Burger, with his basket on his arm. "No doubt you are quite right not to answer, and no doubt I am quite right also – and so again, my dear Kennedy, good night!"

The Englishman watched Burger cross the room, and he had his hand on the handle of the door before his host sprang up with the air of a man who is making the best of that which cannot be helped.

"Hold on, old fellow," said he; "I think you are behaving in a most ridiculous fashion; but still; if this is your condition, I suppose that I must submit to it. I hate saying anything about a girl, but, as you say, it is all over Rome, and I don't suppose I can tell you anything which you do not know already. What was it you wanted to know?"

The German came back to the stove, and, laying down his basket, he sank into his chair once more.

"May I have another cigar?" said he. "Thank you very much! I never smoke when I work, but I enjoy a chat much more when I am under the influence of tobacco. Now, as regards this young lady, with whom you had this little adventure. What in the world has become of her?"

"She is at home with her own people."

"Oh, really – in England?"

"Yes."

"What part of England – London?"

"No, Twickenham."

"You must excuse my curiosity, my dear Kennedy, and you must put it down to my ignorance of the world. No doubt it is quite a simple thing to persuade a young lady to go off with you for three weeks or so, and then to hand her over to her own family at – what did you call the place?"

"Twickenham."

"Quite so – at Twickenham. But it is something so entirely outside my own experience that I cannot even imagine how you set about it. For example, if you had loved this girl your love could hardly disappear in three weeks, so I presume that you could not have loved her at all. But if you did not love her why should you make this great scandal which has damaged you and ruined her?"

Kennedy looked moodily into the red eye of the stove.

"That's a logical way of looking at it, certainly," said he. "Love is a big word, and it represents a good many different shades of feeling. I liked her, and – well, you say you've seen her – you know how charming she could look. But still I am willing to admit, looking back, that I could never have really loved her."

"Then, my dear Kennedy, why did you do it?"

"The adventure of the thing had a great deal to do with it."

"What! You are so fond of adventures!"

"Where would the variety of life be without them? It was for an adventure that I first began to pay my attentions to her. I've chased a good deal of game in my time, but there's no chase like that of a pretty woman. There was the piquant difficulty of it also, for, as she was the companion of Lady Emily Rood, it was almost impossible to see her alone. On the top of all the other obstacles which attracted me, I learned from her own lips very early in the proceedings that she was engaged."

"*Mein Gott*! To whom?"

"She mentioned no names."

"I do not think that anyone knows that. So that made the adventure more alluring, did it?"

"Well, it did certainly give a spice to it. Don't you think so?"

"I tell you that I am very ignorant about these things."

"My dear fellow, you can remember that the apple you stole from your neighbour's tree was always sweeter than that which fell from your own. And then I found that she cared for me."

"What – at once?"

"Oh, no, it took about three months of sapping and mining. But at last I won her over. She understood that my judicial separation from my wife made it impossible for me to do the right thing by her – but she came all the same, and we had a delightful time, as long as it lasted."

"But how about the other man?"

Kennedy shrugged his shoulders.

"I suppose it is the survival of the fittest," said he. "If he had been the better man she would not have deserted him. Let's drop the subject, for I have had enough of it!"

"Only one other thing. How did you get rid of her in three weeks?"

"Well, we had both cooled down a bit, you understand. She absolutely refused, under any circumstances, to come back to face the people she had known in Rome. Now, of course, Rome is necessary to me, and I was already pining to be back at my work – so there was one obvious cause of separation. Then, again, her old father turned up at the hotel in London, and there was a scene, and the whole thing became so unpleasant that really – though I missed her dreadfully at first – I was very glad to slip out of it. Now, I rely upon you not to repeat anything of what I have said."

"My dear Kennedy, I should not dream of repeating it. But all that you say interests me very much, for it gives me an insight into your way of looking at things, which is entirely different from mine, for I have seen so little of life. And now you want to know about my new catacomb. There's no use my trying to describe it, for you would never find it by that. There is only one thing, and that is for me to take you there."

"That would be splendid."

"When would you like to come?"

"The sooner the better. I am all impatience to see it."

"Well, it is a beautiful night – though a trifle cold. Suppose we start in an hour. We must be very careful to keep the matter to ourselves. If anyone saw us hunting in couples they would suspect that there was something going on."

"We can't be too cautious," said Kennedy. "Is it far?"

"Some miles."

"Not too far to walk?"

"Oh, no, we could walk there easily."

"We had better do so, then. A cabman's suspicions would be aroused if he dropped us both at some lonely spot in the dead of the night."

"Quite so. I think it would be best for us to meet at the Gate of the Appian Way at midnight. I must go back to my lodgings for the matches and candles and things."

"All right, Burger! I think it is very kind of you to let me into this secret, and I promise you that I will write nothing about it until you have published your report. Good-bye for the present! You will find me at the Gate at twelve."

The cold, clear air was filled with the musical chimes from that city of clocks as Burger, wrapped in an Italian overcoat, with a lantern hanging from his hand, walked up to the rendezvous. Kennedy stepped out of the shadow to meet him.

"You are ardent in work as well as in love!" said the German, laughing.

"Yes; I have been waiting here for nearly half an hour."

"I hope you left no clue as to where we were going."

"Not such a fool! By Jove, I am chilled to the bone! Come on, Burger, let us warm ourselves by a spurt of hard walking."

Their footsteps sounded loud and crisp upon the rough stone paving of the disappointing road which is all that is left of the most famous highway of the world. A peasant or two going home from the wine-shop, and a few carts of country produce coming up to Rome, were the only things which they met. They swung along, with the huge tombs looming up through the darkness upon each side of them, until they had come as far as the Catacombs of St. Calixtus, and saw against a rising moon the great circular bastion of Cecilia Metella in front of them. Then Burger stopped with his hand to his side.

"Your legs are longer than mine, and you are more accustomed to walking," said he, laughing. "I think that the place where we turn off is somewhere here. Yes, this is it, round the corner of the trattoria. Now, it is a very narrow path, so perhaps I had better go in front and you can follow."

He had lit his lantern, and by its light they were enabled to follow a narrow and devious track which wound across the marshes of the Campagna. The great Aqueduct of old Rome lay like a monstrous caterpillar across the moonlit landscape, and their road led them under one of its huge arches, and past the circle of crumbling bricks which marks the old arena. At last Burger stopped at a solitary wooden cow-house, and he drew a key from his pocket. "Surely your catacomb is not inside a house!" cried Kennedy.

"The entrance to it is. That is just the safeguard which we have against anyone else discovering it."

"Does the proprietor know of it?"

"Not he. He had found one or two objects which made me almost certain that his house was built on the entrance to such a place. So I rented it from him, and did my excavations for myself. Come in, and shut the door behind you."

It was a long, empty building, with the mangers of the cows along one wall. Burger put his lantern down on the ground, and shaded its light in all directions save one by draping his overcoat round it.

"It might excite remark if anyone saw a light in this lonely place," said he. "Just help me to move this boarding."

The flooring was loose in the corner, and plank by plank the two savants raised it and leaned it against the wall. Below there was a square aperture and a stair of old stone steps which led away down into the bowels of the earth.

"Be careful!" cried Burger, as Kennedy, in his impatience, hurried down them. "It is a perfect rabbits'-warren below, and if you were once to lose your way there the chances would be a hundred to one against your ever coming out again. Wait until I bring the light."

"How do you find your own way if it is so complicated?"

"I had some very narrow escapes at first, but I have gradually learned to go about. There is a certain system to it, but it is one which a lost man, if he were in the dark, could not possibly find out. Even now I always spin out a ball of string behind me when I am going far into the catacomb. You can see for yourself that it is difficult, but every one of these passages divides and subdivides a dozen times before you go a hundred yards."

They had descended some twenty feet from the level of the byre, and they were standing now in a square chamber cut out of the soft tufa. The lantern cast a flickering light, bright below and dim above, over the cracked brown walls. In every direction were the black openings of passages which radiated from this common centre.

"I want you to follow me closely, my friend," said Burger. "Do not loiter to look at anything upon the way, for the place to which I will take you contains all that you can see, and more. It will save time for us to go there direct."

He led the way down one of the corridors, and the Englishman followed closely at his heels. Every now and then the passage bifurcated, but Burger was evidently following some secret marks of his own, for he neither stopped nor hesitated. Everywhere along the walls, packed like the berths upon an emigrant ship, lay the Christians of old Rome. The yellow light flickered over the shrivelled features of the mummies, and gleamed upon rounded skulls and long, white armbones crossed over fleshless chests. And everywhere as he passed Kennedy looked with wistful eyes upon inscriptions, funeral vessels, pictures, vestments, utensils, all lying as pious hands had placed them so many centuries ago. It was apparent to him, even in those hurried, passing glances, that this was the earliest and finest of the catacombs, containing such a storehouse of Roman remains as had never before come at one time under the observation of the student.

"What would happen if the light went out?" he asked, as they hurried onwards.

"I have a spare candle and a box of matches in my pocket. By the way, Kennedy, have you any matches?"

"No; you had better give me some."

"Oh, that is all right. There is no chance of our separating."

"How far are we going? It seems to me that we have walked at least a quarter of a mile."

"More than that, I think. There is really no limit to the tombs – at least, I have never been able to find any. This is a very difficult place, so I think that I will use our ball of string."

He fastened one end of it to a projecting stone and he carried the coil in the breast of his coat, paying it out as he advanced. Kennedy saw that it was no unnecessary precaution, for the passages had become more complex and tortuous than ever, with a perfect network of intersecting corridors. But these all ended in one large circular hall with a square pedestal of tufa topped with a slab of marble at one end of it.

"By Jove!" cried Kennedy in an ecstasy, as Burger swung his lantern over the marble. "It is a Christian altar – probably the first one in existence. Here is the little consecration cross cut upon the corner of it. No doubt this circular space was used as a church."

"Precisely," said Burger. "If I had more time I should like to show you all the bodies which are buried in these niches upon the walls, for they are the early popes and bishops of the Church, with their mitres, their croziers, and full canonicals. Go over to that one and look at it!"

Kennedy went across, and stared at the ghastly head which lay loosely on the shredded and mouldering mitre.

"This is most interesting," said he, and his voice seemed to boom against the concave vault. "As far as my experience goes, it is unique. Bring the lantern over, Burger, for I want to see them all."

But the German had strolled away, and was standing in the middle of a yellow circle of light at the other side of the hall.

"Do you know how many wrong turnings there are between this and the stairs?" he asked. "There are over two thousand. No doubt it was one of the means of protection which the Christians adopted. The odds are two thousand to one against a man getting out, even if he had a light; but if he were in the dark it would, of course, be far more difficult."

"So I should think."

"And the darkness is something dreadful. I tried it once for an experiment. Let us try it again!" He stooped to the lantern, and in an instant it was as if an invisible hand was squeezed tightly over each of Kennedy's eyes. Never had he known what such darkness was. It seemed to press upon him and to smother him. It was a solid obstacle against which the body shrank from advancing. He put his hands out to push it back from him.

"That will do, Burger," said he, "let's have the light again."

But his companion began to laugh, and in that circular room the sound seemed to come from every side at once.

"You seem uneasy, friend Kennedy," said he.

"Go on, man, light the candle!" said Kennedy impatiently.

"It's very strange, Kennedy, but I could not in the least tell by the sound in which direction you stand. Could you tell where I am?"

"No; you seem to be on every side of me."

"If it were not for this string which I hold in my hand I should not have a notion which way to go."

"I dare say not. Strike a light, man, and have an end of this nonsense."

"Well, Kennedy, there are two things which I understand that you are very fond of. The one is an adventure, and the other is an obstacle to surmount. The adventure must be the finding of your way out of this catacomb. The obstacle will be the darkness and the two thousand wrong turns which make the way a little difficult to find. But you need not hurry, for you have plenty of time, and when you halt for a rest now and then, I should like you just to think of Miss Mary Saunderson, and whether you treated her quite fairly."

"You devil, what do you mean?" roared Kennedy. He was running about in little circles and clasping at the solid blackness with both hands.

"Good-bye," said the mocking voice, and it was already at some distance. "I really do not think, Kennedy, even by your own showing that you did the right thing by that girl. There was only one little thing which you appeared not to know, and I can supply it. Miss Saunderson was engaged to a poor ungainly devil of a student, and his name was Julius Burger."

There was a rustle somewhere, the vague sound of a foot striking a stone, and then there fell silence upon that old Christian church – a stagnant, heavy silence which closed round Kennedy and shut him in like water round a drowning man.

Some two months afterwards the following paragraph made the round of the European Press:

"One of the most interesting discoveries of recent years is that of the new catacomb in Rome, which lies some distance to the east of the well-known vaults of St. Calixtus. The finding of this important burial-place, which is exceeding rich in most interesting early Christian remains, is due to the energy and sagacity of Dr Julius Burger, the young German specialist, who is rapidly taking the first place as an authority upon ancient Rome. Although the first to publish his discovery, it appears that a less fortunate adventurer had anticipated Dr Burger. Some months ago Mr Kennedy, the well-known English student, disappeared suddenly from his rooms in the Corso, and it was conjectured that his association with a recent scandal had driven him to leave Rome. It appears now that he had in reality fallen a victim to that fervid love of archaeology which had raised him to a distinguished place among living scholars. His body was discovered in the heart of the new catacomb, and it was evident from the condition of his feet and boots that he had tramped for days through the tortuous corridors which make these subterranean tombs so dangerous to explorers. The deceased gentleman had, with inexplicable rashness, made his way into this labyrinth without, as far as can be discovered, taking with him either candles or matches, so that his sad fate was the natural result of his own temerity. What makes the matter more painful is that Dr Julius Burger was an intimate friend of the deceased. His joy at the extraordinary find which he has been so fortunate as to make has been greatly marred by the terrible fate of his comrade and fellow-worker."

Mourners

Kurt Bachard

"TO THY SERVANT DEPARTED..."

Miriam's attention wandered from the tired-eyed priest's droning prayer and the small band of friends and relatives gathered around the grave. She had heard it all a thousand times before, or so it seemed. Besides, the churchyard was far more interesting than the boring priest's petition.

Picturesque in its rustic charm, the churchyard was one of the loveliest yet. Below a pale blue sky, the air was a trifle chilly for early September, the leaves falling by the grave, turning brown at their edges. A little robin redbreast hopped up on to the hoary stone wall that ran alongside a little brook, where sunrays falling through the oaks and willows played a chiaroscuro of shade and light upon the water. Delightedly she watched the robin's little throat chirping before the ghost of a breeze ruffled its feathers and it fluttered away. Miriam sighed contentedly and wished such a sweet afternoon could last forever. The priest droned on in the background, his voice becoming a soft burr. Such a pleasant day for a funeral, she thought. She looked forward to the church luncheon, dreaming of Cherry Bakewells and Battenberg – her favourites.

* * *

Miriam lay in bed, staring at the weak yellow circle of lamplight on the ceiling. The buffet at today's luncheon had left her feeling bloated, full of pickles and hams, flavoured teas, and spiced ginger cake that grumbled noisily in her weary bowels. Worse, she couldn't stop worrying about some of the mourners, the same faces she had seen at last week's funeral: there was the one she had nicknamed Sour Granny Smith, the rosy-cheeked pensioner with a face like a ripening apple; Gin-Mill Lil, the thin-faced middle-aged woman whose patrician nose was riddled with the broken veins of a heavy drinker; Old War Horse, the moustachioed, bent-backed retired Colonel; and Pince-Nez, the tall, thin-lipped, grey-faced lady whose rheumy eyes lurked behind antiquated lenses, her pearls jangling against a bronze fibula. Were they really the same faces at every funeral, or was she losing her marbles in her dotage?

If only my poor Henry were here, she thought, still saddened by the loss six long months after his passing. She had first encountered the mourners at Henry's funeral. They were like a band of familiar faces she had known her entire life but never spoken to – like neighbours. The more she thought about them, the more their faces blurred in her memory until she was no longer sure they were the same people she had seen at other funerals after all.

The following day, she went to see her only friend, Edith, at the hospice and nagged her about symptoms, hoping to gain a clue as to how her Alzheimer's had started. "Don't worry, lovey," Edith crooned, touching Miriam's liver-spotted hand. "If worst comes to worst, you can come join me here. I could do with the company." She was only half joking as she nodded her head with disdain at the doddering half minds snoozing and dribbling in the lounge armchairs. Miriam left, feeling worse. Nothing Edith said had reassured her, and there was nobody with whom she could discuss her fears. She wished she had a daughter to confide in, like those undeserving women who took their children for granted.

On the way out, she passed one such – a young mother who thought nothing of yelling abusively at her three-year-old in his pram. Miriam bent down and picked up the knitted lamb from the pavement, even though it hurt her back to do so, and placed it back into the child's mucky little hands. The mother gave Miriam a look of reproof, telling her child the toy was now dirty; begrimed, her look implied, by the pensioner's touch.

* * *

At the midweek funeral, one of the mourners approached her for the first time. It was Sour Granny Smith.

Other mourners were turning away from the open grave and following the priest back into the church. Miriam had lingered a moment. She had enjoyed the humble graveside service and looked forward to a modest luncheon befitting the cheaply attired relatives of the deceased. No doubt they would buffet cheap supermarket brands of cake, she thought. Oh yes, a weak tea affair, but it wouldn't spoil her day. In the frosty air and winter sunshine, the service had an added solemnity, and she had forgotten her loneliness, glad that the quartet of familiar faces seemed to be absent.

She was looking down at the coffin and muttering her own private prayer, respectfully expressing her genuine sorrow as usual whilst asking forgiveness for what must seem to the dead an intrusion, when the old woman touched her sleeve.

"What a scandal in the end," she said, apparently apropos of nothing.

Miriam turned sharply, startled by the trespass on her tranquillity. Even if she had understood what the stranger had meant by her remark, she doubted she could have replied at that moment.

"Secrets don't always go to the grave," Sour Granny Smith said, even more cryptically, speaking as though this explained her previous comment. Her shrivelled eyes twinkled with purpose above those fat, shiny apple cheeks.

Miriam tried to remember what she had learned of the deceased. Heat flushed her face. Under the scrutiny, Miriam stammered, suddenly feeling shamefully close to exposure.

"I've seen you before," said Sour Granny Smith, eyes narrowing.

Miriam replied in the only way that offered an excuse. "I've had reason to attend a number of funerals recently." She clutched her burgundy handbag between them, like a wall of defence. "In fact, my husband –"

But Sour Granny Smith cut her off and went on undeterred. "You have no idea who that young man was, do you?" she said, pointing unnecessarily at the white pall in the grave below. "You're no relation of his."

"That's not true," Miriam lied, taking several steps back in the grass. Her heels bumped the roots of a tree behind her, and, for an instant, she swayed dazedly.

The woman grabbed her forearm to stop her from falling over backwards, her grip firm, but not unfriendly. "We don't need you to go just yet," she said, smiling now, but it was a cold smile that matched her cold tone. The woman's teeth were yellow and crooked. The arcs of plaque close to her shrivelled gums were like bars of lichen on gravestones.

Gathering her wits and her balance, Miriam shook the woman's hand from her sleeve, somewhat disgustedly. "I haven't the slightest idea what you mean," she said. "And I'd prefer if you kindly left me alone." Having been noticed, her anonymity lost, the thought of standing in the luncheon with this woman watching her did not appeal; she no longer felt she could enjoy herself. Reluctantly, she left the little churchyard to hurry home.

* * *

At the weekend, she chose her outing from the paper with an increased diligence. Nevertheless, she wasn't sure her caution was necessary. One glance in the obituaries revealed a surplus of choice; such a bumper crop of funerals, lately. By no means was the popularity of death declining. Furthermore, it seemed unlikely those awful people would pick the same funeral, she decided. She chose the funeral farthest from her home: an afternoon burial in a riverside churchyard in London.

As usual, she intended to arrive early, to catch important titbits of information on the deceased from the tittle-tattle as the mourners gathered before the graveside service was in full swing, but the bus must have run late because when she alighted, the service was already over. The churchyard was deserted. She crossed the grass verge purposefully, trying to march out the nervousness in her stomach.

Glancing about, she wondered where all the relatives and friends who usually gathered by their cars at the church's driveway had gone. Where were the mourners, ripe for eavesdropping, who chattered as they filed inside for the church service? Perhaps, she thought, with a mingled thrill of excitement and unease, the mourners had already convened inside. Reaching the unfilled grave, Miriam hurried to catch up.

Moments later, she faltered in the middle of the graveyard as Sour Granny Smith sidled out from behind a tree and stepped into her path. She grinned coldly again.

Surprised by the woman's appearance, Miriam lurched to a full stop with a gasp, her heart fluttering.

"'Attend not on a corpse unless ye be invited,'" quoted Sour Granny Smith.

A crow screeched in the branches overhead, as though panic stricken, and fluttered away heavily. Miriam tried to step around the woman, to escape, when Pince-Nez joined her companion, blocking Miriam's path. She stood a foot taller than Miriam and peered snootily down at her over the thick lenses.

From behind Miriam, another voice said, "She's been disrespecting the dead for some time, hasn't she?" The accusation made her tremble as she turned to find Gin-Mill Lil had stepped into the fray, blocking her retreat. The long drinker's nose probed forward beneath languid, accusing eyes.

"She's a ghoul." It was Old War Horse, the curmudgeonly old Colonel, his moustache bristling. His war medals flashed to shame her. "You're a Ghoul, Madam," he emphasised, a stubby finger stabbing the frosty air. "Madam, a Ghoul!"

The quartet closed ranks around her.

"Leave me alone," Miriam croaked, turning on them. Her eyes stung; she felt close to tears, but also defiant and angry. Bullies, that's what they are. Cowardly bullies. "If I'm a ghoul, then what are you lot?" she asked. "You… you eat as much cake as I." The pitiable confession released the tears at last, tears she had not shed since the passing of her husband.

"But we're mourners, dear," said Granny Smith with false sympathy. Finally, the consolation she had missed, but too late and from strangers. She did not want it now.

"If you're mourners then so am I."

"But we have the blessings of the dead, dear."

"What are you saying?" Wiping her eyes, Miriam backed away, frightened by the woman's words. "Just let me be," she moaned.

The church was within sight, but its sanctuary appeared unreachable.

Eyes burning with indignation, the four mourners closed in, forcing Miriam to retreat further, backing her to the edge of the open grave where Miriam's heels slipped.

For a horrible timeless moment, she teetered on the edge of the grave before falling back, screaming, her stomach churning as she fell away from the solid vision of the church in the distance, the cloudy sky tilting to meet her.

The loud crack she heard was her back breaking as she hit the ground. The sound cut short Miriam's scream. Agony clouded her eyes as she tried to move in vain. The damp ground seemed to hold her in position, demanding her body for the soil. She stared up, mouth open in dumb torment.

And she saw not the wide open sky, but the four faces of the mourners. They peered down upon the grave, grinning evilly. Miriam heard their last words sang like the antiphon as the first shovel full of worm-wriggling dirt splattered her lips.

"We'll have a lovely luncheon," said one.

"Yes," agreed another, "with lots of cake for poor Miriam."

The Figure on the Sidewalk

Tim Foley

AT A SMALL TABLE at the café, Theodore ordered some tea and sat across from me, draping his long coat over the chair at his back. He had grown thin and did not look well, not at all. Noting his dull, unhealthy skin and stooped posture, I was discomforted by the awareness that we were the same age. His hair, close cropped, held a great deal of white, and his forehead displayed a deep horizontal furrow that made his face, with its straight nose and long, unshaved jaw, resemble a capital T. He looked at me with restless, sunken eyes.

"It's been difficult," he said. His tea arrived and he stirred sugar into it, the spoon circling again and again, long after the swirling movement had lost its efficacy. I waited for him to clarify. Was it the weather that was difficult? His finances? The world at large? But he seemed to have forgotten me, his eyes scanning the corners of the café, searching. I felt compelled, and curious.

"What, Theodore? What has been difficult?"

His gaze settled on me. "I'm being followed."

"Followed? Explain." I couldn't help executing a look around the café myself, but I saw only the usual evening patrons, engaged in quiet conversation or computer-screen self-hypnosis.

Theodore lifted his cup to his lips, his trembling hands spilling the tea down the sides. "It's difficult," he repeated, after he had taken a tentative sip. And then: "I haven't spoken of this to anyone."

I smiled, hoping to lessen his obvious difficulty. "Well, I've known you longer than anyone, Theodore, so speak of it to me."

"Very well," he said, as he guided the cup into the saucer.

* * *

I'm sure you know that little coffee place over on 21st Street in midtown, he began. It is not unlike this establishment, but a bit scruffier, and without table service. The room has two wings, an L-shape, with the counter at the crux. A few sofas are mixed in with the tables and chairs and, while a bit shabby, it is a calm, comfortable venue to pass some time, especially in the evening. Because of the shape of the room, however, you can't see the entire space from a given spot, so you might miss a friend, or an enemy, I suppose, if you were sitting in one of the wings and he in the other. Of course, this means you can hide a bit, which is nice, and such small mysteries actually lend a bit of charm to the place. One September evening, about a month ago, I was there, reviewing a manuscript, sitting in a quiet corner. The editing dominated my attention, and I was oblivious to the comings and goings around me. Just before ten o'clock, I roused myself, packed up my satchel, and prepared to walk home. I stood, moved to the door, and stepped outside. It was a dull night, with some overcast, clouds obscuring the stars.

As I was leaving the coffeehouse, I had the impression that another patron was also stirring, rising, and approaching the doorway. It was just a vague notion, untargeted. I don't recall actually seeing a person. And, as I felt the door swing shut behind me, I was alone.

I began to walk south on 21st Street, toward Broadway, through that residential stretch of small, close houses and squat apartments. Despite the structures of urban habitation that surrounded me, a desolation seemed to rise from the street. No cars drove past me, no people sat on stoops or balconies. Only a few steps took me into the quiet and dark, leaving the light and society of the coffeehouse behind. The streets seemed deserted, the streetlights unaccountably dim. As you know, my own apartment is on Second Avenue, on the other side of the expressway from midtown, and 21st Street leads to an underpass beneath the six lanes of raised asphalt that bisect our city.

The September night was warm, a suggestive humidity in the air. I allowed my thoughts to ramble unfocused. I walked on the sidewalk, past the little porches of the homes, beneath the crooked branches of the old trees.

After a few blocks, I felt a small but insistent sensation of foreboding. I found myself listening intently and I heard something behind me. Not footsteps but, rather, the more subtle sounds of someone walking. A twig underfoot, leaves resettling after a leg swings past, the almost indecipherable noise of clothing shifting as its wearer moves forward. The whispers of a being passing through space.

I stopped, turned, and looked back.

There, maybe two blocks, perhaps a hundred yards, behind me, on the sidewalk, in the shadows, was a figure moving toward me with a slow and steady gait. Because of the darkness and the distance, I could not make out much detail. I had the impression of an overcoat – something excessive given the warmth of the evening – concealing the figure from the shoulder to the lower leg. And a cap, or a mound of thick hair, on the head. The face was invisible to me. The man – for it must have been a man, surely – was walking down the sidewalk, in the late evening, the same as me, behind me.

As I turned back and continued my walk, I dismissed the figure from my mind. Or tried to, without success. Something about the situation alarmed me. To my annoyance, the presence of this walker, behind me, invaded, and soon dominated, my otherwise commonplace, undirected thoughts. I could not help anticipating: if he was walking at a faster pace than me, he would soon come up behind me, a notion that unaccountably disturbed me. If he walked at the same pace, something I thought he might be intentionally doing, he would go on tracking my path, a notion no less disturbing. After crossing another silent street, I turned and looked back again.

The figure was still behind me, slightly closer, perhaps a block and a half back. I stood and stared, still unable to make out any details. As I looked at him, though, his movements took on an abnormal aspect, without the familiar side to side shifting of a normal purposeful stride. Indeed, I remember thinking, it was as if he was floating toward me, slowly.

I had no plan or intention, and considered the awkwardness of the situation. Should I wait for him to approach me? Should I address him? What would I say?

Then the figure also stopped abruptly. Still well behind me, I could see the shoulders outlined against the half-light of the houses behind. The head seemed to move in such a way as to convey the impression that he was looking at me, waiting for me to act. I was frightened, and I did not know why. Moments passed, both of us standing there.

I turned away and, quickly, continued south. I found myself drawn into an internal debate. My concern, my fear, was absurd. This was nothing more sinister than another pedestrian walking through the streets of midtown at ten in the evening. Hardly cause for alarm. Why did I feel certain that he was tracking me? I felt my heart beating rapidly and my pace quickened almost to a run.

I found myself dreading the underpass, that stretch of road that resembled a long concrete tunnel. At the next intersection – S Street, I think it was – I abruptly turned left and further quickened my pace. Soon I was on 22nd Street, paralleling my earlier path. I did not look back.

Of course, I eventually had to return to 21st Street and the underpass. There was no reasonable alternative to get across town to Second Avenue. The fear in my chest settled into a feeling of dread. I found myself slowing down, creeping forward like a spy. Eventually I slipped back to 21st Street, moving from shadow to shadow, with stealth. I looked both ways, standing on the corner, perspiring. The street was empty and silent. The figure was gone, or hiding. I wiped my slick forehead with my sleeve, hitched up the shoulderstrap on my satchel, and stepped quickly toward the underpass.

The drone of traffic, always present, flowed down from the roadway above. Though vaguely reassuring, the noise surely masked the sounds of anyone following me. I walked through the tunnel, my ears attuned, my breath short. I was determined not to break into a run, and kept my gaze forward. Finally, I emerged, and turned down Second Avenue, passing the city cemetery. I resisted the temptation to look anywhere except straight ahead.

A feeling of foolishness slowly replaced the dread. Still, I had my key ready long before I approached the door to my building, and did not pause until I was in my apartment and behind a bolted door. I sighed and almost fell into a chair, relieved but also quite confused.

I thought no more of this singular incident for several days. Naturally, I hoped to forget the entire affair. But, maybe four days later, I had another experience that disturbed me a great deal.

I was at home and it was late. I had just completed a phone conversation with my daughter. We were discussing the possibility of my coming for a visit. It thrilled me, in a small but uplifting way, to have my daughter supporting me, helping convince my ex-wife that I might join them for a few days. You cannot imagine the comfort I get from any indication that I am valued by my only child.

In the grip of this warm feeling, I stepped to the window, looking out over Second Avenue. My window faces north from three floors up, and in the autumn after the leaves have fallen from the sycamore trees, I can see the traffic below, and the asphalt of the parking lot across the street that accompanies that hideous box-like gray building on the corner of Riverside Drive. I stood there, my eyes following the red and white lights of the cars driving down the avenue, my mind contemplating the prospect of a good night's sleep, when I saw someone standing, on the sidewalk, near the entrance of my building.

With a shudder, I recognized the figure as the same individual who had followed me, from the coffeehouse, on that night not long before. Even though I was looking down, and even with the distance between us, I had no doubt that it was the same person. He wore the same overcoat; he had the same shape. The cap on his head seemed to shadow his eyes and, as before, I could see no detail of his face. This time, he was not moving. Rather, he was standing stock still, immobile, next to several news racks, not far from the curb. As cars passed, their headlights moved across and up his body, then fell away. There was a disturbing rigidity to his stance, and an accompanying determination.

He was facing my building and, to my extreme discomfort, the angle of his neck and posture of his shoulders made it certain, in my mind at least, that he was looking directly at my window. He was watching me as I watched him.

I felt a flutter in my chest and a rising terror. My mind groped for an explanation. I could think of no reason why this person was here, or what purpose he could possibly have.

I stepped back, retreating from the window, out of his range of vision. I turned off the only lamp in the room and felt the darkness surround me. A wave of nausea passed over me. I drank some water from the kitchen sink.

Slowly, I moved to the window, holding my breath, and looked out. The figure was still there. His posture and pose had not changed at all. Even in the dark of my apartment, I knew, with an unreasonable certainty, that he could see me. I backed up again, out of his line of sight. The idea of sleep, now, was inconceivable. My thoughts raced incoherently, my head throbbed.

Some moments passed while I stood there, time slipping away, before I had the courage to approach the window once more. This time, when I peered down, the figure was gone. I felt a shock, and I was suddenly more afraid of his absence than his presence. With a dismal suddenness, my mind seized upon the idea that he was coming for me, that he had entered the building and was walking – floating – slowly up the steps. I could picture him rising, with an inevitable, persistent stealth, up the central stairway. I rushed to the door and checked the locks and the bolt. I peered out through the wide-angled peephole.

I could see little except the wall across the hallway from my door. I listened hard for the sound of him creeping down the hall, not sure I'd be able to hear his approach. I held my breath, afraid to make a sound.

Of course, nothing happened. Except that I stood there, at my door, waiting, for a very long time.

For a week, I avoided going out at night. I drew all the blinds, kept my windows shut tight. I ate little. I slept little. I think I suffered from some illness as well, for I felt lethargic, feverish, and slightly dizzy. Any contemplated trip to see my daughter had to be put off.

Gradually, my state of anxiety lessened a little, especially in the daylight hours. I tried to forget. I told myself that my fears were nonsensical. No one cared what I did. No one would bother to watch me, to follow me. I told myself that there was nothing sinister about a man standing on a sidewalk for a few minutes, nothing sinister about a man walking through midtown on a September evening. I told myself that it was entirely possible that I had imagined all of it.

One night, annoyed at myself for my lack of fortitude, I went to a film at the midtown art-house theater. For an hour or two, the film succeeded in helping me escape from the prison of my own disturbed thoughts.

I was calm when I left the theater and began the walk home. Once I had left the reassuring brightness of the lobby, with its colorful posters and milling patrons, however, I felt my level of anxiety begin to rise. My chest felt constricted; I could not seem to take a full breath. I began to listen intently, my vigilance rising with my pulse.

October had come and, with the new month, colder nights. The sky was clear, without a moon, and the light of the stars was inconsequential. Telephone wires dissected the urban sky, the streetlights revealed small patches of order amid the clusters of shadow.

I made my way over toward 21st, leaving the activity of the theater far behind. I found myself on a dark, quiet street lined with small bungalow houses. Trees rose up, their branches cloaking the dull rays cast by the streetlights. I felt a sudden, forlorn, acute loneliness. No cars passed, and the silence around me made me feel deserted, as if the houses around me were facades, empty of inhabitants, as if this part of the city had been abandoned, deprived of any human touch. No one lived here. No one slept here. No one walked here.

Except for me, and, of course, the other. For I felt him behind me. I had not seen him, or heard him, but I knew he was there, walking slowly, following, watching me.

I did not turn, nor did I stop. I willed myself to continue, my pace unchanged. I lowered my head, made myself small and self-contained.

I was a few blocks from 21st, where I would have to turn and walk through the underpass, beneath the concrete. Suddenly, I was captured by a stark, clear realization: I knew I could not make it through the tunnel beneath the expressway. The acknowledgment of this certainty paralyzed me. My determination disappeared and I stopped walking. A moment passed and, unable now to resist the temptation, I turned to look behind me.

He stood there, in the shadows, on the sidewalk, about twenty-five yards away. He was closer than he had ever been, and I felt my heart roll in my chest.

I could see that the overcoat was frayed and old, too large for the body beneath it. The sleeves almost covered his hands, exposing only the tips of fingers thin and filthy. His black cap had a short bill that cast a shadow over his face. Hair, long and black, lay on his shoulders framing the space where his face should be. But I could still see no expression, no features, only a vague darkness.

He stood still, but I could tell that he had stopped short, pulling up as I halted. He swayed slightly, the motion of one who has ceased walking unexpectedly, and intends only to continue after the reason for the interruption has passed.

The silence settled around us, the moment cloaked in anticipation. He looked at me. I looked at him.

The thoughts in my mind seemed to drain away, without replacement. We stood there, in the night, on the sidewalk, both of us waiting. I was controlled by a single commanding notion: I would not go on. I would not continue, not if it meant that his lurking presence would follow, intent on some purpose hidden to me. I was terribly frightened, and confused, but I clung to this single directive. I don't know how long we stood there, myself and the figure on the sidewalk, but it seemed like a long time.

The moment was broken when the figure moved. He took a single step toward me. His posture remained the same. His shadowed countenance did not change.

My surprise translated into an action. I took a step also. But not in the direction I had been going, for I could not go on. Instead: back. I took a step toward my pursuer, a movement that surprised me. I detected a mirroring surprise in the figure. And, in my near-paralytic terror, I felt a strange and unanticipated surge of relief. Boldly, I took a second step.

The figure moved, swayed, as if he was experiencing an involuntary shudder. Then, he turned around, his back to me, and began a retreat. His pace was measured, unhurried, but he was fleeing from me. I felt feverish, a rising flush that made my face and neck burn. I began to follow him.

He was only twenty yards or so in front of me. I stared at the broad, soft back of the coat, my pace the same as his. I had no purpose, no intent. I only knew that I had broken the spell, that he was no longer behind me, no longer watching me, no longer following me. Instead, I had become the shadowed figure, following him.

We continued down the sidewalk, moving beneath the branches of the trees and the overhead wires, illuminated by the weak streetlights and the partial light from the houses. The figure in front of me began to accelerate, moving in the same odd, floating motion, and the distance between us increased. I grew afraid, now, that he would elude me, and disappear. I hurried in response.

He approached the next intersection and turned right. He had gained enough distance, in an almost magical way, that I lost sight of him as he moved past a cluster of birch trees and the corner of a garage attached to a small house. I continued to the corner, and turned to follow.

The sidewalk before me, and the street, were empty. My pursuer, who I was now pursuing, had disappeared. He must be hiding, I thought, behind some fence or shrub. Perhaps he was crouched behind one of the parked cars or lurking behind a tree. He will fall upon me, I thought, and I will be lost.

This sudden new terror deprived me of my strength. My legs begin to crumple. I felt abandoned and alone. My vision failed, the world became cloudy and black. It was as if my heart had ceased to beat.

"Why are you following me?" came a cold, distinct voice from nearby. For the briefest of moments, I had the odd notion that it might be my own voice, speaking involuntarily. But no, the accusatory question came from a figure standing in shadow on a small patch of lawn, only a few feet away. I remember a broken tree, a crumbling wall of stucco. I became horribly afraid that he would touch me.

"What do you want?" The voice came louder this time, angry, slicing through the fog that was enveloping my mind, uttering a question that should have been mine to ask.

I tried to speak in response, but could not. I think I made some noise, an unintelligible grunting. It was outrageous: he had been following me, not I him.

I think I collapsed. At least I descended to one knee. Something moved past me as I swooned. I caught a musty scent of ashes. I placed my hand on the cold concrete and felt nausea rise in my stomach. I cowered there, trying to steady myself.

Slowly, my mind cleared. My equilibrium returned. I rose and looked about. A dark and desolate street, an empty sidewalk, buckled and cracked by the roots of the old trees rising up into the night sky. The squat, bare houses, with their dark lifeless windows and indifferent facades, around me. Somehow, I managed my way home.

* * *

Theodore took a final sip of tea, which must have gone quite cold. He looked around the café, his eyes bright with fear. I watched him, slow to speak.

"I'm not sure I understand," I ventured, finally.

Theodore seemed to have again forgotten I was there. The café had grown quiet, the hour was late.

After a moment, Theodore said, quickly: "I must go now. Maybe I can slip away before he can trace me." He rose, lifting his coat from the chair, slipping his arms into the sleeves. I noted, with some surprise, how frayed and large was the overcoat he clasped around him. He was away and through the door before I could articulate a farewell, leaving me with an uncomfortable feeling and a cold, half-empty cup of coffee.

Not long after, plagued by disconcerting thoughts, I rose and left the café.

As I walked through the door into the night, I had the distinct impression that someone else was rising from a table and moving, behind me, toward the exit.

The Shadows on the Wall

Mary Eleanor Wilkins Freeman

"HENRY HAD WORDS with Edward in the study the night before Edward died," said Caroline Glynn.

She spoke not with acrimony, but with grave severity. Rebecca Ann Glynn gasped by way of assent. She sat in a wide flounce of black silk in the corner of the sofa, and rolled terrified eyes from her sister Caroline to her sister Mrs Stephen Brigham, who had been Emma Glynn, the one beauty of the family. The latter was beautiful still, with a large, splendid, full-blown beauty, she filled a great rocking-chair with her superb bulk of femininity, and swayed gently back and forth, her black silks whispering and her black frills fluttering. Even the shock of death – for her brother Edward lay dead in the house – could not disturb her outward serenity of demeanor.

But even her expression of masterly placidity changed before her sister Caroline's announcement and her sister Rebecca Ann's gasp of terror and distress in response.

"I think Henry might have controlled his temper, when poor Edward was so near his end," she said with an asperity which disturbed slightly the roseate curves of her beautiful mouth.

"Of course he did not *know*," murmured Rebecca Ann in a faint tone.

"Of course he did not know it," said Caroline quickly. She turned on her sister with a strange, sharp look of suspicion. Then she shrank as if from the other's possible answer.

Rebecca gasped again. The married sister, Mrs Emma Brigham, was now sitting up straight in her chair; she had ceased rocking, and was eyeing them both intently with a sudden accentuation of family likeness in her face.

"What do you mean?" said she impartially to them both. Then she, too, seemed to shrink before a possible answer. She even laughed an evasive sort of laugh.

"Nobody means anything," said Caroline firmly. She rose and crossed the room toward the door with grim decisiveness.

"Where are you going?" asked Mrs Brigham.

"I have something to see to," replied Caroline, and the others at once knew by her tone that she had some solemn and sad duty to perform in the chamber of death.

"Oh," said Mrs Brigham.

After the door had closed behind Caroline, she turned to Rebecca.

"Did Henry have many words with him?" she asked.

"They were talking very loud," replied Rebecca evasively.

Mrs Brigham looked at her. She had not resumed rocking. She still sat up straight, with a slight knitting of intensity on her fair forehead, between the pretty rippling curves of her auburn hair.

"Did you – ever hear anything?" she asked in a low voice with a glance toward the door.

"I was just across the hall in the south parlor, and that door was open and this door ajar," replied Rebecca with a slight flush.

"Then you must have –"

"I couldn't help it."

"Everything?"

"Most of it."

"What was it?"

"The old story."

"I suppose Henry was mad, as he always was, because Edward was living on here for nothing, when he had wasted all the money father left him."

Rebecca nodded, with a fearful glance at the door.

When Emma spoke again her voice was still more hushed. "I know how he felt," said she. "It must have looked to him as if Edward was living at his expense, but he wasn't."

"No, he wasn't."

"And Edward had a right here according to the terms of father's will, and Henry ought to have remembered it."

"Yes, he ought."

"Did he say hard things?"

"Pretty hard, from what I heard."

"What?"

"I heard him tell Edward that he had no business here at all, and he thought he had better go away."

"What did Edward say?"

"That he would stay here as long as he lived and afterward, too, if he was a mind to, and he would like to see Henry get him out; and then –"

"What?"

"Then he laughed."

"What did Henry say?"

"I didn't hear him say anything, but –"

"But what?"

"I saw him when he came out of this room."

"He looked mad?"

"You've seen him when he looked so."

Emma nodded. The expression of horror on her face had deepened.

"Do you remember that time he killed the cat because she had scratched him?"

"Yes. Don't!"

Then Caroline reentered the room; she went up to the stove, in which a wood fire was burning – it was a cold, gloomy day of fall – and she warmed her hands, which were reddened from recent washing in cold water.

Mrs Brigham looked at her and hesitated. She glanced at the door, which was still ajar; it did not easily shut, being still swollen with the damp weather of the summer. She rose and pushed it together with a sharp thud, which jarred the house. Rebecca started painfully with a half-exclamation. Caroline looked at her disapprovingly.

"It is time you controlled your nerves, Rebecca," she said.

Mrs Brigham, returning from the closed door, said imperiously that it ought to be fixed, it shut so hard.

"It will shrink enough after we have had the fire a few days," replied Caroline.

"I think Henry ought to be ashamed of himself for talking as he did to Edward," said Mrs Brigham abruptly, but in an almost inaudible voice.

"Hush," said Caroline, with a glance of actual fear at the closed door.

"Nobody can hear with the door shut."

"He must have heard it shut, and –"

"Well, I can say what I want to before he comes down, and I am not afraid of him."

"I don't know who is afraid of him! What reason is there for anybody to be afraid of Henry?" demanded Caroline.

Mrs Brigham trembled before her sister's look. Rebecca gasped again.

"There isn't any reason, of course. Why should there be?"

"I wouldn't speak so, then. Somebody might overhear you and think it was queer. Miranda Joy is in the south parlor sewing, you know."

"I thought she went upstairs to stitch on the machine."

"She did, but she has come down again."

"Well, she can't hear."

"I say again I think Henry ought to be ashamed of himself. I shouldn't think he'd ever get over it, having words with poor Edward the very night before he died. Edward was enough sight better disposition than Henry, with all his faults."

"I never heard him speak a cross word, unless he spoke cross to Henry that last night. I don't know but he did from what Rebecca overheard."

"Not so much cross, as sort of soft, and sweet, and aggravating," sniffed Rebecca.

"What do you really think ailed Edward?" asked Emma in hardly more than a whisper. She did not look at her sister.

"I know you said that he had terrible pains in his stomach, and had spasms, but what do you think made him have them?"

"Henry called it gastric trouble. You know Edward has always had dyspepsia."

Mrs Brigham hesitated a moment. "Was there any talk of an – examination?" said she.

Then Caroline turned on her fiercely.

"No," said she in a terrible voice. "No."

The three sisters' souls seemed to meet on one common ground of terrified understanding through their eyes.

The old-fashioned latch of the door was heard to rattle, and a push from without made the door shake ineffectually. "It's Henry," Rebecca sighed rather than whispered. Mrs Brigham settled herself, after a noiseless rush across the floor, into her rocking-chair again, and was swaying back and forth with her head comfortably leaning back, when the door at last yielded and Henry Glynn entered. He cast a covertly sharp, comprehensive glance at Mrs Brigham with her elaborate calm; at Rebecca quietly huddled in the corner of the sofa with her handkerchief to her face and only one small uncovered reddened ear as attentive as a dog's, and at Caroline sitting with a strained composure in her armchair by the stove. She met his eyes quite firmly with a look of inscrutable fear, and defiance of the fear and of him.

Henry Glynn looked more like this sister than the others. Both had the same hard delicacy of form and aquilinity of feature. They confronted each other with the pitiless immovability of two statues in whose marble lineaments emotions were fixed for all eternity.

Then Henry Glynn smiled and the smile transformed his face. He looked suddenly years younger, and an almost boyish recklessness appeared in his face. He flung himself into a chair with a gesture which was bewildering from its incongruity with his general appearance. He leaned his head back, flung one leg over the other, and looked laughingly at Mrs Brigham.

"I declare, Emma, you grow younger every year," he said.

She flushed a little, and her placid mouth widened at the corners. She was susceptible to praise.

"Our thoughts today ought to belong to the one of us who will *never* grow older," said Caroline in a hard voice.

Henry looked at her, still smiling. "Of course, we none of us forget that," said he, in a deep, gentle voice; "but we have to speak to the living, Caroline, and I have not seen Emma for a long time, and the living are as dear as the dead."

"Not to me," said Caroline.

She rose and went abruptly out of the room again. Rebecca also rose and hurried after her, sobbing loudly.

Henry looked slowly after them.

"Caroline is completely unstrung," said he.

Mrs Brigham rocked. A confidence in him inspired by his manner was stealing over her. Out of that confidence she spoke quite easily and naturally.

"His death was very sudden," said she.

Henry's eyelids quivered slightly but his gaze was unswerving.

"Yes," said he, "it was very sudden. He was sick only a few hours."

"What did you call it?"

"Gastric."

"You did not think of an examination?"

"There was no need. I am perfectly certain as to the cause of his death."

Suddenly Mrs Brigham felt a creep as of some live horror over her very soul. Her flesh prickled with cold, before an inflection of his voice. She rose, tottering on weak knees.

"Where are you going?" asked Henry in a strange, breathless voice.

Mrs Brigham said something incoherent about some sewing which she had to do – some black for the funeral – and was out of the room. She went up to the front chamber which she occupied. Caroline was there. She went close to her and took her hands, and the two sisters looked at each other.

"Don't speak, don't, I won't have it!" said Caroline finally in an awful whisper.

"I won't," replied Emma.

That afternoon the three sisters were in the study.

Mrs Brigham was hemming some black material. At last she laid her work on her lap.

"It's no use, I cannot see to sew another stitch until we have a light," said she.

Caroline, who was writing some letters at the table, turned to Rebecca, in her usual place on the sofa.

"Rebecca, you had better get a lamp," she said.

Rebecca started up; even in the dusk her face showed her agitation.

"It doesn't seem to me that we need a lamp quite yet," she said in a piteous, pleading voice like a child's.

"Yes, we do," returned Mrs Brigham peremptorily. "I can't see to sew another stitch."

Rebecca rose and left the room. Presently she entered with a lamp. She set it on the table, an old-fashioned card-table which was placed against the opposite wall from the window. That opposite wall was taken up with three doors; the one small space was occupied by the table.

"What have you put that lamp over there for?" asked Mrs Brigham, with more of impatience than her voice usually revealed. "Why didn't you set it in the hall, and have done with it? Neither Caroline nor I can see if it is on that table."

"I thought perhaps you would move," replied Rebecca hoarsely.

"If I do move, we can't both sit at that table. Caroline has her paper all spread around. Why don't you set the lamp on the study table in the middle of the room, then we can both see?"

Rebecca hesitated. Her face was very pale. She looked with an appeal that was fairly agonizing at her sister Caroline.

"Why don't you put the lamp on this table, as she says?" asked Caroline, almost fiercely. "Why do you act so, Rebecca?"

Rebecca took the lamp and set it on the table in the middle of the room without another word. Then she seated herself on the sofa and placed a hand over her eyes as if to shade them, and remained so.

"Does the light hurt your eyes, and is that the reason why you didn't want the lamp?" asked Mrs Brigham kindly.

"I always like to sit in the dark," replied Rebecca chokingly. Then she snatched her handkerchief hastily from her pocket and began to weep. Caroline continued to write, Mrs Brigham to sew.

Suddenly Mrs Brigham as she sewed glanced at the opposite wall. The glance became a steady stare. She looked intently, her work suspended in her hands. Then she looked away again and took a few more stitches, then she looked again, and again turned to her task. At last she laid her work in her lap and stared concentratedly. She looked from the wall round the room, taking note of the various objects. Then she turned to her sisters.

"What *is* that?" said she.

"What?" asked Caroline harshly.

"That strange shadow on the wall," replied Mrs Brigham.

Rebecca sat with her face hidden; Caroline dipped her pen in the inkstand.

"Why don't you turn around and look?" asked Mrs Brigham in a wondering and somewhat aggrieved way.

"I am in a hurry to finish this letter," replied Caroline shortly.

Mrs Brigham rose, her work slipping to the floor, and began walking round the room, moving various articles of furniture, with her eyes on the shadow.

Then suddenly she shrieked out:

"Look at this awful shadow! What is it? Caroline, look, look! Rebecca, look! What is it?"

All Mrs Brigham's triumphant placidity was gone. Her handsome face was livid with horror. She stood stiffly pointing at the shadow.

Then after a shuddering glance at the wall Rebecca burst out in a wild wail.

"Oh, Caroline, there it is again, there it is again!"

"Caroline Glynn, you look!" said Mrs Brigham. "Look! What is that dreadful shadow?"

Caroline rose, turned, and stood confronting the wall.

"How should I know?" she said.

"It has been there every night since he died!" cried Rebecca.

"Every night?"

"Yes; he died Thursday and this is Saturday; that makes three nights," said Caroline rigidly. She stood as if holding her calm with a vise of concentrated will.

"It – it looks like – like –" stammered Mrs Brigham in a tone of intense horror.

"I know what it looks like well enough," said Caroline. "I've got eyes in my head."

"It looks like Edward," burst out Rebecca in a sort of frenzy of fear. "Only –"

"Yes, it does," assented Mrs Brigham, whose horror-stricken tone matched her sisters', "only – Oh, it is awful! What is it, Caroline?"

"I ask you again, how should I know?" replied Caroline. "I see it there like you. How should I know any more than you?"

"It *must* be something in the room," said Mrs Brigham, staring wildly around.

"We moved everything in the room the first night it came," said Rebecca; "it is not anything in the room."

Caroline turned upon her with a sort of fury. "Of course it is something in the room," said she. "How you act! What do you mean talking so? Of course it is something in the room."

"Of course it is," agreed Mrs Brigham, looking at Caroline suspiciously. "It must be something in the room."

"It is not anything in the room," repeated Rebecca with obstinate horror.

The door opened suddenly and Henry Glynn entered. He began to speak, then his eyes followed the direction of the others. He stood staring at the shadow on the wall.

"What is that?" he demanded in a strange voice.

"It must be due to something in the room," Mrs Brigham said faintly.

Henry Glynn stood and stared a moment longer. His face showed a gamut of emotions. Horror, conviction, then furious incredulity. Suddenly he began hastening hither and thither about the room. He moved the furniture with fierce jerks, turning ever to see the effect upon the shadow on the wall. Not a line of its terrible outlines wavered.

"It must be something in the room!" he declared in a voice which seemed to snap like a lash.

His face changed, the inmost secrecy of his nature seemed evident upon his face, until one almost lost sight of his lineaments. Rebecca stood close to her sofa, regarding him with woeful, fascinated eyes. Mrs Brigham clutched Caroline's hand. They both stood in a corner out of his way. For a few moments he raged about the room like a caged wild animal. He moved every piece of furniture; when the moving of a piece did not affect the shadow he flung it to the floor.

Then suddenly he desisted. He laughed.

"What an absurdity," he said easily. "Such a to-do about a shadow."

"That's so," assented Mrs Brigham, in a scared voice which she tried to make natural. As she spoke she lifted a chair near her.

"I think you have broken the chair that Edward was fond of," said Caroline.

Terror and wrath were struggling for expression on her face. Her mouth was set, her eyes shrinking. Henry lifted the chair with a show of anxiety.

"Just as good as ever," he said pleasantly. He laughed again, looking at his sisters. "Did I scare you?" he said. "I should think you might be used to me by this time. You know my way of wanting to leap to the bottom of a mystery, and that shadow does look – queer, like – and I thought if there was any way of accounting for it I would like to without any delay."

"You don't seem to have succeeded," remarked Caroline dryly, with a slight glance at the wall.

Henry's eyes followed hers and he quivered perceptibly.

"Oh, there is no accounting for shadows," he said, and he laughed again. "A man is a fool to try to account for shadows."

Then the supper bell rang, and they all left the room, but Henry kept his back to the wall – as did, indeed, the others.

Henry led the way with an alert motion like a boy; Rebecca brought up the rear. She could scarcely walk, her knees trembled so.

"I can't sit in that room again this evening," she whispered to Caroline after supper.

"Very well; we will sit in the south room," replied Caroline. "I think we will sit in the south parlor," she said aloud; "it isn't as damp as the study, and I have a cold."

So they all sat in the south room with their sewing. Henry read the newspaper, his chair drawn close to the lamp on the table. About nine o'clock he rose abruptly and crossed the hall to the study. The three sisters looked at one another. Mrs Brigham rose, folded her rustling skirts compactly round her, and began tiptoeing toward the door.

"What are you going to do?" inquired Rebecca agitatedly.

"I am going to see what he is about," replied Mrs Brigham cautiously.

As she spoke she pointed to the study door across the hall; it was ajar. Henry had striven to pull it together behind him, but it had somehow swollen beyond the limit with curious speed. It was still ajar and a streak of light showed from top to bottom.

Mrs Brigham folded her skirts so tightly that her bulk with its swelling curves was revealed in a black silk sheath, and she went with a slow toddle across the hall to the study door. She stood there, her eye at the crack.

In the south room Rebecca stopped sewing and sat watching with dilated eyes. Caroline sewed steadily. What Mrs Brigham, standing at the crack in the study door, saw was this:

Henry Glynn, evidently reasoning that the source of the strange shadow must be between the table on which the lamp stood and the wall, was making systematic passes and thrusts with an old sword which had belonged to his father all over and through the intervening space. Not an inch was left unpierced. He seemed to have divided the space into mathematical sections. He brandished the sword with a sort of cold fury and calculation; the blade gave out flashes of light, the shadow remained unmoved. Mrs Brigham, watching, felt herself cold with horror.

Finally Henry ceased and stood with the sword in hand and raised as if to strike, surveying the shadow on the wall threateningly. Mrs Brigham toddled back across the hall and shut the south room door behind her before she related what she had seen.

"He looked like a demon," she said again. "Have you got any of that old wine in the house, Caroline? I don't feel as if I could stand much more."

"Yes, there's plenty," said Caroline; "you can have some when you go to bed."

"I think we had all better take some," said Mrs Brigham. "Oh, Caroline, what –"

"Don't ask; don't speak," said Caroline.

"No, I'm not going to," replied Mrs Brigham; "but –"

Soon the three sisters went to their chambers and the south parlor was deserted. Caroline called to Henry in the study to put out the light before he came upstairs. They had been gone about an hour when he came into the room bringing the lamp which had stood in the study. He set it on the table, and waited a few minutes, pacing up and down. His face was terrible, his fair complexion showed livid, and his blue eyes seemed dark blanks of awful reflections.

Then he took up the lamp and returned to the library. He set the lamp on the center table and the shadow sprang out on the wall. Again he studied the furniture and moved it about, but deliberately, with none of his former frenzy. Nothing affected the shadow.

Then he returned to the south room with the lamp and again waited. Again he returned to the study and placed the lamp on the table, and the shadow sprang out upon the wall. It was midnight before he went upstairs. Mrs Brigham and the other sisters, who could not sleep, heard him.

The next day was the funeral. That evening the family sat in the south room. Some relatives were with them. Nobody entered the study until Henry carried a lamp in there after the others had retired for the night. He saw again the shadow on the wall leap to an awful life before the light.

The next morning at breakfast Henry Glynn announced that he had to go to the city for three days. The sisters looked at him with surprise. He very seldom left home, and just now his practice had been neglected on account of Edward's death.

"How can you leave your patients now?" asked Mrs Brigham wonderingly.

"I don't know how to, but there is no other way," replied Henry easily. "I have had a telegram from Doctor Mitford."

"Consultation?" inquired Mrs Brigham.

"I have business," replied Henry.

Doctor Mitford was an old classmate of his who lived in a neighboring city and who occasionally called upon him in the case of a consultation.

After he had gone, Mrs Brigham said to Caroline that, after all, Henry had not said that he was going to consult with Doctor Mitford, and she thought it very strange.

"Everything is very strange," said Rebecca with a shudder.

"What do you mean?" inquired Caroline.

"Nothing," replied Rebecca.

Nobody entered the study that day, nor the next. The third day Henry was expected home, but he did not arrive and the last train from the city had come.

"I call it pretty queer work," said Mrs Brigham. "The idea of a doctor leaving his patients at such a time as this, and the idea of a consultation lasting three days! There is no sense in it, and *now* he has not come. I don't understand it, for my part."

"I don't either," said Rebecca.

They were all in the south parlor. There was no light in the study; the door was ajar.

Presently Mrs Brigham rose – she could not have told why; something seemed to impel her – some will outside her own. She went out of the room, again wrapping her rustling skirts round that she might pass noiselessly, and began pushing at the swollen door of the study.

"She has not got any lamp," said Rebecca in a shaking voice.

Caroline, who was writing letters, rose again, took the only remaining lamp in the room, and followed her sister. Rebecca had risen, but she stood trembling, not venturing to follow.

The doorbell rang, but the others did not hear it; it was on the south door on the other side of the house from the study. Rebecca, after hesitating until the bell rang the second time, went to the door; she remembered that the servant was out.

Caroline and her sister Emma entered the study. Caroline set the lamp on the table. They looked at the wall, and there were two shadows. The sisters stood clutching each other, staring at the awful things on the wall. Then Rebecca came in, staggering, with a telegram in her hand. "Here is – a telegram," she gasped. "Henry is – dead."

The Wind in the Rose-Bush

Mary Eleanor Wilkins Freeman

FORD VILLAGE HAS NO RAILROAD STATION, being on the other side of the river from Porter's Falls, and accessible only by the ford which gives it its name, and a ferry line.

The ferry-boat was waiting when Rebecca Flint got off the train with her bag and lunch basket. When she and her small trunk were safely embarked she sat stiff and straight and calm in the ferry-boat as it shot swiftly and smoothly across stream. There was a horse attached to a light country wagon on board, and he pawed the deck uneasily. His owner stood near, with a wary eye upon him, although he was chewing, with as dully reflective an expression as a cow. Beside Rebecca sat a woman of about her own age, who kept looking at her with furtive curiosity; her husband, short and stout and saturnine, stood near her. Rebecca paid no attention to either of them. She was tall and spare and pale, the type of a spinster, yet with rudimentary lines and expressions of matronhood. She all unconsciously held her shawl, rolled up in a canvas bag, on her left hip, as if it had been a child. She wore a settled frown of dissent at life, but it was the frown of a mother who regarded life as a froward child, rather than as an overwhelming fate.

The other woman continued staring at her; she was mildly stupid, except for an over-developed curiosity which made her at times sharp beyond belief. Her eyes glittered, red spots came on her flaccid cheeks; she kept opening her mouth to speak, making little abortive motions. Finally she could endure it no longer; she nudged Rebecca boldly.

"A pleasant day," said she.

Rebecca looked at her and nodded coldly.

"Yes, very," she assented.

"Have you come far?"

"I have come from Michigan."

"Oh!" said the woman, with awe. "It's a long way," she remarked presently.

"Yes, it is," replied Rebecca, conclusively.

Still the other woman was not daunted; there was something which she determined to know, possibly roused thereto by a vague sense of incongruity in the other's appearance. "It's a long ways to come and leave a family," she remarked with painful slyness.

"I ain't got any family to leave," returned Rebecca shortly.

"Then you ain't –"

"No, I ain't."

"Oh!" said the woman.

Rebecca looked straight ahead at the race of the river.

It was a long ferry. Finally Rebecca herself waxed unexpectedly loquacious. She turned to the other woman and inquired if she knew John Dent's widow who lived in Ford Village. "Her husband died about three years ago," said she, by way of detail.

The woman started violently. She turned pale, then she flushed; she cast a strange glance at her husband, who was regarding both women with a sort of stolid keenness.

"Yes, I guess I do," faltered the woman finally.

"Well, his first wife was my sister," said Rebecca with the air of one imparting important intelligence.

"Was she?" responded the other woman feebly. She glanced at her husband with an expression of doubt and terror, and he shook his head forbiddingly.

"I'm going to see her, and take my niece Agnes home with me," said Rebecca.

Then the woman gave such a violent start that she noticed it.

"What is the matter?" she asked.

"Nothin', I guess," replied the woman, with eyes on her husband, who was slowly shaking his head, like a Chinese toy.

"Is my niece sick?" asked Rebecca with quick suspicion.

"No, she ain't sick," replied the woman with alacrity, then she caught her breath with a gasp.

"When did you see her?"

"Let me see; I ain't seen her for some little time," replied the woman. Then she caught her breath again.

"She ought to have grown up real pretty, if she takes after my sister. She was a real pretty woman," Rebecca said wistfully.

"Yes, I guess she did grow up pretty," replied the woman in a trembling voice.

"What kind of a woman is the second wife?"

The woman glanced at her husband's warning face. She continued to gaze at him while she replied in a choking voice to Rebecca:

"I – guess she's a nice woman," she replied. "I – don't know, I – guess so. I – don't see much of her."

"I felt kind of hurt that John married again so quick," said Rebecca; "but I suppose he wanted his house kept, and Agnes wanted care. I wasn't so situated that I could take her when her mother died. I had my own mother to care for, and I was school-teaching. Now mother has gone, and my uncle died six months ago and left me quite a little property, and I've given up my school, and I've come for Agnes. I guess she'll be glad to go with me, though I suppose her stepmother is a good woman, and has always done for her."

The man's warning shake at his wife was fairly portentous.

"I guess so," said she.

"John always wrote that she was a beautiful woman," said Rebecca.

Then the ferry-boat grated on the shore.

John Dent's widow had sent a horse and wagon to meet her sister-in-law. When the woman and her husband went down the road, on which Rebecca in the wagon with her trunk soon passed them, she said reproachfully:

"Seems as if I'd ought to have told her, Thomas."

"Let her find it out herself," replied the man. "Don't you go to burnin' your fingers in other folks' puddin', Maria."

"Do you s'pose she'll see anything?" asked the woman with a spasmodic shudder and a terrified roll of her eyes.

"See!" returned her husband with stolid scorn. "Better be sure there's anything to see."

"Oh, Thomas, they say –"

"Lord, ain't you found out that what they say is mostly lies?"

"But if it should be true, and she's a nervous woman, she might be scared enough to lose her wits," said his wife, staring uneasily after Rebecca's erect figure in the wagon disappearing over the crest of the hilly road.

"Wits that so easy upset ain't worth much," declared the man. "You keep out of it, Maria."

Rebecca in the meantime rode on in the wagon, beside a flaxen-headed boy, who looked, to her understanding, not very bright. She asked him a question, and he paid no attention. She repeated it, and he responded with a bewildered and incoherent grunt. Then she let him alone, after making sure that he knew how to drive straight.

They had traveled about half a mile, passed the village square, and gone a short distance beyond, when the boy drew up with a sudden *Whoa!* before a very prosperous-looking house. It had been one of the aboriginal cottages of the vicinity, small and white, with a roof extending on one side over a piazza, and a tiny "L" jutting out in the rear, on the right hand. Now the cottage was transformed by dormer windows, a bay window on the piazzaless side, a carved railing down the front steps, and a modern hard-wood door.

"Is this John Dent's house?" asked Rebecca.

The boy was as sparing of speech as a philosopher. His only response was in flinging the reins over the horse's back, stretching out one foot to the shaft, and leaping out of the wagon, then going around to the rear for the trunk. Rebecca got out and went toward the house. Its white paint had a new gloss; its blinds were an immaculate apple green; the lawn was trimmed as smooth as velvet, and it was dotted with scrupulous groups of hydrangeas and cannas.

"I always understood that John Dent was well-to-do," Rebecca reflected comfortably. "I guess Agnes will have considerable. I've got enough, but it will come in handy for her schooling. She can have advantages."

The boy dragged the trunk up the fine gravel-walk, but before he reached the steps leading up to the piazza, for the house stood on a terrace, the front door opened and a fair, frizzled head of a very large and handsome woman appeared. She held up her black silk skirt, disclosing voluminous ruffles of starched embroidery, and waited for Rebecca. She smiled placidly, her pink, double-chinned face widened and dimpled, but her blue eyes were wary and calculating. She extended her hand as Rebecca climbed the steps.

"This is Miss Flint, I suppose," said she.

"Yes, ma'am," replied Rebecca, noticing with bewilderment a curious expression compounded of fear and defiance on the other's face.

"Your letter only arrived this morning," said Mrs Dent, in a steady voice. Her great face was a uniform pink, and her china-blue eyes were at once aggressive and veiled with secrecy.

"Yes, I hardly thought you'd get my letter," replied Rebecca. "I felt as if I could not wait to hear from you before I came. I supposed you would be so situated that you could have me a little while without putting you out too much, from what John used to write me about his circumstances, and when I had that money so unexpected I felt as if I must come for Agnes. I suppose you will be willing to give her up. You know she's my own blood, and of course she's no relation to you, though you must have got attached to her. I know from her picture what a sweet girl she must be, and John always said she looked like her own mother, and Grace was a beautiful woman, if she was my sister."

Rebecca stopped and stared at the other woman in amazement and alarm. The great handsome blonde creature stood speechless, livid, gasping, with her hand to her heart, her lips parted in a horrible caricature of a smile.

"Are you sick!" cried Rebecca, drawing near. "Don't you want me to get you some water!"

Then Mrs Dent recovered herself with a great effort. "It is nothing," she said. "I am subject to – spells. I am over it now. Won't you come in, Miss Flint?"

As she spoke, the beautiful deep-rose color suffused her face, her blue eyes met her visitor's with the opaqueness of turquoise – with a revelation of blue, but a concealment of all behind.

Rebecca followed her hostess in, and the boy, who had waited quiescently, climbed the steps with the trunk. But before they entered the door a strange thing happened. On the upper terrace close to the piazza-post, grew a great rose-bush, and on it, late in the season though it was, one small red, perfect rose.

Rebecca looked at it, and the other woman extended her hand with a quick gesture. "Don't you pick that rose!" she brusquely cried.

Rebecca drew herself up with stiff dignity.

"I ain't in the habit of picking other folks' roses without leave," said she.

As Rebecca spoke she started violently, and lost sight of her resentment, for something singular happened. Suddenly the rose-bush was agitated violently as if by a gust of wind, yet it was a remarkably still day. Not a leaf of the hydrangea standing on the terrace close to the rose trembled.

"What on earth –" began Rebecca, then she stopped with a gasp at the sight of the other woman's face. Although a face, it gave somehow the impression of a desperately clutched hand of secrecy.

"Come in!" said she in a harsh voice, which seemed to come forth from her chest with no intervention of the organs of speech. "Come into the house. I'm getting cold out here."

"What makes that rose-bush blow so when there isn't any wind?" asked Rebecca, trembling with vague horror, yet resolute.

"I don't see as it is blowing," returned the woman calmly. And as she spoke, indeed, the bush was quiet.

"It was blowing," declared Rebecca.

"It isn't now," said Mrs Dent. "I can't try to account for everything that blows out-of-doors. I have too much to do."

She spoke scornfully and confidently, with defiant, unflinching eyes, first on the bush, then on Rebecca, and led the way into the house.

"It looked queer," persisted Rebecca, but she followed, and also the boy with the trunk.

Rebecca entered an interior, prosperous, even elegant, according to her simple ideas. There were Brussels carpets, lace curtains, and plenty of brilliant upholstery and polished wood.

"You're real nicely situated," remarked Rebecca, after she had become a little accustomed to her new surroundings and the two women were seated at the tea-table.

Mrs Dent stared with a hard complacency from behind her silver-plated service. "Yes, I be," said she.

"You got all the things new?" said Rebecca hesitatingly, with a jealous memory of her dead sister's bridal furnishings.

"Yes," said Mrs Dent; "I was never one to want dead folks' things, and I had money enough of my own, so I wasn't beholden to John. I had the old duds put up at auction. They didn't bring much."

"I suppose you saved some for Agnes. She'll want some of her poor mother's things when she is grown up," said Rebecca with some indignation.

The defiant stare of Mrs Dent's blue eyes waxed more intense. "There's a few things up garret," said she.

"She'll be likely to value them," remarked Rebecca. As she spoke she glanced at the window. "Isn't it most time for her to be coming home?" she asked.

"Most time," answered Mrs Dent carelessly; "but when she gets over to Addie Slocum's she never knows when to come home."

"Is Addie Slocum her intimate friend?"

"Intimate as any."

"Maybe we can have her come out to see Agnes when she's living with me," said Rebecca wistfully. "I suppose she'll be likely to be homesick at first."

"Most likely," answered Mrs Dent.

"Does she call you mother?" Rebecca asked.

"No, she calls me Aunt Emeline," replied the other woman shortly. "When did you say you were going home?"

"In about a week, I thought, if she can be ready to go so soon," answered Rebecca with a surprised look.

She reflected that she would not remain a day longer than she could help after such an inhospitable look and question.

"Oh, as far as that goes," said Mrs Dent, "it wouldn't make any difference about her being ready. You could go home whenever you felt that you must, and she could come afterward."

"Alone?"

"Why not? She's a big girl now, and you don't have to change cars."

"My niece will go home when I do, and not travel alone; and if I can't wait here for her, in the house that used to be her mother's and my sister's home, I'll go and board somewhere," returned Rebecca with warmth.

"Oh, you can stay here as long as you want to. You're welcome," said Mrs Dent.

Then Rebecca started. "There she is!" she declared in a trembling, exultant voice. Nobody knew how she longed to see the girl.

"She isn't as late as I thought she'd be," said Mrs Dent, and again that curious, subtle change passed over her face, and again it settled into that stony impassiveness.

Rebecca stared at the door, waiting for it to open. "Where is she?" she asked presently.

"I guess she's stopped to take off her hat in the entry," suggested Mrs Dent.

Rebecca waited. "Why don't she come? It can't take her all this time to take off her hat."

For answer Mrs Dent rose with a stiff jerk and threw open the door.

"Agnes!" she called. "Agnes!" Then she turned and eyed Rebecca. "She ain't there."

"I saw her pass the window," said Rebecca in bewilderment.

"You must have been mistaken."

"I know I did," persisted Rebecca.

"You couldn't have."

"I did. I saw first a shadow go over the ceiling, then I saw her in the glass there" – she pointed to a mirror over the sideboard opposite – "and then the shadow passed the window."

"How did she look in the glass?"

"Little and light-haired, with the light hair kind of tossing over her forehead."

"You couldn't have seen her."

"Was that like Agnes?"

"Like enough; but of course you didn't see her. You've been thinking so much about her that you thought you did."

"You thought *you* did."

"I thought I saw a shadow pass the window, but I must have been mistaken. She didn't come in, or we would have seen her before now. I knew it was too early for her to get home from Addie Slocum's, anyhow."

When Rebecca went to bed Agnes had not returned. Rebecca had resolved that she would not retire until the girl came, but she was very tired, and she reasoned with herself that she was foolish. Besides, Mrs Dent suggested that Agnes might go to the church social with Addie Slocum. When Rebecca suggested that she be sent for and told that her aunt had come, Mrs Dent laughed meaningly.

"I guess you'll find out that a young girl ain't so ready to leave a sociable, where there's boys, to see her aunt," said she.

"She's too young," said Rebecca incredulously and indignantly.

"She's sixteen," replied Mrs Dent; "and she's always been great for the boys."

"She's going to school four years after I get her before she thinks of boys," declared Rebecca.

"We'll see," laughed the other woman.

After Rebecca went to bed, she lay awake a long time listening for the sound of girlish laughter and a boy's voice under her window; then she fell asleep.

The next morning she was down early. Mrs Dent, who kept no servants, was busily preparing breakfast.

"Don't Agnes help you about breakfast?" asked Rebecca.

"No, I let her lay," replied Mrs Dent shortly.

"What time did she get home last night?"

"She didn't get home."

"What?"

"She didn't get home. She stayed with Addie. She often does."

"Without sending you word?"

"Oh, she knew I wouldn't worry."

"When will she be home?"

"Oh, I guess she'll be along pretty soon."

Rebecca was uneasy, but she tried to conceal it, for she knew of no good reason for uneasiness. What was there to occasion alarm in the fact of one young girl staying overnight with another? She could not eat much breakfast. Afterward she went out on the little piazza, although her hostess strove furtively to stop her.

"Why don't you go out back of the house? It's real pretty – a view over the river," she said.

"I guess I'll go out here," replied Rebecca. She had a purpose: to watch for the absent girl.

Presently Rebecca came hustling into the house through the sitting-room, into the kitchen where Mrs Dent was cooking.

"That rose-bush!" she gasped.

Mrs Dent turned and faced her.

"What of it?"

"It's a-blowing."

"What of it?"

"There isn't a mite of wind this morning."

Mrs Dent turned with an inimitable toss of her fair head. "If you think I can spend my time puzzling over such nonsense as –" she began, but Rebecca interrupted her with a cry and a rush to the door.

"There she is now!" she cried. She flung the door wide open, and curiously enough a breeze came in and her own gray hair tossed, and a paper blew off the table to the floor with a loud rustle, but there was nobody in sight.

"There's nobody here," Rebecca said.

She looked blankly at the other woman, who brought her rolling-pin down on a slab of pie-crust with a thud.

"I didn't hear anybody," she said calmly.

"*I saw somebody pass that window!*"

"You were mistaken again."

"I *know* I saw somebody."

"You couldn't have. Please shut that door."

Rebecca shut the door. She sat down beside the window and looked out on the autumnal yard, with its little curve of footpath to the kitchen door.

"What smells so strong of roses in this room?" she said presently. She sniffed hard.

"I don't smell anything but these nutmegs."

"It is not nutmeg."

"I don't smell anything else."

"Where do you suppose Agnes is?"

"Oh, perhaps she has gone over the ferry to Porter's Falls with Addie. She often does. Addie's got an aunt over there, and Addie's got a cousin, a real pretty boy."

"You suppose she's gone over there?"

"Mebbe. I shouldn't wonder."

"When should she be home?"

"Oh, not before afternoon."

Rebecca waited with all the patience she could muster. She kept reassuring herself, telling herself that it was all natural, that the other woman could not help it, but she made up her mind that if Agnes did not return that afternoon she should be sent for.

When it was four o'clock she started up with resolution. She had been furtively watching the onyx clock on the sitting-room mantel; she had timed herself. She had said that if Agnes was not home by that time she should demand that she be sent for. She rose and stood before Mrs Dent, who looked up coolly from her embroidery.

"I've waited just as long as I'm going to," she said. "I've come 'way from Michigan to see my own sister's daughter and take her home with me. I've been here ever since yesterday – twenty-four hours – and I haven't seen her. Now I'm going to. I want her sent for."

Mrs Dent folded her embroidery and rose.

"Well, I don't blame you," she said. "It is high time she came home. I'll go right over and get her myself."

Rebecca heaved a sigh of relief. She hardly knew what she had suspected or feared, but she knew that her position had been one of antagonism if not accusation, and she was sensible of relief.

"I wish you would," she said gratefully, and went back to her chair, while Mrs Dent got her shawl and her little white head-tie. "I wouldn't trouble you, but I do feel as if I couldn't wait any longer to see her," she remarked apologetically.

"Oh, it ain't any trouble at all," said Mrs Dent as she went out. "I don't blame you; you have waited long enough."

Rebecca sat at the window watching breathlessly until Mrs Dent came stepping through the yard alone. She ran to the door and saw, hardly noticing it this time, that the rose-bush was again violently agitated, yet with no wind evident elsewhere.

"Where is she?" she cried.

Mrs Dent laughed with stiff lips as she came up the steps over the terrace. "Girls will be girls," said she. "She's gone with Addie to Lincoln. Addie's got an uncle who's conductor on the train, and lives there, and he got 'em passes, and they're goin' to stay to Addie's Aunt Margaret's a few days. Mrs Slocum said Agnes didn't have time to come over and ask me before the train went, but she took it on herself to say it would be all right, and –"

"Why hadn't she been over to tell you?" Rebecca was angry, though not suspicious. She even saw no reason for her anger.

"Oh, she was putting up grapes. She was coming over just as soon as she got the black off her hands. She heard I had company, and her hands were a sight. She was holding them over sulfur matches."

"You say she's going to stay a few days?" repeated Rebecca dazedly.

"Yes; till Thursday, Mrs Slocum said."

"How far is Lincoln from here?"

"About fifty miles. It'll be a real treat to her. Mrs Slocum's sister is a real nice woman."

"It is goin' to make it pretty late about my goin' home."

"If you don't feel as if you could wait, I'll get her ready and send her on just as soon as I can," Mrs Dent said sweetly.

"I'm going to wait," said Rebecca grimly.

The two women sat down again, and Mrs Dent took up her embroidery.

"Is there any sewing I can do for her?" Rebecca asked finally in a desperate way. "If I can get her sewing along some –"

Mrs Dent arose with alacrity and fetched a mass of white from the closet. "Here," she said, "if you want to sew the lace on this nightgown. I was going to put her to it, but she'll be glad enough to get rid of it. She ought to have this and one more before she goes. I don't like to send her away without some good underclothing."

Rebecca snatched at the little white garment and sewed feverishly.

That night she wakened from a deep sleep a little after midnight and lay a minute trying to collect her faculties and explain to herself what she was listening to. At last she discovered that it was the then popular strains of "The Maiden's Prayer" floating up through the floor from the piano in the sitting-room below. She jumped up, threw a shawl over her nightgown, and hurried downstairs trembling. There was nobody in the sitting-room; the piano was silent. She ran to Mrs Dent's bedroom and called hysterically:

"Emeline! Emeline!"

"What is it?" asked Mrs Dent's voice from the bed. The voice was stern, but had a note of consciousness in it.

"Who – who was that playing 'The Maiden's Prayer' in the sitting-room, on the piano?"

"I didn't hear anybody."

"There was someone."

"I didn't hear anything."

"I tell you there was someone. But – *there ain't anybody there*."

"I didn't hear anything."

"I did – somebody playing 'The Maiden's Prayer' on the piano. Has Agnes got home? *I want to know*."

"Of course Agnes hasn't got home," answered Mrs Dent with rising inflection. "Be you gone crazy over that girl? The last boat from Porter's Falls was in before we went to bed. Of course she ain't come."

"I heard –"

"You were dreaming."

"I wasn't; I was broad awake."

Rebecca went back to her chamber and kept her lamp burning all night.

The next morning her eyes upon Mrs Dent were wary and blazing with suppressed excitement. She kept opening her mouth as if to speak, then frowning, and setting her lips hard. After breakfast she went upstairs, and came down presently with her coat and bonnet.

"Now, Emeline," she said, "I want to know where the Slocums live."

Mrs Dent gave a strange, long, half-lidded glance at her. She was finishing her coffee.

"Why?" she asked.

"I'm going over there and find out if they have heard anything from her daughter and Agnes since they went away. I don't like what I heard last night."

"You must have been dreaming."

"It don't make any odds whether I was or not. Does she play 'The Maiden's Prayer' on the piano? I want to know."

"What if she does? She plays it a little, I believe. I don't know. She don't half play it, anyhow; she ain't got an ear."

"That wasn't half played last night. I don't like such things happening. I ain't superstitious, but I don't like it. I'm going. Where do the Slocums live?"

"You go down the road over the bridge past the old grist mill, then you turn to the left; it's the only house for half a mile. You can't miss it. It has a barn with a ship in full sail on the cupola."

"Well, I'm going. I don't feel easy."

About two hours later Rebecca returned. There were red spots on her cheeks. She looked wild. "I've been there," she said, "and there isn't a soul at home. Something *has* happened."

"What has happened?"

"I don't know. Something. I had a warning last night. There wasn't a soul there. They've been sent for to Lincoln."

"Did you see anybody to ask?" asked Mrs Dent with thinly concealed anxiety.

"I asked the woman that lives on the turn of the road. She's stone deaf. I suppose you know. She listened while I screamed at her to know where the Slocums were, and then she said, 'Mrs Smith don't live here.' I didn't see anybody on the road, and that's the only house. What do you suppose it means?"

"I don't suppose it means much of anything," replied Mrs Dent coolly. "Mr Slocum is conductor on the railroad, and he'd be away anyway, and Mrs Slocum often goes early when he does, to spend the day with her sister in Porter's Falls. She'd be more likely to go away than Addie."

"And you don't think anything has happened?" Rebecca asked with diminishing distrust before the reasonableness of it.

"Land, no!"

Rebecca went upstairs to lay aside her coat and bonnet. But she came hurrying back with them still on.

"Who's been in my room?" she gasped. Her face was pale as ashes.

Mrs Dent also paled as she regarded her.

"What do you mean?" she asked slowly.

"I found when I went upstairs that – little nightgown of – Agnes's on – the bed, laid out. It was – *laid out*. The sleeves were folded across the bosom, and there was that little red rose between them. Emeline, what is it? Emeline, what's the matter? Oh!"

Mrs Dent was struggling for breath in great, choking gasps. She clung to the back of a chair. Rebecca, trembling herself so she could scarcely keep on her feet, got her some water.

As soon as she recovered herself Mrs Dent regarded her with eyes full of the strangest mixture of fear and horror and hostility.

"What do you mean talking so?" she said in a hard voice.

"It *is there*."

"Nonsense. You threw it down and it fell that way."

"It was folded in my bureau drawer."

"It couldn't have been."

"Who picked that red rose?"

"Look on the bush," Mrs Dent replied shortly.

Rebecca looked at her; her mouth gaped. She hurried out of the room. When she came back her eyes seemed to protrude. (She had in the meantime hastened upstairs, and come down with tottering steps, clinging to the banisters.)

"Now I want to know what all this means?" she demanded.

"What what means?"

"The rose is on the bush, and it's gone from the bed in my room! Is this house haunted, or what?"

"I don't know anything about a house being haunted. I don't believe in such things. Be you crazy?" Mrs Dent spoke with gathering force. The color flashed back to her cheeks.

"No," said Rebecca shortly. "I ain't crazy yet, but I shall be if this keeps on much longer. I'm going to find out where that girl is before night."

Mrs Dent eyed her.

"What be you going to do?"

"I'm going to Lincoln."

A faint triumphant smile overspread Mrs Dent's large face.

"You can't," said she; "there ain't any train."

"No train?"

"No; there ain't any afternoon train from the Falls to Lincoln."

"Then I'm going over to the Slocums' again tonight."

However, Rebecca did not go; such a rain came up as deterred even her resolution, and she had only her best dresses with her. Then in the evening came the letter from the Michigan village which she had left nearly a week ago. It was from her cousin, a single woman, who had come to keep her house while she was away. It was a pleasant unexciting letter enough, all the first of it, and related mostly how she missed Rebecca; how she hoped she was having pleasant weather and kept her health; and how her friend, Mrs Greenaway, had come to stay with her since she had felt lonesome the first night in the house; how she hoped Rebecca would have no objections to this, although nothing had been said about it, since she had not realized that she might be nervous alone. The cousin was painfully conscientious, hence the letter. Rebecca smiled in spite of her disturbed mind as she read it, then her eye caught the postscript. That was in a different hand, purporting to be written by the friend, Mrs Hannah Greenaway, informing her that the cousin had fallen down the cellar stairs and broken her hip, and was in a dangerous condition, and begging Rebecca to return at once, as she herself was rheumatic and unable to nurse her properly, and no one else could be obtained.

Rebecca looked at Mrs Dent, who had come to her room with the letter quite late; it was half-past nine, and she had gone upstairs for the night.

"Where did this come from?" she asked.

"Mr Amblecrom brought it," she replied.

"Who's he?"

"The postmaster. He often brings the letters that come on the late mail. He knows I ain't anybody to send. He brought yours about your coming. He said he and his wife came over on the ferry-boat with you."

"I remember him," Rebecca replied shortly. "There's bad news in this letter."

Mrs Dent's face took on an expression of serious inquiry.

"Yes, my Cousin Harriet has fallen down the cellar stairs – they were always dangerous – and she's broken her hip, and I've got to take the first train home tomorrow."

"You don't say so. I'm dreadfully sorry."

"No, you ain't sorry!" said Rebecca, with a look as if she leaped. "You're glad. I don't know why, but you're glad. You've wanted to get rid of me for some reason ever since I came. I don't know why. You're a strange woman. Now you've got your way, and I hope you're satisfied."

"How you talk."

Mrs Dent spoke in a faintly injured voice, but there was a light in her eyes.

"I talk the way it is. Well, I'm going tomorrow morning, and I want you, just as soon as Agnes Dent comes home, to send her out to me. Don't you wait for anything. You pack what clothes she's got, and don't wait even to mend them, and you buy her ticket. I'll leave the money, and you send her along. She don't have to change cars. You start her off, when she gets home, on the next train!"

"Very well," replied the other woman. She had an expression of covert amusement.

"Mind you do it."

"Very well, Rebecca."

Rebecca started on her journey the next morning. When she arrived, two days later, she found her cousin in perfect health. She found, moreover, that the friend had not written the postscript in the cousin's letter. Rebecca would have returned to Ford Village the next morning, but the fatigue and nervous strain had been too much for her. She was not able to move from her bed. She had a species of low fever induced by anxiety and fatigue. But she could write, and she did, to the Slocums, and she received no answer. She also wrote to Mrs Dent; she even sent numerous telegrams, with no response. Finally she wrote to the postmaster, and an answer arrived by the first possible mail. The letter was short, curt, and to the purpose. Mr Amblecrom, the postmaster, was a man of few words, and especially wary as to his expressions in a letter.

"Dear madam," he wrote, "your favor rec'ed. No Slocums in Ford's Village. All dead. Addie ten years ago, her mother two years later, her father five. House vacant. Mrs John Dent said to have neglected stepdaughter. Girl was sick. Medicine not given. Talk of taking action. Not enough evidence. House said to be haunted. Strange sights and sounds. Your niece, Agnes Dent, died a year ago, about this time.

"Yours truly,

"*Thomas Amblecrom*."

The Overcoat

by Nikolai Gogol

IN THE DEPARTMENT OF – but it is better not to mention the department. There is nothing more irritable than departments, regiments, courts of justice, and, in a word, every branch of public service. Each individual attached to them nowadays thinks all society insulted in his person. Quite recently a complaint was received from a justice of the peace, in which he plainly demonstrated that all the imperial institutions were going to the dogs, and that the Czar's sacred name was being taken in vain; and in proof he appended to the complaint a romance in which the justice of the peace is made to appear about once every ten lines, and sometimes in a drunken condition. Therefore, in order to avoid all unpleasantness, it will be better to describe the department in question only as a certain department.

So, in a certain department there was a certain official – not a very high one, it must be allowed – short of stature, somewhat pock-marked, red-haired, and short-sighted, with a bald forehead, wrinkled cheeks, and a complexion of the kind known as sanguine. The St. Petersburg climate was responsible for this. As for his official status, he was what is called a perpetual titular councillor, over which, as is well known, some writers make merry, and crack their jokes, obeying the praiseworthy custom of attacking those who cannot bite back.

His family name was Bashmatchkin. This name is evidently derived from "bashmak" (shoe); but when, at what time, and in what manner, is not known. His father and grandfather, and all the Bashmatchkins, always wore boots, which only had new heels two or three times a year. His name was Akakiy Akakievitch. It may strike the reader as rather singular and far-fetched, but he may rest assured that it was by no means far-fetched, and that the circumstances were such that it would have been impossible to give him any other.

This is how it came about.

Akakiy Akakievitch was born, if my memory fails me not, in the evening of the 23rd of March. His mother, the wife of a Government official and a very fine woman, made all due arrangements for having the child baptised. She was lying on the bed opposite the door; on her right stood the godfather, Ivan Ivanovitch Eroshkin, a most estimable man, who served as presiding officer of the senate, and the godmother, Anna Semenovna Byelobrushkova, the wife of an officer of the quarter, and a woman of rare virtues. They offered the mother her choice of three names, Mokiya, Sossiya, or that the child should be called after the martyr Khozdazat. "No," said the good woman, "all those names are poor." In order to please her they opened the calendar to another place; three more names appeared, Triphiliy, Dula, and Varakhasiy. "This is a judgment," said the old woman. "What names! I truly never heard the like. Varada or Varukh might have been borne, but not Triphiliy and

Varakhasiy!" They turned to another page and found Pavsikakhiy and Vakhtisiy. "Now I see," said the old woman, "that it is plainly fate. And since such is the case, it will be better to name him after his father. His father's name was Akakiy, so let his son's be Akakiy too." In this manner he became Akakiy Akakievitch. They christened the child, whereat he wept and made a grimace, as though he foresaw that he was to be a titular councillor.

In this manner did it all come about. We have mentioned it in order that the reader might see for himself that it was a case of necessity, and that it was utterly impossible to give him any other name. When and how he entered the department, and who appointed him, no one could remember. However much the directors and chiefs of all kinds were changed, he was always to be seen in the same place, the same attitude, the same occupation; so that it was afterwards affirmed that he had been born in undress uniform with a bald head. No respect was shown him in the department. The porter not only did not rise from his seat when he passed, but never even glanced at him, any more than if a fly had flown through the reception-room. His superiors treated him in coolly despotic fashion. Some sub-chief would thrust a paper under his nose without so much as saying, "Copy," or "Here's a nice interesting affair," or anything else agreeable, as is customary amongst well-bred officials. And he took it, looking only at the paper and not observing who handed it to him, or whether he had the right to do so; simply took it, and set about copying it.

The young officials laughed at and made fun of him, so far as their official wit permitted; told in his presence various stories concocted about him, and about his landlady, an old woman of seventy; declared that she beat him; asked when the wedding was to be; and strewed bits of paper over his head, calling them snow. But Akakiy Akakievitch answered not a word, any more than if there had been no one there besides himself. It even had no effect upon his work: amid all these annoyances he never made a single mistake in a letter. But if the joking became wholly unbearable, as when they jogged his hand and prevented his attending to his work, he would exclaim, "Leave me alone! Why do you insult me?" And there was something strange in the words and the voice in which they were uttered. There was in it something which moved to pity; so much that one young man, a new-comer, who, taking pattern by the others, had permitted himself to make sport of Akakiy, suddenly stopped short, as though all about him had undergone a transformation, and presented itself in a different aspect. Some unseen force repelled him from the comrades whose acquaintance he had made, on the supposition that they were well-bred and polite men. Long afterwards, in his gayest moments, there recurred to his mind the little official with the bald forehead, with his heart-rending words, "Leave me alone! Why do you insult me?" In these moving words, other words resounded – "I am thy brother." And the young man covered his face with his hand; and many a time afterwards, in the course of his life, shuddered at seeing how much inhumanity there is in man, how much savage coarseness is concealed beneath delicate, refined worldliness, and even, O God! in that man whom the world acknowledges as honourable and noble.

It would be difficult to find another man who lived so entirely for his duties. It is not enough to say that Akakiy laboured with zeal: no, he laboured with love. In his copying, he found a varied and agreeable employment. Enjoyment was written on his face: some letters were even favourites with him; and when he encountered these, he smiled, winked, and worked with his lips, till it seemed as though each letter might be read in his face, as his pen traced it. If his pay had been in proportion to his zeal, he would, perhaps, to his great surprise, have been made even a councillor of state. But he worked, as his companions, the wits, put it, like a horse in a mill.

Moreover, it is impossible to say that no attention was paid to him. One director being a kindly man, and desirous of rewarding him for his long service, ordered him to be given something more important than mere copying. So he was ordered to make a report of an already concluded affair to another department: the duty consisting simply in changing the heading and altering a few words from the first to the third person. This caused him so much toil that he broke into a perspiration, rubbed his forehead, and finally said, "No, give me rather something to copy." After that they let him copy on forever.

Outside this copying, it appeared that nothing existed for him. He gave no thought to his clothes: his undress uniform was not green, but a sort of rusty-meal colour. The collar was low, so that his neck, in spite of the fact that it was not long, seemed inordinately so as it emerged from it, like the necks of those plaster cats which wag their heads, and are carried about upon the heads of scores of image sellers. And something was always sticking to his uniform, either a bit of hay or some trifle. Moreover, he had a peculiar knack, as he walked along the street, of arriving beneath a window just as all sorts of rubbish were being flung out of it: hence he always bore about on his hat scraps of melon rinds and other such articles. Never once in his life did he give heed to what was going on every day in the street; while it is well known that his young brother officials train the range of their glances till they can see when anyone's trouser straps come undone upon the opposite sidewalk, which always brings a malicious smile to their faces. But Akakiy Akakievitch saw in all things the clean, even strokes of his written lines; and only when a horse thrust his nose, from some unknown quarter, over his shoulder, and sent a whole gust of wind down his neck from his nostrils, did he observe that he was not in the middle of a page, but in the middle of the street.

On reaching home, he sat down at once at the table, supped his cabbage soup up quickly, and swallowed a bit of beef with onions, never noticing their taste, and gulping down everything with flies and anything else which the Lord happened to send at the moment. His stomach filled, he rose from the table, and copied papers which he had brought home. If there happened to be none, he took copies for himself, for his own gratification, especially if the document was noteworthy, not on account of its style, but of its being addressed to some distinguished person.

Even at the hour when the grey St. Petersburg sky had quite dispersed, and all the official world had eaten or dined, each as he could, in accordance with the salary he received and his own fancy; when all were resting from the departmental jar of pens, running to and fro from their own and other people's indispensable occupations, and from all the work that an uneasy man makes willingly for himself, rather than what is necessary; when officials hasten to dedicate to pleasure the time which is left to them, one bolder than the rest going to the theatre; another, into the street looking under all the bonnets; another wasting his evening in compliments to some pretty girl, the star of a small official circle; another – and this is the common case of all – visiting his comrades on the fourth or third floor, in two small rooms with an ante-room or kitchen, and some pretensions to fashion, such as a lamp or some other trifle which has cost many a sacrifice of dinner or pleasure trip; in a word, at the hour when all officials disperse among the contracted quarters of their friends, to play whist, as they sip their tea from glasses with a kopek's worth of sugar, smoke long pipes, relate at times some bits of gossip which a Russian man can never, under any circumstances, refrain from, and, when there is nothing else to talk of, repeat eternal anecdotes about the commandant to whom they had sent word that the tails of the horses on the Falconet Monument had been cut off, when all strive to divert themselves, Akakiy Akakievitch indulged in no kind of diversion. No one could ever say that he had seen him at any kind of evening party. Having written to his heart's content, he lay down to sleep, smiling at the thought of the coming day – of what God might send him to copy on the morrow.

Thus flowed on the peaceful life of the man, who, with a salary of four hundred rubles, understood how to be content with his lot; and thus it would have continued to flow on, perhaps, to extreme old age, were it not that there are various ills strewn along the path of life for titular councillors as well as for private, actual, court, and every other species of councillor, even for those who never give any advice or take any themselves.

There exists in St. Petersburg a powerful foe of all who receive a salary of four hundred rubles a year, or thereabouts. This foe is no other than the Northern cold, although it is said to be very healthy. At nine o'clock in the morning, at the very hour when the streets are filled with men bound for the various official departments, it begins to bestow such powerful and piercing nips on all noses impartially that the poor officials really do not know what to do with them. At an hour when the foreheads of even those who occupy exalted positions ache with the cold, and tears start to their eyes, the poor titular councillors are sometimes quite unprotected. Their only salvation lies in traversing as quickly as possible, in their thin little cloaks, five or six streets, and then warming their feet in the porter's room, and so thawing all their talents and qualifications for official service, which had become frozen on the way.

Akakiy Akakievitch had felt for some time that his back and shoulders suffered with peculiar poignancy, in spite of the fact that he tried to traverse the distance with all possible speed. He began finally to wonder whether the fault did not lie in his cloak. He examined it thoroughly at home, and discovered that in two places, namely, on the back and shoulders, it had become thin as gauze: the cloth was worn to such a degree that he could see through it, and the lining had fallen into pieces. You must know that Akakiy Akakievitch's cloak served as an object of ridicule to the officials: they even refused it the noble name of cloak, and called it a cape. In fact, it was of singular make: its collar diminishing year by year, but serving to patch its other parts. The patching did not exhibit great skill on the part of the tailor, and was, in fact, baggy and ugly. Seeing how the matter stood, Akakiy Akakievitch decided that it would be necessary to take the cloak to Petrovitch, the tailor, who lived somewhere on the fourth floor up a dark staircase, and who, in spite of his having but one eye, and pock-marks all over his face, busied himself with considerable success in repairing the trousers and coats of officials and others; that is to say, when he was sober and not nursing some other scheme in his head.

It is not necessary to say much about this tailor; but, as it is the custom to have the character of each personage in a novel clearly defined, there is no help for it, so here is Petrovitch the tailor. At first he was called only Grigoriy, and was some gentleman's serf; he commenced calling himself Petrovitch from the time when he received his free papers, and further began to drink heavily on all holidays, at first on the great ones, and then on all church festivities without discrimination, wherever a cross stood in the calendar. On this point he was faithful to ancestral custom; and when quarrelling with his wife, he called her a low female and a German. As we have mentioned his wife, it will be necessary to say a word or two about her. Unfortunately, little is known of her beyond the fact that Petrovitch has a wife, who wears a cap and a dress; but cannot lay claim to beauty, at least, no one but the soldiers of the guard even looked under her cap when they met her.

Ascending the staircase which led to Petrovitch's room – which staircase was all soaked with dish-water, and reeked with the smell of spirits which affects the eyes, and is an inevitable adjunct to all dark stairways in St. Petersburg houses – ascending the stairs, Akakiy Akakievitch pondered how much Petrovitch would ask, and mentally resolved not to give more than two rubles. The door was open; for the mistress, in cooking some fish, had raised such a smoke in the kitchen that not even the beetles were visible. Akakiy Akakievitch passed through the kitchen unperceived, even by the housewife, and at length reached a room where he beheld Petrovitch seated on a large unpainted table, with his legs tucked under him like a Turkish pasha. His feet were bare, after the fashion of tailors who sit at work; and the first thing which caught the eye was his thumb, with a deformed nail thick and strong as a turtle's shell. About Petrovitch's neck hung a skein of silk and thread, and upon his knees lay some old garment. He had been trying unsuccessfully for three minutes to thread his needle, and was enraged at the darkness and even at the thread, growling in a low voice, "It won't go through, the barbarian! you pricked me, you rascal!"

Akakiy Akakievitch was vexed at arriving at the precise moment when Petrovitch was angry; he liked to order something of Petrovitch when the latter was a little downhearted, or, as his wife expressed it, "when he had settled himself with brandy, the one-eyed devil!" Under such circumstances, Petrovitch generally came down in his price very readily, and even bowed and returned thanks. Afterwards, to be sure, his wife would come, complaining that her husband was drunk, and so had fixed the price too low; but, if only a ten-kopek piece were added, then the matter was settled. But now it appeared that Petrovitch was in a sober condition, and therefore rough, taciturn, and inclined to demand, Satan only knows what price. Akakiy Akakievitch felt this, and would gladly have beat a retreat; but he was in for it. Petrovitch screwed up his one eye very intently at him, and Akakiy Akakievitch involuntarily said: "How do you do, Petrovitch?"

"I wish you a good morning, sir," said Petrovitch, squinting at Akakiy Akakievitch's hands, to see what sort of booty he had brought.

"Ah! I – to you, Petrovitch, this –" It must be known that Akakiy Akakievitch expressed himself chiefly by prepositions, adverbs, and scraps of phrases which had no meaning whatever. If the matter was a very difficult one, he had a habit of never completing his sentences; so that frequently, having begun a phrase with the words, "This, in fact, is quite –" he forgot to go on, thinking that he had already finished it.

"What is it?" asked Petrovitch, and with his one eye scanned Akakievitch's whole uniform from the collar down to the cuffs, the back, the tails and the button-holes, all of which were well known to him, since they were his own handiwork. Such is the habit of tailors; it is the first thing they do on meeting one.

"But I, here, this – Petrovitch – a cloak, cloth – here you see, everywhere, in different places, it is quite strong – it is a little dusty, and looks old, but it is new, only here in one place it is a little – on the back, and here on one of the shoulders, it is a little worn, yes, here on this shoulder it is a little – do you see? that is all. And a little work –"

Petrovitch took the cloak, spread it out, to begin with, on the table, looked hard at it, shook his head, reached out his hand to the window-sill for his snuff-box, adorned with the portrait of some general, though what general is unknown, for the place where the face should have been had been rubbed through by the finger, and a square bit of paper had been pasted over it. Having taken a pinch of snuff, Petrovitch held up the cloak, and inspected it against the light, and again shook his head once more. After which he again lifted the general-adorned lid with its bit of pasted paper, and having stuffed his nose with snuff, closed and put away the snuff-box, and said finally, "No, it is impossible to mend it; it's a wretched garment!"

Akakiy Akakievitch's heart sank at these words.

"Why is it impossible, Petrovitch?" he said, almost in the pleading voice of a child; "all that ails it is, that it is worn on the shoulders. You must have some pieces –"

"Yes, patches could be found, patches are easily found," said Petrovitch, "but there's nothing to sew them to. The thing is completely rotten; if you put a needle to it – see, it will give way."

"Let it give way, and you can put on another patch at once."

"But there is nothing to put the patches on to; there's no use in strengthening it; it is too far gone. It's lucky that it's cloth; for, if the wind were to blow, it would fly away."

"Well, strengthen it again. How will this, in fact –"

"No," said Petrovitch decisively, "there is nothing to be done with it. It's a thoroughly bad job. You'd better, when the cold winter weather comes on, make yourself some gaiters out of it, because stockings are not warm. The Germans invented them in order to make more money." Petrovitch loved, on all occasions, to have a fling at the Germans. "But it is plain you must have a new cloak."

At the word "new," all grew dark before Akakiy Akakievitch's eyes, and everything in the room began to whirl round. The only thing he saw clearly was the general with the paper face on the lid of Petrovitch's snuff-box. "A new one?" said he, as if still in a dream: "why, I have no money for that."

"Yes, a new one," said Petrovitch, with barbarous composure.

"Well, if it came to a new one, how would it –?"

"You mean how much would it cost?"

"Yes."

"Well, you would have to lay out a hundred and fifty or more," said Petrovitch, and pursed up his lips significantly. He liked to produce powerful effects, liked to stun utterly and suddenly, and then to glance sideways to see what face the stunned person would put on the matter.

"A hundred and fifty rubles for a cloak!" shrieked poor Akakiy Akakievitch, perhaps for the first time in his life, for his voice had always been distinguished for softness.

"Yes, sir," said Petrovitch, "for any kind of cloak. If you have a marten fur on the collar, or a silk-lined hood, it will mount up to two hundred."

"Petrovitch, please," said Akakiy Akakievitch in a beseeching tone, not hearing, and not trying to hear, Petrovitch's words, and disregarding all his "effects," "some repairs, in order that it may wear yet a little longer."

"No, it would only be a waste of time and money," said Petrovitch; and Akakiy Akakievitch went away after these words, utterly discouraged. But Petrovitch stood for some time after his departure, with significantly compressed lips, and without betaking himself to his work, satisfied that he would not be dropped, and an artistic tailor employed.

Akakiy Akakievitch went out into the street as if in a dream. "Such an affair!" he said to himself: "I did not think it had come to –" and then after a pause, he added, "Well, so it is! see what it has come to at last! and I never imagined that it was so!" Then followed a long silence, after which he exclaimed, "Well, so it is! see what already – nothing unexpected that – it would be nothing – what a strange circumstance!" So saying, instead of going home, he went in exactly the opposite direction without himself suspecting it. On the way, a chimney-sweep bumped up against him, and blackened his shoulder, and a whole hatful of rubbish landed on him from the top of a house which was building. He did not notice it; and only when he ran against a watchman, who, having planted his halberd beside him, was shaking some snuff from his box into his horny hand, did he recover himself a little, and that because the watchman said, "Why are you poking yourself into a man's very face? Haven't you the pavement?" This caused him to look about him, and turn towards home.

There only, he finally began to collect his thoughts, and to survey his position in its clear and actual light, and to argue with himself, sensibly and frankly, as with a reasonable friend with whom one can discuss private and personal matters. "No," said Akakiy Akakievitch, "it is impossible to reason with Petrovitch now; he is that – evidently his wife has been beating him. I'd better go to him on Sunday morning; after Saturday night he will be a little cross-eyed and sleepy, for he will want to get drunk, and his wife won't give him any money; and at such a time, a ten-kopek piece in his hand will – he will become more fit to reason with, and then the cloak, and that –" Thus argued Akakiy Akakievitch with himself, regained his courage, and waited until the first Sunday, when, seeing from afar that Petrovitch's wife had left the house, he went straight to him.

Petrovitch's eye was, indeed, very much askew after Saturday: his head drooped, and he was very sleepy; but for all that, as soon as he knew what it was a question of, it seemed as though Satan jogged his memory. "Impossible," said he: "please to order a new one." Thereupon Akakiy Akakievitch handed over the ten-kopek piece. "Thank you, sir; I will drink your good health," said Petrovitch: "but as for the cloak, don't trouble yourself about it; it is good for nothing. I will make you a capital new one, so let us settle about it now."

Akakiy Akakievitch was still for mending it; but Petrovitch would not hear of it, and said, "I shall certainly have to make you a new one, and you may depend upon it that I shall do my best. It may even be, as the fashion goes, that the collar can be fastened by silver hooks under a flap."

Then Akakiy Akakievitch saw that it was impossible to get along without a new cloak, and his spirit sank utterly. How, in fact, was it to be done? Where was the money to come from? He might, to be sure, depend, in part, upon his present at Christmas; but that money had long been allotted beforehand. He must have some new trousers, and pay a debt of long standing to the shoemaker for putting new tops to his old boots, and he must order three shirts from the seamstress, and a couple of pieces of linen. In short, all his money must be spent; and even if the director should be so kind as to order him to receive forty-five rubles instead of forty, or even fifty, it would be a mere nothing, a mere drop in the ocean towards the funds necessary for a cloak: although he knew that Petrovitch was often wrong-headed enough to blurt out some outrageous price, so that even his own wife could not refrain from exclaiming, "Have you lost your senses, you fool?" At one time he would not work at any price, and now it was quite likely that he had named a higher sum than the cloak would cost.

But although he knew that Petrovitch would undertake to make a cloak for eighty rubles, still, where was he to get the eighty rubles from? He might possibly manage half, yes, half might be procured, but where was the other half to come from? But the reader must first be told where the first half came from. Akakiy Akakievitch had a habit of putting, for every ruble he spent, a groschen into a small box, fastened with a lock and key, and with a slit in the top for the reception of money. At the end of every half-year he counted over the heap of coppers, and changed it for silver. This he had done for a long time, and in the course of years, the sum had mounted up to over forty rubles. Thus he had one half on hand; but where was he to find the other half? where was he to get another forty rubles from? Akakiy Akakievitch thought and thought, and decided that it would be necessary to curtail his ordinary expenses, for the space of one year at least, to dispense with tea in the evening;

to burn no candles, and, if there was anything which he must do, to go into his landlady's room, and work by her light. When he went into the street, he must walk as lightly as he could, and as cautiously, upon the stones, almost upon tiptoe, in order not to wear his heels down in too short a time; he must give the laundress as little to wash as possible; and, in order not to wear out his clothes, he must take them off, as soon as he got home, and wear only his cotton dressing-gown, which had been long and carefully saved.

To tell the truth, it was a little hard for him at first to accustom himself to these deprivations; but he got used to them at length, after a fashion, and all went smoothly. He even got used to being hungry in the evening, but he made up for it by treating himself, so to say, in spirit, by bearing ever in mind the idea of his future cloak. From that time forth his existence seemed to become, in some way, fuller, as if he were married, or as if some other man lived in him, as if, in fact, he were not alone, and some pleasant friend had consented to travel along life's path with him, the friend being no other than the cloak, with thick wadding and a strong lining incapable of wearing out. He became more lively, and even his character grew firmer, like that of a man who has made up his mind, and set himself a goal. From his face and gait, doubt and indecision, all hesitating and wavering traits disappeared of themselves. Fire gleamed in his eyes, and occasionally the boldest and most daring ideas flitted through his mind; why not, for instance, have marten fur on the collar? The thought of this almost made him absent-minded. Once, in copying a letter, he nearly made a mistake, so that he exclaimed almost aloud, "Ugh!" and crossed himself. Once, in the course of every month, he had a conference with Petrovitch on the subject of the cloak, where it would be better to buy the cloth, and the colour, and the price. He always returned home satisfied, though troubled, reflecting that the time would come at last when it could all be bought, and then the cloak made.

The affair progressed more briskly than he had expected. Far beyond all his hopes, the director awarded neither forty nor forty-five rubles for Akakiy Akakievitch's share, but sixty. Whether he suspected that Akakiy Akakievitch needed a cloak, or whether it was merely chance, at all events, twenty extra rubles were by this means provided. This circumstance hastened matters. Two or three months more of hunger and Akakiy Akakievitch had accumulated about eighty rubles. His heart, generally so quiet, began to throb. On the first possible day, he went shopping in company with Petrovitch. They bought some very good cloth, and at a reasonable rate too, for they had been considering the matter for six months, and rarely let a month pass without their visiting the shops to inquire prices. Petrovitch himself said that no better cloth could be had. For lining, they selected a cotton stuff, but so firm and thick that Petrovitch declared it to be better than silk, and even prettier and more glossy. They did not buy the marten fur, because it was, in fact, dear, but in its stead, they picked out the very best of cat-skin which could be found in the shop, and which might, indeed, be taken for marten at a distance.

Petrovitch worked at the cloak two whole weeks, for there was a great deal of quilting: otherwise it would have been finished sooner. He charged twelve rubles for the job, it could not possibly have been done for less. It was all sewed with silk, in small, double seams; and Petrovitch went over each seam afterwards with his own teeth, stamping in various patterns.

It was – it is difficult to say precisely on what day, but probably the most glorious one in Akakiy Akakievitch's life, when Petrovitch at length brought home the cloak. He brought it in the morning, before the hour when it was necessary to start for the department. Never did a cloak arrive so exactly in the nick of time; for the severe cold had set in, and it seemed to threaten to increase. Petrovitch brought the cloak himself as befits a good tailor. On his countenance was a significant expression, such as Akakiy Akakievitch had never beheld there. He seemed fully sensible that he had done no small deed, and crossed a gulf separating tailors who only put in linings, and execute repairs, from those who make new things. He took the cloak out of the pocket handkerchief in which he had brought it. The handkerchief was fresh from the laundress, and he put it in his pocket for use. Taking out the cloak, he gazed proudly at it, held it up with both hands, and flung it skilfully over the shoulders of Akakiy Akakievitch. Then he pulled it and fitted it down behind with his hand, and he draped it around Akakiy Akakievitch without buttoning it. Akakiy Akakievitch, like an experienced man, wished to try the sleeves. Petrovitch helped him on with them, and it turned out that the sleeves were satisfactory also. In short, the cloak appeared to be perfect, and most seasonable. Petrovitch did not neglect to observe that it was only because he lived in a narrow street, and had no signboard, and had known Akakiy Akakievitch so long, that he had made it so cheaply; but that if he had been in business on the Nevsky Prospect, he would have charged seventy-five rubles for the making alone. Akakiy Akakievitch did not care to argue this point with Petrovitch. He paid him, thanked him, and set out at once in his new cloak for the department. Petrovitch followed him, and, pausing in the street, gazed long at the cloak in the distance, after which he went to one side expressly to run through a crooked alley, and emerge again into the street beyond to gaze once more upon the cloak from another point, namely, directly in front.

Meantime Akakiy Akakievitch went on in holiday mood. He was conscious every second of the time that he had a new cloak on his shoulders; and several times he laughed with internal satisfaction. In fact, there were two advantages, one was its warmth, the other its beauty. He saw nothing of the road, but suddenly found himself at the department. He took off his cloak in the ante-room, looked it over carefully, and confided it to the especial care of the attendant. It is impossible to say precisely how it was that everyone in the department knew at once that Akakiy Akakievitch had a new cloak, and that the "cape" no longer existed. All rushed at the same moment into the ante-room to inspect it. They congratulated him and said pleasant things to him, so that he began at first to smile and then to grow ashamed. When all surrounded him, and said that the new cloak must be "christened," and that he must give a whole evening at least to this, Akakiy Akakievitch lost his head completely, and did not know where he stood, what to answer, or how to get out of it. He stood blushing all over for several minutes, and was on the point of assuring them with great simplicity that it was not a new cloak, that it was so and so, that it was in fact the old "cape."

At length one of the officials, a sub-chief probably, in order to show that he was not at all proud, and on good terms with his inferiors, said, "So be it, only I will give the party instead of Akakiy Akakievitch; I invite you all to tea with me tonight; it happens quite apropos, as it is my name-day." The officials naturally at once offered the sub-chief their congratulations and accepted the invitations with pleasure. Akakiy Akakievitch would have declined, but all declared that it was discourteous, that it was simply a sin and a shame, and that he could not possibly refuse. Besides, the notion became pleasant to him when he recollected that he should thereby have a chance of wearing his new cloak in the evening also.

That whole day was truly a most triumphant festival day for Akakiy Akakievitch. He returned home in the most happy frame of mind, took off his cloak, and hung it carefully on the wall, admiring afresh the cloth and the lining. Then he brought out his old, worn-out cloak, for comparison. He looked at it and laughed, so vast was the difference. And long after dinner he laughed again when the condition of the "cape" recurred to his mind. He dined cheerfully, and after dinner wrote nothing, but took his ease for a while on the bed, until it got dark. Then he dressed himself leisurely, put on his cloak, and stepped out into the street. Where the host lived, unfortunately we cannot say: our memory begins to fail us badly; and the houses and streets in St. Petersburg have become so mixed up in our head that it is very difficult to get anything out of it again in proper form. This much is certain, that the official lived in the best part of the city; and therefore it must have been anything but near to Akakiy Akakievitch's residence. Akakiy Akakievitch was first obliged to traverse a kind of wilderness of deserted, dimly-lighted streets; but in proportion as he approached the official's quarter of the city, the streets became more lively, more populous, and more brilliantly illuminated. Pedestrians began to appear; handsomely dressed ladies were more frequently encountered; the men had otter-skin collars to their coats; peasant waggoners, with their grate-like sledges stuck over with brass-headed nails, became rarer; whilst on the other hand, more and more drivers in red velvet caps, lacquered sledges and bear-skin coats began to appear, and carriages with rich hammer-cloths flew swiftly through the streets, their wheels scrunching the snow. Akakiy Akakievitch gazed upon all this as upon a novel sight. He had not been in the streets during the evening for years. He halted out of curiosity before a shop-window to look at a picture representing a handsome woman, who had thrown off her shoe, thereby baring her whole foot in a very pretty way; whilst behind her the head of a man with whiskers and a handsome moustache peeped through the doorway of another room. Akakiy Akakievitch shook his head and laughed, and then went on his way. Why did he laugh? Either because he had met with a thing utterly unknown, but for which everyone cherishes, nevertheless, some sort of feeling; or else he thought, like many officials, as follows: "Well, those French! What is to be said? If they do go in for anything of that sort, why –" But possibly he did not think at all.

Akakiy Akakievitch at length reached the house in which the sub-chief lodged. The sub-chief lived in fine style: the staircase was lit by a lamp; his apartment being on the second floor. On entering the vestibule, Akakiy Akakievitch beheld a whole row of goloshes on the floor. Among them, in the centre of the room, stood a samovar or tea-urn, humming and emitting clouds of steam. On the walls hung all sorts of coats and cloaks, among which there were even some with beaver collars or velvet facings. Beyond, the buzz of conversation was audible, and became clear and loud when the servant came out with a trayful of empty glasses, cream-jugs, and sugar-bowls. It was evident that the officials had arrived long before, and had already finished their first glass of tea.

Akakiy Akakievitch, having hung up his own cloak, entered the inner room. Before him all at once appeared lights, officials, pipes, and card-tables; and he was bewildered by the sound of rapid conversation rising from all the tables, and the noise of moving chairs. He halted very awkwardly in the middle of the room, wondering what he ought to do. But they had seen him. They received him with a shout, and all thronged at once into the ante-room, and there took another look at his cloak. Akakiy Akakievitch, although somewhat confused, was frank-hearted, and could not refrain from rejoicing when he saw how they praised his cloak. Then, of course, they all dropped him and his cloak, and returned, as was proper, to the tables set out for whist.

All this, the noise, the talk, and the throng of people was rather overwhelming to Akakiy Akakievitch. He simply did not know where he stood, or where to put his hands, his feet, and his whole body. Finally he sat down by the players, looked at the cards, gazed at the face of one and another, and after a while began to gape, and to feel that it was wearisome, the more so as the hour was already long past when he usually went to bed. He wanted to take leave of the host; but they would not let him go, saying that he must not fail to drink a glass of champagne in honour of his new garment. In the course of an hour, supper, consisting of vegetable salad, cold veal, pastry, confectioner's pies, and champagne, was served. They made Akakiy Akakievitch drink two glasses of champagne, after which he felt things grow livelier.

Still, he could not forget that it was twelve o'clock, and that he should have been at home long ago. In order that the host might not think of some excuse for detaining him, he stole out of the room quickly, sought out, in the ante-room, his cloak, which, to his sorrow, he found lying on the floor, brushed it, picked off every speck upon it, put it on his shoulders, and descended the stairs to the street.

In the street all was still bright. Some petty shops, those permanent clubs of servants and all sorts of folk, were open. Others were shut, but, nevertheless, showed a streak of light the whole length of the door-crack, indicating that they were not yet free of company, and that probably some domestics, male and female, were finishing their stories and conversations whilst leaving their masters in complete ignorance as to their whereabouts. Akakiy Akakievitch went on in a happy frame of mind: he even started to run, without knowing why, after some lady, who flew past like a flash of lightning. But he stopped short, and went on very quietly as before, wondering why he had quickened his pace. Soon there spread before him those deserted streets, which are not cheerful in the daytime, to say nothing of the evening. Now they were even more dim and lonely: the lanterns began to grow rarer, oil, evidently, had been less liberally supplied. Then came wooden houses and fences: not a soul anywhere; only the snow sparkled in the streets, and mournfully veiled the low-roofed cabins with their closed shutters. He approached the spot where the street crossed a vast square with houses barely visible on its farther side, a square which seemed a fearful desert.

Afar, a tiny spark glimmered from some watchman's box, which seemed to stand on the edge of the world. Akakiy Akakievitch's cheerfulness diminished at this point in a marked degree. He entered the square, not without an involuntary sensation of fear, as though his heart warned him of some evil. He glanced back and on both sides, it was like a sea about him. "No, it is better not to look," he thought, and went on, closing his eyes. When he opened them, to see whether he was near the end of the square, he suddenly beheld, standing just before his very nose, some bearded individuals of precisely what sort he could not make out. All grew dark before his eyes, and his heart throbbed.

"But, of course, the cloak is mine!" said one of them in a loud voice, seizing hold of his collar. Akakiy Akakievitch was about to shout "watch," when the second man thrust a fist, about the size of a man's head, into his mouth, muttering, "Now scream!"

Akakiy Akakievitch felt them strip off his cloak and give him a push with a knee: he fell headlong upon the snow, and felt no more. In a few minutes he recovered consciousness and rose to his feet; but no one was there. He felt that it was cold in the square, and that his cloak was gone; he began to shout, but his voice did not appear to reach to the outskirts of the square. In despair, but without ceasing to shout, he started at a run across the square, straight towards the watchbox, beside which stood the watchman, leaning on his halberd, and apparently curious to know what kind of a customer was running towards him and shouting. Akakiy Akakievitch ran up to him, and began in a sobbing voice to shout that he was asleep, and attended to nothing, and did not see when a man was robbed. The watchman replied that he had seen two men stop him in the middle of the square, but supposed that they were friends of his; and that, instead of scolding vainly, he had better go to the police on the morrow, so that they might make a search for whoever had stolen the cloak.

Akakiy Akakievitch ran home in complete disorder; his hair, which grew very thinly upon his temples and the back of his head, wholly disordered; his body, arms, and legs covered with snow. The old woman, who was mistress of his lodgings, on hearing a terrible knocking, sprang hastily from her bed, and, with only one shoe on, ran to open the door, pressing the sleeve of her chemise to her bosom out of modesty; but when she had opened it, she fell back on beholding Akakiy Akakievitch in such a state. When he told her about the affair, she clasped her hands, and said that he must go straight to the district chief of police, for his subordinate would turn up his nose, promise well, and drop the matter there. The very best thing to do, therefore, would be to go to the district chief, whom she knew, because Finnish Anna, her former cook, was now nurse at his house. She often saw him passing the house; and he was at church every Sunday, praying, but at the same time gazing cheerfully at everybody; so that he must be a good man, judging from all appearances. Having listened to this opinion, Akakiy Akakievitch betook himself sadly to his room; and how he spent the night there anyone who can put himself in another's place may readily imagine.

Early in the morning, he presented himself at the district chief's; but was told that this official was asleep. He went again at ten and was again informed that he was asleep; at eleven, and they said: "The superintendent is not at home;" at dinner time, and the clerks in the ante-room would not admit him on any terms, and insisted upon knowing his business. So that at last, for once in his life, Akakiy Akakievitch felt an inclination to show some spirit, and said curtly that he must see the chief in person; that they ought not to presume to refuse him entrance; that he came from the department of justice, and that when he complained of them, they would see.

The clerks dared make no reply to this, and one of them went to call the chief, who listened to the strange story of the theft of the coat. Instead of directing his attention to the principal points of the matter, he began to question Akakiy Akakievitch: Why was he going home so late? Was he in the habit of doing so, or had he been to some disorderly house? So that Akakiy Akakievitch got thoroughly confused, and left him without knowing whether the affair of his cloak was in proper train or not.

All that day, for the first time in his life, he never went near the department. The next day he made his appearance, very pale, and in his old cape, which had become even more shabby. The news of the robbery of the cloak touched many; although there were some officials present who never lost an opportunity, even such a one as the present, of ridiculing Akakiy Akakievitch. They decided to make a collection for him on the spot, but the officials had already spent a great deal in subscribing for the director's portrait, and for some book, at the suggestion of the head of that division, who was a friend of the author; and so the sum was trifling.

One of them, moved by pity, resolved to help Akakiy Akakievitch with some good advice at least, and told him that he ought not to go to the police, for although it might happen that a police-officer, wishing to win the approval of his superiors, might hunt up the cloak by some means, still his cloak would remain in the possession of the police if he did not offer legal proof that it belonged to him. The best thing for him, therefore, would be to apply to a certain prominent personage; since this prominent personage, by entering into relations with the proper persons, could greatly expedite the matter.

As there was nothing else to be done, Akakiy Akakievitch decided to go to the prominent personage. What was the exact official position of the prominent personage remains unknown to this day. The reader must know that the prominent personage had but recently become a prominent personage, having up to that time been only an insignificant person. Moreover, his present position was not considered prominent in comparison with others still more so. But there is always a circle of people to whom what is insignificant in the eyes of others, is important enough. Moreover, he strove to increase his importance by sundry devices; for instance, he managed to have the inferior officials meet him on the staircase when he entered upon his service; no one was to presume to come directly to him, but the strictest etiquette must be observed; the collegiate recorder must make a report to the government secretary, the government secretary to the titular councillor, or whatever other man was proper, and all business must come before him in this manner. In Holy Russia all is thus contaminated with the love of imitation; every man imitates and copies his superior. They even say that a certain titular councillor, when promoted to the head of some small separate room, immediately partitioned off a private room for himself, called it the audience chamber, and posted at the door a lackey with red collar and braid, who grasped the handle of the door and opened to all comers; though the audience chamber could hardly hold an ordinary writing-table.

The manners and customs of the prominent personage were grand and imposing, but rather exaggerated. The main foundation of his system was strictness. "Strictness, strictness, and always strictness!" he generally said; and at the last word he looked significantly into the face of the person to whom he spoke. But there was no necessity for this, for the half-score of subordinates who formed the entire force of the office were properly afraid; on catching sight of him afar off they left their work and waited, drawn up in line, until he had passed through the room. His ordinary converse with his inferiors smacked of sternness, and consisted chiefly of three phrases: "How dare you?" "Do you know whom you are speaking to?" "Do you realise who stands before you?"

Otherwise he was a very kind-hearted man, good to his comrades, and ready to oblige; but the rank of general threw him completely off his balance. On receiving anyone of that rank, he became confused, lost his way, as it were, and never knew what to do. If he chanced to be amongst his equals he was still a very nice kind of man, a very good fellow in many respects, and not stupid; but the very moment that he found himself in the society of people but one rank lower than himself he became silent; and his situation aroused sympathy, the more so as he felt himself that he might have been making an incomparably better use of his time. In his eyes there was sometimes visible a desire to join some interesting conversation or group; but he was kept back by the thought, "Would it not be a very great condescension on his part? Would it not be familiar? and would he not thereby lose his importance?" And in consequence of such reflections he always remained in the same dumb state, uttering from time to time a few monosyllabic sounds, and thereby earning the name of the most wearisome of men.

To this prominent personage Akakiy Akakievitch presented himself, and this at the most unfavourable time for himself though opportune for the prominent personage. The prominent personage was in his cabinet conversing gaily with an old acquaintance and companion of his childhood whom he had not seen for several years and who had just arrived when it was announced to him that a person named Bashmatchkin had come. He asked abruptly, "Who is he?" – "Some official," he was informed. "Ah, he can wait! this is no time for him to call," said the important man.

It must be remarked here that the important man lied outrageously: he had said all he had to say to his friend long before; and the conversation had been interspersed for some time with very long pauses, during which they merely slapped each other on the leg, and said, "You think so, Ivan Abramovitch!" "Just so, Stepan Varlamitch!" Nevertheless, he ordered that the official should be kept waiting, in order to show his friend, a man who had not been in the service for a long time, but had lived at home in the country, how long officials had to wait in his ante-room.

At length, having talked himself completely out, and more than that, having had his fill of pauses, and smoked a cigar in a very comfortable arm-chair with reclining back, he suddenly seemed to recollect, and said to the secretary, who stood by the door with papers of reports, "So it seems that there is a tchinovnik waiting to see me. Tell him that he may come in." On perceiving Akakiy Akakievitch's modest mien and his worn undress uniform, he turned abruptly to him and said, "What do you want?" in a curt hard voice, which he had practised in his room in private, and before the looking-glass, for a whole week before being raised to his present rank.

Akakiy Akakievitch, who was already imbued with a due amount of fear, became somewhat confused: and as well as his tongue would permit, explained, with a rather more frequent addition than usual of the word "that," that his cloak was quite new, and had been stolen in the most inhuman manner; that he had applied to him in order that he might, in some way, by his intermediation – that he might enter into correspondence with the chief of police, and find the cloak.

For some inexplicable reason this conduct seemed familiar to the prominent personage. "What, my dear sir!" he said abruptly, "are you not acquainted with etiquette? Where have you come from? Don't you know how such matters are managed? You should first have entered a complaint about this at the court below: it would have gone to the head of the department, then to the chief of the division, then it would have been handed over to the secretary, and the secretary would have given it to me."

"But, your excellency," said Akakiy Akakievitch, trying to collect his small handful of wits, and conscious at the same time that he was perspiring terribly, "I, your excellency, presumed to trouble you because secretaries – are an untrustworthy race."

"What, what, what!" said the important personage. "Where did you get such courage? Where did you get such ideas? What impudence towards their chiefs and superiors has spread among the young generation!" The prominent personage apparently had not observed that Akakiy Akakievitch was already in the neighbourhood of fifty. If he could be called a young man, it must have been in comparison with someone who was twenty. "Do you know to whom you speak? Do you realise who stands before you? Do you realise it? do you realise it? I ask you!" Then he stamped his foot and raised his voice to such a pitch that it would have frightened even a different man from Akakiy Akakievitch.

Akakiy Akakievitch's senses failed him; he staggered, trembled in every limb, and, if the porters had not run to support him, would have fallen to the floor. They carried him out insensible. But the prominent personage, gratified that the effect should have surpassed his expectations, and quite intoxicated with the thought that his word could even deprive a man of his senses, glanced sideways at his friend in order to see how he looked upon this, and perceived, not without satisfaction, that his friend was in a most uneasy frame of mind, and even beginning, on his part, to feel a trifle frightened.

Akakiy Akakievitch could not remember how he descended the stairs and got into the street. He felt neither his hands nor feet. Never in his life had he been so rated by any high official, let alone a strange one. He went staggering on through the snow-storm, which was blowing in the streets, with his mouth wide open; the wind, in St. Petersburg fashion, darted upon him from all quarters, and down every cross-street. In a twinkling it had blown a quinsy into his throat, and he reached home unable to utter a word. His throat was swollen, and he lay down on his bed. So powerful is sometimes a good scolding!

The next day a violent fever showed itself. Thanks to the generous assistance of the St. Petersburg climate, the malady progressed more rapidly than could have been expected: and when the doctor arrived, he found, on feeling the sick man's pulse, that there was nothing to be done, except to prescribe a fomentation, so that the patient might not be left entirely without the beneficent aid of medicine; but at the same time, he predicted his end in thirty-six hours. After this he turned to the landlady, and said, "And as for you, don't waste your time on him: order his pine coffin now, for an oak one will be too expensive for him." Did Akakiy Akakievitch hear these fatal words? and if he heard them, did they produce any overwhelming effect upon him? Did he lament the bitterness of his life? – We know not, for he continued in a delirious condition. Visions incessantly appeared to him, each stranger than the other. Now he saw Petrovitch, and ordered him to make a cloak, with some traps for robbers, who seemed to him to be always under the bed; and cried every moment to the landlady to pull one of them from under his coverlet. Then he inquired why his old mantle hung before him when he had a new cloak. Next he fancied that he was standing before the prominent person, listening to a thorough setting-down, and saying, "Forgive me, your excellency!" but at last he began to curse, uttering the most horrible words, so that his aged landlady crossed herself, never in her life having heard anything of the kind from him, the more so as those words followed directly after the words "your excellency." Later on he talked utter nonsense, of which nothing could be made: all that was evident being, that his incoherent words and thoughts hovered ever about one thing, his cloak.

At length poor Akakiy Akakievitch breathed his last. They sealed up neither his room nor his effects, because, in the first place, there were no heirs, and, in the second, there was very little to inherit beyond a bundle of goose-quills, a quire of white official paper, three pairs of socks, two or three buttons which had burst off his trousers, and the mantle already known to the reader. To whom all this fell, God knows. I confess that the person who told me this tale took no interest in the matter. They carried Akakiy Akakievitch out and buried him.

And St. Petersburg was left without Akakiy Akakievitch, as though he had never lived there. A being disappeared who was protected by none, dear to none, interesting to none, and who never even attracted to himself the attention of those students of human nature who omit no opportunity of thrusting a pin through a common fly, and examining it under the microscope. A being who bore meekly the jibes of the department, and went to his grave without having done one unusual deed, but to whom, nevertheless, at the close of his life appeared a bright visitant in the form of a cloak, which momentarily cheered his poor life, and upon whom, thereafter, an intolerable misfortune descended, just as it descends upon the mighty of this world!

Several days after his death, the porter was sent from the department to his lodgings, with an order for him to present himself there immediately; the chief commanding it. But the porter had to return unsuccessful, with the answer that he could not come; and to the question, "Why?" replied, "Well, because he is dead! he was buried four days ago." In this manner did they hear of Akakiy Akakievitch's death at the department, and the next day a new official sat in his place, with a handwriting by no means so upright, but more inclined and slanting.

But who could have imagined that this was not really the end of Akakiy Akakievitch, that he was destined to raise a commotion after death, as if in compensation for his utterly insignificant life? But so it happened, and our poor story unexpectedly gains a fantastic ending.

A rumour suddenly spread through St. Petersburg that a dead man had taken to appearing on the Kalinkin Bridge and its vicinity at night in the form of a tchinovnik seeking a stolen cloak, and that, under the pretext of its being the stolen cloak, he dragged, without regard to rank or calling, everyone's cloak from his shoulders, be it cat-skin, beaver, fox, bear, sable; in a word, every sort of fur and skin which men adopted for their covering. One of the department officials saw the dead man with his own eyes and immediately recognised in him Akakiy Akakievitch. This, however, inspired him with such terror that he ran off with all his might, and therefore did not scan the dead man closely, but only saw how the latter threatened him from afar with his finger. Constant complaints poured in from all quarters that the backs and shoulders, not only of titular but even of court councillors, were exposed to the danger of a cold on account of the frequent dragging off of their cloaks.

Arrangements were made by the police to catch the corpse, alive or dead, at any cost, and punish him as an example to others in the most severe manner. In this they nearly succeeded; for a watchman, on guard in Kirushkin Alley, caught the corpse by the collar on the very scene of his evil deeds, when attempting to pull off the frieze coat of a retired musician. Having seized him by the collar, he summoned, with a shout, two of his comrades, whom he enjoined to hold him fast while he himself felt for a moment in his boot, in order to draw out his snuff-box and refresh his frozen nose. But the snuff was of a sort which even a corpse could not endure. The watchman having closed his right nostril with his finger, had no sooner succeeded in holding half a handful up to the left than the corpse sneezed so violently that he completely filled the eyes of all three. While they raised their hands to wipe them, the dead man vanished completely, so that they positively did not know whether they had actually had him in their grip at all. Thereafter the watchmen conceived such a terror of dead men that they were afraid even to seize the living, and only screamed from a distance, "Hey, there! go your way!" So the dead tchinovnik began to appear even beyond the Kalinkin Bridge, causing no little terror to all timid people.

But we have totally neglected that certain prominent personage who may really be considered as the cause of the fantastic turn taken by this true history. First of all, justice compels us to say that after the departure of poor, annihilated Akakiy Akakievitch he felt something like remorse. Suffering was unpleasant to him, for his heart was accessible to many good impulses, in spite of the fact that his rank often prevented his showing his true self. As soon as his friend had left his cabinet, he began to think about poor Akakiy Akakievitch. And from that day forth, poor Akakiy Akakievitch, who could not bear up under an official reprimand, recurred to his mind almost every day. The thought troubled him to such an extent that a week later he even resolved to send an official to him, to learn whether he really could assist him; and when it was reported to him that Akakiy Akakievitch had died suddenly of fever, he was startled, hearkened to the reproaches of his conscience, and was out of sorts for the whole day.

Wishing to divert his mind in some way, and drive away the disagreeable impression, he set out that evening for one of his friends' houses, where he found quite a large party assembled. What was better, nearly everyone was of the same rank as himself, so that he need not feel in the least constrained. This had a marvellous effect upon his mental state. He grew expansive, made himself agreeable in conversation, in short, he passed a delightful evening. After supper he drank a couple of glasses of champagne – not a bad recipe for cheerfulness, as everyone knows. The champagne inclined him to various adventures; and he determined not to return home, but to go and see a certain well-known lady of German extraction, Karolina Ivanovna, a lady, it appears, with whom he was on a very friendly footing.

It must be mentioned that the prominent personage was no longer a young man, but a good husband and respected father of a family. Two sons, one of whom was already in the service, and a good-looking, sixteen-year-old daughter, with a rather retroussé but pretty little nose, came every morning to kiss his hand and say, "Bonjour, papa." His wife, a still fresh and good-looking woman, first gave him her hand to kiss, and then, reversing the procedure, kissed his. But the prominent personage, though perfectly satisfied in his domestic relations, considered it stylish to have a friend in another quarter of the city. This friend was scarcely prettier or younger than his wife; but there are such puzzles in the world, and it is not our place to judge them. So the important personage descended the stairs, stepped into his sledge, said to the coachman, "To Karolina Ivanovna's," and, wrapping himself luxuriously in his warm cloak, found himself in that delightful frame of mind than which a Russian can conceive no better, namely, when you think of nothing yourself, yet when the thoughts creep into your mind of their own accord, each more agreeable than the other, giving you no trouble either to drive them away or seek them. Fully satisfied, he recalled all the gay features of the evening just passed, and all the mots which had made the little circle laugh. Many of them he repeated in a low voice, and found them quite as funny as before; so it is not surprising that he should laugh heartily at them. Occasionally, however, he was interrupted by gusts of wind, which, coming suddenly, God knows whence or why, cut his face, drove masses of snow into it, filled out his cloak-collar like a sail, or suddenly blew it over his head with supernatural force, and thus caused him constant trouble to disentangle himself.

Suddenly the important personage felt someone clutch him firmly by the collar. Turning round, he perceived a man of short stature, in an old, worn uniform, and recognised, not without terror, Akakiy Akakievitch. The official's face was white as snow, and looked just like a corpse's. But the horror of the important personage transcended all bounds when he saw the dead man's mouth open, and, with a terrible odour of the grave, gave vent to the following remarks: "Ah, here you are at last! I have you, that – by the collar! I need your cloak; you took no trouble about mine, but reprimanded me; so now give up your own."

The pallid prominent personage almost died of fright. Brave as he was in the office and in the presence of inferiors generally, and although, at the sight of his manly form and appearance, everyone said, "Ugh! how much character he had!" at this crisis, he, like many possessed of an heroic exterior, experienced such terror, that, not without cause, he began to fear an attack of illness. He flung his cloak hastily from his shoulders and shouted to his coachman in an unnatural voice, "Home at full speed!" The coachman, hearing the tone which is generally employed at critical moments and even accompanied by something much more tangible, drew his head down between his shoulders in case of an emergency, flourished his whip, and flew on like an arrow. In a little more than six minutes the prominent personage was at the entrance of his own house. Pale, thoroughly scared, and cloakless, he went home instead of to Karolina Ivanovna's, reached his room somehow or other, and passed the night in the direst distress; so that the next morning over their tea his daughter said, "You are very pale today, papa."

But papa remained silent, and said not a word to anyone of what had happened to him, where he had been, or where he had intended to go.

This occurrence made a deep impression upon him. He even began to say: "How dare you? do you realise who stands before you?" less frequently to the under-officials, and if he did utter the words, it was only after having first learned the bearings of the matter. But the most noteworthy point was, that from that day forward the apparition of the dead tchinovnik ceased to be seen. Evidently the prominent personage's cloak just fitted his shoulders; at all events, no more instances of his dragging cloaks from people's shoulders were heard of. But many active and apprehensive persons could by no means reassure themselves, and asserted that the dead tchinovnik still showed himself in distant parts of the city.

In fact, one watchman in Kolomna saw with his own eyes the apparition come from behind a house. But being rather weak of body, he dared not arrest him, but followed him in the dark, until, at length, the apparition looked round, paused, and inquired, "What do you want?" at the same time showing a fist such as is never seen on living men. The watchman said, "It's of no consequence," and turned back instantly. But the apparition was much too tall, wore huge moustaches, and, directing its steps apparently towards the Obukhoff Bridge, disappeared in the darkness of the night.

The Waiting Room

Philip Brian Hall

TO A MAN UTTERLY LOST, walking forward seems preferable to standing still; somehow movement gives purpose to a stateless existence.

Around Harold, the darkness was Stygian; neither moon nor star illumined the blackness. For all his eyes could tell him he might have been entombed within the bowels of the earth. Carried on the stiff breeze that flapped a long trench coat around his unsteady legs was the sweet smell of decay, suggestive of manure recently spread over the fields. He felt rather than saw tall, spiky, hawthorn hedgerows that bounded on either side the narrow country lane along which he tentatively groped his way.

Although it was bitterly cold, Harold was grateful for the wind; its buffeting helped him maintain a sense of direction as he stumbled along. All his being was focused within himself, shrinking back from an external world of which his data-deprived senses could form no coherent picture.

He walked. Therefore he was going somewhere. Strangely he could not remember where, but he supposed he would know it when he arrived. It was not the first time he had been forced to navigate by instinct.

Nevertheless, it was with relief that at length he discerned a tiny point of yellow light in the sepulchral gloom ahead. Artificial light must mean human habitation. His step became surer. He strode on determinedly through the darkness towards the light.

In due course the point grew larger, assumed a rectangular shape and revealed itself to be a window. He made out the silhouette of an isolated country railway station, distinguished from the blackness of the sky and the blackness of the ground by a feeble and diffuse glow emanating from the platform beyond. He discerned a bridge over the line and an old-style semaphore signal. As Harold walked up to the dark exterior of the buildings, the light from the window spilled out across the station approach like a welcome mat, enabling him to see the ground beneath his feet for the first time.

Embossed lettering on the window panes informed him he had arrived at the improbably-named Half Way Halt. Since it offered him a haven from the cold and dark, for the moment it was enough that he had arrived *somewhere*. He stepped through the door, entering a room that was comfortably warm, with a real coal fire burning in an open hearth.

Closing the door quickly behind him, Harold rubbed his hands vigorously together as he glanced around. Clean, upholstered chairs, tables for waiting travellers to put down their tea, the tea itself served as it should be in proper earthenware cups with saucers.

On the walls were beautifully framed coloured prints of hand-painted tourism posters. Into each the artist had introduced a picturesque steam engine puffing along ahead of three or four liveried carriages, somehow enhancing the scene.

Strangely there was no timetable on display, though a traditional round, white-faced, wooden-cased clock on the wall ticked loudly and regularly. Its black, Gothic hands indicated ten minutes to midnight. Harold was rarely out so late.

On the far side of the room was a ticket desk. A clerk sat behind it, smartly attired in a dark blue uniform, waistcoat, blue-and-white striped shirt and maroon tie. He was wearing a peaked cap and looking alert despite the hour.

Into the opposite corner was squeezed an open serving-hatch, giving access to a little kitchen. From this a large, florid brunette in a white pinafore, clearly well versed in the role of ministering angel, dispensed the tea.

Pleased to have gained sanctuary, Harold did not immediately question his surroundings. Had he done so it might have occurred to him to wonder how such an old fashioned station had survived to the turn of the twentieth century. He might have thought Half Way Halt stuck in a time warp.

Walking up to the ticket desk, he reflected on his good fortune to find it staffed in the middle of the night. It was not until he stood there, looking at the clerk, that he realized he had no more idea of where he was going than of what he was doing there. The clerk looked up expectantly.

"I seem to be lost," Harold said. "I suppose I couldn't just rest here for a while?"

"Are you waiting for someone?"

"No. I've no one to wait for."

"Then you need to get on the train. There's nowhere else to go from here. They'll be expecting you."

"They will?"

"Of course. One single." He passed a thick piece of card across the counter.

Harold studied it hesitantly. "It doesn't say where to."

"No. It's a single track line, just a terminus at each end and us here in the middle."

"But I don't even know which direction I'm supposed to be travelling."

"Only two directions: up and down."

"I see. Well then, how much is the ticket, please?"

"You've already paid," said the clerk.

"Have I?" Harold asked. "My memory must be worse than I thought. So, could you perhaps tell me when the next up train is?"

"That's not how it works," said the clerk. "You just get on the first train, whichever direction it's going."

Like all seasoned railway travellers, Harold was used to ignorance of when such unpredictable occurrences as the *arrival* of trains might be expected, but ignorance of its *direction* seemed preposterous. Nevertheless, the prospect of turning around and leaving was daunting. The night had been dreadfully dark and he was unsure how to get home.

"Which way was it going when it passed through here last?"

"That, I'm afraid, I couldn't say," replied the clerk.

"But good god, man, it's your job! You must know!"

"Please mind your language," said the clerk sternly. "You'll offend the other passengers."

Harold had paid little attention to the room's other occupants. Standard equipment for waiting rooms included people waiting. He turned around and surveyed his companions.

There were five, assuming you counted as two a young mother who sat gently rocking a child asleep on her knee. She wore a long coat and a cloche hat, from beneath which long red hair hung down below her shoulders, screening her face from Harold's gaze as she bent forward over the infant.

Sitting on his own was a blond young man, perhaps a motor cyclist. He wore a leather jacket, padded trousers and calf-length boots. On his knees he clutched a cardboard folder. The edge of a map peeped out from one corner.

A dark-haired, middle-aged man was wearing yellow oilskins and sea-boots, for all the world as though he had stepped straight from the dockside. Under his sou'wester his eyes were red-rimmed and his face caked with salt. A faint odour of brine wafted across the room.

Lastly, sitting on his own in a corner, was a young soldier in camouflage, his head bandaged. There were stains on his uniform that might have been dried blood.

"Tea, dear?" Harold heard the large lady speaking to him from behind the hatch.

"Yes, please," he replied, "I could do with one. It's b –, I mean, it's very cold out there tonight. How much?"

"You've already paid, dear," the tea lady replied, flipping the tap on her urn and holding a cup underneath it. "Milk and sugar?"

"Milk please, no sugar," said Harold. Had he twice in the space of a couple of minutes forgotten handing over money? She handed him the cup and saucer and Harold thanked her, taking a sip as he walked over to a chair beside the young soldier.

"Anyone sitting here?" he inquired, in the arcane way the British always do in order to be polite.

The soldier shook his head and grimaced, but said nothing. He looked in pain. There was an unpleasant smell about him that Harold recognized only too well from long ago. Gangrene. Why was the young man not in hospital? Harold sat down and placed his cup and saucer on the table between them.

"Wounded?" he inquired, as the soldier still remained silent.

The soldier nodded, touching his bandage with an anguished expression. "Creased by a sniper; don't remember anything after. Medevac, I suppose. Don't even remember how I got here. Just need to get back to my unit."

"You look as if you need convalescent leave, at the very least," said Harold solicitously.

"No time. They'll need me back as soon as I'm fit to fly out."

"That's the spirit!" Harold replied. He admired the young soldier's courage. It reminded him of other young men he had known; of when *he* had been a young man.

"I was a pilot myself. Mosquito – night fighter - back in 'forty-three. You wouldn't have thought it to see me struggling to find my way in the dark outside just now!"

The image of the Dornier came unbidden to Harold's mind. You were not supposed to enjoy killing. He recalled the triumph that had flooded through him as the machine in his sights caught fire and then exploded.

There, you swine! That's for Margie!

"I'm hurt, not stupid," the soldier replied, suddenly less friendly. "That was sixty years ago and you're not a day over thirty." He got up and went to the serving hatch for another cup of tea, limping badly.

Harold was astonished; he had always looked young for his age, but nowadays that meant looking seventy despite being nearly ninety.

There was no mirror, but he was able to make out his reflection in the glazing of one of the travel posters. It *was* his face, but not the face he was used to seeing of late in the shaving mirror. Gone were the wrinkles of old age. His hair was a youthful black and he sported once again the handlebar moustache that had marked him out as a fighter pilot, attracting all the girls back in those dark days.

To be honest, for Harold those days had not been so dark; the prospect of imminent death had projected him into vivid reality; every experience, every sight, every sound imprinted indelibly on his memory.

The smell of aviation spirit as you walked over to dispersal in the twilight, sheepskin-lined flying boots padding softly on the newly mowed grass. Listening to the first calls of the nightingale; trying not to think that the bird would sing again tomorrow night but you might not be around to hear it. The unique woody odour you always got inside a Mosquito; the shuddering of the whole aircraft as the nose cannon blasted shells in the direction of that half-seen Dornier, twisting and weaving as it attempted to escape.

And of course Margie, the auburn haired, freckled barmaid he'd met in the village pub, romanced and married in a whirlwind, always living in the present, never making plans for the future because a fighter pilot never did.

It should have been me. I should have died that night, not her.

Instead he'd been airborne, searching in the darkness for a hit-and-run Messerschmitt fighter-bomber that mistakenly dropped its bomb on her pub.

With a start Harold dragged himself back from the past. What he should be asking was how on earth his appearance had been rejuvenated.

Makes no sense.

He gently pinched the skin of his cheek; he was not asleep.

What had happened before he found himself walking along that dark road? For the life of him he could not recall leaving home. In fact the last few days were a bit of a blur.

He had been up to London the previous week. The final reunion dinner of the old squadron. Obvious to them all it made no sense to arrange another.

Working in the rose garden; very hot in the sun. Felt tired; went to get a lemonade; sat in the conservatory. Emily came round from next door and fussed over him. After that – a few incoherent bits and pieces, people coming and going, light and darkness, soup in someone's hands, fed to him in bed.

And now? Had he died, was that it? Hardly surprising at his age. Yet Harold was not a believer, not since Margie. He'd never expected any conscious experience to follow death. Was it even remotely credible that Half Way Halt was a gateway to some sort of afterlife?

He needed more evidence. Neither he nor the soldier could remember how they got there; two amnesiacs in one waiting room might be a coincidence, three would be strong circumstantial evidence of the supernatural.

He went over and sat down opposite the man in oilskins, speaking softly so as not to upset the young woman and her child.

"Please don't take this the wrong way," he began, "but do you know what you're doing here?"

"Waitin' for a train, o' course." The fisherman, by his voice Aberdonian, gave him a funny look. "This bein' a *railway* waitin' room, Ah'd no' be waitin' for a *bus*, would I?"

"No, you don't understand, I mean do you know *why* you're waiting for a train?"

"Because it hasnae come yet!" exclaimed the fisherman in irritation. "What's yer game, Jimmy? Are ye anither ane o' they pen-pushers wi' nothin' better tae dae than ask stupit questions?"

"Not at all," said Harold hastily. "I was just hoping you might be able to help me sort out what's happening here."

"All ah ken is we was in collision somewhere off the Dogger Bank. Doon she went in two minutes. Next thing Ah'm washed up on the beach – heard a train whistle – made ma way here."

The man's clothes were perfectly dry. There was no beach within eighty miles of Harold's home.

"You were fortunate to survive," he said. "I didn't hear of any sinking. I'd have remembered, you see; I was in marine insurance for forty years after the second war."

"Whit d'ye mean?" demanded the fisherman. "Och, mon, yon' Hitler's nobbut eight years deed! You're oot o' some loony bin, are ye no'? Awa' wi' ye an' leave a man in peace the noo!"

Harold stood up. Eight years after the war. 1953. The trawler *Katarina* out of Stonehaven. The sinking resulted in multiple claims against his company and as a young loss adjuster trying to impress he worked hard to cut back the size of the awards, establishing contributory negligence on the part of the trawler's owners. The small firm went out of business with the loss of a good many livelihoods. Harold had made suffering worse than it need have been. And why? Because that was his job.

His theory seemed confirmed. He must be dead. And just when he should at long last have been consigned to welcome oblivion there was something more. Harold was not sure how to bear it.

"*Guten Abend, Herr Flugleutnant*. I was told to wait here for you."

Harold turned to see the man he had taken for a biker. "You were? That's strange, I didn't know I was coming here myself. I'm sorry, have we met?"

"No."

"And you're German?"

"Yes."

"And they told you to wait for me?"

"Yes."

"You're not helping me, are you Herr…?"

Silently, the man looked Harold straight in the eye with the sort of stubborn defiance that can sometimes mask insecurity. From close up he looked not much more than a boy; maybe nineteen or twenty.

"Well, are you going to tell me what this is all about? I assume the people who told you to wait for me also told you why?"

"Yes."

"Do you expect me to guess or are you going to save us both some time and tell me?"

"You flew a pathfinder aircraft to Hamburg in July 1943?"

"Ah. Yes, I did. My squadron marked the target for the big raid."

"You dropped incendiaries along with your flares?"

"Of course. The flares wouldn't have burned for long enough."

"My parents lived in Hamburg. Close to the docks. Your bombs hit their house. They were both killed."

"I see." Harold shook his head sadly. "I'm very sorry to hear that. I know it's no consolation, but we weren't aiming for civilian casualties. Bombing was not accurate in those days. I only got so close to the docks because I came in very low; wouldn't have been doing my job if I'd put the markers into the water, you see. Had to hit something solid. I tried to put them on a big freighter. I was just travelling too fast to be accurate."

"Too fast?"

"Your flak gunners *were* shooting at me."

"So an accident? You are trying to say my parents died in an accident?"

"Not exactly. They were casualties of war. But you must know the house would have been destroyed a few minutes later anyway. The heavies behind us were at 10,000 feet. They flattened everything around the markers."

"The firestorm."

"Look," Harold protested, "it was war. A war we didn't start. I'm sorry about your parents. But if you're looking for someone to blame, you need to look closer to home, my friend. *We* didn't invade Poland."

"You are sorry, but you do not apologize?"

"That's correct."

"And the pilot who killed your wife? You would accept from him the same reasoning?"

Harold's eyes narrowed. He looked intently at the young German. The same defiant look, but this time something else behind the eyes.

Only long after the war had it occurred to Harold that the Dornier he'd shot down had been crewed by men like himself rather than the Nazi caricatures that populated war films; that the people he'd killed with his bombs were not all fighting men. They were people, his anonymous victims in the war, with their own lives, families, hopes and dreams. And the fishermen whose livelihoods he'd destroyed in peacetime were ordinary people too.

I was only obeying orders. I was just doing my job.

He nodded. The same excuse the Nazis themselves had used at Nuremberg. He understood. The down train must go to a place where the guilty would at long last be held to account.

"The 109E was a terrible bomber," he said to the young man. "With all that weight slung under its belly it must have flown like a brick. A sitting duck for any night fighter. And you'd lost so many pilots. I can understand a nervous young fighter pilot with no experience being only too eager to get rid of that bomb."

"And so?"

"Yes," Harold sighed. "I would accept from him the same reasoning."

"Then it is good," the young man said with relief. "We can both forgive."

Harold extended his hand and the young man took it.

"We harmed each other, but without malice," Harold said. "We can forgive each other. Whether others will forgive *us* remains to be seen."

The defiance had gone from the young man's eyes, but he still held himself ramrod straight as he turned back towards his seat.

Harold thought he now understood why the young German pilot was here; perhaps also the soldier. But why should the fisherman be taking the down train? And even if he too was condemned for sins of which Harold was ignorant, that still left the young mother and her child.

He was filled with righteous indignation. He would accept his own punishment like a man, but he would not accept the punishment of a child. He turned towards the ticket desk, meaning to remonstrate with the clerk. The railwayman had disappeared. The kitchen hatch had also quietly shut; there was no representative of officialdom to whom he could appeal.

Very well. He had fought for a cause before, he could fight again. These innocents would board the down train over his dead body. He smiled grimly; the irony was not lost upon him. But, for the moment at least, he was a dead man walking.

He cast a glance up at the clock. It was one minute to midnight. A subtle clunk from within the mechanism indicated it was about to strike. Even within the confines of the waiting room, he could hear a singing sound resonating along the tracks and the distant huffing of a steam exhaust heralding the approach of a train. He turned urgently towards the young mother.

"You mustn't get on the down train!" he exclaimed. "There's an innocent child to protect. I'll help you!"

"Well! And hello yourself, Harold! What sort of a greeting is that after all this time?"

The young woman smiled and stood up, gathering the sleepy child in her arms. Her auburn hair shone even in the weak light from the electric bulbs; there were the freckles he knew so well, sprinkled liberally over her snub nose; her eyes were laughing.

"It's all right. They wouldn't let you recognize me until you passed the test, and you've passed it. I knew you would. That's why I insisted on being here when you came."

"Margie?" Harold stammered.

"Yes, Harold, it's me. And say hello to your son. You didn't know I was pregnant when the bomb fell, did you? We both waited for you. Now we can all board the train together."

"I can't believe it…" Then he recollected himself. "But it will be the down train… I… I haven't… I mean, I didn't…"

"No one ever does, Harold," smiled Margie. "That's the reason for the test."

The singing of the lines grew to a rumble, then a rushing, hissing roar. The platform lights brightened suddenly, bathing the whole scene in an electric glow as a great black steam locomotive thundered into the station drawing four liveried carriages behind it, seeming to shake the very fabric of the building in which they stood.

The platform door of the waiting room opened and the ticket clerk came in.

"Up train!" he announced. "All aboard, please. Up train!"

Harold's eyes filled with tears.

The Legend of Sleepy Hollow

by Washington Irving

A pleasing land of drowsy head it was,
Of dreams that wave before the half-shut eye;
And of gay castles in the clouds that pass,
Forever flushing round a summer sky.
Castle of Indolence

IN THE BOSOM of one of those spacious coves which indent the eastern shore of the Hudson, at that broad expansion of the river denominated by the ancient Dutch navigators the Tappan Zee, and where they always prudently shortened sail and implored the protection of St. Nicholas when they crossed, there lies a small market town or rural port, which by some is called Greensburgh, but which is more generally and properly known by the name of Tarry Town. This name was given, we are told, in former days, by the good housewives of the adjacent country, from the inveterate propensity of their husbands to linger about the village tavern on market days. Be that as it may, I do not vouch for the fact, but merely advert to it, for the sake of being precise and authentic. Not far from this village, perhaps about two miles, there is a little valley or rather lap of land among high hills, which is one of the quietest places in the whole world. A small brook glides through it, with just murmur enough to lull one to repose; and the occasional whistle of a quail or tapping of a woodpecker is almost the only sound that ever breaks in upon the uniform tranquility.

I recollect that, when a stripling, my first exploit in squirrel-shooting was in a grove of tall walnut-trees that shades one side of the valley. I had wandered into it at noontime, when all nature is peculiarly quiet, and was startled by the roar of my own gun, as it broke the Sabbath stillness around and was prolonged and reverberated by the angry echoes. If ever I should wish for a retreat whither I might steal from the world and its distractions, and dream quietly away the remnant of a troubled life, I know of none more promising than this little valley.

From the listless repose of the place, and the peculiar character of its inhabitants, who are descendants from the original Dutch settlers, this sequestered glen has long been known by the name of *Sleepy Hollow*, and its rustic lads are called the Sleepy Hollow Boys throughout all the neighboring country. A drowsy, dreamy influence seems to hang over the land, and to pervade the very atmosphere. Some say that the place was bewitched by a High German doctor, during the early days of the settlement; others, that an old Indian chief, the prophet or wizard of his tribe, held his powwows there before the country was discovered by Master Hendrick Hudson. Certain it is, the place still continues under the sway of some witching power, that holds a spell over the minds of the good people, causing them to walk in a continual reverie. They are given to all kinds of marvelous beliefs, are subject to trances and visions, and frequently see strange sights, and hear music and voices in the air. The whole neighborhood abounds with local tales, haunted spots, and twilight superstitions; stars shoot and meteors glare oftener across the valley than in any other part of the country, and the nightmare, with her whole ninefold, seems to make it the favorite scene of her gambols.

The dominant spirit, however, that haunts this enchanted region, and seems to be commander-in-chief of all the powers of the air, is the apparition of a figure on horseback, without a head. It is said by some to be the ghost of a Hessian trooper, whose head had been carried away by a cannon-ball, in some nameless battle during the Revolutionary War, and who is ever and anon seen by the country folk hurrying along in the gloom of night, as if on the wings of the wind. His haunts are not confined to the valley, but extend at times to the adjacent roads, and especially to the vicinity of a church at no great distance. Indeed, certain of the most authentic historians of those parts, who have been careful in collecting and collating the floating facts concerning this specter, allege that the body of the trooper having been buried in the churchyard, the ghost rides forth to the scene of battle in nightly quest of his head, and that the rushing speed with which he sometimes passes along the Hollow, like a midnight blast, is owing to his being belated, and in a hurry to get back to the churchyard before daybreak.

Such is the general purport of this legendary superstition, which has furnished materials for many a wild story in that region of shadows; and the specter is known at all the country firesides, by the name of the Headless Horseman of Sleepy Hollow.

It is remarkable that the visionary propensity I have mentioned is not confined to the native inhabitants of the valley, but is unconsciously imbibed by everyone who resides there for a time. However wide awake they may have been before they entered that sleepy region, they are sure, in a little time, to inhale the witching influence of the air, and begin to grow imaginative, to dream dreams, and see apparitions.

I mention this peaceful spot with all possible laud, for it is in such little retired Dutch valleys, found here and there embosomed in the great State of New York, that population, manners, and customs remain fixed, while the great torrent of migration and improvement, which is making such incessant changes in other parts of this restless country, sweeps by them unobserved. They are like those little nooks of still water, which border a rapid stream, where we may see the straw and bubble riding quietly at anchor, or slowly revolving in their mimic harbor, undisturbed by the rush of the passing current. Though many years have elapsed since I trod the drowsy shades of Sleepy Hollow, yet I question whether I should not still find the same trees and the same families vegetating in its sheltered bosom.

In this by-place of nature there abode, in a remote period of American history, that is to say, some thirty years since, a worthy wight of the name of Ichabod Crane, who sojourned, or, as he expressed it, "tarried," in Sleepy Hollow, for the purpose of instructing the children of the vicinity. He was a native of Connecticut, a State which supplies the Union with pioneers for the mind as well as for the forest, and sends forth yearly its legions of frontier woodmen and country schoolmasters. The cognomen of Crane was not inapplicable to his person. He was tall, but exceedingly lank, with narrow shoulders, long arms and legs, hands that dangled a mile out of his sleeves, feet that might have served for shovels, and his whole frame most loosely hung together. His head was small, and flat at top, with huge ears, large green glassy eyes, and a long snipe nose, so that it looked like a weather-cock perched upon his spindle neck to tell which way the wind blew. To see him striding along the profile of a hill on a windy day, with his clothes bagging and fluttering about him, one might have mistaken him for the genius of famine descending upon the earth, or some scarecrow eloped from a cornfield.

His schoolhouse was a low building of one large room, rudely constructed of logs; the windows partly glazed, and partly patched with leaves of old copybooks. It was most ingeniously secured at vacant hours, by a withe twisted in the handle of the door, and stakes set against the window shutters; so that though a thief might get in with perfect ease, he would find some embarrassment in getting out – an idea most probably borrowed by the architect, Yost Van Houten, from the mystery of an eelpot. The schoolhouse stood in a rather lonely but pleasant situation, just at the foot of a woody hill, with a brook running close by, and a formidable birch-tree growing at one end of it. From hence the low murmur of his pupils' voices, conning over their lessons, might be heard in a drowsy summer's day, like the hum of a beehive; interrupted now and then by the authoritative voice of the master, in the tone of menace or command, or, peradventure, by the appalling sound of the birch, as he urged some tardy loiterer along the flowery path of knowledge. Truth to say, he was a conscientious man, and ever bore in mind the golden maxim, "Spare the rod and spoil the child." Ichabod Crane's scholars certainly were not spoiled.

I would not have it imagined, however, that he was one of those cruel potentates of the school who joy in the smart of their subjects; on the contrary, he administered justice with discrimination rather than severity; taking the burden off the backs of the weak, and laying it on those of the strong. Your mere puny stripling, that winced at the least flourish of the rod, was passed by with indulgence; but the claims of justice were satisfied by inflicting a double portion on some little tough wrong-headed, broad-skirted Dutch urchin, who sulked and swelled and grew dogged and sullen beneath the birch. All this he called "doing his duty by their parents;" and he never inflicted a chastisement without following it by the assurance, so consolatory to the smarting urchin, that "he would remember it and thank him for it the longest day he had to live."

When school hours were over, he was even the companion and playmate of the larger boys; and on holiday afternoons would convoy some of the smaller ones home, who happened to have pretty sisters, or good housewives for mothers, noted for the comforts of the cupboard. Indeed, it behooved him to keep on good terms with his pupils. The revenue arising from his school was small, and would have been scarcely sufficient to furnish him with daily bread, for he was a huge feeder, and, though lank, had the dilating powers of an anaconda; but to help out his maintenance, he was, according to country custom in those parts, boarded and lodged at the houses of the farmers whose children he instructed. With these he lived successively a week at a time, thus going the rounds of the neighborhood, with all his worldly effects tied up in a cotton handkerchief.

That all this might not be too onerous on the purses of his rustic patrons, who are apt to consider the costs of schooling a grievous burden, and schoolmasters as mere drones, he had various ways of rendering himself both useful and agreeable. He assisted the farmers occasionally in the lighter labors of their farms, helped to make hay, mended the fences, took the horses to water, drove the cows from pasture, and cut wood for the winter fire. He laid aside, too, all the dominant dignity and absolute sway with which he lorded it in his little empire, the school, and became wonderfully gentle and ingratiating. He found favor in the eyes of the mothers by petting the children, particularly the youngest; and like the lion bold, which whilom so magnanimously the lamb did hold, he would sit with a child on one knee, and rock a cradle with his foot for whole hours together.

In addition to his other vocations, he was the singing-master of the neighborhood, and picked up many bright shillings by instructing the young folks in psalmody. It was a matter of no little vanity to him on Sundays, to take his station in front of the church gallery, with a band of chosen singers; where, in his own mind, he completely carried away the palm from the parson. Certain it is, his voice resounded far above all the rest of the congregation; and there are peculiar quavers still to be heard in that church, and which may even be heard half a mile off, quite to the opposite side of the millpond, on a still Sunday morning, which are said to be legitimately descended from the nose of Ichabod Crane. Thus, by divers little makeshifts, in that ingenious way which is commonly denominated "by hook and by crook," the worthy pedagogue got on tolerably enough, and was thought, by all who understood nothing of the labor of headwork, to have a wonderfully easy life of it.

The schoolmaster is generally a man of some importance in the female circle of a rural neighborhood; being considered a kind of idle, gentlemanlike personage, of vastly superior taste and accomplishments to the rough country swains, and, indeed, inferior in learning only to the parson. His appearance, therefore, is apt to occasion some little stir at the tea-table of a farmhouse, and the addition of a supernumerary dish of cakes or sweetmeats, or, peradventure, the parade of a silver teapot. Our man of letters, therefore, was peculiarly happy in the smiles of all the country damsels. How he would figure among them in the churchyard, between services on Sundays; gathering grapes for them from the wild vines that overran the surrounding trees; reciting for their amusement all the epitaphs on the tombstones; or sauntering, with a whole bevy of them, along the banks of the adjacent millpond; while the more bashful country bumpkins hung sheepishly back, envying his superior elegance and address.

From his half-itinerant life, also, he was a kind of traveling gazette, carrying the whole budget of local gossip from house to house, so that his appearance was always greeted with satisfaction. He was, moreover, esteemed by the women as a man of great erudition, for he had read several books quite through, and was a perfect master of Cotton Mather's *History of New England Witchcraft*, in which, by the way, he most firmly and potently believed.

He was, in fact, an odd mixture of small shrewdness and simple credulity. His appetite for the marvelous, and his powers of digesting it, were equally extraordinary; and both had been increased by his residence in this spell-bound region. No tale was too gross or monstrous for his capacious swallow. It was often his delight, after his school was dismissed in the afternoon, to stretch himself on the rich bed of clover bordering the little brook that whimpered by his schoolhouse, and there con over old Mather's direful tales, until the gathering dusk of evening made the printed page a mere mist before his eyes. Then, as he wended his way by swamp and stream and awful woodland, to the farmhouse where he happened to be quartered, every sound of nature, at that witching hour, fluttered his excited imagination – the moan of the whip-poor-will from the hillside, the boding cry of the tree toad, that harbinger of storm, the dreary hooting of the screech owl, or the sudden rustling in the thicket of birds frightened from their roost. The fireflies, too, which sparkled most vividly in the darkest places, now and then startled him, as one of uncommon brightness would stream across his path; and if, by chance, a huge blockhead of a beetle came winging his blundering flight against him, the poor varlet was ready to give up the ghost, with the idea that he was struck with a witch's token. His only resource on such occasions, either to drown thought or drive away evil spirits, was to sing psalm tunes and the good people of Sleepy Hollow, as they sat by their doors of an evening, were often filled with awe at hearing his nasal melody, "in linked sweetness long drawn out," floating from the distant hill, or along the dusky road.

Another of his sources of fearful pleasure was to pass long winter evenings with the old Dutch wives, as they sat spinning by the fire, with a row of apples roasting and spluttering along the hearth, and listen to their marvelous tales of ghosts and goblins, and haunted fields, and haunted brooks, and haunted bridges, and haunted houses, and particularly of the headless horseman, or Galloping Hessian of the Hollow, as they sometimes called him. He would delight them equally by his anecdotes of witchcraft, and of the direful omens and portentous sights and sounds in the air, which prevailed in the earlier times of Connecticut; and would frighten them woefully with speculations upon comets and shooting stars; and with the alarming fact that the world did absolutely turn round, and that they were half the time topsy-turvy!

But if there was a pleasure in all this, while snugly cuddling in the chimney corner of a chamber that was all of a ruddy glow from the crackling wood fire, and where, of course, no specter dared to show its face, it was dearly purchased by the terrors of his subsequent walk homewards. What fearful shapes and shadows beset his path, amidst the dim and ghastly glare of a snowy night! With what wistful look did he eye every trembling ray of light streaming across the waste fields from some distant window! How often was he appalled by some shrub covered with snow, which, like a sheeted specter, beset his very path! How often did he shrink with curdling awe at the sound of his own steps on the frosty crust beneath his feet; and dread to look over his shoulder, lest he should behold some uncouth being tramping close behind him! And how often was he thrown into complete dismay by some rushing blast, howling among the trees, in the idea that it was the Galloping Hessian on one of his nightly scourings!

All these, however, were mere terrors of the night, phantoms of the mind that walk in darkness; and though he had seen many specters in his time, and been more than once beset by Satan in divers shapes, in his lonely perambulations, yet daylight put an end to all these evils; and he would have passed a pleasant life of it, in despite of the Devil and all his works, if his path had not been crossed by a being that causes more perplexity to mortal man than ghosts, goblins, and the whole race of witches put together, and that was – a woman.

Among the musical disciples who assembled, one evening in each week, to receive his instructions in psalmody, was Katrina Van Tassel, the daughter and only child of a substantial Dutch farmer. She was a blooming lass of fresh eighteen; plump as a partridge; ripe and melting and rosy-cheeked as one of her father's peaches, and universally famed, not merely for her beauty, but her vast expectations. She was withal a little of a coquette, as might be perceived even in her dress, which was a mixture of ancient and modern fashions, as most suited to set off her charms. She wore the ornaments of pure yellow gold, which her great-great-grandmother had brought over from Saardam; the tempting stomacher of the olden time, and withal a provokingly short petticoat, to display the prettiest foot and ankle in the country round.

Ichabod Crane had a soft and foolish heart towards the sex; and it is not to be wondered at that so tempting a morsel soon found favor in his eyes, more especially after he had visited her in her paternal mansion. Old Baltus Van Tassel was a perfect picture of a thriving, contented, liberal-hearted farmer. He seldom, it is true, sent either his eyes or his thoughts beyond the boundaries of his own farm; but within those everything was snug, happy and well-conditioned. He was satisfied with his wealth, but not proud of it; and piqued himself upon the hearty abundance, rather than the style in which he lived. His stronghold was situated on the banks of the Hudson, in one of those green, sheltered, fertile nooks in which the Dutch farmers are so fond of nestling. A great elm tree spread its broad branches over it, at the foot of which bubbled up a spring of the softest and sweetest water, in a little well formed of a barrel; and then stole sparkling away through the grass, to a neighboring brook, that babbled along among alders and dwarf willows. Hard by the farmhouse was a vast barn, that might have served for a church; every window and crevice of which seemed bursting forth with the treasures of the farm; the flail was busily resounding within it from morning to night; swallows and martins skimmed twittering about the eaves; and rows of pigeons, some with one eye turned up, as if watching the weather, some with their heads under their wings or buried in their bosoms, and others swelling, and cooing, and bowing about their dames, were enjoying the sunshine on the roof. Sleek unwieldy porkers were grunting in the repose and abundance of their pens, from whence sallied forth, now and then, troops of sucking pigs, as if to snuff the air. A stately squadron of snowy geese were riding in an adjoining pond, convoying whole fleets of ducks; regiments of turkeys were gobbling through the farmyard, and Guinea fowls fretting about it, like ill-tempered housewives, with their peevish, discontented cry. Before the barn door strutted the gallant cock, that pattern of a husband, a warrior and a fine gentleman, clapping his burnished wings and crowing in the pride and gladness of his heart –sometimes tearing up the earth with his feet, and then generously calling his ever-hungry family of wives and children to enjoy the rich morsel which he had discovered.

The pedagogue's mouth watered as he looked upon this sumptuous promise of luxurious winter fare. In his devouring mind's eye, he pictured to himself every roasting-pig running about with a pudding in his belly, and an apple in his mouth; the pigeons were snugly put to bed in a comfortable pie, and tucked in with a coverlet of crust; the geese were swimming in their own gravy; and the ducks pairing cozily in dishes, like snug married couples, with a decent competency of onion sauce. In the porkers he saw carved out the future sleek side of bacon, and juicy relishing ham; not a turkey but he beheld daintily trussed up, with its gizzard under its wing, and, peradventure, a necklace of savory sausages; and even bright chanticleer himself lay sprawling on his back, in a side dish, with uplifted claws, as if craving that quarter which his chivalrous spirit disdained to ask while living.

As the enraptured Ichabod fancied all this, and as he rolled his great green eyes over the fat meadow lands, the rich fields of wheat, of rye, of buckwheat, and Indian corn, and the orchards burdened with ruddy fruit, which surrounded the warm tenement of Van Tassel, his heart yearned after the damsel who was to inherit these domains, and his imagination expanded with the idea, how they might be readily turned into cash, and the money invested in immense tracts of wild land, and shingle palaces in the wilderness. Nay, his busy fancy already realized his hopes, and presented to him the blooming Katrina, with a whole family of children, mounted on the top of a wagon loaded with household trumpery, with pots and kettles dangling beneath; and he beheld himself bestriding a pacing mare, with a colt at her heels, setting out for Kentucky, Tennessee – or the Lord knows where!

When he entered the house, the conquest of his heart was complete. It was one of those spacious farmhouses, with high-ridged but lowly sloping roofs, built in the style handed down from the first Dutch settlers; the low projecting eaves forming a piazza along the front, capable of being closed up in bad weather. Under this were hung flails, harness, various utensils of husbandry, and nets for fishing in the neighboring river. Benches were built along the sides for summer use; and a great spinning-wheel at one end, and a churn at the other, showed the various uses to which this important porch might be devoted. From this piazza the wondering Ichabod entered the hall, which formed the center of the mansion, and the place of usual residence. Here rows of resplendent pewter, ranged on a long dresser, dazzled his eyes. In one corner stood a huge bag of wool, ready to be spun; in another, a quantity of linsey-woolsey just from the loom; ears of Indian corn, and strings of dried apples and peaches, hung in gay festoons along the walls, mingled with the gaud of red peppers; and a door left ajar gave him a peep into the best parlor, where the claw-footed chairs and dark mahogany tables shone like mirrors; andirons, with their accompanying shovel and tongs, glistened from their covert of asparagus tops; mock-oranges and conch shells decorated the mantelpiece; strings of various-colored birds' eggs were suspended above it; a great ostrich egg was hung from the center of the room, and a corner cupboard, knowingly left open, displayed immense treasures of old silver and well-mended china.

From the moment Ichabod laid his eyes upon these regions of delight, the peace of his mind was at an end, and his only study was how to gain the affections of the peerless daughter of Van Tassel. In this enterprise, however, he had more real difficulties than generally fell to the lot of a knight-errant of yore, who seldom had anything but giants, enchanters, fiery dragons, and such like easily conquered adversaries, to contend with and had to make his way merely through gates of iron and brass, and walls of adamant to the castle keep, where the lady of his heart was confined; all which he achieved as easily as a man would carve his way to the center of a Christmas pie; and then the lady gave him her hand as a matter of course. Ichabod, on the contrary, had to win his way to the heart of a country coquette, beset with a labyrinth of whims and caprices, which were forever presenting new difficulties and impediments; and he had to encounter a host of fearful adversaries of real flesh and blood, the numerous rustic admirers, who beset every portal to her heart, keeping a watchful and angry eye upon each other, but ready to fly out in the common cause against any new competitor.

Among these, the most formidable was a burly, roaring, roystering blade, of the name of Abraham, or, according to the Dutch abbreviation, Brom Van Brunt, the hero of the country round, which rang with his feats of strength and hardihood. He was broad-shouldered and double-jointed, with short curly black hair, and a bluff but not unpleasant countenance, having a mingled air of fun and arrogance. From his Herculean frame and great powers of limb he had received the nickname of *Brom Bones*, by which he was universally known. He was famed for great knowledge and skill in horsemanship, being as dexterous on horseback as a Tartar. He was foremost at all races and cock fights; and, with the ascendancy which bodily strength always acquires in rustic life, was the umpire in all disputes, setting his hat on one side, and giving his decisions with an air and tone that admitted of no gainsay or appeal. He was always ready for either a fight or a frolic; but had more mischief than ill-will in his composition; and with all his over-bearing roughness, there was a strong dash of waggish good humor at bottom. He had three or four boon companions, who regarded him as their model, and at the head of whom he scoured the country, attending every scene of feud or merriment for miles round. In cold weather he was distinguished by a fur cap, surmounted with a flaunting fox's tail; and when the folks at a country gathering descried this well-known crest at a distance, whisking about among a squad of hard riders, they always stood by for a squall. Sometimes his crew would be heard dashing along past the farmhouses at midnight, with whoop and halloo, like a troop of Don Cossacks; and the old dames, startled out of their sleep, would listen for a moment till the hurry-scurry had clattered by, and then exclaim, "Ay, there goes Brom Bones and his gang!" The neighbors looked upon him with a mixture of awe, admiration, and good-will; and, when any madcap prank or rustic brawl occurred in the vicinity, always shook their heads, and warranted Brom Bones was at the bottom of it.

This rantipole hero had for some time singled out the blooming Katrina for the object of his uncouth gallantries, and though his amorous toyings were something like the gentle caresses and endearments of a bear, yet it was whispered that she did not altogether discourage his hopes. Certain it is, his advances were signals for rival candidates to retire, who felt no inclination to cross a lion in his amours; insomuch, that when his horse was seen tied to Van Tassel's paling, on a Sunday night, a sure sign that his master was courting, or, as it is termed, "sparking," within, all other suitors passed by in despair, and carried the war into other quarters.

Such was the formidable rival with whom Ichabod Crane had to contend, and, considering all things, a stouter man than he would have shrunk from the competition, and a wiser man would have despaired. He had, however, a happy mixture of pliability and perseverance in his nature; he was in form and spirit like a supple-jack – yielding, but tough; though he bent, he never broke; and though he bowed beneath the slightest pressure, yet, the moment it was away – jerk! – he was as erect, and carried his head as high as ever.

To have taken the field openly against his rival would have been madness; for he was not a man to be thwarted in his amours, any more than that stormy lover, Achilles. Ichabod, therefore, made his advances in a quiet and gently insinuating manner. Under cover of his character of singing-master, he made frequent visits at the farmhouse; not that he had anything to apprehend from the meddlesome interference of parents, which is so often a stumbling-block in the path of lovers. Balt Van Tassel was an easy indulgent soul; he loved his daughter better even than his pipe, and, like a reasonable man and an excellent father, let her have her way in everything. His notable little wife, too, had enough to do to attend to her housekeeping and manage her poultry; for, as she sagely observed, ducks and geese are foolish things, and must be looked after, but girls can take care of themselves. Thus, while the busy dame bustled about the house, or plied her spinning-wheel at one end of the piazza, honest Balt would sit smoking his evening pipe at the other, watching the achievements of a little wooden warrior, who, armed with a sword in each hand, was most valiantly fighting the wind on the pinnacle of the barn. In the mean time, Ichabod would carry on his suit with the daughter by the side of the spring under the great elm, or sauntering along in the twilight, that hour so favorable to the lover's eloquence.

I profess not to know how women's hearts are wooed and won. To me they have always been matters of riddle and admiration. Some seem to have but one vulnerable point, or door of access; while others have a thousand avenues, and may be captured in a thousand different ways. It is a great triumph of skill to gain the former, but a still greater proof of generalship to maintain possession of the latter, for man must battle for his fortress at every door and window. He who wins a thousand common hearts is therefore entitled to some renown; but he who keeps undisputed sway over the heart of a coquette is indeed a hero. Certain it is, this was not the case with the redoubtable Brom Bones; and from the moment Ichabod Crane made his advances, the interests of the former evidently declined: his horse was no longer seen tied to the palings on Sunday nights, and a deadly feud gradually arose between him and the preceptor of Sleepy Hollow.

Brom, who had a degree of rough chivalry in his nature, would fain have carried matters to open warfare and have settled their pretensions to the lady, according to the mode of those most concise and simple reasoners, the knights-errant of yore – by single combat; but Ichabod was too conscious of the superior might of his adversary to enter the lists against him; he had overheard a boast of Bones, that he would "double the schoolmaster up, and lay him on a shelf of his own schoolhouse;" and he was too wary to give him an opportunity. There was something extremely provoking in this obstinately pacific system; it left Brom no alternative but to draw upon the funds of rustic waggery in his disposition, and to play off boorish practical jokes upon his rival. Ichabod became the object of whimsical persecution to Bones and his gang of rough riders. They harried his hitherto peaceful domains; smoked out his singing school by stopping up the chimney; broke into the schoolhouse at night, in spite of its formidable fastenings of withe and window stakes, and turned everything topsy-turvy, so that the poor schoolmaster began to think all the witches in the country held their meetings there. But what was still more annoying, Brom took all opportunities of turning him into ridicule in presence of his mistress, and had a scoundrel dog whom he taught to whine in the most ludicrous manner, and introduced as a rival of Ichabod's, to instruct her in psalmody.

In this way matters went on for some time, without producing any material effect on the relative situations of the contending powers. On a fine autumnal afternoon, Ichabod, in pensive mood, sat enthroned on the lofty stool from whence he usually watched all the concerns of his little literary realm. In his hand he swayed a ferule, that scepter of despotic power; the birch of justice reposed on three nails behind the throne, a constant terror to evil doers, while on the desk before him might be seen sundry contraband articles and prohibited weapons, detected upon the persons of idle urchins, such as half-munched apples, popguns, whirligigs, fly-cages, and whole legions of rampant little paper gamecocks. Apparently there had been some appalling act of justice recently inflicted, for his scholars were all busily intent upon their books, or slyly whispering behind them with one eye kept upon the master; and a kind of buzzing stillness reigned throughout the schoolroom. It was suddenly interrupted by the appearance of a negro in tow-cloth jacket and trowsers, a round-crowned fragment of a hat, like the cap of Mercury, and mounted on the back of a ragged, wild, half-broken colt, which he managed with a rope by way of halter. He came clattering up to the school door with an invitation to Ichabod to attend a merry-making or "quilting frolic," to be held that evening at Mynheer Van Tassel's; and having delivered his message with that air of importance, and effort at fine language, which a negro is apt to display on petty embassies of the kind, he dashed over the brook, and was seen scampering away up the hollow, full of the importance and hurry of his mission.

All was now bustle and hubbub in the late quiet schoolroom. The scholars were hurried through their lessons without stopping at trifles; those who were nimble skipped over half with impunity, and those who were tardy had a smart application now and then in the rear, to quicken their speed or help them over a tall word. Books were flung aside without being put away on the shelves, inkstands were overturned, benches thrown down, and the whole school was turned loose an hour before the usual time, bursting forth like a legion of young imps, yelping and racketing about the green in joy at their early emancipation.

The gallant Ichabod now spent at least an extra half hour at his toilet, brushing and furbishing up his best, and indeed only suit of rusty black, and arranging his locks by a bit of broken looking-glass that hung up in the schoolhouse. That he might make his appearance before his mistress in the true style of a cavalier, he borrowed a horse from the farmer with whom he was domiciliated, a choleric old Dutchman of the name of Hans Van Ripper, and, thus gallantly mounted, issued forth like a knight-errant in quest of adventures. But it is meet I should, in the true spirit of romantic story, give some account of the looks and equipments of my hero and his steed. The animal he bestrode was a broken-down plow-horse, that had outlived almost everything but its viciousness. He was gaunt and shagged, with a ewe neck, and a head like a hammer; his rusty mane and tail were tangled and knotted with burs; one eye had lost its pupil, and was glaring and spectral, but the other had the gleam of a genuine devil in it. Still he must have had fire and mettle in his day, if we may judge from the name he bore of Gunpowder. He had, in fact, been a favorite steed of his master's, the choleric Van Ripper, who was a furious rider, and had infused, very probably, some of his own spirit into the animal; for, old and broken-down as he looked, there was more of the lurking devil in him than in any young filly in the country.

Ichabod was a suitable figure for such a steed. He rode with short stirrups, which brought his knees nearly up to the pommel of the saddle; his sharp elbows stuck out like grasshoppers'; he carried his whip perpendicularly in his hand, like a scepter, and as his horse jogged on, the motion of his arms was not unlike the flapping of a pair of wings. A small wool hat rested on the top of his nose, for so his scanty strip of forehead might be called, and the skirts of his black coat fluttered out almost to the horse's tail. Such was the appearance of Ichabod and his steed as they shambled out of the gate of Hans Van Ripper, and it was altogether such an apparition as is seldom to be met with in broad daylight.

It was, as I have said, a fine autumnal day; the sky was clear and serene, and nature wore that rich and golden livery which we always associate with the idea of abundance. The forests had put on their sober brown and yellow, while some trees of the tenderer kind had been nipped by the frosts into brilliant dyes of orange, purple, and scarlet. Streaming files of wild ducks began to make their appearance high in the air; the bark of the squirrel might be heard from the groves of beech and hickory-nuts, and the pensive whistle of the quail at intervals from the neighboring stubble field.

The small birds were taking their farewell banquets. In the fullness of their revelry, they fluttered, chirping and frolicking from bush to bush, and tree to tree, capricious from the very profusion and variety around them. There was the honest cock robin, the favorite game of stripling sportsmen, with its loud querulous note; and the twittering blackbirds flying in sable clouds; and the golden-winged woodpecker with his crimson crest, his broad black gorget, and splendid plumage; and the cedar bird, with its red-tipt wings and yellow-tipt tail and its little monteiro cap of feathers; and the blue jay, that noisy coxcomb, in his gay light blue coat and white underclothes, screaming and chattering, nodding and bobbing and bowing, and pretending to be on good terms with every songster of the grove.

As Ichabod jogged slowly on his way, his eye, ever open to every symptom of culinary abundance, ranged with delight over the treasures of jolly autumn. On all sides he beheld vast stores of apples; some hanging in oppressive opulence on the trees; some gathered into baskets and barrels for the market; others heaped up in rich piles for the cider-press. Farther on he beheld great fields of Indian corn, with its golden ears peeping from their leafy coverts, and holding out the promise of cakes and hasty-pudding; and the yellow pumpkins lying beneath them, turning up their fair round bellies to the sun, and giving ample prospects of the most luxurious of pies; and anon he passed the fragrant buckwheat fields breathing the odor of the beehive, and as he beheld them, soft anticipations stole over his mind of dainty slapjacks, well buttered, and garnished with honey or treacle, by the delicate little dimpled hand of Katrina Van Tassel.

Thus feeding his mind with many sweet thoughts and "sugared suppositions," he journeyed along the sides of a range of hills which look out upon some of the goodliest scenes of the mighty Hudson. The sun gradually wheeled his broad disk down in the west. The wide bosom of the Tappan Zee lay motionless and glassy, excepting that here and there a gentle undulation waved and prolonged the blue shadow of the distant mountain. A few amber clouds floated in the sky, without a breath of air to move them. The horizon was of a fine golden tint, changing gradually into a pure apple green, and from that into the deep blue of the mid-heaven. A slanting ray lingered on the woody crests of the precipices that overhung some parts of the river, giving greater depth to the dark gray and purple of their rocky sides. A sloop was loitering in the distance, dropping slowly down with the tide, her sail hanging uselessly against the mast; and as the reflection of the sky gleamed along the still water, it seemed as if the vessel was suspended in the air.

It was toward evening that Ichabod arrived at the castle of the Heer Van Tassel, which he found thronged with the pride and flower of the adjacent country. Old farmers, a spare leathern-faced race, in homespun coats and breeches, blue stockings, huge shoes, and magnificent pewter buckles. Their brisk, withered little dames, in close-crimped caps, long-waisted short gowns, homespun petticoats, with scissors and pincushions, and gay calico pockets hanging on the outside. Buxom lasses, almost as antiquated as their mothers, excepting where a straw hat, a fine ribbon, or perhaps a white frock, gave symptoms of city innovation. The sons, in short square-skirted coats, with rows of stupendous brass buttons, and their hair generally queued in the fashion of the times, especially if they could procure an eel-skin for the purpose, it being esteemed throughout the country as a potent nourisher and strengthener of the hair.

Brom Bones, however, was the hero of the scene, having come to the gathering on his favorite steed Daredevil, a creature, like himself, full of mettle and mischief, and which no one but himself could manage. He was, in fact, noted for preferring vicious animals, given to all kinds of tricks which kept the rider in constant risk of his neck, for he held a tractable, well-broken horse as unworthy of a lad of spirit.

Fain would I pause to dwell upon the world of charms that burst upon the enraptured gaze of my hero, as he entered the state parlor of Van Tassel's mansion. Not those of the bevy of buxom lasses, with their luxurious display of red and white; but the ample charms of a genuine Dutch country tea-table, in the sumptuous time of autumn. Such heaped up platters of cakes of various and almost indescribable kinds, known only to experienced Dutch housewives! There was the doughty doughnut, the tender oly koek, and the crisp and crumbling cruller; sweet cakes and short cakes, ginger cakes and honey cakes, and the whole family of cakes. And then there were apple pies, and peach pies, and pumpkin pies; besides slices of ham and smoked beef; and moreover delectable dishes of preserved plums, and peaches, and pears, and quinces; not to mention broiled shad and roasted chickens; together with bowls of milk and cream, all mingled higgledy-piggledy, pretty much as I have enumerated them, with the motherly teapot sending up its clouds of vapor from the midst – Heaven bless the mark! I want breath and time to discuss this banquet as it deserves, and am too eager to get on with my story. Happily, Ichabod Crane was not in so great a hurry as his historian, but did ample justice to every dainty.

He was a kind and thankful creature, whose heart dilated in proportion as his skin was filled with good cheer, and whose spirits rose with eating, as some men's do with drink. He could not help, too, rolling his large eyes round him as he ate, and chuckling with the possibility that he might one day be lord of all this scene of almost unimaginable luxury and splendor. Then, he thought, how soon he'd turn his back upon the old schoolhouse; snap his fingers in the face of Hans Van Ripper, and every other niggardly patron, and kick any itinerant pedagogue out of doors that should dare to call him comrade!

Old Baltus Van Tassel moved about among his guests with a face dilated with content and good humor, round and jolly as the harvest moon. His hospitable attentions were brief, but expressive, being confined to a shake of the hand, a slap on the shoulder, a loud laugh, and a pressing invitation to "fall to, and help themselves."

And now the sound of the music from the common room, or hall, summoned to the dance. The musician was an old gray-headed negro, who had been the itinerant orchestra of the neighborhood for more than half a century. His instrument was as old and battered as himself. The greater part of the time he scraped on two or three strings, accompanying every movement of the bow with a motion of the head; bowing almost to the ground, and stamping with his foot whenever a fresh couple were to start.

Ichabod prided himself upon his dancing as much as upon his vocal powers. Not a limb, not a fiber about him was idle; and to have seen his loosely hung frame in full motion, and clattering about the room, you would have thought St. Vitus himself, that blessed patron of the dance, was figuring before you in person. He was the admiration of all the negroes; who, having gathered, of all ages and sizes, from the farm and the neighborhood, stood forming a pyramid of shining black faces at every door and window, gazing with delight at the scene, rolling their white eyeballs, and showing grinning rows of ivory from ear to ear. How could the flogger of urchins be otherwise than animated and joyous? The lady of his heart was his partner in the dance, and smiling graciously in reply to all his amorous oglings; while Brom Bones, sorely smitten with love and jealousy, sat brooding by himself in one corner.

When the dance was at an end, Ichabod was attracted to a knot of the sager folks, who, with Old Van Tassel, sat smoking at one end of the piazza, gossiping over former times, and drawing out long stories about the war.

This neighborhood, at the time of which I am speaking, was one of those highly favored places which abound with chronicle and great men. The British and American line had run near it during the war; it had, therefore, been the scene of marauding and infested with refugees, cowboys, and all kinds of border chivalry. Just sufficient time had elapsed to enable each storyteller to dress up his tale with a little becoming fiction, and, in the indistinctness of his recollection, to make himself the hero of every exploit.

There was the story of Doffue Martling, a large blue-bearded Dutchman, who had nearly taken a British frigate with an old iron nine-pounder from a mud breastwork, only that his gun burst at the sixth discharge. And there was an old gentleman who shall be nameless, being too rich a mynheer to be lightly mentioned, who, in the battle of White Plains, being an excellent master of defence, parried a musket-ball with a small sword, insomuch that he absolutely felt it whiz round the blade, and glance off at the hilt; in proof of which he was ready at any time to show the sword, with the hilt a little bent. There were several more that had been equally great in the field, not one of whom but was persuaded that he had a considerable hand in bringing the war to a happy termination.

But all these were nothing to the tales of ghosts and apparitions that succeeded. The neighborhood is rich in legendary treasures of the kind. Local tales and superstitions thrive best in these sheltered, long-settled retreats; but are trampled under foot by the shifting throng that forms the population of most of our country places. Besides, there is no encouragement for ghosts in most of our villages, for they have scarcely had time to finish their first nap and turn themselves in their graves, before their surviving friends have traveled away from the neighborhood; so that when they turn out at night to walk their rounds, they have no acquaintance left to call upon. This is perhaps the reason why we so seldom hear of ghosts except in our long-established Dutch communities.

The immediate cause, however, of the prevalence of supernatural stories in these parts, was doubtless owing to the vicinity of Sleepy Hollow. There was a contagion in the very air that blew from that haunted region; it breathed forth an atmosphere of dreams and fancies infecting all the land. Several of the Sleepy Hollow people were present at Van Tassel's, and, as usual, were doling out their wild and wonderful legends. Many dismal tales were told about funeral trains, and mourning cries and wailings heard and seen about the great tree where the unfortunate Major André was taken, and which stood in the neighborhood. Some mention was made also of the woman in white, that haunted the dark glen at Raven Rock, and was often heard to shriek on winter nights before a storm, having perished there in the snow. The chief part of the stories, however, turned upon the favorite specter of Sleepy Hollow, the Headless Horseman, who had been heard several times of late, patrolling the country; and, it was said, tethered his horse nightly among the graves in the churchyard.

The sequestered situation of this church seems always to have made it a favorite haunt of troubled spirits. It stands on a knoll, surrounded by locust-trees and lofty elms, from among which its decent, whitewashed walls shine modestly forth, like Christian purity beaming through the shades of retirement. A gentle slope descends from it to a silver sheet of water, bordered by high trees, between which, peeps may be caught at the blue hills of the Hudson. To look upon its grass-grown yard, where the sunbeams seem to sleep so quietly, one would think that there at least the dead might rest in peace. On one side of the church extends a wide woody dell, along which raves a large brook among broken rocks and trunks of fallen trees. Over a deep black part of the stream, not far from the church, was formerly thrown a wooden bridge; the road that led to it, and the bridge itself, were thickly shaded by overhanging trees, which cast a gloom about it, even in the daytime; but occasioned a fearful darkness at night. Such was one of the favorite haunts of the Headless Horseman, and the place where he was most frequently encountered. The tale was told of old Brouwer, a most heretical disbeliever in ghosts, how he met the Horseman returning from his foray into Sleepy Hollow, and was obliged to get up behind him; how they galloped over bush and brake, over hill and swamp, until they reached the bridge; when the Horseman suddenly turned into a skeleton, threw old Brouwer into the brook, and sprang away over the tree-tops with a clap of thunder.

This story was immediately matched by a thrice marvelous adventure of Brom Bones, who made light of the Galloping Hessian as an arrant jockey. He affirmed that on returning one night from the neighboring village of Sing Sing, he had been overtaken by this midnight trooper; that he had offered to race with him for a bowl of punch, and should have won it too, for Daredevil beat the goblin horse all hollow, but just as they came to the church bridge, the Hessian bolted, and vanished in a flash of fire.

All these tales, told in that drowsy undertone with which men talk in the dark, the countenances of the listeners only now and then receiving a casual gleam from the glare of a pipe, sank deep in the mind of Ichabod. He repaid them in kind with large extracts from his invaluable author, Cotton Mather, and added many marvelous events that had taken place in his native State of Connecticut, and fearful sights which he had seen in his nightly walks about Sleepy Hollow.

The revel now gradually broke up. The old farmers gathered together their families in their wagons, and were heard for some time rattling along the hollow roads, and over the distant hills. Some of the damsels mounted on pillions behind their favorite swains, and their light-hearted laughter, mingling with the clatter of hoofs, echoed along the silent woodlands, sounding fainter and fainter, until they gradually died away – and the late scene of noise and frolic was all silent and deserted. Ichabod only lingered behind, according to the custom of country lovers, to have a tête-à-tête with the heiress; fully convinced that he was now on the high road to success. What passed at this interview I will not pretend to say, for in fact I do not know. Something, however, I fear me, must have gone wrong, for he certainly sallied forth, after no very great interval, with an air quite desolate and chapfallen. Oh, these women! these women! Could that girl have been playing off any of her coquettish tricks? Was her encouragement of the poor pedagogue all a mere sham to secure her conquest of his rival? Heaven only knows, not I! Let it suffice to say, Ichabod stole forth with the air of one who had been sacking a henroost, rather than a fair lady's heart. Without looking to the right or left to notice the scene of rural wealth, on which he had so often gloated, he went straight to the stable, and with several hearty cuffs and kicks roused his steed most uncourteously from the comfortable quarters in which he was soundly sleeping, dreaming of mountains of corn and oats, and whole valleys of timothy and clover.

It was the very witching time of night that Ichabod, heavyhearted and crestfallen, pursued his travels homewards, along the sides of the lofty hills which rise above Tarry Town, and which he had traversed so cheerily in the afternoon. The hour was as dismal as himself. Far below him the Tappan Zee spread its dusky and indistinct waste of waters, with here and there the tall mast of a sloop, riding quietly at anchor under the land. In the dead hush of midnight, he could even hear the barking of the watchdog from the opposite shore of the Hudson; but it was so vague and faint as only to give an idea of his distance from this faithful companion of man. Now and then, too, the long-drawn crowing of a cock, accidentally awakened, would sound far, far off, from some farmhouse away among the hills – but it was like a dreaming sound in his ear. No signs of life occurred near him, but occasionally the melancholy chirp of a cricket, or perhaps the guttural twang of a bullfrog from a neighboring marsh, as if sleeping uncomfortably and turning suddenly in his bed.

All the stories of ghosts and goblins that he had heard in the afternoon now came crowding upon his recollection. The night grew darker and darker; the stars seemed to sink deeper in the sky, and driving clouds occasionally hid them from his sight. He had never felt so lonely and dismal. He was, moreover, approaching the very place where many of the scenes of the ghost stories had been laid. In the center of the road stood an enormous tulip-tree, which towered like a giant above all the other trees of the neighborhood, and formed a kind of landmark. Its limbs were gnarled and fantastic, large enough to form trunks for ordinary trees, twisting down almost to the earth, and rising again into the air. It was connected with the tragical story of the unfortunate André, who had been taken prisoner hard by; and was universally known by the name of Major André's tree. The common people regarded it with a mixture of respect and superstition, partly out of sympathy for the fate of its ill-starred namesake, and partly from the tales of strange sights, and doleful lamentations, told concerning it.

As Ichabod approached this fearful tree, he began to whistle; he thought his whistle was answered; it was but a blast sweeping sharply through the dry branches. As he approached a little nearer, he thought he saw something white, hanging in the midst of the tree: he paused and ceased whistling but, on looking more narrowly, perceived that it was a place where the tree had been scathed by lightning, and the white wood laid bare. Suddenly he heard a groan – his teeth chattered, and his knees smote against the saddle: it was but the rubbing of one huge bough upon another, as they were swayed about by the breeze. He passed the tree in safety, but new perils lay before him.

About two hundred yards from the tree, a small brook crossed the road, and ran into a marshy and thickly-wooded glen, known by the name of Wiley's Swamp. A few rough logs, laid side by side, served for a bridge over this stream. On that side of the road where the brook entered the wood, a group of oaks and chestnuts, matted thick with wild grape-vines, threw a cavernous gloom over it. To pass this bridge was the severest trial. It was at this identical spot that the unfortunate André was captured, and under the covert of those chestnuts and vines were the sturdy yeomen concealed who surprised him. This has ever since been considered a haunted stream, and fearful are the feelings of the schoolboy who has to pass it alone after dark.

As he approached the stream, his heart began to thump; he summoned up, however, all his resolution, gave his horse half a score of kicks in the ribs, and attempted to dash briskly across the bridge; but instead of starting forward, the perverse old animal made a lateral movement, and ran broadside against the fence. Ichabod, whose fears increased with the delay, jerked the reins on the other side, and kicked lustily with the contrary foot: it was all in vain; his steed started, it is true, but it was only to plunge to the opposite side of the road into a thicket of brambles and alder bushes. The schoolmaster now bestowed both whip and heel upon the starveling ribs of old Gunpowder, who dashed forward, snuffling and snorting, but came to a stand just by the bridge, with a suddenness that had nearly sent his rider sprawling over his head. Just at this moment a plashy tramp by the side of the bridge caught the sensitive ear of Ichabod. In the dark shadow of the grove, on the margin of the brook, he beheld something huge, misshapen and towering. It stirred not, but seemed gathered up in the gloom, like some gigantic monster ready to spring upon the traveler.

The hair of the affrighted pedagogue rose upon his head with terror. What was to be done? To turn and fly was now too late; and besides, what chance was there of escaping ghost or goblin, if such it was, which could ride upon the wings of the wind? Summoning up, therefore, a show of courage, he demanded in stammering accents, "Who are you?" He received no reply. He repeated his demand in a still more agitated voice. Still there was no answer. Once more he cudgeled the sides of the inflexible Gunpowder, and, shutting his eyes, broke forth with involuntary fervor into a psalm tune. Just then the shadowy object of alarm put itself in motion, and with a scramble and a bound stood at once in the middle of the road. Though the night was dark and dismal, yet the form of the unknown might now in some degree be ascertained. He appeared to be a horseman of large dimensions, and mounted on a black horse of powerful frame. He made no offer of molestation or sociability, but kept aloof on one side of the road, jogging along on the blind side of old Gunpowder, who had now got over his fright and waywardness.

Ichabod, who had no relish for this strange midnight companion, and bethought himself of the adventure of Brom Bones with the Galloping Hessian, now quickened his steed in hopes of leaving him behind. The stranger, however, quickened his horse to an equal pace. Ichabod pulled up, and fell into a walk, thinking to lag behind – the other did the same. His heart began to sink within him; he endeavored to resume his psalm tune, but his parched tongue clove to the roof of his mouth, and he could not utter a stave. There was something in the moody and dogged silence of this pertinacious companion that was mysterious and appalling. It was soon fearfully accounted for. On mounting a rising ground, which brought the figure of his fellow-traveler in relief against the sky, gigantic in height, and muffled in a cloak, Ichabod was horror-struck on perceiving that he was headless! – but his horror was still more increased on observing that the head, which should have rested on his shoulders, was carried before him on the pommel of his saddle! His terror rose to desperation; he rained a shower of kicks and blows upon Gunpowder, hoping by a sudden movement to give his companion the slip; but the specter started full jump with him. Away, then, they dashed through thick and thin; stones flying and sparks flashing at every bound. Ichabod's flimsy garments fluttered in the air, as he stretched his long lank body away over his horse's head, in the eagerness of his flight.

They had now reached the road which turns off to Sleepy Hollow; but Gunpowder, who seemed possessed with a demon, instead of keeping up it, made an opposite turn, and plunged headlong downhill to the left. This road leads through a sandy hollow shaded by trees for about a quarter of a mile, where it crosses the bridge famous in goblin story; and just beyond swells the green knoll on which stands the whitewashed church.

As yet the panic of the steed had given his unskillful rider an apparent advantage in the chase, but just as he had got half way through the hollow, the girths of the saddle gave way, and he felt it slipping from under him. He seized it by the pommel, and endeavored to hold it firm, but in vain; and had just time to save himself by clasping old Gunpowder round the neck, when the saddle fell to the earth, and he heard it trampled underfoot by his pursuer. For a moment the terror of Hans Van Ripper's wrath passed across his mind – for it was his Sunday saddle; but this was no time for petty fears; the goblin was hard on his haunches; and (unskillful rider that he was!) he had much ado to maintain his seat; sometimes slipping on one side, sometimes on another, and sometimes jolted on the high ridge of his horse's backbone, with a violence that he verily feared would cleave him asunder.

An opening in the trees now cheered him with the hopes that the church bridge was at hand. The wavering reflection of a silver star in the bosom of the brook told him that he was not mistaken. He saw the walls of the church dimly glaring under the trees beyond. He recollected the place where Brom Bones's ghostly competitor had disappeared. "If I can but reach that bridge," thought Ichabod, "I am safe." Just then he heard the black steed panting and blowing close behind him; he even fancied that he felt his hot breath. Another convulsive kick in the ribs, and old Gunpowder sprang upon the bridge; he thundered over the resounding planks; he gained the opposite side; and now Ichabod cast a look behind to see if his pursuer should vanish, according to rule, in a flash of fire and brimstone. Just then he saw the goblin rising in his stirrups, and in the very act of hurling his head at him.

Ichabod endeavored to dodge the horrible missile, but too late. It encountered his cranium with a tremendous crash – he was tumbled headlong into the dust, and Gunpowder, the black steed, and the goblin rider, passed by like a whirlwind.

The next morning the old horse was found without his saddle, and with the bridle under his feet, soberly cropping the grass at his master's gate. Ichabod did not make his appearance at breakfast; dinner-hour came, but no Ichabod. The boys assembled at the schoolhouse, and strolled idly about the banks of the brook; but no schoolmaster. Hans Van Ripper now began to feel some uneasiness about the fate of poor Ichabod, and his saddle. An inquiry was set on foot, and after diligent investigation they came upon his traces. In one part of the road leading to the church was found the saddle trampled in the dirt; the tracks of horses' hoofs deeply dented in the road, and evidently at furious speed, were traced to the bridge, beyond which, on the bank of a broad part of the brook, where the water ran deep and black, was found the hat of the unfortunate Ichabod, and close beside it a shattered pumpkin.

The brook was searched, but the body of the schoolmaster was not to be discovered. Hans Van Ripper as executor of his estate, examined the bundle which contained all his worldly effects. They consisted of two shirts and a half; two stocks for the neck; a pair or two of worsted stockings; an old pair of corduroy small-clothes; a rusty razor; a book of psalm tunes full of dog's-ears; and a broken pitch-pipe. As to the books and furniture of the schoolhouse, they belonged to the community, excepting Cotton Mather's *History of Witchcraft*, a *New England Almanac*, and a book of dreams and fortune-telling; in which last was a sheet of foolscap much scribbled and blotted in several fruitless attempts to make a copy of verses in honor of the heiress of Van Tassel. These magic books and the poetic scrawl were forthwith consigned to the flames by Hans Van Ripper; who, from that time forward, determined to send his children no more to school, observing that he never knew any good come of this same reading and writing. Whatever money the schoolmaster possessed, and he had received his quarter's pay but a day or two before, he must have had about his person at the time of his disappearance.

The mysterious event caused much speculation at the church on the following Sunday. Knots of gazers and gossips were collected in the churchyard, at the bridge, and at the spot where the hat and pumpkin had been found. The stories of Brouwer, of Bones, and a whole budget of others were called to mind; and when they had diligently considered them all, and compared them with the symptoms of the present case, they shook their heads, and came to the conclusion that Ichabod had been carried off by the Galloping Hessian. As he was a bachelor, and in nobody's debt, nobody troubled his head any more about him; the school was removed to a different quarter of the hollow, and another pedagogue reigned in his stead.

It is true, an old farmer, who had been down to New York on a visit several years after, and from whom this account of the ghostly adventure was received, brought home the intelligence that Ichabod Crane was still alive; that he had left the neighborhood partly through fear of the goblin and Hans Van Ripper, and partly in mortification at having been suddenly dismissed by the heiress; that he had changed his quarters to a distant part of the country; had kept school and studied law at the same time; had been admitted to the bar; turned politician; electioneered; written for the newspapers; and finally had been made a justice of the Ten Pound Court. Brom Bones, too, who, shortly after his rival's disappearance conducted the blooming Katrina in triumph to the altar, was observed to look exceedingly knowing whenever the story of Ichabod was related, and always burst into a hearty laugh at the mention of the pumpkin; which led some to suspect that he knew more about the matter than he chose to tell.

The old country wives, however, who are the best judges of these matters, maintain to this day that Ichabod was spirited away by supernatural means; and it is a favorite story often told about the neighborhood round the winter evening fire. The bridge became more than ever an object of superstitious awe; and that may be the reason why the road has been altered of late years, so as to approach the church by the border of the millpond. The schoolhouse being deserted soon fell to decay, and was reported to be haunted by the ghost of the unfortunate pedagogue and the plowboy, loitering homeward of a still summer evening, has often fancied his voice at a distance, chanting a melancholy psalm tune among the tranquil solitudes of Sleepy Hollow.

The Monkey's Paw

by W.W. Jacobs

I

WITHOUT, THE NIGHT WAS COLD and wet, but in the small parlour of Laburnam Villa the blinds were drawn and the fire burned brightly. Father and son were at chess, the former, who possessed ideas about the game involving radical changes, putting his king into such sharp and unnecessary perils that it even provoked comment from the white-haired old lady knitting placidly by the fire.

"Hark at the wind," said Mr White, who, having seen a fatal mistake after it was too late, was amiably desirous of preventing his son from seeing it.

"I'm listening," said the latter, grimly surveying the board as he stretched out his hand. "Check."

"I should hardly think that he'd come tonight," said his father, with his hand poised over the board.

"Mate," replied the son.

"That's the worst of living so far out," bawled Mr White, with sudden and unlooked-for violence; "of all the beastly, slushy, out-of-the-way places to live in, this is the worst. Pathway's a bog, and the road's a torrent. I don't know what people are thinking about. I suppose because only two houses in the road are let, they think it doesn't matter."

"Never mind, dear," said his wife, soothingly; "perhaps you'll win the next one."

Mr White looked up sharply, just in time to intercept a knowing glance between mother and son. The words died away on his lips, and he hid a guilty grin in his thin grey beard.

"There he is," said Herbert White, as the gate banged to loudly and heavy footsteps came toward the door.

The old man rose with hospitable haste, and opening the door, was heard condoling with the new arrival. The new arrival also condoled with himself, so that Mrs White said, "Tut, tut!" and coughed gently as her husband entered the room, followed by a tall, burly man, beady of eye and rubicund of visage.

"Sergeant-Major Morris," he said, introducing him.

The sergeant-major shook hands, and taking the proffered seat by the fire, watched contentedly while his host got out whiskey and tumblers and stood a small copper kettle on the fire.

At the third glass his eyes got brighter, and he began to talk, the little family circle regarding with eager interest this visitor from distant parts, as he squared his broad shoulders in the chair and spoke of wild scenes and doughty deeds; of wars and plagues and strange peoples.

"Twenty-one years of it," said Mr White, nodding at his wife and son. "When he went away he was a slip of a youth in the warehouse. Now look at him."

"He don't look to have taken much harm," said Mrs White, politely.

"I'd like to go to India myself," said the old man, "just to look round a bit, you know."

"Better where you are," said the sergeant-major, shaking his head. He put down the empty glass, and sighing softly, shook it again.

"I should like to see those old temples and fakirs and jugglers," said the old man. "What was that you started telling me the other day about a monkey's paw or something, Morris?"

"Nothing," said the soldier, hastily. "Leastways nothing worth hearing."

"Monkey's paw?" said Mrs White, curiously.

"Well, it's just a bit of what you might call magic, perhaps," said the sergeant-major, offhandedly.

His three listeners leaned forward eagerly. The visitor absent-mindedly put his empty glass to his lips and then set it down again. His host filled it for him.

"To look at," said the sergeant-major, fumbling in his pocket, "it's just an ordinary little paw, dried to a mummy."

He took something out of his pocket and proffered it. Mrs White drew back with a grimace, but her son, taking it, examined it curiously.

"And what is there special about it?" inquired Mr White as he took it from his son, and having examined it, placed it upon the table.

"It had a spell put on it by an old fakir," said the sergeant-major, "a very holy man. He wanted to show that fate ruled people's lives, and that those who interfered with it did so to their sorrow. He put a spell on it so that three separate men could each have three wishes from it."

His manner was so impressive that his hearers were conscious that their light laughter jarred somewhat.

"Well, why don't you have three, sir?" said Herbert White, cleverly.

The soldier regarded him in the way that middle age is wont to regard presumptuous youth. "I have," he said, quietly, and his blotchy face whitened.

"And did you really have the three wishes granted?" asked Mrs White.

"I did," said the sergeant-major, and his glass tapped against his strong teeth.

"And has anybody else wished?" persisted the old lady.

"The first man had his three wishes. Yes," was the reply; "I don't know what the first two were, but the third was for death. That's how I got the paw."

His tones were so grave that a hush fell upon the group.

"If you've had your three wishes, it's no good to you now, then, Morris," said the old man at last. "What do you keep it for?"

The soldier shook his head. "Fancy, I suppose," he said, slowly. "I did have some idea of selling it, but I don't think I will. It has caused enough mischief already. Besides, people won't buy. They think it's a fairy tale; some of them, and those who do think anything of it want to try it first and pay me afterward."

"If you could have another three wishes," said the old man, eyeing him keenly, "would you have them?"

"I don't know," said the other. "I don't know."

He took the paw, and dangling it between his forefinger and thumb, suddenly threw it upon the fire. White, with a slight cry, stooped down and snatched it off.

"Better let it burn," said the soldier, solemnly.

"If you don't want it, Morris," said the other, "give it to me."

"I won't," said his friend, doggedly. "I threw it on the fire. If you keep it, don't blame me for what happens. Pitch it on the fire again like a sensible man."

The other shook his head and examined his new possession closely. "How do you do it?" he inquired.

"Hold it up in your right hand and wish aloud," said the sergeant-major, "but I warn you of the consequences."

"Sounds like the *Arabian Nights*," said Mrs White, as she rose and began to set the supper. "Don't you think you might wish for four pairs of hands for me?"

Her husband drew the talisman from his pocket, and then all three burst into laughter as the sergeant-major, with a look of alarm on his face, caught him by the arm.

"If you must wish," he said, gruffly, "wish for something sensible."

Mr White dropped it back in his pocket, and placing chairs, motioned his friend to the table. In the business of supper the talisman was partly forgotten, and afterward the three sat listening in an enthralled fashion to a second instalment of the soldier's adventures in India.

"If the tale about the monkey's paw is not more truthful than those he has been telling us," said Herbert, as the door closed behind their guest, just in time for him to catch the last train, "we shan't make much out of it."

"Did you give him anything for it, father?" inquired Mrs White, regarding her husband closely.

"A trifle," said he, colouring slightly. "He didn't want it, but I made him take it. And he pressed me again to throw it away."

"Likely," said Herbert, with pretended horror. "Why, we're going to be rich, and famous and happy. Wish to be an emperor, father, to begin with; then you can't be henpecked."

He darted round the table, pursued by the maligned Mrs White armed with an antimacassar.

Mr White took the paw from his pocket and eyed it dubiously. "I don't know what to wish for, and that's a fact," he said, slowly. "It seems to me I've got all I want."

"If you only cleared the house, you'd be quite happy, wouldn't you?" said Herbert, with his hand on his shoulder. "Well, wish for two hundred pounds, then; that'll just do it."

His father, smiling shamefacedly at his own credulity, held up the talisman, as his son, with a solemn face, somewhat marred by a wink at his mother, sat down at the piano and struck a few impressive chords.

"I wish for two hundred pounds," said the old man distinctly.

A fine crash from the piano greeted the words, interrupted by a shuddering cry from the old man. His wife and son ran toward him.

"It moved," he cried, with a glance of disgust at the object as it lay on the floor.

"As I wished, it twisted in my hand like a snake."

"Well, I don't see the money," said his son as he picked it up and placed it on the table, "and I bet I never shall."

"It must have been your fancy, father," said his wife, regarding him anxiously.

He shook his head. "Never mind, though; there's no harm done, but it gave me a shock all the same."

They sat down by the fire again while the two men finished their pipes. Outside, the wind was higher than ever, and the old man started nervously at the sound of a door banging upstairs. A silence unusual and depressing settled upon all three, which lasted until the old couple rose to retire for the night.

"I expect you'll find the cash tied up in a big bag in the middle of your bed," said Herbert, as he bade them good-night, "and something horrible squatting up on top of the wardrobe watching you as you pocket your ill-gotten gains."

He sat alone in the darkness, gazing at the dying fire, and seeing faces in it. The last face was so horrible and so simian that he gazed at it in amazement. It got so vivid that, with a little uneasy laugh, he felt on the table for a glass containing a little water to throw over it. His hand grasped the monkey's paw, and with a little shiver he wiped his hand on his coat and went up to bed.

II

IN THE BRIGHTNESS OF THE WINTRY SUN next morning as it streamed over the breakfast table he laughed at his fears. There was an air of prosaic wholesomeness about the room which it had lacked on the previous night, and the dirty, shrivelled little paw was pitched on the sideboard with a carelessness which betokened no great belief in its virtues.

"I suppose all old soldiers are the same," said Mrs White. "The idea of our listening to such nonsense! How could wishes be granted in these days? And if they could, how could two hundred pounds hurt you, father?"

"Might drop on his head from the sky," said the frivolous Herbert.

"Morris said the things happened so naturally," said his father, "that you might if you so wished attribute it to coincidence."

"Well, don't break into the money before I come back," said Herbert as he rose from the table. "I'm afraid it'll turn you into a mean, avaricious man, and we shall have to disown you."

His mother laughed, and following him to the door, watched him down the road; and returning to the breakfast table, was very happy at the expense of her husband's credulity. All of which did not prevent her from scurrying to the door at the postman's knock, nor prevent her from referring somewhat shortly to retired sergeant-majors of bibulous habits when she found that the post brought a tailor's bill.

"Herbert will have some more of his funny remarks, I expect, when he comes home," she said, as they sat at dinner.

"I dare say," said Mr White, pouring himself out some beer; "but for all that, the thing moved in my hand; that I'll swear to."

"You thought it did," said the old lady soothingly.

"I say it did," replied the other. "There was no thought about it; I had just – What's the matter?"

His wife made no reply. She was watching the mysterious movements of a man outside, who, peering in an undecided fashion at the house, appeared to be trying to make up his mind to enter. In mental connection with the two hundred pounds, she noticed that the stranger was well dressed, and wore a silk hat of glossy newness. Three times he paused at the gate, and then walked on again. The fourth time he stood with his hand upon it, and then with sudden resolution flung it open and walked up the path. Mrs White at the same moment placed her hands behind her, and hurriedly unfastening the strings of her apron, put that useful article of apparel beneath the cushion of her chair.

She brought the stranger, who seemed ill at ease, into the room. He gazed at her furtively, and listened in a preoccupied fashion as the old lady apologized for the appearance of the room, and her husband's coat, a garment which he usually reserved for the garden. She then waited as patiently as her sex would permit, for him to broach his business, but he was at first strangely silent.

"I – was asked to call," he said at last, and stooped and picked a piece of cotton from his trousers. "I come from 'Maw and Meggins.'"

The old lady started. "Is anything the matter?" she asked, breathlessly. "Has anything happened to Herbert? What is it? What is it?"

Her husband interposed. "There, there, mother," he said, hastily. "Sit down, and don't jump to conclusions. You've not brought bad news, I'm sure, sir;" and he eyed the other wistfully.

"I'm sorry –" began the visitor.

"Is he hurt?" demanded the mother, wildly.

The visitor bowed in assent. "Badly hurt," he said, quietly, "but he is not in any pain."

"Oh, thank God!" said the old woman, clasping her hands. "Thank God for that! Thank –"

She broke off suddenly as the sinister meaning of the assurance dawned upon her and she saw the awful confirmation of her fears in the other's averted face. She caught her breath, and turning to her slower-witted husband, laid her trembling old hand upon his. There was a long silence.

"He was caught in the machinery," said the visitor at length in a low voice.

"Caught in the machinery," repeated Mr White, in a dazed fashion, "yes."

He sat staring blankly out at the window, and taking his wife's hand between his own, pressed it as he had been wont to do in their old courting-days nearly forty years before.

"He was the only one left to us," he said, turning gently to the visitor. "It is hard."

The other coughed, and rising, walked slowly to the window. "The firm wished me to convey their sincere sympathy with you in your great loss," he said, without looking round. "I beg that you will understand I am only their servant and merely obeying orders."

There was no reply; the old woman's face was white, her eyes staring, and her breath inaudible; on the husband's face was a look such as his friend the sergeant might have carried into his first action.

"I was to say that 'Maw and Meggins' disclaim all responsibility," continued the other. "They admit no liability at all, but in consideration of your son's services, they wish to present you with a certain sum as compensation."

Mr White dropped his wife's hand, and rising to his feet, gazed with a look of horror at his visitor. His dry lips shaped the words, "How much?"

"Two hundred pounds," was the answer.

Unconscious of his wife's shriek, the old man smiled faintly, put out his hands like a sightless man, and dropped, a senseless heap, to the floor.

III

IN THE HUGE new cemetery, some two miles distant, the old people buried their dead, and came back to a house steeped in shadow and silence. It was all over so quickly that at first they could hardly realize it, and remained in a state of expectation as though of something else to happen – something else which was to lighten this load, too heavy for old hearts to bear.

But the days passed, and expectation gave place to resignation – the hopeless resignation of the old, sometimes miscalled, apathy. Sometimes they hardly exchanged a word, for now they had nothing to talk about, and their days were long to weariness.

It was about a week after that the old man, waking suddenly in the night, stretched out his hand and found himself alone. The room was in darkness, and the sound of subdued weeping came from the window. He raised himself in bed and listened.

"Come back," he said, tenderly. "You will be cold."

"It is colder for my son," said the old woman, and wept afresh.

The sound of her sobs died away on his ears. The bed was warm, and his eyes heavy with sleep. He dozed fitfully, and then slept until a sudden wild cry from his wife awoke him with a start.

"The paw!" she cried wildly. "The monkey's paw!"

He started up in alarm. "Where? Where is it? What's the matter?"

She came stumbling across the room toward him. "I want it," she said, quietly. "You've not destroyed it?"

"It's in the parlour, on the bracket," he replied, marvelling. "Why?"

She cried and laughed together, and bending over, kissed his cheek.

"I only just thought of it," she said, hysterically. "Why didn't I think of it before? Why didn't you think of it?"

"Think of what?" he questioned.

"The other two wishes," she replied, rapidly. "We've only had one."

"Was not that enough?" he demanded, fiercely.

"No," she cried, triumphantly; "we'll have one more. Go down and get it quickly, and wish our boy alive again."

The man sat up in bed and flung the bedclothes from his quaking limbs. "Good God, you are mad!" he cried, aghast.

"Get it," she panted; "get it quickly, and wish – Oh, my boy, my boy!"

Her husband struck a match and lit the candle. "Get back to bed," he said, unsteadily. "You don't know what you are saying."

"We had the first wish granted," said the old woman, feverishly; "why not the second?"

"A coincidence," stammered the old man.

"Go and get it and wish," cried his wife, quivering with excitement.

The old man turned and regarded her, and his voice shook. "He has been dead ten days, and besides he – I would not tell you else, but – I could only recognize him by his clothing. If he was too terrible for you to see then, how now?"

"Bring him back," cried the old woman, and dragged him toward the door. "Do you think I fear the child I have nursed?"

He went down in the darkness, and felt his way to the parlour, and then to the mantelpiece. The talisman was in its place, and a horrible fear that the unspoken wish might bring his mutilated son before him ere he could escape from the room seized upon him, and he caught his breath as he found that he had lost the direction of the door. His brow cold with sweat, he felt his way round the table, and groped along the wall until he found himself in the small passage with the unwholesome thing in his hand.

Even his wife's face seemed changed as he entered the room. It was white and expectant, and to his fears seemed to have an unnatural look upon it. He was afraid of her.

"Wish!" she cried, in a strong voice.

"It is foolish and wicked," he faltered.

"Wish!" repeated his wife.

He raised his hand. "I wish my son alive again."

The talisman fell to the floor, and he regarded it fearfully. Then he sank trembling into a chair as the old woman, with burning eyes, walked to the window and raised the blind.

He sat until he was chilled with the cold, glancing occasionally at the figure of the old woman peering through the window. The candle-end, which had burned below the rim of the china candlestick, was throwing pulsating shadows on the ceiling and walls, until, with a flicker larger than the rest, it expired. The old man, with an unspeakable sense of relief at the failure of the talisman, crept back to his bed, and a minute or two afterward the old woman came silently and apathetically beside him.

Neither spoke, but lay silently listening to the ticking of the clock. A stair creaked, and a squeaky mouse scurried noisily through the wall. The darkness was oppressive, and after lying for some time screwing up his courage, he took the box of matches, and striking one, went downstairs for a candle.

At the foot of the stairs the match went out, and he paused to strike another; and at the same moment a knock, so quiet and stealthy as to be scarcely audible, sounded on the front door.

The matches fell from his hand and spilled in the passage. He stood motionless, his breath suspended until the knock was repeated. Then he turned and fled swiftly back to his room, and closed the door behind him. A third knock sounded through the house.

"What's that?" cried the old woman, starting up.

"A rat," said the old man in shaking tones – "a rat. It passed me on the stairs."

His wife sat up in bed listening. A loud knock resounded through the house.

"It's Herbert!" she screamed. "It's Herbert!"

She ran to the door, but her husband was before her, and catching her by the arm, held her tightly.

"What are you going to do?" he whispered hoarsely.

"It's my boy; it's Herbert!" she cried, struggling mechanically. "I forgot it was two miles away. What are you holding me for? Let go. I must open the door."

"For God's sake don't let it in," cried the old man, trembling.

"You're afraid of your own son," she cried, struggling. "Let me go. I'm coming, Herbert; I'm coming."

There was another knock, and another. The old woman with a sudden wrench broke free and ran from the room. Her husband followed to the landing, and called after her appealingly as she hurried downstairs. He heard the chain rattle back and the bottom bolt drawn slowly and stiffly from the socket. Then the old woman's voice, strained and panting.

"The bolt," she cried, loudly. "Come down. I can't reach it."

But her husband was on his hands and knees groping wildly on the floor in search of the paw. If he could only find it before the thing outside got in. A perfect fusillade of knocks reverberated through the house, and he heard the scraping of a chair as his wife put it down in the passage against the door. He heard the creaking of the bolt as it came slowly back, and at the same moment he found the monkey's paw, and frantically breathed his third and last wish.

The knocking ceased suddenly, although the echoes of it were still in the house. He heard the chair drawn back, and the door opened. A cold wind rushed up the staircase, and a long loud wail of disappointment and misery from his wife gave him courage to run down to her side, and then to the gate beyond. The street lamp flickering opposite shone on a quiet and deserted road.

The Altar of the Dead

by Henry James

Chapter I

HE HAD A MORTAL DISLIKE, poor Stransom, to lean anniversaries, and loved them still less when they made a pretence of a figure. Celebrations and suppressions were equally painful to him, and but one of the former found a place in his life. He had kept each year in his own fashion the date of Mary Antrim's death. It would be more to the point perhaps to say that this occasion kept *him*: it kept him at least effectually from doing anything else. It took hold of him again and again with a hand of which time had softened but never loosened the touch. He waked to his feast of memory as consciously as he would have waked to his marriage-morn. Marriage had had of old but too little to say to the matter: for the girl who was to have been his bride there had been no bridal embrace. She had died of a malignant fever after the wedding-day had been fixed, and he had lost before fairly tasting it an affection that promised to fill his life to the brim.

Of that benediction, however, it would have been false to say this life could really be emptied: it was still ruled by a pale ghost, still ordered by a sovereign presence. He had not been a man of numerous passions, and even in all these years no sense had grown stronger with him than the sense of being bereft. He had needed no priest and no altar to make him for ever widowed. He had done many things in the world – he had done almost all but one: he had never, never forgotten. He had tried to put into his existence whatever else might take up room in it, but had failed to make it more than a house of which the mistress was eternally absent. She was most absent of all on the recurrent December day that his tenacity set apart. He had no arranged observance of it, but his nerves made it all their own. They drove him forth without mercy, and the goal of his pilgrimage was far. She had been buried in a London suburb, a part then of Nature's breast, but which he had seen lose one after another every feature of freshness. It was in truth during the moments he stood there that his eyes beheld the place least. They looked at another image, they opened to another light. Was it a credible future? Was it an incredible past? Whatever the answer it was an immense escape from the actual.

It's true that if there weren't other dates than this there were other memories; and by the time George Stransom was fifty-five such memories had greatly multiplied. There were other ghosts in his life than the ghost of Mary Antrim. He had perhaps not had more losses than most men, but he had counted his losses more; he hadn't seen death more closely, but had in a manner felt it more deeply. He had formed little by little the habit of numbering his Dead: it had come to him early in life that there was something one had to do for them.

They were there in their simplified intensified essence, their conscious absence and expressive patience, as personally there as if they had only been stricken dumb. When all sense of them failed, all sound of them ceased, it was as if their purgatory were really still on earth: they asked so little that they got, poor things, even less, and died again, died every day, of the hard usage of life. They had no organised service, no reserved place, no honour, no shelter, no safety. Even ungenerous people provided for the living, but even those who were called most generous did nothing for the others. So on George Stransom's part had grown up with the years a resolve that he at least would do something, do it, that is, for his own – would perform the great charity without reproach. Every man *had* his own, and every man had, to meet this charity, the ample resources of the soul.

It was doubtless the voice of Mary Antrim that spoke for them best; as the years at any rate went by he found himself in regular communion with these postponed pensioners, those whom indeed he always called in his thoughts the Others. He spared them the moments, he organised the charity. Quite how it had risen he probably never could have told you, but what came to pass was that an altar, such as was after all within everybody's compass, lighted with perpetual candles and dedicated to these secret rites, reared itself in his spiritual spaces. He had wondered of old, in some embarrassment, whether he had a religion; being very sure, and not a little content, that he hadn't at all events the religion some of the people he had known wanted him to have. Gradually this question was straightened out for him: it became clear to him that the religion instilled by his earliest consciousness had been simply the religion of the Dead. It suited his inclination, it satisfied his spirit, it gave employment to his piety. It answered his love of great offices, of a solemn and splendid ritual; for no shrine could be more bedecked and no ceremonial more stately than those to which his worship was attached. He had no imagination about these things but that they were accessible to anyone who should feel the need of them. The poorest could build such temples of the spirit – could make them blaze with candles and smoke with incense, make them flush with pictures and flowers. The cost, in the common phrase, of keeping them up fell wholly on the generous heart.

Chapter II

HE HAD THIS YEAR, on the eve of his anniversary, as happened, an emotion not unconnected with that range of feeling. Walking home at the close of a busy day he was arrested in the London street by the particular effect of a shop-front that lighted the dull brown air with its mercenary grin and before which several persons were gathered. It was the window of a jeweller whose diamonds and sapphires seemed to laugh, in flashes like high notes of sound, with the mere joy of knowing how much more they were "worth" than most of the dingy pedestrians staring at them from the other side of the pane. Stransom lingered long enough to suspend, in a vision, a string of pearls about the white neck of Mary Antrim, and then was kept an instant longer by the sound of a voice he knew. Next him was a mumbling old woman, and beyond the old woman a gentleman with a lady on his arm. It was from him, from Paul Creston, the voice had proceeded: he was talking with the lady of some precious object in the window. Stransom had no sooner recognised him than the old woman turned away; but just with this growth of opportunity came a felt strangeness that stayed him in the very act of laying his hand on his friend's arm. It lasted but the instant, only that space sufficed for the flash of a wild question. Was *not* Mrs Creston dead? – the ambiguity met him there in the short drop of her husband's voice, the drop conjugal, if it ever was, and in the way the two figures leaned to each other. Creston, making a step to look at something else, came nearer, glanced at him, started and exclaimed – behaviour the effect of which was at first only to leave Stransom staring, staring back across the months at the different face, the wholly other face, the poor man had shown him last, the blurred ravaged mask bent over the open grave by which they had stood together. That son of affliction wasn't in mourning now; he detached his arm from his companion's to grasp the hand of the older friend. He coloured as well as smiled in the strong light of the shop when Stransom raised a tentative hat to the lady. Stransom had just time to see she was pretty before he found himself gaping at a fact more portentous. "My dear fellow, let me make you acquainted with my wife."

Creston had blushed and stammered over it, but in half a minute, at the rate we live in polite society, it had practically become, for our friend, the mere memory of a shock. They stood there and laughed and talked; Stransom had instantly whisked the shock out of the way, to keep it for private consumption. He felt himself grimace, he heard himself exaggerate the proper, but was conscious of turning not a little faint. That new woman, that hired performer, Mrs Creston? Mrs Creston had been more living for him than any woman but one. This lady had a face that shone as publicly as the jeweller's window, and in the happy candour with which she wore her monstrous character was an effect of gross immodesty. The character of Paul Creston's wife thus attributed to her was monstrous for reasons Stransom could judge his friend to know perfectly that he knew. The happy pair had just arrived from America, and Stransom hadn't needed to be told this to guess the nationality of the lady. Somehow it deepened the foolish air that her husband's confused cordiality was unable to conceal. Stransom recalled that he had heard of poor Creston's having, while his bereavement was still fresh, crossed the sea for what people in such predicaments call a little change. He had found the little change indeed, he had brought the little change back; it was the little change that stood there and that, do what he would, he couldn't, while he showed those high front teeth of his, look other than a conscious ass about. They were going into the shop, Mrs Creston said, and she begged Mr Stransom to come with them and help to decide. He thanked her, opening his watch and pleading an engagement for which he was already late, and they parted while she shrieked into the fog, "Mind now you come to see me right away!" Creston had had the delicacy not to suggest that, and Stransom hoped it hurt him somewhere to hear her scream it to all the echoes.

He felt quite determined, as he walked away, never in his life to go near her. She was perhaps a human being, but Creston oughtn't to have shown her without precautions, oughtn't indeed to have shown her at all. His precautions should have been those of a forger or a murderer, and the people at home would never have mentioned extradition. This was a wife for foreign service or purely external use; a decent consideration would have spared her the injury of comparisons. Such was the first flush of George Stransom's reaction; but as he sat alone that night – there were particular hours he always passed alone – the harshness dropped from it and left only the pity. *He* could spend an evening with Kate Creston, if the man to whom she had given everything couldn't. He had known her twenty years, and she was the only woman for whom he might perhaps have been unfaithful. She was all cleverness and sympathy and charm; her house had been the very easiest in all the world and her friendship the very firmest. Without accidents he had loved her, without accidents everyone had loved her: she had made the passions about her as regular as the moon makes the tides. She had been also of course far too good for her husband, but he never suspected it, and in nothing had she been more admirable than in the exquisite art with which she tried to keep everyone else (keeping Creston was no trouble) from finding it out. Here was a man to whom she had devoted her life and for whom she had given it up – dying to bring into the world a child of his bed; and she had had only to submit to her fate to have, ere the grass was green on her grave, no more existence for him than a domestic servant he had replaced. The frivolity, the indecency of it made Stransom's eyes fill; and he had that evening a sturdy sense that he alone, in a world without delicacy, had a right to hold up his head. While he smoked, after dinner, he had a book in his lap, but he had no eyes for his page: his eyes, in the swarming void of things, seemed to have caught Kate Creston's, and it was into their sad silences he looked. It was to him her sentient spirit had turned, knowing it to be of her he would think. He thought for a long time of how the closed eyes of dead women could still live – how they could open again, in a quiet lamplit room, long after they had looked their last. They had looks that survived – had them as great poets had quoted lines.

The newspaper lay by his chair – the thing that came in the afternoon and the servants thought one wanted; without sense for what was in it he had mechanically unfolded and then dropped it. Before he went to bed he took it up, and this time, at the top of a paragraph, he was caught by five words that made him start. He stood staring, before the fire, at the "Death of Sir Acton Hague, K.C.B.," the man who ten years earlier had been the nearest of his friends and whose deposition from this eminence had practically left it without an occupant. He had seen him after their rupture, but hadn't now seen him for years. Standing there before the fire he turned cold as he read what had befallen him. Promoted a short time previous to the governorship of the Westward Islands, Acton Hague had died, in the bleak honour of this exile, of an illness consequent on the bite of a poisonous snake. His career was compressed by the newspaper into a dozen lines, the perusal of which excited on George Stransom's part no warmer feeling than one of relief at the absence of any mention of their quarrel, an incident accidentally tainted at the time, thanks to their joint immersion in large affairs, with a horrible publicity. Public indeed was the wrong Stransom had, to his own sense, suffered, the insult he had blankly taken from the only man with whom he had ever been intimate; the friend, almost adored, of his University years, the subject, later, of his passionate loyalty: so public that he had never spoken of it to a human creature, so public that he had completely overlooked it. It had made the difference for him that friendship too was all over, but it had only made just that one. The shock of interests had been private, intensely so; but the action taken by Hague had been in the face of men. Today it all seemed to have occurred merely to the end that George Stransom should think of him as "Hague" and measure exactly how much he himself could resemble a stone. He went cold, suddenly and horribly cold, to bed.

Chapter III

THE NEXT DAY, in the afternoon, in the great grey suburb, he knew his long walk had tired him. In the dreadful cemetery alone he had been on his feet an hour. Instinctively, coming back, they had taken him a devious course, and it was a desert in which no circling cabman hovered over possible prey. He paused on a corner and measured the dreariness; then he made out through the gathered dusk that he was in one of those tracts of London which are less gloomy by night than by day, because, in the former case of the civil gift of light. By day there was nothing, but by night there were lamps, and George Stransom was in a mood that made lamps good in themselves. It wasn't that they could show him anything, it was only that they could burn clear. To his surprise, however, after a while, they did show him something: the arch of a high doorway approached by a low terrace of steps, in the depth of which – it formed a dim vestibule – the raising of a curtain at the moment he passed gave him a glimpse of an avenue of gloom with a glow of tapers at the end. He stopped and looked up, recognising the place as a church. The thought quickly came to him that since he was tired he might rest there; so that after a moment he had in turn pushed up the leathern curtain and gone in. It was a temple of the old persuasion, and there had evidently been a function – perhaps a service for the dead; the high altar was still a blaze of candles. This was an exhibition he always liked, and he dropped into a seat with relief. More than it had ever yet come home to him it struck him as good there should be churches.

This one was almost empty and the other altars were dim; a verger shuffled about, an old woman coughed, but it seemed to Stransom there was hospitality in the thick sweet air. Was it only the savour of the incense or was it something of larger intention? He had at any rate quitted the great grey suburb and come nearer to the warm centre. He presently ceased to feel intrusive, gaining at last even a sense of community with the only worshipper in his neighbourhood, the sombre presence of a woman, in mourning unrelieved, whose back was all he could see of her and who had sunk deep into prayer at no great distance from him. He wished he could sink, like her, to the very bottom, be as motionless, as rapt in prostration. After a few moments he shifted his seat; it was almost indelicate to be so aware of her. But Stransom subsequently quite lost himself, floating away on the sea of light. If occasions like this had been more frequent in his life he would have had more present the great original type, set up in a myriad temples, of the unapproachable shrine he had erected in his mind. That shrine had begun in vague likeness to church pomps, but the echo had ended by growing more distinct than the sound. The sound now rang out, the type blazed at him with all its fires and with a mystery of radiance in which endless meanings could glow. The thing became as he sat there his appropriate altar and each starry candle an appropriate vow. He numbered them, named them, grouped them – it was the silent roll-call of his Dead. They made together a brightness vast and intense, a brightness in which the mere chapel of his thoughts grew so dim that as it faded away he asked himself if he shouldn't find his real comfort in some material act, some outward worship.

This idea took possession of him while, at a distance, the black-robed lady continued prostrate; he was quietly thrilled with his conception, which at last brought him to his feet in the sudden excitement of a plan. He wandered softly through the aisles, pausing in the different chapels, all save one applied to a special devotion. It was in this clear recess, lampless and unapplied, that he stood longest – the length of time it took him fully to grasp the conception of gilding it with his bounty. He should snatch it from no other rites and associate it with nothing profane; he would simply take it as it should be given up to him and make it a masterpiece of splendour and a mountain of fire. Tended sacredly all the year, with the sanctifying church round it, it would always be ready for his offices. There would be difficulties, but from the first they presented themselves only as difficulties surmounted. Even for a person so little affiliated the thing would be a matter of arrangement. He saw it all in advance, and how bright in especial the place would become to him in the intermissions of toil and the dusk of afternoons; how rich in assurance at all times, but especially in the indifferent world. Before withdrawing he drew nearer again to the spot where he had first sat down, and in the movement he met the lady whom he had seen praying and who was now on her way to the door.

She passed him quickly, and he had only a glimpse of her pale face and her unconscious, almost sightless eyes. For that instant she looked faded and handsome.

This was the origin of the rites more public, yet certainly esoteric, that he at last found himself able to establish. It took a long time, it took a year, and both the process and the result would have been – for any who knew – a vivid picture of his good faith. No one did know, in fact – no one but the bland ecclesiastics whose acquaintance he had promptly sought, whose objections he had softly overridden, whose curiosity and sympathy he had artfully charmed, whose assent to his eccentric munificence he had eventually won, and who had asked for concessions in exchange for indulgences. Stransom had of course at an early stage of his enquiry been referred to the Bishop, and the Bishop had been delightfully human, the Bishop had been almost amused. Success was within sight, at any rate from the moment the attitude of those whom it concerned became liberal in response to liberality. The altar and the sacred shell that half encircled it, consecrated to an ostensible and customary worship, were to be splendidly maintained; all that Stransom reserved to himself was the number of his lights and the free enjoyment of his intention. When the intention had taken complete effect the enjoyment became even greater than he had ventured to hope. He liked to think of this effect when far from it, liked to convince himself of it yet again when near. He was not often indeed so near as that a visit to it hadn't perforce something of the patience of a pilgrimage; but the time he gave to his devotion came to seem to him more a contribution to his other interests than a betrayal of them. Even a loaded life might be easier when one had added a new necessity to it.

How much easier was probably never guessed by those who simply knew there were hours when he disappeared and for many of whom there was a vulgar reading of what they used to call his plunges. These plunges were into depths quieter than the deep sea-caves, and the habit had at the end of a year or two become the one it would have cost him most to relinquish. Now they had really, his Dead, something that was indefensibly theirs; and he liked to think that they might in cases be the Dead of others, as well as that the Dead of others might be invoked there under the protection of what he had done. Whoever bent a knee on the carpet he had laid down appeared to him to act in the spirit of his intention. Each of his lights had a name for him, and from time to time a new light was kindled. This was what he had fundamentally agreed for, that there should always be room for them all. What those who passed or lingered saw was simply the most resplendent of the altars called suddenly into vivid usefulness, with a quiet elderly man, for whom it evidently had a fascination, often seated there in a maze or a doze; but half the satisfaction of the spot for this mysterious and fitful worshipper was that he found the years of his life there, and the ties, the affections, the struggles, the submissions, the conquests, if there had been such, a record of that adventurous journey in which the beginnings and the endings of human relations are the lettered mile-stones. He had in general little taste for the past as a part of his own history; at other times and in other places it mostly seemed to him pitiful to consider and impossible to repair; but on these occasions he accepted it with something of that positive gladness with which one adjusts one's self to an ache that begins to succumb to treatment. To the treatment of time the malady of life begins at a given moment to succumb; and these were doubtless the hours at which that truth most came home to him. The day was written for him there on which he had first become acquainted with death and the successive phases of the acquaintance were marked each with a flame.

The flames were gathering thick at present, for Stransom had entered that dark defile of our earthly descent in which someone dies every day. It was only yesterday that Kate

Creston had flashed out her white fire; yet already there were younger stars ablaze on the tips of the tapers. Various persons in whom his interest had not been intense drew closer to him by entering this company. He went over it, head by head, till he felt like the shepherd of a huddled flock, with all a shepherd's vision of differences imperceptible. He knew his candles apart, up to the colour of the flame, and would still have known them had their positions all been changed. To other imaginations they might stand for other things – that they should stand for something to be hushed before was all he desired; but he was intensely conscious of the personal note of each and of the distinguishable way it contributed to the concert. There were hours at which he almost caught himself wishing that certain of his friends would now die, that he might establish with them in this manner a connexion more charming than, as it happened, it was possible to enjoy with them in life. In regard to those from whom one was separated by the long curves of the globe such a connexion could only be an improvement: it brought them instantly within reach. Of course there were gaps in the constellation, for Stransom knew he could only pretend to act for his own, and it wasn't every figure passing before his eyes into the great obscure that was entitled to a memorial. There was a strange sanctification in death, but some characters were more sanctified by being forgotten than by being remembered. The greatest blank in the shining page was the memory of Acton Hague, of which he inveterately tried to rid himself. For Acton Hague no flame could ever rise on any altar of his.

Chapter IV

EVERY YEAR, the day he walked back from the great graveyard, he went to church as he had done the day his idea was born. It was on this occasion, as it happened, after a year had passed, that he began to observe his altar to be haunted by a worshipper at least as frequent as himself. Others of the faithful, and in the rest of the church, came and went, appealing sometimes, when they disappeared, to a vague or to a particular recognition; but this unfailing presence was always to be observed when he arrived and still in possession when he departed. He was surprised, the first time, at the promptitude with which it assumed an identity for him – the identity of the lady whom two years before, on his anniversary, he had seen so intensely bowed, and of whose tragic face he had had so flitting a vision. Given the time that had passed, his recollection of her was fresh enough to make him wonder. Of himself she had of course no impression, or rather had had none at first: the time came when her manner of transacting her business suggested her having gradually guessed his call to be of the same order. She used his altar for her own purpose – he could only hope that sad and solitary as she always struck him, she used it for her own Dead. There were interruptions, infidelities, all on his part, calls to other associations and duties; but as the months went on he found her whenever he returned, and he ended by taking pleasure in the thought that he had given her almost the contentment he had given himself. They worshipped side by side so often that there were moments when he wished he might be sure, so straight did their prospect stretch away of growing old together in their rites. She was younger than he, but she looked as if her Dead were at least as numerous as his candles. She had no colour, no sound, no fault, and another of the things about which he had made up his mind was that she had no fortune. Always black-robed, she must have had a succession of sorrows. People weren't poor, after all, whom so many losses could overtake; they were positively rich when they had had so much to give up. But the air of this devoted and indifferent woman, who always made, in any attitude, a beautiful accidental line, conveyed somehow to Stransom that she had known more kinds of trouble than one.

He had a great love of music and little time for the joy of it; but occasionally, when workaday noises were muffled by Saturday afternoons, it used to come back to him that there were glories. There were moreover friends who reminded him of this and side by side with whom he found himself sitting out concerts. On one of these winter afternoons, in St. James's Hall, he became aware after he had seated himself that the lady he had so often seen at church was in the place next him and was evidently alone, as he also this time happened to be. She was at first too absorbed in the consideration of the programme to heed him, but when she at last glanced at him he took advantage of the movement to speak to her, greeting her with the remark that he felt as if he already knew her. She smiled as she said "Oh yes, I recognise you"; yet in spite of this admission of long acquaintance it was the first he had seen of her smile. The effect of it was suddenly to contribute more to that acquaintance than all the previous meetings had done. He hadn't "taken in," he said to himself, that she was so pretty. Later, that evening – it was while he rolled along in a hansom on his way to dine out – he added that he hadn't taken in that she was so interesting. The next morning in the midst of his work he quite suddenly and irrelevantly reflected that his impression of her, beginning so far back, was like a winding river that had at last reached the sea.

His work in fact was blurred a little all that day by the sense of what had now passed between them. It wasn't much, but it had just made the difference. They had listened together to Beethoven and Schumann; they had talked in the pauses, and at the end, when at the door, to which they moved together, he had asked her if he could help her in the matter of getting away. She had thanked him and put up her umbrella, slipping into the crowd without an allusion to their meeting yet again and leaving him to remember at leisure that not a word had been exchanged about the usual scene of that coincidence. This omission struck him now as natural and then again as perverse. She mightn't in the least have allowed his warrant for speaking to her, and yet if she hadn't he would have judged her an underbred woman. It was odd that when nothing had really ever brought them together he should have been able successfully to assume they were in a manner old friends – that this negative quantity was somehow more than they could express. His success, it was true, had been qualified by her quick escape, so that there grew up in him an absurd desire to put it to some better test. Save in so far as some other poor chance might help him, such a test could be only to meet her afresh at church. Left to himself he would have gone to church the very next afternoon, just for the curiosity of seeing if he should find her there. But he wasn't left to himself, a fact he discovered quite at the last, after he had virtually made up his mind to go. The influence that kept him away really revealed to him how little to himself his Dead *ever* left him. He went only for *them* – for nothing else in the world.

The force of this revulsion kept him away ten days: he hated to connect the place with anything but his offices or to give a glimpse of the curiosity that had been on the point of moving him. It was absurd to weave a tangle about a matter so simple as a custom of devotion that might with ease have been daily or hourly; yet the tangle got itself woven. He was sorry, he was disappointed: it was as if a long happy spell had been broken and he had lost a familiar security. At the last, however, he asked himself if he was to stay away for ever from the fear of this muddle about motives. After an interval neither longer nor shorter than usual he re-entered the church with a clear conviction that he should scarcely heed the presence or the absence of the lady of the concert. This indifference didn't prevent his at once noting that for the only time since he had first seen her she wasn't on the spot. He had now no scruple about giving her time to arrive, but she didn't arrive, and when he went away still missing her he was profanely and consentingly sorry. If her absence made the tangle more intricate, that was all her own doing. By the end of another year it was very intricate indeed; but by that time he didn't in the least care, and it was only his cultivated consciousness that had given him scruples. Three times in three months he had gone to church without finding her, and he felt he hadn't needed these occasions to show him his suspense had dropped. Yet it was, incongruously, not indifference, but a refinement of delicacy that had kept him from asking the sacristan, who would of course immediately have recognised his description of her, whether she had been seen at other hours. His delicacy had kept him from asking any question about her at any time, and it was exactly the same virtue that had left him so free to be decently civil to her at the concert.

This happy advantage now served him anew, enabling him when she finally met his eyes – it was after a fourth trial – to predetermine quite fixedly his awaiting her retreat. He joined her in the street as soon as she had moved, asking her if he might accompany her a certain distance. With her placid permission he went as far as a house in the neighbourhood at which she had business: she let him know it was not where she lived. She lived, as she said, in a mere slum, with an old aunt, a person in connexion with whom she spoke of the engrossment of humdrum duties and regular occupations. She wasn't, the mourning niece, in her first youth, and her vanished freshness had left something behind that, for Stransom, represented the proof it had been tragically sacrificed. Whatever she gave him the assurance of she gave without references. She might have been a divorced duchess – she might have been an old maid who taught the harp.

Chapter V

THEY FELL AT LAST into the way of walking together almost every time they met, though for a long time still they never met but at church. He couldn't ask her to come and see him, and as if she hadn't a proper place to receive him she never invited her friend. As much as himself she knew the world of London, but from an undiscussed instinct of privacy they haunted the region not mapped on the social chart. On the return she always made him leave her at the same corner. She looked with him, as a pretext for a pause, at the depressed things in suburban shop-fronts; and there was never a word he had said to her that she hadn't beautifully understood. For long ages he never knew her name, any more than she had ever pronounced his own; but it was not their names that mattered, it was only their perfect practice and their common need.

These things made their whole relation so impersonal that they hadn't the rules or reasons people found in ordinary friendships. They didn't care for the things it was supposed necessary to care for in the intercourse of the world. They ended one day – they never knew which of them expressed it first – by throwing out the idea that they didn't care for each other. Over this idea they grew quite intimate; they rallied to it in a way that marked a fresh start in their confidence. If to feel deeply together about certain things wholly distinct from themselves didn't constitute a safety, where was safety to be looked for? Not lightly nor often, not without occasion nor without emotion, any more than in any other reference by serious people to a mystery of their faith; but when something had happened to warm, as it were, the air for it, they came as near as they could come to calling their Dead by name. They felt it was coming very near to utter their thought at all.

The word "they" expressed enough; it limited the mention, it had a dignity of its own, and if, in their talk, you had heard our friends use it, you might have taken them for a pair of pagans of old alluding decently to the domesticated gods. They never knew – at least Stransom never knew – how they had learned to be sure about each other. If it had been with each a question of what the other was there for, the certitude had come in some fine way of its own. Any faith, after all, has the instinct of propagation, and it was as natural as it was beautiful that they should have taken pleasure on the spot in the imagination of a following. If the following was for each but a following of one it had proved in the event sufficient. Her debt, however, of course was much greater than his, because while she had only given him a worshipper he had given her a splendid temple. Once she said she pitied him for the length of his list – she had counted his candles almost as often as himself – and this made him wonder what could have been the length of hers. He had wondered before at the coincidence of their losses, especially as from time to time a new candle was set up. On some occasion some accident led him to express this curiosity, and she answered as if in surprise that he hadn't already understood. "Oh for me, you know, the more there are the better – there could never be too many. I should like hundreds and hundreds – I should like thousands; I should like a great mountain of light."

Then of course in a flash he understood. "Your Dead are only One?"

She hung back at this as never yet. "Only One," she answered, colouring as if now he knew her guarded secret. It really made him feel he knew less than before, so difficult was it for him to reconstitute a life in which a single experience had so belittled all others. His own life, round its central hollow, had been packed close enough. After this she appeared to have regretted her confession, though at the moment she spoke there had been pride in her very embarrassment. She declared to him that his own was the larger, the dearer possession – the portion one would have chosen if one had been able to choose; she assured him she could perfectly imagine some of the echoes with which his silences were peopled. He knew she couldn't: one's relation to what one had loved and hated had been a relation too distinct from the relations of others. But this didn't affect the fact that they were growing old together in their piety. She was a feature of that piety, but even at the ripe stage of acquaintance in which they occasionally arranged to meet at a concert or to go together to an exhibition she was not a feature of anything else. The most that happened was that his worship became paramount. Friend by friend dropped away till at last there were more emblems on his altar than houses left him to enter. She was more than any other the friend who remained, but she was unknown to all the rest. Once when she had discovered, as they called it, a new star, she used the expression that the chapel at last was full.

"Oh no," Stransom replied, "there is a great thing wanting for that! The chapel will never be full till a candle is set up before which all the others will pale. It will be the tallest candle of all."

Her mild wonder rested on him. "What candle do you mean?"

"I mean, dear lady, my own."

He had learned after a long time that she earned money by her pen, writing under a pseudonym she never disclosed in magazines he never saw. She knew too well what he couldn't read and what she couldn't write, and she taught him to cultivate indifference with a success that did much for their good relations. Her invisible industry was a convenience to him; it helped his contented thought of her, the thought that rested in the dignity of her proud obscure life, her little remunerated art and her little impenetrable home.

Lost, with her decayed relative, in her dim suburban world, she came to the surface for him in distant places. She was really the priestess of his altar, and whenever he quitted England he committed it to her keeping. She proved to him afresh that women have more of the spirit of religion than men; he felt his fidelity pale and faint in comparison with hers. He often said to her that since he had so little time to live he rejoiced in her having so much; so glad was he to think she would guard the temple when he should have been called. He had a great plan for that, which of course he told her too, a bequest of money to keep it up in undiminished state. Of the administration of this fund he would appoint her superintendent, and if the spirit should move her she might kindle a taper even for him.

"And who will kindle one even for me?" she then seriously asked.

Chapter VI

SHE WAS ALWAYS IN MOURNING, yet the day he came back from the longest absence he had yet made her appearance immediately told him she had lately had a bereavement. They met on this occasion as she was leaving the church, so that postponing his own entrance he instantly offered to turn round and walk away with her. She considered, then she said: "Go in now, but come and see me in an hour." He knew the small vista of her street, closed at the end and as dreary as an empty pocket, where the pairs of shabby little houses, semi-detached but indissolubly united, were like married couples on bad terms. Often, however, as he had gone to the beginning he had never gone beyond. Her aunt was dead – that he immediately guessed, as well as that it made a difference; but when she had for the first time mentioned her number he found himself, on her leaving him, not a little agitated by this sudden liberality. She wasn't a person with whom, after all, one got on so very fast: it had taken him months and months to learn her name, years and years to learn her address. If she had looked, on this reunion, so much older to him, how in the world did he look to her? She had reached the period of life he had long since reached, when, after separations, the marked clock-face of the friend we meet announces the hour we have tried to forget. He couldn't have said what he expected as, at the end of his waiting, he turned the corner where for years he had always paused; simply not to pause was an efficient cause for emotion. It was an event, somehow; and in all their long acquaintance there had never been an event. This one grew larger when, five minutes later, in the faint elegance of her little drawing-room, she quavered out a greeting that showed the measure she took of it. He had a strange sense of having come for something in particular; strange because literally there was nothing particular between them, nothing save that they were at one on their great point, which had long ago become a magnificent matter of course. It was true that after she had said "You can always come now, you know," the thing he was there for seemed already to have happened. He asked her if it was the death of her aunt that made the difference; to which she replied: "She never knew I knew you. I wished her not to." The beautiful clearness of her candour – her faded beauty was like a summer twilight – disconnected the words from any image of deceit. They might have struck him as the record of a deep dissimulation; but she had always given him a sense of noble reasons. The vanished aunt was present, as he looked about him, in the small complacencies of the room, the beaded velvet and the fluted moreen; and though, as we know, he had the worship of the Dead, he found himself not definitely regretting this lady. If she wasn't in his long list, however, she was in her niece's short one, and Stransom presently observed to the latter that now at least, in the place they haunted together, she would have another object of devotion.

"Yes, I shall have another. She was very kind to me. It's that that's the difference."

He judged, wondering a good deal before he made any motion to leave her, that the difference would somehow be very great and would consist of still other things than her having let him come in. It rather chilled him, for they had been happy together as they were. He extracted from her at any rate an intimation that she should now have means less limited, that her aunt's tiny fortune had come to her, so that there was henceforth only one to consume what had formerly been made to suffice for two. This was a joy to Stransom, because it had hitherto been equally impossible for him either to offer her presents or contentedly to stay his hand. It was too ugly to be at her side that way, abounding himself and yet not able to overflow – a demonstration that would have been signally a false note. Even her better situation too seemed only to draw out in a sense the loneliness of her future. It would merely help her to live more and more for their small ceremonial, and this at a time when he himself had begun wearily to feel that, having set it in motion, he might depart. When they had sat a while in the pale parlour she got up – "This isn't my room: let us go into mine." They had only to cross the narrow hall, as he found, to pass quite into another air. When she had closed the door of the second room, as she called it, he felt at last in real possession of her. The place had the flush of life – it was expressive; its dark red walls were articulate with memories and relics. These were simple things – photographs and water-colours, scraps of writing framed and ghosts of flowers embalmed; but a moment sufficed to show him they had a common meaning. It was here she had lived and worked, and she had already told him she would make no change of scene. He read the reference in the objects about her – the general one to places and times; but after a minute he distinguished among them a small portrait of a gentleman. At a distance and without their glasses his eyes were only so caught by it as to feel a vague curiosity. Presently this impulse carried him nearer, and in another moment he was staring at the picture in stupefaction and with the sense that some sound had broken from him. He was further conscious that he showed his companion a white face when he turned round on her gasping: "Acton Hague!"

She matched his great wonder. "Did you know him?"

"He was the friend of all my youth – of my early manhood. And *you* knew him?"

She coloured at this and for a moment her answer failed; her eyes embraced everything in the place, and a strange irony reached her lips as she echoed: "Knew him?"

Then Stransom understood, while the room heaved like the cabin of a ship, that its whole contents cried out with him, that it was a museum in his honour, that all her later years had been addressed to him and that the shrine he himself had reared had been passionately converted to this use. It was all for Acton Hague that she had kneeled every day at his altar. What need had there been for a consecrated candle when he was present in the whole array? The revelation so smote our friend in the face that he dropped into a seat and sat silent. He had quickly felt her shaken by the force of his shock, but as she sank on the sofa beside him and laid her hand on his arm he knew almost as soon that she mightn't resent it as much as she'd have liked.

Chapter VII

HE LEARNED IN THAT INSTANT two things: one being that even in so long a time she had gathered no knowledge of his great intimacy and his great quarrel; the other that in spite of this ignorance, strangely enough, she supplied on the spot a reason for his stupor. "How extraordinary," he presently exclaimed, "that we should never have known!"

She gave a wan smile which seemed to Stransom stranger even than the fact itself. "I never, never spoke of him."

He looked again about the room. "Why then, if your life had been so full of him?"

"Mayn't I put you that question as well? Hadn't your life also been full of him?"

"Anyone's, everyone's life who had the wonderful experience of knowing him. *I* never spoke of him," Stransom added in a moment, "because he did me – years ago – an unforgettable wrong." She was silent, and with the full effect of his presence all about them it almost startled her guest to hear no protest escape her. She accepted his words, he turned his eyes to her again to see in what manner she accepted them. It was with rising tears and a rare sweetness in the movement of putting out her hand to take his own. Nothing more wonderful had ever appeared to him than, in that little chamber of remembrance and homage, to see her convey with such exquisite mildness that as from Acton Hague any injury was credible. The clock ticked in the stillness – Hague had probably given it to her – and while he let her hold his hand with a tenderness that was almost an assumption of responsibility for his old pain as well as his new, Stransom after a minute broke out: "Good God, how he must have used *you*!"

She dropped his hand at this, got up and, moving across the room, made straight a small picture to which, on examining it, he had given a slight push. Then turning round on him with her pale gaiety recovered, "I've forgiven him!" she declared.

"I know what you've done," said Stransom "I know what you've done for years." For a moment they looked at each other through it all with their long community of service in their eyes. This short passage made, to his sense, for the woman before him, an immense, an absolutely naked confession; which was presently, suddenly blushing red and changing her place again, what she appeared to learn he perceived in it. He got up and "How you must have loved him!" he cried.

"Women aren't like men. They can love even where they've suffered."

"Women are wonderful," said Stransom. "But I assure you I've forgiven him too."

"If I had known of anything so strange I wouldn't have brought you here."

"So that we might have gone on in our ignorance to the last?"

"What do you call the last?" she asked, smiling still.

At this he could smile back at her. "You'll see – when it comes."

She thought of that. "This is better perhaps; but as we were – it was good."

He put her the question. "Did it never happen that he spoke of me?"

Considering more intently she made no answer, and he then knew he should have been adequately answered by her asking how often he himself had spoken of their terrible friend. Suddenly a brighter light broke in her face and an excited idea sprang to her lips in the appeal: "You *have* forgiven him?"

"How, if I hadn't, could I linger here?"

She visibly winced at the deep but unintended irony of this; but even while she did so she panted quickly: "Then in the lights on your altar –?"

"There's never a light for Acton Hague!"

She stared with a dreadful fall, "But if he's one of your Dead?"

"He's one of the world's, if you like – he's one of yours. But he's not one of mine. Mine are only the Dead who died possessed of me. They're mine in death because they were mine in life."

"*He* was yours in life then, even if for a while he ceased to be. If you forgave him you went back to him. Those whom we've once loved –"

"Are those who can hurt us most," Stransom broke in.

"Ah it's not true – you've *not* forgiven him!" she wailed with a passion that startled him.

He looked at her as never yet. "What was it he did to you?"

"Everything!" Then abruptly she put out her hand in farewell. "Good-bye."

He turned as cold as he had turned that night he read the man's death. "You mean that we meet no more?"

"Not as we've met – not *there*!"

He stood aghast at this snap of their great bond, at the renouncement that rang out in the word she so expressively sounded. "But what's changed – for you?"

She waited in all the sharpness of a trouble that for the first time since he had known her made her splendidly stern. "How can you understand now when you didn't understand before?"

"I didn't understand before only because I didn't know. Now that I know, I see what I've been living with for years," Stransom went on very gently.

She looked at him with a larger allowance, doing this gentleness justice. "How can I then, on this new knowledge of my own, ask you to continue to live with it?"

"I set up my altar, with its multiplied meanings," Stransom began; but she quietly interrupted him.

"You set up your altar, and when I wanted one most I found it magnificently ready. I used it with the gratitude I've always shown you, for I knew it from of old to be dedicated to Death. I told you long ago that my Dead weren't many. Yours were, but all you had done for them was none too much for *my* worship! You had placed a great light for Each – I gathered them together for One!"

"We had simply different intentions," he returned. "That, as you say, I perfectly knew, and I don't see why your intention shouldn't still sustain you."

"That's because you're generous – you can imagine and think. But the spell is broken."

It seemed to poor Stransom, in spite of his resistance, that it really was, and the prospect stretched grey and void before him. All he could say, however, was: "I hope you'll try before you give up."

"If I had known you had ever known him I should have taken for granted he had his candle," she presently answered. "What's changed, as you say, is that on making the discovery I find he never has had it. That makes *my* attitude" – she paused as thinking how to express it, then said simply – "all wrong."

"Come once again," he pleaded.

"Will you give him his candle?" she asked.

He waited, but only because it would sound ungracious; not because of a doubt of his feeling. "I can't do that!" he declared at last.

"Then good-bye." And she gave him her hand again.

He had got his dismissal; besides which, in the agitation of everything that had opened out to him, he felt the need to recover himself as he could only do in solitude. Yet he lingered – lingered to see if she had no compromise to express, no attenuation to propose. But he only met her great lamenting eyes, in which indeed he read that she was as sorry for him as for anyone else. This made him say: "At least, in any case, I may see you here."

"Oh yes, come if you like. But I don't think it will do."

He looked round the room once more, knowing how little he was sure it would do. He felt also stricken and more and more cold, and his chill was like an ague in which he had to make an effort not to shake. Then he made doleful reply: "I must try on my side – if you can't try on yours." She came out with him to the hall and into the doorway, and here he put her the question he held he could least answer from his own wit. "Why have you never let me come before?"

"Because my aunt would have seen you, and I should have had to tell her how I came to know you."

"And what would have been the objection to that?"

"It would have entailed other explanations; there would at any rate have been that danger."

"Surely she knew you went every day to church," Stransom objected.

"She didn't know what I went for."

"Of me then she never even heard?"

"You'll think I was deceitful. But I didn't need to be!"

He was now on the lower door-step, and his hostess held the door half-closed behind him. Through what remained of the opening he saw her framed face. He made a supreme appeal. "What *did* he do to you?"

"It would have come out – *she* would have told you. That fear at my heart – that was my reason!" And she closed the door, shutting him out.

Chapter VIII

HE HAD RUTHLESSLY abandoned her – that of course was what he had done. Stransom made it all out in solitude, at leisure, fitting the unmatched pieces gradually together and dealing one by one with a hundred obscure points. She had known Hague only after her present friend's relations with him had wholly terminated; obviously indeed a good while after; and it was natural enough that of his previous life she should have ascertained only what he had judged good to communicate. There were passages it was quite conceivable that even in moments of the tenderest expansion he should have withheld. Of many facts in the career of a man so in the eye of the world there was of course a common knowledge; but this lady lived apart from public affairs, and the only time perfectly clear to her would have been the time following the dawn of her own drama. A man in her place would have "looked up" the past – would even have consulted old newspapers. It remained remarkable indeed that in her long contact with the partner of her retrospect no accident had lighted a train; but there was no arguing about that; the accident had in fact come: it had simply been that security had prevailed. She had taken what Hague had given her, and her blankness in respect of his other connexions was only a touch in the picture of that plasticity Stransom had supreme reason to know so great a master could have been trusted to produce.

This picture was for a while all our friend saw: he caught his breath again and again as it came over him that the woman with whom he had had for years so fine a point of contact was a woman whom Acton Hague, of all men in the world, had more or less fashioned. Such as she sat there today she was ineffaceably stamped with him. Beneficent, blameless as Stransom held her, he couldn't rid himself of the sense that he had been, as who should say, swindled. She had imposed upon him hugely, though she had known it as little as he. All this later past came back to him as a time grotesquely misspent. Such at least were his first reflexions; after a while he found himself more divided and only, as the end of it, more troubled. He imagined, recalled, reconstituted, figured out for himself the truth she had refused to give him; the effect of which was to make her seem to him only more saturated with her fate. He felt her spirit, through the whole strangeness, finer than his own to the very degree in which she might have been, in which she certainly had been, more wronged. A woman, when wronged, was always more wronged than a man, and there were conditions when the least she could have got off with was more than the most he could have to bear. He was sure this rare creature wouldn't have got off with the least. He was awestruck at the thought of such a surrender – such a prostration. Moulded indeed she had been by powerful hands, to have converted her injury into an exaltation so sublime. The fellow had only had to die for everything that was ugly in him to be washed out in a torrent. It was vain to try to guess what had taken place, but nothing could be clearer than that she had ended by accusing herself. She absolved him at every point, she adored her very wounds. The passion by which he had profited had rushed back after its ebb, and now the tide of tenderness, arrested for ever at flood, was too deep even to fathom. Stransom sincerely considered that he had forgiven him; but how little he had achieved the miracle that she had achieved! His forgiveness was silence, but hers was mere unuttered sound. The light she had demanded for his altar would have broken his silence with a blare; whereas all the lights in the church were for her too great a hush.

She had been right about the difference – she had spoken the truth about the change: Stransom was soon to know himself as perversely but sharply jealous. *His* tide had ebbed, not flowed; if he had "forgiven" Acton Hague, that forgiveness was a motive with a broken spring. The very fact of her appeal for a material sign, a sign that should make her dead lover equal there with the others, presented the concession to her friend as too handsome for the case. He had never thought of himself as hard, but an exorbitant article might easily render him so. He moved round and round this one, but only in widening circles – the more he looked at it the less acceptable it seemed. At the same time he had no illusion about the effect of his refusal; he perfectly saw how it would make for a rupture. He left her alone a week, but when at last he again called this conviction was cruelly confirmed. In the interval he had kept away from the church, and he needed no fresh assurance from her to know she hadn't entered it. The change was complete enough: it had broken up her life. Indeed it had broken up his, for all the fires of his shrine seemed to him suddenly to have been quenched. A great indifference fell upon him, the weight of which was in itself a pain; and he never knew what his devotion had been for him till in that shock it ceased like a dropped watch. Neither did he know with how large a confidence he had counted on the final service that had now failed: the mortal deception was that in this abandonment the whole future gave way.

These days of her absence proved to him of what she was capable; all the more that he never dreamed she was vindictive or even resentful. It was not in anger she had forsaken him; it was in simple submission to hard reality, to the stern logic of life. This came home to him when he sat with her again in the room in which her late aunt's conversation lingered like the tone of a cracked piano. She tried to make him forget how much they were estranged, but in the very presence of what they had given up it was impossible not to be sorry for her. He had taken from her so much more than she had taken from him. He argued with her again, told her she could now have the altar to herself; but she only shook her head with pleading sadness, begging him not to waste his breath on the impossible, the extinct. Couldn't he see that in relation to her private need the rites he had established were practically an elaborate exclusion? She regretted nothing that had happened; it had all been right so long as she didn't know, and it was only that now she knew too much and that from the moment their eyes were open they would simply have to conform. It had doubtless been happiness enough for them to go on together so long. She was gentle, grateful, resigned; but this was only the form of a deep immoveability. He saw he should never more cross the threshold of the second room, and he felt how much this alone would make a stranger of him and give a conscious stiffness to his visits. He would have hated to plunge again into that well of reminders, but he enjoyed quite as little the vacant alternative.

After he had been with her three or four times it struck him that to have come at last into her house had had the horrid effect of diminishing their intimacy. He had known her better, had liked her in greater freedom, when they merely walked together or kneeled together. Now they only pretended; before they had been nobly sincere. They began to try their walks again, but it proved a lame imitation, for these things, from the first, beginning or ending, had been connected with their visits to the church. They had either strolled away as they came out or gone in to rest on the return. Stransom, besides, now faltered; he couldn't walk as of old. The omission made everything false; it was a dire mutilation of their lives. Our friend was frank and monotonous, making no mystery of his remonstrance and no secret of his predicament. Her response, whatever it was, always came to the same thing – an implied invitation to him to judge, if he spoke of predicaments, of how much comfort she had in hers. For him indeed was no comfort even in complaint, since every allusion to what had befallen them but made the author of their trouble more present. Acton Hague was between them – that was the essence of the matter, and never so much between them as when they were face to face. Then Stransom, while still wanting to banish him, had the strangest sense of striving for an ease that would involve having accepted him. Deeply disconcerted by what he knew, he was still worse tormented by really not knowing. Perfectly aware that it would have been horribly vulgar to abuse his old friend or to tell his companion the story of their quarrel, it yet vexed him that her depth of reserve should give him no opening and should have the effect of a magnanimity greater even than his own.

He challenged himself, denounced himself, asked himself if he were in love with her that he should care so much what adventures she had had. He had never for a moment allowed he was in love with her; therefore nothing could have surprised him more than to discover he was jealous. What but jealousy could give a man that sore contentious wish for the detail of what would make him suffer? Well enough he knew indeed that he should never have it from the only person who today could give it to him. She let him press her with his sombre eyes, only smiling at him with an exquisite mercy and breathing equally little the word that would expose her secret and the word that would appear to deny his literal right to bitterness. She told nothing, she judged nothing; she accepted everything but the possibility of her return to the old symbols. Stransom divined that for her too they had been vividly individual, had stood for particular hours or particular attributes – particular links in her chain. He made it clear to himself, as he believed, that his difficulty lay in the fact that the very nature of the plea for his faithless friend constituted a prohibition; that it happened to have come from *her* was precisely the vice that attached to it. To the voice of impersonal generosity he felt sure he would have listened; he would have deferred to an advocate who, speaking from abstract justice, knowing of his denial without having known Hague, should have had the imagination to say: "Ah, remember only the best of him; pity him; provide for him." To provide for him on the very ground of having discovered another of his turpitudes was not to pity but to glorify him. The more Stransom thought the more he made out that whatever this relation of Hague's it could only have been a deception more or less finely practised. Where had it come into the life that all men saw? Why had one never heard of it if it had had the frankness of honourable things? Stransom knew enough of his other ties, of his obligations and appearances, not to say enough of his general character, to be sure there had been some infamy. In one way or another this creature had been coldly sacrificed. That was why at the last as well as the first he must still leave him out and out.

Chapter IX

AND YET THIS WAS NO SOLUTION, especially after he had talked again to his friend of all it had been his plan she should finally do for him. He had talked in the other days, and she had responded with a frankness qualified only by a courteous reluctance, a reluctance that touched him, to linger on the question of his death. She had then practically accepted the charge, suffered him to feel he could depend upon her to be the eventual guardian of his shrine; and it was in the name of what had so passed between them that he appealed to her not to forsake him in his age. She listened at present with shining coldness and all her habitual forbearance to insist on her terms; her deprecation was even still tenderer, for it expressed the compassion of her own sense that he was abandoned. Her terms, however, remained the same, and scarcely the less audible for not being uttered; though he was sure that secretly even more than he she felt bereft of the satisfaction his solemn trust was to have provided her. They both missed the rich future, but she missed it most, because after all it was to have been entirely hers; and it was her acceptance of the loss that gave him the full measure of her preference for the thought of Acton Hague over any other thought whatever. He had humour enough to laugh rather grimly when he said to himself: "Why the deuce does she like him so much more than she likes me?" – the reasons being really so conceivable. But even his faculty of analysis left the irritation standing, and this irritation proved perhaps the greatest misfortune that had ever overtaken him. There had been nothing yet that made him so much want to give up. He had of course by this time well reached the age of renouncement; but it had not hitherto been vivid to him that it was time to give up everything.

Practically, at the end of six months, he had renounced the friendship once so charming and comforting. His privation had two faces, and the face it had turned to him on the occasion of his last attempt to cultivate that friendship was the one he could look at least. This was the privation he inflicted; the other was the privation he bore. The conditions she never phrased he used to murmur to himself in solitude: "One more, one more – only just one." Certainly he was going down; he often felt it when he caught himself, over his work, staring at vacancy and giving voice to that inanity. There was proof enough besides in his being so weak and so ill. His irritation took the form of melancholy, and his melancholy that of the conviction that his health had quite failed. His altar moreover had ceased to exist; his chapel, in his dreams, was a great dark cavern. All the lights had gone out – all his Dead had died again. He couldn't exactly see at first how it had been in the power of his late companion to extinguish them, since it was neither for her nor by her that they had been called into being. Then he understood that it was essentially in his own soul the revival had taken place, and that in the air of this soul they were now unable to breathe. The candles might mechanically burn, but each of them had lost its lustre. The church had become a void; it was his presence, her presence, their common presence, that had made the indispensable medium. If anything was wrong everything was – her silence spoiled the tune.

Then when three months were gone he felt so lonely that he went back; reflecting that as they had been his best society for years his Dead perhaps wouldn't let him forsake them without doing something more for him. They stood there, as he had left them, in their tall radiance, the bright cluster that had already made him, on occasions when he was willing to compare small things with great, liken them to a group of sea-lights on the edge of the ocean of life. It was a relief to him, after a while, as he sat there, to feel they had still a virtue. He was more and more easily tired, and he always drove now; the action of his heart was weak and gave him none of the reassurance conferred by the action of his fancy. None the less he returned yet again, returned several times, and finally, during six months, haunted the place with a renewal of frequency and a strain of impatience. In winter the church was unwarmed and exposure to cold forbidden him, but the glow of his shrine was an influence in which he could almost bask. He sat and wondered to what he had reduced his absent associate and what she now did with the hours of her absence. There were other churches, there were other altars, there were other candles; in one way or another her piety would still operate; he couldn't absolutely have deprived her of her rites. So he argued, but without contentment; for he well enough knew there was no other such rare semblance of the mountain of light she had once mentioned to him as the satisfaction of her need. As this semblance again gradually grew great to him and his pious practice more regular, he found a sharper and sharper pang in the imagination of her darkness; for never so much as in these weeks had his rites been real, never had his gathered company seemed so to respond and even to invite. He lost himself in the large lustre, which was more and more what he had from the first wished it to be – as dazzling as the vision of heaven in the mind of a child. He wandered in the fields of light; he passed, among the tall tapers, from tier to tier, from fire to fire, from name to name, from the white intensity of one clear emblem, of one saved soul, to another. It was in the quiet sense of having saved his souls that his deep strange instinct rejoiced. This was no dim theological rescue, no boon of a contingent world; they were saved better than faith or works could save them, saved for the warm world they had shrunk from dying to, for actuality, for continuity, for the certainty of human remembrance.

By this time he had survived all his friends; the last straight flame was three years old, there was no one to add to the list. Over and over he called his roll, and it appeared to him compact and complete. Where should he put in another, where, if there were no other objection, would it stand in its place in the rank? He reflected, with a want of sincerity of which he was quite conscious, that it would be difficult to determine that place. More and more, besides, face to face with his little legion, over endless histories, handling the empty shells and playing with the silence – more and more he could see that he had never introduced an alien. He had had his great companions, his indulgences – there were cases in which they had been immense; but what had his devotion after all been if it hadn't been at bottom a respect? He was, however, himself surprised at his stiffness; by the end of the winter the responsibility of it was what was uppermost in his thoughts. The refrain had grown old to them, that plea for just one more. There came a day when, for simple exhaustion, if symmetry should demand just one he was ready so far to meet symmetry. Symmetry was harmony, and the idea of harmony began to haunt him; he said to himself that harmony was of course everything. He took, in fancy, his composition to pieces, redistributing it into other lines, making other juxtapositions and contrasts. He shifted this and that candle, he made the spaces different, he effaced the disfigurement of a possible gap. There were subtle and complex relations, a scheme of cross-reference, and moments in which he seemed to catch a glimpse of the void so sensible to the woman who wandered in exile or sat where he had seen her with the portrait of Acton Hague. Finally, in this way, he arrived at a conception of the total, the ideal, which left a clear opportunity for just another figure. "Just one more – to round it off; just one more, just one," continued to hum in his head. There was a strange confusion in the thought, for he felt the day to be near when he too should be one of the Others. What in this event would the Others matter to him, since they only mattered to the living? Even as one of the Dead what would his altar matter to him, since his particular dream of keeping it up had melted away? What had harmony to do with the case if his lights were all to be quenched? What he had hoped for was an instituted thing. He might perpetuate it on some other pretext, but his special meaning would have dropped. This meaning was to have lasted with the life of the one other person who understood it.

In March he had an illness during which he spent a fortnight in bed, and when he revived a little he was told of two things that had happened. One was that a lady whose name was not known to the servants (she left none) had been three times to ask about him; the other was that in his sleep and on an occasion when his mind evidently wandered he was heard to murmur again and again: "Just one more – just one." As soon as he found himself able to go out, and before the doctor in attendance had pronounced him so, he drove to see the lady who had come to ask about him. She was not at home; but this gave him the opportunity, before his strength should fall again, to take his way to the church. He entered it alone; he had declined, in a happy manner he possessed of being able to decline effectively, the company of his servant or of a nurse. He knew now perfectly what these good people thought; they had discovered his clandestine connexion, the magnet that had drawn him for so many years, and doubtless attached a significance of their own to the odd words they had repeated to him. The nameless lady was the clandestine connexion – a fact nothing could have made clearer than his indecent haste to rejoin her. He sank on his knees before his altar while his head fell over on his hands. His weakness, his life's weariness overtook him. It seemed to him he had come for the great surrender. At first he asked himself how he should get away; then, with the failing belief in the power, the very desire to move gradually left him. He had come, as he always came, to lose himself; the fields of light were still there to stray in; only this time, in straying, he would never come back. He had given himself to his Dead, and it was good: this time his Dead would keep him. He couldn't rise from his knees; he believed he should never rise again; all he could do was to lift his face and fix his eyes on his lights. They looked unusually, strangely splendid, but the one that always drew him most had an unprecedented lustre. It was the central voice of the choir, the glowing heart of the brightness, and on this occasion it seemed to expand, to spread great wings of flame. The whole altar flared – dazzling and blinding; but the source of the vast radiance burned clearer than the rest, gathering itself into form, and the form was human beauty and human charity, was the far-off face of Mary Antrim. She smiled at him from the glory of heaven – she brought the glory down with her to take him. He bowed his head in submission and at the same moment another wave rolled over him. Was it the quickening of joy to pain? In the midst of his joy at any rate he felt his buried face grow hot as with some communicated knowledge that had the force of a reproach. It suddenly made him contrast that very rapture with the bliss he had refused to another. This breath of the passion immortal was all that other had asked; the descent of Mary Antrim opened his spirit with a great compunctious throb for the descent of Acton Hague. It was as if Stransom had read what her eyes said to him.

After a moment he looked round in a despair that made him feel as if the source of life were ebbing. The church had been empty – he was alone; but he wanted to have something done, to make a last appeal. This idea gave him strength for an effort; he rose to his feet with a movement that made him turn, supporting himself by the back of a bench. Behind him was a prostrate figure, a figure he had seen before; a woman in deep mourning, bowed in grief or in prayer. He had seen her in other days – the first time of his entrance there, and he now slightly wavered, looking at her again till she seemed aware he had noticed her. She raised her head and met his eyes: the partner of his long worship had come back. She looked across at him an instant with a face wondering and scared; he saw he had made her afraid. Then quickly rising she came straight to him with both hands out.

"Then you *could* come? God sent you!" he murmured with a happy smile.

"You're very ill – you shouldn't be here," she urged in anxious reply.

"God sent me too, I think. I was ill when I came, but the sight of you does wonders." He held her hands, which steadied and quickened him. "I've something to tell you."

"Don't tell me!" she tenderly pleaded; "let me tell you. This afternoon, by a miracle, the sweetest of miracles, the sense of our difference left me. I was out – I was near, thinking, wandering alone, when, on the spot, something changed in my heart. It's my confession – there it is. To come back, to come back on the instant – the idea gave me wings. It was as if I suddenly saw something – as if it all became possible. I could come for what you yourself came for: that was enough. So here I am. It's not for my own – that's over. But I'm here for *them*." And breathless, infinitely relieved by her low precipitate explanation, she looked with eyes that reflected all its splendour at the magnificence of their altar.

"They're here for you," Stransom said, "they're present tonight as they've never been. They speak for you – don't you see? – in a passion of light; they sing out like a choir of angels. Don't you hear what they say? – they offer the very thing you asked of me."

"Don't talk of it – don't think of it; forget it!" She spoke in hushed supplication, and while the alarm deepened in her eyes she disengaged one of her hands and passed an arm round him to support him better, to help him to sink into a seat.

He let himself go, resting on her; he dropped upon the bench and she fell on her knees beside him, his own arm round her shoulder. So he remained an instant, staring up at his shrine. "They say there's a gap in the array – they say it's not full, complete. Just one more," he went on, softly – "isn't that what you wanted? Yes, one more, one more."

"Ah no more – no more!" she wailed, as with a quick new horror of it, under her breath.

"Yes, one more," he repeated, simply; "just one!" And with this his head dropped on her shoulder; she felt that in his weakness he had fainted. But alone with him in the dusky church a great dread was on her of what might still happen, for his face had the whiteness of death.

Count Magnus

M.R. James

BY WHAT MEANS the papers out of which I have made a connected story came into my hands is the last point which the reader will learn from these pages. But it is necessary to prefix to my extracts from them a statement of the form in which I possess them.

They consist, then, partly of a series of collections for a book of travels, such a volume as was a common product of the forties and fifties. Horace Marryat's *Journal of a Residence in Jutland and the Danish Isles* is a fair specimen of the class to which I allude. These books usually treated of some unknown district on the Continent. They were illustrated with woodcuts or steel plates. They gave details of hotel accommodation and of means of communication, such as we now expect to find in any well-regulated guide-book, and they dealt largely in reported conversations with intelligent foreigners, racy innkeepers, and garrulous peasants. In a word, they were chatty.

Begun with the idea of furnishing material for such a book, my papers as they progressed assumed the character of a record of one single personal experience, and this record was continued up to the very eve, almost, of its termination.

The writer was a Mr Wraxall. For my knowledge of him I have to depend entirely on the evidence his writings afford, and from these I deduce that he was a man past middle age, possessed of some private means, and very much alone in the world. He had, it seems, no settled abode in England, but was a denizen of hotels and boarding-houses. It is probable that he entertained the idea of settling down at some future time which never came; and I think it also likely that the Pantechnicon fire in the early seventies must have destroyed a great deal that would have thrown light on his antecedents, for he refers once or twice to property of his that was warehoused at that establishment.

It is further apparent that Mr Wraxall had published a book, and that it treated of a holiday he had once taken in Brittany. More than this I cannot say about his work, because a diligent search in bibliographical works has convinced me that it must have appeared either anonymously or under a pseudonym.

As to his character, it is not difficult to form some superficial opinion. He must have been an intelligent and cultivated man. It seems that he was near being a Fellow of his college at Oxford – Brasenose, as I judge from the Calendar. His besetting fault was pretty clearly that of over-inquisitiveness, possibly a good fault in a traveller, certainly a fault for which this traveller paid dearly enough in the end.

On what proved to be his last expedition, he was plotting another book. Scandinavia, a region not widely known to Englishmen forty years ago, had struck him as an interesting field. He must have alighted on some old books of Swedish history or memoirs, and the idea had struck him that there was room for a book descriptive of travel in Sweden, interspersed with episodes from the history of some of the great Swedish families. He procured letters of introduction, therefore, to some persons of quality in Sweden, and set out thither in the early summer of 1863.

Of his travels in the North there is no need to speak, nor of his residence of some weeks in Stockholm. I need only mention that some *savant* resident there put him on the track of an important collection of family papers belonging to the proprietors of an ancient manor-house in Vestergothland, and obtained for him permission to examine them.

The manor-house, or *herrgard*, in question is to be called Råbäck (pronounced something like Roebeck), though that is not its name. It is one of the best buildings of its kind in all the country, and the picture of it in Dahlenberg's *Suecia antiqua et moderna*, engraved in 1694, shows it very much as the tourist may see it today. It was built soon after 1600, and is, roughly speaking, very much like an English house of that period in respect of material – red-brick with stone facings – and style. The man who built it was a scion of the great house of De la Gardie, and his descendants possess it still. De la Gardie is the name by which I will designate them when mention of them becomes necessary.

They received Mr Wraxall with great kindness and courtesy, and pressed him to stay in the house as long as his researches lasted. But, preferring to be independent, and mistrusting his powers of conversing in Swedish, he settled himself at the village inn, which turned out quite sufficiently comfortable, at any rate during the summer months. This arrangement would entail a short walk daily to and from the manor-house of something under a mile. The house itself stood in a park, and was protected – we should say grown up – with large old timber. Near it you found the walled garden, and then entered a close wood fringing one of the small lakes with which the whole country is pitted. Then came the wall of the demesne, and you climbed a steep knoll – a knob of rock lightly covered with soil – and on the top of this stood the church, fenced in with tall dark trees. It was a curious building to English eyes. The nave and aisles were low, and filled with pews and galleries. In the western gallery stood the handsome old organ, gaily painted, and with silver pipes. The ceiling was flat, and had been adorned by a seventeenth-century artist with a strange and hideous "Last Judgement", full of lurid flames, falling cities, burning ships, crying souls, and brown and smiling demons. Handsome brass coronae hung from the roof; the pulpit was like a doll's-house covered with little painted wooden cherubs and saints; a stand with three hour-glasses was hinged to the preacher's desk. Such sights as these may be seen in many a church in Sweden now, but what distinguished this one was an addition to the original building. At the eastern end of the north aisle the builder of the manor-house had erected a mausoleum for himself and his family. It was a largish eight-sided building, lighted by a series of oval windows, and it had a domed roof, topped by a kind of pumpkin-shaped object rising into a spire, a form in which Swedish architects greatly delighted. The roof was of copper externally, and was painted black, while the walls, in common with those of the church, were staringly white. To this mausoleum there was no access from the church. It had a portal and steps of its own on the northern side.

Past the churchyard the path to the village goes, and not more than three or four minutes bring you to the inn door.

On the first day of his stay at Råbäck Mr Wraxall found the church door open, and made these notes of the interior which I have epitomized. Into the mausoleum, however, he could not make his way. He could by looking through the keyhole just descry that there were fine marble effigies and sarcophagi of copper, and a wealth of armorial ornament, which made him very anxious to spend some time in investigation.

The papers he had come to examine at the manor-house proved to be of just the kind he wanted for his book. There were family correspondence, journals, and account-books of the earliest owners of the estate, very carefully kept and clearly written, full of amusing and picturesque detail. The first De la Gardie appeared in them as a strong and capable man. Shortly after the building of the mansion there had been a period of distress in the district, and the peasants had risen and attacked several châteaux and done some damage. The owner of Råbäck took a leading part in suppressing trouble, and there was reference to executions of ring-leaders and severe punishments inflicted with no sparing hand.

The portrait of this Magnus de la Gardie was one of the best in the house, and Mr Wraxall studied it with no little interest after his day's work. He gives no detailed description of it, but I gather that the face impressed him rather by its power than by its beauty or goodness; in fact, he writes that Count Magnus was an almost phenomenally ugly man.

On this day Mr Wraxall took his supper with the family, and walked back in the late but still bright evening.

"I must remember," he writes, "to ask the sexton if he can let me into the mausoleum at the church. He evidently has access to it himself, for I saw him tonight standing on the steps, and, as I thought, locking or unlocking the door."

I find that early on the following day Mr Wraxall had some conversation with his landlord. His setting it down at such length as he does surprised me at first; but I soon realized that the papers I was reading were, at least in their beginning, the materials for the book he was meditating, and that it was to have been one of those quasi-journalistic productions which admit of the introduction of an admixture of conversational matter.

His object, he says, was to find out whether any traditions of Count Magnus de la Gardie lingered on in the scenes of that gentleman's activity, and whether the popular estimate of him were favourable or not. He found that the Count was decidedly not a favourite. If his tenants came late to their work on the days which they owed to him as Lord of the Manor, they were set on the wooden horse, or flogged and branded in the manor-house yard. One or two cases there were of men who had occupied lands which encroached on the lord's domain, and whose houses had been mysteriously burnt on a winter's night, with the whole family inside. But what seemed to dwell on the innkeeper's mind most – for he returned to the subject more than once – was that the Count had been on the Black Pilgrimage, and had brought something or someone back with him.

You will naturally inquire, as Mr Wraxall did, what the Black Pilgrimage may have been. But your curiosity on the point must remain unsatisfied for the time being, just as his did. The landlord was evidently unwilling to give a full answer, or indeed any answer, on the point, and, being called out for a moment, trotted out with obvious alacrity, only putting his head in at the door a few minutes afterwards to say that he was called away to Skara, and should not be back till evening.

So Mr Wraxall had to go unsatisfied to his day's work at the manor-house. The papers on which he was just then engaged soon put his thoughts into another channel, for he had to occupy himself with glancing over the correspondence between Sophia Albertina in Stockholm and her married cousin Ulrica Leonora at Råbäck in the years 1705–10. The letters were of exceptional interest from the light they threw upon the culture of that period in Sweden, as anyone can testify who has read the full edition of them in the publications of the Swedish Historical Manuscripts Commission.

In the afternoon he had done with these, and after returning the boxes in which they were kept to their places on the shelf, he proceeded, very naturally, to take down some of the volumes nearest to them, in order to determine which of them had best be his principal subject of investigation next day. The shelf he had hit upon was occupied mostly by a collection of account-books in the writing of the first Count Magnus. But one among them was not an account-book, but a book of alchemical and other tracts in another sixteenth-century hand. Not being very familiar with alchemical literature, Mr Wraxall spends much space which he might have spared in setting out the names and beginnings of the various treatises: The book of the Phoenix, book of the Thirty Words, book of the Toad, book of Miriam, Turba philosophorum, and so forth; and then he announces with a good deal of circumstance his delight at finding, on a leaf originally left blank near the middle of the book, some writing of Count Magnus himself headed "Liber nigrae peregrinationis". It is true that only a few lines were written, but there was quite enough to show that the landlord had that morning been referring to a belief at least as old as the time of Count Magnus, and probably shared by him. This is the English of what was written:

"If any man desires to obtain a long life, if he would obtain a faithful messenger and see the blood of his enemies, it is necessary that he should first go into the city of Chorazin, and there salute the prince…" Here there was an erasure of one word, not very thoroughly done, so that Mr Wraxall felt pretty sure that he was right in reading it as *aeris* ("of the air"). But there was no more of the text copied, only a line in Latin: *Quaere reliqua hujus materiei inter secretiora* (see the rest of this matter among the more private things).

It could not be denied that this threw a rather lurid light upon the tastes and beliefs of the Count; but to Mr Wraxall, separated from him by nearly three centuries, the thought that he might have added to his general forcefulness alchemy, and to alchemy something like magic, only made him a more picturesque figure, and when, after a rather prolonged contemplation of his picture in the hall, Mr Wraxall set out on his homeward way, his mind was full of the thought of Count Magnus. He had no eyes for his surroundings, no perception of the evening scents of the woods or the evening light on the lake; and when all of a sudden he pulled up short, he was astonished to find himself already at the gate of the churchyard, and within a few minutes of his dinner. His eyes fell on the mausoleum.

"Ah," he said, "Count Magnus, there you are. I should dearly like to see you."

"Like many solitary men," he writes, "I have a habit of talking to myself aloud; and, unlike some of the Greek and Latin particles, I do not expect an answer. Certainly, and perhaps fortunately in this case, there was neither voice nor any that regarded: only the woman who, I suppose, was cleaning up the church, dropped some metallic object on the floor, whose clang startled me. Count Magnus, I think, sleeps sound enough."

That same evening the landlord of the inn, who had heard Mr Wraxall say that he wished to see the clerk or deacon (as he would be called in Sweden) of the parish, introduced him to that official in the inn parlour. A visit to the De la Gardie tomb-house was soon arranged for the next day, and a little general conversation ensued.

Mr Wraxall, remembering that one function of Scandinavian deacons is to teach candidates for Confirmation, thought he would refresh his own memory on a Biblical point.

"Can you tell me," he said, "anything about Chorazin?"

The deacon seemed startled, but readily reminded him how that village had once been denounced.

"To be sure," said Mr Wraxall; "it is, I suppose, quite a ruin now?"

"So I expect," replied the deacon. "I have heard some of our old priests say that Antichrist is to be born there; and there are tales –"

"Ah! what tales are those?" Mr Wraxall put in.

"Tales, I was going to say, which I have forgotten," said the deacon; and soon after that he said good night.

The landlord was now alone, and at Mr Wraxall's mercy; and that inquirer was not inclined to spare him.

"Herr Nielsen," he said, "I have found out something about the Black Pilgrimage. You may as well tell me what you know. What did the Count bring back with him?"

Swedes are habitually slow, perhaps, in answering, or perhaps the landlord was an exception. I am not sure; but Mr Wraxall notes that the landlord spent at least one minute in looking at him before he said anything at all. Then he came close up to his guest, and with a good deal of effort he spoke:

"Mr Wraxall, I can tell you this one little tale, and no more – not any more. You must not ask anything when I have done. In my grandfather's time – that is, ninety-two years ago – there were two men who said: 'The Count is dead; we do not care for him. We will go tonight and have a free hunt in his wood' – the long wood on the hill that you have seen behind Råbäck. Well, those that heard them say this, they said: 'No, do not go; we are sure you will meet with persons walking who should not be walking. They should be resting, not walking.' These men laughed. There were no forestmen to keep the wood, because no one wished to live there. The family were not here at the house. These men could do what they wished.

"Very well, they go to the wood that night. My grandfather was sitting here in this room. It was the summer, and a light night. With the window open, he could see out to the wood, and hear.

"So he sat there, and two or three men with him, and they listened. At first they hear nothing at all; then they hear someone – you know how far away it is – they hear someone scream, just as if the most inside part of his soul was twisted out of him. All of them in the room caught hold of each other, and they sat so for three-quarters of an hour. Then they hear someone else, only about three hundred ells off. They hear him laugh out loud: it was not one of those two men that laughed, and, indeed, they have all of them said that it was not any man at all. After that they hear a great door shut.

"Then, when it was just light with the sun, they all went to the priest. They said to him:

"'Father, put on your gown and your ruff, and come to bury these men, Anders Bjornsen and Hans Thorbjorn.'

"You understand that they were sure these men were dead. So they went to the wood – my grandfather never forgot this. He said they were all like so many dead men themselves. The priest, too, he was in a white fear. He said when they came to him:

"'I heard one cry in the night, and I heard one laugh afterwards. If I cannot forget that, I shall not be able to sleep again.'

"So they went to the wood, and they found these men on the edge of the wood. Hans Thorbjorn was standing with his back against a tree, and all the time he was pushing with his hands – pushing something away from him which was not there. So he was not dead. And they led him away, and took him to the house at Nykjoping, and he died before the winter; but he went on pushing with his hands. Also Anders Bjornsen was there; but he was dead. And I tell you this about Anders Bjornsen, that he was once a beautiful man, but now his face was not there, because the flesh of it was sucked away off the bones.

You understand that? My grandfather did not forget that. And they laid him on the bier which they brought, and they put a cloth over his head, and the priest walked before; and they began to sing the psalm for the dead as well as they could. So, as they were singing the end of the first verse, one fell down, who was carrying the head of the bier, and the others looked back, and they saw that the cloth had fallen off, and the eyes of Anders Bjornsen were looking up, because there was nothing to close over them. And this they could not bear. Therefore the priest laid the cloth upon him, and sent for a spade, and they buried him in that place."

The next day Mr Wraxall records that the deacon called for him soon after his breakfast, and took him to the church and mausoleum. He noticed that the key of the latter was hung on a nail just by the pulpit, and it occurred to him that, as the church door seemed to be left unlocked as a rule, it would not be difficult for him to pay a second and more private visit to the monuments if there proved to be more of interest among them than could be digested at first. The building, when he entered it, he found not unimposing. The monuments, mostly large erections of the seventeenth and eighteenth centuries, were dignified if luxuriant, and the epitaphs and heraldry were copious. The central space of the domed room was occupied by three copper sarcophagi, covered with finely-engraved ornament. Two of them had, as is commonly the case in Denmark and Sweden, a large metal crucifix on the lid. The third, that of Count Magnus, as it appeared, had, instead of that, a full-length effigy engraved upon it, and round the edge were several bands of similar ornament representing various scenes. One was a battle, with cannon belching out smoke, and walled towns, and troops of pikemen. Another showed an execution. In a third, among trees, was a man running at full speed, with flying hair and outstretched hands. After him followed a strange form; it would be hard to say whether the artist had intended it for a man, and was unable to give the requisite similitude, or whether it was intentionally made as monstrous as it looked. In view of the skill with which the rest of the drawing was done, Mr Wraxall felt inclined to adopt the latter idea. The figure was unduly short, and was for the most part muffled in a hooded garment which swept the ground. The only part of the form which projected from that shelter was not shaped like any hand or arm. Mr Wraxall compares it to the tentacle of a devil-fish, and continues: "On seeing this, I said to myself, 'This, then, which is evidently an allegorical representation of some kind – a fiend pursuing a hunted soul – may be the origin of the story of Count Magnus and his mysterious companion. Let us see how the huntsman is pictured: doubtless it will be a demon blowing his horn.'" But, as it turned out, there was no such sensational figure, only the semblance of a cloaked man on a hillock, who stood leaning on a stick, and watching the hunt with an interest which the engraver had tried to express in his attitude.

Mr Wraxall noted the finely-worked and massive steel padlocks – three in number – which secured the sarcophagus. One of them, he saw, was detached, and lay on the pavement. And then, unwilling to delay the deacon longer or to waste his own working-time, he made his way onward to the manor-house.

"It is curious," he notes, "how, on retracing a familiar path, one's thoughts engross one to the absolute exclusion of surrounding objects. Tonight, for the second time, I had entirely failed to notice where I was going (I had planned a private visit to the tomb-house to copy the epitaphs), when I suddenly, as it were, awoke to consciousness, and found myself (as before) turning in at the churchyard gate, and, I believe, singing or chanting some such words as, 'Are you awake, Count Magnus? Are you asleep, Count Magnus?' and then something more which I have failed to recollect. It seemed to me that I must have been behaving in this nonsensical way for some time."

He found the key of the mausoleum where he had expected to find it, and copied the greater part of what he wanted; in fact, he stayed until the light began to fail him.

"I must have been wrong," he writes, "in saying that one of the padlocks of my Count's sarcophagus was unfastened; I see tonight that two are loose. I picked both up, and laid them carefully on the window-ledge, after trying unsuccessfully to close them. The remaining one is still firm, and, though I take it to be a spring lock, I cannot guess how it is opened. Had I succeeded in undoing it, I am almost afraid I should have taken the liberty of opening the sarcophagus. It is strange, the interest I feel in the personality of this, I fear, somewhat ferocious and grim old noble."

The day following was, as it turned out, the last of Mr Wraxall's stay at Råbäck. He received letters connected with certain investments which made it desirable that he should return to England; his work among the papers was practically done, and travelling was slow. He decided, therefore, to make his farewells, put some finishing touches to his notes, and be off.

These finishing touches and farewells, as it turned out, took more time than he had expected. The hospitable family insisted on his staying to dine with them – they dined at three – and it was verging on half past six before he was outside the iron gates of Råbäck. He dwelt on every step of his walk by the lake, determined to saturate himself, now that he trod it for the last time, in the sentiment of the place and hour. And when he reached the summit of the churchyard knoll, he lingered for many minutes, gazing at the limitless prospect of woods near and distant, all dark beneath a sky of liquid green. When at last he turned to go, the thought struck him that surely he must bid farewell to Count Magnus as well as the rest of the De la Gardies. The church was but twenty yards away, and he knew where the key of the mausoleum hung. It was not long before he was standing over the great copper coffin, and, as usual, talking to himself aloud: "You may have been a bit of a rascal in your time, Magnus," he was saying, "but for all that I should like to see you, or, rather –"

"Just at that instant," he says, "I felt a blow on my foot. Hastily enough I drew it back, and something fell on the pavement with a clash. It was the third, the last of the three padlocks which had fastened the sarcophagus. I stooped to pick it up, and – Heaven is my witness that I am writing only the bare truth – before I had raised myself there was a sound of metal hinges creaking, and I distinctly saw the lid shifting upwards. I may have behaved like a coward, but I could not for my life stay for one moment. I was outside that dreadful building in less time than I can write – almost as quickly as I could have said – the words; and what frightens me yet more, I could not turn the key in the lock. As I sit here in my room noting these facts, I ask myself (it was not twenty minutes ago) whether that noise of creaking metal continued, and I cannot tell whether it did or not. I only know that there was something more than I have written that alarmed me, but whether it was sound or sight I am not able to remember. What is this that I have done?"

* * *

Poor Mr Wraxall! He set out on his journey to England on the next day, as he had planned, and he reached England in safety; and yet, as I gather from his changed hand and inconsequent jottings, a broken man. One of the several small note-books that have come to me with his papers gives, not a key to, but a kind of inkling of, his experiences. Much of his journey was made by canal-boat, and I find not less than six painful attempts to enumerate and describe his fellow-passengers. The entries are of this kind:

24. Pastor of village in Skane. Usual black coat and soft black hat.
25. Commercial traveller from Stockholm going to Trollhättan. Black cloak, brown hat.
26. Man in long black cloak, broad-leafed hat, very old-fashioned.

This entry is lined out, and a note added: "Perhaps identical with No. 13. Have not yet seen his face." On referring to No. 13, I find that he is a Roman priest in a cassock.

The net result of the reckoning is always the same. Twenty-eight people appear in the enumeration, one being always a man in a long black cloak and broad hat, and another a "short figure in dark cloak and hood". On the other hand, it is always noted that only twenty-six passengers appear at meals, and that the man in the cloak is perhaps absent, and the short figure is certainly absent.

On reaching England, it appears that Mr Wraxall landed at Harwich, and that he resolved at once to put himself out of the reach of some person or persons whom he never specifies, but whom he had evidently come to regard as his pursuers. Accordingly he took a vehicle – it was a closed fly – not trusting the railway and drove across country to the village of Belchamp St. Paul. It was about nine o'clock on a moonlight August night when he neared the place. He was sitting forward, and looking out of the window at the fields and thickets – there was little else to be seen – racing past him. Suddenly he came to a cross-road. At the corner two figures were standing motionless; both were in dark cloaks; the taller one wore a hat, the shorter a hood. He had no time to see their faces, nor did they make any motion that he could discern. Yet the horse shied violently and broke into a gallop, and Mr Wraxall sank back into his seat in something like desperation. He had seen them before.

Arrived at Belchamp St. Paul, he was fortunate enough to find a decent furnished lodging, and for the next twenty-four hours he lived, comparatively speaking, in peace. His last notes were written on this day. They are too disjointed and ejaculatory to be given here in full, but the substance of them is clear enough. He is expecting a visit from his pursuers – how or when he knows not – and his constant cry is "What has he done?" and "Is there no hope?" Doctors, he knows, would call him mad, policemen would laugh at him. The parson is away. What can he do but lock his door and cry to God?

People still remember last year at Belchamp St. Paul how a strange gentleman came one evening in August years back; and how the next morning but one he was found dead, and there was an inquest; and the jury that viewed the body fainted, seven of 'em did, and none of 'em wouldn't speak to what they see, and the verdict was visitation of God; and how the people as kep' the 'ouse moved out that same week, and went away from that part. But they do not, I think, know that any glimmer of light has ever been thrown, or could be thrown, on the mystery. It so happened that last year the little house came into my hands as part of a legacy. It had stood empty since 1863, and there seemed no prospect of letting it; so I had it pulled down, and the papers of which I have given you an abstract were found in a forgotten cupboard under the window in the best bedroom.

Lost Hearts

by M.R. James

IT WAS, AS FAR AS I CAN ASCERTAIN, in September of the year 1811 that a post-chaise drew up before the door of Aswarby Hall, in the Heart of Lincolnshire. The little boy who jumped out as soon as it had stopped, looked about him with the keenest curiosity during the short interval that elapsed between the ringing of the bell and the opening of the hall door. He saw a tall, square, red-brick house, built in the reign of Anne; a stone-pillared porch had been added in the purest classical style of 1790; the windows of the house were many, tall and narrow, with small panes and thick white woodwork. A pediment, pierced with a round window, crowned the front. There were wings to right and left, connected by curious glazed galleries, supported by colonnades, with the central block. These wings plainly contained the stables and offices of the house. Each was surmounted by an ornamental cupola with a gilded vane.

An evening light shone on the building, making the window-panes glow like so many fires. Away from the Hall in front stretched a flat park studded with oaks and fringed with firs, which stood out against the sky. The clock in the church-tower, buried in trees on the edge of the park, only its golden weather-cock catching the light, was striking six, and the sound came gently beating down the wind. It was altogether a pleasant impression, though tinged with the sort of melancholy appropriate to an evening in early autumn, that was conveyed to the mind of the boy who was standing in the porch waiting for the door to open to him.

The post-chaise had brought him from Warwickshire, where, some six months before, he had been left an orphan. Now, owing to the generous offer of his elderly cousin, Mr Abney, he had come to live at Aswarby. The offer was unexpected, because all who knew anything of Mr Abney looked upon him as a somewhat austere recluse, into whose steady-going household the advent of a small boy would import a new and, it seemed, incongruous element. The truth is that very little was known of Mr Abney's pursuits or temper. The Professor of Greek at Cambridge had been heard to say that no one knew more of the religious beliefs of the later pagans than did the owner of Aswarby. Certainly his library contained all the then available books bearing on the Mysteries, the Orphic poems, the worship of Mithras, and the Neo-Platonists. In the marble-paved hall stood a fine group of Mithras slaying a bull, which had been imported from the Levant at great expense by the owner. He had contributed a description of it to the *Gentleman's Magazine*, and he had written a remarkable series of articles in the *Critical Museum* on the superstitions of the Romans of the Lower Empire. He was looked upon, in fine, as a man wrapped up in his books, and it was a matter of great surprise among his neighbours that he should even have heard of his cousin, Stephen Elliot, much more that he should have volunteered to make him an inmate of Aswarby Hall.

Whatever may have been expected by his neighbours, it is certain that Mr Abney – the tall, the thin, the austere – seemed inclined to give his young cousin a kindly reception. The moment the front door was opened he darted out of his study, rubbing his hands with delight.

"How are you, my boy? – how are you? How old are you?" said he – "that is, you are not too much tired, I hope, by your journey to eat your supper?"

"No, thank you, sir," said Master Elliot; "I am pretty well."

"That's a good lad," said Mr Abney. "And how old are you, my boy?"

It seemed a little odd that he should have asked the question twice in the first two minutes of their acquaintance.

"I'm twelve years old next birthday, sir," said Stephen.

"And when is your birthday, my dear boy? Eleventh of September, eh? That's well – that's very well. Nearly a year hence, isn't it? I like – ha, ha! – I like to get these things down in my book. Sure it's twelve? Certain?"

"Yes, quite sure, Sir."

"Well, Well! Take him to Mrs Bunch's room, Parkes, and let him have his tea – supper – whatever it is."

"Yes, sir," answered the staid Mr Parkes: and conducted Stephen to the lower regions.

Mrs Bunch was the most comfortable and human person whom Stephen had as yet met in Aswarby. She made him completely at home: they were great friends in a quarter of an hour: and great friends they remained. Mrs Bunch had been born in the neighbourhood some fifty-five years before the date of Stephen's arrival, and her residence at the Hall was of twenty years standing. Consequently, if anyone knew the ins and outs of the house and the district, Mrs Bunch knew them; and she was by no means disinclined to communicate her information.

Certainly there were plenty of things about the Hall and the Hall gardens which Stephen, who was of an adventurous and enquiring turn, was anxious to have explained to him. Who built the temple at the end of the laurel walk? Who was the old man whose picture hung on the staircase, sitting at a table, with a skull under his hand? These and many similar points were cleared up by the resources of Mrs Bunch's powerful intellect. There were others, however, of which the explanations furnished were less satisfactory.

One November evening Stephen was sitting by the fire in the housekeeper's room reflecting on his surroundings.

"Is Mr Abney a good man, and will he go to heaven?" he suddenly asked, with the peculiar confidence which children possess in the ability of their elders to settle these questions, the decision of which is believed to be reserved for other tribunals.

"Good? – bless the child!" said Mrs Bunch. "Master's as kind a soul as ever I see! Didn't I never tell you of the little boy as he took in out of the street, as you may say, this seven years back? and the little girl, two years after I first come here?"

"No. Do tell me all about them, Mrs Bunch – now this minute!"

"Well," said Mrs Bunch, "the little girl I don't seem to recollect so much about. I know master brought her back with him from his walk one day, and give orders to Mrs Ellis, as was housekeeper then, as she should be took every care with. And the pore child hadn't no one belonging to her – she telled me so her own self – and here she lived with us a matter of three weeks it might be; and then, whether she were somethink of a gipsy in her blood or what not, but one morning she out of her bed afore any of us had opened a eye, and neither track nor yet trace of her have I set eyes on since. Master was wonderful put about, and had all the ponds dragged; but it's my belief she was had away by them gypsies, for there was singing round the house for as much as an hour the night she went, and Parkes, he declares he heard them a-calling in the woods all that afternoon. Dear, dear! a hodd child she was, so silent in her ways and all, but I was wonderful taken up with her, so domesticated she was – surprising."

"And what about the little boy?" said Stephen.

"Ah, that poor boy!" sighed Mrs Bunch. "He were a foreigner – Jevanny he called himself – and he come a-tweakin' his hurdy-gurdy round and about the drive one winter day, and master 'ad him in that minute, and ast all about where he came from, and how old he was, and how he made his way, and where was his relatives, and all as kind as heart could wish. But it went the same way with him. They're a hunruly lot, them foreign nations, I do suppose, and he was off one fine morning just the same as the girl. Why he went and what he done was our question for as much as a year after; for he never took his 'urdy-gurdy, and there it lays on the shelf."

The remainder of the evening was spent by Stephen in miscellaneous cross-examination of Mrs Bunch and in efforts to extract a tune from the hurdy-gurdy.

That night he had a curious dream. At the end of the passage at the top of the house, in which his bedroom was situated, there was an old disused bathroom. It was kept locked, but the upper half of the door was glazed, and, since the muslin curtains which used to hang there had long been gone, you could look in and see the lead-lined bath affixed to the wall on the right hand, with its head towards the window. On the night of which I am speaking, Stephen Elliot found himself, as he thought, looking through the glazed door. The moon was shining through the window, and he was gazing at a figure which lay in the bath.

His description of what he saw reminds me of what I once beheld myself in the famous vaults of St. Michan's Church in Dublin, which possess the horrid property of preserving corpses from decay for centuries. A figure inexpressibly thin and pathetic, of a dusty leaden colour, enveloped in a shroud-like garment, the thin lips crooked into a faint and dreadful smile, the hands pressed tightly over the region of the heart.

As he looked upon it, a distant, almost inaudible moan seemed to issue from its lips, and the arms began to stir. The terror of the sight forced Stephen backwards, and he awoke to the fact that he was indeed standing on the cold boarded floor of the passage in the full light of the moon. With a courage which I do not think can be common among boys of his age, he went to the door of the bathroom to ascertain if the figure of his dream were really there. It was not, and he went back to bed.

Mrs Bunch was much impressed next morning by his story, and went so far as to replace the muslin curtain over the glazed door of the bathroom. Mr Abney, moreover, to whom he confided his experiences at breakfast, was greatly interested, and made notes of the matter in what he called "his book."

The spring equinox was approaching, as Mr Abney frequently reminded his cousin, adding that this had been always considered by the ancients to be a critical time for the young: that Stephen would do well to take care of himself, and shut his bedroom window at night; and that Censorinus had some valuable remarks on the subject. Two incidents that occurred about this time made an impression upon Stephen's mind.

The first was after an unusually uneasy and oppressed night that he had passed – though he could not recall any particular dream that he had had.

The following evening Mrs Bunch was occupying herself in mending his nightgown.

"Gracious me, Master Stephen!" she broke forth rather irritably, "how do you manage to tear your nightdress all to flinders this way? Look here, sir, what trouble you do give to poor servants that have to darn and mend after you!"

There was indeed a most destructive and apparently wanton series of slits or scorings in the garment, which would undoubtedly require a skilful needle to make good. They were confined to the left side of the chest – long, parallel slits, about six inches in length, some of them not quite piercing the texture of the linen. Stephen could only express his entire ignorance of their origin: he was sure that they were not there the night before.

"But," he said, "Mrs Bunch, they are just the same as the scratches on the outside of my bedroom door; and I'm sure I never had anything to do with making them."

Mrs Bunch gazed at him open-mouthed, then snatched up a candle, departed hastily from the room, and was heard making her way upstairs. In a few minutes she came down.

"Well," she said," Master Stephen, it's a funny thing to me how them marks and scratches can 'a' come there – too high up for any cat or dog to 'ave made 'em, much less a rat; for all the world like a Chinaman's finger-nails, as my uncle in the tea-trade used to tell us of when we was girls together. I wouldn't say nothing to master, not if I was you, Master Stephen, my dear; and just turn the key of your door when you go to your bed."

"I always do, Mrs Bunch, as soon as I've said my prayers."

"Ah, that's a good child: always say your prayers, and then no one can't hurt you."

Herewith Mrs Bunch addressed herself to mending the injured nightgown, with intervals of meditation, until bed-time. This was on a Friday night in March, 1812.

On the following evening the usual duet of Stephen and Mrs Bunch was augmented by the sudden arrival of Mr Parkes, the butler, who as a rule kept himself rather to himself in the pantry. He did not see that Stephen was there: he was, moreover, flustered, and less slow of speech than was his wont.

"Master may get up his own wine, if he likes, of an evening," was his first remark. "Either I do it in the daytime or not at all, Mrs Bunch. I don't know what it may be: very like it's the rats, or the wind got into the cellars; but I'm not as young as I was, and I can't go through with it as I have done."

"Well, Mr Parkes, you know it is a surprising place for the rats, is the Hall."

"I'm not denying that, Mrs Bunch; and to be sure, many a time I've heard the tale from the men in the shipyards about the rat that could speak. I never laid no confidence in that before; but tonight, if I'd demeaned myself to lay my ear to the door of the further bin, I could pretty much have heard what they was saying."

"Oh, there, Mr Parkes, I've no patience with your fancies! Rats talking in the wine-cellar indeed!"

"Well, Mrs Bunch, I've no wish to argue with you: all I say is, if you choose to go to the far bin, and lay your ear to the door, you may prove my words this minute."

"What nonsense you do talk, Mr Parkes – not fit for children to listen to! Why, you'll be frightening Master Stephen there out of his wits."

"What! Master Stephen?" said Parkes, awaking to the consciousness of the boy's presence. "Master Stephen knows well enough when I'm a-playing a joke with you, Mrs Bunch."

In fact, Stephen knew much too well to suppose that Mr Parkes had in the first instance intended a joke. He was interested, not altogether pleasantly, in the situation; but all his questions were unsuccessful in inducing the butler to give any more detailed account of his experiences in the wine-cellar.

* * *

We have now arrived at March 24, 1812. It was a day of curious experiences for Stephen: a windy, noisy day, which filled the house and the gardens with a restless impression. As Stephen stood by the fence of the grounds, and looked out into the park, he felt as if an endless procession of unseen people were sweeping past him on the wind, borne on restlessly and aimlessly, vainly striving to stop themselves, to catch at something that might arrest their flight and bring them once again into contact with the living world of which they had formed a part. After luncheon that day Mr Abney said:

"Stephen, my boy, do you think you could manage to come to me tonight as late as eleven o'clock in my study? I shall be busy until that time, and I wish to show you something connected with your future life which it is most important that you should know. You are not to mention this matter to Mrs Bunch nor to anyone else in the house; and you had better go to your room at the usual time."

Here was a new excitement added to life; Stephen eagerly grasped at the opportunity of sitting up till eleven o'clock. He looked in at the library door on his way upstairs that evening, and saw a brazier, which he had often noticed in the corner of the room, moved out before the fire; an old silver-gilt cup stood on the table, filled with red wine, and some written sheets of paper lay near it. Mr Abney was sprinkling some incense on the brazier from a round silver box as Stephen passed, but did not seem to notice his step.

The wind had fallen, and there was a still night and a full moon. At about ten o'clock Stephen was standing at the open window of his bedroom, looking out over the country. Still as the night was, the mysterious population of the distant moonlit woods was not yet lulled to rest. From time to time strange cries as of lost and despairing wanderers sounded from across the mere. They might be the notes of owls or water-birds, yet they did not quite resemble either sound. Were not they coming nearer? Now they sounded from the nearer side of the water, and in a few moments they seemed to be floating about among the shrubberies. Then they ceased; but just as Stephen was thinking of shutting the window and resuming his reading of *Robinson Crusoe*, he caught sight of two figures standing on the gravelled terrace that ran along the garden side of the Hall – the figures of a boy and girl, as it seemed; they stood side by side, looking up at the windows. Something in the form of the girl recalled irresistibly his dream of the figure in the bath. The boy inspired him with more acute fear.

Whilst the girl stood still, half smiling, with her hands clasped over her heart, the boy, a thin shape, with black hair and ragged clothing, raised his arms in the air with an appearance of menace and of unappeasable hunger and longing. The moon shone upon his almost transparent hands, and Stephen saw that the nails were fearfully long and that the light shone through them. As he stood with his arms thus raised, he disclosed a terrifying spectacle. On the left side of his chest there opened a black and gaping rent; and there fell upon Stephen's brain, rather than upon his ear, the impression of one of those hungry and desolate cries that he had heard resounding over the woods of Aswarby all that evening. In another moment this dreadful pair had moved swiftly and noiselessly over the dry grass and he saw them no more.

Inexpressibly frightened as he was, he determined to take his candle and go down to Mr Abney's study, for the hour appointed for their meeting was near at hand. The study or library opened out of the front hall on one side, and Stephen, urged on by his terrors, did not take long in getting there. To effect an entrance was not so easy. The door was not locked, he felt sure, for the key was on the outside of it as usual. His repeated knocks produced no answer. Mr Abney was engaged: he was speaking. What! why did he try to cry out? and why was the cry choked in his throat? Had, he, too, seen the mysterious children? But now everything was quiet, and the door yielded to Stephen's terrified and frantic pushing.

* * *

On the table in Mr Abney's study certain papers were found which explained the situation to Stephen Elliot when he was of an age to understand them. The most important sentences were as follows:

"It was a belief very strongly and generally held by the ancients – of whose wisdom in these matters I have had such experience as induces me to place confidence in their assertions – that by enacting certain processes, which to us moderns have something of a barbaric complexion, a very remarkable enlightenment of the spiritual faculties in man may be attained: that, for example, by absorbing the personalities of a certain number of his fellow-creatures, an individual may gain a complete ascendancy over those orders of spiritual beings which control the elemental forces of our universe.

"It is recorded of Simon Magus that he was able to fly in the air, to become invisible, or to assume any form he pleased, by the agency of the soul of a boy whom, to use the libellous phrase employed by the author of the *Clementine Recognitions*, he had 'murdered'. I find it set down, moreover, with considerable detail in the writings of Hermes Trismegistus, that similar happy results may be produced by the absorption of the hearts of not less than three human beings below the age of twenty-one years. To the testing of the truth of this receipt I have devoted the greater part of the last twenty years, selecting as the *corpora vilia* of my experiment such persons as could conveniently be removed without occasioning a sensible gap in society. The first step I effected by the removal of one Phoebe Stanley, a girl of gipsy extraction, on March 24, 1792. The second, by the removal of a wandering Italian lad, named Giovanni Paoli, on the night of March 23, 1805. The final 'victim' – to employ a word repugnant in the highest degree to my feelings – must be my cousin, Stephen Elliott. His day must be this March 24, 1812.

"The best means of effecting the required absorption is to remove the heart from the living subject, to reduce it to ashes, and to mingle them with about a pint of red wine, preferably port. The remains of the first two subjects, at least, it will be well to conceal: a disused bathroom or wine-cellar will be found convenient for such a purpose. Some annoyance may be experienced from the psychic portion of the subjects, which popular language dignifies with the name of ghosts. But the man of philosophic temperament – to whom alone the experiment is appropriate – will be little prone to attach importance to the feeble efforts of these beings to wreak their vengeance on him. I contemplate with the liveliest satisfaction the enlarged and emancipated existence which the experiment, if successful, will confer on me; not only placing me beyond the reach of human justice (so-called) but eliminating to a great extent the prospect of death itself."

* * *

MR ABNEY WAS FOUND in his chair, his head thrown back, his face stamped with an expression of rage, fright and mortal pain. In his left side was a terrible lacerated wound, exposing the heart. There was no blood on his hands, and a long knife that lay on the table was perfectly clean. A savage wild-cat might have inflicted the injuries. The window of the study was open, and it was the opinion of the coroner that Mr Abney had met his death by the agency of some wild creature. But Stephen Elliot's study of the papers I have quoted led him to a very different conclusion.

The Five Jars

by M.R. James

I: The Discovery

MY DEAR JANE,

You remember that you were puzzled when I told you I had heard something from the owls – or if not puzzled (for I know you have some experience of these things), you were at any rate anxious to know exactly how it happened. Perhaps the time has now come for you to be told.

It was really luck, and not any skill of mine, that put me in the way of it; luck, and also being ready to believe more than I could see. I have promised not to put down on paper the name of the wood where it happened: that can keep till we meet; but all the rest I can tell exactly as it came about.

It is a wood with a stream at the edge of it; the water is brown and clear. On the other side of it are flat meadows, and beyond these a hillside quite covered with an oak wood. The stream has alder-trees along it, and is pretty well shaded over; the sun hits it in places and makes flecks of light through the leaves.

The day I am thinking of was a very hot one in early September. I had come across the meadows with some idea of sitting by the stream and reading. The only change in my plans that I made was that instead of sitting down I lay down, and instead of reading I went to sleep.

You know how sometimes – but very, very seldom – you see something in a dream which you are quite sure is real. So it was with me this time. I did not dream any story or see any people; I only dreamt of a plant. In the dream no one told me anything about it: I just saw it growing under a tree: a small bit of the tree root came into the picture, an old gnarled root covered with moss, and with three sorts of eyes in it, round holes trimmed with moss – you know the kind. The plant was not one I should have thought much about, though certainly it was not one that I knew: it had no flowers or berries, and grew quite squat in the ground; more like a yellow aconite without the flower than anything else. It seemed to consist of a ring of six leaves spread out pretty flat with nine points on each leaf. As I say, I saw this quite clearly, and remembered it because six times nine makes fifty-four, which happens to be a number which I had a particular reason for remembering at that moment.

Well, there was no more in the dream than that: but, such as it was, it fixed itself in my mind like a photograph, and I was sure that if ever I saw that tree root and that plant, I should know them again. And, though I neither saw nor heard anything more of them than I have told you, it was borne in upon my mind that the plant *was* worth finding.

When I woke up I still lay, feeling very lazy, on the grass with my head within a foot or two of the edge of the stream and listened to its noise, until in five or six minutes – whether I began to doze off again or not does not much matter – the water-sound became like words, and said, "*Trickle-up, trickle-up*," an immense number of times. It pleased me, for though in poetry we hear a deal about babbling brooks, and though I am particularly fond of the noise they make, I never was able before to pretend that I could hear any words. And when I did finally get up and shake myself awake I thought I would anyhow pay so much attention to what the water said as to stroll up the stream instead of down. So I did: it took me through the flat meadows, but still along the edge of the wood, and still every now and then I heard the same peculiar noise which sounded like *Trickle-up*.

Not so very long after, I came to a place where another stream ran out of the wood into the one I had been following, and just below the place where the two joined there was – not a bridge, but a pole across, and another pole to serve as a rail, by which you could cross, without trouble. I did cross, not thinking much about it, but with some idea of looking at this new little stream, which went at a very quick pace and seemed to promise small rapids and waterfalls a little higher up. Now when I got to the edge of it, there was no mistake: it was saying "*Trickle-up*," or even "*Track-up*," much plainer than the old one. I stepped across it and went a few yards up the old stream. Before the new one joined it, it was saying nothing of the kind. I went back to the new one: it was talking as plain as print. Of course there were no two words about what must be done now. Here was something quite new, and even if I missed my tea, it had got to be looked into. So I went up the new stream into the wood.

Though I was well on the look-out for unusual things – in particular the plant, which I could not help thinking about – I cannot say there was anything peculiar about the stream or the plants or the insects or the trees (except the words which the water kept saying) so long as I was in the flat part of the wood. But soon I came to a steepish bank – the land began to slope up suddenly and the rapids and waterfalls of the brook were very gay and interesting. Then, besides *Track-up*, which was now its word always instead of *Trickle*, I heard every now and then *All right*, which was encouraging and exciting. Still, there was nothing out of the way to be seen, look as I might.

The climb up the slope or bank was fairly long. At the top was a kind of terrace, pretty level and with large old trees growing upon it, mainly oaks. Behind there was a further slope up and still more woodland: but that does not matter now. For the present I was at the end of my wanderings. There was no more stream, and I had found what of all natural things I think pleases me best, a real spring of water quite untouched.

Five or six oaks grew in something like a semicircle, and in the middle of the flat ground in front of them was an almost perfectly round pool, not more than four or five feet across. The bottom of it in the middle was pale sand which was continually rising up in little egg-shaped mounds and falling down again. It was the clearest and strongest spring of the kind I had ever seen, and I could have watched it for hours. I did sit down by it and watch it for some time without thinking of anything but the luck I had had to find it. But then I began to wonder if it would say anything. Naturally I could not expect it to say "*Track-up*" any more, for here I was at the end of it. So I listened with some curiosity. It hardly made so much noise as the stream: the pool was deeper. But I thought it must say something, and I put my head down as close as I could to the surface of the water. If I am not mistaken (and as things turned out I am sure I was right) the words were: *Gather gather, pick pick*, or *quick quick*.

Now I had not been thinking about the plant for a little time; but, as you may suppose, this brought it back to my mind and I got up and began to look about at the roots of the old oaks which grew just round the spring. No, none of the roots on this side which faced towards the water were like that which I had seen – still, the feeling was strong upon me that this, if any, was the kind of place, and even the very place, where the plant must be. So I walked to the back of the trees, being careful to go from right to left, according to the course of the sun.

Well, I was not mistaken. At the back of the middlemost oak-tree there were the roots I had dreamt of with the moss and the holes like eyes, and between them was the plant. I think the only thing which was new to me in the look of it was that it was so extraordinarily *green*. It seemed to have in it all the greenness that was possible or that would be wanted for a whole field of grass.

I had some scruples about touching it. In fact, I actually went back to the spring and listened, to make sure that it was still saying the same thing. Yes, it was: "*Gather gather, pick*." But there was something else every now and then which I could *not* for the life of me make out at first. I lay down, put my hand round my ear and held my breath. It might have been *bark tree* or *dark tree* or *cask free*. I got impatient at last and said:

"Well, I'm very sorry, but do what I will I *cannot* make out what you are trying to say."

Instantly a little spirt of water hit me on the ear, and I heard, as clear as possible, what it was: "*Ask tree*."

I got up at once. "I *beg* your pardon," I said, "of course. Thank you very much;" and the water went on saying "*Gather gather, all right, dip dip*."

After thinking how best to greet it, I went back to the oak, stood in front of it and said (of course baring my head):

"Oak, I humbly desire your good leave to gather the green plant which grows between your roots. If an acorn falls into this my right hand" (which I held out) "I will count it that you answer yes – and give you thanks." The acorn fell straight into the palm of my hand. I said, "I thank you, Oak: good growth to you. I will lay this your acorn in the place whence I gather the plant."

Then very carefully I took hold of the stalk of the plant (which was very short, for, as I said, it grew rather flat on the ground) and pulled, and to my surprise it came up as easily as a mushroom. It had a clean round bulb without any rootlets and left a smooth neat hole in the ground, in which, according to promise, I laid the acorn, and covered it in with earth. I think it very likely that it will turn into a second plant.

Then I remembered the last word of the spring and went back to dip the plant in it. I had a shock when I did so, and it was lucky I was holding it firm, for when it touched the water it struggled in my hand like a fish or a newt and almost slipped out. I dipped it three times and thought I felt it growing smaller in my hand: and indeed when I looked at it I found it had shut up its leaves and curled them in quite close, so that the whole thing was little more than a bulb. As I looked at it I thought the water changed its note and said, "*That'll do, that'll do*."

I thought it was time to thank the spring for all it had done for me, though, as you may suppose, I did not yet know in the least what was to be done with the plant, or what use it was going to be.

So I went over and said in the politest words I could how much I was obliged, and if there was anything I had or could do which would be agreeable, how glad I should be. Then I listened carefully, for it seemed by this time quite natural that I should get some sort of answer. It came. There was a sudden change in the sound, and the water said clearly and rapidly, "*Silver silver silver silver.*" I felt in my pocket. Luckily I had several shillings, sixpences and half-crowns. I thought the best way was to offer them all, so I put them in the palm of my right hand and held it under the water, open, just over the dancing sand. For a few seconds the water ran over the silver without doing anything: only the coins seemed to grow very bright and clean. Then one of the shillings was very neatly and smoothly slid off, and then another and a sixpence. I waited, but no more happened, and the water seemed to draw itself down and away from my hand, and to say "*All right.*" So I got up.

The three coins lay on the bottom of the pool looking brighter than even the newest I have ever seen, and gradually as they lay there they began to appear larger. The shillings looked like half-crowns and the sixpence like a shilling. I thought for a moment that it was because water magnifies, but I soon saw that this could not be the reason, for they went on growing larger, and of course thinner, until they finally spread into a kind of silver film all over the bottom of the pool; and as they did so the water began to take on a musical sound, much like the singing that comes when you wet your finger and draw it round the edge of a finger glass at dessert (which some people's idea of table manners allows them to do). It was a pretty sight and sound, and I listened and looked for a long time.

But all this time what had become of the plant? Why, when I gave the silver to the spring I had wrapped the plant carefully in a silk handkerchief and put it safe in my breast pocket. I took the handkerchief out now, and for a moment I was afraid the plant was gone; but it was not. It had shrunk to a very small whity-green ball. Now what was to be done with it, or rather what could it do? It was plain to me that it must have a strange and valuable property or virtue, since I had been put on its track in such a remarkable way. I thought I could not do better than ask the spring. I said, "O Spring of water, have I your good leave to ask what I should do with this precious plant to put it to the best use?" The silver lining of the spring made its words much easier to catch when it said anything – for I should tell you that for the most part now it did not speak, or not in any language that I could understand, but rather sang – and it now said, "*Swallow swallow, drink, swallow.*"

Prompt obedience, dear Jane, has always been my motto, as it is doubtless yours, and I at once laid myself down, drank a mouthful of water from the spring, and put the little bulb in my mouth. It instantly grew soft and slipped down my throat. How prosaic! I have no idea what it tasted like.

And again I addressed the spring: "Is there anything more for me to do?"

"*No no, no no, you'll see, you'll see – good-bye, good-bye,*" was the answer which came at once.

Accordingly I once more thanked the spring, wished it clear water, no mud, no tramplings of cattle, and bade it farewell. But, I said, I should hope to visit it again.

Then I turned away and looked about me, wondering whether, now that I had swallowed the mysterious plant, I should see anything different. The only thing I noticed was due, I suppose, not to the plant, but to the spring; but it was odd enough. All the trees hard by were crowded with little birds of all kinds sitting in rows on the branches as they do on telegraph wires. I have no doubt they were listening to the silver bell in the spring. They were quite still, and did not take any notice when I began to walk away.

I said, you will remember, that the ground I was on was a sort of flat terrace at the top of a steep slope. Now at one end this terrace just went down into the wood, but at the other end there was a little mound or hillock with thick underwood behind it. I felt a curiosity, and inclination, to walk that way: I have very little doubt that the plant was at the bottom of it. As I walked I looked at the ground, and noticed a curious thing: the roots of the plants and grasses seemed to show more than I was accustomed to see them.

It was not a great way to the hillock. When I got to it I wondered why I had gone, for there was nothing odd about it. Still I stepped on to the top, and then I did see something, namely, a square flat stone just in front of my feet. I poked at it with my walking-stick, but somehow I did not seem to touch it, nor was there any scraping noise. This was funny. I tried again, and now I saw that my stick was not touching it at all; there was something in between. I felt with my hands, and they met with what seemed like grass and earth, certainly not like stone. *Then* I understood. The plant was the one which makes you able to see what is under the ground!

I need not tell you all I thought, or how surprising and delightful it was. The first thing was to get at the flat stone and find out what was underneath it.

Accordingly, what with a knife and what with my fingers, I soon had it uncovered: it was four or five inches under the surface. There were no marks on it; it measured more than a foot each way. I lifted it. It was the cover of a sort of box with bottom and sides each made of a slab just like the lid. In this box was another, made of some dark metal, which I took to be lead. I pulled it out and found that the lid of the box was all of one piece with the rest, like a sardine tin. Evidently I could not open it there and then. It was rather heavy, but I did not care, and I managed without too much inconvenience to carry it home to the place I was lodging in. Of course I put back the stone neatly and covered it up with earth and grass again.

I was late for tea, but I had found what was better than tea.

II: The First Jar

THAT NIGHT I WAITED till the moon was up before trying to open the box. I do not well know why, but it seemed the right thing, and I followed my instinct, feeling that it might be the plant that made me think as I did. I drew up the blind and laid the box on a table near the window, where the moon shone full on it, and waited to see if anything else occurred to me. Suddenly I heard a sort of metallic snap. I went and looked at the box. Nothing appeared on the side nearest to me – but when I turned it round I saw that all along the side which the moon had shone upon there was a line along the metal. I turned another side to the moonlight, and another snap came in two or three minutes. Of course I went on. When the moon had made a groove on all four sides, I tried the lid. It would not come off yet, so there was nothing to be done but continue the process. Three times I did it: every side I turned to the moon thrice, and when that was done the lid was free. I lifted it, and what did I see in the box? All this writing would be very little use if I did not tell you, so it must be done.

There were five compartments in the box: in each of them was a little jar or vase of glass with a round body, a narrow neck, and spreading out a little at the top. The top of each was covered with a plate of metal and on each plate was a word or two in capital letters. On the one in the middle there were the words *unge oculos*, the other jars had one word apiece, *aures, linguam, frontem, pectus.*

Now, years ago, I took great pains to learn the Latin language, and on many occasions I have found it *most useful*, whatever you may see to the contrary in the newspaper: but seldom or never have I found it more useful than now. I saw at once that the words meant *anoint the eyes, the ears, the tongue, the forehead, the chest.* What would be the result of my doing this, of course I knew no more than you: but I was pretty sure that it would not do to try them all at once, and another thing I felt, that it would be better to wait till next day before trying any of them. It was past midnight now, so I went to bed: but first I locked up the box in a cupboard, for I did not want anyone to see it as yet.

Next day I woke bright and early, looked at my watch, found there was no need to think about getting up yet, and, like a wise creature, went to sleep again. I mention this, not merely by way of being jocose, but because after I went to sleep I had a dream which most likely came from the plant and certainly had to do with the box.

I seemed to see a room, or to be in a room about which I only noticed that the floor was paved with mosaic in a pattern mostly red and white, that there were no pictures on the walls and no fireplace, no sashes or indeed panes in the window, and the moon was shining in very bright. There was a table and a chest. Then I saw an old man, rather badly shaved and bald, in a Roman dress, white for the most part, with a purple stripe somewhere, and sandals. He looked by no means a wicked or designing old man. I was glad of that. He opened the chest, took out my box, and placed it carefully on the table in the moonlight. Then he went to a part of the room I could not see, and I heard a sound of water being poured into a metal basin, and he came into sight again, wiping his hands on a white towel. He opened the box, took out a little silver spoon and one of the jars, took off the lid and dipped the spoon in the jar and touched first his right eye and then his left with it. Then he put the jar and the spoon back, laid the lid on the box and put it back in the chest. After that he went to the window and stood there looking out, and seemed to be very much amused with what he saw. That was all.

"Hints for me," I remember thinking. "Perhaps it will be best not to touch the box before the moon is up tonight, and always with washed hands." I suppose I woke up immediately, for it was all very fresh in my mind when I did.

It was something of a disappointment to have to put off my experiments till the night came round. But it was all for the best, for letters came by the post which I had to attend to: in fact, I was obliged to go to the town a little way off to see someone and to send telegrams and so on. I was a little doubtful about the seeing things underground, but I soon found that unless I – so to say – turned on the tap, and specially wished and tried to use the power, it did not interfere with my ordinary seeing. When I did, it seemed to come forward from the back of my eyes, and was stronger than the day before. I could see rabbits in their burrows and followed the roots of one oak-tree very deep down. Once it threatened to be awkward, when I stooped to pick up a silver coin in the street, and grazed my knuckle against a paving stone, under which, of course, it was.

So much for that. By the way, I had taken a look at the box after breakfast, I found (not very much to my surprise) that the lid was as tight on it as when I found it first.

After dinner that evening I put out the light – the moon being now bright – placed the box on the table, washed my hands, opened it and, shutting my eyes, put my hand on one of the jars at random and took it out. As I had rather expected, I heard a little rattle as I did so, and feeling in the compartment, I found a little, a very little, spoon. All was well. Now to see which jar chance or the plant had chosen for my first experiment. I took it to the window: it was the one marked *aures* – ears – and the spoon had on the handle a letter A. I opened the jar. The lid fitted close but not over tightly. I put in the spoon as the old man had done, as near as I could remember. It brought out a very small drop of thick stuff with which I touched first my right ear and then my left. When I had done so I looked at the spoon.

It was perfectly dry. I put it and the jar back, closed the box, locked it up, and, not knowing in the least what to expect, went to the open window and put my head out.

For some little time I heard nothing. That was to be expected, and I was not in the least inclined to distrust the jar. Then I was rewarded; a bat flew by, and I, who have not heard a bat even squeak these twenty years, now heard this one say in a whistling angry tone, "Would you, would you, *I've* got you – no, drat, drat." It was not a very exciting remark, but it was enough to show me that a whole new world (as the books say) was open to me.

This, of course, was only a beginning. There were some plants and flowering shrubs under the window, and though I could see nothing, I began to hear voices – two voices – talking among them. They sounded young: of course they were anyhow very small, but they seemed to belong to young creatures of their kind.

"Hullo, I say, what have you got there? Do let's look; you might as well."

Then a pause – another voice: "I believe it's a bad one."

Number one: "Taste it."

Number two, after another pause, with a slight sound (very diminutive) of spitting: "Heugh! bad! I should rather think it was. Maggot!"

Number one (after laughing rather longer than I thought kind): "Look here – don't chuck it away – let's give it to the old man. Here – shove the piece in again and rub it over – here he is!" (Very demurely): "O sir, we've got such a nice-looking –" (*I could not catch what it was*) "here; we thought you might perhaps like it, sir. Would you, sir?... Oh no, thank you, sir, we've had plenty, sir, but this was the biggest we found."

A third voice said something; it was a deeper one and less easy to hear.

Number two: "Bitten, sir? Oh no, I don't think so. Do you –?" (*a name which I did not make out*).

Number one: "Why, how could it be?"

Number three again – angry, I thought.

Number two (rather anxiously): "But, sir, really, sir, I don't much like them... Must I really, sir?... O *sir*, it's got a maggot in it, and I believe they're poison." (*Smack, smack, smack, smack.*)

Two voices, very lamentable: "O *sir*, sir, please sir!"

A considerable pause, and sniffing. Then *Number two*, in a broken voice: "You silly fool, why did you go laughing like that right under his snout? You might have known he'd cog it." ("Cog." I had not heard the word since 1876.) "There'll be an awful row tomorrow. Look here, I shall go to bed."

The voices died away; I thought *Number one* seemed to be apologising.

That was all I heard *that* night. After eleven o'clock things seemed to get very still, and I began to feel just a little apprehensive lest something of a less innocent kind should come along. So I went to bed.

III: The Second Jar

NEXT DAY, I MUST SAY, was very amusing. I spent the whole of it in the fields just strolling about and sitting down, as the fancy took me, listening to what went on in the trees and hedges. I will not write down yet the kind of thing I heard, for it was only the beginning. I had not yet found out the way of using the new power to the very best advantage. I felt the want of being able to put in a remark or a question of my own every now and then. But I was pretty sure that the jar which had *linguam* on it would manage that.

Very nearly all the talking I heard was done by the birds and animals – especially the birds; but perhaps half a dozen times, as I sat under a tree or walked along the road, I was aware of voices which sounded exactly like those of people (some grown-up and some children) passing by or coming towards me and talking to each other as they went along. Needless to say, there was nothing to be *seen*: no movement of the grass and no track on the dusty road, even when I could tell exactly where the people who owned the voices must be. It interested me more than anything else to guess what sort of creatures they were, and I determined that the next jar I tried should be the Eye one. Once, I must tell you, I ventured to say "Good afternoon" when I heard a couple of these voices within a yard of me. I think the owners must nearly have had a fit. They stopped dead: one of them gave a sort of cry of surprise, and then, I believe, they ran or flew away. I felt a little breath of wind on my face, and heard no more. It wasn't (as I know now) that they couldn't see me: but they felt much as you would if a tree or a cow were to say "Good afternoon" to you.

When I was at supper that evening, the cat came in, as she usually did, to see what was going. I had always been accustomed to think that cats talk when they mew, dogs when they bark, and so on. It is not so at all. Their talking is almost all done (except when they are in a great state of mind) in a tone which you cannot possibly hear without help. Mewing is for the most part only shouting without saying any words. Purring is, as we often say, singing.

Well, this cat was an ordinary nice creature, tabby, and in she came, and sat watching me while I had soup. To all appearance she was as innocent as a lamb – but no matter for that. What she was saying was something of this kind:

"Get on with it, do: shove it down, lap it up! Who cares about soup? Get to business. I know there's fish coming."

When the fish actually came, there was a great deal of good feeling shown at first. "Oh, *how* much we have to be thankful for, all of us, have we not? Fish, fish: what a thought! Dear, kind, generous people all around us, all striving to supply us with what is best and pleasantest for us."

Then there was a silence for a short time, then in a somewhat different tone I heard: "Ah dear! the longer I live, the wiser I find it is not to expect too much consideration from others! Self-love! how few, how terribly few, are really free from it! The nature that knows how to take a hint, how rare it is!"

Another short silence, and then: "There you go – another great bit. I wonder you don't choke or burst! Disgusting! A good scratch all down your horrible fat cheek is what you want, and I know some cats that would give it you. No more notion how to behave than a cockroach."

About this time I rang the bell and the fish was taken away. The cat went too, circling round the maid with trusting and childlike glances, and I heard her saying in the former tone:

"Well, I daresay after all there are *some* kind hearts in the world, some that can feel for a poor weary creature, and know what a deal of strength and nourishment even the least bit of fish can give –" And I lost the rest.

When the time came and the box was open once more, I duly anointed my eyes and went to the window. I knew something of what I might expect to see, but I had not realised at all how much of it there would be. In the first place there were a great many buildings, in fact a regular village, all about the little lawn on which my window looked. They were, of course, not big; perhaps three feet high was the largest size. The roofs seemed to be of tiles, the walls were white, the windows were brightly lighted, and I could see people moving about inside. But there were plenty of people outside, too – people about six inches high – walking about, standing about, talking, running, playing some game which might have been hockey. These were on levelled spaces, for the grass, neatly kept as it was, would have come half-way up their legs; and there were some driving along smooth tracks in carriages drawn by horses of the right size, which were really the most charming little animals I ever saw.

You may suppose that I should not soon have got tired of watching them and listening to the little treble buzz of voices that went on, but I was interrupted. Just in front of me I heard what I can only call a snigger. I looked down, and saw four heads supported by four pairs of elbows leaning on the window-sill and looking up at me. They belonged to four boys who were standing on the twigs of a bush that grew up against the wall, and who seemed to be very much amused. Every now and again one of them nudged another and pointed towards me; and then, for some unexplained reason, they sniggered again. I felt my ears growing warm and red.

"Well, young gentlemen," I said, "you seem to be enjoying yourselves." No answer. "I appear to be so fortunate as to afford you some gratification," I went on, in my sarcastic manner. "Perhaps you would do me the honour of stepping into my poor apartment?" Again no answer, but more undisguised amusement. I was thinking out a really withering remark, when one of them said:

"Do look at his nose. I wonder if they know how ridiculous they are. I *should* like to talk to one of them for five minutes."

"Well," I said, "that can be managed very easily, and I assure you I should be equally glad of the opportunity. *My* remarks would deal with the subject of good manners."

Another one spoke this time, but did not answer me. "Oh, I don't know," he said, "I expect they're pretty stupid. They look it – at least this one does."

"Can they talk?" said the third. "I've never heard 'em."

"No, but you can see them moving their jaws and mouths and things. This one did just now."

I saw how it was now, and, becoming cooler, I recognised that these youths were behaving very much as I might have done myself in the presence of someone who I was sure could neither see nor hear me. I even smiled. One of them pointed at me at once:

"Thought of a joke, I s'pose. Don't keep it all to yourself, old chap."

At this moment the fourth, who had not said anything so far, but seemed to have been listening, piped up: "I say! I believe I know what it is that makes that hammering noise: it's something he has got in his clothes."

I could not resist this. "Right again," I said; "it's my watch, and you're very welcome to look at it." And I took it out and put it on the window-sill.

An awful horror and surprise came into their faces. In a second they had dived down like so many ducks. In another second I saw them walking across the grass, and each of them threw his arms round the waist or the neck of one of the elder people who were walking about among the houses. The person so attacked pulled himself up and listened attentively to what the boy was saying. The particular one I was watching looked towards my window and then burst out laughing, slapped the boy on the back, and resumed his walk. The boy went slowly off towards one of the houses. One or two of the other "men" came and stood nearer to the window, looking up. I thought I would venture a bow, and made one rather ceremoniously. It did not produce much effect, and I could not at the moment think of anything I could do that would show them quite clearly that I saw them. They went on looking at me quietly enough, and then I heard a deep low bell, seemingly very far off, toll five times. They heard it too, turned sharply round and walked off to the houses. Soon after that the lights in the windows died down and everything became very still. I looked at my watch. It was ten o'clock.

I waited for a while to see if anything would happen, but there was nothing; so I got some books out (which took a few minutes) and before I settled down to them I thought I would just take one more look out of the window. Where were all the little houses? At the first glance I thought they had vanished, but it was not exactly so. I found I could still see the chimneys above the grass, but as I looked they too disappeared. It was done very neatly: there was no hole, the turf closed in upon the roofs as they sank down, just as if it was of india-rubber. There was not a trace left of houses or roads or playgrounds or anything.

I was strongly tempted to go out and walk over the site of the village, but I did not. For one thing I was afraid I might disturb the people of the house, and besides there was a mist coming up over the meadows which sloped away outside the garden. So I stopped where I was.

But what a very odd mist, I began to think. It was not coming in all in one piece as it should. It was more in patches or even pillars of a smoky grey which moved at different rates, some of them occasionally standing still, others even seeming to go to and fro. And now I began to hear something like a hollow whispering coming from their direction. It was not conversation, for it went on quite continuously in the same tone: it sounded more as if something was being recited. I did not like it.

Then I saw what I liked less. Seven of these pillars of mist, each about the size of a man, were standing in a row just outside the garden fence, and in each I thought I saw two dull red eyes; and the hollow whispering grew louder.

Just then I heard a noise behind me in the room, as if the fire-irons had suddenly fallen down. So they had: and the reason why they had was that an old horseshoe which was on the mantelpiece had, for no reason that I could see, tumbled over and knocked them. Something I had heard came into my mind. I took the horseshoe and laid it on the window-sill. The pillars of mist swayed and quivered as if a sudden gust of wind had struck them, and seemed all at once to go farther off; and the hollow murmur was no longer to be heard. I shut the window and went to bed. But, the last thing, I looked out once again. The meadow was clear of mist and bright beneath the light of the moon.

As I lay in bed I thought and thought over what I had seen last. I was quite sure that the pillars of mist concealed some beings who wished me no good: but why should they have any spite against me? I was also sure that they wanted to get into the house: but again, why? You may think I was slow in the wits, but I must confess that some few minutes passed before I guessed. Of course they wanted to get hold of the box with the five jars. The thought disturbed me so much that I got up, lighted a candle, and went to the cupboard to see if all was safe. Yes, the box was there, but the cupboard door, which I knew I had locked, was unfastened, and when I had to turn the key it became plain that the lock was hampered and useless. How could this have come about? Earlier in the evening it had been perfectly right, and nobody had been in the room since I locked it last.

Whoever had done it, they had made the cupboard no safe place for the box. I took it into the bedroom and after a minute's thought cleared out a space in a suitcase which I had brought with me, locked it in that, and put the key on the ring of my watch-chain. Watch and all went under my pillow, and once more I got into bed.

IV: The Small People

YOU WILL HAVE MADE SURE that the next jar I meant to try was the one for the tongue, in hopes that it would help me to speak to some of the creatures. Though I looked forward to the experiment very much, and felt somewhat restless until I had made it, I did get a good deal of amusement out of what I saw and heard the next day. The small people were not to be seen – at least not in the morning. No, I am wrong: I found a bunch of three of them – young ones – asleep in a hollow tree. They woke up and looked at me without much interest, and when I was withdrawing my head they blew kisses to me. I am afraid there is no doubt they did so in derision. But there were others. I passed a cottage garden in which a little dog was barking most furiously. It seemed to be barking at a clothes-line, on which, with a lot of other things, was a print dress with rather a staring pattern of flowers. The dress caught my eye, and so did something red at the top which stuck up above the line. I gave it another glance, and really I had a most dreadful shock. It was a face. I gazed at it in horror, and was just gathering my wits to run and call for help or something, when I saw that it was laughing. Then I realised that it could not be an ordinary person, hanging as it was on a thin bit of cord and blowing to and fro in the breeze. I went nearer, staring at it with all my eyes, and made out that it was the face of an old woman, very cheerful and ruddy, and, as I said, laughing and swinging to and fro. Suddenly she seemed to catch my eye and to see that I saw her, and in a flash she was off the line and round the corner of the house, nearly tumbling over the dog as she went. It rushed after her, still very angry, but soon came trotting back, rather out of breath, and *that* incident was over.

I walked on. Among the village people I met, there were one or two whom I didn't think I had seen before – elderly, bright-eyed people they were – who seemed very much surprised when I said "Good morning" to them, and stopped still, looking after me, when I passed on. At last, some little way outside the village, I saw in the distance the same bright-coloured dress that had been on the clothes-line. The person who wore it was going slowly, and looking in the grass and hedges, and sometimes stooping to pick a plant, as it seemed. I quickened my pace and came up with her, and when I was just behind her, I cleared my throat rather loudly and said, "Fine day," or words to that effect.

You should have seen her jump! I was well paid for the fright she had given me just before. However, the startled look cleared away from her face, and she drew herself up and looked at me very calmly.

"Yes," she said, "it's a fine day." Then she actually blushed and went on: "I think I ought to beg your pardon for giving you such a turn just now."

"Well," I said, "I certainly was a good deal startled, but no harm was done. The dog took it more to heart than I did."

She gave a short laugh. "Yes," she said. "I hardly know why I was behaving like that. I suppose we all of us feel skittish at times." She paused and said with some little hesitation, "You have them, I suppose?" and at the same time she rapidly touched her ears, eyes and mouth with her forefinger.

I looked at her in some doubt, for I thought, might not she be one of the unknown who wished to get hold of the Five Jars? But her eye was honest, and my instinct was to trust her: so I nodded, and put my finger on my lips.

"Of course," she said. "Well, you are the first since I was a little thing, and that's fourteen hundred years ago." (You may think I opened my eyes.) "Yes, Vitalis was the last, and he lived in the villa – they called it so – down by the stream. You'll find the place some of these days if you look. I heard talk yesterday that someone had got them, and I'm told the mist was about last night. Perhaps you saw it?"

"Yes," I said, "I did, and I guessed what it meant." And I told her all that had happened, and ended by asking if she could kindly advise me what to do.

She thought for a moment, and then handed me a little bunch of the leaves she held in her hand. "Four-leaved clover," she said. "I know nothing better. Lay it on the box itself. You'll hear of them again, be sure."

"Who are *they*?" I asked in a whisper.

She shook her head. "Not allowed," was all she would say. "I must be going"; and she was gone, sure enough. You might suppose (as I did, when I came to think of it) that my new sight ought to have been able to see what became of her. I think it would, if she had gone straight away from me; but what I believe she did was to dart round behind me and then go away in a straight line, so that I was left looking in front of me while she was travelling away behind me like a bullet from a gun. You need practice with these things, and I had only been at it a couple of days.

I turned and walked rather quickly homewards, for I thought it would be wise to protect my box as soon as possible now that I had the means. I think it was fortunate that I did.

As I opened the garden gate I saw an old woman coming down the path – an old woman very unlike the last. "Old" was not the word for her face: she might have been born before the history-books begin. As to her expression, if ever you saw a snake with red rims to its eyes and the expression of a parrot, you might have some idea of it. She was hobbling along with a stick, in quite the proper manner, but I felt certain that all that was put on, and that she could have glided as swift as an adder if she pleased. I confess I was afraid of her. I had a feeling that she knew everything and hated everybody.

"And what," I suddenly thought, "has she been up to? If she has got at the box, where am I? and more than that, what mischief will she and her company work among the small people and the birds and beasts?" There would be no mercy for them; a glance at her eye told me that.

It was an immense relief to see that she could not possibly have got the box about her, and another relief when my eye travelled to the door of the house and I saw no fewer than three horseshoes nailed above it. I smiled to myself. Oh, how angry she looked! But she had to act her part, and with feeble curtseys and in a very small hoarse trembling voice she wished me a good day (though I noticed her pointing to the ground with her thumb as she said the words) and would be very obliged if I could tell her the right time. I was going to pull out my watch (and if I had, she would have seen a certain key we know of), when something said suddenly and clearly to my brain, "Look out," and by good luck I heard a clock inside the house strike one before I could answer.

"Just struck one," was my reply accordingly, and I said it as innocently as I could. She drew her breath in hard and quivered all over, and her mouth remained open like a cat's when it is using its worst expressions, and when she eventually thanked me I leave it to you to imagine how gracefully she did it.

Well, she had no more cards to play at the moment, and no excuse for remaining. I stood my ground and watched her out of the gate. A path led down the meadow, and, much against her will no doubt, she had to keep up the pretence and toil painfully along it until she reached another hedge and could reckon on being out of my sight. After that I neither saw nor expected to see anything more of her. I went up to my room and found all safe, and laid the four-leaved clover on the box. At luncheon I took occasion to find out from the maid, without asking her in so many words, whether the old woman had been visible to her; evidently she had not: evidently also, the evil creatures were really on the track of the Five Jars, knew that I had them, and had a very fair idea of where they were kept.

However, if the maid had not seen her, the cat had, and murmured a good deal to herself, and was in a rather nervous state. She sat, with her ears turned different ways, on the window-sill, looking out, and twitching her back uncomfortably, like an old lady who feels a draught. When I was available, she came and sat on my knee (a very uncommon attention on her part) with an air half of wishing to be protected and half of undertaking to protect me.

"If there is fish tonight," I said, "you shall have some." But I was not yet in a position to make myself understood.

"Pussy's been sleepin' on your box all the afternoon, sir," said the maid when I came in to tea. "I couldn't get her to come off; and when I did turn her out of the room, I do believe she climbed up and got in again by the winder."

"I don't mind at all," I said; "let her be there if she likes." And indeed I felt quite grateful to the cat. I don't know that she could have done much if there had been any attempt on the box, but I was sure her intentions were good.

There was fish that evening, and she had a good deal of it. She did not say much that I could follow, but chiefly sang songs without words.

* * *

NOT TO GO OVER the preliminaries again, I did, when the proper time came, touch my tongue with the contents of the third jar. I found that it worked in this way: I could not hear what I was saying myself, when I was talking to an animal: I only *thought* the remark very clearly, and then I felt my tongue and lips moving in an odd fashion, which I can't describe. But with the small people in human shape it was different. I spoke in the ordinary way to them, and though I dare say my voice went up an octave or two, I can't say I perceived it.

The village was there again tonight, and the life going on in it seemed much the same. I was set upon making acquaintance in a natural sort of way with the people, and as it would not do to run any risk of startling them, I just took my place near the window and made some pretence of playing Patience. I thought it likely that some of the young people would come and watch me, in spite of the fright they had had the night before. And it was not long before I heard a rustling in the shrubs under the window and voices saying:

"Is he in there? Can you see? Oh, I say, *do* look out: you all but had me over that time!"

They were suddenly quiet after this, and apparently one must have, very cautiously, climbed up and looked into the room. When he got down again there was a great fuss.

"No, is he really?" "What d'you say he was doing?" "What sort of charm?" "I say, d'you think we'd better get down?" "No, but what is he really doing?" "Laying out rows of flat things on the table, with marks on them." "I don't believe it." "Well, you go and look yourself." "All right, I shall." "Yes, but, I say, do look out: suppose you get shut in and we're late for the bell?" "Why, you fool, I shan't go into the room, only stop on the window-sill." "Well, I don't know, but I do believe he saw us last night, and my father said he thought so too." "Oh, well, he can't move very quick, anyway, and he's some way off the window. *I* shall go up."

I managed, without altering my position too much, to keep my eye on the window-sill, and, sure enough, in a second or two a small round head came into sight. I went on with my game. At first I could see that the watcher was ready to duck down at the slightest provocation, but as I took no sort of notice, he gained confidence, leant his elbows on the sill, and then actually pulled himself up and sat down on it. He bent over and whispered to the others below, and it was not long before I saw a whole row of heads filling up the window-sill from end to end. There must have been a dozen of them. I thought the time was come, and without moving, and in as careless a tone as I could, I said:

"Come in, gentlemen, come in; don't be shy." There was a rustle, and two or three heads disappeared, but nobody said anything. "Come in, if you like," I said again; "you can hear the bell quite well from here, and I shan't shut the window."

"Promise!" said the one who was sitting on the sill.

"I promise, honour bright," I said, whereupon he made the plunge. First he dropped on to the seat of a chair by the window, and from that to the floor. Then he wandered about the room, keeping at a distance from me at first, and, I have no doubt, watching very anxiously to see whether I had any intention of pouncing on him. The others followed, first one by one and then two or three at a time. Some remained sitting on the window-sill, but most plucked up courage to get down on to the floor and explore.

I had now my first good chance of seeing what they were like. They all wore the same fashion of clothes – a tunic and close-fitting hose and flat caps – seemingly very much what a boy would have worn in Queen Elizabeth's time. The colours were sober – dark blue, dark red, grey, brown – and each one's clothes were of one colour all through. They had some white linen underneath; it showed a little at the neck. There were both fair and dark among them: all were clean and passably good-looking, one or two certainly handsome. The firstcomer was ruddy and auburn-haired and evidently a leader. They called him Wag.

I heard whispers from corners of the room, and appeals to Wag to explain what this and that unfamiliar object was, and noticed that he was never at a loss for an answer of some kind, correct or not. The fireplace, which had its summer dressing, was, it appeared, a rock garden; an old letter lying on the floor was a charm ("Better not touch it"); the waste-paper basket (not unnaturally) a prison; the pattern on the carpet was – "Oh, you wouldn't understand it if I was to tell you."

Soon a voice – Wag's voice – came from somewhere near my foot.

"I say, could I get up on the top?" I offered to lift him, but he declined rather hastily and said my leg would be all right if I didn't mind putting it out a bit sloping: and he then ran up it on all fours – he was quite a perceptible weight – and got on to the table from my knee without any difficulty.

Once there, there was a great deal to interest him – books, papers, ink, pens, pipes, matches and cards. He was full of questions about them, and his being so much at his ease encouraged the others to follow him, so that before very long the whole lot were perambulating the table and making me very nervous lest they should fall off, while Wag was standing close up to me and putting me through a catechism.

"What do you have such *little* spears for?" he wanted to know, brandishing a pen at me. "Is that blood on the end? whose blood? Well then, what do you do with it? Let's see – only that?" (when I wrote a word or two). "Well, you can tell me about it another time. Now I want to know what these clubs in the chest are."

I said, "We make fire with them; if you like I'll show you – but it makes a little noise."

"Go on," said Wag; and I struck a match, rather expecting a stampede. But no, they were quite unmoved, and Wag said, "Beastly row and smell – why don't you do the ordinary way?"

He brushed the palm of his left hand along the tips of the fingers on his right hand, put them to his lips and then to his eyes, and behold! his eyes began to glow from behind with a light which would have been quite bright enough for him to read by. "Quite simple," he said; "don't you know it?" Then he did the same thing in reverse order, touching eyes, lips and hand, and the light was gone. I didn't like to confess that this was beyond me.

"Yes, that's all very well," I said, "but how do you manage about your houses? I am sure I saw lights in the windows."

"Course," he said, "put as many as you want;" and he ran round the table dabbing his hand here and there on the cloth, or on anything that lay on it, and at every place a little round bud or drop of very bright but also soft light came out. "See?" he said, and darted round again, passing his hands over the lights and touching his lips; and they were gone. He came back and said, "It's a *much* better way; it is *really*," as if it were only my native stupidity that prevented me from using it myself.

A smaller one, who looked to me rather a quieter sort than Wag, had come up and was standing by him: he now said in a low voice:

"P'raps they can't."

It seemed a new idea to Wag: he made his eyes very round. "Can't? Oh, rot! it's quite simple."

The other shook his head and pointed to my hand which rested on the table. Wag looked at it too, and then at my face.

"Could I see it spread out?" he said.

"Yes, if you'll promise not to spoil it."

He laughed slightly, and then both he and the other – whom he called Slim – bent over and looked closely at the tips of my fingers. "Other side, please," he said after a time, and they subjected my nails to a like examination. The others, who had been at the remoter parts of the table, wandered up and looked over their shoulders. After tapping my nails and lifting up one or more fingers, Wag stood upright and said:

"Well, I s'pose it's true, and you can't. I thought your sort could do anything."

"I thought much the same about you," I said in self-defence. "I always thought you could fly, but you –"

"So we can," said Wag very sharply, and his face grew red.

"Oh," I said, "then why haven't you been doing it tonight?"

He kicked one foot with the other and looked quickly at Slim. The rest said nothing and edged away, humming to themselves.

"Well, we *can* fly perfectly well, only –"

"Only not tonight, I suppose," said I, rather unkindly.

"No, *not* tonight," said Wag; "and you needn't laugh, either – we'll soon show you."

"That *will* be nice," I said; "and when will you show me?"

"Let's see" (he turned to Slim), "two nights more, isn't it? All right then (to me), in two nights more you'll see."

Just then a moth which flew in caused a welcome diversion – for I could see that somehow I had touched on a sore subject, and that he was feeling awkward – and he first jumped at it and then ran after it. Slim lingered. I raised my eyebrows and pointed at Wag. Slim nodded.

"The fact is," he said in a low voice, "he got us into rather a row yesterday and we're all stopped flying for three nights."

"Oh," said I. "I *see*: you must tell him I am very sorry for being so stupid. May I ask who stopped you?"

"Oh, just the old man, not the owls."

"You do go to the owls for something, then?" I asked, trying to appear intelligent.

"Yes, history and geography."

"To be sure," I said; "of course they've seen a lot, haven't they?"

"So they say," said Slim, "but –"

Just then the low toll of the bell was wafted through the window and there was an instant scurry to the edge of the table, then to the seat of the chair, and up to the window-sill; small arms waved caps at me, the shrubs rustled, and I was left alone.

V: Danger to the Jars

NOW MY EARS and eyes and tongue had been dealt with, and what remained were the forehead and the chest. I could not guess what would come of treating these with the ointment, but I thought I would try the forehead first. There was still a day or two when the moon would be bright enough for the trial. I hoped that perhaps the effect of these two last jars might be to make me able to go on with my experiences – to keep in touch with the new people I had come across – during the time when she – the moon, I mean – was out of sight.

I had one anxiety. The precious box must be guarded from those who were after it. About this I had a conviction, that if I could keep them off until I had used each of the five jars, the box and I would be safe. Why I felt sure of this I could not say, but my experience had led me to trust these beliefs that came into my head, and I meant to trust this one. It would be best, I thought, if I did not go far from the house – perhaps even if I did not leave it at all till the time of danger was past.

Several things happened in the course of the morning which confirmed me in my belief. I took up a position at the table by the window of my sitting-room. I had put the box in my suitcase, which I had locked, and I now laid it beside me where I could keep an eye upon it. The view from my window showed me, first, the garden of the cottage, with its lawn and little flower beds, its hedge and back gate, and beyond that a path leading down across a field. More fields, I knew, came after that one, and sloped pretty sharply down to a stream in the valley, which I could not see; but I could see the steep slope of fields, partly pasture, and then clothed with green woods towards the top. There were no other houses in sight: the road was behind me, passing the front of the cottage, and my bedroom looked out that way. I had some writing and reading to do, and I had not long finished breakfast before I settled down to it, and heard the maid "doing out" the bedroom as usual, accompanied every now and then by a slight mew from the cat, who (also as usual) was watching her at work. These mews meant nothing in particular, I may say; they were only intended to be met by an encouraging remark, such as "There you are, then, pussy," or "Don't get in my way, now," or "All in good time." Finally I heard "Come along then, and let's see what we've got for you downstairs," and the door was shut. I mention this because of what happened about a quarter of an hour later.

There was suddenly a fearful crash in the bedroom, a fall, a breaking of glass and crockery and snapping of wood, and then, fainter, sobbings and moans of pain. I started up.

"Goodness!" I thought, "she must have been dusting that heavy shelf high up on the wall with all the china on it, and the whole thing has given way. She must be badly hurt! But why doesn't her mistress come rushing upstairs? and what was that rasping noise just beside me?"

I looked at my suitcase, which lay on the table just inside the open window. Across the new smooth top of it there were three deep scratches running towards the window, which had not been there before. I moved it to the other side of me and sat down. There had been an attempt to decoy me out of the room, and it had failed. Certainly there would be more.

I waited; but everything was quiet in the house: no more noise from the bedroom and no one moving about, upstairs or downstairs; nothing but the pump clanking in the scullery. I turned to my work again.

Half an hour must have gone by, and, though on the look-out, I was not fidgety. Then I was aware of a confused noise from the field outside.

"Help! help! Keep off, you brute! Help, you there!" as well as I could make out, again and again. Towards the far end of the field, which was a pretty large one, a poor old man was trying to get to a gate in the hedge at a staggering run, and striking now and then with his stick at a great deer-hound which was leaping up at him with hollow barks. It seemed as if nothing but the promptest dash to the spot could save him; it seemed, too, as if he had caught sight of me at the window, for he beckoned. How strange the cries sounded! It was as if someone was shouting into an empty jug. My field-glasses were by me on the table, and I thought I would take just *one* look before I rushed out. I am glad I did; for, do you know, when I had the glasses focused on the dog and the man, all that I could see was a sort of fuzz of dancing vapour, much as if the shimmering air that you see on the heath on a hot day had been gathered up and rolled into a shape.

"Ha! ha!" I said, as I put down the glasses; and something in the air, about four yards off, made a sharp hissing sound. No doubt there were words, but I could not distinguish them. A second attempt had failed; you may be sure I was well on the alert for the next.

I put away my books now, and sat looking out of the window, and wondering as I watched whether there was anything out of the common to be noticed. For one thing, I thought there were more little birds about than I expected. At first I did not see them, for they were not hopping about on the lawn; but as I stared at the hedge of the garden, and at that of the field, I became aware that these were full of life. On almost every twig that could hold a bird in shelter – not on the top of the hedges – a bird was sitting, quite still, and they were all looking towards the window, as if they were expecting something to happen there. Occasionally one would flutter its wings a little and turn its head towards its neighbour; but this was all they did.

I picked up my glasses and began to study the bottom of the hedges and the bushes, where there was some quantity of dead leaves, and here, too, I could see that there were spectators. A small bright eye or a bit of a nose was visible almost wherever I looked; in short, the mice, and, I don't doubt, some of the rats, hedgehogs, and toads as well, were collected there and were as intently on the watch as the birds. "What a chance for the cat, if only she knew!" I put my head cautiously out of the window, and looking down on the sill of the window below, I could see her head, with the ears pushed forward; she was looking earnestly at the hedge, but she did not move. Only, at the slight noise I made, she turned her face upwards and crowed to me in a modest but encouraging manner.

Time passed on. Luncheon was laid – on another table – and was over, before anything else happened.

The next thing was that I heard the maid saying sharply:

"What business 'ave you got going round to the back? We don't want none of your rubbish here."

A hoarse voice answered inaudibly.

Maid: "No, nor the gentleman don't want none of your stuff neither; and how do you know there's a gentleman here at all I should like to know? What? Don't mean no offence? I dare say. That's more than I know. Well, that's the last word I've got to say."

In a minute more there was a knock at my door, and at the same time a step on the gravel path under my window, and a loud hiss from the cat. As I said "Come in" to the knock, I hastily looked out of the window, but saw nothing. It was the maid who had knocked. She had come to ask if there was anything I should like from the village, or anything I should want before tea-time, because the mistress was going out, and wanted her to go over and fetch something from the shop. I said there was nothing except the letters and perhaps a small parcel from the post office. She lingered a moment before going, and finally said:

"You'll excuse me naming it, sir, but there seems to be some funny people about the roads today, if you'd please to be what I mean to say a bit on the look-out, if you're not a-going out yourself."

"Certainly," I said. "No, I don't mean to go out. By the way, who was it came to the door just now?"

"Oh, it was one of these 'awking men, not one I've seen before, and he must be a stranger in this part, I think, because he began going round to the garden door, only I stopped him. He'd got these cheap rubbishing 'atpins and what not; leastways, if you understand me, what I thought to myself I shouldn't like to be seen with 'em, whatever others might."

"Yes, I see," I answered; and she went, and I turned to my books once more.

Within a very few minutes I began to suspect that I was getting sleepy. Yes, it was undoubtedly so. What with the warmth of the day, and lunch, and not having been out… There was a curious smell in the room, too, not exactly nasty, like something burning. What did it remind me of? Wood smoke from a cottage fire, that one smells on an autumn evening as one comes bicycling down the hill into a village? Not quite so nice as that; something more like a chemist's shop. I wondered: and as I wondered, my eyes closed and my head went forward.

A sharp pain on the back of my hand, and a crash of glass! Up I jumped, and which of three or four things I realised first I don't know now. But I did realise in a second or two that my hand was bleeding from a scratch all down the back of it, that a pane of the window was broken and that the whole window was darkened with little birds that were bumping their chests against it; that the cat was on the table gazing into my face with intense expression, that a little smoke was drifting into the room, and that my suitcase was on the point of slipping out over the window-sill. A despairing dash at it I made, and managed to clutch it; but for the life of me I could not pull it back. I could see no string or cord, much less any hand that was dragging at it. I hardly dared to take my hand from it to catch up something and hack at the thief I could not see. Besides, there was nothing within reach.

Then I remembered the knife in my pocket. Could I get it out and open it without losing hold? "They hate steel," I thought. Somehow – frantically holding on with one hand – I got out the knife, and opened it, goodness knows how, for it was horribly small and stiff, with my teeth, and sheared and stabbed indiscriminately all round the farther end of the suitcase. Thank goodness, the strain relaxed. I got the thing inside the window, dropped it, and stood on it, craning over the garden path and round the corner of the house. Of course there was nothing to be seen. The birds were gone. The cat was still on the table saying "O you owl! O you owl!" The sole and only clue to what had been happening was a small earthenware saucer that lay on the path immediately below the window, with a little heap of ashes in it, from which a thin column of smoke was coming straight up and curling over when it reached the window level. That, I could not doubt, was the cause of my sudden sleepiness. I dropped a large book straight on to it, and had the satisfaction of hearing it crush to bits and of seeing the smoke go four ways along the ground and vanish.

I was perfectly awake now. I looked at the cat, and showed her the back of my hand. She sat quite still and said:

"Well, what did you expect? I had to do something. I'll lick it if you like, but I'd rather not. No particular ill-feeling, you understand; all the same a hundred years hence."

I was not in a position to answer her, so I shook my head at her, wound up my hand in a handkerchief, and then stroked her. She took it agreeably, jumped off the table, and requested to be let out.

So the third attack had failed. I sat down and looked out. The hedges were empty; not a bird, not a mouse was left. I took this to mean that the dangerous time was past, and great was the relief. Soon I heard the maid come back from her errands in the village, then the mistress's chaise, then the clock striking five. I felt it would be all right for me to go out after tea.

And so I did; first, however, concealing the suitcase in my bedroom – not that I supposed hiding it would be of much use – and piling upon it poker, tongs, knife, horseshoe, and anything else I could find which I thought would keep off trespassers. I had, by the way, to explain to the maid that a bird had flown against the window and broken it, and when she said "Stupid, tiresome little things they are," I am afraid I did not contradict her.

I went out by way of the garden and crossed the field, near the middle of which stands a large old oak. I went up to this, for no particular reason, and stood gazing at the trunk. As I did so I became aware that my eyes were beginning to "see through," and behold! a family of owls was inside. As it was near evening, they were getting wakeful, stirring, smacking their beaks and opening their wings a little from time to time. At last one of them said:

"Time's nearly up. Out and about! Out and about!"

"Anyone outside?" said another.

"No harm there," said the first.

This short way of talking, I believe, was due to the owls not being properly awake and consequently sulky. As they brightened up and got their eyes open, they began to be more easy in manner.

"Oop! Oop! Oop! I've had a very good day of it. You have, too, I hope?"

"Sound as a rock, I thank you, except when they were carrying on at the cottage."

"Oh goodness! I forgot! They didn't bring it off, I hope."

"Not they; the watch was too well set, but it was wanted. I had a leaf about it a few minutes after, and it seems they got him asleep."

"Well! I never heard anyone bring a leaf."

"I dare say not, but I was expecting it; pigeon dropped it. There it is, on that child's back."

I saw the hen-owl stoop and examine a dead chestnut leaf which lay, as the other had said, on an owlet's back.

"Fa-a-ther!" said this owlet suddenly, in a shrill voice, "mayn't I go out tonight?"

But all that Father did was to clasp its head in his claw and push it to and fro several times. When he let go, the owlet made no sound, but crept away and hid its face in a corner, and heaved as if with sobs. Father closed his eyes slowly and opened them slowly – amused, I thought. The mother had been reading the leaf all the time.

"Dear me! *very* interesting!" she said. "I suppose now the worst of it is over."

"All's quiet for tonight, anyhow," said Father, "but I wish he could see someone about tomorrow; that's their last chance, and they *may* –" He ruffled up his feathers, lifted first one foot and then the other. "The awkwardness is," he went on, "if I say too much and they do get the jars, there's one risk; and if there's no warning and they get them, there's another risk."

"But if there *is* a warning and they *don't* get them," said she, very sensibly.

"Well, to be sure, that would be better, even though we don't know much about him."

"But where do you suppose he is, and whom ought he to see?" (It was just what I wanted to know, and I thanked her.)

"Why, as to the first, I suspect he's outside; there is someone there, and why they should stop there all this time unless they're listening, I don't know."

"Good gracious! listening to our private conversation! and me with my feathers all anyhow!" She began to peck at herself vigorously; but this was straying from the point, and annoyed me. However, Father went slowly on:

"As to that, I don't much care whether he's listening or not. As to whom he ought to see, that's rather more difficult. If he's got as far as talking to any of the Right People (he said this as if they had capital letters), they'd know, of course; and some of them down about the village, they'd know; and the Old Mother knows, and –"

"What about the boys?" said she, pausing in the middle of her toilet and poking her head up at him. He wholly disdained to answer, and merely butted at her with his head, so that she slipped down off her ledge several inches, with a great scrabbling. "Oh, *don't*!" she said peevishly, as she climbed back. "I'm all untidy again."

"Well then, don't ask such ridiculous questions. I shall buffle you with both wings next time. And now, as soon as the coast is clear, I shall be out and about."

I took the hint and moved off, for I had learnt as much perhaps as I could expect, even if all was not yet plain; and before I had gone many paces I was aware of the pair both sailing smoothly off in the opposite direction.

I was "seeing through" a good deal that evening; it is surprising what a lot of coppers people drop, even on a field path; surprising, too, in how many places there lie, unsuspected, bones of men. Some things I saw which were ugly and sad, like that, but more that were amusing and even exciting. There is one spot I could show where four gold cups stand round what was once a book, but the book is no more than earth now. That, however, I did not see on this particular evening.

What I remember best is a family of young rabbits huddled round their parents in a burrow, and the mother telling a story: "And so then he went a little farther and found a dandelion, and stopped and sat up and began to eat it. And when he had eaten two large leaves and one little one, he saw a fly on it – no, two flies; and then he thought he had had enough of that dandelion, and he went a little farther and found another dandelion…" And so it went on interminably, and entirely stupid, like everything else I ever heard a rabbit say, for they have forgotten all about their ancestor, Brer Rabbit. However, the children were absorbed in the story, so much so that they never heard a stoat making its way down the burrow. But I heard it, and by stamping and driving my stick in I was able to make it turn tail and go off, cursing. All stoats, weasels, ferrets, polecats, are of the wrong people, as you may imagine, and so are most rats and bats.

At last I left off seeing through, by trying not to do so, and went back to the house, where I found all safe and quiet.

I ought to say that I had not as yet tried speaking to any animal, even to the cat when she scratched me, but I thought I would try it now. So when she came in at dinner-time and circled about, with what I may call pious aspirations about fish and other such things,

I summoned up my courage and said (using my voice in the way I described, or rather did not describe, before):

"I used to be told, 'If you are hungry, you can eat dry bread.'"

She was certainly horribly startled. At first I thought she would have dashed up the chimney or out of the window; but she recovered pretty quickly and sat down, still looking at me with intense surprise.

"I suppose I might have guessed," she said; "but dear! what a turn you did give me! I feel quite faint; and gracious! what a day it has been! When I found you dozing off like a great – Well, no one wants to be rude, do they? but I can tell you I had more than half a mind to go at your face."

"I am glad you didn't," I said; "and really, you know, it wasn't my fault: it was that stuff they were burning on the path."

"I know that well enough," she said; "but to come back to the point, all this anxiety has made me as empty in myself as a clean saucer."

"Just what I was saying; if you are hungry, you can –"

"Say that again, say it just once more," she said, and her eyes grew narrow as she said it, "and I shall –"

"What shall you do?" I asked, for she stopped suddenly.

She calmed herself. "Oh, you know how it is when one's been all excited-like and worked up; we all say more than we mean. But that about dry bread! Well, there! I simply can't bear it. It's a wicked, cruel untruth, that's what it is; and besides, you *can't* be going to eat all the whole of what she's put down for you." Excitement was coming on again, and she ended with a loud ill-tempered mew.

Well, I gave her what she seemed to want, and shortly after, worn out doubtless with the fatigues of the day, she went to sleep on a chair, not even caring to follow the maid downstairs when things were cleared away.

VI: The Cat, Wag, Slim and Others

I GOT OUT my precious casket. I sat by the window and watched. The moon shone out, the lid of the box loosened in due course, and I touched my forehead with the ointment. But neither at once nor for some little time after did I notice any fresh power coming to me.

With the moon, up came also the little town, and no sooner were the doors of the houses level with the grass than the boys were out of them and running in some numbers towards my window; in fact, some slipped out of their own windows, not waiting for the doors to be available. Wag was the first. Slim, more sedate, came among the crowd that followed. These were still the only two who felt no hesitation about talking to me. The others were all fully occupied in exploring the room.

"Tomorrow," I said (after some sort of how-do-you-do's had been exchanged), "you'll be flying all over the place, I suppose."

"Yes," said Wag, shortly. "But I want to know – I say, Slim, what was it we wanted first?"

"Wasn't there a message from your father?" said Slim.

"Oh, yes, of course. 'If they're about the house,' he said, 'give them horseshoes; if there's a bat-ball, squirt at it': he thinks there's a squirt in the tool-house – Oh, there's the cat; I must –" After delivering all this in one sentence, he rushed to the edge of the table and took a kind of header into the midst of the unfortunate animal, who, however, only moaned or crowed without waking, and turned partly over on her back.

Slim remained sitting on a book and gazing soberly at me.

"Well," I said, "it's very kind of Wag's father to send me a message, but I must say I can't make much of it."

Slim nodded. "So he said, and he said you'd see when the time came; of course I don't know, myself; I've never seen a bat-ball. Wag says he has, but you never know with Wag."

"Well, I must do the best I can, I suppose; but look here, Slim, I wish you could tell me one or two things. What *are* you? What do they call you?"

"They call me Slim: and the whole of us they call the Right People," said Slim; "but it's no good asking us much, because we don't know, and besides, it isn't good for us."

"How do you mean?"

"Why, you see, our job is to keep the little things right, and if we do more than that, or if we try to find out much more, then we burst."

"And is that the end of you?"

"Oh, no!" he said cheerfully, "but that's one of the things it's no good asking."

"And if you don't do your job, what then?"

"Oh, then they get smaller and have no sense." (He said *they*, not *we*, I noticed.)

"I see. Well now, you go to school, don't you?" He nodded. "What for? Isn't that likely to be bad for you?" (I hardly liked to say "make you burst.")

"No," he said; "you see, it's to learn our job. We have to be told what used to go on, so as we can put things right, or keep them right. And the owls, you see, they remember a long way back, but they don't know any more than we do about the swell things."

I was very shy about putting the next question I had in mind, but I felt I must. "Now do you know how old you are, or how long it takes you to grow up, or how – how long you go on when you *are* grown up!"

He pressed his hands to his head, and I was dreadfully afraid for the moment that it might be swelling and would burst; but it was not so bad as that. After a few seconds he looked up and said:

"I think it's seven times seven moons since I went to school and seven times seven times seven moons before I grow up; and the rest is no good asking. But it's all right"; upon which he smiled.

And this, I may say, was the most part of what I ventured to ask any of them about themselves. But at other times I gathered that as long as they "did their job" nothing could injure them; and they were regularly measured – all of them – to see if they were getting smaller, and a careful record kept. But if anyone lost as much as a quarter of his height, he was doomed, and he crept off out of the settlement. Whether such a one ever came back I could not be sure; most of the failures (and they were not common) went and lived in hollow trees or by brooks, and were happy enough, but in a feeble way, not remembering much, nor able to make anything; and it was supposed that very slowly they shrunk to the size of a pin's point, and probably to nothing. All the same, it was believed that they *could* recover. Many other things that *you* would have asked, I did not, being anxious to avoid giving trouble.

But this time, anyhow, I felt I had catechised Slim long enough, so I broke off and said:

"What can Wag be doing all this while?"

"There's no knowing," said Slim. "But he's very quiet for him; either he's doing something awful, or he's asleep."

"I saw him with the cat last," I said; "you might go and look at her."

He walked to the edge of the table, and said, "Why, he *is* asleep!" And so he was, with his head on the cat's chest, under her chin, which she had turned up; and she had put her front paws together over the top of his head. As for the others, I descried them sitting in a circle in a corner of the room, also very quiet. (I imagine they were a little afraid of doing much without Wag, and also of waking him.) But I could not make out what they were doing, so I asked Slim.

"Racing earwigs, I should think," he said, with something of contempt.

"Well, I hope they won't leave them about when they go. I don't like earwigs."

"Who does?" he said; "but they'll take them away all right; they're prize ones, some of them."

I went over and looked at the racing for a little. The course was neatly marked out with small lights sprouting out of the boards, and the circle was at the winning-post, the starters being at the other end, some six feet away. I watched one heat. The earwigs seemed to me neither very speedy nor very intelligent, and all except one were apt to stop in mid-course and engage in personal encounters with each other.

I was beginning to wonder how long this would go on, when Wag woke up. Like most of us, he was not willing to allow that he had been asleep.

"I thought I'd just lie down a bit," he said, "and then I didn't want to bustle your cat, so I stopped there. And now I want to know – Slim, I say, what was it you were asking me?"

"Me asking you? I don't know."

"Oh, yes, you do; what he was doing the other time before we came in."

"I didn't ask you that; you asked me."

"Well, it doesn't matter who asked." (Turning to me): "What *were* you doing?"

"I don't know," I said. "Was it these things I was using" (taking up a pack of cards), "or something like this?" (I held up a book.)

"Yes, that one. What were you doing with it? What's it for?"

"We call it reading a book," and I tried to explain what the idea was, and read out a few lines; it happened to be *Pickwick*. They were absorbed. Slim said, half to himself, "Something like a glass," which I thought quite meaningless at the time. Then I showed them a picture in another book. That they made out very quickly.

"But when's it going to move on?" said Slim.

"Never," I said. "Ours stop just like that always. Do yours move on?"

"Of course they do; look here." He lay down on the tablecloth and pressed his forehead on it, but evidently could make nothing of it. "It's all rough," he said. I gave him a sheet of paper. "That's better;" and he lay down again in the same posture for a few seconds. Then he got up and began rubbing the paper all over with the palms of his hands. As he did so a coloured picture came out pretty quickly, and when it was finished he drew aside to let me see, and said, somewhat bashfully, "I don't think I've got it *quite* right, but I meant it for what happened the other evening." He had certainly not got it right as far as I was concerned. It was a view of the window of the house, seen from outside by moonlight, and there was a back view of a row of figures with their elbows on the sill. So far, so good; but inside the open window was standing a figure which was plainly – much too plainly, I thought – meant for me; far too short and fat, far too red-faced, and with an owlish expression which I am sure I never wear. This person was now seen to move his hand – a very poor hand, with only about three fingers – to his side, and pull, apparently, out of his body, a round object more or less like a watch (at any rate it was white on one side with black marks, and yellow on the other) and lay it down in front of him. At this the figures at the window-sill threw up their arms in all directions and fell or slid down like so many dolls. Then the picture began to get fainter, and disappeared from the paper. Slim looked at me expectantly.

"Well," I said, "it's very interesting to see how you do it, but is that the best likeness of me that you can make?"

"What's wrong with it?" said he. "Isn't it handsome enough or something?"

I heard Wag throw himself down on the table, and, looking at him, I saw that he had got both hands pressed over his mouth.

"May I ask what the joke is?" I said rather dryly (for it is surprising how touchy one can be over one's personal appearance, even at my time of life). He looked up for an instant at me, and then gasped and hid his face again. Slim went up to him and kicked him in the ribs.

"Where's your manners?" he said in a loud whisper. Wag rolled over and sat up, wiping his eyes.

"I'm very sorry," he said. "I'm sure I don't know what I was laughing for." Slim whistled. "Well," said Wag, "what *was* I?"

"Him, of course, and you know perfectly well!"

"Oh, was I? Well, perhaps you'll tell me what there is to laugh at about him?" said Wag, rather basely, I thought; so, as Slim put his finger to his lip and looked unhappy, I interrupted.

"Get up a minute, Wag," I said. "I want to see something."

"What?" said he, jumping up at once.

"Stand back to back with Slim, if you don't mind. That's it. Dear me! I thought you were taller than that – you looked to me taller last night. My mistake, I dare say. All right, thanks." But there they stood, gazing at each other with horror, and I felt I had been trifling with a most serious subject, so I laughed and said, "Don't disturb yourselves. I was only chaffing you, Wag, because you seemed to be doing something of the kind to me."

Slim understood, and heaved a sigh of relief. Wag sat down on a book and looked reproachfully upon me. Neither said a word. I was very much ashamed, and begged their pardon as nicely as I knew how. Luckily Wag was soon convinced that I was not in earnest, and he recovered his spirits directly.

"All *right*," he said, nodding at me; "did I hear you say you didn't like earwigs? That's worth remembering, Slim."

This reduced me at once; I tried to point out that he had begun it, and that it would be a mean revenge, and very hard on the earwigs, if he filled my room with them, for I should be obliged to kill all I could.

"Why," he said, "they needn't be real earwigs; my own tickle every bit as much as real ones."

This was no better for me, and I tried to make more appeals to his better feelings. He did not seem to be listening very attentively, though his eyes were fixed on me.

"What's that on your neck?" he said suddenly, and at the same moment I felt a procession of legs walking over my skin. I brushed at it hastily, and something seemed to fall on the table. "No, the other side I mean," said he, and again I felt the same horrid tickling and went through the same exercises, with a face, I've no doubt, contorted with terror. Anyhow, it seemed to amuse them very much; Wag, in fact, was quite unable to speak, and could only point. It was dull of me not to have realized at once that these were "his" earwigs and not real ones. But now I did, and though I still felt the tickling, I did not move, but sat down and gazed severely at him. Soon he got the better of his mirth and said, "I think we are quits now." Then, with sudden alarm, "I say, what's become of the others? The bell hasn't gone, has it?"

"How should I know?" I said. "If you hadn't been making all this disturbance, perhaps we might have heard it."

He took a flying leap – an extraordinary feat it was – from the edge of the table to a chair in the window, scrambled up to the sill, and gazed out. "It's all right," he said, in a faint voice of infinite relief; let himself down limply to the floor, and climbed slowly up my leg to his former place.

"Well," I said, "the bell hasn't gone, it seems, but where are the rest? I've hardly seen anything of them."

"Oh, *you* go and find 'em, Slim; I'm worn out with all these frights."

Slim went to the farther end of the table, prospected, and returned. He reported them "all right, but they're having rather a slow time of it, I think." I, too, got up, walked round, and looked; they were seated in a solemn circle on the floor round the cat, who was now curled up and fast asleep on a round footstool. Not a word was being said by anybody. I thought I had better address them, so I said:

"Gentlemen, I'm afraid I've been very inattentive to you this evening. Isn't there anything I can do to amuse you? Won't you come up on the table? You're welcome to walk up my leg if you find that convenient."

I was almost sorry I had spoken the moment after, for they made but one rush at my legs as I stood by the table, and the sensation was rather like that, I imagine, of a swarm of rats climbing up one's trousers. However, it was over in a few seconds, and all of them – over a dozen – were with Wag and Slim on the table, except one, who, whether by mistake or on purpose, went on climbing me by way of my waistcoat buttons, rather deliberately, until he reached my shoulder. I didn't object, of course, but I turned round (which made him catch at my ear) and went back to my chair, seated in which I felt rather as if I was presiding at a meeting. The one on my shoulder sat down and, I thought, folded his arms and looked at his friends with some triumph. Wag evidently took this to be a liberty.

"My word!" he said, "what do you mean by it, Wisp? Come off it!"

Wisp was a little daunted, as I judged by his fidgeting somewhat, but put a bold face on it and said, "Why should I come off?"

I put in a word: "I don't mind his being here."

"I dare say not; that's not the point," said Wag. "Are you coming down?"

"No," said Wisp, "not for you." But his tone was rather blustering than brave.

"Very well, don't then," said Wag; and I expected him to run up and pull Wisp down by the legs, but he didn't do that. He took something out of the breast of his tunic, put it in his mouth, lay down on his stomach, and, with his eyes on Wisp, puffed out his cheeks. Two or three seconds passed, during which I felt Wisp shifting about on his perch, and breathing quickly. Then he gave a sharp shriek, which went right through my head, slipped rapidly down my chest and legs and on to the floor, where he continued to squeal and to run about like a mad thing, to the great amusement of everyone on the table.

Then I saw what was the matter. All round his head were a multitude of little sparks, which flew about him like a swarm of bees, every now and then settling and coming off again, and, I suppose, burning him every time; if he beat them off, they attacked his hands, so he was in a bad way. After watching him for about a minute from the edge of the table, Wag called out:

"Do you apologise?"

"Yes!" he screamed.

"All right," said Wag; "stand still! stand still, you bat! How can I get 'em back if you don't?" Wag was back to me and I couldn't see what he did, but Wisp sat down on the carpet free of sparks, and wiped his face and neck with his handkerchief for some time, while the rest gradually recovered from their laughter. "You can come up again now," said Wag; and so he did, though he was slow and shy about it.

"Why didn't he send sparks at Wag?" said I to Slim.

"He hasn't got 'em to send," was the answer. "It's only the Captain of the moon."

"Well now, what about a little peace and quiet?" I said. "And, you know, I've never been introduced to you all properly. Wouldn't it be a good idea to do that, before the bell goes?"

"Very well," said Wag. "We'll *do* it properly. You bring 'em up one at a time, Slim, and" (to me) "you put your sun-hand out on the table."

(*I*: "Sun-hand?"

Wag: "Yes, sun-hand; don't you know?" He held up his right hand, then his left: "Sun-hand, Moon-hand, Day-hand, Night-hand, Star-hand, Cloud-hand, and so on."

I: "Thank you.")

This was done, and meanwhile Slim formed the troop into a queue and beckoned them up one by one. Wag stood on a book on the right and proclaimed the name of each. First he had made me arrange my right hand edgeways on the table, with the forefinger out. Then "Gold!" said Wag. Gold stepped forward and made a lovely bow, which I returned with an inclination of my head, then took as much of my forefinger top joint in his right hand as he could manage, bent over it and shook it or tried to, and then took up a position on the left and watched the next comer. The ceremony was the same for everyone, but not all the bows were equally elegant; some of the boys were jocular, and shook my finger with both hands and a great display of effort. These were frowned upon by Wag. The names (I need not set them all down now) were all of the same kind as you have heard; there was Red, Wise, Dart, Sprat, and so on. After Wisp, who came last and was rather humble, Wag called out Slim, and, after him, descended and presented himself in the same form.

"And now," he said, "perhaps you'll tell us *your* name."

I did so (one is always a little shamefaced about it, I don't know why) in full. He whistled.

"Too much," he said; "what's the easiest you can do?"

After some thought I said, "What about M or N?"

"Much better! If M's all right for you, it'll do for us." So M was agreed upon.

I was still rather afraid that the rank and file had been passing a dull evening and would not come again, and I tried to express as much to them. But they said:

"Dull? Oh no, M; why we've found out all sorts of things!"

"Really? What sort of things?"

"Well, inside the wall in that corner there's the biggest spider I've ever seen for one thing."

"Good gracious!" I said. "I hate 'em. I hope it can't get out?"

"It would have tonight if we hadn't stopped up the hole. Something's been helping it to gnaw through."

"Has it?" said Wag. "My word! that looks bad. What was it made the hole?"

Some called out, "A bat," and some "A rat."

"It doesn't matter much for that," said Slim, "so long as it's safe now. Where is it?"

"Gone down to the bottom and saying awful things," Red answered.

"Well, I *am* obliged to you," I said. "Anything else?"

"There's a lot of this stuff under the floor," said Dart, pointing with his foot at a half-crown which lay on the table.

"Is there? Whereabouts?" said I. "Oh, but I was forgetting; I can look after that myself."

"Yes, of course you can," they said; "and lots of things happened here before you came. We were watching. The old man and the woman, they were the worst, weren't they, Red?"

"Do you mean you've been here before?" I asked.

"No, no, but tonight we were looking at them, like we do at school."

This was beyond me, and I thought it would be of no use to ask for more explanations. Besides, just at this moment we heard the bell. They all clambered down either me or the chairs or the tablecloth. Slim lingered a moment to say, "You'll look out, won't you?" and then followed the rest on to the window-sill, where, taking the time from Captain Wag, they all stood in a row, bowed with their caps off, straightened up again, each sang one note, which combined into a wonderful chord, faced round and disappeared. I followed them to the window and saw the inhabitants of the house separating and going to their homes with the young ones capering round them. One or two of the elders – Wag's father in particular – looked up at me, paused in their walk, and bowed gravely, which courtesy I returned. I went on gazing until the lawn was a blank once more, and then, closing and fastening the sitting-room window, I betook myself to the bedroom.

VII: The Bat-Ball

IT HAD CERTAINLY BEEN an eventful day and evening, and I felt that my adventures could not be quite at an end yet, for I had still to find out what new power or sense the Fourth Jar had brought me. I stood and thought, and tried quite vainly to detect some difference in myself. And then I went to the window and drew the curtain aside and looked out on the road, and within a few minutes I began to understand.

There came walking rapidly along the road a young man, and he turned in at the garden gate and came straight up the path to the house door. I began to be surprised, not at his coming, for it was not so very late, but at the look of him. He was young, as I said, rather red-faced, but not bad-looking; of the class of a farmer, I thought. He wore biggish brown whiskers – which is not common nowadays – and his hair was rather long at the back – which also is not common with young men who want to look smart – but his hat, and his clothes generally, were the really odd part of him. The hat was a sort of low top-hat, with a curved brim; it spread out at the top and it was brushed rough instead of smooth. His coat was a blue swallow-tail with brass buttons. He had a broad tie wound round and round his neck, and a Gladstone collar. His trousers were tight all the way down and had straps under his feet. To put it in the dullest, shortest way, he was "dressed in the fashion of eighty or ninety years ago," as we read in the ghost stories. Evidently he knew his way about very well. He came straight up to the front door and, as far as I could tell, into the house, but I did not hear the door open or shut or any steps on the stairs. He must, I thought, be in my landlady's parlour downstairs.

I turned away from the window, and there was the next surprise. It was as if there was no wall between me and the sitting-room. I saw straight into it. There was a fire in the grate, and by it were sitting face to face an old man and an old woman. I thought at once of what one of the boys had said, and I looked curiously at them. They were, you would have said, as fine specimens of an old-fashioned yeoman and his wife as anyone could wish to see. The man was hale and red-faced, with grey whiskers, smiling as he sat bolt upright in his arm-chair.

The old lady was rosy and smiling too, with a smart silk dress and a smart cap, and tidy ringlets on each side of her face – a regular picture of wholesome old age; and yet I hated them both. The young man, their son, I suppose, was in the room standing at the door with his hat in his hand, looking timidly at them. The old man turned half round in his chair, looked at him, turned down the corners of his mouth, looked across at the old lady, and they both smiled as if they were amused. The son came farther into the room, put his hat down, leaned with both hands on the table, and began to speak (though nothing could be heard) with an earnestness that was painful to see, because I could be certain his pleading would be of no use; sometimes he spread out his hands and shook them, every now and again he brushed his eyes. He was very much moved, and so was I, merely watching him. The old people were not; they leaned forward a little in their chairs and sometimes smiled at each other – again as if they were amused. At last he had done, and stood with his hands before him, quivering all over. His father and mother leaned back in their chairs and looked at each other. I think they said not a single word. The son caught up his hat, turned round, and went quickly out of the room. Then the old man threw back his head and laughed, and the old lady laughed too, not so boisterously.

I turned back to the window. It was as I expected. Outside the garden gate, in the road, a young slight girl in a large poke-bonnet and shawl and rather short-skirted dress was waiting, in great anxiety, as I could see by the way she held to the railings. Her face I could not see. The young man came out; she clasped her hands, he shook his head; they went off together slowly up the road, he with bowed shoulders, supporting her, she, I dare say, crying. Again I looked round to the sitting-room. The wall hid it now.

It sounds a dull ordinary scene enough, but I can assure you it was horribly disturbing to watch, and the cruel calm way in which the father and mother, who looked so nice and worthy and were so abominable, treated their son, was like nothing I had ever seen.

Of course I know now what the effect of the Fourth Jar was; it made me able to see what had happened in any place. I did not yet know how far back the memories would go, or whether I was obliged to see them if I did not want to. But it was clear to me that the boys were sometimes taught in this way. "We were watching them like we do at school," one of them said, and though the grammar was poor, the meaning was plain, and I would ask Slim about it when we next met. Meanwhile I must say I hoped the gift would not go on working instead of letting me go to sleep. It did not.

Next day I met my landlady employing herself in the garden, and asked her about the people who had formerly lived in the house.

"Oh yes," said she. "I can tell you about them, for my father he remembered old Mr and Mrs Eld quite well when he was a slip of a lad. They wasn't liked in the place, neither of them, partly through bein' so hard-like to their workpeople, and partly from them treating their only son so bad – I mean to say turning him right off because he married without asking permission. Well, no doubt, that's what he shouldn't have done, but my father said it was a very nice respectable young girl he married, and it do seem hard for them never to say a word of kindness all those years and leave every penny away from the young people. What become of them, do you say, sir? Why, I believe they emigrated away to the United States of America and never was heard of again, but the old people they lived on here, and I never heard but what they was easy in their minds right up to the day of their death. Nice looking old people they was too, my father used to say; seemed as if butter wouldn't melt in their mouths, as the saying is. Now I don't know when I've thought of them last, but recollect my father speaking of them as well, and the way they're spoke of on their stone that lays just to the right-hand side as you go up the churchyard path – well, you'd think there never was such people. But I believe that was put up by them that got the property; now what was that name again?"

But about that time I thought I must be getting on. I also thought (as before) that it would be well for me not to go very far away from the house.

As I strolled up the road I pondered over the message which Wag's father had been so good as to send me. "If they're about the house, give them horseshoes; if there's a bat-ball, squirt at it. I think there's a squirt in the tool-house." All very well, no doubt. I had one horseshoe, but that was not much, and I could explore the tool-house and borrow the garden squirt. But more horseshoes?

At that moment I heard a squeak and a rustle in the hedge, and could not help poking my stick into it to see what had made the noise. The stick clinked against something with its iron ferrule. An old horseshoe! – evidently shown to me on purpose by a friendly creature. I picked it up, and, not to make a long story of it, I was helped by much the same devices to increase my collection to four. And now I felt it would be wise to turn back.

As I turned into the back garden and came in sight of the little potting-shed or tool-house or whatever it was, I started. Someone was just coming out of it. I gave a loud cough. The party turned round hastily; it was an old man in a sleeved waistcoat, made up, I thought, to look like an "odd man." He touched his hat civilly enough, and showed no surprise; but, oh, horror! he held in his hand the garden squirt.

"Morning," I said; "going to do a bit of watering?" He grinned. "Just stepped up to borrer this off the lady; there's a lot of fly gets on the plants this weather."

"I dare say there is. By the way, what a lot of horseshoes you people leave about. How many do you think I picked up this morning just along the road? Look here!" and I held one out to him, and his hand came slowly out to meet it, as though he could not keep it back.

His face wrinkled up into a horrible scowl, and what he was going to say I don't know, but just then his hand clutched the horseshoe and he gave a shout of pain, dropped the squirt and the horseshoe, whipped round as quick as any young man could, and was off round the corner of the shed before I had really taken in what was happening. Before I tried to see what had become of him, I snatched up the squirt and the horseshoe, and almost dropped them again. Both were pretty hot – the squirt much the hotter of the two; but both of them cooled down in a few seconds. By that time my old man was completely out of sight. And I should not wonder if he was away some time; for perhaps you know, and perhaps you don't know, the effect of an old horseshoe on that sort of people. Not only is it of iron, which they can't abide, but when they see or, still more, touch the shoe, they have to go over all the ground that the shoe went over since it was last in the blacksmith's hands. Only I doubt if the same shoe will work for more than one witch or wizard. Anyway, I put that one aside when I went indoors. And then I sat and wondered what would come next, and how I could best prepare for it. It occurred to me that it would do no harm to put one of the shoes where it couldn't be seen at once, and it also struck me that under the rug just inside the bedroom door would not be a bad place. So there I put it, and then fell to smoking and reading.

A knock at the door.

"Come in," said I, a little curious; but no, it was only the maid. As she passed me (which she did quickly) I heard her mutter something about "'ankerchieves for the wash," and I thought there was something not quite usual about the voice. So I looked round. She was back to me, but the dress and the height and the hair was what I was accustomed to see.

Into the bedroom she hurried, and the next thing was a scream like that of at least two cats in agony! I could just see her leap into the air, come down again on the rug, scream again, and then bundle, hopping, limping – I don't know what – out of the room and down the stairs. I did catch sight of her feet, though; they were bare, they were greenish, and they were webbed, and I think there were some large white blisters on the soles of them. You would have thought that the commotion would have brought the household about my ears; but it did not, and I can only suppose that they heard no more of it than they did of the things which the birds and so on say to each other.

"Next, please!" said I, as I lighted a pipe; but if you will believe it, there was no next. Lunch, the afternoon, tea, all passed by, and I was completely undisturbed. "They must be saving up for the bat-ball," I thought. "What in the world can it be?"

As candle-time came on, and the moon began to make herself felt, I took up my old position at the window, with the garden squirt at hand and two full jugs of water on the floor – plenty more to be got from the bathroom if wanted. The leaden box of the Five Jars was in the right place for the moonbeams to fall on it… But no moonbeams would touch it tonight! Why was this? There were no clouds. Yet, between the orb of the moon and my box, there was some obstruction. High up in the sky was a dancing film, thick enough to cast a shadow on the area of the window; and ever, as the moon rode higher in the heavens, this obstruction became more solid. It seemed gradually to get its bearings and settle into the place where it would shut off the light from the box most completely. I began to guess. It was the bat-ball; neither more nor less than a dense cloud of bats, gradually forming itself into a solid ball, and coming lower, and nearer to my window. Soon they were only about thirty feet off, and I felt that the moment was come.

I have never much liked bats or desired their company, and now, as I studied them through the glass, and saw their horrid little wicked faces and winking wings, I felt justified in trying to make things as unpleasant for them as I could. I charged the squirt and let fly, and again, and again, as quick as I could fill it. The water spread a bit before it reached the ball, but not too much to spoil the effect; and the effect was almost alarming. Some hundreds of bats all shrieking out at once, and shrieking with rage and fear (not merely from the excitement of chasing flies, as they generally do). Dozens of them dropping away, with wings too soaked to fly, some on to the grass, where they hopped and fluttered and rolled in ecstasies of passion, some into bushes, one or two plumb on to the path, where they lay motionless; that was the first tableau. Then came a new feature. From both sides there darted into the heart of the ball two squadrons of figures flying at great speed (though without wings) and perfectly horizontal, with arms joined and straight out in front of them, and almost at the same instant seven or eight more plunged into the ball from above, as if taking headers. The boys were out.

I stopped squirting, for I did not know whether the water would fell them as it felled the bats; but a shrill cry rose from below:

"Go on, M! go on, M!"

So I aimed again, and it was time, for a knot of bats just then detached itself from the main body and flew full-face towards me. My shot caught the middle one on the snout, and as I swung the squirt to left and right, it disabled four or five others, and discouraged the rest. Meanwhile the ball was cloven again and again by the arms of the flying squadrons, which shot through it from side to side and from top to bottom (though never, as appeared later, quite through the middle), and though it kept closing up again, it was plainly growing smaller as more and more of the bats outside, which were exposed to the squirt, dropped away.

I suddenly felt something alight on my shoulder, and a voice said in my ear, "Wag says if you *could* throw a shoe into the middle now, he believes it would finish them. Can you?" It was, I think, Dart who had been sent with the message.

"Horseshoes, I suppose he means," I said. "I'll try."

"Wait till we're out of the way," said Dart, and was off.

In a moment more I heard – not what I was rather expecting, a horn of Elf-land, but two strokes on the bell. I saw the figures of the boys shoot up and away to left and right, leaving the bat-ball clear, and the bats shrieked aloud, I dare say in triumph at the enemy's retreat.

There were two horseshoes left. I had no idea how they would fly, and I had not much confidence in my power of aiming; but it must be tried, and I threw them edgeways, like quoits. The first skimmed the top of the ball, the second went straight through the middle. Something which the bats in the very centre were holding – something soft – was pierced by it, and burst. I think it must have been a globe of jelly-like stuff in a thin skin. The contents spurted out on to some of the bats, and seemed to scald the fur off them in an instant and singe up all the membranes of their wings. They fell down at once, with broken screams. The rest darted off in every direction, and the ball was gone.

"Now don't be long," said a voice from the window-sill.

I thought I knew what was meant, and looked to the leaden casket. As if to make up for lost time, the moonbeam had already made an opening all round the part on which it shone, and I had but to turn the other side towards it – not even very slowly – to get the whole lid free. After cleansing my hands in the water, I made trial of the Fifth Jar, and, as I replaced it, a chorus of applause and cheering came up from below.

The Jars were mine.

VIII: Wag at Home

THERE WAS NO SCRAMBLING up to the window-sill this time. My visitors shot in like so many arrows, and "brought up" on their hands on the tablecloth, or lit on their feet on the top rail of a chair-back or on my shoulder, as the fancy took them. It would be tedious to go through all the congratulations and thanks which I offered, and indeed received, for it was important to them that the Jars should not get into wrong hands.

"Father says," said Wag, who was sitting on a book, as usual – "Oh, what fun it is to be able to fly again!" And he darted straight and level and butted head first into the back of – Sprat, was it? – who was standing near the edge of the table. Sprat was merely propelled into the air a foot or two off, and remained standing, but, of course, turned round and told Wag what he thought of him. Wag returned contentedly to his book. "Father says," he resumed, "he hopes you'll come and see us now. He says you did all right, and he's very glad the stuff got spilt, because they'll take moons and moons to get as much of it together again. He says they meant to squirt some of it on you when they got near enough, and while you were trying to get it off they'd have got hold of –" He pointed to the box of jars; there was a shyness about mentioning it.

"Your father's very kind," I said, "and I hope you'll thank him from me; but I don't quite see how I'm to get into your house."

"Fancy you not knowing that!" said Wag. "I'll tell him you'll come." And he was out of the window. As usual, I had recourse to Slim.

"Why, you did put some on your chest, didn't you?" was Slim's question.

"Yes, but nothing came of it."

"Well, I believe you can go pretty well anywhere with that, if you think you can."

"Can I fly, then?"

"No, I should say not; I mean, if you couldn't fly before, you can't now."

"How do you fly? I don't see any wings."

"No, we never have wings, and I'm rather glad we don't; the things that have them are always going wrong somehow. We just work it in the proper way with our backs, and there you are; like this." He made a slight movement of his shoulders, and was standing in the air an inch off the table. "You never tried that, I suppose?" he went on.

"No," I said, "only in dreams," which evidently meant nothing to him. "Well now," I said, "do you tell me that if I went to Wag's house now, I could get inside it? Look at the size I am!"

"It doesn't look as if you could," he agreed, "but my father said just the same as Wag's father about it."

Here Wag shot on to my shoulder. "Are you coming?"

"Yes, if I knew how."

"Well, come and try, anyhow."

"Very well, as you please; anything to oblige."

I picked up a hat and went downstairs. All the rest followed, if you can call it following, when there was at least as much flying up steps and in and out of banisters as going down. When we were out on the path, Wag said with more seriousness than usual:

"Now you do mean to come into our house, don't you?"

"Certainly I do, if you wish me to."

"Then that's all right. This way. There's Father."

We were on the grass now, and very long it was, and nice and wet I thought I should be with all the dew. As I looked up to see the elder Wag I very nearly fell over a large log which it was very careless of anyone to have left about. But here was Mr Wag within a yard of me, and to my extreme surprise he was quite a sizeable man of middle height, with a sensible, good-humoured face, in which I could see a strong likeness to his son. We both bowed, and then shook hands, and Mr Wag was very complimentary and pleasant about the occurrences of the evening.

"We've pretty well got the mess cleared up, you see. Yes, don't be alarmed," he went on, and took hold of my elbow, for he had, no doubt, seen a bewildered look in my eyes. The fact was, as I suppose you have made out, not that he had grown to my size, but that I had come down to his. "Things right themselves; you'll have no difficulty about getting back when the time comes. But come in, won't you?"

You will expect me to describe the house and the furniture. I shall not, further than to say that it seemed to me to be of a piece with the fashion in which the boys were dressed; that is, it was like my idea of a good citizen's house in Queen Elizabeth's time; and I shall not describe Mrs Wag's costume. She did not wear a ruff, anyhow.

Wag, who had been darting about in the air while we walked to his home, followed us in on foot. He now reached up to my shoulder. Slim, who came in too, was shorter.

"Haven't you got any sisters?" I took occasion to say to Wag.

"Of course," said he; "don't you see 'em? Oh! I forgot. Come out, you sillies!"

Upon which there came forward three nice little girls, each of whom was putting away something into a kind of locket which she wore round her neck. No, it is no use asking me what *their* dresses were like; none at all. All I know is that they curtsied to me very nicely, and that when we all sat down the youngest came and put herself on my knee as if it was a matter of course.

"Why didn't I see you before?" I asked her.

"I suppose because the flowers were in our hair."

"Show him what you mean, my dear," said her father. "He doesn't know our ways yet."

Accordingly she opened her locket and took out of it a small blue flower, looking as if it was made of enamel, and stuck it in her hair over her forehead. As she did so she vanished, but I could still feel the weight of her on my knee. When she took it out again (as no doubt she did) she became visible, put it back in the locket, and smiled agreeably at me. Naturally, I had a good many questions to ask about this, but you will hardly expect me to put them all down. Becoming invisible in this way was a privilege which the girls always had till they were grown up, and I suppose I may say "came out." Of course, if they presumed on it, the lockets were taken away for the time being – just in the same way as the boys were sometimes stopped from flying, as we have seen. But their own families could always see them, or at any rate the flowers in their hair, and they could always see each other.

But dear me! how much am I to tell of the conversation of that evening? One part at least: I remembered to ask about the pictures of the things that had happened in former times in places where I chanced to be. Was I obliged to see them, whether they were pleasant or horrible? "Oh no," they said; if you shut your eyes from below – that meant pushing up the lower eyelids – you would be rid of them; and you would only begin seeing them, either if you wanted to, or else if you left your mind quite blank, and were thinking of nothing in particular. Then they would begin to come, and there was no knowing how old they might be; that depended on how angry or excited or happy or sad the people had been to whom they happened.

And that reminds me of another thing. Wag had got rather fidgety while we were talking, and was flying up to the ceiling and down again, and walking on his hands, and so forth, when his mother said:

"Dear, do be quiet. Why don't you take a glass and amuse yourself with it? Here's the key of the cupboard."

She threw it to him and he caught it and ran to a tall bureau opposite and unlocked it. After humming and flitting about in front of it for a little time, he pulled a thing like a slate off a shelf where there were a large number of them.

"What have you got?" said his mother.

"The one I didn't get to the end of yesterday, about the dragon."

"Oh, that's a very good one," said she. "I used to be very fond of that."

"I liked it awfully as far as I got," he said, and was betaking himself to a settle on the other side of the room when I asked if I might see it, and he brought it to me.

It was just like a small looking-glass in a frame, and the frame had one or two buttons or little knobs on it. Wag put it into my hand and then got behind me and put his chin on my shoulder.

"That's where I'd got to," he said; "he's just going out through the forest."

I thought at the first glance that I was looking at a very good copy of a picture. It was a knight on horseback, in plate-armour, and the armour looked as if it had really seen service. The horse was a massive white beast, rather of the cart-horse type, but not so "hairy in the hoof"; the background was a wood, chiefly of oak-trees; but the undergrowth was wonderfully painted. I felt that if I looked into it I should see every blade of grass and every bramble-leaf.

"Ready?" said Wag, and reached over and moved one of the knobs. The knight shook his rein, and the horse began to move at a foot-pace.

"Well, but he can't *hear* anything, Wag," said his father.

"I thought you wanted to be quiet," said Wag, "but we'll have it aloud if you like."

He slid aside another knob, and I began to hear the tread of the horse and the creaking of the saddle and the chink of the armour, as well as a rising breeze which now came sighing through the wood. Like a cinema, you will say, of course. Well, it was; but there was colour and sound, and you could hold it in your hand, and it wasn't a photograph, but the live thing which you could stop at pleasure, and look into every detail of it.

Well, I went on reading, as you may say, this glass. In a theatre, you know, if you saw a knight riding through a forest, the effect would be managed by making the scenery slide backwards past him; and in a cinema it could all be shortened up by increasing the pace or leaving out part of the film. Here it was not like that; we seemed to be keeping pace and going along with the knight. Presently he began to sing. He had a loud voice and uttered his words crisply, so that I had no difficulty in making out the song. It was about a lady who was very proud and haughty to him and would have nothing to say to his suit, and it declared that the only thing left for him was to lay himself down under a tree. But he seemed quite cheerful about it, and indeed neither his complexion nor the glance of his eye gave any sign that he was suffering the pangs of hopeless love.

Suddenly his horse stopped short and snorted uneasily. The knight left off singing in the middle of a verse, looked earnestly into the wood at the back of the picture, and then out towards us, and then behind him. He patted his horse's neck, and then, humming to himself, put on his gauntlets, which were hanging at his saddle bow, managed somehow to latch or bolt the fastenings of them, slipped down his visor, and took the hilt of his sword in one hand and the sheath in the other and loosened the blade in the sheath. He had hardly done this when the horse shied violently and reared; and out of the thicket on the near side of the road (I suppose) something shot up in front of him on the saddle. We all drew in our breath.

"Don't be frightened, dear," said Mrs Wag to the youngest girl, who had given a sort of jump. "He's quite safe this time."

I must say it did not look like it. The beast that had leapt on to the saddle was tearing with its claws, drawing back its head and driving it forward again with horrid force against the visor, and was at such close quarters that the knight could not possibly either draw or use his sword. It was a horrible beast, too; evidently a young dragon. As it sat on the saddle-bow, its head was just about on a level with the knight's. It had four short legs with long toes and claws. It clung to the saddle with the hind feet and tore with the fore feet, as I said. Its head was rather long, and had two pointed ears and two small sharp horns. Besides, it had bat wings, with which it buffeted the knight, but its tail was short. I don't know whether it had been bitten or cut off in some previous fight. It was all of a mustard-yellow colour. The knight was for the moment having a bad time of it, for the horse was plunging and the dragon doing its very worst. The crisis was not long, though. The knight took hold of the right wing with both hands and tore the membrane upwards to the root, like parchment. It bled yellow blood, and the dragon gave a grating scream. Then he clutched it hard by the neck and managed to wrench it away from its hold on the saddle; and when it was in the air, he whirled its body, heavy as it was, first over his back and then forwards again, and its neck-bone, I suppose, broke, for it was quite limp when he cast it down. He looked down at it for a little, and seeing it stir, he got off, with the rein over his arm, drew his sword, cut the head off, and kicked it away some yards. The next thing he did was to push up his visor, look upward, mutter something I could not well hear, and cross himself; after which he said aloud, "Where man finds one of a brood, he may look for more," mounted, turned his horse's head and galloped off the way he had come.

We had not followed him far through the wood when –

"Bother!" said Wag, "there's the bell"; and he reached over and slid back the knobs in the frame, and the knight stopped.

I was full of questions, but there was no time to put them. Good-nights had to be said quickly, and Father Wag saw me out of the front door.

I set out on what seemed a considerable walk across the rough grass towards the enormous building in which I lived. I suppose I did not really take many minutes about getting to the path; and as I stepped on to it rather carefully, for it was a longish way down – why, without any shock or any odd feeling, I was my own size again. And I went to bed pondering much upon the events of the day.

Well, I began this communication by saying that I was going to explain to you how it was that I "heard something from the owls," and I think I have explained how it is that I am able to say that I have done so. Exactly what it was that you and I were talking about when I mentioned the owls, I dare say neither of us remembers. As you can see, I have had more exciting experiences than merely conversing with them – interesting, and, I think, unusual as that is. I have not, of course, told you nearly all there is to tell, but perhaps I have said enough for the present. More, if you should wish it, another time.

As to present conditions. Today there is a slight coolness between Wisp and the cat. He made his way into a mouse-hole which she was watching, and enticed her close up to it by scratchings and other sounds, and then, when she came quite near (taking great trouble, of course, to make no noise whatever), he put his head out and blew in her face, which affronted her very much. However, I believe I have persuaded her that he meant no harm.

The room is rather full of them tonight. Wag and most of the rest are rehearsing a play which they mean to present before I go. Slim, who happens not to be wanted for a time, is manœuvring on the table, facing me, and is trying to produce a portrait of me which shall be a little less libellous than his first effort. He has just now shown me the final production, with which he is greatly pleased. I am not.

Farewell. I am, with the usual expressions of regard,

Yours,

M (or N).

An Authentic Narrative of a Haunted House

by Joseph Sheridan Le Fanu

[**THE EDITOR OF** the *University Magazine* submits the following very remarkable statement, with every detail of which he has been for some years acquainted, upon the ground that it affords the most authentic and ample relation of a series of marvellous phenomena, in nowise connected with what is technically termed "spiritualism," which he has anywhere met with. All the persons – and there are many of them living – upon whose separate evidence some parts, and upon whose united testimony others, of this most singular recital depend, are, in their several walks of life, respectable, and such as would in any matter of judicial investigation be deemed wholly unexceptionable witnesses. There is not an incident here recorded which would not have been distinctly deposed to on oath had any necessity existed, by the persons who severally, and some of them in great fear, related their own distinct experiences. The Editor begs most pointedly to meet *in limine* the suspicion, that he is elaborating a trick, or vouching for another ghost of Mrs Veal. As a mere story the narrative is valueless: its sole claim to attention is its absolute truth. For the good faith of its relator he pledges his own and the character of this Magazine. With the Editor's concurrence, the name of the watering-place, and some special circumstances in no essential way bearing upon the peculiar character of the story, but which might have indicated the locality, and possibly annoyed persons interested in house property there, have been suppressed by the narrator. Not the slightest liberty has been taken with the narrative, which is presented precisely in the terms in which the writer of it, who employs throughout the first person, would, if need were, fix it in the form of an affidavit.]

Within the last eight years – the precise date I purposely omit – I was ordered by my physician, my health being in an unsatisfactory state, to change my residence to one upon the sea-coast; and accordingly, I took a house for a year in a fashionable watering-place, at a moderate distance from the city in which I had previously resided, and connected with it by a railway.

Winter was setting in when my removal thither was decided upon; but there was nothing whatever dismal or depressing in the change. The house I had taken was to all appearance and in point of convenience, too, quite a modern one. It formed one in a cheerful row, with small gardens in front, facing the sea, and commanding sea air and sea views in perfection. In the rear it had coach-house and stable, and between them and the house a considerable grass-plot, with some flower-beds, interposed.

Our family consisted of my wife and myself, with three children, the eldest about nine years old, she and the next in age being girls; and the youngest, between six and seven, a boy. To these were added six servants, whom, although for certain reasons I decline giving their real names, I shall indicate, for the sake of clearness, by arbitrary ones. There was a nurse, Mrs Southerland; a nursery-maid, Ellen Page; the cook, Mrs Greenwood; and the housemaid, Ellen Faith; a butler, whom I shall call Smith, and his son, James, about two-and-twenty.

We came out to take possession at about seven o'clock in the evening; everything was comfortable and cheery; good fires lighted, the rooms neat and airy, and a general air of preparation and comfort, highly conducive to good spirits and pleasant anticipations.

The sitting-rooms were large and cheerful, and they and the bedrooms more than ordinarily lofty, the kitchen and servants' rooms, on the same level, were well and comfortably furnished, and had, like the rest of the house, an air of recent painting and fitting up, and a completely modern character, which imparted a very cheerful air of cleanliness and convenience.

There had been just enough of the fuss of settling agreeably to occupy us, and to give a pleasant turn to our thoughts after we had retired to our rooms. Being an invalid, I had a small bed to myself – resigning the four-poster to my wife. The candle was extinguished, but a night-light was burning. I was coming up stairs, and she, already in bed, had just dismissed her maid, when we were both startled by a wild scream from her room; I found her in a state of the extremest agitation and terror. She insisted that she had seen an unnaturally tall figure come beside her bed and stand there. The light was too faint to enable her to define anything respecting this apparition, beyond the fact of her having most distinctly seen such a shape, colourless from the insufficiency of the light to disclose more than its dark outline.

We both endeavoured to re-assure her. The room once more looked so cheerful in the candlelight, that we were quite uninfluenced by the contagion of her terrors. The movements and voices of the servants downstairs still getting things into their places and completing our comfortable arrangements, had also their effect in steeling us against any such influence, and we set the whole thing down as a dream, or an imperfectly-seen outline of the bed-curtains. When, however, we were alone, my wife reiterated, still in great agitation, her clear assertion that she had most positively seen, being at the time as completely awake as ever she was, precisely what she had described to us. And in this conviction she continued perfectly firm.

A day or two after this, it came out that our servants were under an apprehension that, somehow or other, thieves had established a secret mode of access to the lower part of the house. The butler, Smith, had seen an ill-looking woman in his room on the first night of our arrival; and he and other servants constantly saw, for many days subsequently, glimpses of a retreating figure, which corresponded with that so seen by him, passing through a passage which led to a back area in which were some coal-vaults.

This figure was seen always in the act of retreating, its back turned, generally getting round the corner of the passage into the area, in a stealthy and hurried way, and, when closely followed, imperfectly seen again entering one of the coal-vaults, and when pursued into it, nowhere to be found.

The idea of anything supernatural in the matter had, strange to say, not yet entered the mind of any one of the servants. They had heard some stories of smugglers having secret passages into houses, and using their means of access for purposes of pillage, or with a view to frighten superstitious people out of houses which they needed for their own objects, and a suspicion of similar practices here, caused them extreme uneasiness. The apparent anxiety also manifested by this retreating figure to escape observation, and her always appearing to make her egress at the same point, favoured this romantic hypothesis. The men, however, made a most careful examination of the back area, and of the coal-vaults, with a view to discover some mode of egress, but entirely without success. On the contrary, the result was, so far as it went, subversive of the theory; solid masonry met them on every hand.

I called the man, Smith, up, to hear from his own lips the particulars of what he had seen; and certainly his report was very curious. I give it as literally as my memory enables me: –

His son slept in the same room, and was sound asleep; but he lay awake, as men sometimes will on a change of bed, and having many things on his mind. He was lying with his face towards the wall, but observing a light and some little stir in the room, he turned round in his bed, and saw the figure of a woman, squalid, and ragged in dress; her figure rather low and broad; as well as I recollect, she had something – either a cloak or shawl – on, and wore a bonnet. Her back was turned, and she appeared to be searching or rummaging for something on the floor, and, without appearing to observe him, she turned in doing so towards him. The light, which was more like the intense glow of a coal, as he described it, being of a deep red colour, proceeded from the hollow of her hand, which she held beside her head, and he saw her perfectly distinctly. She appeared middle-aged, was deeply pitted with the smallpox, and blind of one eye. His phrase in describing her general appearance was, that she was "a miserable, poor-looking creature."

He was under the impression that she must be the woman who had been left by the proprietor in charge of the house, and who had that evening, after having given up the keys, remained for some little time with the female servants. He coughed, therefore, to apprize her of his presence, and turned again towards the wall. When he again looked round she and the light were gone; and odd as was her method of lighting herself in her search, the circumstances excited neither uneasiness nor curiosity in his mind, until he discovered next morning that the woman in question had left the house long before he had gone to his bed.

I examined the man very closely as to the appearance of the person who had visited him, and the result was what I have described. It struck me as an odd thing, that even then, considering how prone to superstition persons in his rank of life usually are, he did not seem to suspect anything supernatural in the occurrence; and, on the contrary, was thoroughly persuaded that his visitant was a living person, who had got into the house by some hidden entrance.

On Sunday, on his return from his place of worship, he told me that, when the service was ended, and the congregation making their way slowly out, he saw the very woman in the crowd, and kept his eye upon her for several minutes, but such was the crush, that all his efforts to reach her were unavailing, and when he got into the open street she was gone. He was quite positive as to his having distinctly seen her, however, for several minutes, and scouted the possibility of any mistake as to identity; and fully impressed with the substantial and living reality of his visitant, he was very much provoked at her having escaped him. He made inquiries also in the neighbourhood, but could procure no information, nor hear of any other persons having seen any woman corresponding with his visitant.

The cook and the housemaid occupied a bedroom on the kitchen floor. It had whitewashed walls, and they were actually terrified by the appearance of the shadow of a woman passing and repassing across the side wall opposite to their beds. They suspected that this had been going on much longer than they were aware, for its presence was discovered by a sort of accident, its movements happening to take a direction in distinct contrariety to theirs.

This shadow always moved upon one particular wall, returning after short intervals, and causing them extreme terror. They placed the candle, as the most obvious specific, so close to the infested wall, that the flame all but touched it; and believed for some time that they had effectually got rid of this annoyance; but one night, notwithstanding this arrangement of the light, the shadow returned, passing and repassing, as heretofore, upon the same wall, although their only candle was burning within an inch of it, and it was obvious that no substance capable of casting such a shadow could have interposed; and, indeed, as they described it, the shadow seemed to have no sort of relation to the position of the light, and appeared, as I have said, in manifest defiance of the laws of optics.

I ought to mention that the housemaid was a particularly fearless sort of person, as well as a very honest one; and her companion, the cook, a scrupulously religious woman, and both agreed in every particular in their relation of what occurred.

Meanwhile, the nursery was not without its annoyances, though as yet of a comparatively trivial kind. Sometimes, at night, the handle of the door was turned hurriedly as if by a person trying to come in, and at others a knocking was made at it. These sounds occurred after the children had settled to sleep, and while the nurse still remained awake. Whenever she called to know "who is there," the sounds ceased; but several times, and particularly at first, she was under the impression that they were caused by her mistress, who had come to see the children, and thus impressed she had got up and opened the door, expecting to see her, but discovering only darkness, and receiving no answer to her inquiries.

With respect to this nurse, I must mention that I believe no more perfectly trustworthy servant was ever employed in her capacity; and, in addition to her integrity, she was remarkably gifted with sound common sense.

One morning, I think about three or four weeks after our arrival, I was sitting at the parlour window which looked to the front, when I saw the little iron door which admitted into the small garden that lay between the window where I was sitting and the public road, pushed open by a woman who so exactly answered the description given by Smith of the woman who had visited his room on the night of his arrival as instantaneously to impress me with the conviction that she must be the identical person. She was a square, short woman, dressed in soiled and tattered clothes, scarred and pitted with smallpox, and blind of an eye. She stepped hurriedly into the little enclosure, and peered from a distance of a few yards into the room where I was sitting. I felt that now was the moment to clear the matter up; but there was something stealthy in the manner and look of the woman which convinced me that I must not appear to notice her until her retreat was fairly cut off. Unfortunately, I was suffering from a lame foot, and could not reach the bell as quickly as I wished. I made all the haste I could, and rang violently to bring up the servant Smith. In the short interval that intervened, I observed the woman from the window, who having in a leisurely way, and with a kind of scrutiny, looked along the front windows of the house, passed quickly out again, closing the gate after her, and followed a lady who was walking along the footpath at a quick pace, as if with the intention of begging from her. The moment the man entered

I told him – "the blind woman you described to me has this instant followed a lady in that direction, try to overtake her." He was, if possible, more eager than I in the chase, but returned in a short time after a vain pursuit, very hot, and utterly disappointed. And, thereafter, we saw her face no more.

All this time, and up to the period of our leaving the house, which was not for two or three months later, there occurred at intervals the only phenomenon in the entire series having any resemblance to what we hear described as "Spiritualism." This was a knocking, like a soft hammering with a wooden mallet, as it seemed in the timbers between the bedroom ceilings and the roof. It had this special peculiarity, that it was always rhythmical, and, I think, invariably, the emphasis upon the last stroke. It would sound rapidly "one, two, three, *four* – one, two, three, *four*;" or "one, two, *three* – one, two, *three*," and sometimes "one, *two* – one, *two*," &c., and this, with intervals and resumptions, monotonously for hours at a time.

At first this caused my wife, who was a good deal confined to her bed, much annoyance; and we sent to our neighbours to inquire if any hammering or carpentering was going on in their houses but were informed that nothing of the sort was taking place. I have myself heard it frequently, always in the same inaccessible part of the house, and with the same monotonous emphasis. One odd thing about it was, that on my wife's calling out, as she used to do when it became more than usually troublesome, "stop that noise," it was invariably arrested for a longer or shorter time.

Of course none of these occurrences were ever mentioned in hearing of the children. They would have been, no doubt, like most children, greatly terrified had they heard anything of the matter, and known that their elders were unable to account for what was passing; and their fears would have made them wretched and troublesome.

They used to play for some hours every day in the back garden – the house forming one end of this oblong inclosure, the stable and coach-house the other, and two parallel walls of considerable height the sides. Here, as it afforded a perfectly safe playground, they were frequently left quite to themselves; and in talking over their days' adventures, as children will, they happened to mention a woman, or rather the woman, for they had long grown familiar with her appearance, whom they used to see in the garden while they were at play. They assumed that she came in and went out at the stable door, but they never actually saw her enter or depart. They merely saw a figure – that of a very poor woman, soiled and ragged – near the stable wall, stooping over the ground, and apparently grubbing in the loose clay in search of something. She did not disturb, or appear to observe them; and they left her in undisturbed possession of her nook of ground. When seen it was always in the same spot, and similarly occupied; and the description they gave of her general appearance – for they never saw her face – corresponded with that of the one-eyed woman whom Smith, and subsequently as it seemed, I had seen.

The other man, James, who looked after a mare which I had purchased for the purpose of riding exercise, had, like everyone else in the house, his little trouble to report, though it was not much. The stall in which, as the most comfortable, it was decided to place her, she peremptorily declined to enter. Though a very docile and gentle little animal, there was no getting her into it. She would snort and rear, and, in fact, do or suffer anything rather than set her hoof in it. He was fain, therefore, to place her in another. And on several occasions he found her there, exhibiting all the equine symptoms of extreme fear. Like the rest of us, however, this man was not troubled in the particular case with any superstitious qualms.

The mare had evidently been frightened; and he was puzzled to find out how, or by whom, for the stable was well-secured, and had, I am nearly certain, a lock-up yard outside.

One morning I was greeted with the intelligence that robbers had certainly got into the house in the night; and that one of them had actually been seen in the nursery. The witness, I found, was my eldest child, then, as I have said, about nine years of age. Having awoke in the night, and lain awake for some time in her bed, she heard the handle of the door turn, and a person whom she distinctly saw – for it was a light night, and the window-shutters unclosed – but whom she had never seen before, stepped in on tiptoe, and with an appearance of great caution. He was a rather small man, with a very red face; he wore an oddly cut frock coat, the collar of which stood up, and trousers, rough and wide, like those of a sailor, turned up at the ankles, and either short boots or clumsy shoes, covered with mud. This man listened beside the nurse's bed, which stood next to the door, as if to satisfy himself that she was sleeping soundly; and having done so for some seconds, he began to move cautiously in a diagonal line, across the room to the chimney-piece, where he stood for a while, and so resumed his tiptoe walk, skirting the wall, until he reached a chest of drawers, some of which were open, and into which he looked, and began to rummage in a hurried way, as the child supposed, making search for something worth taking away. He then passed on to the window, where was a dressing-table, at which he also stopped, turning over the things upon it, and standing for some time at the window as if looking out, and then resuming his walk by the side wall opposite to that by which he had moved up to the window, he returned in the same way toward the nurse's bed, so as to reach it at the foot. With its side to the end wall, in which was the door, was placed the little bed in which lay my eldest child, who watched his proceedings with the extremest terror. As he drew near she instinctively moved herself in the bed, with her head and shoulders to the wall, drawing up her feet; but he passed by without appearing to observe, or, at least, to care for her presence. Immediately after the nurse turned in her bed as if about to waken; and when the child, who had drawn the clothes about her head, again ventured to peep out, the man was gone.

The child had no idea of her having seen anything more formidable than a thief. With the prowling, cautious, and noiseless manner of proceeding common to such marauders, the air and movements of the man whom she had seen entirely corresponded. And on hearing her perfectly distinct and consistent account, I could myself arrive at no other conclusion than that a stranger had actually got into the house. I had, therefore, in the first instance, a most careful examination made to discover any traces of an entrance having been made by any window into the house. The doors had been found barred and locked as usual; but no sign of anything of the sort was discernible. I then had the various articles – plate, wearing apparel, books, &c., counted; and after having conned over and reckoned up everything, it became quite clear that nothing whatever had been removed from the house, nor was there the slightest indication of anything having been so much as disturbed there. I must here state that this child was remarkably clear, intelligent, and observant; and that her description of the man, and of all that had occurred, was most exact, and as detailed as the want of perfect light rendered possible.

I felt assured that an entrance had actually been effected into the house, though for what purpose was not easily to be conjectured. The man, Smith, was equally confident upon this point; and his theory was that the object was simply to frighten us out of the house by making us believe it haunted; and he was more than ever anxious and on the alert to discover the conspirators. It often since appeared to me odd. Every year, indeed, more odd, as this cumulative case of the marvellous becomes to my mind more and more inexplicable – that underlying my sense of mystery and puzzle, was all along the quiet assumption that all these occurrences were one way or another referable to natural causes. I could not account for them, indeed, myself; but during the whole period I inhabited that house, I never once felt, though much alone, and often up very late at night, any of those tremors and thrills which everyone has at times experienced when situation and the hour are favourable. Except the cook and housemaid, who were plagued with the shadow I mentioned crossing and recrossing upon the bedroom wall, we all, without exception, experienced the same strange sense of security, and regarded these phenomena rather with a perplexed sort of interest and curiosity, than with any more unpleasant sensations.

The knockings which I have mentioned at the nursery door, preceded generally by the sound of a step on the lobby, meanwhile continued. At that time (for my wife, like myself, was an invalid) two eminent physicians, who came out occasionally by rail, were attending us. These gentlemen were at first only amused, but ultimately interested, and very much puzzled by the occurrences which we described. One of them, at last, recommended that a candle should be kept burning upon the lobby. It was in fact a recurrence to an old woman's recipe against ghosts – of course it might be serviceable, too, against impostors; at all events, seeming, as I have said, very much interested and puzzled, he advised it, and it was tried. We fancied that it was successful; for there was an interval of quiet for, I think, three or four nights. But after that, the noises – the footsteps on the lobby – the knocking at the door, and the turning of the handle recommenced in full force, notwithstanding the light upon the table outside; and these particular phenomena became only more perplexing than ever.

The alarm of robbers and smugglers gradually subsided after a week or two; but we were again to hear news from the nursery. Our second little girl, then between seven and eight years of age, saw in the night time – she alone being awake – a young woman, with black, or very dark hair, which hung loose, and with a black cloak on, standing near the middle of the floor, opposite the hearthstone, and fronting the foot of her bed. She appeared quite unobservant of the children and nurse sleeping in the room. She was very pale, and looked, the child said, both "sorry and frightened," and with something very peculiar and terrible about her eyes, which made the child conclude that she was dead. She was looking, not at, but in the direction of the child's bed, and there was a dark streak across her throat, like a scar with blood upon it. This figure was not motionless; but once or twice turned slowly, and without appearing to be conscious of the presence of the child, or the other occupants of the room, like a person in vacancy or abstraction. There was on this occasion a night-light burning in the chamber; and the child saw, or thought she saw, all these particulars with the most perfect distinctness. She got her head under the bed-clothes; and although a good many years have passed since then, she cannot recall the spectacle without feelings of peculiar horror.

One day, when the children were playing in the back garden, I asked them to point out to me the spot where they were accustomed to see the woman who occasionally showed herself as I have described, near the stable wall. There was no division of opinion as to this precise point, which they indicated in the most distinct and confident way. I suggested that, perhaps, something might be hidden there in the ground; and advised them digging a hole there with their little spades, to try for it. Accordingly, to work they went, and by my return in the evening they had grubbed up a piece of a jawbone, with several teeth in it. The bone was very much decayed, and ready to crumble to pieces, but the teeth were quite sound. I could not tell whether they were human grinders; but I showed the fossil to one of the physicians I have mentioned, who came out the next evening, and he pronounced them human teeth. The same conclusion was come to a day or two later by the other medical man. It appears to me now, on reviewing the whole matter, almost unaccountable that, with such evidence before me, I should not have got in a labourer, and had the spot effectually dug and searched. I can only say, that so it was. I was quite satisfied of the moral truth of every word that had been related to me, and which I have here set down with scrupulous accuracy. But I experienced an apathy, for which neither then nor afterwards did I quite know how to account. I had a vague, but immovable impression that the whole affair was referable to natural agencies. It was not until some time after we had left the house, which, by-the-by, we afterwards found had had the reputation of being haunted before we had come to live in it, that on reconsideration I discovered the serious difficulty of accounting satisfactorily for all that had occurred upon ordinary principles. A great deal we might arbitrarily set down to imagination. But even in so doing there was, *in limine*, the oddity, not to say improbability, of so many different persons having nearly simultaneously suffered from different spectral and other illusions during the short period for which we had occupied that house, who never before, nor so far as we learned, afterwards were troubled by any fears or fancies of the sort. There were other things, too, not to be so accounted for. The odd knockings in the roof I frequently heard myself.

There were also, which I before forgot to mention, in the daytime, rappings at the doors of the sitting-rooms, which constantly deceived us; and it was not till our "come in" was unanswered, and the hall or passage outside the door was discovered to be empty, that we learned that whatever else caused them, human hands did not. All the persons who reported having seen the different persons or appearances here described by me, were just as confident of having literally and distinctly seen them, as I was of having seen the hard-featured woman with the blind eye, so remarkably corresponding with Smith's description.

About a week after the discovery of the teeth, which were found, I think, about two feet under the ground, a friend, much advanced in years, and who remembered the town in which we had now taken up our abode, for a very long time, happened to pay us a visit. He good-humouredly pooh-poohed the whole thing; but at the same time was evidently curious about it. "We might construct a sort of story," said I (I am giving, of course, the substance and purport, not the exact words, of our dialogue), "and assign to each of the three figures who appeared their respective parts in some dreadful tragedy enacted in this house. The male figure represents the murderer; the ill-looking, one-eyed woman his accomplice, who, we will suppose, buried the body where she is now so often seen grubbing in the earth, and where the human teeth and jawbone have so lately been disinterred; and the young woman with dishevelled tresses, and black cloak, and the bloody scar across her throat, their victim. A difficulty, however, which I cannot get over, exists in the cheerfulness, the great publicity, and the evident very recent date of the house." "Why, as to that," said he, "the house is *not* modern; it and those beside it formed an old government store, altered and fitted up recently as you see. I remember it well in my young days, fifty years ago, before the town had grown out in this direction, and a more entirely lonely spot, or one more fitted for the commission of a secret crime, could not have been imagined."

I have nothing to add, for very soon after this my physician pronounced a longer stay unnecessary for my health, and we took our departure for another place of abode. I may add, that although I have resided for considerable periods in many other houses, I never experienced any annoyances of a similar kind elsewhere; neither have I made (stupid dog! you will say), any inquiries respecting either the antecedents or subsequent history of the house in which we made so disturbed a sojourn. I was content with what I knew, and have here related as clearly as I could, and I think it a very pretty puzzle as it stands.

[Thus ends the statement, which we abandon to the ingenuity of our readers, having ourselves no satisfactory explanation to suggest; and simply repeating the assurance with which we prefaced it, namely, that we can vouch for the perfect good faith and the accuracy of the narrator. – E.D.U.M.]

The Spirit's Whisper

by Joseph Sheridan Le Fanu

YES, I HAVE BEEN HAUNTED! – haunted so fearfully that for some little time I thought myself insane. I was no raving maniac; I mixed in society as heretofore, although perhaps a trifle more grave and taciturn than usual; I pursued my daily avocations; I employed myself even on literary work. To all appearance I was one of the sanest of the sane; and yet all the while I considered myself the victim of such strange delusions that, in my own mind, I fancied my senses – and one sense in particular – so far erratic and beyond my own control that I was, in real truth, a madman. How far I was then insane it must be for others, who hear my story, to decide. My hallucinations have long since left me, and, at all events, I am now as sane as I suppose most men are.

My first attack came on one afternoon when, being in a listless and an idle mood, I had risen from my work and was amusing myself with speculating at my window on the different personages who were passing before me. At that time I occupied apartments in the Brompton Road. Perhaps, there is no thoroughfare in London where the ordinary passengers are of so varied a description or high life and low life mingle in so perpetual a medley. South-Kensington carriages there jostle costermongers' carts; the clerk in the public office, returning to his suburban dwelling, brushes the labourer coming from his work on the never-ending modern constructions in the new district; and the ladies of some of the surrounding squares flaunt the most gigantic of *chignons*, and the most exuberant of motley dresses, before the envying eyes of the ragged girls with their vegetable-baskets.

There was, as usual, plenty of material for observation and conjecture in the passengers, and their characters or destinations, from my window on that day. Yet I was not in the right cue for the thorough enjoyment of my favourite amusement. I was in a rather melancholy mood. Somehow or other, I don't know why, my memory had reverted to a pretty woman whom I had not seen for many years. She had been my first love, and I had loved her with a boyish passion as genuine as it was intense. I thought my heart would have broken, and I certainly talked seriously of dying, when she formed an attachment to an ill-conditioned, handsome young adventurer, and, on her family objecting to such an alliance, eloped with him. I had never seen the fellow, against whom, however, I cherished a hatred almost as intense as my passion for the infatuated girl who had flown from her home for his sake. We had heard of her being on the Continent with her husband, and learned that the man's shifty life had eventually taken him to the East. For some years nothing more had been heard of the poor girl. It was a melancholy history, and its memory ill-disposed me for amusement.

A sigh was probably just escaping my lips with the half-articulated words, "Poor Julia!" when my eyes fell on a man passing before my window. There was nothing particularly striking about him. He was tall, with fine features, and a long, fair beard, contrasting somewhat with his bronzed complexion. I had seen many of our officers on their return from the Crimea look much the same. Still, the man's aspect gave me a shuddering feeling, I didn't know why. At the same moment, a whispering, low voice uttered aloud in my ear the words, "It is he!" I turned, startled; there was no one near me, no one in the room. There was no fancy in the sound; I had heard the words with painful distinctness. I ran to the door, opened it – not a sound on the staircase, not a sound in the whole house – nothing but the hum from the street. I came back and sat down. It was no use reasoning with myself; I had the ineffaceable conviction that I had heard the voice. Then first the idea crossed my mind that I might be the victim of hallucinations. Yes, it must have been so, for now I recalled to mind that the voice had been that of my poor lost Julia; and at the moment I heard it I had been dreaming of her. I questioned my own state of health. I was well; at least I had been so, I felt fully assured, up to that moment. Now a feeling of chilliness and numbness and faintness had crept over me, a cold sweat was on my forehead. I tried to shake off this feeling by bringing back my thoughts to some other subject. But, involuntarily as it were, I again uttered the words, "Poor Julia!" aloud. At the same time a deep and heavy sigh, almost a groan, was distinctly audible close by me. I sprang up; I was alone – quite alone. It was, once more, an hallucination.

By degrees the first painful impression wore away. Some days had passed, and I had begun to forget my singular delusion. When my thoughts did revert to it, the recollection was dismissed as that of a ridiculous fancy. One afternoon I was in the Strand, coming from Charing Cross, when I was once more overcome by that peculiar feeling of cold and numbness which I had before experienced. The day was warm and bright and genial, and yet I positively shivered. I had scarce time to interrogate my own strange sensations when a man went by me rapidly. How was it that I recognised him at once as the individual who had only passed my window so casually on that morning of the hallucination? I don't know, and yet I was aware that this man was the tall, fair passer-by of the Brompton Road. At the same moment the voice I had previously heard whispered distinctly in my ear the words, "Follow him!" I stood stupefied. The usual throngs of indifferent persons were hurrying past me in that crowded thoroughfare, but I felt convinced that not one of these had spoken to me. I remained transfixed for a moment. I was bent on a matter of business in the contrary direction to the individual I had remarked, and so, although with unsteady step, I endeavoured to proceed on my way. Again that voice said, still more emphatically, in my ear, "Follow him!" I stopped involuntarily. And a third time, "Follow him!" I told myself that the sound was a delusion, a cheat of my senses, and yet I could not resist the spell. I turned to follow. Quickening my pace, I soon came up with the tall, fair man, and, unremarked by him, I followed him. Whither was this foolish pursuit to lead me? It was useless to ask myself the question – I was impelled to follow.

I was not destined to go very far, however. Before long the object of my absurd chase entered a well-known insurance-office. I stopped at the door of the establishment. I had no business within, why should I continue to follow? Had I not already been making a sad fool of myself by my ridiculous conduct? These were my thoughts as I stood heated by my quick walk. Yes, heated; and yet, once more, came the sudden chill. Once more that same low but now awful voice spoke in my ear: "Go in!" it said. I endeavoured to resist the spell, and yet I felt that resistance was in vain. Fortunately, as it seemed to me, the thought crossed my mind that an old acquaintance was a clerk in that same insurance-office. I had not seen the fellow for a great length of time, and I never had been very intimate with him. But here was a pretext; and so I went in and inquired for Clement Stanley. My acquaintance came forward. He was very busy, he said. I invented, on the spur of the moment, some excuse of the most frivolous and absurd nature, as far as I can recollect, for my intrusion.

"By the way," I said, as I turned to take my leave, although my question was "by the way" of nothing at all, "who was that tall, fair man who just now entered the office?"

"Oh, that fellow?" was the indifferent reply; "a Captain Campbell, or Canton, or some such name; I forget what. He is gone in before the board insured his wife's life – and she is dead; comes for a settlement, I suppose."

There was nothing more to be gained, and so I left the office. As soon as I came without into the scorching sunlight, again the same feeling of cold, again the same voice – "Wait!" Was I going mad? More and more the conviction forced itself upon me that I was decidedly a monomaniac already. I felt my pulse. It was agitated and yet not feverish. I was determined not to give way to this absurd hallucination; and yet, so far was I out of my senses, that my will was no longer my own. Resolved as I was to go, I listened to the dictates of that voice and waited. What was it to me that this Campbell or Canton had insured his wife's life, that she was dead, and that he wanted a settlement of his claim? Obviously nothing; and I yet waited.

So strong was the spell on me that I had no longer any count of time. I had no consciousness whether the period was long or short that I stood there near the door, heedless of all the throng that passed, gazing on vacancy. The fiercest of policemen might have told me to "move on," and I should not have stirred, spite of all the terrors of the "station." The individual came forth. He paid no heed to me. Why should he? What was I to him? This time I needed no warning voice to bid me follow. I was a madman, and I could not resist the impulses of my madness. It was thus, at least I reasoned with myself. I followed into Regent Street. The object of my insensate observation lingered, and looked around as if in expectation. Presently a fine-looking woman, somewhat extravagantly dressed, and obviously not a lady, advanced toward him on the pavement. At the sight of her he quickened his step, and joined her rapidly. I shuddered again, but this time a sort of dread was mingled with that strange shivering. I knew what was coming, and it came. Again that voice in my ear. "Look and remember!" it said. I passed the man and woman as they stopped at their first meeting!

"Is all right, George?" said the female.

"All right, my girl," was the reply.

I looked. An evil smile, as if of wicked triumph, was on the man's face, I thought. And on the woman's? I looked at her, and I remembered. I could not be mistaken. Spite of her change in manner, dress, and appearance, it was Mary Simms. This woman some years before, when she was still very young, had been a sort of humble companion to my mother. A simple-minded, honest girl, we thought her. Sometimes I had fancied that she had paid me, in a sly way, a marked attention. I had been foolish enough to be flattered by her stealthy glances and her sighs. But I had treated these little demonstrations of partiality as due only to a silly girlish fancy. Mary Simms, however, had come to grief in our household. She had been detected in the abstraction of sundry jewels and petty ornaments. The morning after discovery she had left the house, and we had heard of her no more. As these recollections passed rapidly through my mind I looked behind me. The couple had turned back. I turned to follow again; and spite of carriages and cabs, and shouts and oaths of drivers, I took the middle of the street in order to pass the man and woman at a little distance unobserved. No; I was not mistaken. The woman was Mary Simms, though without any trace of all her former simple-minded airs; Mary Simms, no longer in her humble attire, but flaunting in all the finery of overdone fashion. She wore an air of reckless joyousness in her face; and yet, spite of that, I pitied her. It was clear she had fallen on the evil ways of bettered fortune – bettered, alas! for the worse.

I had an excuse now, in my own mind, for my continued pursuit, without deeming myself an utter madman – the excuse of curiosity to know the destiny of one with whom I had been formerly familiar, and in whom I had taken an interest. Presently the game I was hunting down stopped at the door of the Grand Café. After a little discussion they entered. It was a public place of entertainment; there was no reason why I should not enter also. I found my way to the first floor. They were already seated at a table, Mary holding the *carte* in her hand. They were about to dine. Why should not I dine there too? There was but one little objection, – I had an engagement to dinner. But the strange impulse which overpowered me, and seemed leading me on step by step, spite of myself, quickly overruled all the dictates of propriety toward my intended hosts. Could I not send a prettily devised apology? I glided past the couple, with my head averted, seeking a table, and I was unobserved by my old acquaintance. I was too agitated to eat, but I made a semblance, and little heeded the air of surprise and almost disgust on the bewildered face of the waiter as he bore away the barely touched dishes. I was in a very fever of impatience and doubt what next to do. They still sat on, in evident enjoyment of their meal and their constant draughts of sparkling wine. My impatience was becoming almost unbearable when the man at last rose. The woman seemed to have uttered some expostulation, for he turned at the door and said somewhat harshly aloud, "Nonsense; only one game and I shall be back. The waiter will give you a paper – a magazine – something to while away the time." And he left the room for the billiard-table, as I surmised.

Now was my opportunity. After a little hesitation, I rose, and planted myself abruptly on the vacant seat before the woman.

"Mary," I said.

She started, with a little exclamation of alarm, and dropped the paper she had held. She knew me at once.

"Master John!" she exclaimed, using the familiar term still given me when I was long past boyhood; and then, after a lengthened gaze, she turned away her head. I was embarrassed at first how to address her.

"Mary," I said at last, "I am grieved to see you thus."

"Why should you be grieved for me?" she retorted, looking at me sharply, and speaking in a tone of impatient anger. "I am happy as I am."

"I don't believe you," I replied.

She again turned away her head.

"Mary," I pursued, "can you doubt, that, spite of all, I have still a strong interest in the companion of my youth?"

She looked at me almost mournfully, but did not speak. At that moment I probably grew pale; for suddenly that chilly fit seized me again, and my forehead became clammy. That voice sounded again in my ear: "Speak of him!" were the words it uttered. Mary gazed on me with surprise, and yet I was assured that *she* had not heard that voice, so plain to me. She evidently mistook the nature of my visible emotion.

"O Master John!" she stammered, with tears gathering in her eyes, reverting again to that name of bygone times, "if you had loved me then – if you had consoled my true affection with one word of hope, one look of loving-kindness – if you had not spurned and crushed me, I should not have been what I am now."

I was about to make some answer to this burst of unforgotten passion, when the voice came again: "Speak of him!"

"You have loved others since," I remarked, with a coldness which seemed cruel to myself. "You love *him* now." And I nodded my head toward the door by which the man had disappeared.

"Do I?" she said, with a bitter smile. "Perhaps; who knows?"

"And yet no good can come to you from a connection with that man," I pursued.

"Why not? He adores me, and he is free," was her answer, given with a little triumphant air.

"Yes," I said, "I know he is free: he has lately lost his wife. He has made good his claim to the sum for which he insured her life."

Mary grew deadly pale. "How did you learn this? what do you know of him?" she stammered.

I had no reply to give. She scanned my face anxiously for some time; then in a low voice she added, "What do you suspect?"

I was still silent, and only looked at her fixedly.

"You do not speak," she pursued nervously. "Why do you not speak? Ah, you know more than you would say! Master John, Master John, you might set my tortured mind at rest, and clear or confirm those doubts which *will* come into my poor head, spite of myself. Speak out – O, do speak out!"

"Not here; it is impossible," I replied, looking around. The room as the hour advanced, was becoming more thronged with guests, and the full tables gave a pretext for my reticence, when in truth I had nothing to say.

"Will you come and see me – will you?" she asked with earnest entreaty.

I nodded my head.

"Have you a pocketbook? I will write you my address; and you will come – yes, I am sure you will come!" she said in an agitated way.

I handed her my pocketbook and pencil; she wrote rapidly.

"Between the hours of three and five," she whispered, looking uneasily at the door; "*he* is sure not to be at home."

I rose; Mary held out her hand to me, then withdrew it hastily with an air of shame, and the tears sprang into her eyes again. I left the room hurriedly, and met her companion on the stairs.

That same evening, in the solitude of my own room, I pondered over the little event of the day. I had calmed down from my state of excitement. The living apparition of Mary Simms occupied my mind almost to the exclusion of the terrors of the ghostly voice which had haunted me, and my own fears of coming insanity. In truth, what was that man to me? Nothing. What did his doings matter to such a perfect stranger as myself? Nothing. His connection with Mary Simms was our only link; and in what should that affect me? Nothing again. I debated with myself whether it were not foolish of me to comply with my youthful companion's request to visit her; whether it were not imprudent in me to take any further interest in the lost woman; whether there were not even danger in seeking to penetrate mysteries which were no concern of mine. The resolution to which I came pleased me, and I said aloud, "No, I will not go!"

At the same moment came again the voice like an awful echo to my words – "Go!" It came so suddenly and so imperatively, almost without any previous warning of the usual shudder, that the shock was more than I could bear. I believe I fainted; I know I found myself, when I came to consciousness, in my arm-chair, cold and numb, and my candles had almost burned down into their sockets.

The next morning I was really ill. A sort of low fever seemed to have prostrated me, and I would have willingly seized so valid a reason for disobeying, at least for that day – for some days, perhaps – the injunction of that ghostly voice. But all that morning it never left me. My fearful chilly fit was of constant recurrence, and the words "Go! go! go!" were murmured so perpetually in my ears – the sound was one of such urgent entreaty – that all force of will gave way completely. Had I remained in that lone room, I should have gone wholly mad. As yet, to my own feelings, I was but partially out of my senses.

I dressed hastily; and, I scarce know how – by no effort of my own will, it seemed to me – I was in the open air. The address of Mary Simms was in a street not far from my own suburb. Without any power of reasoning, I found myself before the door of the house. I knocked, and asked a slipshod girl who opened the door to me for "Miss Simms." She knew no such person, held a brief shrill colloquy with some female in the back-parlour, and, on coming back, was about to shut the door in my face, when a voice from above – the voice of her I sought – called down the stairs, "Let the gentleman come up!"

I was allowed to pass. In the front drawing-room I found Mary Simms.

"They do not know me under that name," she said with a mournful smile, and again extended, then withdrew, her hand.

"Sit down," she went on to say, after a nervous pause. "I am alone now; and I adjure you, if you have still one latent feeling of old kindness for me, explain your words of yesterday to me."

I muttered something to the effect that I had no explanation to give. No words could be truer; I had not the slightest conception what to say.

"Yes, I am sure you have; you must, you will," pursued Mary excitedly; "you have some knowledge of that matter."

"What matter?" I asked.

"Why, the insurance," she replied impatiently. "You know well what I mean. My mind has been distracted about it. Spite of myself, terrible suspicions have forced themselves on me. No; I don't mean that," she cried, suddenly checking herself and changing her tone; "don't heed what I said; it was madness in me to say what I did. But do, do, do tell me all you know."

The request was a difficult one to comply with, for I knew nothing. It is impossible to say what might have been the end of this strange interview, in which I began to feel myself an unwilling impostor; but suddenly Mary started.

"The noise of the latchkey in the lock!" she cried, alarmed; "He has returned; he must not see you; you must come another time. Here, here, be quick! I'll manage him."

And before I could utter another word she had pushed me into the back drawing-room and closed the door. A man's step on the stairs; then voices. The man was begging Mary to come out with him, as the day was so fine. She excused herself; he would hear no refusal. At last she appeared to consent, on condition that the man would assist at her toilet. There was a little laughter, almost hysterical on the part of Mary, whose voice evidently quivered with trepidation.

Presently both mounted the upper stairs. Then the thought struck me that I had left my hat in the front room – a sufficient cause for the woman's alarm. I opened the door cautiously, seized my hat, and was about to steal down the stairs, when I was again spellbound by that numb cold.

"Stay!" said the voice. I staggered back to the other room with my hat, and closed the door.

Presently the couple came down. Mary was probably relieved by discovering that my hat was no longer there, and surmised that I had departed; for I heard her laughing as they went down the lower flight. Then I heard them leave the house.

I was alone in that back drawing-room. Why? what did I want there? I was soon to learn. I felt the chill invisible presence near me; and the voice said, "Search!"

The room belonged to the common representative class of back drawing-rooms in "apartments" of the better kind. The only one unfamiliar piece of furniture was an old Indian cabinet; and my eye naturally fell on that. As I stood and looked at it with a strange unaccountable feeling of fascination, again came the voice – "Search!"

I shuddered and obeyed. The cabinet was firmly locked; there was no power of opening it except by burglarious infraction; but still the voice said, "Search!"

A thought suddenly struck me, and I turned the cabinet from its position against the wall. Behind, the woodwork had rotted, and in many portions fallen away, so that the inner drawers were visible. What could my ghostly monitor mean – that I should open those drawers? I would not do such a deed of petty treachery. I turned defiantly, and addressing myself to the invisible as if it were a living creature by my side, I cried, "I must not, will not, do such an act of baseness."

The voice replied, "Search!"

I might have known that, in my state of what I deemed insanity, resistance was in vain. I grasped the most accessible drawer from behind, and pulled it toward me. Uppermost within it lay letters: they were addressed to "Captain Cameron," – "Captain George Cameron." That name! – the name of Julia's husband, the man with whom she had eloped; for it was he who was the object of my pursuit.

My shuddering fit became so strong that I could scarce hold the papers; and "Search!" was repeated in my ear.

Below the letters lay a small book in a limp black cover. I opened this book with trembling hand; it was filled with manuscript – Julia's well-known handwriting.

"Read!" muttered the voice. I read. There were long entries by poor Julia of her daily life; complaints of her husband's unkindness, neglect, then cruelty. I turned to the last pages: her hand had grown very feeble now, and she was very ill. "George seems kinder now," she wrote; "he brings me all my medicines with his own hand." Later on: "I am dying; I know I am dying: he has poisoned me. I saw him last night through the curtains pour something in my cup; I saw it in his evil eye. I would not drink; I will drink no more; but I feel that I must die."

These were the last words. Below were written, in a man's bold hand, the words "Poor fool!"

This sudden revelation of poor Julia's death and dying thoughts unnerved me quite. I grew colder in my whole frame than ever.

"Take it!" said her voice. I took the book, pushed back the cabinet into its place against the wall, and, leaving that fearful room, stole down the stairs with trembling limbs, and left the house with all the feelings of a guilty thief.

For some days I perused my poor lost Julia's diary again and again. The whole revelation of her sad life and sudden death led but to one conclusion – she had died of poison by the hands of her unworthy husband. He had insured her life, and then –

It seemed evident to me that Mary Simms had vaguely-shared suspicions of the same foul deed. On my own mind came conviction. But what could I do next? how bring this evil man to justice? what proof would be deemed to exist in those writings? I was bewildered, weak, irresolute. Like Hamlet, I shrank back and temporised. But I was not feigning madness; my madness seemed but all too real for me. During all this period the wailing of that wretched voice in my ear was almost incessant. O, I must have been mad!

I wandered about restlessly, like the haunted thing I had become. One day I had come unconsciously and without purpose into Oxford Street. My troubled thoughts were suddenly broken in upon by the solicitations of a beggar. With a heart hardened against begging impostors, and under the influence of the shock rudely given to my absorbing dreams, I answered more hardly than was my wont. The man heaved a heavy sigh, and sobbed forth, "Then Heaven help me!" I caught sight of him before he turned away. He was a ghastly object, with fever in his hollow eyes and sunken cheeks, and fever on his dry, chapped lips. But I knew, or fancied I knew, the tricks of the trade, and I was obdurate. Why, I asked myself, should the cold shudder come over me at such a moment? But it was so strong on me as to make me shake all over. It came – that maddening voice. "Succour!" it said now. I had become so accustomed already to address the ghostly voice that I cried aloud, "Why, Julia, why?" I saw people laughing in my face at this strange cry, and I turned in the direction in which the beggar had gone. I just caught sight of him as he was tottering down a street toward Soho. I determined to have pity for this once, and followed the poor man. He led me on through I know not what streets. His steps were hurried now. In one street I lost sight of him; but I felt convinced he must have turned into a dingy court. I made inquiries, but for a time received only rude jeering answers from the rough men and women whom I questioned. At last a little girl informed me that I must mean the strange man who lodged in the garret of a house she pointed out to me. It was an old dilapidated building, and I had much repugnance on entering it. But again I was no master of my will. I mounted some creaking stairs to the top of the house, until I could go no further. A shattered door was open; I entered a wretched garret; the object of my search lay now on a bundle of rags on the bare floor. He opened his wild eyes as I approached.

"I have come to succour," I said, using unconsciously the word of the voice; "what ails you?"

"Ails me?" gasped the man; "hunger, starvation, fever."

I was horrified. Hurrying to the top of the stairs, I shouted till I had roused the attention of an old woman. I gave her money to bring me food and brandy, promising her a recompense for her trouble.

"Have you no friends?" I asked the wretched man as I returned.

"None," he said feebly. Then as the fever rose in his eyes and even flushed his pallid face, he said excitedly, "I had a master once – one I perilled my soul for. He knows I am dying; but, spite of all my letters, he will not come. He wants me dead, he wants me dead – and his wish is coming to pass now."

"Cannot I find him – bring him here?" I asked.

The man stared at me, shook his head, and at last, as if collecting his faculties with much exertion, muttered, "Yes; it is a last hope; perhaps you may, and I can be revenged on him at least. Yes, revenged. I have threatened him already." And the fellow laughed a wild laugh.

"Control yourself," I urged, kneeling by his side; "give me his name – his address."

"Captain George Cameron," he gasped, and then fell back.

"Captain George Cameron!" I cried. "Speak! what of him?"

But the man's senses seemed gone; he only muttered incoherently. The old woman returned with the food and spirits. I had found one honest creature in that foul region. I gave her money – provide her more if she would bring a doctor. She departed on her new errand.

I raised the man's head, moistened his lips with the brandy, and then poured some of the spirit down his throat. He gulped at it eagerly, and opened his eyes; but he still raved incoherently, "I did not do it, it was he. He made me buy the poison; he dared not risk the danger himself, the coward! I knew what he meant to do with it, and yet I did not speak; I was her murderer too. Poor Mrs Cameron! poor Mrs Cameron! do you forgive? – can you forgive?" And the man screamed aloud and stretched out his arms as if to fright away a phantom.

I had drunk in every word, and knew the meaning of those broken accents well. Could I have found at last the means of bringing justice on the murderer's head? But the man was raving in a delirium, and I was obliged to hold him with all my strength. A step on the stairs. Could it be the medical man I had sent for? That would be indeed a blessing. A man entered – it was Cameron!

He came in jauntily, with the words, "How now, Saunders, you rascal! What more do you want to get out of me?"

He started at the sight of a stranger.

I rose from my kneeling posture like an accusing spirit. I struggled for calm; but passion beyond my control mastered me, and was I not a madman? I seized him by the throat, with the words, "Murderer! poisoner! where is Julia?" He shook me off violently.

"And who the devil are you, sir?" he cried.

"That murdered woman's cousin!" I rushed at him again.

"Lying hound!" he shouted, and grappled me. His strength was far beyond mine. He had his hand on my throat; a crimson darkness was in my eyes; I could not see, I could not hear; there was a torrent of sound pouring in my ears. Suddenly his grasp relaxed. When I recovered my sight, I saw the murderer struggling with the fever-stricken man, who had risen from the floor, and seized him from behind. This unexpected diversion saved my life; but the ex-groom was soon thrown back on the ground.

"Captain George Cameron," I cried, "kill me, but you will only heap another murder on your head!"

He advanced on me with something glittering in his hand. Without a word he came and stabbed at me; but at the same moment I darted at him a heavy blow. What followed was too confused for clear remembrance. I saw – no, I will say I fancied that I saw – the dim form of Julia Staunton standing between me and her vile husband. Did he see the vision too? I cannot say. He reeled back, and fell heavily to the floor. Maybe it was only my blow that felled him. Then came confusion – a dream of a crowd of people – policemen – muttered accusations. I had fainted from the wound in my arm.

Captain George Cameron was arrested. Saunders recovered, and lived long enough to be the principal witness on his trial. The murderer was found guilty. Poor Julia's diary, too, which I had abstracted, told fearfully against him. But he contrived to escape the gallows; he had managed to conceal poison on his person, and he was found dead in his cell. Mary Simms I never saw again. I once received a little scrawl, "I am at peace now, Master John. God bless you!"

I have had no more hallucinations since that time; the voice has never come again. I found out poor Julia's grave, and, as I stood and wept by its side, the cold shudder came over me for the last time. Who shall tell me whether I was once really mad, or whether I was not?

An Englishman in St. Louis

by Raymond Little

YOU SHOULD *not be here.*

"What?" Martin opened his eyes and looked at the air-hostess leaning over him.

"Hi." She flashed her perfect teeth in an apologetic smile. "I didn't like to disturb you, but we're making our descent." She pointed at the illuminated seat-belt sign above his head.

"Oh, right, sorry. I must have dropped off." He clipped the buckle across his waist, pushed his lap tray up into its seat back and looked through the little porthole at the swell of cotton ball clouds below.

You should not be here.

Where did that come from? He rubbed his eyes as if to erase the mantra repeating itself in his mind. The plane dropped into the low clouds, their wisps and tendrils swirling past his window, and then they were through and Martin caught his first glimpse of Missouri, a mass of lush plains and greenery that gave way to the gradual advance of urbanisation, and then they were down, the bump and squeak of rubber on tarmac as final as it was familiar.

You should not be here.

Goose bumps tickled his arms as another phrase, unbidden, came to his mind.

Too late, now. Too late.

* * *

"Wow. It's amazing." Martin gazed down into the roar of foam from the top of the dam.

"Sure is when the gates are open." Tom Barnes removed his sunglasses and gave them a wipe. "You got nothing like this in the UK?"

"No, not really."

"So what do you think? Can you help us?"

"I'd have to see the plans, but I don't see why not. If we can conserve even one more percent of its energy output, that'll make a huge difference."

"Well, I was told you were the man."

Martin blushed. "Oh, I wouldn't say that."

"Come on," Tom laughed and slapped him on the back. "Stop being so goddamned English. Let's go look at the control room. Where're you staying, by the way?"

"Up in St. Louis," Martin said as they made their way down from the walkway.

"It's a great city. You should enjoy yourself a little while you're here."

The control room was set back among the low level complex of buildings on the bank, the din of the gushing water from the barrier muffled almost to silence by its walls.

"Here," Tom passed Martin a memory stick and a plastic card. "It's all on there. You're welcome to come look at the full size drawings any time, though. Just swipe that pass."

"Thank you." Martin gazed through the wide viewing window at the spray cascading down the sloped concrete walls of the dam, then above at the parapet where they had stood a few minutes before. At its mid-point, staring into the drop, Martin noticed a figure. "There's somebody up there," he muttered.

"Huh?"

"At the top of the dam." He moved closer to the glass and saw that it was a young woman, slim with dark cropped hair. "Should she be up there?" He got no reply from Tom and glanced sideways at him. Tom was also looking through the window, but in the opposite direction. "Tom?"

"Ain't nobody up there," he said, his eyes set firmly on the view downstream.

"There's a girl," Martin pointed and looked back at the dam. The grey wall cut a horizontal line against the cerulean sky, but there was no figure. "She was right there." He felt his face redden for the second time in Tom's presence.

"I think you got a touch of jet-lag, buddy. Get yourself back up to St. Louis and have yourself a couple of beers."

Martin peered through the window. "I could have sworn..."

He felt Tom's hand on his shoulder. "Forget about it," the American said in his deep Missouri accent, and Martin saw an expression in the man's eyes of such sincere concern that the mantra – forgotten since he'd touched down that morning – began to repeat itself.

You should not be here. You should not be here.

* * *

The beer tasted good, and Martin felt any tension drop from his shoulders as he relaxed in his booth by the window. Tom was right, he'd just needed a little leisure time to get over the flight. He'd taken a nap and a shower back at the hotel before going for a stroll along the river past the Gateway Arch, the edge of its curved steel a burnt orange in the fading sunlight. The city was buzzing with Friday night revellers and he'd found a little bar and grill where he'd eaten what was probably the biggest T-bone he'd ever seen. As he glanced through his window at the locals – groups of friends and couples in love – he felt a pang deep inside. He was in a crowded bar in a beautiful city but he'd never felt more alone. He pulled out his wallet and looked at the photograph in the clear plastic insert, a head shot of him with Susan. Her face was pressed close to his with her lips pursed in a playful kiss at the camera, her blue eyes so alive and mischievous. She was wearing a purple bandana; the snap had been taken after her shock of red hair had gone, probably a month or so before the end. The familiar emptiness of grief filled his insides as he slipped the wallet back inside his pocket, and he was about to take a sip of his beer when he heard a raised voice by the door.

"You can't come in. Please go away."

Martin straightened and peered over his booth at the doorway, where a stout bald headed man who seemed to be the manager was standing with his hands on his hips, facing somebody beyond his view on the threshold. He heard a reply, a woman's voice, but it was too quiet to decipher her words.

"No, no. Go away," the manager replied. "You should not be here."

Martin leaned close to the window and saw the back of a woman with her shoulders hunched and the hood of her top pulled up as she walked away, oblivious to anyone one else on the sidewalk. He looked back at the bald man who touched his fingertips from his brow to his torso and across his chest in the shape of the Holy Cross. A group of locals at a nearby table who had watched the scene copied his gesture.

You should not be here. Martin felt a wave of nausea and looked back through the window. Between the heads of pedestrians crossing his view he caught a glimpse of the girl. She was on the opposite side of the avenue, her arms wrapped around herself as she stood staring at the entrance to the bar. Her shoulders seemed to tremble as if she were sobbing, and a moment later as the girl turned and stalked off she dropped her hood to reveal a spiky crop of dark hair. By the time Martin thrust some notes at a passing waitress and rushed outside, the girl was gone.

* * *

The cell phone buzzed sometime after two, and Martin grabbed it from his bedside table without turning the lamp on. "Hello?" He heard breathing, shallow and quiet. "Who is this?"

"It's me, Martin."

He sat straight, his heart pounding, his throat too dry to talk, and wondered if he were dreaming. He held the phone away from his ear for a moment to check the caller ID, which read *unknown* on the illuminated face, and felt a tremble in his legs. When he spoke at last he realised his cheeks were wet with tears. "Susan? Is that you?" He waited for a reply. "Where are you?"

"I'm in Delete."

"What? I don't understand."

"It's where you put me. You deleted me."

"No, it isn't like that," he pleaded, remembering the guilt he'd felt on the anniversary of Susan's death when he'd finally had the strength to erase her number from his phone.

"Go home, now. You shouldn't be here."

The line clicked and he turned on the light and cried into his hands until his eyes were sore. After that it seemed a good idea to drain the mini bar, and by the time he fell into a drunken stupor he'd convinced himself that he was losing it again, the way he had when Susan had died.

* * *

"Hey, how you doing?"

Martin glanced up from the blueprints. "Hello, Tom."

"Whoa, when I said get a beer, buddy, I didn't mean the whole barrel."

"Do I look that bad?"

Tom laughed. "I've seen worse, but not by much. I'll make you a coffee."

"Thanks, that'd be great." Martin looked at the plans and tapped out some calculations on his laptop as Tom busied himself with the electric kettle. A dull throb had embedded itself behind his eyes since he'd woke late that morning, but he'd somehow managed the long drive in the hire car down to Table Rock. It was quieter than on his first visit – the dam gates were shut – and Martin let his attention drift from his work to the top of its grey walls.

"Here." Tom placed a steaming St. Louis Cardinals mug on the desk and sat opposite.

"So, you had a good time?"

Martin forced a thin smile. "It's kind of lonely hitting the town on your own."

"I'm sure a good looking guy like you could meet a girl while you're here."

"Pick one up?" Martin laughed. "That's not really my…" he stuttered, "I'm not great at that kind of thing."

"You only gotta open your mouth. Some girls really go for that English accent."

"Maybe." Martin sipped his coffee. "I did see one girl. It was kind of strange. I'm almost sure it was the girl I saw on the dam, yesterday." He glanced over the rim of his mug at Tom.

"Oh, Martin, Martin." Tom sighed deeply, put his mug on the table and rubbed his eyes. "There was no girl."

Martin leaned forward and lowered his voice. "Tom, I swear to you I saw her up there yesterday. And I think you know I did, too. Please tell me I'm not going mad."

Tom stared at him for some time before he spoke. "You're not crazy, Martin. I know you saw something, but as far as I'm concerned, that *thing* ain't no girl."

* * *

Martin waited and watched from the same booth he'd occupied the previous two nights, and at last, just before midnight, he saw her approach the bar's entrance. A group of five friends drinking at a table by the door became agitated, one young man in particular, who hid his face in his hands as the woman next to him hugged him close. "Mike!" she called. "She's back!"

The manager came from behind the bar and strode across the room. "Get out of here. Go away. There's nothing for you here."

Martin jumped from his seat and crossed to the doorway as the girl was turned away, and regretted the fifth beer he'd downed as the warm night air hit him. He steadied himself one handed against a lamp-post as the girl crossed the avenue.

"Hey, wait."

She ignored him and took her place on the opposite sidewalk where she turned and faced the bar as she had before, her arms wrapped around her thin trembling frame. As he approached, Martin saw that her eyes were red with tears. He pulled a tissue from his pocket and held it out. "Here," he said.

The girl turned her dark eyes with a deliberate slowness to meet his gaze.

"I don't mean to impose, I just… you look distressed. I wondered if I might help."

The corner of her mouth twitched in a sign of amusement. "A real English gentleman. And how are you going to help me?"

Martin lowered the tissue. "I couldn't help over-hearing. That guy was pretty awful to you. Maybe I could buy you a drink elsewhere."

"I don't want a drink. I just want to see my friends."

Martin glanced over his shoulder at the bar where the manager was watching him from the doorway. "Those guys at the table?" He looked back at the girl. "Why won't they talk to you?"

"Because I had an accident. They're superstitious nut-jobs. They say I couldn't have survived, so now they won't see me."

Martin felt the beginning of a nausea deep in his stomach. "You jumped from the dam, didn't you?"

"I fell."

"I've been there. I have to say, it seems pretty impossible that anybody could survive a fall like that."

Her mouth stretched into a thin, humourless smile. "So what, you think I'm a ghost as well?" She pulled the hood of her jacket up and stood on tip-toes to whisper in his ear. "I'm alive, Martin. My friends have just deleted me."

She strode off then, and left him shaking on the sidewalk. It wasn't until she was out of sight that he realised he'd never told her his name.

* * *

Martin looked out through the open window of his room at the Millennium. No river traffic travelled the Mississippi – it was approaching three in the morning – and the massive arch that dominated the view was a black curve against the moonlit skyline. He swigged from the cold beer bottle in his hand and staggered across to the bed where he sat and looked at his cell phone on the table. The tears that had been so near welled and ran from the corners of his bloodshot eyes.

"Call me, Susan, please." The sound of his own voice freaked him out, but he guessed talking to himself was just another step, along with alcohol abuse and sleep deprivation, on the road to madness. He'd heard her voice last time, was sure it was real, but if the alternative was the loss of his sanity he would give it up in an instant to hear her speak once more. "*Go home now*," she'd said, "*you shouldn't be here*." Maybe she was right. He grabbed his phone and the keys to his hire car.

* * *

The pre-dawn sky was a dark shade of blue with a hint of gold on the eastern horizon that told him it was minutes from sun-up as he made his way up to the parapet. He expected her to be there, almost knew that she would be, but still took a sharp intake of breath at the sight of her when he reached the walkway.

"You came," she said.

"Yes." He walked across to the girl, who was staring down the sloped concrete wall to the base of the dam. Her hood was pulled up and her hands were in her jacket pockets. "You knew my name," he said.

"Did I?"

"Yes."

The girl continued to look down, her face obscured from his view by her hood. When she spoke at last it was hesitant, as if she were explaining to herself as well as to him. "Sometimes I know things. I just know."

"Because you're dead."

Her shoulders began to rise and fall. "Don't say that," she managed through her sobs. "Please, don't say that."

"I want to talk to Susan."

She took one hand from her pocket and wiped her cuff across her face. "Well, you can't. Too bad."

"But I spoke to her the other night. She called me."

"Did you love her?"

"Yes."

"Then maybe you should have taken her advice."

"How could you know…?" Martin didn't bother to finish his question. "I want to see her again. I miss her."

"Then she's lucky. My friends won't even talk to me." Her sobs became anguished. "Because every time they see me, they see this." She turned her head to him, and the rising sun gave just enough light to see her face, the left side of which was a mess of torn and bloody flesh lacerated down to the bone. "I guess I hit the wall on my way down. But I survived. I'm alive."

Martin placed his hands on her shoulders and pulled her close into a gentle embrace. "You didn't survive," he said. "You're dead."

"I'm alive!"

"No," his voice cracked as the sound of his own quiet sobs mingled with the girl's. "You're dead." He was speaking to her, and to Susan, and, he realised, to himself. "You have to say it."

"I won't! I can't!"

"You have to."

He felt her hands reach around and cling tight to his jacket. "I'm scared," she said.

"It'll be okay." His voice was gentle. "You shouldn't be here. You know that."

Her grip loosened as she pulled back and turned her half formed face up to his. "I'm dead," she said, her voice barely audible. She lowered her head and rested it on his shoulder. "I'm dead," she repeated. "I shouldn't be here."

"I know," he said, "I know." And as the sun's first rays fought back the night her body became nothing in his arms, and he prayed for her, and for Susan, and had the feeling that things were at last as they were supposed to be.

Death and Champagne

by Luke Murphy

THE PREACHER STOOD before the gates, his scarlet face rising above the helmets of the police. The great slopes of his gut shook with fury.

"The Lord will not be mocked!"

I heard his roar through my closed car windows. Spittle shot in ropes from his lips.

"What you do here is an abomination!"

I slowed as I came closer to the gates of the lab. Reverend Smallings and a dozen of his church had been here all week, but they'd never blocked the entrance before. *Scientists Pornographers and Socialists You Will Burn* read a new sign.

Holding it was a young man in a military buzz cut and black combat fatigues. I'd heard he was the preacher's son. Jonah Smallings, wasn't that his name?

The senior officer nodded to me and gestured to the Reverend to get away from the gate.

"Repent of your sins!" he shouted, eyes glaring at me. My skin prickled as if spiders were crawling on me. "You're building a tower of Babel!"

The cop grabbed one of his thick arms above the elbow. The preacher wrenched, tried to shake him off. Another officer grabbed his wrist. Smallings barked. His son sprang with a fist cocked. A nightstick flashed, a meaty smack: Jonah crumpled. His father twisted in rage against the hands that held him. A cop pressed something at the preacher's neck. It buzzed like when a fly lands on those fatal blue lights and the Reverend fell to the earth.

The latte I'd finished ten minutes ago burst into my throat in a bitter gush. Everything was suddenly wrong. I put my fingers around the neck of the champagne bottle that lay on the passenger seat and gripped it like a club.

The little crowd of protesters surged, placards like pitchforks. The police formed a line. Clubs rose and fell with steady thuds. Two officers dragged the preacher's still body to the grass verge. The head of security waved a frantic hand at me. The gate whined open. I let go of the bottle and slammed the gas.

As I passed through, Jonah Smallings crawled to where his father lay. He pressed a finger to the old man's neck. A shout broke from him. He looked up, locked my eyes and pointed at me. His face was melting with tears and fury. Around him was a chaos of brawling bodies but in that instant he and I were the only people in the world.

Then I was through the gate and it closed behind me, my hands tight on the wheel to keep them from shaking. Time to start my workday.

* * *

I nodded to the guard at the landing on my floor. "That preacher at the gate. Is he hurt?"

"They're getting an ambulance, ma'am," he said. He nodded at his screen. "Looks like it's arrived."

"Let me know if you hear anything, could you?"

"Morning, Selma."

That was Carlos, the lead physicist on my team, and my boss.

"Carlos. Did you see what happened out there? It's like a war zone."

He shrugged. "If they don't like science, they should throw out their cellphones and wear bearskins. We're making history here."

"'Scuse me, doctor," the guard said. A crackling was coming over his headset. We both turned around to him.

"The paramedics are using those paddle things on that preacher guy," he said. "Looks like he might be dead."

My hands jumped up to my mouth to cram in the scream that wanted to rush out. "What happened?" I said. "I think I saw one of the police tasering him."

"That can kill you if your heart's weak," Carlos said.

The three of us stood in a triangle for stilted seconds, trying to think of something nice to say about a man we had only seen from our cars and hated anyway.

Carlos shrugged. "Can't change what's done."

"You sure?" I said.

* * *

Temple Laboratories was established by a couple of Internet billionaires who hadn't much interest in luxury yachts, so they found a deeper hole in which to bury their money. I'd been there since the early days, and finally this: Project Osiris. The first thing we'd done that worked. After our first successful test – a loop of three nanoseconds – the billionaires got excited.

Bad news. They should have kept the PR team out of it. Instead they sent out press releases that launched a million florid listicles and got the attention of Reverend Smallings and his church, who'd got bored of gay marriage and climatology and needed a new Unnatural Thing to be outraged by. Project Osiris was it.

The focus of their hate was what we called the chamber: a metal room the size of a meat locker built inside Lab Two. Twenty-four of us worked in that lab and we were all there that morning. It was the day we'd prove the technology viable. It was the day we'd do a loop of nearly thirteen minutes.

I spent the morning drinking too much tea and rechecking figures that were already sound. The lab had an unsettling quietness about it, the researchers murmuring to each other in small groups and checking news sites constantly. Occasionally someone would drop something or laugh and we'd all look up in irritation. I kept hearing Smallings' name. His death had been confirmed, family and church would issue statements in due course. Carlos warned us: no interviews. A couple of media people got hold of my number. I hung up on them and turned my phone off.

Zero hour was eleven. At ten minutes to, Carlos stood up to make a desultory speech. He addressed the fire alarm on the back wall and spoke with many pauses that he filled with his irritating long hum. This was a historical moment, umm, and we were making, umm, a great contribution to science. He didn't mention Reverend Smallings but the dead man occupied the silences.

We checked watches and cellphones as the seconds ticked closer to eleven.

"Power it up," Carlos said.

Initiate startup procedure? said my computer. I clicked *Yes*. From inside the chamber came a whirr of machinery. Numbers fluttered across two dozen monitors. Carlos walked from one to another. Sit down, I wanted to shout at him.

"Ten seconds to go," he said. "Nine..." His voice faded out and he watched the metal walls of the chamber.

Two computers made competing beeps.

"The object –" Carlos coughed, cleared his throat. "The object is in the chamber."

"Woo hoo," said someone, too quietly to inspire anyone. Someone else clapped twice, and looked at their shoes when nobody joined in.

"Save the champagne until we complete sending," Carlos said.

The champagne. I'd forgotten the champagne. It was still lying on the passenger seat of my car. That was okay. I had twelve minutes to get it.

Someone touched me. I felt it, a light hand on my shoulder. I snapped around. Nobody there. Heads turned at my sudden movement and I pretended to be absorbed in the clock on the wall.

Just nerves firing randomly. Too much tension.

I felt it again. Hands on my face. A cool sensation, like a shaped breeze, but there were distinct fingers, palms, left and right, as if a person was seizing my head. A sudden memory: Smallings staring at me through the windshield, shouting his drivel. A vine of dread grew in my belly, sent shoots through my guts. He was not here: he was dead.

Faces were staring at me. Someone had just said something.

"Selma? The door," Carlos repeated.

I fluttered some buttons. Low hisses came from within the chamber's steel walls. On its door, a light went from red to green. It swung open, a ton of metal moving in silence.

Hands on me again. My body jerked, spine snapping like a whip. There's nobody here, I screamed silently. It was as if the air was disturbed by the shape of a person next to me, the currents of its flow all wrong. I stood hastily to cover up my spasm.

Carlos came out of the chamber holding up a coin-sized iron disk. I heard distant shouting. It came from no direction. I couldn't make out any words.

"What's the code?" I said to cover up the non-sound. Carlos glared. I'd spoiled his moment. He held up the engraved surface of the disk.

"Five, three, R..." He put on his reading glasses. "Seven, Q, B, nine, Y."

In the middle of the room, a lone desk was home to the usual laptop, plus a laser engraver. And, sitting on it, another little disk of iron, this one blank. Carlos tapped the computer. I'd written a random code generator for this purpose, ten lines of Javascript. Bodies pressed forward to gather around. The designated videographer, a grad student, pushed his way to the front. I lingered at the back. That distant shout was still coming from nowhere. Were there words? All I could make out was anguish.

Selma, I heard, like a distant cry in a storm. *I* –

Madness. This is how it starts: you pay attention to your mindvomit. I was in shock, I'd seen a man killed, and my brain, trying to digest it, was madly chewing on the gristle of that scene (electrical buzz, body falling) and trying to swallow it, but it kept coming back up. A breakthrough in science was happening in front of me and all I could think of was a dead nutcase.

The videographer framed the laptop as Carlos hit the *Return* key.

"Generating a new code now," he said. "The code is..."

A hiss as breath was sucked in.

"Five, three, R, seven, Q, B, nine, Y. Perfect match."

Sporadic cheers. Someone clapped Carlos on the back as he put the blank disk under the laser, copied and pasted the code and set the engraver running.

The cold hands were on my neck, my shoulders. What do you want? I shouted inside. It wasn't Smallings' ghost; that idea was insane. I was making this up.

Selma! The voice, pleading, mad with anguish.

"I'm now putting the engraved disk back into the chamber," Carlos declared to the video camera. "For the next several minutes, until we send it, this item exists in two places at once." He held the freshly engraved disk next to the one that had materialized in the chamber.

I lurched to my feet. My left arm was twitching, trying to fight the cold grip on it.

"I'm going to get the champagne," I said. "Left it in my car."

Carlos stopped. "You want to be here for this. We'll send someone."

I was already at the exit. "It's fine," I said, and was outside in the corridor a second later.

I walked, head down and staring like a bull. Too many doors. I swiped my card through one reader after another, waited for tiny lights to turn green. Those cold hands followed me all the way. They were moulded from winter and trailed down my neck, touched shoulders and arms.

"Leave me alone," I whispered to the faint voice shouting my name. "You're not real. I'm not listening to you."

The air in my lungs was hot and thick. At the end of the corridor, daylight dazzled through the door to the parking lot. I broke into a trot. Three puzzled faces looked up as I passed the coffee room. I swiped the card, waited for the green, and was out. I stood on the grass and threw my head back and breathed in deep.

No! Help –

The shouting voice was almost clear for a moment, then a distant siren wailed and the voice was gone.

"Go away," I said. "You're dead. It's not my fault. I can't help you."

I walked towards my car through the rows of silent metal. The sun lay on my face like a blanket, but the cold hands were here again, grabbing, stroking, clutching. My skin jumped at every touch.

"What do you want?" I whispered. "You're not real. I don't feel anything."

I was at the car. The ghost hands were on my shoulders. They pressed into me, inside me, as if I were soft dough. Through bone and fat and blood they crawled, a shocking cold in my lungs, then scraping through my heart. I could not draw breath to scream.

Look! cried the voice.

I turned and saw. A man in black was coming for me. Eyes blazed under a shaved head. He crouched low between lines of parked cars to hide from the security cameras.

"What do you want?" I said to the preacher's son. "How did you get in here?"

In two steps Jonah Smallings was on me. A leather glove stopped my cry.

"Quiet, bitch." He shoved me against the car. "Want to mock God now?"

I bit, thrashed, body lurching. His fingers were cables. My heel found his knee, I drove it in. He grunted, dropped one hand. I twisted, kicked again. His loose hand found something at his belt. Something shiny. But I was off, one foot down, another step –

His arm was a snake around my neck, crushing. I tried to haul in breath, heard a whistle in my throat. Sun flashed on metal. A sound I'd heard at the butcher's block, and something cold was inside my chest. An alien thing, like a thief in my home. Metal bit deeper. My limbs were too heavy to carry. Falling, no fear now. The ground was surely below me but I never felt it, just softness and silence and sleep.

* * *

Light burst in. I gazed at the clouds waltzing overhead. I felt weightless, as if I was floating in warm water.

I looked down. Below me, a body lay on the ground next to a car. Dirt was smeared on waxlike skin and scarlet spread on silk. A broken necklace lay nearby, the one my mother gave me when I graduated.

I stared at the body, curious and sad. Such a broken thing, just a doll thrown away.

And crouched next to it, a young man, eyes huge with fear. His fingers were white on the knife he held. He stared around; his gaze passed through me but saw only sky. He broke and ran for the fence. Pity surged up in me for the fear he was full of and how it had ruined him, but he wasn't mine to save.

"But you can still save yourself."

I heard the voice, familiar but strange, and I turned.

She hung in the air before me like a sculpture carved from pale light.

It was her all along. How did I ever imagine she was the preacher? She had only wanted to warn me. My hand seemed made of mist; I touched hers. A current of warmth spread between us.

"You know what you need to do," she said.

My new body turned like a weightless machine and I flitted through the air to the laboratory building. Here was the door, and by silly habit I reached for my card, but I was made of finer stuff now. I pressed forward. My body sank into layers of steel and wood that felt like a faint coolness inside, and I was through. In the coffee room, three colleagues laughed at something on a phone. I flew, shimmering through doors, willing myself to go faster. I shot through a wall – a momentary chill of dark and concrete and I burst into the light of Lab Two. I dragged myself through scratchy desks and shelves. Nobody looked at me.

Carlos stood between me and the chamber, his phone pressed to his ear.

"I think she turned hers off," someone said.

"Selma's fault if she misses it," Carlos said, and put his phone away. "We ready to send it back?"

"Ten seconds."

I brushed through his body, feeling jealous of the hot blood and firm bones that the living own. He shivered and a spasm of confusion ran over his face. I pressed myself through the chamber's cold steel walls, shimmering through the fizz of ticking circuits and bursts of glowing electricity. Would it work? I pushed myself onto the altar where the iron disk waited to be sent thirteen minutes back in time. The humming in the chamber grew.

I didn't have to do this. I could push myself out of the chamber and find the natural path, the way all the dead must go. It wasn't too late. This couldn't be right, what I wanted to do.

Then I thought of the pale broken body that I used to own. The taste of chocolate truffles, the feel of a warm bath, the way it had always served me faithfully. I'd do whatever it took to let it go on living.

"Sending now," came a voice over a speaker.

I stared at the engraved letters and numbers on the iron disk. Please, please, let it work.

Machinery rose to a whine. The world tilted in strange ways and folded at angles unknown.

Muffled from outside the chamber, two computers made competing beeps and Carlos spoke. "The object –" He coughed, cleared his throat. "The object is in the chamber."

I floated back through the metal walls and stared around Lab Two, looking for my desk. There was Selma, flesh glowing with life, eyes on her laptop as always. Oh lovely Selma, you'll listen to me this time, won't you?

"Save the champagne until we complete sending," Carlos was saying.

"Selma!" I called. I touched her shoulder. Her head snapped around and she stared at me, through me. "Selma, listen!"

A line of annoyance appeared in the middle of her forehead. I took her face in my hands. "Listen to me!" I shouted.

This time she'd hear me.

Or I'd watch her stabbed again, and see my duplicate emerge from her cooling flesh, and I'd send her back to the lab to try again.

And again. And again.

How many times had I done this? How many times had I lived and died in these minutes? I didn't care. This time would be different. She would know her own ghost.

"I won't give up on you," I whispered. "Listen to me."

The Mystery of the Semi-Detached

by Edith Nesbit

HE WAS WAITING FOR HER, he had been waiting an hour and a half in a dusty suburban lane, with a row of big elms on one side and some eligible building sites on the other – and far away to the south-west the twinkling yellow lights of the Crystal Palace. It was not quite like a country lane, for it had a pavement and lamp-posts, but it was not a bad place for a meeting all the same: and farther up, towards the cemetery, it was really quite rural, and almost pretty, especially in twilight But twilight had long deepened into the night, and still he waited. He loved her, and he was engaged to be married to her, with the complete disapproval of every reasonable person who had been consulted. And this half-clandestine meeting was tonight to take the place of the grudgingly sanctioned weekly interview – because a certain rich uncle was visiting at her house, and her mother was not the woman to acknowledge to a moneyed uncle, who might "go off" any day, a match so deeply ineligible as hers with him.

So he waited for her, and the chill of an unusually severe May evening entered into his bones.

The policeman passed him with a surly response to his "Good night". The bicyclists went by him like grey ghosts with foghorns; and it was nearly ten o'clock, and she had not come.

He shrugged his shoulders and turned towards his lodgings. His road led him by her house – desirable, commodious, semidetached – and he walked slowly as he neared it. She might, even now, be coming out. But she was not. There was no sign of movement about the house, no sign of life, no lights even in the windows. And her people were not early people.

He paused by the gate, wondering.

Then he noticed that the front door was open – wide open – and the street lamp shone a little way into the dark hall. There was something about all this that did not please him – that scared him a little, indeed. The house had a gloomy and deserted air. It was obviously impossible that it harboured a rich uncle. The old man must have left early. In which case –

He walked up the path of patent glazed dies, and listened. No sign of life. He passed into the hall. There was no light anywhere. Where was everybody, and why was the front door open? There was no one in the drawing room; the dining room and the study (nine feet by seven) were equally blank.

Everyone was out, evidently. But the unpleasant sense that he was, perhaps, not the first casual visitor to walk through that open door impelled him to look through the house before he went away and closed it after him. So he went upstairs, and at the door of the first bedroom he came to he struck a wax match, as he had done in the sitting rooms. Even as he did so he felt that he was not alone. And he was prepared to see something but for what he saw he was not prepared. For what he saw lay on the bed, in a white loose gown – and it was his sweetheart, and its throat was cut from ear to ear. He doesn't know what happened then, nor how he got downstairs and into the street; but he got out somehow, and the policeman found him in a fit, under the lamp-post at the corner of the street. He couldn't speak when they picked him up, and he passed the night in the police cells, because the policeman had seen plenty of drunken men before, but never one in a fit.

The next morning he was better, though still very white and shaky. But the tale he told the magistrate was convincing, and they sent a couple of constables with him to her house.

There was no crowd about it as he had fancied there would be, and the blinds were not down.

He held on to the door-post for support…

"She's all right, you see," said the constable, who had found him under the lamp. "I told you you was drunk, but you would know best –"

When he was alone with her he told her – not all – for that would not bear telling – but how he had come into the commodious semi-detached, and how he had found the door open and the lights out, and that he had been into that long back room facing the stairs, and had seen something – in even trying to hint at which he turned sick and broke down and had to have brandy given him.

"But, my dearest," she said, "I dare say the house was dark, for we were all at the Crystal Palace with my uncle, and no doubt the door was open, for the maids will run out if they're left. But you could not have been in that room, because I locked it when I came away, and the key was in my pocket. I dressed in a hurry and I left all my odds and ends lying about."

"I know," he said; "I saw a green scarf on a chair, and some long brown gloves, and a lot of hairpins and ribbons, and a prayerbook, and a lace handkerchief on the dressing table. Why, I even noticed the almanack on the mantelpiece – 21 October. At least it couldn't be that, because this is May. And yet it was. Your almanack is at 21 October, isn't it?"

"No, of course it isn't," she said, smiling rather anxiously; "but all the other things were just as you say. You must have had a dream, or a vision, or something."

He was a very ordinary, commonplace, City young man, and he didn't believe in visions, but he never rested day or night till he got his sweetheart and her mother away from that commodious semi-detached, and settled them in a quiet distant suburb. In the course of the removal he incidentally married her, and the mother went on living with them.

His nerves must have been a good bit shaken, because he was very queer for a long time, and was always enquiring if anyone had taken the desirable semi-detached; and when an old stockbroker with a family took it, he went the length of calling on the old gentleman and imploring him by all that he held dear, not to live in that fatal house.

"Why?" said the stockbroker, not unnaturally.

And then he got so vague and confused, between trying to tell why and trying not to tell why, that the stockbroker showed him out, and thanked his God he was not such a fool as to allow a lunatic to stand in the way of his taking that really remarkably cheap and desirable semi-detached residence.

Now the curious and quite inexplicable part of this story is that when she came down to breakfast on the morning of the 22 October she found him looking like death, with the morning paper in his hand. He caught hers – he couldn't speak, and pointed to the paper. And there she read that on the night of the 21st a young lady, the stockbroker's daughter, had been found, with her throat cut from ear to ear, on the bed in the long back bedroom facing the stairs of that desirable semi-detached.

Lost Souls

by Jeff Parsons

May 24, 1944

THE DAMP AIR SMOTHERED HANS with a slow asphyxiation of hot sweat, carbon dioxide, and diesel fuel. Each breath grew more and more tortured, not so much from the pervasive soggy drip of foul moisture clogging his lungs, but from the thought of what caused the U-292 German submarine to shudder, as if in anticipated pleasure.

The U-boat was cruising along the surface in attack mode with other subs in the wolf pack. They preyed upon the merchant cargo ships that crossed the unforgiving sea from Newfoundland to England. Each time the ship shook, a torpedo was sent away through the frigid North Atlantic Ocean towards its hapless convoy target.

Hans sat in the narrow toilet stall behind a flimsy curtain screen, leaning forward with his head cradled by his trembling hands, ashamed of his behavior, but unable to control it any more. He carefully eased a photograph from his uniform's breast pocket. Stroking the portrait of his love, Greta, he wondered yet again how he was going to stay sane – U-boat service extracted a heavy toll upon him.

He winced yet again…

Hans thought he could hear the harsh shriek of the enemy vessels tearing apart after each torpedo hit, but he knew that was unlikely, for the submarine's twin diesel engines were humming along at low throttle in the nearby bulkhead compartment.

He had heard that sound before, the dreadful shearing metal sound of sinking ships, and it haunted him. Like being underneath a waterfall, thunderous bubbling accompanied the dying throes of a merchant ship as it cracked open like a fragile egg shell, the deadly water flooding inside and the sailors within… he swore that he could hear the sounds of their lost souls screaming, just like in his nightmares.

Gott im Himmel… they were dying, he thought. Even if the sailors survived the sudden tumultuous sinking, they'd be cast adrift into the freezing wave-wracked water to die with little hope of rescue.

"Hans! Get your butt outta there now!" Gruber, the head mechanic, bellowed from the engine room.

Hans sighed. He kissed Greta's snapshot and slid it back into his pocket. Standing up, he wiped off the sweat streaking down his face, and left his safe haven. Back to work. The endless war needed him…

Gruber frowned at him, "Did you get lost?"

"No. I just felt sick. Queasy," he lied. "Must be something I ate."

"Uh-huh," Gruber said, tapping on a pressure gauge for the noisy diesel engines.

Hans knew how lame his response sounded. They had just been restocked with fresh food from a submarine supply ship. It was unlikely that the food had been spoiled.

He didn't hear the sound of torpedoes being fired any more. "Is the attack over?"

Gruber was busy starting the electric engines. They were used for quiet running engines, instead of the diesels, which would be shut off before the submarine slid beneath the waves.

"No more torpedoes left. We'll have to connect with the supply ship again." Gruber looked up at Hans, then smiled slightly, not unkindly. "Hans, this is what we do. Best get used to it. And don't let the Oberleutnant or anyone else know about your… feelings, okay?"

"Ja… thanks, Gruber. I'll do my best."

* * *

The submarine had left the oil-slicked scene of floating carnage and escaped unharmed into the vast rolling sea. Later that evening, Oberleutnant zur See, Herr Werner Schmidt, their commander, gave an announcement over the ship's comm: "We have fought with great valor. Each torpedo struck a mighty blow to the enemy's supply lines. We have saved the lives of many a valiant German soldier. On behalf of the Fatherland, I commend you once again for your selfless acts of bravery."

Hans cringed on the inside. He didn't want to share his emotions with the other crewmates settled around him in the aft sleeping quarters. The crowded room contained bunks stacked three high, filled with crewmen lying on their off-hours, too restless to sleep. The hypnotic tempo of water condensate dripping from the ceiling, piping and curved walls encouraged Hans' mind to wander into places he'd rather not consider, such as the meaning behind Schmidt's words.

Schmidt was right about bravery. Kriegsmarine U-boat service was dangerous. An encounter with an enemy destroyer was lethal in most cases, let alone the technical problems associated with repeatedly diving deep into the briny depths. The experience was unnatural – it took a certain amount of mental fortitude to be a submariner. Even so, everyone was always so solemn after a battle. Perhaps they realized that sooner or later, their luck could run out and death could overtake them.

His friend Fadi broke the silent gloom… He said, "Looks like we've single-handedly saved the Fatherland again."

Several tired smirks were exchanged at Fadi's remark. He smiled ruefully, then said, "I talked with some of the supply ship crew when their officers weren't looking. They said supplies were running short, no one was getting what they needed."

Rudi, one of the pipefitters, said, "Ja, and they also said something else…"

"Rudi, no need to bring that up," Johanne, another pipefitter, grumbled.

"I think it's important. Did you see the expressions on their faces?" Rudi asked.

"They were scared," Rudi said, his voice going low, "…afraid to talk much. One of them said they were being hunted…"

"Ha!" Fadi said. "What do they expect? It's a war! We're all combatants here, even the merchant ships."

"That's true," Johanne said, sadly. "We must kill our fellow mariners to win this war. Then, if it's our time, we can go home."

Hans thought… *What would we say when we met our maker? That we were following orders?*

* * *

The boat waited at the predesignated rendezvous coordinates for the supply ship's restocking of torpedoes and other essentials.

The crew was kept busy with the many routine tasks of maintenance, operations and testing, part of which involved quick certification dives to check for leaks that inevitably sprouted.

During the dives, Hans dreaded hearing the hull's metal shrinking due to the enormous forces crushing against the ship. If the seawater pressure could compress the submarine's high-strength steel, what would it do to him if the ship imploded?

The ship continued to complain like an old woman shuffling across a kitchen floor on a winter morning. In fact, it sounded like his beloved grandmother, Brunhilda, God rest her soul.

Hans had been trained to know the sounds of the ship, so when he heard something new amidst the hull's normal groaning, popping and creaking, he was quick to investigate it. It was a rhythmic tinkling sound that traveled along the piping of the ship's water cooling system.

He had to fix whatever was making the sound. An unexpected mechanical failure could potentially sink the boat. Also, excessive spurious noise was dangerous on a submarine. The enemy destroyers had hydrophones that could detect underwater sound. If they knew where you were, they could kill you.

Listening carefully, he patiently tracked the sound towards its source, ducking and squeezing through crowded spaces full of machinery, support struts and piping systems. It wasn't much different than working on the plumbing under his grandmother's sink back in Dresden. Except now, he rarely hit his head when he moved without thinking.

The sound originated inside the main ballast area, a large hollow tank situated within the hull underneath the control room. Inside the tank, a careful balance of air and water was maintained to raise and lower the ship's depth, and incidentally, it was used as a backup reserve for breathing air. There were also four other ballast tanks located outside of the hull, fore and aft, and along each side; without sufficient air in the ballast tanks, the ship would sink like a weighted corpse.

What the hell was that? It was almost like a glass bottle bouncing against metal. Perhaps one of the shipyard fitters had left their stash of liquor in there?

He'd have to tell Gruber about it. Gruber wouldn't be happy. The reasons behind mysterious sounds were elusive at times; they might not be able to repair this type of problem at sea.

* * *

The supply ship never showed up. Schmidt decided to travel back to port. It was a disgraceful waste of diesel, but the ship needed torpedoes.

Hans thought, *Even the angel of death has its limits…*

Still, the crew's morale was high. Back to merry Spain, where shore leave, booze and women awaited them, while the ship underwent an overhaul and torpedo reload.

Then, the unthinkable happened.

A man didn't show up at his work station. The cook, Alfred, who was also an assistant electrician, hadn't been seen since last night. The crewmen methodically searched the ship, section by section, bulkhead door by bulkhead door. No one could slip past them. When the crew met up in the command center, Schmidt announced that the cook was nowhere to be found. Everyone was to keep a lookout for him.

Where could he have gone while submerged under the sea?

Gruber whispered something into Schmidt's ear. Schmidt looked at Hans, then said, "Prepare for ascent to surface. We need to recharge the air. While we're doing that, we'll check the internal ballast compartment. We probably have a sound short."

The Captain gave the command. The ship rose to periscope depth. Schmidt scanned the surrounding sea and gave the order to surface.

Hans and another crewman, Dieter, were chosen to enter the main ballast tank.

Hans' slight frame made it easier for him to squeeze through confined spaces, so he was regularly chosen for tasks like these.

The tank's hatchway was unlocked and opened. After ten minutes of letting the tank air out, they entered one at a time through the narrow hatchway. He took a final deep breath before submerging himself into the cloying darkness.

The lights from their electric lanterns did little to dispel his anxiety.

They split up, searching for the cause of the mysterious sound.

Hans left behind the one way in and out of this foul smelling area, cramped with interconnecting metal supporting baffles, struts and piping. Good thing the sea weather was relatively mild, it was difficult enough walking on the slippery surfaces without the boat rocking wildly.

A few minutes later, Dieter yelped. Not a typical sound that one would hear from a seasoned sailor. Hans moved towards his partner, stepping over and bending around obstructions until he got to where Dieter leaned against the wall, breathing deeply.

Dieter's sickened expression said it all – Hans wasn't going to like this.

He saw a head. Just a head. No body.

The head rolled with the shifting of the boat and kept hitting a pipe that passed through the wall structure. *Mein Gott, his teeth*… the teeth hit the pipe, making the tinkling noise.

Hans shuddered – it was Alfred's head. Alfred… who had once told Hans how he missed his wife, his childhood sweetheart, and their two young girls, who would squeal with delight when he pushed them on their tire swing.

Dieter trudged back to the hatchway to ask for direction on what to do next. Hans stood awkwardly in silence, his lantern light playing across what remained of his shipmate, knowing that the only access into this area, the hatchway, had been padlocked closed…

How the hell did Alfred get in here? What the hell happened to him?

* * *

They never found the rest of the body, so they once again submerged, traveling on a course back to port.

Morale was low. Schmidt authorized a ration of Schnapps for the crewmen, but the drink seemed to make everyone feel melancholy.

Several hours later, loud noises started to bang intermittently against the outside length of the ship.

Fadi joked with Hans, saying that the boat must be looking very sexy to some of the amorous whales in the region.

Hans laughed nervously, knowing that wouldn't be a first in naval history, but it was highly unlikely.

The noises continued to disturb everyone's sanity… Schmidt described the anomaly as a mechanical problem that would need to get fixed at the port shipyard.

Then, another person went missing. It was Gebhard, the ship's best navigator, last seen going to his bunk for a quick nap.

Again, the crewmen went through the same drill. Gebhard couldn't be found, so after verifying that no other ships were in the area, the submarine was raised to the surface.

When the top hatch was popped opened, a brief waterfall of cold seawater spilled inside.

The banging noise stopped.

A storm was brewing outside. Some crewmen were sent topside, tasked with inspecting the outside of the ship to see what had been causing the raucous banging noises.

Hans was called to duty again, along with Dieter, to search the main ballast tank. He dreaded going in there again. *Will we find what's left of Gebhard?*

Sweating in the dark, even though the air was damp and chilly, Hans groped his way around cold metal and over slippery surfaces. The ship's rocking slowed his progress through the ballast tank.

About halfway through his search, he heard the call to return to the hatchway.

Schmidt wanted them to come see something.

They were directed towards the torpedo room where the nervous crewmen were assembled. What Hans saw shocked him to the core. It was Gebhard, strung up, suspended in midair, electrical wires woven deep into his flesh and connected to the piping overheard, looking like the sacrifice portrayed on the cross he wore around his neck.

Gebhard's skin was a fish-white color, his waxy eyes were bugged out, and seawater still dripped from his body, obviously drowned, yet trussed up here before the group.

They had searched this area not long ago – impossible as it was, it must've happened recently.

Mechanical problem, my ass…

Schmidt took control of the paralyzing situation. "Take him down. Gently. Put him in the machine shop. Men, stay sharp, go back to your stations, make sure that we're running safe and secure, then reassemble in a quarter of an hour at operations. We'll get to the bottom of this. Dismissed." He then motioned for his officers to confer with him, as if seeking counsel on what to do next.

Hans was alarmed that the order wasn't given to submerge the ship – they were extremely vulnerable to the enemy on the surface. Then again, being below the waves had definitely proven to be lethal.

* * *

Hans went back to the engine room with Gruber and Michael, the machinist mate who assisted with engine repair.

Gruber fussed with the diesels and electric motors. Of course, everything was operating perfectly. They were designed and manufactured by Germans – the best craftsmen in the world.

Hans and Michael talked, faces close to each other, at the aft end of the engine room, near a diesel fuel storage tank, out of sight and earshot from Gruber.

"Are we being hunted as well?" Michael asked softly, reminding Hans of what was said by sailors on the supply ship.

"I don't know. What could do this? And why?"

Michael was about to answer when he was suddenly jerked backward into the inky shadows behind the storage tank. It was so quick that only impressions lingered with Hans: Michael's eyes bulging with surprise, a sudden whoosh of displaced air, and outstretched arms, the last thing Hans saw of him.

No scream. No sound. Just a haloed afterimage of Michael...

Hans hesitated, trembling, then reached forward into the darkness. Nothing there except the sticky bulkhead wall. There was blood coating his fingertips when he pulled his hand back.

"Gruber!" he screamed like a frightened schoolgirl.

* * *

Hans stared into the darkness, shivering and unmoving, for what seemed like an eternity.

His body jerked at Gruber's touch.

Gruber saw the blood and cursed.

"Michael... he's gone," Hans whispered, "something... he's gone."

"Hans!" Gruber yelled. His grip on Hans' shoulder tightened. "We need to leave. Now!"

Hans snapped out of his mental fog.

"Just... just follow me, okay?" Gruber said.

Hans nodded.

They bolted out of the engine room to the all-hands meeting.

Not everyone was there yet. The men kept a wary distance from each other, no longer behaving as comrades, anxious with suspicious looks. Some glared at Hans when they saw the blood dripping from his hands.

At this point, the pounding against the ship's hull had started again. Also, there were scratching noises like nails being drawn across the outer skin of the ship. The sounds unnerved the already tense crew.

When Schmidt arrived, Gruber began, "We lost Michael... Hans said that something –"

Schmidt gruffly said, "That's enough, Gruber."

Hans didn't know what was scarier, Schmidt's suddenly harsh voice holding fast to his Prussian emotional control or the knowing frightened looks of the other crewmen staring back at him. *Something happened to even more of the others... that's why everyone isn't here.*

There was a sudden flash to Han's left. Others saw it happen too. Officer Waldemar was grabbed by something, a sky-blue misty blur – there he was one moment, and gone the next, pulled through the metal-lattice floor like cheese through a grater, drawn out of sight into the dark decks below. Nothing was left of the man except thin strands of ropy red-brown liquids that spilled into the darkness below.

There was a brief stillness of awful silence, then all hell broke loose. Screaming crewmen, mindless with terror, pushed and clawed each other in a raging chaos to escape until...

Schmidt's loud commanding voice quickly brought the remainder of the panicked crew under disciplined control. "We're leaving. Launch the lifeboats, prepare to scuttle the boat.

On my orders. Move it!"

Shocked as they were by the unusual order, the crew instinctively knew that it was suicidal to remain onboard and, as one, they scrambled to complete their preassigned emergency tasks.

Visibly shaking, Hans put on raingear and helped lift one of the rectangular lifeboat packages up the top hatch ladder. The lifeboat was damned heavy, but he had the strength of adrenaline driving him.

The weather topside rocked the boat from side to side even with its heavy ballast.

Wind whipped the night-time waves to smash against the lower conning tower. Electric lantern lights lanced wildly into the rain-soaked deluge of Atlantic darkness. Sailors on the outside deck tried to deploy their rafts while holding onto tether ropes. The treacherous wave action almost made some lose their footing, making it more difficult. One raft was almost ready to go.

He heard the sound of an airplane approaching fast from the overcast sky above. He glanced upward. It was probably an enemy dive bomber.

What! No no no, not now...

Hans' teeth chattered. The cold was brutal, especially after being inside the humid ship, but he'd also been traumatized by the insanity of recent events.

With trembling hands, he and his partner gripped their section of the tether rope while they placed their lifeboat on the deck. They held the lifeboat package in place with their knees and, fumbling, started to undo the straps that held it together.

Something heavy splashed nearby into the water, portside of the ship's aft end.

Mein Gott, not a depth charge!

The explosion was deafening, cracking against the ship with a huge wave that swept along the ship's surface.

The wave slapped him hard, forcing saltwater into his eyes and mouth. He lost hold of the tether rope as the boat began to list to one side. When he glanced along the ship's waterline rising out of the rough sea, he saw a myriad of long, thick furrows cut into the metal, like claw marks gutting the belly of a dying beast.

Overhead, the plane's engine roared away from the ship into the dark night.

There was no scuttle charge detonation... the ship was sinking of its own accord, with help by a near-hit from the depth charge. The ship rolled suddenly on its port side as it sank into the sea, throwing everyone off balance and flailing into the torrential high-water waves.

The cold gripped him mercilessly, squeezing the breath from him and sapping the heat from his shocked body. His heavy raingear made it impossible to stay surfaced for long as tall waves and fierce undercurrents dashed him about and yanked him under repeatedly, forcing burning saltwater down his nose and throat.

Where's the raft... the raft... the raft...

The raft was lost to his sight long ago in the endless swirling darkness and gurgle of struggled breathing. From a great distance, he heard screams off and on when his head broke above the water for moments at a time.

He knew he wouldn't last long.

The saltwater in his eyes distorted his vision, but he thought he saw a flicker of light. The raft? He was saved!

The light was closer now. But it wasn't above the waves, it traveled below. Moving swiftly, as if unaffected by the weather or waves.

The spectral form of light glowed a pale blue and more followed it, maybe several dozens of them, coming towards him. When he saw what they were, he knew that his time was at an end.

The specters of foreign sailors had come to claim their vengeance.

The Skeleton Crew

Michael Penkas

THERE COMES A POINT in every woman's life when she just has to accept that the sexy witch costume isn't an option any longer. Georgia Slazynski sighed as she considered herself in the full-length mirror. Gone were the nylons and low-cut blouses. Now her sagging breasts were concealed in a high-cut blouse, her wrinkled legs obscured by an ankle-length broomstick dress. The low-heels were replaced with black sneakers. Pretty much, the hat was all she'd kept from her glory days.

Staring at her reflection, she asked, "Are you ready?"

A stilted chorus of children answered, "Yes, Ms Slazynski."

Turning, she saw ten children lined up like soldiers, each dressed in a black and white skeleton costume, skull masks pulled on and pumpkin-shaped treat baskets held in their left hands. Several of them shifted nervously from one foot to the other. The costumes included black gloves with little bones etched across the fingers. The masks had white fabric flaps that fell in back to conceal their hair. Aside from height, there was no way to tell one child from another, not even boys from girls.

"Now, remember, we all stay together. No one running ahead or lagging behind. Absolutely no one walking in the streets. If any of you do, then I'll make you all hold hands. Is that understood?"

The children nodded. They heard the same thing from her every year.

"No one takes off their mask or gloves. And no one takes off anyone else's mask or gloves. None of you talk to any of the other trick-or-treaters, even if you recognize them. And if a stranger says something to you, what do you say?"

Again, the stilted chorus responded, "Happy Halloween."

"And what else?"

Ten hands ran across ten mouths in a zipper pantomime.

"That's right. So let's go." She picked up her own pumpkin basket. Sifting through the contents, she made sure everything was there: an eleventh costume, complete with gloves, mask and even black slippers with bony toes sewn on. It had taken her a month of spare hours to put the costume together, but she hadn't minded. She'd sewn all the other costumes with as much care, even molding the skull masks out of papier-mâché.

She heard several gasps from the children and knew it was because of the basket she held. "That's right. We're picking up another trick-or-treater this year. I want you all to be polite to him." She smiled as they nodded.

They were good children, every last one, and she was always glad to give them this night's adventure. Looking outside, she could see that the sun had just set, leaving only a hazy red horizon behind. Opening the door, she let the ten children march out single file, then followed the last one out. Her house was on Leland Street, near Damen, and their route would take them through most of the Ravenswood neighborhood, as well as east into the edge of Uptown. In all, they would probably walk a total of twenty blocks before the night was finished; but the children never complained and Georgia kept herself in shape.

The first house was only two blocks away, near Montrose and Damen. The Fosters. As usual, they kept their lights off. As usual, Georgia and the children went up to the door anyway. One of the skeletons pressed the door buzzer. There was shuffling from within the house, then slow footsteps. Two sets of footsteps. A quick curtain peek from a window beside the door, then the porchlight came on.

Mr and Mrs Foster were dressed in jeans and sweatshirts. They looked more or less the same as they'd looked last year. Mr Foster might have been a little pudgier and Mrs Foster's hair might have been a little thinner; but they were more or less the same. It was Mrs Foster who spoke. "Well, Happy Halloween."

The children replied, "Happy Halloween, Mrs Foster," which made her tremble just a little. She pulled a candy dish off a side table and held it out to the children. There were two-dozen candy bars piled on it. Snickers. Milky Way. Mars. Three Musketeers. Full-sized bars. Not those tiny "fun-sized" ones you bought twenty to a bag.

Each of the children picked one bar. Mrs Foster's hands were trembling as she held the tray, flinching whenever an eager child brushed against them. As each child took a bar, he or she would mutter a "thank you."

The final child to take a bar paused before thanking her. He looked up at Mrs Foster, who quickly put the tray back on the counter, as if afraid she would drop it. Mr Foster said nothing as he took hold of his wife's shoulder. He looked down at the last child as well. While Mrs Foster trembled, Georgia could actually see tears forming in Mr Foster's eyes.

Georgia was about to guide the children away when Mr Foster looked behind him and yelled, "Go back to your room!"

Tilting her head, Georgia saw a girl standing at the top of the stairway, looking down on them. She couldn't have been older than twelve. She was dressed in blue jeans and a t-shirt with the name of a band Georgia had never heard of. "Is that them?" she asked, setting foot on the top stair.

Mrs Foster also turned and screamed, "Get back in your room! Don't even look at them!"

Mr Foster had let go of his wife and was heading for the stairs. "So help me God, Stacey, if you don't go back in your room right now –"

One of the skeleton children asked, "Stacey?"

Mr and Mrs Foster both turned back to look at the boy they'd been staring at before. It was Stacey who asked, "Joey?"

She was running down the stairs as her father ran up. When they met in the middle, he scooped the girl up and carried her back to her room. She was screaming at the boy, "Joey! Why did you leave? They're even worse now."

Before Joey could offer any answer, Mrs Foster closed the door without another word. The porchlight went out.

Joey turned to look at Georgia, as if she could offer some answer or word of comfort. But there was nothing to say. Eventually, they left the Fosters' porch and made their way to the next house on their route. No one paused as the screams from inside the house began to be punctuated with slaps.

The next house, the Riveras, had its porchlight on and a bucket on the top step, overflowing with M&M bags with a note reading *Take One* taped to it. But one of the children rang the doorbell anyway. And when no one answered, she rang it again. And again. And again. Until finally, Mr and Mrs Rivera came to the door to hear the children's greeting and accept their thanks for the candy.

Georgia reminded them of the rules. Parents couldn't just leave candy out. They had to come to the door. They had to see the children. Every year, they had to see the children.

Bad things happened to the parents who decided to go out for Halloween. Worse things happened to parents who tried to move out of the neighborhood. Those were the rules.

The Keyes and the Morrises didn't offer any trouble, leaving their lights on and coming to the door on the first ring. Snickers and Butterfingers, respectively. They were the two oldest stops on the route and had long ago resigned themselves to it.

The Hendricks, on the other hand, were always a problem. They were the only couple who actually tried to touch the children, reaching for their masks. While not expressly forbidden, Georgia had explained more than once that it would be a bad idea. Better to pretend that this was just an elaborate Halloween prank rather than see what lay beneath the masks. The skulls were a morbid touch added to a great mercy.

This year, only Mrs Hendrick answered the door. The children offered their usual "Trick or Treat" and she reached for a dish of Mounds and Almond Joys.

As the children took their pick of the candy, Georgia reminded her, "You both have to come to the door, Mrs Hendrick. It's not fair to make just one of you do it."

She began to cry as the children finished taking their candy. "He can't... he can't come to the door. Mr... Ernie died in August."

Georgia closed her eyes. "I'm sorry to hear that."

"No, you're not," Mrs Hendrick snapped back. When Georgia opened her eyes, she saw the woman's face tightened with hate. "You come here every year and you know it kills us a little more. But you don't care. You fucking bitch!"

"Don't," Georgia whispered, nodding to the children.

Mrs Hendrick laughed at her concern. "If you gave a damn about these kids, you'd leave them... where they belong."

One of the children offered a hushed, "Mom?"

Mrs Hendrick dropped the dish, which shattered when it hit the floor. "Damn it damn it damn it," was all she had to say as she shut the door and turned off the porchlight. Georgia heard her running up a flight of stairs as she guided the children away from the house.

The Taylors had only been on the route for three years, but had already adjusted well to it. Porchlight, there after one ring, and even smiles. None of that was absolutely required. Just as it wasn't required that they give good candy. It would have been enough to offer apples or carrots or even sticks of gum. But every one of the houses always gave out good treats. The Taylors had Skittles.

And then there was the next house. The Bakers. It was the new house on the route, where they were scheduled to pick up the new child. This was always the hardest part of the routine for her. There was no point in calling ahead. The situation would have been explained to the Bakers in the same way it had been explained to Georgia. And if they didn't believe before her arrival... well, they would have to accept the proof of what they saw.

It was Georgia who rang the bell this time. The porchlight was on, which was unusual for a first time house. So maybe they hadn't believed.

It was Mrs Baker who answered the door, dressed in yellow pajamas with a pair of yellow cat-ears perched on her head and some painted whiskers. "Happy Halloween!" she said with a wide smile that died as she looked down on the ten skulls looking back up at her.

The children replied, "Trick or Treat."

Mrs Baker just stared at the children silently, mouth open. The children waited patiently for their candy.

Finally, Georgia asked, "Mrs Baker, did someone explain to you –"

"No," she whispered, then began to cry. She sank to her knees in front of the children and leaned against the open door. She just whispered over and over, "No."

When Mr Baker came to the door, he knelt beside his wife and wrapped his arms around her before even looking at the children. When he did look at them, he shouted, "Get out of here! We don't deserve this!"

Georgia said nothing. They were actually handling it better than some had done. Eight years ago, Mr Rivera had actually pointed a gun at her when she'd first appeared at his door. She wondered briefly how Mr Rivera had died.

She couldn't speak to what was deserved and what wasn't. It wasn't her decision what children came on the route, after all.

The thirteen of them, Georgia, the ten children and the Bakers, all waited quietly for some answer. It finally came as a thumping sound from inside the house. Both Mr and Mrs Baker turned to look at their stairway. A wall obscured everything but the base of the stairs from Georgia's view on the porch. But the thumping sound was unmistakable. Someone was falling down the stairs.

The sound ended as a boy came into view, toppling down the last step and coming to rest on the floor. His neck was bent at a sharp right angle so that his ear was flattened against his shoulder. One arm was twisted back behind him while the other obscured his face. His legs were folded at uncomfortable angles.

Mrs Baker screamed as the jumble of limbs straightened themselves slowly, cracking and popping as the boy stood up. His neck was the last thing to snap back into an appropriate position. He was maybe ten, eleven at the most, his hair an unruly blond mop flattened on one side. He was dressed in blue pajamas that were a shade lighter than the bruises that covered his face and hands.

As the boy stumbled towards the door, Mr Baker whispered, "Please, God."

Neither parent made a move to stop the boy as he walked past them and stood before Georgia. He offered a timid, expectant smile. She offered a smile that was far more confident as she handed him a basket. "Danny?" He nodded. "That's your costume, Danny. Do you want to put it on now?"

Again, he nodded and she looked away from him as he slid off his pajamas. Facing the Bakers, she said, "We'll be back next Halloween. It will be some time after sunset. You'll have to be here when we come. Don't try to run. It's better if you just… it's better if you just open the door when we come."

Mr Baker was nodding, but something seemed to waken in Mrs Baker as she pleaded, "It wasn't me. Reed pushed him. Not me. I never… I never did anything."

Georgia nodded. "I'm sure you didn't, Mrs Baker. But that's why you both have to answer the door next Halloween. Because of everything your husband did. And everything you didn't do."

When she turned away from them, she saw Danny was already suited up, pulling his skull mask over his face. "Ready to go?" The boy nodded. Turning back to the rest of the children, she asked, "What do we say?"

"Thank you, Mr and Mrs Baker." The children hadn't taken any candy from the house, but parents didn't have to give out candy their first year on the route. The first year, they always gave something much more precious.

Like the others, Danny was a good child, staying with the group, not talking to strangers and saying "thank you" at each house without any problem. The others accepted him immediately.

When they'd finished the route, Georgia took them back to their home. The gates to Saint Boniface Cemetery were always locked after sunset, but she'd been given a key decades ago. Opening the gate, she walked each child to a grave. Once the candy had been emptied onto the earth, each costume was taken off and folded into a pumpkin basket, skull mask on top. Each child offered a sincere, "Thank you, Ms Slazynski," before going back to sleep.

The last grave she found was Daniel Baker's. As the boy took off his costume, she asked him, "Are you going to be all right here?"

Putting everything into the basket, same as he'd seen the other children do, he nodded. "Yes, ma'am. I'm actually… I'm glad I don't have to stay there anymore. Thank you."

"It's all right. I'm glad to do it."

Looking around the cemetery, he asked, "Where, um, where are you buried?"

And she laughed just a little. "I'm not buried anywhere, dear. I live in a house a few blocks from here. Next Halloween, I'll come over and bring you all there to change."

Danny shook his head. "If you're not… then why do you do it? I mean, is one of them your…"

"No. I never had children. But I had a sister. Her name was Audrey. We were twins. And when we were eight years old, Audrey… well, had an accident. Like yours. And then she started visiting our house every year with other children like her. Like you."

"So one of the other kids is –"

"No. When my parents died, she went away. That's how it works. When your parents die, you'll move on to… whatever comes next. Until then, you can visit them once a year, on the night when doors are left open to all children."

That seemed to satisfy Danny because he said, "Okay," then, "Good night, Ms Slazynski."

She smiled as he finally went to sleep.

Then she took all eleven of the pumpkin baskets in her arms, five handles looped on one arm, six handles on the other. If she took any more children on this route next year, she decided that she'd bring a garbage bag with her to carry all the baskets back to her house.

She remembered the woman who used to bring her sister to the door every year. She'd seemed so impossibly old to Georgia back then, maybe fifty. She remembered peeking at her from behind doorways, not wanting her parents to catch her. The way Stacey Foster had been staring at her this year. And she wondered how many more years she could make the trip through the neighborhood before someone younger had to take over.

After all, it was only the dead who weren't getting any older.

Ligeia

Edgar Allan Poe

And the will therein lieth, which dieth not. Who knoweth the mystery of the will, with its vigor? For God is but a great will pervading all things by nature of its intentness. Man doth not yield himself to the angels, nor unto death utterly, save only through the weakness of his feeble will.

Joseph Glanvill.

I CANNOT, for my soul, remember how, when, or even precisely where, I first became acquainted with the lady Ligeia. Long years have since elapsed, and my memory is feeble through much suffering. Or, perhaps, I cannot *now* bring these points to mind, because, in truth, the character of my beloved, her rare learning, her singular yet placid cast of beauty, and the thrilling and enthralling eloquence of her low musical language, made their way into my heart by paces so steadily and stealthily progressive, that they have been unnoticed and unknown. Yet I believe that I met her first and most frequently in some large, old, decaying city near the Rhine. Of her family – I have surely heard her speak. That it is of a remotely ancient date cannot be doubted. Ligeia! Ligeia! Buried in studies of a nature more than all else adapted to deaden impressions of the outward world, it is by that sweet word alone – by Ligeia – that I bring before mine eyes in fancy the image of her who is no more. And now, while I write, a recollection flashes upon me that I have *never known* the paternal name of her who was my friend and my betrothed, and who became the partner of my studies, and finally the wife of my bosom. Was it a playful charge on the part of my Ligeia? or was it a test of my strength of affection, that I should institute no inquiries upon this point? or was it rather a caprice of my own – a wildly romantic offering on the shrine of the most passionate devotion? I but indistinctly recall the fact itself – what wonder that I have utterly forgotten the circumstances which originated or attended it? And, indeed, if ever that spirit which is entitled *Romance* – if ever she, the wan misty-winged *Ashtophet* of idolatrous Egypt, presided, as they tell, over marriages ill-omened, then most surely she presided over mine.

There is one dear topic, however, on which my memory fails me not. It is the *person* of Ligeia. In stature she was tall, somewhat slender, and, in her latter days, even emaciated. I would in vain attempt to portray the majesty, the quiet ease of her demeanor, or the incomprehensible lightness and elasticity of her footfall. She came and departed as a shadow. I was never made aware of her entrance into my closed study, save by the dear music of her low sweet voice, as she placed her marble hand upon my shoulder. In beauty of face no maiden ever equaled her. It was the radiance of an opium-dream – an airy and spirit-lifting vision more wildly divine than the phantasies which hovered about the slumbering souls of the daughters of Delos. Yet her features were not of that regular mold which we have been falsely taught to worship in the classical labors of the heathen. "There is no exquisite beauty," says Bacon, Lord Verulam, speaking truly of all the forms and *genera* of beauty, "without some *strangeness* in the proportion." Yet, although I saw that the features of Ligeia were not of a classic regularity – although I perceived that her loveliness was indeed "exquisite," and felt that there was much of "strangeness" pervading it, yet I have tried in vain to detect the irregularity and to trace home my own perception of "the strange." I examined the contour of the lofty and pale forehead – it was faultless – how cold indeed that word when applied to a majesty so divine! – the skin rivaling the purest ivory, the commanding extent and repose, the gentle prominence of the regions above the temples; and then the raven-black, the glossy, the luxuriant, and naturally-curling tresses, setting forth the full force of the Homeric epithet, "hyacinthine!" I looked at the delicate outlines of the nose – and nowhere but in the graceful medallions of the Hebrews had I beheld a similar perfection. There were the same luxurious smoothness of surface, the same scarcely perceptible tendency to the aquiline, the same harmoniously curved nostrils speaking the free spirit. I regarded the sweet mouth. Here was indeed the triumph of all things heavenly – the magnificent turn of the short upper lip – the soft, voluptuous slumber of the under – the dimples which sported, and the color which spoke – the teeth glancing back, with a brilliancy almost startling, every ray of the holy light which fell upon them in her serene and placid yet most exultingly radiant of all smiles. I scrutinized the formation of the chin – and, here, too, I found the gentleness of breadth, the softness and the majesty, the fullness and the spirituality, of the Greek – the contour which the god Apollo revealed but in a dream, to Cleomenes, the son of the Athenian. And then I peered into the large eyes of Ligeia.

For eyes we have no models in the remotely antique. It might have been, too, that in these eyes of my beloved lay the secret to which Lord Verulam alludes. They were, I must believe, far larger than the ordinary eyes of our own race. They were even fuller than the fullest of the gazelle eyes of the tribe of the valley of Nourjahad. Yet it was only at intervals – in moments of intense excitement – that this peculiarity became more than slightly noticeable in Ligeia. And at such moments was her beauty – in my heated fancy thus it appeared perhaps – the beauty of beings either above or apart from the earth – the beauty of the fabulous Houri of the Turk. The hue of the orbs was the most brilliant of black, and, far over them, hung jetty lashes of great length. The brows, slightly irregular in outline, had the same tint. The "strangeness," however, which I found in the eyes was of a nature distinct from the formation, or the color, or the brilliancy of the features, and must, after all, be referred to the *expression*. Ah, word of no meaning! behind whose vast latitude of mere sound we intrench our ignorance of so much of the spiritual. The expression of the eyes of Ligeia! How for long hours have I pondered upon it! How have I, through the whole of a midsummer night, struggled to fathom it! What was it – that something more profound than the well of Democritus – which lay far within the pupils of my beloved? What *was* it? I was possessed with a passion to discover. Those eyes! those large, those shining, those divine orbs! they became to me twin stars of Leda, and I to them devoutest of astrologers.

There is no point, among the many incomprehensible anomalies of the science of mind, more thrillingly exciting than the fact – never, I believe, noticed in the schools – than in our endeavors to recall to memory something long forgotten, we often find ourselves *upon the very verge* of remembrance, without being able, in the end, to remember. And thus how frequently, in my intense scrutiny of Ligeia's eyes, have I felt approaching the full knowledge of their expression – felt it approaching – yet not quite be mine – and so at length entirely depart! And (strange, oh, strangest mystery of all!) I found, in the commonest objects of the universe, a circle of analogies to that expression. I mean to say that, subsequently to the period when Ligeia's beauty passed into my spirit, there dwelling as in a shrine, I derived, from many existences in the material world, a sentiment such as I felt always around, within me, by her large and luminous orbs. Yet not the more could I define that sentiment, or analyze, or even steadily view it. I recognized it, let me repeat, sometimes in the survey of a rapidly growing vine – in the contemplation of a moth, a butterfly, a chrysalis, a stream of running water. I have felt it in the ocean – in the falling of a meteor. I have felt it in the glances of unusually aged people. And there are one or two stars in heaven (one especially, a star of the sixth magnitude, double and changeable, to be found near the large star in Lyra) in a telescopic scrutiny of which I have been made aware of the feeling. I have been filled with it by certain sounds from stringed instruments, and not unfrequently by passages from books. Among innumerable other instances, I well remember something in a volume of Joseph Glanvill, which (perhaps merely from its quaintness – who shall say?) never failed to inspire me with the sentiment: "And the will therein lieth, which dieth not. Who knoweth the mysteries of the will, with its vigor? For God is but a great will pervading all things by nature of its intentness. Man doth not yield him to the angels, nor unto death utterly, save only through the weakness of his feeble will."

Length of years and subsequent reflection have enabled me to trace, indeed, some remote connection between this passage in the English moralist and a portion of the character of Ligeia. An *intensity* in thought, action, or speech was possibly, in her, a result, or at least an index, of that gigantic volition which, during our long intercourse, failed to give other and more immediate evidence of its existence. Of all the women whom I have ever known, she, the outwardly calm, the ever-placid Ligeia, was the most violently a prey to the tumultuous vultures of stern passion. And of such passion I could form no estimate, save by the miraculous expansion of those eyes which at once so delighted and appalled me – by the almost magical melody, modulation, distinctness, and placidity of her very low voice – and by the fierce energy (rendered doubly effective by contrast with her manner of utterance) of the wild words which she habitually uttered.

I have spoken of the learning of Ligeia: it was immense – such as I have never known in woman. In the classical tongues was she deeply proficient, and as far as my own acquaintance extended in regard to the modern dialects of Europe, I have never known her at fault. Indeed upon any theme of the most admired because simply the most abstruse of the boasted erudition of the Academy, have I *ever* found Ligeia at fault? How singularly – how thrillingly, this one point in the nature of my wife has forced itself, at this late period only, upon my attention! I said her knowledge was such as I have never known in woman – but where breathes the man who has traversed, and successfully, *all* the wide areas of moral, physical, and mathematical science? I saw not then what I now clearly perceive that the acquisitions of Ligeia were gigantic, were astounding; yet I was sufficiently aware of her infinite supremacy to resign myself, with a child-like confidence, to her guidance through the chaotic world of metaphysical investigation at which I was most busily occupied during the earlier years of our marriage. With how vast a triumph – with how vivid a delight – with how much of all that is ethereal in hope did I *feel*, as she bent over me in studies but little sought – but less known – that delicious vista by slow degrees expanding before me, down whose long, gorgeous, and all untrodden path, I might at length pass onward to the goal of a wisdom too divinely precious not to be forbidden.

How poignant, then, must have been the grief with which, after some years, I beheld my well-grounded expectations take wings to themselves and fly away! Without Ligeia I was but as a child groping benighted. Her presence, her readings alone, rendered vividly luminous the many mysteries of the transcendentalism in which we were immersed. Wanting the radiant luster of her eyes, letters, lambent and golden, grew duller than Saturnian lead. And now those eyes shone less and less frequently upon the pages over which I pored. Ligeia grew ill. The wild eyes blazed with a too – too glorious effulgence; the pale fingers became of the transparent waxen hue of the grave; and the blue veins upon the lofty forehead swelled and sank impetuously with the tides of the most gentle emotion. I saw that she must die – and I struggled desperately in spirit with the grim Azrael. And the struggles of the passionate wife were, to my astonishment, even more energetic than my own. There had been much in her stern nature to impress me with the belief that, to her, death would have come without its terrors; but not so. Words are impotent to convey any just idea of the fierceness of resistance with which she wrestled with the Shadow. I groaned in anguish at the pitiable spectacle. I would have soothed – I would have reasoned; but in the intensity of her wild desire for life – for life – *but* for life – solace and reason were alike the uttermost of folly. Yet not until the last instance, amid the most convulsive writhings of her fierce spirit, was shaken the external placidity of her demeanor. Her voice grew more gentle – grew more low – yet I would not wish to dwell upon the wild meaning of the quietly uttered words. My brain reeled as I hearkened, entranced, to a melody more than mortal – to assumptions and aspirations which mortality had never before known.

That she loved me I should not have doubted; and I might have been easily aware that, in a bosom such as hers, love would have reigned no ordinary passion. But in death only was I fully impressed with the strength of her affection. For long hours, detaining my hand, would she pour out before me the overflowing of a heart whose more than passionate devotion amounted to idolatry. How had I deserved to be so blessed by such confessions? – how had I deserved to be so cursed with the removal of my beloved in the hour of my making them? But upon this subject I cannot bear to dilate. Let me say only, that in Ligeia's more than womanly abandonment to a love, alas! all unmerited, all unworthily bestowed, I at length, recognized the principle of her longing, with so wildly earnest a desire, for the life which was now fleeing so rapidly away. It is this wild longing – it is this eager vehemence of desire for life – *but* for life – that I have no power to portray – no utterance capable of expressing.

At high noon of the night in which she departed, beckoning me, peremptorily, to her side, she bade me repeat certain verses composed by herself not many days before. I obeyed her. They were these: –

Lo! 'tis a gala night
Within the lonesome latter years!
An angel throng, bewinged, bedight
In veils, and drowned in tears,
Sit in a theatre, to see
A play of hopes and fears,
While the orchestra breathes fitfully
The music of the spheres.

Mimes, in the form of God on high,
Mutter and mumble low,
And hither and thither fly;
Mere puppets they, who come and go
At bidding of vast formless things
That shift the scenery to and fro,
Flapping from out their condor wings
Invisible Wo!
That motley drama! – oh, be sure
It shall not be forgot!
With its Phantom chased for evermore
By a crowd that seize it not,
Through a circle that ever returneth in
To the self-same spot;
And much of Madness, and more of Sin
And Horror, the soul of the plot!
But see, amid the mimic rout,
A crawling shape intrude!
A blood-red thing that writhes from out
The scenic solitude!
It writhes! – it writhes! – with mortal pangs
The mimes become its food,
And the seraphs sob at vermin fangs
In human gore imbued.
Out – out are the lights – out all:
And over each quivering form,
The curtain, a funeral pall,
Comes down with the rush of a storm –
And the angels, all pallid and wan,
Uprising, unveiling, affirm
That the play is the tragedy, "Man,"
And its hero, the conqueror Worm.

"O God!" half shrieked Ligeia, leaping to her feet and extending her arms aloft with a spasmodic movement, as I made an end of these lines – "O God! O Divine Father! – shall these things be undeviatingly so? – shall this conqueror be not once conquered? Are we not part and parcel in Thee? Who – who knoweth the mysteries of the will with its vigor? Man doth not yield him to the angels, *nor unto death utterly*, save only through the weakness of his feeble will."

And now, as if exhausted with emotion, she suffered her white arms to fall, and returned solemnly to her bed of death. And as she breathed her last sighs, there came mingled with them a low murmur from her lips. I bent to them my ear, and distinguished, again, the concluding words of the passage in Glanvill: *"Man doth not yield him to the angels, nor unto death utterly, save only through the weakness of his feeble will."*

She died: and I, crushed into the very dust with sorrow, could no longer endure the lonely desolation of my dwelling in the dim and decaying city by the Rhine. I had no lack of what the world calls wealth. Ligeia had brought me far more, very far more, than ordinarily falls to the lot of mortals. After a few months, therefore, of weary and aimless wandering, I purchased and put in some repair, an abbey, which I shall not name, in one of the wildest and least frequented portions of fair England. The gloomy and dreary grandeur of the building, the almost savage aspect of the domain, the many melancholy and time-honored memories connected with both, had much in unison with the feelings of utter abandonment which had driven me into that remote and unsocial region of the country. Yet although the external abbey, with its verdant decay hanging about it, suffered but little alteration, I gave way, with a child-like perversity, and perchance with a faint hope of alleviating my sorrows, to a display of more than regal magnificence within. For such follies, even in childhood, I had imbibed a taste, and now they came back to me as if in the dotage of grief. Alas, I feel how much even of incipient madness might have been discovered in the gorgeous and fantastic draperies, in the solemn carvings of Egypt, in the wild cornices and furniture, in the Bedlam patterns of the carpets of tufted gold! I had become a bounden slave in the trammels of opium, and my labors and my orders had taken a coloring from my dreams. But these absurdities I must not pause to detail. Let me speak only of that one chamber, ever accursed, whither, in a moment of mental alienation, I led from the altar as my bride – as the successor of the unforgotten Ligeia – the fair-haired and blue-eyed Lady Rowena Trevanion, of Tremaine.

There is no individual portion of the architecture and decoration of that bridal chamber which is not visibly before me. Where were the souls of the haughty family of the bride, when, through thirst of gold, they permitted to pass the threshold of an apartment *so* bedecked, a maiden and a daughter so beloved? I have said, that I minutely remember the details of the chamber – yet I am sadly forgetful on topics of deep moment; and here there was no system, no keeping, in the fantastic display to take hold upon the memory. The room lay in a high turret of the castellated abbey, was pentagonal in shape, and of capacious size. Occupying the whole southern face of the pentagonal was the sole window – an immense sheet of unbroken glass from Venice – a single pane, and tinted of a leaden hue, so that the rays of either the sun or moon passing through it, fell with a ghastly luster on the objects within. Over the upper portion of this huge window extended the trellis-work of an aged vine, which clambered up the massy walls of the turret. The ceiling, of gloomy-looking oak, was excessively lofty, vaulted, and elaborately fretted with the wildest and most grotesque specimens of a semi-Gothic, semi-Druidical device. From out the most central recess of this melancholy vaulting, depended, by a single chain of gold with long links, a huge censer of the same metal, Saracenic in pattern, and with many perforations so contrived that there writhed in and out of them, as if endued with a serpent vitality, a continual succession of parti-colored fires.

Some few ottomans and golden candelabra, of Eastern figure, were in various stations about; and there was the couch, too – the bridal couch – of an Indian model, and low, and sculptured of solid ebony, with a pall-like canopy above. In each of the angles of the chamber stood on end a gigantic sarcophagus of black granite, from the tombs of the kings over against Luxor, with their aged lids full of immemorial sculpture. But in the draping of the apartment lay, alas! the chief phantasy of all. The lofty walls, gigantic in height – even unproportionably so – were hung from summit to foot, in vast folds, with a heavy and massive-looking tapestry – tapestry of a material which was found alike as a carpet on the floor, as a covering for the ottomans and the ebony bed, as a canopy for the bed, and as the gorgeous volutes of the curtains which partially shaded the window. The material was the richest cloth of gold. It was spotted all over, at irregular intervals, with arabesque figures, about a foot in diameter, and wrought upon the cloth in patterns of the most jetty black. But these figures partook of the true character of the arabesque only when regarded from a single point of view. By a contrivance now common, and indeed traceable to a very remote period of antiquity, they were made changeable in aspect. To one entering the room, they bore the appearance of simple monstrosities; but upon a farther advance, this appearance gradually departed; and, step by step, as the visitor moved his station in the chamber, he saw himself surrounded by an endless succession of the ghastly forms which belong to the superstition of the Norman, or arise in the guilty slumbers of the monk. The phantasmagoric effect was vastly heightened by the artificial introduction of a strong continual current of wind behind the draperies – giving a hideous and uneasy animation to the whole.

In halls such as these – in a bridal chamber such as this – I passed, with the Lady of Tremaine, the unhallowed hours of the first month of our marriage – passed them with but little disquietude. That my wife dreaded the fierce moodiness of my temper – that she shunned me, and loved me but little – I could not help perceiving; but it gave me rather pleasure than otherwise. I loathed her with a hatred belonging more to demon than to man. My memory flew back (oh, with what intensity of regret!) to Ligeia, the beloved, the august, the beautiful, the entombed. I reveled in recollections of her purity, of her wisdom, of her lofty – her ethereal nature, of her passionate, her idolatrous love. Now, then, did my spirit fully and freely burn with more than all the fires of her own. In the excitement of my opium dreams (for I was habitually fettered in the shackles of the drug), I would call aloud upon her name, during the silence of the night, or among the sheltered recesses of the glens by day, as if, through the wild eagerness, the solemn passion, the consuming ardor of my longing for the departed, I could restore her to the pathways she had abandoned – ah, *could* it be forever? – upon the earth.

About the commencement of the second month of the marriage, the Lady Rowena was attacked with sudden illness, from which her recovery was slow. The fever which consumed her rendered her nights uneasy; and in her perturbed state of half-slumber, she spoke of sounds, and of motions, in and about the chamber of the turret, which I concluded had no origin save in the distemper of her fancy, or perhaps in the phantasmagoric influences of the chamber itself. She became at length convalescent – finally, well. Yet but a second more violent disorder again threw her upon a bed of suffering; and from this attack her frame, at all times feeble, never altogether recovered. Her illnesses were, after this epoch, of alarming character, and of more alarming recurrence, defying alike the knowledge and the great exertions of her physicians. With the increase of the chronic disease, which had thus, apparently, taken too sure hold upon her constitution to be eradicated by human means, I could not fail to observe a similar increase in the nervous irritation of her temperament, and in her excitability by trivial causes of fear. She spoke again, and now more frequently and pertinaciously, of the sounds – of the slight sounds – and of the unusual motions among the tapestries, to which she had formerly alluded.

One night, near the closing in of September, she pressed this distressing subject with more than usual emphasis upon my attention. She had just awakened from an unquiet slumber, and I had been watching, with feelings half of anxiety, half of vague terror, the workings of her emaciated countenance. I sat by the side of her ebony bed, upon one of the ottomans of India. She partly arose, and spoke, in an earnest low whisper, of sounds which she *then* heard, but which I could not hear – of motions which she *then* saw, but which I could not perceive. The wind was rushing hurriedly behind the tapestries, and I wished to show her (what, let me confess it, I could not *all* believe) that those almost inarticulate breathings, and those very gentle variations of the figures upon the wall, were but the natural effects of that customary rushing of the wind. But a deadly pallor, overspreading her face, had proved to me that my exertions to reassure her would be fruitless. She appeared to be fainting, and no attendants were within call. I remembered where was deposited a decanter of light wine which had been ordered by her physicians, and hastened across the chamber to procure it. But, as I stepped beneath the light of the censer, two circumstances of a startling nature attracted my attention. I had felt that some palpable although invisible object had passed lightly by my person; and I saw that there lay upon the golden carpet, in the very middle of the rich luster thrown from the censer, a shadow – a faint, indefinite shadow of angelic aspect – such as might be fancied for the shadow of a shade. But I was wild with the excitement of an immoderate dose of opium, and heeded these things but little, nor spoke of them to Rowena. Having found the wine, I recrossed the chamber, and poured out a gobletful, which I held to the lips of the fainting lady. She had now partially recovered, however, and took the vessel herself, while I sank upon an ottoman near me, with my eyes fastened upon her person. It was then that I became distinctly aware of a gentle footfall upon the carpet, and near the couch; and in a second thereafter, as Rowena was in the act of raising the wine to her lips, I saw, or may have dreamed that I saw, fall within the goblet, as if from some invisible spring in the atmosphere of the room, three or four large drops of a brilliant and ruby colored fluid. If this I saw – not so Rowena. She swallowed the wine unhesitatingly, and I forebore to speak to her of a circumstance which must, after all, I considered, have been but the suggestion of a vivid imagination, rendered morbidly active by the terror of the lady, by the opium, and by the hour.

Yet I cannot conceal it from my own perception that, immediately subsequent to the fall of the ruby drops, a rapid change for the worse took place in the disorder of my wife; so that, on the third subsequent night, the hands of her menials prepared her for the tomb, and on the fourth, I sat alone, with her shrouded body, in that fantastic chamber which had received her as my bride. Wild visions, opium-engendered, flitted, shadow-like, before me. I gazed with unquiet eye upon the sarcophagi in the angles of the room, upon the varying figures of the drapery, and upon the writhing of the parti-colored fires in the censer overhead. My eyes then fell, as I called to mind the circumstances of a former night, to the spot beneath the glare of the censer where I had seen the faint traces of the shadow. It was there, however, no longer; and breathing with greater freedom, I turned my glances to the pallid and rigid figure upon the bed. Then rushed upon me a thousand memories of Ligeia – and then came back upon my heart, with the turbulent violence of a flood, the whole of that unutterable woe with which I had regarded *her* thus enshrouded. The night waned; and still, with a bosom full of bitter thoughts of the one only and supremely beloved, I remained gazing upon the body of Rowena.

It might have been midnight, or perhaps earlier, or later, for I had taken no note of time, when a sob, low, gentle, but very distinct, startled me from my revery. I *felt* that it came from the bed of ebony – the bed of death. I listened in an agony of superstitious terror – but there was no repetition of the sound. I strained my vision to detect any motion in the corpse – but there was not the slightest perceptible. Yet I could not have been deceived. I *had* heard the noise, however faint, and my soul was awakened within me. I resolutely and perseveringly kept my attention riveted upon the body. Many minutes elapsed before any circumstance occurred tending to throw light upon the mystery. At length it became evident that a slight, a very feeble, and barely noticeable tinge of color had flushed up within the cheeks, and along the sunken small veins of the eyelids. Through a species of unutterable horror and awe, for which the language of mortality has no sufficiently energetic expression, I felt my heart cease to beat, my limbs grow rigid where I sat. Yet a sense of duty finally operated to restore my self-possession. I could no longer doubt that we had been precipitate in our preparations – that Rowena still lived. It was necessary that some immediate exertion be made; yet the turret was altogether apart from the portion of the abbey tenanted by the servants – there were none within call – I had no means of summoning them to my aid without leaving the room for many minutes – and this I could not venture to do. I therefore struggled alone in my endeavors to call back the spirit still hovering. In a short period it was certain, however, that a relapse had taken place; the color disappeared from both eyelid and cheek, leaving a wanness even more than that of marble; the lips became doubly shriveled and pinched up in the ghastly expression of death; a repulsive clamminess and coldness overspread rapidly the surface of the body; and all the usual rigorous stiffness immediately supervened. I fell back with a shudder upon the couch from which I had been so startlingly aroused, and again gave myself up to passionate waking visions of Ligeia.

An hour thus elapsed, when (could it be possible?) I was a second time aware of some vague sound issuing from the region of the bed. I listened – in extremity of horror. The sound came again – it was a sigh. Rushing to the corpse, I saw – distinctly saw – a tremor upon the lips. In a minute afterward they relaxed, disclosing a bright line of the pearly teeth. Amazement now struggled in my bosom with the profound awe which had hitherto reigned there alone. I felt that my vision grew dim, that my reason wandered; and it was only by a violent effort that I at length succeeded in nerving myself to the task which duty thus once more had pointed out. There was now a partial glow upon the forehead and upon the cheek and throat; a perceptible warmth pervaded the whole frame; there was even a slight pulsation at the heart. The lady *lived*; and with redoubled ardor I betook myself to the task of restoration. I chafed and bathed the temples and the hands and used every exertion which experience, and no little medical reading, could suggest. But in vain. Suddenly, the color fled, the pulsation ceased, the lips resumed the expression of the dead, and, in an instant afterward, the whole body took upon itself the icy chilliness, the livid hue, the intense rigidity, the sunken outline, and all the loathsome peculiarities of that which has been, for many days, a tenant of the tomb.

And again I sunk into visions of Ligeia – and again (what marvel that I shudder while I write?), *again* there reached my ears a low sob from the region of the ebony bed. But why shall I minutely detail the unspeakable horrors of that night? Why shall I pause to relate how, time after time, until near the period of the gray dawn, this hideous drama of revivification was repeated; how each terrific relapse was only into a sterner and apparently more irredeemable death; how each agony wore the aspect of a struggle with some invisible foe; and how each struggle was succeeded by I know not what of wild change in the personal appearance of the corpse? Let me hurry to a conclusion.

The greater part of the fearful night had worn away, and she who had been dead once again stirred – and now more vigorously than hitherto, although arousing from a dissolution more appalling in its utter hopelessness than any. I had long ceased to struggle or to move, and remained sitting rigidly upon the ottoman, a helpless prey to a whirl of violent emotions, of which extreme awe was perhaps the least terrible, the least consuming. The corpse, I repeat, stirred, and now more vigorously than before.

The hues of life flushed up with unwonted energy into the countenance – the limbs relaxed – and, save that the eyelids were yet pressed heavily together, and that the bandages and draperies of the grave still imparted their charnel character to the figure, I might have dreamed that Rowena had indeed shaken off, utterly, the fetters of Death. But if this idea was not, even then, altogether adopted, I could at least doubt no longer, when, arising from the bed, tottering, with feeble steps, with closed eyes, and with the manner of one bewildered in a dream, the thing that was enshrouded advanced boldly and palpably into the middle of the apartment.

I trembled not – I stirred not – for a crowd of unutterable fancies connected with the air, the stature, the demeanor, of the figure, rushing hurriedly through my brain, had paralyzed – had chilled me into stone. I stirred not – but gazed upon the apparition. There was a mad disorder in my thoughts – a tumult unappeasable. Could it, indeed, be the *living* Rowena who confronted me? Could it, indeed, be Rowena *at all* – the fair-haired, the blue-eyed Lady Rowena Trevanion of Tremaine? Why, *why* should I doubt it? The bandage lay heavily about the mouth – but then might it not be the mouth of the breathing Lady of Tremaine? And the cheeks – there were the roses as in her noon of life – yes, these might indeed be the fair cheeks of the living Lady of Tremaine. And the chin, with its dimples, as in health, might it not be hers? – but *had she then grown taller since her malady?* What inexpressible madness seized me with that thought? One bound, and I had reached her feet! Shrinking from my touch, she let fall from her head, unloosened, the ghastly cerements which had confined it, and there streamed forth into the rushing atmosphere of the chamber huge masses of long and disheveled hair; *it was blacker than the raven wings of midnight*. And now slowly opened *the eyes* of the figure which stood before me. "Here then, at least," I shrieked aloud, "can I never – can I never be mistaken – these are the full, and the black, and the wild eyes – of my lost love – of the Lady – of the *Lady Ligeia*."

The Black Cat

by Edgar Allan Poe

FOR THE MOST WILD, yet most homely narrative which I am about to pen, I neither expect nor solicit belief. Mad indeed would I be to expect it, in a case where my very senses reject their own evidence. Yet, mad am I not – and very surely do I not dream. But tomorrow I die, and today I would unburthen my soul. My immediate purpose is to place before the world, plainly, succinctly, and without comment, a series of mere household events. In their consequences, these events have terrified – have tortured – have destroyed me. Yet I will not attempt to expound them. To me, they have presented little but Horror – to many they will seem less terrible than *baroques*. Hereafter, perhaps, some intellect may be found which will reduce my phantasm to the common-place – some intellect more calm, more logical, and far less excitable than my own, which will perceive, in the circumstances I detail with awe, nothing more than an ordinary succession of very natural causes and effects.

From my infancy I was noted for the docility and humanity of my disposition. My tenderness of heart was even so conspicuous as to make me the jest of my companions. I was especially fond of animals, and was indulged by my parents with a great variety of pets. With these I spent most of my time, and never was so happy as when feeding and caressing them. This peculiarity of character grew with my growth, and, in my manhood, I derived from it one of my principal sources of pleasure. To those who have cherished an affection for a faithful and sagacious dog, I need hardly be at the trouble of explaining the nature or the intensity of the gratification thus derivable. There is something in the unselfish and self-sacrificing love of a brute, which goes directly to the heart of him who has had frequent occasion to test the paltry friendship and gossamer fidelity of mere *Man*.

I married early, and was happy to find in my wife a disposition not uncongenial with my own. Observing my partiality for domestic pets, she lost no opportunity of procuring those of the most agreeable kind. We had birds, goldfish, a fine dog, rabbits, a small monkey and *a cat*.

This latter was a remarkably large and beautiful animal, entirely black, and sagacious to an astonishing degree. In speaking of her intelligence, my wife, who at heart was not a little tinctured with superstition, made frequent allusion to the ancient popular notion, which regarded all black cats as witches in disguise. Not that she was ever *serious* upon this point – and I mention the matter at all for no better reason than that it happens, just now, to be remembered.

Pluto – this was the cat's name – was my favorite pet and playmate. I alone fed him, and he attended me wherever I went about the house. It was even with difficulty that I could prevent him from following me through the streets.

Our friendship lasted, in this manner, for several years, during which my general temperament and character – through the instrumentality of the Fiend Intemperance had – (I blush to confess it) experienced a radical alteration for the worse. I grew, day by day, more moody, more irritable, more regardless of the feelings of others. I suffered myself to use intemperate language to my wife. At length, I even offered her personal violence. My pets, of course, were made to feel the change in my disposition. I not only neglected, but ill-used them. For Pluto, however, I still retained sufficient regard to restrain me from maltreating him, as I made no scruple of maltreating the rabbits, the monkey, or even the dog, when by accident, or through affection, they came in my way. But my disease grew upon me – for what disease is like Alcohol! – and at length even Pluto, who was now becoming old, and consequently somewhat peevish – even Pluto began to experience the effects of my ill temper.

One night, returning home, much intoxicated, from one of my haunts about town, I fancied that the cat avoided my presence. I seized him; when, in his fright at my violence, he inflicted a slight wound upon my hand with his teeth. The fury of a demon instantly possessed me. I knew myself no longer. My original soul seemed, at once, to take its flight from my body; and a more than fiendish malevolence, gin-nurtured, thrilled every fiber of my frame. I took from my waistcoat-pocket a pen-knife, opened it, grasped the poor beast by the throat, and deliberately cut one of its eyes from the socket! I blush, I burn, I shudder, while I pen the damnable atrocity.

When reason returned with the morning – when I had slept off the fumes of the night's debauch – I experienced a sentiment half of horror, half of remorse, for the crime of which I had been guilty; but it was, at best, a feeble and equivocal feeling, and the soul remained untouched. I again plunged into excess, and soon drowned in wine all memory of the deed.

In the meantime the cat slowly recovered. The socket of the lost eye presented, it is true, a frightful appearance, but he no longer appeared to suffer any pain. He went about the house as usual, but, as might be expected, fled in extreme terror at my approach. I had so much of my old heart left, as to be, at first, grieved by this evident dislike on the part of a creature which had once so loved me. But this feeling soon gave place to irritation. And then came, as if to my final and irrevocable overthrow, the spirit of *perverseness*. Of this spirit philosophy takes no account. Phrenology finds no place for it among its organs. Yet I am not more sure that my soul lives, than I am that perverseness is one of the primitive impulses of the human heart – one of the indivisible primary faculties, or sentiments, which give direction to the character of Man. Who has not, a hundred times, found himself committing a vile or a silly action, for no other reason than because he knows he should *not*? Have we not a perpetual inclination, in the teeth of our best judgment, to violate that which is *Law*, merely because we understand it to be such? This spirit of perverseness, I say, came to my final overthrow. It was this unfathomable longing of the soul *to vex itself* – to offer violence to its own nature – to do wrong for the wrong's sake only – that urged me to continue and finally to consummate the injury I had inflicted upon the unoffending brute. One morning, in cool blood, I slipped a noose about its neck and hung it to the limb of a tree; – hung it with the tears streaming from my eyes, and with the bitterest remorse at my heart; – hung it *because* I knew that it had loved me, and *because* I felt it had given me no reason of offence; – hung it *because* I knew that in so doing I was committing a sin – a deadly sin that would so jeopardize my immortal soul as to place it – if such a thing were possible – even beyond the reach of the infinite mercy of the Most Merciful and Most Terrible God.

On the night of the day on which this cruel deed was done, I was aroused from sleep by the cry of fire. The curtains of my bed were in flames. The whole house was blazing. It was with great difficulty that my wife, a servant, and myself, made our escape from the conflagration. The destruction was complete. My entire worldly wealth was swallowed up, and I resigned myself thenceforward to despair.

I am above the weakness of seeking to establish a sequence of cause and effect, between the disaster and the atrocity. But I am detailing a chain of facts – and wish not to leave even a possible link imperfect. On the day succeeding the fire, I visited the ruins. The walls, with one exception, had fallen in. This exception was found in a compartment wall, not very thick, which stood about the middle of the house, and against which had rested the head of my bed. The plastering had here, in great measure, resisted the action of the fire – a fact which I attributed to its having been recently spread. About this wall a dense crowd were collected, and many persons seemed to be examining a particular portion of it with very minute and eager attention. The words "strange!" "singular!" and other similar expressions, excited my curiosity. I approached and saw, as if graven in *bas relief* upon the white surface, the figure of a gigantic *cat*. The impression was given with an accuracy truly marvelous. There had been a rope about the animal's neck.

When I first beheld this apparition – for I could scarcely regard it as less – my wonder and my terror were extreme. But at length reflection came to my aid. The cat, I remembered, had been hung in a garden adjacent to the house. Upon the alarm of fire, this garden had been immediately filled by the crowd – by some one of whom the animal must have been cut from the tree and thrown, through an open window, into my chamber. This had probably been done with the view of arousing me from sleep. The falling of other walls had compressed the victim of my cruelty into the substance of the freshly-spread plaster; the lime of which, with the flames, and the *ammonia* from the carcass, had then accomplished the portraiture as I saw it.

Although I thus readily accounted to my reason, if not altogether to my conscience, for the startling fact just detailed, it did not the less fail to make a deep impression upon my fancy. For months I could not rid myself of the phantasm of the cat; and, during this period, there came back into my spirit a half-sentiment that seemed, but was not, remorse. I went so far as to regret the loss of the animal, and to look about me, among the vile haunts which I now habitually frequented, for another pet of the same species, and of somewhat similar appearance, with which to supply its place.

One night as I sat, half stupefied, in a den of more than infamy, my attention was suddenly drawn to some black object, reposing upon the head of one of the immense hogsheads of Gin, or of Rum, which constituted the chief furniture of the apartment. I had been looking steadily at the top of this hogshead for some minutes, and what now caused me surprise was the fact that I had not sooner perceived the object thereupon. I approached it, and touched it with my hand. It was a black cat – a very large one – fully as large as Pluto, and closely resembling him in every respect but one. Pluto had not a white hair upon any portion of his body; but this cat had a large, although indefinite splotch of white, covering nearly the whole region of the breast.

Upon my touching him, he immediately arose, purred loudly, rubbed against my hand, and appeared delighted with my notice. This, then, was the very creature of which I was in search. I at once offered to purchase it of the landlord; but this person made no claim to it – knew nothing of it – had never seen it before.

I continued my caresses, and, when I prepared to go home, the animal evinced a disposition to accompany me. I permitted it to do so; occasionally stooping and patting it as I proceeded. When it reached the house it domesticated itself at once, and became immediately a great favorite with my wife.

For my own part, I soon found a dislike to it arising within me. This was just the reverse of what I had anticipated; but – I know not how or why it was – its evident fondness for myself rather disgusted and annoyed. By slow degrees, these feelings of disgust and annoyance rose into the bitterness of hatred. I avoided the creature; a certain sense of shame, and the remembrance of my former deed of cruelty, preventing me from physically abusing it. I did not, for some weeks, strike, or otherwise violently ill use it; but gradually – very gradually – I came to look upon it with unutterable loathing, and to flee silently from its odious presence, as from the breath of a pestilence.

What added, no doubt, to my hatred of the beast, was the discovery, on the morning after I brought it home, that, like Pluto, it also had been deprived of one of its eyes. This circumstance, however, only endeared it to my wife, who, as I have already said, possessed, in a high degree, that humanity of feeling which had once been my distinguishing trait, and the source of many of my simplest and purest pleasures.

With my aversion to this cat, however, its partiality for myself seemed to increase. It followed my footsteps with a pertinacity which it would be difficult to make the reader comprehend. Whenever I sat, it would crouch beneath my chair, or spring upon my knees, covering me with its loathsome caresses. If I arose to walk, it would get between my feet and thus nearly throw me down, or, fastening its long and sharp claws in my dress, clamber, in this manner, to my breast. At such times, although I longed to destroy it with a blow, I was yet withheld from so doing, partly by a memory of my former crime, but chiefly – let me confess it at once – by absolute *dread* of the beast.

This dread was not exactly a dread of physical evil – and yet I should be at a loss how otherwise to define it. I am almost ashamed to own – yes, even in this felon's cell, I am almost ashamed to own – that the terror and horror with which the animal inspired me, had been heightened by one of the merest chimæras it would be possible to conceive. My wife had called my attention, more than once, to the character of the mark of white hair, of which I have spoken, and which constituted the sole visible difference between the strange beast and the one I had destroyed. The reader will remember that this mark, although large, had been originally very indefinite; but, by slow degrees – degrees nearly imperceptible, and which for a long time my Reason struggled to reject as fanciful – it had, at length, assumed a rigorous distinctness of outline. It was now the representation of an object that I shudder to name – and for this, above all, I loathed, and dreaded, and would have rid myself of the monster *had I dared* – it was now, I say, the image of a hideous – of a ghastly thing – of the *gallows*! – oh, mournful and terrible engine of Horror and of Crime – of Agony and of Death!

And now was I indeed wretched beyond the wretchedness of mere Humanity. And a *brute beast* – whose fellow I had contemptuously destroyed – a *brute beast* to work out for *me* – for me a man, fashioned in the image of the High God – so much of insufferable wo! Alas! neither by day nor by night knew I the blessing of Rest any more! During the former the creature left me no moment alone; and, in the latter, I started, hourly, from dreams of unutterable fear, to find the hot breath of the *thing* upon my face, and its vast weight – an incarnate Night-Mare that I had no power to shake off – incumbent eternally upon my *heart*!

Beneath the pressure of torments such as these, the feeble remnant of the good within me succumbed. Evil thoughts became my sole intimates – the darkest and most evil of thoughts.

The moodiness of my usual temper increased to hatred of all things and of all mankind; while, from the sudden, frequent, and ungovernable outbursts of a fury to which I now blindly abandoned myself, my uncomplaining wife, alas! was the most usual and the most patient of sufferers.

One day she accompanied me, upon some household errand, into the cellar of the old building which our poverty compelled us to inhabit. The cat followed me down the steep stairs, and, nearly throwing me headlong, exasperated me to madness. Uplifting an axe, and forgetting, in my wrath, the childish dread which had hitherto stayed my hand, I aimed a blow at the animal which, of course, would have proved instantly fatal had it descended as I wished. But this blow was arrested by the hand of my wife. Goaded, by the interference, into a rage more than demoniacal, I withdrew my arm from her grasp and buried the axe in her brain. She fell dead upon the spot, without a groan.

This hideous murder accomplished, I set myself forthwith, and with entire deliberation, to the task of concealing the body. I knew that I could not remove it from the house, either by day or by night, without the risk of being observed by the neighbors. Many projects entered my mind. At one period I thought of cutting the corpse into minute fragments, and destroying them by fire. At another, I resolved to dig a grave for it in the floor of the cellar. Again, I deliberated about casting it in the well in the yard – about packing it in a box, as if merchandize, with the usual arrangements, and so getting a porter to take it from the house. Finally, I hit upon what I considered a far better expedient than either of these. I determined to wall it up in the cellar – as the monks of the middle ages are recorded to have walled up their victims.

For a purpose such as this the cellar was admirably adapted. Its walls were loosely constructed, and had lately been plastered throughout with a rough plaster, which the dampness of the atmosphere had prevented from hardening. Moreover, in one of the walls was a projection, caused by a false chimney, or fire-place, that had been filled, or walled up, and made to resemble the rest of the cellar. I made no doubt that I could readily displace the bricks at this point, insert the corpse, and wall the whole up as before, so that no eye could detect anything suspicious.

And in this calculation I was not deceived. By means of a crowbar I easily dislodged the bricks, and, having carefully deposited the body against the inner wall, I propped it in that position, while, with little trouble, I re-laid the whole structure as it originally stood. Having procured mortar, sand, and hair, with every possible precaution, I prepared a plaster which could not be distinguished from the old, and with this I very carefully went over the new brick-work. When I had finished, I felt satisfied that all was right. The wall did not present the slightest appearance of having been disturbed. The rubbish on the floor was picked up with the minutest care. I looked around triumphantly, and said to myself – "Here at least, then, my labor has not been in vain."

My next step was to look for the beast which had been the cause of so much wretchedness; for I had, at length, firmly resolved to put it to death. Had I been able to meet with it, at the moment, there could have been no doubt of its fate; but it appeared that the crafty animal had been alarmed at the violence of my previous anger, and forebore to present itself in my present mood. It is impossible to describe, or to imagine, the deep, the blissful sense of relief which the absence of the detested creature occasioned in my bosom. It did not make its appearance during the night – and thus for one night at least, since its introduction into the house, I soundly and tranquilly slept; aye, *slept* even with the burden of murder upon my soul!

The second and the third day passed and still my tormentor came not. Once again I breathed as a freeman. The monster, in terror, had fled the premises forever! I should behold it no more! My happiness was supreme! The guilt of my dark deed disturbed me but little. Some few inquiries had been made, but these had been readily answered. Even a search had been instituted – but of course nothing was to be discovered. I looked upon my future felicity as secured.

Upon the fourth day of the assassination, a party of the police came, very unexpectedly, into the house, and proceeded again to make rigorous investigation of the premises. Secure, however, in the inscrutability of my place of concealment, I felt no embarrassment whatever. The officers bade me accompany them in their search. They left no nook or corner unexplored. At length, for the third or fourth time, they descended into the cellar. I quivered not in a muscle. My heart beat calmly as that of one who slumbers in innocence. I walked the cellar from end to end. I folded my arms upon my bosom and roamed easily to and fro. The police were thoroughly satisfied and prepared to depart. The glee at my heart was too strong to be restrained. I burned to say if but one word, by way of triumph, and to render doubly sure their assurance of my guiltlessness.

"Gentlemen," I said at last, as the party ascended the steps, "I delight to have allayed your suspicions. I wish you all health, and a little more courtesy. By the bye, gentlemen, this – this is a very well-constructed house." [In the rabid desire to say something easily, I scarcely knew what I uttered at all.] – "I may say an *excellently* well-constructed house. These walls – are you going, gentlemen? – these walls are solidly put together;" and here, through the mere phrenzy of bravado, I rapped heavily, with a cane which I held in my hand, upon that very portion of the brick-work behind which stood the ghastly corpse of the wife of my bosom.

But may God shield and deliver me from the fangs of the Arch-Fiend! No sooner had the reverberation of my blows sunk into silence, than I was answered by a voice from within the tomb! – by a cry, at first muffled and broken, like the sobbing of a child, and then quickly swelling into one long, loud, and continuous scream, utterly anomalous and inhuman – a howl – a wailing shriek, half of horror and half of triumph, such as might have arisen only out of hell, conjointly from the throats of the dammed in their agony and of the demons that exult in the damnation!

Of my own thoughts it is folly to speak. Swooning, I staggered to the opposite wall. For one instant the party upon the stairs remained motionless, through extremity of terror and of awe. In the next, a dozen stout arms were toiling at the wall. It fell bodily. The corpse, already greatly decayed and clotted with gore, stood erect before the eyes of the spectators. Upon its head, with red extended mouth and solitary eye of fire, sat the hideous beast whose craft had seduced me into murder, and whose informing voice had consigned me to the hangman. I had walled the monster up within the tomb!

Songs for the Lost

by Brian Rappatta

THE OLD BASTARD couldn't even die quickly, so it was a relief when the angel of death appeared at the threshold.

The creature hovered silently in the doorframe, head bowed, entreating entrance, its little wings fluttering like those of a dragonfly, keeping it at her eye level.

Tirsa's breath caught in her throat at its beauty. This one had a full head of golden, curly hair, and its skin shone with that otherworldly radiance for which they were fabled. Tirsa had to forcibly remind herself not to try to reach out and touch it, to attempt to cup it in her hand like a firefly.

When Tirsa did not speak the ritual words of welcome, the angel looked up. A slight frown of puzzlement crossed its luminescent face. It looked straight at her, its eyes a liquid violet. Tirsa gasped; the violet-eyed angels were rumored to have the most enchanting voices of all.

So beautiful. And for such an ugly man.

Tirsa looked behind her, where deeper inside the hut, behind the hide blanket, her mother sat vigil with her father. She considered for a moment, then turned back to the angel. "Get out of here," she whispered.

The creature's frown deepened, as if it hadn't heard correctly. It cocked its head to the side just a fraction, and its wings beat a little faster, causing it to bob unsteadily in the air.

"You heard me," Tirsa whispered again. "Go on. Get out of here."

The angel's golden eyebrows rose slightly, and its violet eyes widened. Its head shook slowly as if to say *I don't understand*.

"You're not wanted here," Tirsa said, just low enough for her mother not to hear. She took a step nearer the angel of death, hefting the large metal pot she'd been washing.

The angel backed out of the threshold in alarm, but stopped short only a pace or so outside the door. Its mouth opened, but no sound emerged. Of course it had no voice. Not yet.

"You heard me," Tirsa hissed, brandishing the pot once again. "I said go."

The angel hovered another moment, its confusion now plain. Tirsa charged forward and took a swing with the pot. The angel dodged it easily, flitting several paces beyond her reach. It paused only a moment to gape at her in horror, then flew away, leaving Tirsa standing at the stoop, her chest heaving.

When she was sure it was gone, Tirsa lowered her pot. And from within, behind the blanket, came her mother's cry of anguish and loss.

Father had passed.

* * *

The village held a small ceremony for Father, but it was without joy. Without an angel to sing his passing, it was a somber affair, full of tears and snuffles and downcast looks, unlike any passing in any of the villagers' memories. The villagers talked among themselves, wondering what it could mean that the Lord of the Dead had sent no angel to sing her father's passing. There was much talk, and much speculation – had the Lord of the Dead abandoned them? Would there be no more angels to sing their passings? The villagers were uneasy, and Wana, the priest, was hard-pressed to maintain their faith. But when an angel appeared to sing goodwife Bertin's passing only a few weeks later, everyone was much relieved.

Over the remaining winter months, the gossip turned to other topics – always just outside of Tirsa's hearing. Every time she walked by a cluster of goodwives at their washing or braiding, they would fall silent, and abruptly change their topic. They were too courteous to talk about her bulging stomach in front of her, but she was no fool. She knew they were wondering who the father was. And as the winter wore on and turned to spring and none of the boys of the village, who'd used to flatter her with their appreciative eyes, claimed to be the father, the gossip grew worse. Perhaps out of respect for Tirsa, Cüna, Lott's wife, started the rumor that the baby belonged to the son of a neighboring tribe. Tirsa knew none of the wives believed this, but it was far better than the truth, so she did what she could to encourage it, making sure to cast near-improper gazes at the other clans' sons when they came around to barter.

Tirsa and her mother withdrew into their hut, and spent most of the days there, leaving only when absolutely necessary. Some of the clansmen took pity on them and gave them meat when they could spare it, which was rarely; it was a rough year for everyone.

Toward the end of the spring, the same hacking cough that had taken Father settled into Tirsa's mother. Tirsa had expected it. Mother had always been frail, and since Father's passing had taken poorer care of herself, had eaten less and less every day. When the cold rains came and Mother's hacking cough grew into a fever, all Tirsa could do was wait.

There had been three passings in the village since Father's, all of them beautifully sung by angels, just as always. But when Mother's eyes closed forever and her bowels loosened for the last time, there was no angel of death to sing her passing.

The Lord of the Dead had a long memory. He must surely remember the rude greeting one of his servants had found at the threshold to the hut that Tirsa now lived in alone.

* * *

Her baby was small at his birth, and yellow. She nursed him faithfully, however, and when he made it past his first month of life she named him Sildur. It was a new name, one none of her fathers or father's fathers had had, and as such caused another round of gossip among the villagers.

As spring warmed into full summer and Sildur put on weight, Tirsa knew the villagers spoke of her almost nightly. She gathered the thrust of most of their conversations from snatches of dialogue overheard just before the other wives realized she was there: they begrudged her her hut. So much space for only herself and her baby; she, who had no more living family members, should be asked to move into one of the other huts. There were other families who were crowded.

But no one made any move to challenge her ownership of it. It was, after all, the hut where the angels had failed to arrive – twice now. No one wanted to incur that curse.

So she was all alone, rocking Sildur in her arms, when the angel appeared again on the threshold. At first she was alarmed – had the angel come for her child? But no, Sildur was perfectly healthy, and sleeping contentedly in her arms. But then she realized that it had been one year since her father's passing. The angel had come, just as they always did, to remind the living of the dead's passing.

Only this one had nothing to sing. It flitted on the threshold and peered nervously inside the hut, perhaps wary of a cookpot.

"It's all right," Tirsa called to it. "I won't hurt you anymore."

It considered her warily.

"You can come in. It's all right. My hands are full, at any rate."

It fluttered into the room and hovered, considering her. It looked haggard, unlike any angel she'd ever seen. Its deep violet eyes had lost their luster and were now little more than a faded lilac. Its vibrant complexion was now sallow, and its tightly curled golden hair now hung loose on its head. Even its wings seemed heavier, like a weight on its back. It hovered in the air with great effort.

"I'm surprised you came back," Tirsa told it. "I wouldn't be in such a hurry to see me again." She chuckled ruefully.

It drew nearer, and its eyes fixed on hers. It looked so much like a child, with eyes begging for understanding. Tirsa sighed. "Well, I suppose I do owe you an explanation."

The angel waited patiently.

The words were harder than she thought. She never thought she'd face such accusation from one of these benevolent creatures. "I – I was angry. I didn't… I couldn't bear listening to a song of passing for such an awful man." She paused. The angel continued staring at her patiently. "It just didn't seem right."

In response, the angel merely blinked.

"I suppose I got what I deserved. There was no one to sing my mother's passing. I suppose she'll go forgotten."

Another blink.

"And I… I suppose when it's my time… there will be no one to sing my passing?"

It blinked twice.

* * *

The summer came and went again, along with the anniversary of her mother's passing. Winter came again, too, seemingly harsher than the last. Tirsa caught the fever and lay abed for several days. Cüna, one of the few villagers who would dare to enter Tirsa's cursed hut, tended to her, bringing her broths and blankets to ward off the chill. And the good woman stayed by Tirsa's side and listened to her ravings about the angel of death who had no song to sing, who came anyway. The woman surely thought they were the ravings of a madwoman, but she listened nevertheless.

After nearly a week, the fever left her. She began to sit up, and then stand up, and then she was back at her work, weaving baskets for the other villagers. She took Sildur in her arms and dutifully attended the singings for all the departed villagers, where everybody in the village pretended not to notice that her tears were far too bitter to be tears of joy produced by the sweet strains of the angels' voices.

The season progressed, and she tried hard to keep her hut warm and her fingers useful. Until the fever settled into Sildur.

He made it three days of fussy, rattling breathing before his tiny chest stuttered mid-breath and rose no more.

The villagers buried him at the edge of town, along with all the rest. Tirsa weathered their half-hearted condolences and offers of support.

And of course, no angel came.

* * *

Tirsa stopped attending even the annual singings for the other members of the village. She could not bear to witness their joy at hearing the haunting melodies of their loved ones again, especially could not bear to see the vibrant faces of the angels that came to sing their songs. She shut herself up in her hut and came out less and less, sometimes not even bothering to eat.

She'd lost all track of the days, so it was a surprise to see the angel appearing at her threshold again, on the second anniversary of her father's passing.

Did angels age? Surely they must, if they had no song of life to sing. This one was even more haggard than last she'd seen it. Its back was hunched over under the weight of its wings, and it flew low to the ground. Its hair had receded, like that of an old man's, and its face was wrinkled.

"Come in," she said to it, and held out her hand. It fluttered its wings, arcing up into the air, and came down to settle into the palm of her hand. It panted a little at the exertion.

Up close, she could see that its eyes were almost completely clear, like the pupils of a blind man. "You look like I feel," she said.

It nodded.

"Will you die?" she asked.

It shrugged, and spread its arms out, palms upward. *Who can tell?* it seemed to say.

She would have liked to cry for it, for its sad visage, but she had no tears left. "I'm sorry," she told it. "I didn't know this would happen."

It smiled halfheartedly, as if to say it understood.

A single tear slid down her cheek then, though in truth it was not for the creature; it was for herself, and for Sildur, and her mother. "Is there anything I can do?" she asked it.

The creature cocked its head to one side. Its expression turned… was it hopeful?

"Is there?" she asked louder, and her volume made the creature wince. "What is it? What can I do?"

The creature's expressions grew pensive. It considered for a few moments, then shook its head.

"What do you mean? What is it? Can you help me or not?"

It considered further, then gave a resigned nod. Far more tentative than she would have liked, but it was something.

"Show me," she said. "Whatever it is, I'll do it. Show me how to get the songs back."

In response it held up a tiny index finger as if to tell her to *wait*, then flew away, out of the hut and into the village beyond.

* * *

It returned carrying something in its arms. The load was almost too much for its little body to bear. It fluttered erratically over to her, and when she held out her hand, it dropped its burden into her palm.

She stared down at it – *them*, actually – for a few seconds, uncomprehending. Two twin orbs, slightly sticky to the touch –

She dropped them with a startled cry when she realized what they were. She stood and backed up a few paces until her back rattled the wall of her hut.

They were small, and the irises were blue. At first she thought they must have belonged to Sildur, but that wouldn't make sense. Sildur had passed almost two months ago; they could not belong to him. And then she remembered that Morva's toddler Renick had passed only a few days ago; she'd not gone to his passing ceremony.

The angel looked from the two eyes lying in the dirt to her face. It nodded its head and with its hand mimicked putting food in its mouth.

The meaning was clear. Black legend held that you could peer into the realm of the dead by consuming the eyeballs of the departed. Tirsa had thought that was a tale for old, bored wives. She knew of no one who had ever tried it.

And yet…

She looked once again to the angel. It repeated the gesture of putting food into its mouth, more insistently this time.

"You mean for me to go into your realm myself? For what purpose?"

The angel hopped up into her hand. There, in her palm, it fell to its knees and clasped its hands together and turned up its face, and she could see the pleading in its eyes. At first she thought it was pleading with her, but then its meaning became clear. She sighed. "Must I beg forgiveness of the Lord of the Dead himself?"

The angel nodded.

Tirsa fought down her revulsion. The angel seemed eager. And surely a creature spawned in the land of the dead, who crossed over into the other realm as part of its existence, would know the rites that must be followed for her to cross over.

"This had better work," she muttered. She bent down, retrieved the eyeballs, considered brushing the dirt off them, but then reasoned that the taste of dirt might be preferable.

She popped the first one in her mouth and swallowed it whole. And then she followed it with the second.

* * *

The next night, the angel brought her another pair. She looked into them as they rested in the palm of her hand, trying to discern whose they might be. The village was no stranger to harsh winters, and newly departed dead were easy to come by. She wondered what the rest of the villagers would think if they knew the angel was desecrating graves on her behalf.

She took them nevertheless, and on the third night the angel brought her another set. Although the thought of what she was doing made her want to vomit, she couldn't wait to swallow them. Three pairs, consumed on three consecutive nights. These were the ones that would seal the passage.

At first, she felt nothing. She looked askance at the angel. Its look was reassuring, approving, even. Was it her imagination, or was the glow returning to its eyes, just a little bit?

She held her stomach and waited. "How long?" she asked. "How long does it –"

Perception took a sickening lurch to the side. Her senses reeled out of her control. She had the vague sensation of hitting the floor, and after that, nothing.

She came awake again slowly, as if awakening from a deep sleep. She stretched and rolled over, then opened her eyes.

It was dark, but fluttering in her field of vision directly above her was the angel. Its eyes were indeed more luminous, beginning to regain their healthy violet luster. When it saw that she was awake, it smiled.

"Am I here?" she asked. "Is this…?" She struggled to sit up. In the darkness, she could vaguely make out the walls of her hut. Her heart sank. She hadn't left at all. She still beheld all the trappings of the living.

But the angel beckoned to her excitedly. It flitted over to the threshold, its anxiousness belying its apparent age, and it beckoned her to follow. She got to her feet –

– and swayed precariously. The hut's interior reeled for a moment, but she did not overbalance. It was rather that she no longer knew what balance was. She looked down at her feet. They were there, and yet she felt disconnected to them. The hut's dirt floor seemed very far away indeed.

The angel fluttered back to her side. It held out its arm to guide her. She did likewise, and it wrapped its tiny hand around her little finger. Its touch was chill, yet reassuring at the same time.

Following its lead, she crossed the floor to stand at the threshold. Walking was more like floating; like willing your essence to move, and it did.

She'd made it after all. Was this the land of the dead? Was this – this freedom from the encumbrance of limbs – what being dead felt like?

Under the angel's lead, she passed over the threshold without having to pull aside the flap. The material world was little impediment here.

Outside, she beheld her village. Only, the other huts were mere outlines of themselves, suggestions of structures, the shadows rather than the substance. What stood out in clear detail were the people, literally hundreds of them. Their bodies were resplendent, like those of the angels that fluttered in the air around them like fireflies. All of them were dancing, swaying in unison to some song that Tirsa couldn't hear.

Tirsa stared in wonder. "They're beautiful."

As one, the deadfolk sensed her presence. They turned to her, and their smiles were radiant.

Most of them Tirsa didn't recognize, but amidst the group of faces she saw Danë and Fulda, two of the recently departed members of the village. And as she looked more carefully she saw familiar features among the faces, hints of cheekbones like those of Höxte's family, and round, pudgy faces that reminded her of Hamel's children. These were the village's ancestors, and somehow she knew the names of every single one of them.

"Amazing," she breathed. She turned to look at the angel. "But why can't I hear the song?"

The angel didn't have time to answer. The dancing throng rushed forward and carried her into it. She found herself among hundreds of figures, all of them dancing in a choreographed wave around her. The tempo picked up, and so did their rhythm. She longed to dance with them, but she could not hear the melody.

So she pushed through the mass of bodies. They parted before her, taking no notice of her. She was looking for a handful of departed in particular, she reminded herself; that was her mission here.

She clung tightly to the angel's hand as she made her way through the endless mass of bodies. They seemed to go on without end, constantly parting around her until they seemed like tides crashing around her while she stood still.

At last the bodies thinned out, and before her stood those she had come to see. She recognized her mother, though a version far younger than any she had ever known. This one had long, black hair, olive skin that glowed like everyone's here. Her father, also younger, stood next to her. His hands were resting on the shoulder of a boy, maybe of thirteen summers, with sandy brown hair and bright blue eyes. She recognized him immediately, though he had never lived to be this age: Sildur.

She wanted to run to her son and wrap him in her arms and kiss him, but she still wasn't fully in command of her own motion in this place. Led by her angel, she drift-walked over to him, tears streaming down her face, and wrapped her arms around him.

She felt nothing. His shoulders to her felt like nothing more than wispy puffs of air, but he seemed to understand her sentiment. He stepped back, flashed her a bright smile, and lifted his phantom finger to wipe away one of her tears. She felt his touch as only a vague tingle on her cheek.

"He's beautiful," she said, and the angel nodded its agreement.

Her son stood back, shifting the reunion to her father. She stiffened, and swallowed instinctively. He stood with his arms outstretched, waiting for her to come to him.

She did not go. Uneasily, she shot a look at the angel. It squeezed her finger reassuringly.

Slowly, she drifted over to him. She did not open her embrace to him, but he wrapped his arms around her anyway, and with his left hand he pushed a strand of hair out of her face, just as he'd used to do, though he didn't have the physical form to move it.

And even though his touch was insubstantial, she flinched because she couldn't help it. She closed her eyes against what she knew was to come.

Nothing happened.

When she opened her eyes again, Sildur and her mother were gone. She was alone with only her father. And this time, he was older, the father she remembered, with the peppery gray beard and the lines of age on his face.

He smiled at her. "I've been waiting a long time for someone like you," he said.

She frowned. "I – I can hear you." So far she'd been unable to hear anything in this realm. "Why?"

"Because I wished to speak to you."

She considered. "You're not really my father, are you?"

He shook his head. "Of course not. But I can take any form I wish. And you seemed to have a reaction to this one."

"Take another form. Please."

"Hmm. Not yet."

"I don't want to see him again. Please."

"I don't understand. You came here to see him, did you not?"

"I came here to find my family."

"And you found it. He is a part of your family, whether you wish it or not."

"I – I made a mistake. I should go."

He conjured a throne and lounged in it with his feet draping over the side. "Surely you did not make this trip for nothing. You had something to ask of me, I believe?"

She looked uncertainly to the angel, who was still holding onto her finger. The need she saw in its eyes decided her.

She sank to her knees and lowered her head. "Forgive me, lord, please. I was wrong to turn away your servant."

"And?" he prodded.

She took this realm's equivalent of a deep breath. "And I wish to reclaim the songs of my family, if I may."

He didn't respond for some time, long moments in which she felt the weight of her physical heart hammering in her chest.

When he broke the silence, his voice was kind. "Come, child. You no longer need to kneel in front of me."

She got to her feet, and he was there before her. He reached out his hand, and she felt it this time. His touch was icy, yet exhilarating at the same time.

"I understand why you turned away my servant," he said, and plucked a strand of hair from her face. "But there are always consequences. Our two worlds need each other much more than either of us might realize."

"Please." She looked up into his eyes. "Will you restore the songs of my family?"

He smiled. "Of course. You are very brave to come here and make this request of me in person. No one from your realm has been here for dozens of your lifetimes. But I have a condition. Are you willing to meet it?"

"Name it."

For the first time he seemed unsure of himself – awkward, as if afraid she would refuse. "I want you to come back here. Once every year. To lie with me."

The full import of his words was slow to sink in. But when they did, she made sure to look him straight in the eye and say without hesitation, "I will."

* * *

That year, the angel showed up at her threshold exactly at the correct date to sing Sildur's passing. The villagers thought it strange that the same angel now had arrived three times in the same year to sing three different passings, but they were beginning to take the strangeness in stride. Which was a good thing, because she had no idea how they would react to the child that was now growing inside of her. For that matter, she had no idea herself what the child would be like, the product of an odd union, but she knew it filled her with warmth, and bearing it made her happy.

The angel was looking well. It'd been granted its voice, and the vitality that came from singing three passings a year sat well on it. Its hair was the same mass of golden curls she remembered from the first time it'd appeared, and its eyes were deep violet, and brimming with ebullience.

It nodded to her, and smiled. It was time for the public ceremony of Sildur's passing. She got to her feet and crossed her hut to where the angel fluttered. She would go to the ceremony, as she had the previous two, although she could not hear the angel's song.

In fact, she heard nothing anymore – not in this realm, at any rate – not even the loudest crashes of thunder on stormy nights. Nothing came without a price. Those who would walk in two worlds were doomed to be incomplete in both.

But it did not matter to her. She would hear the songs of her family soon enough, on that one night of the year she could spend with her lord, the Lord of the Dead.

The angel took her little finger, and together they stepped across the threshold.

An Unquiet Slumber

Rhiannon Rasmussen

GREYSON SET THE PLIERS DOWN and leaned heavily against the table to stand. Every move brought a stiff jolt of pain into his ossified joints. He had to cut and squeeze to extract blood from his desiccating body, to get even a fingertip's worth of that rust. Not good, no good at all. Only the dead don't bleed. He had lived longer than most, true, as stones do, but he had no desire to flicker out after a mayfly's lifespan. Short and worthless, like the rest of humanity.

He ran his fingers along his chin while he examined the day's work on the doll. Stubble scratched under his dull nails. He needed to wash up and shave. No good to walk around unshaven and disgusting. He might have *company*, after all. Greyson hadn't been in the washroom long before something out of the corner of his eye startled him. When he glanced back at the door, it was empty, just the dim hallway stretching out to the study. He turned back to the mirror. A silhouette stood behind him where there had been the wall's reflection; a woman, her wet hair clinging to her face. Her features were obscured by shadow, but something about the tilt of her head and the lay of her hair was wrong. There was less substance than she should have possessed, and faint glistening. She was angry with him.

He put the razor down, leaned forward, and breathed on the glass. The ghost reached past his reflection.

You slept through our anniversary, she wrote, letter by painstaking letter. They faded as he watched. The whole room chilled. Ghosts, or at least Abigail, had scent. Not as a person did, not the distasteful pungency of the byproducts of living, but as a room long abandoned to the desert, a remembrance of her self. She was too old to have the fragrance of turned earth or the deep draught of the river Thames. He never had pegged her exact date of death, but it was long before he had been born. No, Abigail was the faint breath of old ink, the fragile grain of aging paper as it crumbled under touch. His dear wife.

"Well, I believe we'll have another next year," Greyson said. "And it will be five times as grand. I doubt it matters if we miss one of one hundred ten." In the cold room, his breath frosted the glass easily.

You slept for three days. Abigail retraced her earlier words. He had. And dreamed. She'd been there. She'd danced with him.

Greyson picked the razor back up. Certainly, were their positions reversed, he would be livid with her.

"The dreams weren't enough?" The memories faded like the words she traced on the mirror. "They were so lovely that I lost track of time. I wouldn't mind wandering in those gardens forever with you, for… how did it go? 'The moon never beams without bringing me dreams…'" Abigail didn't respond. "I need to finish shaving now, my dear."

When she did not stir, he went back to shaving. The chill sharpened, made his bones ache. The cold distracted him, or his hand slipped, or something shoved him; either way, the razor sliced through his skin, and deep. He swore and threw it into the sink. It clattered shut. "Abigail!"

Her fingers pinched the wound on his cheek, drawing out his drying, silty blood. She smeared it across the mirror. The blood was too thick for her to get far.

Greyson clapped his hand over the cut. It stung. He met his own gaze in the mirror. He looked haggard and weary and half-shaven. His spectacles hid the worst of the shadows under his eyes. "It's not our wedding anniversary, is it? No, only the anniversary of when we met. Did I deserve that? All right? Darling? I know it's important to you. What are we all but creatures of habit? I'll make it up to you. What would you like me to say? 'I love you yet; you are in my soul.'" The line was a bit bastardized, perhaps, but he would recite the scene in full if she asked him to. They had both read her favorite book so many times, so often aloud. "If I could touch you, if you could come to me, then you would know."

The silhouette lifted her head and smiled. Her visage was less ghastly than he had feared; she still had both her eyes. He touched her reflection's cheek and she vanished, left him with his hand pressed to smooth, empty glass.

She was hungry again. She grew hungrier as she grew older. The hunger of a ghost that no longer had the volition to temper desire, the narrow-mindedness of a soul stripped to the emotions of her death throes. Not that it mattered. They were both desperate. Cruel to think that he might be the one trapped in a dying routine, a living fossil, slower to adapt than a ghost. How long until he couldn't clear the dust collecting on the shelves of his own home? How long until the dust would settle on his own self? Living forever had turned out to be the falsely optimistic term for dying forever. It was bearable, as long as he had her.

Greyson finished shaving, splashed his face with stale water from the basin, and threw the razor into the bin next to it. Blades wore down fast, or perhaps it was just how cheaply they were manufactured now.

"I'm going back downstairs," he said, all cheer, to the air. "To finish your gift, my dear. A few days late, but with you by my side, who would count the time?" No answer, save for the light brush of a breeze on the back of his neck. He touched the locket he wore. It was cool, but not cold.

A memento, so Abigail could accompany him always. Her wedding ring was strung on the chain, and inside, instead of a portrait, nestled a folded page from her beloved book. Her focus and sole grounding tie to the living world, to his dismay; if only he were the tie, she wouldn't speak so fondly of Heathcliff.

He closed the bathroom door and then reopened it as a door to the basement, his workshop, and stepped through. Upper floor to lower floor. Alchemy had myriad uses; in this case, a forged trinket wound in copper and embedded under his skin allowed a reroute from one room to another. Door to door, he could go anywhere he pleased. Around the world, even. But everything he cared about was in this manor. Most of the doors in the house now opened to walls and mirrors and beds of nails and other such distractions. No one besides himself and spirits could navigate the maze.

The manor's air carried the stifling must of a catacomb. Greyson flicked the light switch on and off until the lamp decided to cooperate. He took off his glasses and blinked until his vision adjusted, then replaced them and closed the door. A table and work tools took up this half of the room, his study. A large life-sized doll lay across the table, fabric stretched across its wooden frame. Abigail's body. An object to return the solidity he'd never known her to have.

He stepped over the smeared remains of two white chalk circles across the stone floor. The books stored here were shelved well away from the ground so that moisture wouldn't warp their pages.

Books held no interest for him today, save for one. *Wuthering Heights* lay across the body Abigail would inhabit; the last remnant of her past life and the artifact that would be her future. Greyson leaned forward, kissed the book along the spine, inhaled the sharp scent of the leather cover, soft as human skin, and murmured Abigail's name. She was there, the shadow of a breath on his cheek, a cool touch slipping under the collar of his shirt. Not in body, never in body, but in spirit. She never strayed far from his side. Even if he couldn't see her, she was there. She would brush her fingers down his neck, a chill too cold and sudden to be a breeze in this windowless house.

Greyson picked *Wuthering Heights* off the doll's chest and set it to the side. Pages fell out, the companions to those ripped out of their bindings, burned and scattered into the body, to tie it to Abigail. He stacked them back on the desk.

Glass eyes stared up at the ceiling's beams, clouded gray jewels in her porcelain face. He'd heard of puppets built of flesh, handstitched golems to do their master's bidding, but the thought made him queasy. No doubt Abigail would have objections as well. No disgusting secondhand materials would comprise her earthly vessel. Except the hair; human hair, of course. There was no other substitute.

He ran his hand through the hair, soft and dark and curled, and laid his head on her chest, imagined back to when they had first met, when he could still see her and, after a fashion, touch her. A gift he'd squandered on immortality. Love for life; her love, to extend his life.

Steps that, once danced, could never be undone.

No heartbeat, no breath stirred the doll's frame, nor would it ever. He nestled his hand in the crook of its jaw and murmured sweet platitudes to its still lips: all the night-tide, he'd lay down by the side of his darling, his darling, his life and his bride. The doll couldn't answer, of course. It was almost finished. Almost. All it lacked was the ghost to give it function and some way to give it a smoother semblance of life, more than the jerky, violent movements that she could manage with it now.

Greyson closed his eyes, and then said, quite aloud, "With all the smoke and mirrors I contrive to talk to you, my dear, it makes you wonder if I've simply gone mad, doesn't it? All this to touch you."

A twinge, and then a deeper pain in his neck, the locket's chain digging into his collar.

"I'm joking, darling," Greyson said, his hand on the locket to keep it from trying to burrow its way deeper into his flesh.

"Just words said in jest."

Before her presence faded he got up and began work on the doll again, tweaking the fine jeweler's wire that twined through her limbs, gold and copper to hold the energy that would animate her, silk and steel to hold the physical frame together. Magic and copper stitched together the seams, giving it movement, which was all very pretty and for naught if the wires snapped when it moved.

When he was satisfied with the doll's state, Greyson slid his arms under the doll's body and lifted it up, propped it against his chest and arranged its arms as if it were his partner in a waltz. He let the doll's head loll against his shoulder, cold porcelain lips resting on his collar. The skirts rustled against his legs as he walked it gently to the middle of the room, over the necromancer's array sketched onto the stone floor, and began to dance with it. He didn't need music to keep time; this was only practice for when they could truly dance.

The doll would be finished soon, and they could go out and satiate Abigail's hunger together, both of them, physically embodied. They would go out and feel; she would leave the house, really leave it, not just as a shade trailing the folded words in his locket. Travel wherever she pleased. Anywhere.

With or without him.

He swung the doll around, skirts twirling out. They were both reflected in the mirrors that lined the study's walls, the reflections spiraling out on to eternity. If Abigail watched, she left no shadow. Was she just waiting for him to finish, so that she could travel in physical form without his aid?

She could abandon him; she could walk away and never look back.

Abigail was capricious. Given a chance, she would run after some imagined Heathcliff and forget to return, leave him to rot in his own house. He stopped mid-stride and held the limp thing out in his arms.

The head tipped brokenly to one side, pale face wearing the sheen of fine porcelain, sightlessly gazing over his shoulder, through the walls and away to the far horizon where Heathcliff awaited her.

The doll was the most abhorrent thing he had ever touched. Greyson threw it away from him. It collapsed and clattered across the floor, limbs crooked in ways that no living body would ever move. Three years of his life on this lifeless device that would steal Abigail away from him. He scrambled for a hammer or a saw or any other implement on the table.

The saw would do. He cracked the legs, splinted the wood in rough strokes. It did not yield easily under his hands; he cut gouges, threw the saw aside, bent the legs with the hammer and stomped on the wounds until the hardwood snapped and the cloth ripped.

Shavings covered the floor, two severed stumps stuck out from under the carefully layered petticoats. He stood and brushed his coat up, glanced around the room with sudden dread. Idiot, idiot! He took up the hammer again and smashed the mirrors, too, so that Abigail couldn't see him. If they didn't break when he swung at them he pried them off the wall and tossed them facing down onto the floor. Every creak made him nervous; the house settling, or Abigail? A mouse in the wall, or his wife come to ask what was wrong?

She wouldn't understand. Couldn't understand.

The locket burned. The room creaked. A woman's shadow wavered in the heart of the room. Her visage stared out from every mirror shard. Greyson dropped the saw.

"It was an accident," he said, stepping backwards. Wood crunched under his feet. "The legs were too frail. I'll just have to remake them. It won't take long, my dear."

"And the mirrors?" she hissed. He could hear her, see her lips move in her reflections, all the little shattered pieces, fragments of Abigail.

Anger congealed her form. If only there were more amicable conditions.

"You claim you love me." Her voice echoed, a thin whisper that filled the room like old spiderwebs. "Heathcliff would never betray his love so."

Her reflection reached down and picked up the saw.

"As I recall, he could, and he did," Greyson said, and then regretted every word.

In the mirror, Abigail struck him across the face with the saw. Greyson readjusted his glasses, ignoring the warm rivulet that crawled down his cheek. "Alas, Heathcliff is fictional."

"Fictional!" A rising wail accompanied the word. "I love you, I love you, and this is how you repay me?"

"Swear you'll never leave me," Greyson said. "Because you care so deeply. Isn't that right?"

"Why won't you join me in death? I asked you even before you proposed to me, when you were just a student of the occult and I a lost shade in that depository. You could have joined me then and none of this would have happened. How can you claim to love me?" She grew closer with every word, skeletal, rotting. His beautiful wife. Anger made her vile, and his revulsion made him guilty. She was right; he should be able to love her no matter her petty faults, no matter the situation. And he could, if she would pay attention to him instead of that damned novel.

"You teach me now how cruel you've been – cruel and false. Why did you despise me? Why did you betray your own heart?"

"Stop quoting that infernal book at me!" Greyson yelled back, throwing out his hands. "And you – how can you claim to love me? All you ever profess is your obsession with Heathcliff, with never a thought for me. Me, your husband! I've done everything for you. I carry pieces of your bloody book around next to my heart, for God's sake! But soon enough you'll have naught but a statue to love! Is that steadfast enough?!"

"You broke my body," she said, sadly, so sadly, but at least they were her own words. "You gave it to me, then you take it all away. I wish I could hold you until we both were dead." The fragmented remains of her skeleton reached out, grabbed him around the throat, before melting away completely.

And then came pain, crippling needles and the razor edges of knives. Every clock in the house rang out, a clamor that drowned Greyson's cry even to his own ears.

Greyson tore the locket off and threw it across the room as far as his shaking hands could manage. Abigail shrieked, and her presence left him. Chasing the locket. Maybe there was a God after all and this was Greyson's last reprieve. He sat gasping until the pain subsided some, then staggered across the room, ripped the door open, and stepped through it without looking at his destination. Didn't matter, as long as it was as far away as possible. It wasn't abandonment, or if it was, she had made the first move away.

He slammed the door behind him and then sank to his knees. He was facing the ocean at night, some unwitting person's unlocked beach house at his back. It was too cloudy and dark for stars. Abigail was trying to kill him. Abigail was honestly trying to murder him. After all the sacrifices he had made for her, ungrateful bitch, after all those decades they'd lived together.

Greyson forced himself up and picked his way slowly, unsteadily across the idiot's property and down to the sound of crashing waves. High tide, low tide, who cared? It wasn't as if he were capable of drowning.

When the sand got damp and his boots sunk into the ground, he stopped and lay down, and stared up at the moon's silhouette shifting through the clouds. She should understand that he couldn't just let her leave. What if she decided not to come back?

What if she refused to take him back?

He lay there in the mud until dawn, ruining his suit in the salt water, contemplating how many pretty seashells would purchase Abigail's renewed affection, when some fool spotted his body and approached. He didn't look up when he heard a voice.

"Hey, are you all right?" Yankee accent. A young man, porcine-faced, unsuitable for Abigail.

"Well," Greyson said. "Waiting for the end of the world."

The man leaned over, then stepped back. "I'll get help," the man said, puzzlement creasing his fattened cheeks, before rushing back into the house.

Like Hell he'd wait around. Once the man was back inside, Greyson rolled to his feet, dripping wet, and walked to the house. He opened the door to another locale where he could sulk in peace. It would have been much simpler had he died. They would be together in Heaven or in Hell, or to wander the earth forever as shades until Armageddon came. He wanted to see the end, the war to truly end all wars, but to be without Abigail was another sort of end, a worse one, an empty gouge in his chest that left him listless.

He wandered for weeks aimlessly, ticking off the days in his mind. From city to city, no matter how many people crowded the streets, he was alone.

Of course she would forgive him. She had to. Who else loved her, who else did she love? Anyone she may have had a chance to was long dust by now; just her and him and her damnable beloved book, rotting in the house with her. He would have to be presentable, though. He cleaned himself up in Paris, washed and shaved and changed his suit.

He opened a door in Paris and stepped back though to his study. All but one of the doors in the house yawned open, exposing their nails, their empty portals into adjacent rooms. Useless to him. An opened door could not be opened again until closed, and so could not take him back outside. A trap, most likely. Nothing left to do but fall for her again. He shut the door carefully behind himself and then called out, cheerfully, "Abigail, I'm home!"

Nothing. He sighed and stepped into the room, towards the locket, which still lay untouched on the floor where he had thrown it a week ago.

Beside it lay what remained of the doll, hand stretched out as if it were reaching for the locket. The air in the study stilled.

Abigail was here, waiting, watching him. Forgiving him, he hoped.

"I missed you," Greyson said. The doll stirred.

What little light there was winked out. The air thickened. It stank like mildew and sludge dredged up from the bottom of the Thames. Abigail appeared before him, eyes glittering like bone exposed deep in their sockets, soaked, so solid that silt and water dripped from her hair and clothes and pooled on the floor around her reflections.

"How dare you step foot in this house again," she said. "You promised me, you promised, and you broke the promise and its legs and then abandoned me. I hate you."

"It was an accident."

"Why even pretend I didn't see you?! I see everything you do!"

"Then you'll see how I've been heartbroken, searching for gifts to appease you with. I was afraid that you would leave me."

"Yet you arrive empty-handed," Abigail spat. She was hardly transparent. Solid as flesh. Her voice carried well in the thick air.

"I thought you might forgive me simply because you also missed me."

She fixed him with a hollow glare, reached for him with thin fingers. He would not back away this time. Greyson strode forward; the doll dragged itself upright to meet him, and he knelt, kissed her, twined his hands into her hair. It was just the doll's body, but wasn't this what he had built it for? In the reflections fragmented across the floor it was Abigail herself who embraced him, who returned the kiss, deeper, hungrily. She dug her fingers into his back. Her hair and her brine-soaked dress dampened his suit.

For a moment he thought that in her lust she might have forgiven him, until the pressure blossomed into pain. Greyson tried to pull away.

She dug deeper. Stabbed in the back by his own desperation, perhaps by a sliver from one of the mirrors. Pathetic. Struggling deepened the wound.

She pressed his head to her shoulder and murmured something like the strain of a lullaby, the same words that he had whispered to the doll.

"Abigail, please forgive me," he said, lying limp in her embrace.

"I'll forgive you," she promised. Her cold hand stroked his cheek. "I'll forgive you very soon."

"If you mean that you'll forgive me when I die, I'll take this chance to remind you that I can't, not even for you. I would in a heartbeat, I swear, if I could, but I was young and foolish once, you know."

"Are you frightened?"

"Of course not. I know you wouldn't hurt me."

"I wouldn't," she agreed, and in what would have been the same breath for anyone living, said – "offer me your heart."

"You have my heart, darling. You always have."

"No. Your heart." Her fingers trailed down to rest over his chest.

"Really?" How could she say that after all he'd done for her? "Really, I need that to circulate blood through my decrepit body. Do you know how long it will take me to heal? Months –" She made some small movement that sent pain down his side and he gasped. "If you're just going to leave me bleeding on the floor, Abigail, please, I'll bring you someone else's heart. Please, Abigail."

"I don't want anyone else's heart." She unbuttoned his vest, slid her cold fingers against his skin. "I realized, when you were gone. What's been missing, what I want. Only you."

"Heathcliff," he said. "I'll bring you Heathcliff's heart."

"He doesn't exist, darling. You keep telling me that. But it doesn't matter, because you love me more than Heathcliff ever loved his dear Catherine, don't you? There's no use for the book or the doll, any of that. I want your love to fill me. Don't you want that, too?" She was pleading, the hunger turned to desperation turned on him. Inevitably.

He couldn't leave her to suffer, never let her cry alone without respite. What was one more little sacrifice, to ensure that she wouldn't leave him?

"Of course I do," Greyson said. He closed his eyes, pressed his face against Abigail's damp collar. "And if I give you this, will you never leave me?"

"I will never leave you. I keep all my promises."

Of course she had to make one last dig at him. He smiled crookedly.

"Ah. I'll make the first cut for you."

"Oh, you don't need to." Abigail lifted his chin slightly and kissed him. She held him still, drawing out the caress even as she cut him open, even as she dug into his chest. It hurt. He gripped her tighter, but it wasn't as painful as he had feared. His flesh was clay; no doubt the nerves had hardened and died. Blood and sediment pooled on the floor over his shoes, mixing with her river water. No matter. The suit was long past ruin.

Greyson clutched her in his tight embrace until she held his barely beating heart in her hands. She knelt down with him, laid him on the floor, and lifted his heart to her lips and took a tentative bite.

He hoped it was the sweetest meat she ever tasted.

* * *

Greyson woke lying on the ground like Abigail's broken doll. Abigail sat over his body. He had to squint to focus on her. Her figure seemed odd; she was dressed loosely in his clothes, his glasses tucked neatly into the waistcoat breast-pocket. She fitted together small brass springs and gears and pipes. Though she was by his side, he could only conjure up the vague memories of affection. *Take my heart, and all my love for you, darling.* Dried blood made his skin sticky. The room smelled like wet earth and rot.

"I suppose I didn't need it," he said, through his parched throat. "Maybe you'll have more use for it." He laughed until it turned to coughing, a hollow grating noise, the dying strikes of a wound-down clock, and lifted a hand to probe at the wound in his chest. All the warmth had drained out of him, down into a distant well.

"Hush, darling, Greyson," Abigail said, and traced his lips with her fingertips. The cool band of the wedding ring brushed his chin. The locket's bare chain dangled from her neck. "Lie still. I'm building you a new heart, to tick away the seconds until the world ends. I burnt the book, dear. Only your love sustains us." She sprinkled damp ash among the workings. Greyson locked his fingers around hers, and the ash clung to his fingers and to the wet flesh of his open chest.

She was as warm as life and love.

Almost

M. Regan

I

THE BOY BREATHES.

Crystallized air floats in clouds around his lips, their part as pink as fallen petals and crusted with rime. The cold of it stings. It melts, only to freeze and hurt again. Each silvery exhalation weaves into the mist of predawn smog, escaping the velvet abyss of his mouth in shimmering plumes. Beneath his – their – feet, similarly shimmering pathways shine with spider webs of hoarfrost and ice.

There are mirrors in the frozen surfaces of shallow puddles, their glitter dangerous. The cobblestones are laden with cracks as extensive and dark as those that riddle the mind.

He thinks. That is dangerous, too. He breathes, which is more so.

There is something frightening in the act of respiration. In the simplicity of so integral a need, and in how easily it can all go wrong. His breath haunts, hovering before him in spectral palls that fade to nothingness.

Everything good is dead. Gone. Life is as evanescent as a sigh, and there is none to be found here. The garden cemetery is littered with the shriveled corpses of weeds, nostalgia, and those clawing, persistent memories that are too deeply rooted to be dealt with on one's own. They linger like paranoia, or insanity.

Ice splinters beneath his sole.

Above emaciated bouquets and the jagged teeth of stone markers, gnarled hands are scraping epitaphs into the sky. There is a cry, or a caw, or a cackle. Only when the boy blinks does he realize that those straining arms are branches, and the contorted fingers are twigs. A willowy hand alights upon his shoulder. Or perhaps it is a snowflake.

In the dead of winter, the creature stands too close.

And he breathes.

II

IT BEGAN AT THE BEGINNING, and it will end at the end.

However, as with most dreams, he is unsure of the course that the journey will take between those two junctures. Once, the creature had been little more than a nightmare, flittering in his peripheral. Like a reflection in a half-noticed looking glass, It was only ever seen out of the corner of his eye.

But then he had begun to look. After looking came seeking, and if one seeks, they will find. The pearl of Its toothy maw glistened, reflecting things both horrible and welcoming.

Beckoning, beautiful, that Cheshire smile hung in suspension within a gilded frame, urging him down a rabbit hole that may or may not have led to a rumbling belly.

For a time, the boy could do nothing but resist being gobbled. He would thrash and writhe, buckle and scream, until the strange specter had no choice but to regurgitate him. With a wet retching, he would find himself atop his rumpled bed sheets, drenched in all manner of fluids.

It had been a dream, then.

But that was then. Some point before the end, sometime after the beginning. Then is not now.

Now, when the boy breaks through the clammy skin of midnight-swaddled horror, he finds the hungry nightmare waiting outside of himself, as if the whole of the world has been turned inside-out in mimicry of the creature's stomach.

Sitting by his side, the monster clutches him with the passion of a silhouette, never once letting go. The roseate dim of a lamp casts hellish highlights over the malleable gloom of the creature's chin, nose, cheekbones. Simper.

It is like gazing upon the countenance of an old friend.

The boy can taste salt on his tongue. Spit on his lip. And every gasp and gulp of air scorches his throat as he chokes it down, fighting against the bile that tries to rise, rise, rise. He clings back just as desperately, fists coiling around curls of shade and satin.

The monster stays with him until terror subsides. It escorts mania out the door, leaving the shadowed bedroom quiet, still, and smelling of rotten apples.

III

HE IS A FRAGILE THING, the boy with the dead garden.

He thinks of himself as a sickly sapling: brittle and breakable, wooden and wan. For a decade and three-quarters, he had been protected by the strength of a forest. Then came a man with an axe.

He is no longer part of a family tree. He is exposed, and weaker for it. Since birth, his lungs have been like the parchment that makes up the tomes on his bedside table. They hiss and crackle with each shallow inhale, every raspy exhale.

In, out. Pain, pain.

Though he is lonely, he cannot stand the company of creatures furred or feathered. He barely trusts those who had been hired to dust his home. Sometimes, he'll crack a window for fresh air – the window closest to his wilted plot – but the chill and the damp are a threat to him, as well. Whatever he tries, the boy cannot fully evade the consequences of a delicate constitution.

Asthma, flus. Cold after cold. Perhaps consumption, one day. He comments on the inevitable offhandedly, with the sort of long-suffering nonchalance of his favorite novel heroes. That he earns the reaction he had hoped for is an unexpected surprise.

The nightmare, by nature, is a superficial creature. Its emotions and expressions have never once reflected anything of particular depth. But in this moment, It exudes something akin to genuine concern. It looks as worried as he feels.

With the tinkled grind of icicles, the being's features pinch. It frowns. Already pressed against the boy, the nightmare sweeps a frigid palm over his temple, clearing away the matted sheaves of his bangs.

At first, all he feels are Its fingertips scoring sigils into the perspiration on his brow. Then he feels something else.

There is a finite sound. There is finality. The creature leans forward, pressing Its forehead to his.

He would gasp, were he able.

But in the minute gap of space that lingers between their lips, there are no mingled breaths. How can there be, when neither is breathing?

There are only glassy eyes and darkness.

IV

SOMETIMES, he breathes not at all.

Other times, he breathes too much.

Blunted nails rake at the bedspread, screeching down sweat-slickened silk as fingers scrabble and feet flail and toes curl. Bony heels beat against the back of an arched spine as a paper-thin chest is blotted in beautiful bruises.

Blue. Green. Love-you-red.

After every thrust and shudder, the boy feels his mouth open wider, wider, jaw unhinging like a snake's. The garden outside the window is little more than a collection of husks, its dry leaves rattling like air in his gullet. From the depths of that mortal chasm, silent screams waft over the monster's dew-dappled face, the strings of snapping spittle scented strongly of apples. Other things snap in time. Time itself snaps, too fast and then too slow.

Forelocks flutter, mimicking the countdown of a clock's pendulum: four, three, two, one, back and forth and in and out.

Pain, pain.

The creature loves to make him pant. And whether during waking dreams or waking hours, It is very, very good at it.

V

AFTER HIS NIGHTMARE becomes his monster, and his monster becomes his companion, and his companion becomes in all ways his, the boy allows a kiss.

He does not like kissing, though he is not sure why. Perhaps it is because the creature takes such obvious delight in the act. Predatory talons cleave to his shoulders with the tenacity of a shadow, and he is pulled close – too close – so close that he can hear skin dimpling in each corner of Its smirk. The tip of his lip is teased, his gums cut by the sharpness of a silver tongue.

He does not like kissing. He does not like the way the sexless sensation crashes over him, simple and sweet and toxic. Something within him throbs. His heart, he thinks, before it drops like a stone.

He recalls then the waves of high tide: ripples that start small, but soon surge into a surf. Before he has a chance to escape, the waters have risen and he is caught in the undertow, spinning, swirling, sinking. When he finally breaks the surface with a splutter and a wheeze, arms flailing like one of the half-drowned, he discovers that the heavens have been replaced by his ember-eyed monster.

It looms, starry stare blazing above the sickle moon of Its grin. A crescent strip to start, that same moon begins to wax, bones creaking and teeth unsheathed. Time passes in a blur.

In the spotted haze of his asphyxiated gaze, the creature's wonderland leer grows and grows, grows and grows, until it has swallowed all. Until there is nothing left above the boy but the void of a mouth. A black hole, ravenous and all-consuming.

The vacuum of space suckles oxygen from all hidden places, including the spongy air pockets of secreted lungs. The boy chokes, the sound disagreeably shrill. His face purples; his body seizes. Panic sets in, and he can do no more than cling to his throat, holding to it with the same determination that he does his consciousness.

His plight is acknowledged by a sympathetic coo. Blackness enshrouds more than just the edges of his vision. The smiling creature dips low once more, as if to help resuscitate.

But It is breathing in, not out.

VI

LATELY, he has been very tired.

Lethargic, listless, and limp, there are days when the boy can do little more than lie in the feathery down of his bed, chest rising and falling, rising and falling.

Too weary to lift a book, he passes the endless hours by studying his own story. He turns his gaze inward, diving into the cataleptic depths of his subconscious. Again and again he returns to that place, as if hoping to find something meaningful there. Something lost, or forgotten, or unsullied, or profound. But his sleep remains deep and dreamless.

It makes sense, he supposes. More sense than anything else. After all, he had expunged himself of nightmares long ago. He had let them loose – he had let It loose – and It had been far too happy to begin a life of Its own outside the prison of his thoughts.

And he, in turn, is happy too, because he is no longer alone.

Day after day, when the wheedling light of dawn urges his eyes to open, the first thing the boy sees is his monster waiting at his bedside: body tilted, nostrils flaring, flushed features burning with secret pleasure. As It becomes more humanoid, this is more of a comfort than a terror.

But perhaps it should be the other way around.

When the creature whispers this morning's salutations, the boy cannot help noticing the way It has cocked Its head.

The way Its smile reflects his own.

The way Its eyes seem a little more familiar.

VII

THE MIRROR IS COLD. His breath is hot.

Out of petulance, the boy smears the steamed surface with his withered finger. Doing so will leave stains, he knows, long after the vaporous mist has faded.

The monster arches an eyebrow, but does not speak. Never a complaint from those twitching lips uttered, though a smirk does curl their elastic edges when the design becomes an encircled, five-pointed star. In afterthought, the boy inscribes the familiar symbol with equally-familiar runes: sigils once lifted from the pages of childhood readings.

Condensation drips like transparent blood from the thick, liquidizing lines. His hand is wet, cold, and stolen by the creature.

It bows. It lowers Its head. An elegant tongue laps at the beads of tepid water that have pearled on the tips of knotty digits, as white and frail as the bones that shape them.

Spindly. Spidery. Like a skeleton, half-alive and still writhing within the embalming sheets of semi-translucent skin.

Breaking the mirror would do no good now.

The creature lifts Its looking-glass face, politely patting Its mouth with a captured wrist. It smiles, and Its sire cannot help doing the same, for a smile is a skull's only choice of expression.

Losing strength and air in equal time, the boy gazes upon himself as a ghost might upon its body, and finally makes a connection. Finally realizes something.

It leaves him breathless.

Over the rush of this last exhalation, he hears his voice whisper into his own ear:

"Thank you for the meal."

* * *

EVERY TIME YOU EXHALE, a little bit of your soul escapes. Luckily, you almost always inhale it back before anyone else gets it.

Almost.

Ever fogged up a mirror with your breath?

Don't do that.

The Bulge in the Wall

Annette Siketa

MAXWELL THOMAS COULD NOT have been happier. A rural lad from deepest Devonshire, his sole ambition was to become a professional journalist, and after what he considered "wasted" years writing overly sensational articles for penny papers, his application to join a popular London newspaper was accepted.

Max arrived at King's Cross Station one dull October morning. He deposited his belongings in the left luggage office, and then reported to his new boss. "I possess a keen mind and a ready pen," he said assuringly to the editor, a squat, round-faced man with a perpetual sniff. "I can do good work for the paper."

"Guess we'll have to see about that," said the editor sceptically. "Have you secured lodgings?"

"No, sir."

The editor sighed. "Try the back streets, they're usually cheaper," he advised, pointing over his shoulder towards the back of the building. "Report to me at two o'clock tomorrow afternoon. You can start on the graveyard shift."

Undeterred, Max set off to find a new home. Unfortunately, the few pounds his parents had given him upon departure, coupled with his future meagre income, meant that a respectable hotel was out of the question. Nevertheless, his optimism was high as he began to pound the pavements. The reality, however, soon hit home, and he was astonished and appalled at the squalor in which some people, presumably induced by circumstance, were forced to live.

The best that could be said for the three-storey, grime-smeared boarding house at 34 Baxter Street, was that the windows and front door were clean. The landlady, Mrs Dixon, looked as old as the house. Her nose was large, her green eyes were small, and her face was a network of wrinkles.

The preliminaries having been settled, as Max followed her to the top of the house, he noticed that there was only one mounted gaslight on each landing, and judging from the lack of scorching on the wall, the flame was always kept low. The room was plain in every respect, with basic furniture and threadbare carpet. Still, it was within his price range, and there was very little noise in the street outside.

"Here it is," she said in her snappy, high-pitched cockney accent. "It's the only room I have left, take it or leave it."

"Is there anyone else on this floor?" he asked, taking in a thin partition. It was so crudely made that he could see the outline of the boards under the wallpaper. Clearly at some stage in its history, the room had been much larger.

Mrs Dixon eyed him warily. "What do you want to know for?"

Max shrugged. "No particular reason. It's just nice to know who my neighbours are."

"There's no one except the gentleman next door." She jerked a thumb towards the partition. "But he keeps very much to himself. I doubt you'll ever see him."

"I see," said Max. "So, I'm more or less alone up here."

"Pretty much," said Mrs Dixon, her eyes glistening greedily as Max produced his purse. For better or worse, this was his new home.

As ordered, Max arrived for work the next day, and for the following two nights, did not return home until after one am. At first, Mrs Dixon had complained about being, "Awakened from me bed," but by the fourth night, when she opened the door to hear the nearby church clock striking three, she reluctantly gave Max a key.

The room proved comfortable enough, but Max's irregular hours prevented him from meeting other residents, including the gentleman next door. Except for the man's inclination to move about in the early hours, which he took little care to do quietly, Max had no conception of him.

About the middle of the second week, Max returned home after a long day's work. It was two o'clock in the morning, and the gaslights on the landings were turned low as usual. Being excessively tired, his footing was clumsy in the virtual darkness. Yet nobody seemed disturbed by the undue noise, and the house remained still and quiet.

Peeling off his clothes, he was about to get into bed and read a book, when he suddenly stopped and listened. Someone was coming up the stairs. The heavy tread denoted a man, and the confident footfall announced that he was no stranger to the house.

Deciding that it could only be the gentleman next door, he was about to turn out the light when he was startled by a knock on the door. Was he finally to meet his elusive neighbour?

Max had scarcely taken a step across the room, when he heard the sound of the other door being opened and a man saying peevishly, "Father, you have the wrong room as usual. Come in here."

The door was slammed shut, quickly followed by more heavy footsteps and the sound of scraping chairs. The men seemed completely indifferent to their neighbour's comfort, for they made enough noise to wake the dead, and as they began to talk, Max jumped into bed and buried his head under the pillow. He did not want to listen, but in the quietude and darkness, snatches of conversation reached his ears.

"What do you mean, you can't get it?"

"I might be able to get part of it, but..."

Max heard the sound of a dull thud, as though a fist had been banged on a table. "A part of it!" cried the elder man. "Oscar, we are facing ruin and disgrace. Part of it is next to useless. We need all of it, and only by marrying the girl can you get it. You know she is silly enough to give you anything, and so long as you give her a plausible excuse, she will not suspect. I give you my word that all will be repaid." There was a long pause, and Max guessed that the younger man was thinking. When the older man resumed, his voice was calmer but no less insistent. "Oscar, you must get it. Would you see me arrested for embezzlement when it could be avoided? Is our name to be cursed and spat upon?"

Max realised that he had been listening intensely. Moreover, it was likely that other people in the house had also overheard. Decency dictated that somehow, he convey the fact to the men. He began to cough loudly and persistently, but the voices continued as before, the son protesting and the father growing angrier. Max then groped in the dark for his book, and hoping it would not penetrate the cheap materials, tossed it lightly towards the partition. The voices went on unconcernedly. His attempts to alert the men had fallen on deaf ears.

Max climbed out of bed, turned up the light, and checked his watch. It was nearly three am. More concerned with sleep than the morality of his neighbours, he went into the passageway and knocked on their door. The conversation instantly ceased, and Max expected one of the men to appear and apologise, but the door remained closed. He knocked again, but as he did so, he became aware of a curious sensation. Although there was no light shining under the door, he was absolutely sure that someone was behind it. In addition, the house had taken on an aura of expectancy, as though it was waiting for something to happen.

Max shivered, but whether it was from the cold or the creepiness he could not have said. He put his mouth next to the keyhole. "Gentlemen, please do not talk so loudly. It is very late and I wish to sleep."

He listened but there was no answer. The stillness of the house began to press on him. He looked behind and down the stairs, hoping and yet fearing that something would break the silence.

Returning to his room, he paused to peer over the banister. The space below was a void of deep shadows, where anything or anyone could be concealed. Was it his imagination, or was there something swaying on the very bottom step? Was someone whispering and shuffling near the front door, the faint sound more inarticulate than the usual noises of the night?

"Don't be silly," he murmured to himself, and went to bed, leaving the house and its inmates to themselves.

Peace reigned for the next two nights, but on the third night, when his consciousness was hovering between sleeping and waking, he was disturbed by a sound from the depths of the house. The window suddenly rattled. Max turned his head so sharply that he cricked his neck. Moonlight spread across the floor, highlighting the carpet's shabbiness, but there was nobody forcing an entry. It was the wind, a howling portentous bluster.

Max settled down to sleep again, but a moment later he sat bolt upright. There *was* another sound, growing more distinct every second, and what's more, he'd heard it before.

"The old man," he whispered. He checked his watch by moonlight. It was half past two, roughly the same time as three nights earlier. Perhaps it was the slow rhythmic footfall, but he was suddenly assailed by a feeling of menace, as though the man was coming to get him.

Max stared at the door. Did the handle just move? His skin crawled and his hair seemed to stand on end. He was trembling all over when he heard something brush past the wall, followed by a loud knock on the adjacent door.

"Oh, so it's you." Max recognised the voice as Oscar's.

"Did you get it?" his father demanded, noisily closing the door.

Max, now slightly light-headed with relief, was desirous of stopping the loud conversation, but curiosity and a sense of righteousness got the better of him. He had almost been frightened to death, and he didn't think it impertinent to discover the reason why.

"No, I didn't," said Oscar feebly. "I'm sorry, father, but I just can't do it."

There was a sickening *smack* and then a crash. Max threw back the blankets, ready to jump out of bed, certain that the father had just hit the son.

"You are weak!" the father screeched. "How you came from my loins I will never know. Why, even your air-head fiancée has more gumption than you."

Oscar's voice was steadier as he countered, "Don't you dare speak of Gillian like that. I will not have her dragged into this unholy mess. Your troubles are of your own making, father. I will not allow you to rob the innocent again, even at the cost of my honour."

His father's laugh was mocking and cruel. "Honour? Shall I show you the price of your honour?"

There were ten seconds of dead silence and then... "Father!" A chair toppled over. "You... you... they're Gillian's jewels. You stole them."

"Of course I did. I knew you were too much of a coward to ask her, so I paid her a visit yesterday. The jewel case was lying on a table." He dropped his voice to a malicious growl. "If she was stupid enough to leave them lying about, then she can hardly complain if they're stolen."

Instantly, there were the sounds of a scuffle, the father hurling vile oaths as though they were weapons, his son with short, strenuous gasps. The fight did not last long, and Oscar evidently won, for a moment later he exclaimed, "You scoundrel, you will never have her jewels."

Suddenly, frighteningly, the house fell eerily quiet. Max's blood froze in his veins, and as the seconds ticked past without any more sounds, his instinct screamed that something terrible had happened next door. He jumped out of bed, turned up the light, donned his shoes and a dressing-gown, and darted for the door. Then, as he was about to turn the handle, something caught his eye. A lower portion of the flimsy partition was bulging into his room. Moreover, the wallpaper was splitting under the strain of the bending boards.

Max stared in horrified fascination, for beneath the bulge, which was clearly the size and shape of a man's back, something dark and serpentine was creeping over the carpet. Stretching out a hand to touch it, at the moment of contact he snatched it away. His fingers were covered in blood.

He ran next door and pounded on the door. "Open up! Open up, I say!" There was no response. He tried the door. It was locked. One tremendous kick later and he fell headlong into the room.

Max sprang to his feet. Apart from the moonlight pouring through the uncurtained window, there was no sound, no movement, not even the semblance of a presence. The room was completely empty, horribly and miserably empty.

A light flashed into the room. Max spun around, his arm raised as though to fend off a blow, but it was only Mrs Dixon. Even so, Max took a step backwards. In the dim light cast by the candle in her hand, her expression was one of hideous triumph.

"Fancy a bit of prowling, did ya?"

"My dear woman, something awful has happened in this room."

"No, it didn't. I can never keep anyone on this floor longer than a month, though those who are sensitive catch on sooner. Nothing really happens, it's all sort of in your head."

"Look here," he said, holding out his bloodied hand, "did I imagine this?"

"Imagine what?"

Max looked at his hand. It was perfectly clean and white. "I don't understand. It was covered in blood."

"Not to worry, dearie, it's all over now." Mrs Dixon spoke as if she was soothing a child after a tooth extraction. "Nothing else will happen now. I'm going back to bed."

"Oh no, you're not," said Max determinedly, blocking her path to the stairs. "I want the truth."

Mrs Dixon pulled her shawl more tightly around her shoulders. "Not here. Come into my parlour and I'll explain, but mind you get dressed first. I have my reputation to think of."

Still bewildered, Max returned to his room. On his way downstairs however, he turned up the gaslights on the landings. After what he'd just experienced, nothing could induce him to place his safety in the hands of a penny-pinching hag.

"It's a performance," said Mrs Dixon, her scrawny hands wrapped around a steaming cup. To Max's surprise, she had made two cups of tea. "Once it's played out the spirits go away, that is to say, until the next tenant arrives. I only said there was a gentleman next door in case you heard something."

"Mrs Dixon, that was deceitful, perhaps even fraud."

"And who's going to prove it? The man who last had that room, was found dead in bed. Terribly pale he was, eyes bulging out of his head."

"Good god! How many times has it happened?"

Mrs Dixon put down her cup and began to count on her fingers. "Four times that I know of."

"And they all died in the room next to mine?"

"Yes, which is why I don't rent it out any more." She lowered her voice and spoke in a confidential manner. "The house was getting a bit of a reputation, and being a poor widow, I had to curtail it, even though I can hardly carry the cost."

Max stared at her in disbelief. He did not know which shocked him the more, the number of deaths, or her callous indifference. "Who are the spirits?" he managed to ask.

"Twenty-five years ago, this house was a private residence, owned by a family named Steinbeck. I think they were German. Wilfred Steinbeck, the father, was some bigwig in the city. Well up in society they were. Anyway, one day, his only son Oscar, was found dead in his room."

"I presume you mean the two rooms minus the partition."

"Just so. The son was declared to have committed suicide after robbing his fiancée of her jewels. Mr Steinbeck buried his son and returned to Germany. However, many doubted the verdict."

"Why?"

"Because of the position of the stab wounds. I have never seen the performance myself, though I've heard them moving about often enough."

"So," said Max slowly, an idea forming at the back of his mind, "you've never heard the conversation between the spirits?"

Mrs Dixon shuddered. "Not bloomin' likely. Gives me the willies just thinking about it."

Max returned to his room. There was no sign of blood or the bulge in the wall. He lay awake for some time, half listening for any sound next door, and half deep in thought. He had names, he had an approximate date, and he had a good grasp of the circumstances. Though not vindictive, his face broke into a satisfied smile as he thought of Mrs Dixon. She did not have a clue, and if his guess was right, both she and the house were about to become famous, but for all the wrong reasons. He managed to snatch a few hours' sleep and then went to the office.

"Why, Mr Thomas," said the concierge in surprise, "you're early."

Max did not resent the fact that he was still restricted to the graveyard shift. On the contrary, he enjoyed it. "Things to do," he said evasively, and hurried to a vast underground vault, where a veritable sea of bookcases and shelves stored decades of newspapers.

"The Steinbeck case?" said the archivist, a tall spare man whose gaunt pallor reflected the fact that he rarely saw the sun. He checked his records and then pointed to an aisle. "Down there, third shelf from the top."

Max found the folios. They were covered in dust and had obviously not been opened in years. An hour later, he ran to the editor's office and rapped smartly on the door. "Boss," he panted excitedly, all sense of propriety temporarily forgotten, "have I got a story for you."

Many years later when Max published his memoirs, he declared that, although he had reported many famous and notorious events, his greatest moment of triumph was when, after much persuasion, Scotland Yard lifted the floorboards at 34 Baxter Street.

"It was a most singular honour," he wrote. "Discretion dictates that I not disclose her proper name, but Miss Gillian was still alive, and it was with tears in my eyes that I returned her jewels. She declared that she had always known Oscar to be innocent of the theft, but never imagined the depths to which his father had sunk."

Wilfred Steinbeck was never charged. He survived his son by several years, and died in wretched circumstances. Mrs Dixon dined on her notoriety for some time. Everyone was keen to spend a night in the "haunted room", and although many declared that they'd heard a conversation, the alleged dialogue never came close to Max's experience. He always smiled when he heard of a so-called encounter, for in his heart, he was sure that the spirit of poor Oscar Steinbeck was finally at peace, not that Mrs Dixon would ever have admitted that.

The Psychic Fair

Cathy Smith

NICOLE COLLINS LIKED HER SHOWERS to be so hot that her bathroom was turned into a veritable sauna. It was little wonder she didn't notice there was a draft in the bathroom until she turned the faucets off. She shuddered when the water stopped running, and quickly dried off and wrapped herself in a thick towel. *It's cold.* She shuddered. Definitely cold, not merely in comparison between the hot water and regular air temperature, it was a real draft.

Did I leave a window open? When she stepped out of the stall there was a man in the bathroom.

"Get out of here, you pervert!" she snapped. There was no telling how long he'd been there, what he may've already seen, and the thought infuriated her.

"*Leave!*" she said again.

The man disappeared, along with the draft, which didn't surprise Nicole. Ghosts dropped in whenever they wanted at all hours and places wherever she was around. It was bad enough that she had increased heating costs because of them, but the lack respect for her time and privacy was maddening – *I can't believe he dropped in on me in the bathroom! Don't I have the right to privacy?!*

She looked about herself to see if the man or anyone else was in the room with her. She was alone – for now. She dressed quickly before she had anymore "visitors".

There was a knock on her door, and she groaned at the sight of her landlady Mrs Phillips at her doorstep, "I heard a scream –"

Nicole couldn't deny that she'd cried out so she said, "I saw a spider."

"Spider?" Mrs Phillips asked.

"Yes, a spider," she hoped Mrs Phillips hadn't heard her say "you pervert."

Seeing there wouldn't be any more of an explanation Mrs Phillips sighed, "Tell me if you see any more. I'll call the exterminator –"

"I'll do that –"

Nicole rolled her eyes as she shut the door. Mrs Phillips' concern for her was touching and even heart warming – when she was in the mood for it. She couldn't just tell Mrs Phillips to mind her own business when she exploited Mrs Phillips' maternal instincts to get this apartment in the first place. Nicole's apartment was warm and roomy, the rent was reasonable, and maintenance service was prompt.

The other renters complained about unexpected noises in the night, and cold spots, but no one thought there may be ghosts in the area. They thought it was just the quirks of living in an old house converted into flats. Nicole did her best to make sure the ghosts didn't get too pushy and disruptive, but she didn't always succeed. So far no one was calling Nicole "the Freak" like they did in high school. She was considered a pretty, quiet young woman who kept to herself.

She needed a good laugh to take her mind off her problems so she watched the latest John Zachery special when she was alone. There was the usual disclaimer that this show was only for entertainment purposes. The specials gave her hope that she wouldn't be dismissed as a lunatic if people knew she was a ghost magnet. The people on the show gushed over John Zachery's gifts. Of course, it was possible that the people on the show were actors instead of people willing to display their gullibility on national TV, but Nicole was riveted.

When people who had supposedly known Zachery in his early years came on she felt a wave of bitterness engulf her heart. *An honest interview would be, "I thought he was creepy." "He was always talking to himself." And "I always knew there wasn't something quite right about him."*

Nicole was feeling so cynical and depressed that she ended up turning the TV off early rather than watch anymore. *If only every ghost magnet's life could be like that.* She wished she could turn her ability on or off at will so she could get peace and quiet when she wanted it. Nicole had the Gift, but she could never control when a ghost would make an appearance. Nor could she call a specific ghost to her when she wanted to.

Grandma asks me when I want to see her next time, and that's when she'll visit me, but I'd have a hard time getting some stranger to agree to come when I want. I couldn't have a live person come to me and ask to make a ghost appear at will. That wouldn't work –

She tried to put the envy behind her as she got ready for bed. There was the sound of knocking at a nearby door. *Someone's getting visitors.* By the time she had her jammies on the knocking had gone on non-stop. *That's just rude. You'd think they'd know no one's there or that they're unwanted by now.*

The knocking grew louder and louder, and Nicole knew that the knocks were coming closer – she jumped when there was a knock at her bedroom door.

"*Go away!*"

She sighed in relief when the knocking stopped. *You'd think anyone with half a brain would know not to look someone up this late at night...*

Things had to change so she looked up John Zachery's website on her laptop the next morning. She didn't want to be gullible, but it occurred to her that if John Zachery could summon whatever ghost he wanted when he wanted them to appear he could be more powerful than her. *What if he's not a fake, but someone who has more control over his Gift than I do?* There was a list of upcoming appearances on his website and her eyes alighted on a show at a psychic fair next month.

She clicked on the link to the psychic fair's information and website. Her eyes widened at the list of people making appearances and their purported abilities. *This could be good. Even if John Zachery is a fake, maybe there is someone there who isn't? Someone I can talk to?*

Even if the psychics are phonies what about the people who come here? I will be surrounded by people who are open to the thought of paranormal abilities. Who think it's cool instead of something weird or delusional. Maybe I can find someone to hang with?

If any of the psychics were real she didn't fault them for making money off their Gifts. She hadn't been born independently wealthy herself, and couldn't afford to work for free either. Yet, she wouldn't be able to help ghosts if she had to work a regular nine-to-five job, which is why most of the ghosts found ways to pay her back. The information she picked up from ghosts sometimes had monetary value, they either offered financial expertise or the location of hidden assets. They usually reached an agreement on a percentage that was fair and reasonable for her efforts as a means to compensate her for her time. She'd felt funny accepting this arrangement at first, but Grandma told her, "Don't ask for it, but don't turn it down either."

Some of the ghosts assumed they were still alive, and had to pay her for her time as they would for any other service provider. Some were aware they were dead, but knowing she still had to pay her way were willing to compensate her for running errands for them.

Her cover story to her landlady Mrs Phillips, and anyone else who bothered to ask, was that she was self employed as a freelance writer and researcher. She wasn't sure if Mrs Phillips was satisfied with this story, but it was the best she could give.

* * *

The fair was in full swing by the time Nicole made it there. There was a booth full of John Zachery's products at the front, books and pictures for autographing. There was a life-size picture of John Zachery, and people were taking pictures of themselves with it. *They treat him like he's a superstar!*

Either John Zachery was a fake playing the crowd, or else he was more powerful than she was. She saw that the booth was selling his autobiography. *I may be a sucker, but I'm buying it. I should be able to tell if he's real or not by what it says.* It was too bad she didn't have the time to peruse it right now, but that could wait until later.

If I get it signed it'd be an excuse to get close to him. Maybe I'll sense something if he's nearby? She wondered if her senses could detect someone who had the same sort of abilities as her.

She thought she was heading in early, but found the best seats were taken already. *Did they overbook the place? It's packed! Don't the fire codes put a limit on how many people you can pack into a room?* She may have her doubts about John Zachery's powers, but she trusted his business sense. She thought his handlers would know how to run a professional show.

Some people would take seats, but then allow them to be taken over by other people. They were annoyed, but didn't put up much resistance at being displaced. Nicole saw a young man with curly brown hair take a seat in the middle when a group of old ladies squeezed him out. The way he rolled his eyes made her think he was one who wouldn't allow respect for his elders to cheat him out of a seat, but other than the eye roll he didn't protest.

I don't get it. If he's respectful he wouldn't do the eye roll. If he were pushy he wouldn't allow himself to be unseated.

She'd been looking at him too long, and he noticed it. His brows drew together. *Great, now he's going to think I'm creepy* – when he smiled she rolled her eyes. *No, it's worse, he thinks I'm interested.*

The young man walked up to her and stood directly in front of her. He waved his hand in front of her and she felt a draft. *He's a ghost!* She glanced at all the people who were standing. The organizers hadn't overbooked after all. The extra people were ghosts.

"Hello, can you hear me?" the young man asked.

Nicole merely nodded "yes" because she was in a public place.

"You can hear me! You must be the real deal!"

She couldn't stop herself from asking under her breath, "Ghosts visit psychic fairs too?"

"Yeah, I hope to find someone I can talk to. Most of these 'psychics' are either charlatans or exaggerating," the young man said.

"Exaggerating?" Nicole's brows came together.

"They aren't as powerful or sensitive as they claim to be. Some can tell that I'm in the room, but can't tell what I'm saying or else it takes them a lot of preparation to be able to hear anything."

"Preparation?" Nicole felt like she was completely clueless.

The young man rolled his eyes, "You obviously don't have any problems connecting to ghosts, but some of these psychics need to warm themselves up."

Nicole snorted, "I wish I was able to turn it on and off whenever I wanted."

"They'd wish they had your power if they knew you had it," the young man said.

"I'm Bryce Wilson. I had a blog documenting paranormal research. I was open to the concept of the supernatural, but applied scientific methods to its study. I debunked various quacks and charlatans." He laughed bitterly, "I ended up dying young in a car accident, and am experiencing life after death for myself. Now I know that the mechanics of paranormal activity aren't as cut and dried as I thought they were."

He gestured to the building in general. "When I was living I would've been saying that these people operate by guess work and intuition. Now I know that some are more sensitive than others, but even if they have this sensitivity it waxes and wanes. Sometimes they are only guessing and sometimes they can actually sense things."

He pointed his thumb to the main show room, "If I were still alive I'd create a directory with a rating system for anyone who wants to use their services –"

The lights were turned off and loud music blared. A spotlight fell on a tall man in a dark suit and the announcer spoke breathlessly: "Welcome to this conjunction between planes, between the world of the Living and that of the Dead. Watch as the veil is parted and be amazed!"

The people sitting oohed and awed while the people standing, the ghosts, watched the show with silent intensity. Their stares would've been unnerving to Nicole if they were looking at her. *Good thing he's got all their attention. They look like vultures waiting for their next meal.* Nicole shuddered.

"Why don't we do a test?" Bryce asked.

"Test?" Nicole frowned.

"See if he's real or not?" Bryce grinned.

Nicole sighed and nodded, "Might as well. That's what I'm here for too."

"I am John Zachery and I'm here to help you." The man on the stage said. "Who shall be first?"

Bryce got up and waved his arms, "Pick me!"

His cry was in counterpoint to the reverent hush of the rest of the show's audience.

Bryce got up and ran down the aisles while everyone else stayed in their seats. John Zachery was oblivious to the ruckus he was making, but John Zachery's assistants were coaxing crowd members to go up. A silver-haired woman was chosen and brought forward.

"Nnnn –" Bryce gritted between clenched teeth as the woman was placed in front of a microphone.

Bryce screamed into the microphone. "CHOOSE ME!" If he'd been living his voice would've been amplified, but instead his scream was turned into static. "I'm here!" Bryce said pounding on the microphone with his finger which produced pounding bursts of static.

John Zachery was frowning, "I'm afraid we're experiencing technical difficulties –"

"Ah forget it," Bryce snorted and went back to his seat beside Nicole. "This is a colossal waste of time. I know places where these people could get better service at a better price."

"You know of real psychics?" Nicole asked in a whisper.

Bryce nodded, "You're the best I've seen. They're not up to your level."

"Show me," Nicole said.

"Maureen's got a booth here. I can take you to her," Bryce started to walk out.

As soon as Nicole stood up one of John Zachery's assistants approached her.

"Would you like to go up?" the young woman asked.

Nicole shook her head, "no".

There was a frown as she walked out of the hall, but no one made a move to stop her. Nicole found that she wasn't the only one walking out on John Zachery's show. All the people, ghosts, who'd been standing left too. At first it was a trickle, but as John Zachery kept talking it became a stream. *Whatever you do, don't look anyone in the eye!* Nicole told herself. She was used to handling ghosts one at a time, but now she was fully immersed in a throng. She felt as if she were in a blizzard, but she forced herself not to flinch. They didn't touch her physically, but their minds overlapped with hers. It was all she could do to shut out their thoughts, feelings, memories and regrets. It was too much to ask anyone to handle at once.

She saw Bryce at the side of the hall's doors and drifted to the right. She made a slow gradual shift in order not to be in contact with any of the ghosts. *Slow and steady,* Nicole coached herself. *No sudden moves.* It felt like she walked a mile before she was able to finally emerge from the stream, but she saw she was only six feet from the entrance. The line kept moving on even after she left it. *It's too much! Too much to ask anyone to help that many at once! I can't be the only one out there capable of helping them!* She hoped that there were enough psychics at the fair to deal with them –

Bryce was frowning, "Are you alright?"

Nicole sighed, "You aren't the only one who wanted to leave."

He glanced at the steady stream that he was oblivious to, but said, "Oh –"

"Are you sure you're up to following me?" he asked.

"Give me a minute," Nicole said.

Neither of them moved until her heartbeat and breathing returned to normal. "I'm ready now," Nicole said.

"I better take you to Maureen – she'll know what to do," Bryce said.

She followed Bryce as he led her to a booth. They came to a cream-colored tent with a beaded curtain at its entrance. Bryce walked through the curtain. The beads didn't part for him but they made a rustling noise like a wind-chime as he passed through them.

"I'm only open to paying customers now," a woman's voice said.

"I've got someone to see you, Maureen – someone living," Nicole heard Bryce say.

"Send them in," Maureen said.

The curtain rustled without parting again when Bryce put his head out of the curtain. "You can come in now."

Nicole nodded and followed him in, brushing past him. Images of his life flowed into her mind as their minds overlapped. The monotony of being an office drone was absorbed all at once. Nicole yawned and her energy levels went down as if she'd put in a twenty-four hour shift without any breaks.

"What have you done to this girl!" Maureen said.

Nicole's eyes were closed, but she felt the brush of soft fabric against her face, and a warm hand being placed on her forehead. She forced herself to open her eyes and saw a woman with a mane of long, frosted silver hair, and flowing cream robes in the softest cotton. The woman's face was as rounded as a Buddha, but she didn't look serene at this moment.

"Take a seat," she commanded. "I'll make you some tea," Maureen said.

There was a separate room curtained off away from her table and Nicole heard her rummage around for utensils and pour water. She emerged from the room.

"It'll take a few minutes for the water to heat up." Maureen glanced at Nicole more closely. "You've got a pretty bad case of psychic shock."

"Psychic shock?" Nicole asked with a frown.

She found her curiosity gave her just the dose of interest she needed to stay awake.

"It's when you become fatigued and stressed by psychic over-stimulation. You need a break."

This made Nicole laugh bitterly. "I wish it were as easy as that."

"I want to show you something," Maureen said.

She put up a sign with a clock on it, "Be back –" She positioned the hands for an hour.

Bryce immediately disappeared from sight.

Nicole blinked, "I wish all ghosts were so polite."

"It's not about politeness, it's about erecting a barrier to psychic energy. You can set limits that ghosts have to respect if you apply your will to it," Maureen said.

"Not every ghost is polite and reasonable," Nicole frowned.

"It doesn't matter how pushy or scary a ghost is. They are nothing but free floating psychic energy which is like clay to a strong psychic," Maureen said.

She took out a planner from a desk. "Use this to set limits."

"Use a planner?" Nicole asked.

"Write in your hours of business, and set appointments with ghosts you want to have meetings with, the ghosts will appear at the times you set for them," Maureen said.

"The answer to my problems with ghosts is time management?" Nicole laughed.

"In the old days wards and spells would've been set, but all you need to do is channel your will into an object." She held up the book. "Best to use subtle methods first. This way you don't call attention to yourself. People will just assume it's a regular planner."

"I guess – but how do I get rid of the peeping toms and midnight callers?" Nicole said.

"Do you have your own space that you can arrange to your liking?"

Nicole nodded, "Yes."

"Put up 'keep out' signs on the doors of rooms you want privacy in. Have a business hours sign posted."

Nicole was laughing, "That's all I have to do?"

"You still need to try it out first. You may need something stronger, but you should see a cut down in the number of unwanted visitors you have."

Maureen took a card from the card holder on her table and wrote down a private address.

"Use this to contact with me if you need more help."

Nicole glanced at the fees posted in sight at the booth, and counted out the money.

Maureen blinked, "Thanks, but it's not necessary for a fellow psychic."

"I paid full price for an overpriced ticket and a book from a charlatan, I shouldn't be cheap with you."

Maureen nodded and put up no further arguments.

* * *

Nicole stopped at an office supply store on her way home and bought a large yearly planner and various signs: "keep out", "back by", "no trespassing", "hours of operation", that she could post around her apartment. When she got home she wrote up her schedule for the next day in the datebook and posted all the signs she'd bought at strategic locations.

I feel ridiculous doing this, but it'll be worth it if it works, Nicole thought as she turned herself in for the night.

She was startled awake by the sound of her alarm clock ringing. *I had a full night's sleep, and wasn't awakened by any noises.*

So far, Nicole was impressed, but the ultimate test would be to see what happened when she took her shower. She double checked to see that the perv wasn't lying in wait for her, and took her shower, which was completed without interruptions.

Breakfast was unhurried, but she was startled by the sound of a knock at her door. *I knew it was too good to last!* She rolled her eyes.

She assumed it was the phantom knocker starting up again, but still checked the door just in case it was Mrs Phillips. She saw a strange woman at the door. "You're open for business now?" the woman asked.

Nicole glanced at her clock and saw that it was nine thirty, which was the time she'd scheduled for "drop-ins". "Yes…"

There were more drop-ins, most of which needed more time then she could spare at that moment so she penciled them into later times in the datebook throughout the week.

She already had some chores she had to run when she initially made up the datebook. There were no more interruptions while she completed her tasks. She'd been shocked to be allowed to go her way in peace even when she knew she was looking at a ghost. An old man caught her eye, but instead of crossing her path he let her go her way with a nod of his head. She knew that she'd be seeing him at her next drop in time – Nicole found herself smiling. She finally had a life.

Unclaimed

Lesa Pascavis Smith

Sara Warner twirled the oversized stone that graced her finger. She knew all about hiding secrets. After all, she had been doing it since she was a child. Behind the shimmering beauty of the diamond, the stone was cold, hard, and also hiding a secret. The jeweler had pointed out a tiny fracture hiding beneath the surface of the sparkle and shine. Secrets seemed to be the theme inside the Warner mansion.

Sara picked up the bottle of sherry from her husband's desk. Even through her botulism-laden forehead, lines of disbelief formed. "You bought a what?"

"I believe you heard me the first time. It is really no secret. Not that we have any secrets between us, now, do we?" Her husband smiled while tapping his hand-carved pipe against the antique smoking stand. "I bought a six hundred dollar bottle of sherry and a corpse at an auction last month."

Sara covered her face with her hands before allowing them to slide down to her cheeks. Her skin pulled tighter. "Booth Warner, you have officially snapped."

He reclined in his desk chair, stroking the buttery mahogany leather. "My insanity has afforded you many pleasures, hasn't it? I suggest you tread lightly on my ego or else you might end up fodder for my next novel."

Sara could not deny that Booth's notoriety had afforded her a luxurious lifestyle. However, it was not his writing that had earned him such fame. She owed her gratitude to the television producer that turned his books into a series with a hot lead actor and a crazed cult following. If she were to be brutally honest, she would admit that Booth's checkbook was far more attractive to her than the actual man was.

"Personally, I found Charleston's idea ingenious." He opened the bottle and poured himself a generous glass of the straw-colored liquid. "The city was in dire need of financial help and the council voted to auction off the unclaimed body of a serial killer." He took a sip of the wine before continuing. "How utterly delicious."

"Booth –"

"Now calm down. It is all quite legal and all. I am certain the good folks of Charleston expected researchers and universities to get into a bidding war. A successful study on just what makes a serial killer would be quite an accomplishment for any institution. I am sure they never expected a novelist to place the winning bid."

Sara swatted at the plume of smoke beginning to surround her. "Booth, I swear, smoking is going to kill you, if I don't do it first. Please explain to me just what on earth possessed you to make such a gruesome purchase."

"Possessed. Good one, my dear," he said with a laugh. "It was quite philanthropic of me, don't you think? As for me, please do not waste your time trying to plot my demise. It would take a far craftier spirit than you, I'm afraid."

Sara lowered her head. The multitude of plastic surgeries it had taken to become a trophy of Booth Warner had managed to shield her from his barrage of constant insults; however, sometimes they still stung.

"All right, if you must have the details, I will tell you. Are you sure you want to hear them?" He raised his silvery eyebrows in an eerie dance.

"Stop it, Booth! You know I hate that gory stuff." She stood and adjusted her tiny skirt around her oddly tanned legs. "Please, just tell me where you plan on keeping that thing."

"Larry, if you please."

Sara's ears wiggled as she attempted to wrinkle her brow. "Who?"

"Larry Wingo. That thing has a name and it is Larry. From now on, please do not refer to him as 'the body' or 'the corpse,' or worse, 'that thing.'" Booth moved toward his wife, wrapping his arm around her slender waist. Stale tobacco from his breath slithered around her neck as he whispered in her ear. "They said he murdered four women. Plotted and planned his strategies for years. He was, by all accounts, a genius. His name is Larry. Understand?"

In vain, Sara tried to free herself from her husband's grip. "You don't have that, Larry, in this house, do you?"

"For heaven's sake, Sara. Do you actually think I would keep a corpse inside my own home?" Booth returned to his pipe. A long inhale followed by a short exhale and slight cough interrupted his thoughts. "Oh, yes. Corpse in the house. That is extreme, even for me. Other than your side of the bed, a dead body has never once been here."

Sara glared at him.

"Joking, my dear." Booth swirled the amber liquid inside the glass. "Actually, I've had Larry cremated and have placed his remains somewhere inside these four walls."

Sara's hand traveled to her stomach. "You are sick."

"All in the name of love and money, my dear. I think a little hide and seek with Larry would liven up the old homestead and make for an excellent adventure. Let's play a game, shall we?"

"Booth, please. No more games."

"Ah, all children love to play games and aren't you still that same little orphan girl you once were?" He took his checkbook from the desk drawer and waved it at her. "I will tell you this much, Larry's ashes are somewhere inside this house. I will give you two days to find him. If you do, I will give you fifty thousand dollars. And the game begins now!"

"Always with the orphan thing!" Sara stormed out of the office to the sound of his laughter.

The Venetian mirror in the hallway caught her reflection. She wiped the tears from her cheeks and moved closer, studying her image. Everything about her belonged to him. Her hair, eyes, nose, lips, body – all purchased by Booth. He had managed to take a poor, unclaimed child and turn her into a beautiful woman.

She ran her fingers across her smooth forehead. The Botox injections were as priceless to her as jewelry. The monthly invasion of poison into her skin not only erased years from her appearance, they also dulled the headaches that threatened to reveal her secret. Sara pretended to smooth her tresses in front of the glass at the sound of footsteps.

Lena appeared with a feather duster in hand. "Excuse me, Mrs Warner, but will your guest be staying for another night?"

"Guests?" Sara gave her image one last inspection. "We don't have any guests staying here."

"I'm sorry, Mrs Warner. The guest room looked like someone had been sleeping in there. My mistake."

"Oh, Mr Warner bought some things at the auction last month and had them delivered yesterday. He probably stored them in there."

"Yes, Ma'am," Lena said. "Should I straighten the room or leave it until Mr Warner tells me?"

"Leave it. I will take care of it. Thank you, Lena."

Sara headed to the room at the end of the upstairs hallway to begin her search for Larry. If it was a game Booth wanted, she would play. She would play and win.

Her heartbeat quickened at the thought of winning Booth's money. Not that he didn't give her anything she wanted. He did, but often with a price. This money would be her own and she liked the thought of that. She had discovered throughout her years as Mrs Warner that dollars could fill the vacant space inside her soul.

The door to the guest room was ajar. Sara stood outside it and took in a deep breath trying to recall each item in the room so she could spot anything new. Slowly, she pushed the door open further and went inside. The rumpled silk bedspread gave the appearance that someone or something had been sitting on the bed. Sara dropped to her knees and checked under the bed, finding not even a dust bunny.

She ran her fingers along the shelves of the mahogany bookcase along the far wall. The smoothness of the wood housed a slew of Booth's best sellers, but nothing else. Carved ivory and teak trinkets from their travels and a large stone of South African amethyst adorned the nightstand. From the painting on the walls to the candelabra on the dresser, everything appeared just the same as always.

The closet was empty except for spare pillows, linens and a shoebox. A pit formed in Sara's stomach at the thought of finding Larry's remains inside the cardboard coffin. She lifted the lid and momentarily held her breath. Inside was a brass-plated memory left over from her days as a waitress at the country club. Sara picked up the badge and let her fingers dance across the engraving. SARA. Once she aged out of the orphanage, the waitress job at the club was the first and also her only, thanks to Booth.

In the bottom of the box was an envelope addressed to her husband. Before she could open it, footsteps followed by Booth's muffled voice came from down the hallway. Sara placed the box back on the shelf, then wedged her tiny frame underneath the bed. If he found her, he would tease and torment her relentlessly for even trying to win his money.

At the corner of the bed, she could see the tips of his shoes. She held her breath, afraid even a single exhalation would catch his ear. Her heart thumped inside her chest as she lay against the floor. Booth took a seat on the edge of the bed. She released her breath, timing it perfectly with his movements. Sara stared at the backs of his Berluti shoes. One pair cost almost as much as she was trying to win. No matter, Sara craved the power the money would give her and longed to see her husband's face when she won.

"Ollie, Ollie oxen free," Booth said with a laugh.

Sara remained motionless. The odor of his pipe met with her nose. Without the visual image of Booth, his temples graying, ruggedly tanned skin and wearing his beloved tweed jacket, the tobacco smelled like burning tar. Her stomach turned. Then she spotted it. Another pair of shoes. Lena's.

"Excuse me, Mr Warner." Lena's feet moved foward a few inches inside the room. "Would you like for me to straighten up in here now?"

The bed above Sara shifted as Booth stood.

"Yes, that would be fine." His feet moved toward the door. "Wait. First, find Mrs Warner for me."

"Of course, Mr Warner."

Sara watched as four feet headed out of the room and listened as they made their way back down the hallway. She crawled out from underneath the bed and adjusted her clothing. The servant's stairway provided her escape to the kitchen. She grabbed a bottle of water from the fridge and took a few sips to help slow her racing heart. When Lena entered the kitchen with Booth closely behind, it appeared as if Sara had been there for some time.

"Booth," Sara said moving from the window. "I was just thinking that we should add some gardenias to the flower beds this spring. What do you think?"

Lena made her way past the couple and into the laundry room.

Booth joined his wife at the window. "Gardenias. Yes, they would look nice. I will speak to the gardener. And now, what about our little game of hide and seek?"

Sara smiled and shook her head. "Booth, I am far too busy to play your games."

"Busy. Oh, yes, planning the spring garden." Booth winked and headed outside to the garage.

Sara grabbed her head and sat down at the bar. The pounding behind her left eye had been absent for years, but now it was back and all too familiar. A four-day migraine was imminent unless she gave in to the secret of her past. Her hands pressed against her skull like a vise trying to stop the throbbing and block the voice. Through the chaos inside her head, someone called to her.

Sara. I can help you.

"Mrs Warner. Are you all right?" The housekeeper gently touched Sara's shoulder. "You are as white as a ghost."

"It's one of my dreadful headaches," Sara said. "I just need to lie down for a while."

Lena escorted Sara to the bedroom and pulled the shades. Once Sara was alone, she sat up in bed and called to him. "Larry. Is that you?"

The lamp on her nightstand flickered. Sara's breath suspended. A chill invaded her body, causing her stomach to knot. A serial killer was in the room with her.

Sara, you need to claim your gift. It is the only way you will ever truly be happy. Trust me. I turned to a life of crime trying to avoid my true calling. Don't make the same mistakes I did

"So you did kill all those women."

I didn't mean to. I became so confused. I thought their voices were the ones in my head. I heard spirits and they drove me to insanity.

"I would never. I am not like you. I would never kill anyone."

You are just like me. I, too, tried everything to block the voices and be normal. In the end, I was anything but normal. When I killed those women, for just a moment, I was in total control and no one or any voice could touch me.

Sara squeezed her skull tighter than before.

Your husband is very clever. Not in a million years would you be able to find my ashes. He has scattered them in the fireplace, the ashtray and even in the plants.

He never intended on you finding me. Even if you would have won the money, what would that have proved?

"That he cannot control me."

Even though you have never killed another person, you have killed your true self. Stand up to him. Claim your gift.

Sara knew Larry's spirit was right. It was time. She walked to the door with the intention of finding Booth and telling him her secret. She placed her hand on the crystal doorknob. It turned beneath her hand from an outside force. Her heart jumped.

Booth barged inside. "Lena said you weren't feeling well."

"It was just a headache." She sat down on the bed. "I was actually coming down to talk to you."

Booth leaned against the dresser. "You look so serious."

Sara cleared the years of fear from her throat. "To me, it is very serious. Ever since I was a child, I have had a special gift. At least I thought it was special until it cost me my family."

Booth pulled his pipe from his breast pocket, tapping it against the palm of his hand. "Are you talking about when you thought you could talk to dead people?"

Sara's jaw dropped. "How did you –"

"My dear, you should know by now that nothing escapes me. I had you thoroughly investigated before I ever asked you out on a date." He paused to light the pipe. "Everything is in your file. I know your so-called gift was the reason you were abandoned and never adopted."

Tears rolled down Sara's face. "I can't believe you have known all this time."

"It's not like I believed any of it. Lord, woman. If I had known bringing the remains of that criminal in this house would conjure up all this nonsense, I never would have."

"What if I told you it was true. I can communicate with spirits." She stared at her husband.

"I would say all that Botox has gone to your brain." He moved toward the door. "I have had enough of this for now."

Sara jumped from the bed and blocked the doorway. "I still have something to say. Larry told me where you scattered his ashes. He told me there are bits of his remains in the fireplace and plants."

Booth's face twisted. "Larry told you this?"

"Yes. A ghost told me. Now do you believe me?"

"If this is indeed true, my dear, all it means is you are the freak the couple from the orphanage said you were. No wonder you, as well as Larry, went unclaimed."

Booth turned and walked out of the room. Sara started to follow him.

Sara. Wait. It would be useless for you to follow him. He has made up his mind to let fear control him.

"Booth is not afraid of anything. He writes dark tales of horror, for goodness sake."

You're wrong, Sara. He is afraid of you. You are able to do something he cannot understand and that frightens him. Don't you see? That is why he tries to control you.

"That's enough. I'm tired of listening to you. I did what you said and he told me I was crazy."

Then go. Go after him. Beg his forgiveness and continue living your life with your gift hidden away forever. Leave your precious gift unclaimed. See how far that goes in helping you gain your life back.

"At least it is my decision."

Sara caught her image in the dresser mirror and froze. Before her was a broken woman she barely recognized.

"Larry, you are right. It is time to take control. Will you help me?"

He won't know what happened to him.

* * *

Booth was sitting behind his desk smoking his beloved pipe when Sara approached.

"I refuse to let you control me any longer."

Booth rested the pipe in the smoking stand and walked toward her. "And just how do you intend to do this, my dear?"

"By living my life and fully embracing my gift of communicating with spirits." She slipped her wedding band, flaws and all, from her finger. "And I intend on living it without you."

Booth raised his hand in protest. "I'm afraid that will never happen, my dear. We have this little thing called a prenup. You will be penniless." He tapped his pipe against the brass stand. "Insane and penniless."

Booth leaned over the stand to relight his pipe, sucking in several breaths through the stem. The ashes in the tray began swirling toward the chamber, causing him to inhale them. He clutched his throat as the ashes traveled inside him. He coughed violently, trying to force Larry's remains from his lungs.

Sara briefly turned away. Aspiration was not a pleasant thing to witness. "I told you smoking would kill you."

She stopped and took a final look at her blue-faced husband. "Oh, but you were right about one thing, my dear. Larry Wingo is a genius."

Breathless, Lena met Sara in the hallway. "Is Mr Warner all right?"

"Mr Warner is fine. He is laughing at something I said." Sara took Lena by the arm. "Let's go take a look at where we will plant those gardenias, shall we?"

The Bottle Imp

Robert Louis Stevenson

THERE WAS A MAN of the Island of Hawaii, whom I shall call Keawe; for the truth is, he still lives, and his name must be kept secret; but the place of his birth was not far from Honaunau, where the bones of Keawe the Great lie hidden in a cave. This man was poor, brave, and active; he could read and write like a schoolmaster; he was a first-rate mariner besides, sailed for some time in the island steamers, and steered a whaleboat on the Hamakua coast. At length it came in Keawe's mind to have a sight of the great world and foreign cities, and he shipped on a vessel bound to San Francisco.

This is a fine town, with a fine harbour, and rich people uncountable; and in particular, there is one hill which is covered with palaces. Upon this hill Keawe was one day taking a walk with his pocket full of money, viewing the great houses upon either hand with pleasure. "What fine houses these are!" he was thinking, "and how happy must those people be who dwell in them, and take no care for the morrow!" The thought was in his mind when he came abreast of a house that was smaller than some others, but all finished and beautified like a toy; the steps of that house shone like silver, and the borders of the garden bloomed like garlands, and the windows were bright like diamonds; and Keawe stopped and wondered at the excellence of all he saw. So stopping, he was aware of a man that looked forth upon him through a window so clear that Keawe could see him as you see a fish in a pool upon the reef. The man was elderly, with a bald head and a black beard; and his face was heavy with sorrow, and he bitterly sighed. And the truth of it is, that as Keawe looked in upon the man, and the man looked out upon Keawe, each envied the other.

All of a sudden, the man smiled and nodded, and beckoned Keawe to enter, and met him at the door of the house. "This is a fine house of mine," said the man, and bitterly sighed. "Would you not care to view the chambers?" So he led Keawe all over it, from the cellar to the roof, and there was nothing there that was not perfect of its kind, and Keawe was astonished.

"Truly," said Keawe, "this is a beautiful house; if I lived in the like of it I should be laughing all day long. How comes it, then, that you should be sighing?"

"There is no reason," said the man, "why you should not have a house in all points similar to this, and finer, if you wish. You have some money, I suppose?"

"I have fifty dollars," said Keawe; "but a house like this will cost more than fifty dollars."

The man made a computation. "I am sorry you have no more," said he, "for it may raise you trouble in the future; but it shall be yours at fifty dollars."

"The house?" asked Keawe.

"No, not the house," replied the man; "but the bottle. For, I must tell you, although I appear to you so rich and fortunate, all my fortune, and this house itself and its garden, came out of a bottle not much bigger than a pint. This is it."

And he opened a lockfast place, and took out a round-bellied bottle with a long neck; the glass of it was white like milk, with changing rainbow colours in the grain. Withinsides something obscurely moved, like a shadow and a fire. "This is the bottle," said the man; and, when Keawe laughed, "You do not believe me?" he added. "Try, then, for yourself. See if you can break it."

So Keawe took the bottle up and dashed it on the floor till he was weary; but it jumped on the floor like a child's ball, and was not injured.

"This is a strange thing," said Keawe. "For by the touch of it, as well as by the look, the bottle should be of glass." "Of glass it is," replied the man, sighing more heavily than ever; "but the glass of it was tempered in the flames of hell. An imp lives in it, and that is the shadow we behold there moving; or so I suppose. If any man buy this bottle the imp is at his command; all that he desires – love, fame, money, houses like this house, ay, or a city like this city – all are his at the word uttered. Napoleon had this bottle, and by it he grew to be the king of the world; but he sold it at the last, and fell. Captain Cook had this bottle, and by it he found his way to so many islands; but he, too sold it, and was slain upon Hawaii. For, once it is sold, the power goes and the protection; and unless a man remain content with what he has, ill will befall him."

"And yet you talk of selling it yourself?" Keawe said.

"I have all I wish, and I am growing elderly," replied the man. "There is one thing the imp cannot do – he cannot prolong life; and, it would not be fair to conceal from you, there is a drawback to the bottle; for if a man die before he sells it, he must burn in hell for ever."

"To be sure, that is a drawback and no mistake," cried Keawe. "I would not meddle with the thing. I can do without a house, thank God; but there is one thing I could not be doing with one particle, and that is to be damned." "Dear me, you must not run away with things," returned the man. "All you have to do is to use the power of the imp in moderation, and then sell it to someone else, as I do to you, and finish your life in comfort."

"Well, I observe two things," said Keawe. "All the time you keep sighing like a maid in love, that is one; and, for the other, you sell this bottle very cheap."

"I have told you already why I sigh," said the man. "It is because I fear my health is breaking up; and, as you said yourself, to die and go to the devil is a pity for anyone. As for why I sell so cheap, I must explain to you there is a peculiarity about the bottle. Long ago, when the devil brought it first upon earth, it was extremely expensive, and was sold first of all to Prester John for many millions of dollars; but it cannot be sold at all, unless sold at a loss. If you sell it for as much as you paid for it, back it comes to you again like a homing pigeon. It follows that the price has kept falling in these centuries, and the bottle is now remarkably cheap. I bought it myself from one of my great neighbours on this hill, and the price I paid was only ninety dollars. I could sell it for as high as eighty-nine dollars and ninety-nine cents, but not a penny dearer, or back the thing must come to me. Now, about this there are two bothers. First, when you offer a bottle so singular for eighty odd dollars, people suppose you to be jesting. And second – but there is no hurry about that – and I need not go into it. Only remember it must be coined money that you sell it for."

"How am I to know that this is all true?" asked Keawe.

"Some of it you can try at once," replied the man. "Give me your fifty dollars, take the bottle, and wish your fifty dollars back into your pocket. If that does not happen, I pledge you my honour I will cry off the bargain and restore your money."

"You are not deceiving me?" said Keawe. The man bound himself with a great oath.

"Well, I will risk that much," said Keawe, "for that can do no harm." And he paid over his money to the man, and the man handed him the bottle.

"Imp of the bottle," said Keawe, "I want my fifty dollars back." And sure enough he had scarce said the word before his pocket was as heavy as ever.

"To be sure this is a wonderful bottle," said Keawe.

"And now, good morning to you, my fine fellow, and the devil go with you for me!" said the man.

"Hold on," said Keawe, "I don't want any more of this fun. Here, take your bottle back."

"You have bought it for less than I paid for it," replied the man, rubbing his hands. "It is yours now; and, for my part, I am only concerned to see the back of you." And with that he rang for his Chinese servant, and had Keawe shown out of the house.

Now, when Keawe was in the street, with the bottle under his arm, he began to think. "If all is true about this bottle, I may have made a losing bargain," thinks he. "But perhaps the man was only fooling me." The first thing he did was to count his money; the sum was exact – forty-nine dollars American money, and one Chili piece. "That looks like the truth," said Keawe. "Now I will try another part."

The streets in that part of the city were as clean as a ship's decks, and though it was noon, there were no passengers. Keawe set the bottle in the gutter and walked away. Twice he looked back, and there was the milky, round-bellied bottle where he left it. A third time he looked back, and turned a corner; but he had scarce done so, when something knocked upon his elbow, and behold! it was the long neck sticking up; and as for the round belly, it was jammed into the pocket of his pilot- coat.

"And that looks like the truth," said Keawe.

The next thing he did was to buy a cork-screw in a shop, and go apart into a secret place in the fields. And there he tried to draw the cork, but as often as he put the screw in, out it came again, and the cork as whole as ever. "This is some new sort of cork," said Keawe, and all at once he began to shake and sweat, for he was afraid of that bottle.

On his way back to the port-side, he saw a shop where a man sold shells and clubs from the wild islands, old heathen deities, old coined money, pictures from China and Japan, and all manner of things that sailors bring in their sea-chests. And here he had an idea. So he went in and offered the bottle for a hundred dollars. The man of the shop laughed at him at the first, and offered him five; but indeed, it was a curious bottle – such glass was never blown in any human glass-works, so prettily the colours shown under the milky white, and so strangely the shadow hovered in the midst; so, after he had disputed awhile after the manner of his kind, the shopman gave Keawe sixty silver dollars for the thing, and set it on a shelf in the midst of his window.

"Now," said Keawe, "I have sold that for sixty which I bought for fifty – so, to say truth, a little less, because one of my dollars was from Chili. Now I shall know the truth upon another point."

So he went back on board his ship, and, when he opened his chest, there was the bottle, and had come more quickly than himself. Now Keawe had a mate on board whose name was Lopaka.

"What ails you?" said Lopaka, "that you stare in your chest?"

They were alone in the ship's forecastle, and Keawe bound him to secrecy, and told all.

"This is a very strange affair," said Lopaka; "and I fear you will be in trouble about this bottle. But there is one point very clear – that you are sure of the trouble, and you had better have the profit in the bargain. Make up your mind what you want with it; give the order, and if it is done as you desire, I will buy the bottle myself; for I have an idea of my own to get a schooner, and go trading through the islands."

"That is not my idea," said Keawe; "but to have a beautiful house and garden on the Kona Coast, where I was born, the sun shining in at the door, flowers in the garden, glass in the windows, pictures on the walls, and toys and fine carpets on the tables, for all the world like the house I was in this day – only a storey higher, and with balconies all about like the king's palace; and to live there without care and make merry with my friends and relatives." "Well," said Lopaka, "let us carry it back with us to Hawaii, and if all comes true, as you suppose, I will buy the bottle, as I said, and ask a schooner."

Upon that they were agreed, and it was not long before the ship returned to Honolulu, carrying Keawe and Lopaka, and the bottle. They were scarce come ashore when they met a friend upon the beach, who began at once to condole with Keawe.

"I do not know what I am to be condoled about," said Keawe.

"Is it possible you have not heard," said the friend, "your uncle – that good old man – is dead, and your cousin – that beautiful boy – was drowned at sea?"

Keawe was filled with sorrow, and, beginning to weep and to lament he forgot about the bottle. But Lopaka was thinking to himself, and presently, when Keawe's grief was a little abated, "I have been thinking," said Lopaka. "Had not your uncle lands in Hawaii, in the district of Kau?"

"No," said Keawe, "not in Kau; they are on the mountain-side – a little way south of Hookena."

"These lands will now be yours?" asked Lopaka.

"And so they will," says Keawe, and began again to lament for his relatives.

"No," said Lopaka, "do not lament at present. I have a thought in my mind. How if this should be the doing of the bottle? For here is the place ready for your house."

"If this be so," cried Keawe, "it is a very ill way to serve me by killing my relatives. But it may be, indeed; for it was in just such a station that I saw the house with my mind's eye."

"The house, however, is not yet built," said Lopaka.

"No, nor like to be!" said Keawe, "for though my uncle has some coffee and ava and bananas, it will not be more than will keep me in comfort; and the rest of that land is the black lava."

"Let us go to the lawyer," said Lopaka; "I have still this idea in my mind."

Now, when they came to the lawyer's, it appeared Keawe's uncle had grown monstrous rich in the last days, and there was a fund of money.

"And here is the money for the house!" cried Lopaka.

"If you are thinking of a new house," said the lawyer, "here is the card of a new architect, of whom they tell me great things."

"Better and better!" cried Lopaka. "Here is all made plain for us. Let us continue to obey orders." So they went to the architect, and he had drawings of houses on his table.

"You want something out of the way," said the architect. "How do you like this?" and he handed a drawing to Keawe.

Now, when Keawe set eyes on the drawing, he cried out aloud, for it was the picture of his thought exactly drawn. "I am for this house," thought he. "Little as I like the way it comes to me, I am in for it now, and I may as well take the good along with the evil."

So he told the architect all that he wished, and how he would have that house furnished, and about the pictures on the wall and the knick-knacks on the tables; and he asked the man plainly for how much he would undertake the whole affair.

The architect put many questions, and took his pen and made a computation; and when he had done he named the very sum that Keawe had inherited.

Lopaka and Keawe looked at one another and nodded.

"It is quite clear," thought Keawe, "that I am to have this house, whether or no. It comes from the devil, and I fear I will get little good by that; and of one thing I am sure, I will make no more wishes as long as I have this bottle. But with the house I am saddled, and I may as well take the good along with the evil."

So he made his terms with the architect, and they signed a paper; and Keawe and Lopaka took ship again and sailed to Australia; for it was concluded between them they should not interfere at all, but leave the architect and the bottle imp to build and to adorn that house at their own pleasure.

The voyage was a good voyage, only all the time Keawe was holding in his breath, for he had sworn he would utter no more wishes, and take no more favours from the devil. The time was up when they got back. The architect told them that the house was ready, and Keawe and Lopaka took a passage in the *Hall*, and went down Kona way to view the house, and see if all had been done fitly according to the thought that was in Keawe's mind.

Now, the house stood on the mountain-side, visible to ships. Above, the forest ran up into the clouds of rain; below, the black lava fell in cliffs, where the kings of old lay buried. A garden bloomed about that house with every hue of flowers; and there was an orchard of papaia on the one hand and an orchard of breadfruit on the other, and right in front, toward the sea, a ship's mast had been rigged up and bore a flag. As for the house, it was three storeys high, with great chambers and broad balconies on each. The windows were of glass, so excellent that it was as clear as water and as bright as day. All manner of furniture adorned the chambers. Pictures hung upon the wall in golden frames: pictures of ships, and men fighting, and of the most beautiful women, and of singular places; nowhere in the world are there pictures of so bright a colour as those Keawe found hanging in his house. As for the knick-knacks, they were extraordinary fine; chiming clocks and musical boxes, little men with nodding heads, books filled with pictures, weapons of price from all quarters of the world, and the most elegant puzzles to entertain the leisure of a solitary man. And as no one would care to live in such chambers, only to walk through and view them, the balconies were made so broad that a whole town might have lived upon them in delight; and Keawe knew not which to prefer, whether the back porch, where you got the land breeze, and looked upon the orchards and the flowers, or the front balcony, where you could drink the wind of the sea, and look down the steep wall of the mountain and see the *Hall* going by once a week or so between Kookena and the hills of Pele, or the schooners plying up the coast for wood and ava and bananas.

When they had viewed all, Keawe and Lopaka sat on the porch.

"Well," asked Lopaka, "is it all as you designed?"

"Words cannot utter it," said Keawe. "It is better than I dreamed, and I am sick with satisfaction."

"There is but one thing to consider," said Lopaka; "all this may be quite natural, and the bottle imp have nothing whatever to say to it. If I were to buy the bottle, and got no schooner after all, I should have put my hand in the fire for nothing. I gave you my word, I know; but yet I think you would not grudge me one more proof."

"I have sworn I would take no more favours," said Keawe. "I have gone already deep enough."

"This is no favour I am thinking of," replied Lopaka. "It is only to see the imp himself. There is nothing to be gained by that, and so nothing to be ashamed of; and yet, if I once saw him, I should be sure of the whole matter. So indulge me so far, and let me see the imp; and, after that, here is the money in my hand, and I will buy it."

"There is only one thing I am afraid of," said Keawe. "The imp may be very ugly to view; and if you once set eyes upon him you might be very undesirous of the bottle."

"I am a man of my word," said Lopaka. "And here is the money betwixt us."

"Very well," replied Keawe. "I have a curiosity myself. So come, let us have one look at you, Mr Imp." Now as soon as that was said, the imp looked out of the bottle, and in again, swift as a lizard; and there sat Keawe and Lopaka turned to stone. The night had quite come, before either found a thought to say or voice to say it with; and then Lopaka pushed the money over and took the bottle.

"I am a man of my word," said he, "and had need to be so, or I would not touch this bottle with my foot. Well, I shall get my schooner and a dollar or two for my pocket; and then I will be rid of this devil as fast as I can. For to tell you the plain truth, the look of him has cast me down."

"Lopaka," said Keawe, "do not you think any worse of me than you can help; I know it is night, and the roads bad, and the pass by the tombs an ill place to go by so late, but I declare since I have seen that little face, I cannot eat or sleep or pray till it is gone from me. I will give you a lantern, and a basket to put the bottle in, and any picture or fine thing in all my house that takes your fancy; – and be gone at once, and go sleep at Hookena with Nahinu."

"Keawe," said Lopaka, "many a man would take this ill; above all, when I am doing you a turn so friendly, as to keep my word and buy the bottle; and for that matter, the night and the dark, and the way by the tombs, must be all tenfold more dangerous to a man with such a sin upon his conscience, and such a bottle under his arm. But for my part, I am so extremely terrified myself, I have not the heart to blame you. Here I go then; and I pray God you may be happy in your house, and I fortunate with my schooner, and both get to heaven in the end in spite of the devil and his bottle."

So Lopaka went down the mountain; and Keawe stood in his front balcony, and listened to the clink of the horse's shoes, and watched the lantern go shining down the path, and along the cliff of caves where the old dead are buried; and all the time he trembled and clasped his hands, and prayed for his friend, and gave glory to God that he himself had escaped out of that trouble.

But the next day came very brightly, and that new house of his was so delightful to behold that he forgot his terrors. One day followed another, and Keawe dwelt there in perpetual joy. He had his place on the back porch; it was there he ate and lived, and read the stories in the Honolulu newspapers; but when anyone came by they would go in and view the chambers and the pictures. And the fame of the house went far and wide; it was called *Ka-Hale Nui* – the Great House – in all Kona; and sometimes the Bright House, for Keawe kept a Chinaman, who was all day dusting and furbishing; and the glass and the gilt, and the fine stuffs, and the pictures, shown as bright as the morning. As for Keawe himself, he could not walk in the chambers without singing, his heart was so enlarged; and when ships sailed by upon the sea, he would fly his colours on the mast.

So time went by, until one day Keawe went upon a visit as far as Kailua to certain of his friends. There he was well feasted; and left as soon as he could the next morning, and rode hard, for he was impatient to behold his beautiful house; and, besides, the night then coming on was the night in which the dead of old days go abroad in the sides of Kona; and having already meddled with the devil, he was the more chary of meeting with the dead. A little beyond Honaunau, looking far ahead, he was aware of a woman bathing in the edge of the sea; and she seemed a well grown girl, but he thought no more of it. Then he saw her white shift flutter as she put it on, and then her red holoku; and by the time he came abreast of her she was done with her toilet, and had come up from the sea, and stood by the track-side in her red holoku, and she was all freshened with the bath, and her eyes shone and were kind. Now Keawe no sooner beheld her than he drew rein.

"I thought I knew everyone in this country," said he. "How comes it that I do not know you?"

"I am Kokua, daughter of Kiano," said the girl, "and I have just returned from Oahu. Who are you?" "I will tell you who I am in a little," said Keawe, dismounting from his horse, "but not now. For I have a thought in my mind, and if you knew who I was, you might have heard of me, and would not give me a true answer. But tell me, first of all, one thing: Are you married?"

At this Kokua laughed out aloud. "It is you who ask questions," said she. "Are you married yourself?"

"Indeed, Kokua, I am not," replied Keawe, "and never thought to be until this hour. But here is the plain truth. I have met you here at the roadside, and I saw your eyes, which are like the stars, and my heart went to you as swift as a bird. And so now, if you want none of me, say so, and I will go on to my own place; but if you think me no worse than any other young man, say so, too, and I will turn aside to your father's for the night, and tomorrow I will talk with the good man."

Kokua said never a word, but she looked at the sea and laughed.

"Kokua," said Keawe, "if you say nothing, I will take that for the good answer; so let us be stepping to your father's door."

She went on ahead of him, still without speech; only sometimes she glanced back and glanced away again, and she kept the string of her hat in her mouth.

Now, when they had come to the door, Kiano came out on his verandah, and cried out and welcomed Keawe by name. At that the girl looked over, for the fame of the great house had come to her ears; and, to be sure, it was a great temptation. All that evening they were very merry together; and the girl was as bold as brass under the eyes of her parents, and made a mock of Keawe, for she had a quick wit. The next day he had a word with Kiano, and found the girl alone.

"Kokua," said he, "you made a mock of me all the evening; and it is still time to bid me go. I would not tell you who I was, because I have so fine a house, and I feared you would think too much of that house and too little of the man that loves you. Now you know all, and if you wish to have seen the last of me, say so at once."

"No," said Kokua; but this time she did not laugh, nor did Keawe ask for more.

This was the wooing of Keawe; things had gone quickly; but so an arrow goes, and the ball of a rifle swifter still, and yet both may strike the target. Things had gone fast, but they had gone far also, and the thought of Keawe rang in the maiden's head; she heard his voice in the breach of the surf upon the lava, and for this young man that she had seen but twice she would have left father and mother and her native islands. As for Keawe himself, his horse flew up the path of the mountain under the cliff of tombs, and the sound of the hoofs, and the sound of Keawe singing to himself for pleasure echoed in the caverns of the dead. He came to the Bright House, and still he was singing. He sat and ate in the broad balcony, and the Chinaman wondered at his master, to hear how he sang between the mouthfuls. The sun went down into the sea, and the night came; and Keawe walked the balconies by lamplight, high on the mountains, and the voice of his singing startled men on ships.

"Here am I now upon my high place," he said to himself. "Life may be no better; this is the mountain top; and all shelves about me towards the worse. For the first-time I will light up the chambers, and bathe in my fine bath with the hot water and the cold, and sleep alone in the bed of my bridal chamber."

So the Chinaman had word, and he must rise from sleep and light the furnaces; and as he wrought below, beside the boilers, he heard his master singing and rejoicing above him in the lighted chambers. When the water began to be hot the Chinaman cried to his master; and Keawe went into the bathroom; and the Chinaman heard him sing as he filled the marble basin; and heard him sing, and the singing broken, as he undressed; until of a sudden, the song ceased. The Chinaman listened, and listened; he called up the house to Keawe to ask if all were well, and Keawe answered him "Yes," and bad him go to bed; but there was no more singing in the Bright House; and all night long, the Chinaman heard his master's feet go round and round the balconies without repose.

Now the truth of it was this: as Keawe undressed for his bath, he spied upon his flesh a patch like a patch of lichen on a rock, and it was then that he stopped singing. For he knew the likeness of that patch, and knew that he was fallen in the Chinese Evil. Now, it is a sad thing for any man to fall into this sickness. And it would be a sad thing for anyone to leave a house so beautiful and so commodious, and depart from all his friends to the north coast of Molokai between the mighty cliff and the sea-breakers. But what was that to the case of the man Keawe, he who had met his love but yesterday, and won her but that morning, and now saw all his hopes break, in a moment, like a piece of glass?

Awhile he sat upon the edge of the bath; then sprang, with a cry and ran outside; and to and fro, to and fro, along the balcony, like one despairing.

"Very willingly could I leave Hawaii, the home of my fathers," Keawe was thinking. "Very lightly could I leave my house, the high-placed, the many-windowed, here upon the mountains. Very bravely could I go to Molokai, to Kalaupapa by the cliffs, to live with the smitten and to sleep there, far from my fathers. But what wrong have I done, what sin lies upon my soul, that I should have encountered Kokua coming cool from the sea-water in the evening? Kokua, the soul ensnarer! Kokua, the light of my life! Her may I never wed, her may I look upon no longer, her may I no more handle with my living hand; and it is for this, it is for you, O Kokua! that I pour my lamentations!" Now you are to observe what sort of a man Keawe was, for he might have dwelt there in the Bright House for years, and no one been the wiser of his sickness; but he reckoned nothing of that, if he must lose Kokua. And again, he might have wed Kokua even as he was; and so many would have done, because they have the souls of pigs; but Keawe loved the maid manfully, and he would do her no hurt and bring her in no danger.

A little beyond the midst of the night, there came in his mind the recollection of that bottle. He went round to the back porch, and called to memory the day when the devil had looked forth; and at the thought ice ran in his veins. "A dreadful thing is the bottle," thought Keawe, "and dreadful is the imp, and it is a dreadful thing to risk the flames of hell. But what other hope have I to cure the sickness or to wed Kokua? What!" he thought, "would I beard the devil once, only to get me a house, and not face him again to win Kokua?"

Thereupon he called to mind it was the next day the *Hall* went by on her return to Honolulu. "There must I go first," he thought, "and see Lopaka. For the best hope that I have now is to find that same bottle I was so pleased to be rid of."

Never a wink could he sleep; the food stuck in his throat; but he sent a letter to Kiano, and about the time when the steamer would be coming, rode down beside the cliff of the tombs. It rained; his horse went heavily; he looked up at the black mouths of the caves, and he envied the dead that slept there and were done with trouble; and called to mind how he had galloped by the day before, and was astonished. So he came down to Hookena, and there was all the country gathered for the steamer as usual. In the shed before the store they sat and jested and passed the news; but there was no matter of speech in Keawe's bosom, and he sat in their midst and looked without on the rain falling on the houses, and the surf beating among the rocks, and the sighs arose in his throat.

"Keawe of the Bright House is out of spirits," said one to another. Indeed, and so he was, and little wonder. Then the *Hall* came, and the whaleboat carried him on board. The after-part of the ship was full of Haoles who had been to visit the volcano, as their custom is; and the midst was crowded with Kanakas, and the forepart with wild bulls from Hilo and horses from Kau; but Keawe sat apart from all in his sorrow, and watched for the house of Kiano. There it sat, low upon the shore in the black rocks and shaded by the cocoa palms, and there by the door was a red holoku, no greater than a fly, and going to and fro with a fly's busyness.

"Ah, queen of my heart," he cried, "I'll venture my dear soul to win you!"

Soon after, darkness fell, and the cabins were lit up, and the Haoles sat and played at the cards and drank whisky as their custom is; but Keawe walked the deck all night; and all the next day, as they steamed under the lee of Maui or of Molokai, he was still pacing to and fro like a wild animal in a menagerie.

Towards evening they passed Diamond Head, and came to the pier of Honolulu. Keawe stepped out among the crowd and began to ask for Lopaka. It seemed he had become the owner of a schooner – none better in the islands – and was gone upon an adventure as far as Pola-Pola or Kahiki; so there was no help to be looked for from Lopaka. Keawe called to mind a friend of his, a lawyer in the town (I must not tell his name), and inquired of him. They said he was grown suddenly rich, and had a fine new house upon Waikiki shore; and this put a thought in Keawe's head, and he called a hack and drove to the lawyer's house.

The house was all brand new, and the trees in the garden no greater than walking-sticks, and the lawyer, when he came, had the air of a man well pleased.

"What can I do to serve you?" said the lawyer.

"You are a friend of Lopaka's," replied Keawe, "and Lopaka purchased from me a certain piece of goods that I thought you might enable me to trace."

The lawyer's face became very dark. "I do not profess to misunderstand you, Mr Keawe," said he, "though this is an ugly business to be stirring in. You may be sure I know nothing, but yet I have a guess, and if you would apply in a certain quarter I think you might have news."

And he named the name of a man, which, again, I had better not repeat. So it was for days, and Keawe went from one to another, finding everywhere new clothes and carriages, and fine new houses and men everywhere in great contentment, although, to be sure, when he hinted at his business their faces would cloud over.

"No doubt I am upon the track," thought Keawe. "These new clothes and carriages are all the gifts of the little imp, and these glad faces are the faces of men who have taken their profit and got rid of the accursed thing in safety. When I see pale cheeks and hear sighing, I shall know that I am near the bottle."

So it befell at last that he was recommended to a Haole in Beritania Street. When he came to the door, about the hour of the evening meal, there were the usual marks of the new house, and the young garden, and the electric light shining in the windows; but when the owner came, a shock of hope and fear ran through Keawe; for here was a young man, white as a corpse, and black about the eyes, the hair shedding from his head, and such a look in his countenance as a man may have when he is waiting for the gallows.

"Here it is, to be sure," thought Keawe, and so with this man he no ways veiled his errand. "I am come to buy the bottle," said he.

At the word, the young Haole of Beritania Street reeled against the wall.

"The bottle!" he gasped. "To buy the bottle!" Then he seemed to choke, and seizing Keawe by the arm carried him into a room and poured out wine in two glasses.

"Here is my respects," said Keawe, who had been much about with Haoles in his time. "Yes," he added, "I am come to buy the bottle. What is the price by now?"

At that word the young man let his glass slip through his fingers, and looked upon Keawe like a ghost. "The price," says he; "the price! you do not know the price?"

"It is for that I am asking you," returned Keawe. "But why are you so much concerned? Is there anything wrong about the price?"

"It has dropped a great deal in value since your time, Mr Keawe," said the young man, stammering. "Well, well, I shall have the less to pay for it," said Keawe. "How much did it cost you?" The young man was as white as a sheet. "Two cents," said he.

"What?" cried Keawe, "two cents? Why, then, you can only sell it for one. And he who buys it –" The words died upon Keawe's tongue; he who bought it could never sell it again, the bottle and the bottle imp must abide with him until he died, and when he died must carry him to the red end of hell.

The young man of Beritania Street fell upon his knees. "For God's sake buy it!" he cried. "You can have all my fortune in the bargain. I was mad when I bought it at that price. I had embezzled money at my store; I was lost else; I must have gone to jail."

"Poor creature," said Keawe, "you would risk your soul upon so desperate an adventure, and to avoid the proper punishment of your own disgrace; and you think I could hesitate with love in front of me. Give me the bottle, and the change which I make sure you have all ready. Here is a five-cent piece."

It was as Keawe supposed; the young man had the change ready in a drawer; the bottle changed hands, and Keawe's fingers were no sooner clasped upon the stalk than he had breathed his wish to be a clean man. And, sure enough, when he got home to his room and stripped himself before a glass, his flesh was whole like an infant's. And here was the strange thing: he had no sooner seen this miracle, than his mind was changed within him, and he cared naught for the Chinese Evil, and little enough for Kokua; and had but the one thought, that here he was bound to the bottle imp for time and for eternity, and had no better hope but to be a cinder for ever in the flames of hell. Away ahead of him he saw them blaze with his mind's eye, and his soul shrank, and darkness fell upon the light.

When Keawe came to himself a little, he was aware it was the night when the band played at the hotel. Thither he went, because he feared to be alone; and there, among happy faces, walked to and fro, and heard the tunes go up and down, and saw Berger beat the measure, and all the while he heard the flames crackle, and saw the red fire burning in the bottomless pit. Of a sudden the band played *Kiki-au-ao*; that was a song that he had sung with Kokua, and at the strain courage returned to him.

"It is done now," he thought, "and once more let me take the good along with the evil."

So it befell that he returned to Hawaii by the first steamer, and as soon as it could be managed he was wedded to Kokua, and carried her up the mountain-side to the Bright House.

Now it was so with these two, that when they were together, Keawe's heart was stilled; but so soon as he was alone he fell into a brooding horror, and heard the flames crackle, and saw the red fire burn in the bottomless pit. The girl, indeed, had come to him wholly; her heart leapt in her side at sight of him, her hand clung to his; and she was so fashioned from the hair upon her head to the nails upon her toes that none could see her without joy. She was pleasant in her nature. She had the good word always. Full of song she was, and went to and fro in the Bright House, the brightest thing in its three storeys, carolling like the birds. And Keawe beheld and heard her with delight, and then must shrink upon one side, and weep and groan to think upon the price that he had paid for her; and then he must dry his eyes, and wash his face, and go and sit with her on the broad balconies joining in her songs, and, with a sick spirit, answering her smiles.

There came a day when her feet began to be heavy and her songs more rare; and now it was not Keawe only that would weep apart, but each would sunder from the other and sit in opposite balconies with the whole width of the Bright House betwixt. Keawe was so sunk in his despair, he scarce observed the change, and was only glad he had more hours to sit alone and brood upon his destiny and was not so frequently condemned to pull a smiling face on a sick heart. But one day, coming softly through the house, he heard the sound of a child sobbing, and there was Kokua rolling her face upon the balcony floor, and weeping like the lost.

"You do well to weep in this house, Kokua," he said. "And yet I would give the head off my body that you (at least) might have been happy."

"Happy!" she cried. "Keawe, when you lived alone in your Bright House, you were the word of the island for a happy man; laughter and song were in your mouth, and your face was as bright as the sunrise. Then you wedded pour Kokua; and the good God knows what is amiss in her – but from that day you have not smiled. Ah!" she cried, "what ails me? I thought I was pretty, and I knew I loved him. What ails me that I throw this cloud upon my husband?"

"Poor Kokua," said Keawe. He sat down by her side, and sought to take her hand; but that she plucked away. "Poor Kokua," he said, again. "My poor child – my pretty. And I thought all this while to spare you! Well, you shall know all. Then, at least, you will pity poor Keawe; then you will understand how much he loved you in the past – that he dared hell for your possession – and how much he loves you still (the poor condemned one), that he can yet call up a smile when he beholds you."

With that, he told her all, even from the beginning.

"You have done this for me?" she cried. "Ah, well, then what do I care!" – and she clasped and wept upon him. "Ah, child!" said Keawe, "and yet, when I consider of the fire of hell, I care a good deal!"

"Never tell me," said she; "no man can be lost because he loved Kokua, and no other fault. I tell you, Keawe, I shall save you with these hands, or perish in your company. What! you loved me, and gave your soul, and you think I will not die to save you in return?"

"Ah, my dear! you might die a hundred times, and what difference would that make?" he cried, "except to leave me lonely till the time comes of my damnation?"

"You know nothing," said she. "I was educated in a school in Honolulu; I am no common girl. And I tell you, I shall save my lover. What is this you say about a cent? But all the world is not American. In England they have a piece they call a farthing, which is about half a cent. Ah! sorrow!" she cried, "that makes it scarcely better, for the buyer must be lost, and we shall find none so brave as my Keawe! But, then, there is France; they have a small coin there which they call a centime, and these go five to the cent or thereabout. We could not do better. Come, Keawe, let us go to the French islands; let us go to Tahiti, as fast as ships can bear us. There we have four centimes, three centimes, two centimes, one centime; four possible sales to come and go on; and two of us to push the bargain. Come, my Keawe! kiss me, and banish care. Kokua will defend you."

"Gift of God!" he cried. "I cannot think that God will punish me for desiring aught so good! Be it as you will, then; take me where you please: I put my life and my salvation in your hands."

Early the next day Kokua was about her preparations. She took Keawe's chest that he went with sailoring; and first she put the bottle in a corner; and then packed it with the richest of the clothes and the bravest of the knick-knacks in the house. "For," said she, "we must seem to be rich folks, or who will believe in the bottle?" All the time of her preparation she was as gay as a bird; only when she looked upon Keawe, the tears would spring in her eye, and she must run and kiss him. As for Keawe, a weight was off his soul; now that he had his secret shared, and some hope in front of him, he seemed like a new man, his feet went lightly on the earth, and his breath was good to him again. Yet was terror still at his elbow; and ever and again, as the wind blows out a taper, hope died in him, and he saw the flames toss and the red fire burn in hell.

It was given out in the country they were gone pleasuring to the States, which was thought a strange thing, and yet not so strange as the truth, if any could have guessed it. So they went to Honolulu in the *Hall*, and thence in the *Umatilla* to San Francisco with a crowd of Haoles, and at San Francisco took their passage by the mail brigantine, the *Tropic Bird* for Papeete, the chief place of the French in the south islands. Thither they came, after a pleasant voyage, on a fair day of the Trade Wind, and saw the reef with the surf breaking, and Motuiti with its palms, and the schooner riding within-side, and the white houses of the town low down along the shore among green trees, and overhead the mountains and the clouds of Tahiti, the wise island.

It was judged the most wise to hire a house, which they did accordingly, opposite the British Consul's, to make a great parade of money, and themselves conspicuous with carriages and horses. This it was very easy to do, so long as they had the bottle in their possession; for Kokua was more bold than Keawe, and whenever she had a mind, called on the imp for twenty or a hundred dollars. At this rate they soon grew to be remarked in the town; and the strangers from Hawaii, their riding and their driving, the fine holokus and the rich lace of Kokua, became the matter of much talk.

They got on well after the first with the Tahitian language, which is indeed like to the Hawaiian, with a change of certain letters; and as soon as they had any freedom of speech, began to push the bottle. You are to consider it was not an easy subject to introduce; it was not easy to persuade people you were in earnest, when you offered to sell them for four centimes the spring of health and riches inexhaustible. It was necessary besides to explain the dangers of the bottle; and either people disbelieved the whole thing and laughed or they thought the more of the darker part, became overcast with gravity, and drew away from Keawe and Kokua, as from persons who had dealings with the devil. So far from gaining ground, these two began to find they were avoided in the town; the children ran away from them screaming, a thing intolerable to Kokua; Catholics crossed themselves as they went by; and all persons began with one accord to disengage themselves from their advances.

Depression fell upon their spirits. They would sit at night in their new house, after a day's weariness, and not exchange one word, or the silence would be broken by Kokua bursting suddenly into sobs. Sometimes they would pray together; sometimes they would have the bottle out upon the floor, and sit all evening watching how the shadow hovered in the midst. At such times they would be afraid to go to rest. It was long ere slumber came to them, and if either dozed off, it would be to wake and find the other silently weeping in the dark, or perhaps, to wake alone, the other having fled from the house and the neighbourhood of that bottle, to pace under the bananas in the little garden, or to wander on the beach by moonlight.

One night it was so when Kokua awoke. Keawe was gone. She felt in the bed and his place was cold. Then fear fell upon her, and she sat up in bed. A little moonshine filtered through the shutters. The room was bright, and she could spy the bottle on the floor. Outside it blew high, the great trees of the avenue cried aloud, and the fallen leaves rattled in the verandah. In the midst of this Kokua was aware of another sound; whether of a beast or of a man she could scarce tell, but it was as sad as death, and cut her to the soul. Softly she arose, set the door ajar, and looked forth in the moonlit yard. There, under the bananas, lay Keawe, his mouth in the dust, and as he lay he moaned. It was Kokua's first thought to run forward and console him; her second potently withheld her. Keawe had borne himself before his wife like a brave man; it became her little in the hour of weakness to intrude upon his shame. With the thought she drew back into the house.

"Heavens!" she thought, "how careless have I been – how weak! It is he, not I that stands in this eternal peril; it was he, not I, that took the curse upon his soul. It is for my sake, and for the love of a creature of so little worth and such poor help, that he now beholds so close to him the flames of hell – ay, and smells the smoke of it, lying without there in the wind and moonlight. Am I so dull of spirit that never till now have I surmised my duty, or have I seen it before and turned aside? But now, at least, I take upon my soul in both the hands of my affection; now I say farewell to the white steps of heaven and the waiting faces of my friends. A love for a love, and let mine be equalled with Keawe's! A soul for a soul, and be it mine to perish!"

She was a deft woman with her hands, and was soon apparelled. She took in her hands the change – the precious centimes they kept ever at their side; for this coin is little used, and they had made provision at a Government office. When she was forth in the avenue clouds came on the wind, and the moon was blackened. The town slept, and she knew not whither to turn till she heard one coughing in the shadow of the trees.

"Old man," said Kokua, "what do you here abroad in the cold night?"

The old man could scarce express himself for coughing, but she made out that he was old and poor, and a stranger in the island.

"Will you do me a service?" said Kokua. "As one stranger to another, and as an old man to a young woman, will you help a daughter of Hawaii?"

"Ah," said the old man. "So you are the witch from the eight islands, and even my old soul you seek to entangle. But I have heard of you, and defy your wickedness."

"Sit down here," said Kokua, "and let me tell you a tale." And she told him the story of Keawe from the beginning to the end.

"And now," said she, "I am his wife, whom he bought with his soul's welfare. And what should I do? If I went to him myself and offered to buy it, he would refuse. But if you go, he will sell it eagerly; I will await you here; you will buy it for four centimes, and I will buy it again for three. And the Lord strengthen a poor girl!"

"If you meant falsely," said the old man, "I think God would strike you dead."

"He would!" cried Kokua. "Be sure he would. I could not be so treacherous – God would not suffer it."

"Give me the four centimes and await me here," said the old man.

Now, when Kokua stood alone in the street, her spirit died. The wind roared in the trees, and it seemed to her the rushing of the flames of hell; the shadows tossed in the light of the street lamp, and they seemed to her the snatching hands of evil ones. If she had had the strength, she must have run away, and if she had had the breath she must have screamed aloud; but, in truth, she could do neither, and stood and trembled in the avenue, like an affrighted child. Then she saw the old man returning, and he had the bottle in his hand.

"I have done your bidding," said he. "I left your husband weeping like a child; tonight he will sleep easy." And he held the bottle forth.

"Before you give it me," Kokua panted, "take the good with the evil – ask to be delivered from your cough." "I am an old man," replied the other, "and too near the gate of the grave to take a favour from the devil. But what is this? Why do you not take the bottle? Do you hesitate?"

"Not hesitate!" cried Kokua. "I am only weak. Give me a moment. It is my hand resists, my flesh shrinks back from the accursed thing. One moment only!"

The old man looked upon Kokua kindly. "Poor child!" said he, "you fear; your soul misgives you. Well, let me keep it. I am old and can never more be happy in this world, and as for the next –"

"Give it me!" gasped Kokua. "There is your money. Do you think I am so base as that? Give me the bottle." "God bless you, child," said the old man.

Kokua concealed the bottle under her holoku, said farewell to the old man, and walked off along the avenue, she cared not whither. For all roads were not the same to her, and led equally to hell. Sometimes she walked, and sometimes ran; sometimes she screamed out loud in the night, and sometimes lay by the wayside in the dust and wept. All that she had heard of hell came back to her; she saw the flames blaze, and she smelt the smoke, and her flesh withered on the coals.

Near the day she came to her mind again, and returned to the house. It was even as the old man said – Keawe slumbered like a child. Kokua stood and gazed upon his face.

"Now, my husband," said she, "it is your turn to sleep. When you wake it will be your turn to sing and laugh. But for poor Kokua, alas! that meant no evil – for poor Kokua no more sleep, no more singing, no more delight, whether in earth or heaven."

With that she lay down in the bed by his side, and her misery was so extreme that she fell in a deep slumber instantly.

Late in the morning her husband woke her and gave her the good news. It seemed he was silly with delight, for he paid no heed to her distress, ill though she dissembled it. The words stuck in her mouth, it mattered not; Keawe did the speaking. She ate not a bite, but who was to observe it? for Keawe cleared the dish. Kokua saw and heard him, like some strange thing in a dream; there were times when she forgot or doubted, and put her hands to her brow; to know herself doomed and hear her husband babble, seemed so monstrous. All the while Keawe was eating and talking, and planning the time of their return, and thanking her for saving him, and fondling her, and calling her the true helper after all. He laughed at the old man that was fool enough to buy that bottle.

"A worthy old man he seemed," Keawe said. "But no one can judge by appearances. For why did the old reprobate require the bottle?"

"My husband," said Kokua, humbly, "his purpose may have been good."

Keawe laughed like an angry man.

"Fiddle-de-dee!" cried Keawe. "An old rogue, I tell you; and an old ass to boot. For the bottle was hard enough to sell at four centimes; and at three it will be quite impossible. The margin is not broad enough, the thing begins to smell of scorching – brrr!" said he, and shuddered. "It is true I bought it myself at a cent, when I knew not there were smaller coins. I was a fool for my pains; there will never be found another: and whoever has that bottle now will carry it to the pit."

"O my husband!" said Kokua. "Is it not a terrible thing to save oneself by the eternal ruin of another? It seems to me I could not laugh. I would be humbled. I would be filled with melancholy. I would pray for the poor holder." Then Keawe, because he felt the truth of what she said, grew the more angry. "Heighty-teighty!" cried he. "You may be filled with melancholy if you please. It is not the mind of a good wife. If you thought at all of me, you would sit shamed."

Thereupon he went out, and Kokua was alone.

What chance had she to sell that bottle at two centimes? None, she perceived. And if she had any, here was her husband hurrying her away to a country where there was nothing lower than a cent. And here – on the morrow of her sacrifice – was her husband leaving her and blaming her.

She would not even try to profit by what time she had, but sat in the house, and now had the bottle out and viewed it with unutterable fear, and now, with loathing, hid it out of sight.

By-and-by, Keawe came back, and would have her take a drive.

"My husband, I am ill," she said. "I am out of heart. Excuse me, I can take no pleasure."

Then was Keawe more wroth than ever. With her, because he thought she was brooding over the case of the old man; and with himself, because he thought she was right, and was ashamed to be so happy.

"This is your truth," cried he, "and this your affection! Your husband is just saved from eternal ruin, which he encountered for the love of you – and you take no pleasure! Kokua, you have a disloyal heart."

He went forth again furious, and wandered in the town all day. He met friends, and drank with them; they hired a carriage and drove into the country, and there drank again. All the time Keawe was ill at ease, because he was taking this pastime while his wife was sad, and because he knew in his heart that she was more right than he; and the knowledge made him drink the deeper.

Now there was an old brutal Haole drinking with him, one that had been a boatswain of a whaler, a runaway, a digger in gold mines, a convict in prisons. He had a low mind and a foul mouth; he loved to drink and to see other drunken; and he pressed the glass upon Keawe. Soon there was no more money in the company. "Here, you!" says the boatswain, "you are rich, you have been always saying. You have a bottle or some foolishness."

"Yes," says Keawe, "I am rich; I will go back and get some money from my wife, who keeps it."

"That's a bad idea, mate," said the boatswain. "Never you trust a petticoat with dollars. They're all as false as water; you keep an eye on her."

Now, this word struck in Keawe's mind; for he was muddled with what he had been drinking.

"I should not wonder but she was false, indeed," thought he. "Why else should she be so cast down at my release? But I will show her I am not the man to be fooled, I will catch her in the act."

Accordingly, when they were back in town, Keawe bade the boatswain wait for him at the corner, by the old calaboose, and went forward up the avenue alone to the door of his house. The night had come again; there was a light within, but never a sound; and Keawe crept about the corner, opened the back door softly, and looked in. There was Kokua on the floor, the lamp at her side; before her was a milk-white bottle, with a round belly and a long neck; and as she viewed it, Kokua wrung her hands.

A long time Keawe stood and looked in the doorway. At first he was struck stupid; and then fear fell upon him that the bargain had been made amiss, and the bottle had come back to him as it came at San Francisco; and at that his knees were loosened, and the fumes of the wine departed from his head like mists off a river in the morning. And then he had another thought; and it was a strange one, that made his cheeks to burn.

"I must make sure of this," thought he.

So he closed the door, and went softly round the corner again, and then came noisily in, as though he were but now returned. And, lo! by the time he opened the front door no bottle was to be seen; and Kokua sat in a chair and started up like one awakened out of sleep.

"I have been drinking all day and making merry," said Keawe. "I have been with good companions, and now I only come back for money, and return to drink and carouse with them again."

Both his face and voice were as stern as judgement, but Kokua was too troubled to observe.

"You do well to use your own, my husband," said she, and her words trembled.

"O, I do well in all things," said Keawe, and he went straight to the chest and took out money. But he looked besides in the corner where they kept the bottle, and there was no bottle there.

At that the chest heaved upon the floor like a sea-billow, and the house span about him like a wreath of smoke, for he saw he was lost now, and there was no escape. "It is what I feared," he thought. "It is she who bought it."

And then he came to himself a little and rose up; but the sweat streamed on his face as thick as the rain and as cold as the well-water.

"Kokua," said he, "I said to you today what ill became me. Now I return to carouse with my jolly companions," and at that he laughed a little quietly. "I will take more pleasure in the cup if you forgive me."

She clasped his knees in a moment; she kissed his knees with flowing tears.

"O," she cried, "I asked but a kind word!"

"Let us never one think hardly of the other," said Keawe, and was gone out of the house.

Now, the money that Keawe had taken was only some of that store of centime pieces they had laid in at their arrival. It was very sure he had no mind to be drinking. His wife had given her soul for him, now he must give his for hers; no other thought was in the world with him.

At the corner, by the old calaboose, there was the boatswain waiting.

"My wife has the bottle," said Keawe, "and, unless you help me to recover it, there can be no more money and no more liquor tonight."

"You do not mean to say you are serious about that bottle?" cried the boatswain.

"There is the lamp," said Keawe. "Do I look as if I was jesting?"

"That is so," said the boatswain. "You look as serious as a ghost."

"Well, then," said Keawe, "here are two centimes; you must go to my wife in the house, and offer her these for the bottle, which (if I am not much mistaken) she will give you instantly. Bring it to me here, and I will buy it back from you for one; for that is the law with this bottle, that it still must be sold for a less sum. But whatever you do, never breathe a word to her that you have come from me."

"Mate, I wonder are you making a fool of me?" asked the boatswain.

"It will do you no harm if I am," returned Keawe.

"That is so, mate," said the boatswain.

"And if you doubt me," added Keawe, "you can try. As soon as you are clear of the house, wish to have your pocket full of money, or a bottle of the best rum, or what you please, and you will see the virtue of the thing." "Very well, Kanaka," says the boatswain. "I will try; but if you are having your fun out of me, I will take my fun out of you with a belaying pin."

So the whaler-man went off upon the avenue; and Keawe stood and waited. It was near the same spot where Kokua had waited the night before; but Keawe was more resolved, and never faltered in his purpose; only his soul was bitter with despair.

It seemed a long time he had to wait before he heard a voice singing in the darkness of the avenue. He knew the voice to be the boatswain's; but it was strange how drunken it appeared upon a sudden. Next, the man himself came stumbling into the light of the lamp. He had the devil's bottle buttoned in his coat; another bottle was in his hand; and even as he came in view he raised it to his mouth and drank. "You have it," said Keawe. "I see that."

"Hands off!" cried the boatswain, jumping back. "Take a step near me, and I'll smash your mouth. You thought you could make a cat's-paw of me, did you?"

"What do you mean?" cried Keawe.

"Mean?" cried the boatswain. "This is a pretty good bottle, this is; that's what I mean. How I got it for two centimes I can't make out; but I'm sure you shan't have it for one."

"You mean you won't sell?" gasped Keawe.

"No, sir!" cried the boatswain. "But I'll give you a drink of the rum, if you like."

"I tell you," said Keawe, "the man who has that bottle goes to hell."

"I reckon I'm going anyway," returned the sailor; "and this bottle's the best thing to go with I've struck yet. No, sir!" he cried again, "this is my bottle now, and you can go and fish for another."

"Can this be true?" Keawe cried. "For your own sake, I beseech you, sell it me!"

"I don't value any of your talk," replied the boatswain. "You thought I was a flat; now you see I'm not; and there's an end. If you won't have a swallow of the rum, I'll have one myself. Here's your health, and goodnight to you!"

So off he went down the avenue toward town, and there goes the bottle out of the story.

But Keawe ran to Kokua light as the wind; and great was their joy that night; and great, since then has been the peace of all their days in the Bright House.

Bewitched

Edith Wharton

I

THE SNOW was still falling thickly when Orrin Bosworth, who farmed the land south of Lonetop, drove up in his cutter to Saul Rutledge's gate. He was surprised to see two other cutters ahead of him. From them descended two muffled figures. Bosworth, with increasing surprise, recognized Deacon Hibben, from North Ashmore, and Sylvester Brand, the widower, from the old Bearcliff farm on the way to Lonetop.

It was not often that anybody in Hemlock County entered Saul Rutledge's gate; least of all in the dead of winter, and summoned (as Bosworth, at any rate, had been) by Mrs Rutledge, who passed, even in that unsocial region, for a woman of cold manners and solitary character. The situation was enough to excite the curiosity of a less imaginative man than Orrin Bosworth.

As he drove in between the broken-down white gate-posts topped by fluted urns the two men ahead of him were leading their horses to the adjoining shed. Bosworth followed, and hitched his horse to a post. Then the three tossed off the snow from their shoulders, clapped their numb hands together, and greeted each other.

"Hallo, Deacon."

"Well, well, Orrin –." They shook hands.

"'Day, Bosworth," said Sylvester Brand, with a brief nod. He seldom put any cordiality into his manner, and on this occasion he was still busy about his horse's bridle and blanket.

Orrin Bosworth, the youngest and most communicative of the three, turned back to Deacon Hibben, whose long face, queerly blotched and mouldy-looking, with blinking peering eyes, was yet less forbidding than Brand's heavily-hewn countenance.

"Queer, our all meeting here this way. Mrs Rutledge sent me a message to come," Bosworth volunteered.

The Deacon nodded. "I got a word from her too – Andy Pond come with it yesterday noon. I hope there's no trouble here –."

He glanced through the thickening fall of snow at the desolate front of the Rutledge house, the more melancholy in its present neglected state because, like the gate-posts, it kept traces of former elegance. Bosworth had often wondered how such a house had come to be built in that lonely stretch between North Ashmore and Cold Corners. People said there had once been other houses like it, forming a little township called Ashmore, a sort of mountain colony created by the caprice of an English Royalist officer, one Colonel Ashmore, who had been murdered by the Indians, with all his family, long before the Revolution. This tale was confirmed by the fact that the ruined cellars of several smaller houses were still to be discovered under the wild growth of the adjoining slopes, and that the Communion plate of the moribund Episcopal church of Cold Corners was engraved with the name of Colonel Ashmore, who had given it to the church of Ashmore in the year 1723. Of the church itself no traces remained. Doubtless it had been a modest wooden edifice, built on piles, and the conflagration which had burnt the other houses to the ground's edge had reduced it utterly to ashes. The whole place, even in summer, wore a mournful solitary air, and people wondered why Saul Rutledge's father had gone there to settle.

"I never knew a place," Deacon Hibben said, "as seemed as far away from humanity. And yet it ain't so in miles."

"Miles ain't the only distance," Orrin Bosworth answered; and the two men, followed by Sylvester Brand, walked across the drive to the front door. People in Hemlock County did not usually come and go by their front doors, but all three men seemed to feel that, on an occasion which appeared to be so exceptional, the usual and more familiar approach by the kitchen would not be suitable.

They had judged rightly; the Deacon had hardly lifted the knocker when the door opened and Mrs Rutledge stood before them.

"Walk right in," she said in her usual dead-level tone; and Bosworth, as he followed the others, thought to himself; "Whatever's happened, she's not going to let it show in her face."

It was doubtful, indeed, if anything unwonted could be made to show in Prudence Rutledge's face, so limited was its scope, so fixed were its features. She was dressed for the occasion in a black calico with white spots, a collar of crochet-lace fastened by a gold brooch, and a gray woollen shawl crossed under her arms and tied at the back. In her small narrow head the only marked prominence was that of the brow projecting roundly over pale spectacled eyes. Her dark hair, parted above this prominence, passed tight and flat over the tips of her ears into a small braided coil at the nape; and her contracted head looked still narrower from being perched on a long hollow neck with cord-like throat-muscles. Her eyes were of a pale cold gray, her complexion was an even white. Her age might have been anywhere from thirty-five to sixty.

The room into which she led the three men had probably been the dining-room of the Ashmore house. It was now used as a front parlour, and a black stove planted on a sheet of zinc stuck out from the delicately fluted panels of an old wooden mantel. A newly-lit fire smouldered reluctantly, and the room was at once close and bitterly cold.

"Andy Pond," Mrs Rutledge cried to someone at the back of the house, "step out and call Mr Rutledge. You'll likely find him in the wood-shed, or round the barn somewheres." She rejoined her visitors. "Please suit yourselves to seats," she said.

The three men, with an increasing air of constraint, took the chairs she pointed out, and Mrs Rutledge sat stiffly down upon a fourth, behind a rickety bead-work table. She glanced from one to the other of her visitors.

"I presume you folks are wondering what it is I asked you to come here for," she said in her dead-level voice. Orrin Bosworth and Deacon Hibben murmured an assent; Sylvester Brand sat silent, his eyes, under their great thicket of eyebrows, fixed on the huge boot-tip swinging before him.

"Well, I allow you didn't expect it was for a party," continued Mrs Rutledge.

No one ventured to respond to this chill pleasantry, and she continued: "We're in trouble here, and that's the fact. And we need advice – Mr Rutledge and myself do." She cleared her throat, and added in a lower tone, her pitilessly clear eyes looking straight before her: "There's a spell been cast over Mr Rutledge."

The Deacon looked up sharply, an incredulous smile pinching his thin lips. "A spell?"

"That's what I said: he's bewitched."

Again the three visitors were silent; then Bosworth, more at ease or less tongue-tied than the others, asked with an attempt at humour: "Do you use the word in the strict Scripture sense, Mrs Rutledge?"

She glanced at him before replying: "That's how *he* uses it."

The Deacon coughed and cleared his long rattling throat. "Do you care to give us more particulars before your husband joins us?"

Mrs Rutledge looked down at her clasped hands, as if considering the question. Bosworth noticed that the inner fold of her lids was of the same uniform white as the rest of her skin, so that when she dropped them her rather prominent eyes looked like the sightless orbs of a marble statue. The impression was unpleasing, and he glanced away at the text over the mantelpiece, which read:

The Soul That Sinneth It Shall Die.

"No," she said at length, "I'll wait."

At this moment Sylvester Brand suddenly stood up and pushed back his chair. "I don't know," he said, in his rough bass voice, "as I've got any particular lights on Bible mysteries; and this happens to be the day I was to go down to Starkfield to close a deal with a man."

Mrs Rutledge lifted one of her long thin hands. Withered and wrinkled by hard work and cold, it was nevertheless of the same leaden white as her face. "You won't be kept long," she said. "Won't you be seated?"

Farmer Brand stood irresolute, his purplish underlip twitching. "The Deacon here – such things is more in his line..."

"I want you should stay," said Mrs Rutledge quietly; and Brand sat down again.

A silence fell, during which the four persons present seemed all to be listening for the sound of a step; but none was heard, and after a minute or two Mrs Rutledge began to speak again.

"It's down by that old shack on Lamer's pond; that's where they meet," she said suddenly.

Bosworth, whose eyes were on Sylvester Brand's face, fancied he saw a sort of inner flush darken the farmer's heavy leathern skin. Deacon Hibben leaned forward, a glitter of curiosity in his eyes.

"They – *who*, Mrs Rutledge?"

"My husband, Saul Rutledge... and her..."

Sylvester Brand again stirred in his seat. "Who do you mean by *her*?" he asked abruptly, as if roused out of some far-off musing.

Mrs Rutledge's body did not move; she simply revolved her head on her long neck and looked at him.

"Your daughter, Sylvester Brand."

The man staggered to his feet with an explosion of inarticulate sounds. "My – my daughter? What the hell are you talking about? My daughter? It's a damned lie... it's... it's..."

"Your daughter *Ora*, Mr Brand," said Mrs Rutledge slowly.

Bosworth felt an icy chill down his spine. Instinctively he turned his eyes away from Brand, and they rested on the mildewed countenance of Deacon Hibben. Between the blotches it had become as white as Mrs Rutledge's, and the Deacon's eyes burned in the whiteness like live embers among ashes.

Brand gave a laugh: the rusty creaking laugh of one whose springs of mirth are never moved by gaiety. "My daughter *Ora*?" he repeated.

"Yes."

"My *dead* daughter?"

"That's what he says."

"Your husband?"

"That's what Mr Rutledge says."

Orrin Bosworth listened with a sense of suffocation; he felt as if he were wrestling with long-armed horrors in a dream. He could no longer resist letting his eyes return to Sylvester Brand's face. To his surprise it had resumed a natural imperturbable expression. Brand rose to his feet. "Is that all?" he queried contemptuously.

"All? Ain't it enough? How long is it since you folks seen Saul Rutledge, any of you?" Mrs Rutledge flew out at them.

Bosworth, it appeared, had not seen him for nearly a year; the Deacon had only run across him once, for a minute, at the North Ashmore post office, the previous autumn, and acknowledged that he wasn't looking any too good then. Brand said nothing, but stood irresolute.

"Well, if you wait a minute you'll see with your own eyes; and he'll tell you with his own words. That's what I've got you here for – to see for yourselves what's come over him. Then you'll talk different," she added, twisting her head abruptly toward Sylvester Brand.

The Deacon raised a lean hand of interrogation.

"Does your husband know we've been sent for on this business, Mrs Rutledge?" Mrs Rutledge signed assent.

"It was with his consent, then –?"

She looked coldly at her questioner. "I guess it had to be," she said. Again Bosworth felt the chill down his spine. He tried to dissipate the sensation by speaking with an affectation of energy.

"Can you tell us, Mrs Rutledge, how this trouble you speak of shows itself… what makes you think…?"

She looked at him for a moment; then she leaned forward across the rickety bead-work table. A thin smile of disdain narrowed her colourless lips. "I don't think – I know."

"Well – but how?"

She leaned closer, both elbows on the table, her voice dropping. "I seen 'em."

In the ashen light from the veiling of snow beyond the windows the Deacon's little screwed-up eyes seemed to give out red sparks. "Him and the dead?"

"Him and the dead."

"Saul Rutledge and – and Ora Brand?"

"That's so."

Sylvester Brand's chair fell backward with a crash. He was on his feet again, crimson and cursing. "It's a God-damned fiend-begotten lie…"

"Friend Brand… friend Brand…" the Deacon protested.

"Here, let me get out of this. I want to see Saul Rutledge himself, and tell him –"

"Well, here he is," said Mrs Rutledge.

The outer door had opened; they heard the familiar stamping and shaking of a man who rids his garments of their last snowflakes before penetrating to the sacred precincts of the best parlour. Then Saul Rutledge entered.

II

AS HE CAME IN he faced the light from the north window, and Bosworth's first thought was that he looked like a drowned man fished out from under the ice – "self-drowned," he added. But the snow-light plays cruel tricks with a man's colour, and even with the shape of his features; it must have been partly that, Bosworth reflected, which transformed Saul Rutledge from the straight muscular fellow he had been a year before into the haggard wretch now before them.

The Deacon sought for a word to ease the horror. "Well, now, Saul – you look's if you'd ought to set right up to the stove. Had a touch of ague, maybe?"

The feeble attempt was unavailing. Rutledge neither moved nor answered. He stood among them silent, incommunicable, like one risen from the dead.

Brand grasped him roughly by the shoulder. "See here, Saul Rutledge, what's this dirty lie your wife tells us you've been putting about?"

Still Rutledge did not move. "It's no lie," he said.

Brand's hand dropped from his shoulder. In spite of the man's rough bullying power he seemed to be undefinably awed by Rutledge's look and tone.

"No lie? You've gone plumb crazy, then, have you?"

Mrs Rutledge spoke. "My husband's not lying, nor he ain't gone crazy. Don't I tell you I seen 'em?"

Brand laughed again. "Him and the dead?"

"Yes."

"Down by the Lamer pond, you say?"

"Yes."

"And when was that, if I might ask?"

"Day before yesterday."

A silence fell on the strangely assembled group. The Deacon at length broke it to say to Mr Brand: "Brand, in my opinion we've got to see this thing through."

Brand stood for a moment in speechless contemplation: there was something animal and primitive about him, Bosworth thought, as he hung thus, lowering and dumb, a little foam beading the corners of that heavy purplish underlip. He let himself slowly down into his chair. "I'll see it through."

The two other men and Mrs Rutledge had remained seated. Saul Rutledge stood before them, like a prisoner at the bar, or rather like a sick man before the physicians who were to heal him. As Bosworth scrutinized that hollow face, so wan under the dark sunburn, so sucked inward and consumed by some hidden fever, there stole over the sound healthy man the thought that perhaps, after all, husband and wife spoke the truth, and that they were all at that moment really standing on the edge of some forbidden mystery. Things that the rational mind would reject without a thought seemed no longer so easy to dispose of as one looked at the actual Saul Rutledge and remembered the man he had been a year before. Yes; as the Deacon said, they would have to see it through…

"Sit down then, Saul; draw up to us, won't you?" the Deacon suggested, trying again for a natural tone.

Mrs Rutledge pushed a chair forward, and her husband sat down on it. He stretched out his arms and grasped his knees in his brown bony fingers; in that attitude he remained, turning neither his head nor his eyes.

"Well, Saul," the Deacon continued, "your wife says you thought mebbe we could do something to help you through this trouble, whatever it is."

Rutledge's gray eyes widened a little. "No; I didn't think that. It was her idea to try what could be done."

"I presume, though, since you've agreed to our coming, that you don't object to our putting a few questions?"

Rutledge was silent for a moment; then he said with a visible effort: "No; I don't object."

"Well – you've heard what your wife says?"

Rutledge made a slight motion of assent. "And – what have you got to answer? How do you explain…?"

Mrs Rutledge intervened. "How can he explain? I seen 'em."

There was a silence; then Bosworth, trying to speak in an easy reassuring tone, queried: "That so, Saul?"

"That's so."

Brand lifted up his brooding head. "You mean to say you… you sit here before us all and say…"

The Deacon's hand again checked him. "Hold on, friend Brand. We're all of us trying for the facts, ain't we?" He turned to Rutledge. "We've heard what Mrs Rutledge says. What's your answer?"

"I don't know as there's any answer. She found us."

"And you mean to tell me the person with you was… was what you took to be…" the Deacon's thin voice grew thinner: "Ora Brand?"

Saul Rutledge nodded.

"You knew… or thought you knew… you were meeting with the dead?"

Rutledge bent his head again. The snow continued to fall in a steady unwavering sheet against the window, and Bosworth felt as if a winding-sheet were descending from the sky to envelop them all in a common grave.

"Think what you're saying! It's against our religion! Ora… poor child!… died over a year ago. I saw you at her funeral, Saul. How can you make such a statement?"

"What else can he do?" thrust in Mrs Rutledge.

There was another pause. Bosworth's resources had failed him, and Brand once more sat plunged in dark meditation. The Deacon laid his quivering finger-tips together, and moistened his lips.

"Was the day before yesterday the first time?" he asked.

The movement of Rutledge's head was negative.

"Not the first? Then when…"

"Nigh on a year ago, I reckon."

"God! And you mean to tell us that ever since –?"

"Well… look at him," said his wife. The three men lowered their eyes.

After a moment Bosworth, trying to collect himself, glanced at the Deacon. "Why not ask Saul to make his own statement, if that's what we're here for?"

"That's so," the Deacon assented. He turned to Rutledge. "Will you try and give us your idea… of… of how it began?"

There was another silence. Then Rutledge tightened his grasp on his gaunt knees, and still looking straight ahead, with his curiously clear unseeing gaze: "Well," he said, "I guess it begun away back, afore even I was married to Mrs Rutledge…" He spoke in a low automatic tone, as if some invisible agent were dictating his words, or even uttering them for him. "You know," he added, "Ora and me was to have been married."

Sylvester Brand lifted his head. "Straighten that statement out first, please," he interjected.

"What I mean is, we kept company. But Ora, she was very young. Mr Brand here he sent her away. She was gone nigh to three years, I guess. When she come back I was married."

"That's right," Brand said, relapsing once more into his sunken attitude.

"And after she came back did you meet her again?" the Deacon continued.

"Alive?" Rutledge questioned.

A perceptible shudder ran through the room.

"Well – of course," said the Deacon nervously.

Rutledge seemed to consider. "Once I did – only once. There was a lot of other people round. At Cold Corners fair it was."

"Did you talk with her then?"

"Only a minute."

"What did she say?"

His voice dropped. "She said she was sick and knew she was going to die, and when she was dead she'd come back to me."

"And what did you answer?"

"Nothing."

"Did you think anything of it at the time?"

"Well, no. Not till I heard she was dead I didn't. After that I thought of it – and I guess she drew me." He moistened his lips.

"Drew you down to that abandoned house by the pond?"

Rutledge made a faint motion of assent, and the Deacon added: "How did you know it was there she wanted you to come?"

"She… just drew me…"

There was a long pause. Bosworth felt, on himself and the other two men, the oppressive weight of the next question to be asked. Mrs Rutledge opened and closed her narrow lips once or twice, like some beached shell-fish gasping for the tide. Rutledge waited.

"Well, now, Saul, won't you go on with what you was telling us?" the Deacon at length suggested.

"That's all. There's nothing else."

The Deacon lowered his voice. "She just draws you?"

"Yes."

"Often?"

"That's as it happens…"

"But if it's always there she draws you, man, haven't you the strength to keep away from the place?"

For the first time, Rutledge wearily turned his head toward his questioner. A spectral smile narrowed his colourless lips. "Ain't any use. She follers after me…"

There was another silence. What more could they ask, then and there? Mrs Rutledge's presence checked the next question. The Deacon seemed hopelessly to revolve the matter. At length he spoke in a more authoritative tone. "These are forbidden things. You know that, Saul. Have you tried prayer?"

Rutledge shook his head.

"Will you pray with us now?"

Rutledge cast a glance of freezing indifference on his spiritual adviser. "If you folks want to pray, I'm agreeable," he said. But Mrs Rutledge intervened.

"Prayer ain't any good. In this kind of thing it ain't no manner of use; you know it ain't. I called you here, Deacon, because you remember the last case in this parish. Thirty years ago it was, I guess; but you remember. Lefferts Nash – did praying help him? I was a little girl then, but I used to hear my folks talk of it winter nights. Lefferts Nash and Hannah Cory. They drove a stake through her breast. That's what cured him."

"Oh –" Orrin Bosworth exclaimed.

Sylvester Brand raised his head. "You're speaking of that old story as if this was the same sort of thing?"

"Ain't it? Ain't my husband pining away the same as Lefferts Nash did? The Deacon here knows –"

The Deacon stirred anxiously in his chair. "These are forbidden things," he repeated. "Supposing your husband is quite sincere in thinking himself haunted, as you might say. Well, even then, what proof have we that the… the dead woman… is the spectre of that poor girl?"

"Proof? Don't he say so? Didn't she tell him? Ain't I seen 'em?" Mrs Rutledge almost screamed.

The three men sat silent, and suddenly the wife burst out: "A stake through the breast! That's the old way; and it's the only way. The Deacon knows it!"

"It's against our religion to disturb the dead."

"Ain't it against your religion to let the living perish as my husband is perishing?" She sprang up with one of her abrupt movements and took the family Bible from the what-not in a corner of the parlour. Putting the book on the table, and moistening a livid finger-tip, she turned the pages rapidly, till she came to one on which she laid her hand like a stony paper-weight. "See here," she said, and read out in her level chanting voice:

"'*Thou shalt not suffer a witch to live.*'

"That's in Exodus, that's where it is," she added, leaving the book open as if to confirm the statement.

Bosworth continued to glance anxiously from one to the other of the four people about the table. He was younger than any of them, and had had more contact with the modern world; down in Starkfield, in the bar of the Fielding House, he could hear himself laughing with the rest of the men at such old wives' tales. But it was not for nothing that he had been born under the icy shadow of Lonetop, and had shivered and hungered as a lad through the bitter Hemlock County winters. After his parents died, and he had taken hold of the farm himself, he had got more out of it by using improved methods, and by supplying the increasing throng of summer-boarders over Stotesbury way with milk and vegetables. He had been made a selectman of North Ashmore; for so young a man he had a standing in the county. But the roots of the old life were still in him. He could remember, as a little boy, going twice a year with his mother to that bleak hill-farm out beyond Sylvester Brand's, where Mrs Bosworth's aunt, Cressidora Cheney, had been shut up for years in a cold clean room with iron bars in the windows. When little Orrin first saw Aunt Cressidora she was a small white old woman, whom her sisters used to "make decent" for visitors the day that Orrin and his mother were expected. The child wondered why there were bars to the window. "Like a canary-bird," he said to his mother. The phrase made Mrs Bosworth reflect. "I do believe they keep Aunt Cressidora too lonesome," she said; and the next time she went up the mountain with the little boy he carried to his great-aunt a canary in a little wooden cage. It was a great excitement; he knew it would make her happy.

The old woman's motionless face lit up when she saw the bird, and her eyes began to glitter. "It belongs to me," she said instantly, stretching her soft bony hand over the cage.

"Of course it does, Aunt Cressy," said Mrs Bosworth, her eyes filling.

But the bird, startled by the shadow of the old woman's hand, began to flutter and beat its wings distractedly. At the sight, Aunt Cressidora's calm face suddenly became a coil of twitching features. "You she-devil, you!" she cried in a high squealing voice; and thrusting her hand into the cage she dragged out the terrified bird and wrung its neck. She was plucking the hot body, and squealing "she-devil, she-devil!" as they drew little Orrin from the room. On the way down the mountain his mother wept a great deal, and said: "You must never tell anybody that poor Auntie's crazy, or the men would come and take her down to the asylum at Starkfield, and the shame of it would kill us all. Now promise." The child promised.

He remembered the scene now, with its deep fringe of mystery, secrecy and rumour. It seemed related to a great many other things below the surface of his thoughts, things which stole up anew, making him feel that all the old people he had known, and who "believed in these things," might after all be right. Hadn't a witch been burned at North Ashmore? Didn't the summer folk still drive over in jolly buckboard loads to see the meeting-house where the trial had been held, the pond where they had ducked her and she had floated?... Deacon Hibben believed; Bosworth was sure of it. If he didn't, why did people from all over the place come to him when their animals had queer sicknesses, or when there was a child in the family that had to be kept shut up because it fell down flat and foamed? Yes, in spite of his religion, Deacon Hibben *knew*...

And Brand? Well, it came to Bosworth in a flash: that North Ashmore woman who was burned had the name of Brand. The same stock, no doubt; there had been Brands in Hemlock County ever since the white men had come there. And Orrin, when he was a child, remembered hearing his parents say that Sylvester Brand hadn't ever oughter married his own cousin, because of the blood. Yet the couple had had two healthy girls, and when Mrs Brand pined away and died nobody suggested that anything had been wrong with her mind. And Vanessa and Ora were the handsomest girls anywhere round. Brand knew it, and scrimped and saved all he could to send Ora, the eldest, down to Starkfield to learn book-keeping. "When she's married I'll send you," he used to say to little Venny, who was his favourite. But Ora never married. She was away three years, during which Venny ran wild on the slopes of Lonetop; and when Ora came back she sickened and died – poor girl! Since then Brand had grown more savage and morose. He was a hard-working farmer, but there wasn't much to be got out of those barren Bearcliff acres. He was said to have taken to drink since his wife's death; now and then men ran across him in the "dives" of Stotesbury. But not often. And between times he laboured hard on his stony acres and did his best for his daughters. In the neglected grave-yard of Cold Corners there was a slanting head-stone marked with his wife's name; near it, a year since, he had laid his eldest daughter. And sometimes, at dusk, in the autumn, the village people saw him walk slowly by, turn in between the graves, and stand looking down on the two stones. But he never brought a flower there, or planted a bush; nor Venny either. She was too wild and ignorant...

Mrs Rutledge repeated: "That's in Exodus."

The three visitors remained silent, turning about their hats in reluctant hands. Rutledge faced them, still with that empty pellucid gaze which frightened Bosworth. What was he seeing?

"Ain't any of you folks got the grit –?" his wife burst out again, half hysterically.

Deacon Hibben held up his hand. "That's no way, Mrs Rutledge. This ain't a question of having grit. What we want first of all is... proof..."

"That's so," said Bosworth, with an explosion of relief, as if the words had lifted something black and crouching from his breast. Involuntarily the eyes of both men had turned to Brand. He stood there smiling grimly, but did not speak.

"Ain't it so, Brand?" the Deacon prompted him.

"Proof that spooks walk?" the other sneered.

"Well – I presume you want this business settled too?"

The old farmer squared his shoulders. "Yes – I do. But I ain't a sperritualist. How the hell are you going to settle it?"

Deacon Hibben hesitated; then he said, in a low incisive tone: "I don't see but one way – Mrs Rutledge's."

There was a silence.

"What?" Brand sneered again. "Spying?"

The Deacon's voice sank lower. "If the poor girl *does* walk… her that's your child… wouldn't you be the first to want her laid quiet? We all know there've been such cases… mysterious visitations… Can any one of us here deny it?"

"I seen 'em," Mrs Rutledge interjected.

There was another heavy pause. Suddenly Brand fixed his gaze on Rutledge. "See here, Saul Rutledge, you've got to clear up this damned calumny, or I'll know why. You say my dead girl comes to you." He laboured with his breath, and then jerked out: "When? You tell me that, and I'll be there."

Rutledge's head drooped a little, and his eyes wandered to the window. "Round about sunset, mostly."

"You know beforehand?"

Rutledge made a sign of assent.

"Well, then – tomorrow, will it be?" Rutledge made the same sign.

Brand turned to the door. "I'll be there." That was all he said. He strode out between them without another glance or word. Deacon Hibben looked at Mrs Rutledge. "We'll be there too," he said, as if she had asked him; but she had not spoken, and Bosworth saw that her thin body was trembling all over. He was glad when he and Hibben were out again in the snow.

III

THEY THOUGHT THAT BRAND wanted to be left to himself, and to give him time to unhitch his horse they made a pretense of hanging about in the doorway while Bosworth searched his pockets for a pipe he had no mind to light.

But Brand turned back to them as they lingered. "You'll meet me down by Lamer's pond tomorrow?" he suggested. "I want witnesses. Round about sunset."

They nodded their acquiescence, and he got into his sleigh, gave the horse a cut across the flanks, and drove off under the snow-smothered hemlocks. The other two men went to the shed.

"What do you make of this business, Deacon?" Bosworth asked, to break the silence.

The Deacon shook his head. "The man's a sick man – that's sure. Something's sucking the life clean out of him."

But already, in the biting outer air, Bosworth was getting himself under better control. "Looks to me like a bad case of the ague, as you said."

"Well – ague of the mind, then. It's his brain that's sick."

Bosworth shrugged. "He ain't the first in Hemlock County."

"That's so," the Deacon agreed. "It's a worm in the brain, solitude is."

"Well, we'll know this time tomorrow, maybe," said Bosworth. He scrambled into his sleigh, and was driving off in his turn when he heard his companion calling after him. The Deacon explained that his horse had cast a shoe; would Bosworth drive him down to the forge near North Ashmore, if it wasn't too much out of his way? He didn't want the mare slipping about on the freezing snow, and he could probably get the blacksmith to drive him back and shoe her in Rutledge's shed. Bosworth made room for him under the bearskin, and the two men drove off, pursued by a puzzled whinny from the Deacon's old mare.

The road they took was not the one that Bosworth would have followed to reach his own home. But he did not mind that. The shortest way to the forge passed close by Lamer's pond, and Bosworth, since he was in for the business, was not sorry to look the ground over. They drove on in silence.

The snow had ceased, and a green sunset was spreading upward into the crystal sky. A stinging wind barbed with ice-flakes caught them in the face on the open ridges, but when they dropped down into the hollow by Lamer's pond the air was as soundless and empty as an unswung bell. They jogged along slowly, each thinking his own thoughts.

"That's the house… that tumble-down shack over there, I suppose?" the Deacon said, as the road drew near the edge of the frozen pond.

"Yes: that's the house. A queer hermit-fellow built it years ago, my father used to tell me. Since then I don't believe it's ever been used but by the gipsies."

Bosworth had reined in his horse, and sat looking through pine-trunks purpled by the sunset at the crumbling structure. Twilight already lay under the trees, though day lingered in the open. Between two sharply-patterned pine-boughs he saw the evening star, like a white boat in a sea of green.

His gaze dropped from that fathomless sky and followed the blue-white undulations of the snow. It gave him a curious agitated feeling to think that here, in this icy solitude, in the tumble-down house he had so often passed without heeding it, a dark mystery, too deep for thought, was being enacted. Down that very slope, coming from the grave-yard at Cold Corners, the being they called "Ora" must pass toward the pond. His heart began to beat stiflingly. Suddenly he gave an exclamation: "Look!"

He had jumped out of the cutter and was stumbling up the bank toward the slope of snow. On it, turned in the direction of the house by the pond, he had detected a woman's foot-prints; two; then three; then more. The Deacon scrambled out after him, and they stood and stared.

"God – barefoot!" Hibben gasped. "Then it *is*… the dead…"

Bosworth said nothing. But he knew that no live woman would travel with naked feet across that freezing wilderness. Here, then, was the proof the Deacon had asked for – they held it. What should they do with it?

"Supposing we was to drive up nearer – round the turn of the pond, till we get close to the house," the Deacon proposed in a colourless voice. "Mebbe then…"

Postponement was a relief. They got into the sleigh and drove on. Two or three hundred yards farther the road, a mere lane under steep bushy banks, turned sharply to the right, following the bend of the pond. As they rounded the turn they saw Brand's cutter ahead of them. It was empty, the horse tied to a tree-trunk. The two men looked at each other again. This was not Brand's nearest way home.

Evidently he had been actuated by the same impulse which had made them rein in their horse by the pond-side, and then hasten on to the deserted hovel. Had he too discovered those spectral foot-prints? Perhaps it was for that very reason that he had left his cutter and vanished in the direction of the house. Bosworth found himself shivering all over under his bearskin. "I wish to God the dark wasn't coming on," he muttered. He tethered his own horse near Brand's, and without a word he and the Deacon ploughed through the snow, in the track of Brand's huge feet. They had only a few yards to walk to overtake him. He did not hear them following him, and when Bosworth spoke his name, and he stopped short and turned, his heavy face was dim and confused, like a darker blot on the dusk. He looked at them dully, but without surprise.

"I wanted to see the place," he merely said.

The Deacon cleared his throat. "Just take a look… yes… We thought so… But I guess there won't be anything to *see*…" He attempted a chuckle.

The other did not seem to hear him, but laboured on ahead through the pines. The three men came out together in the cleared space before the house. As they emerged from beneath the trees they seemed to have left night behind. The evening star shed a lustre on the speckless snow, and Brand, in that lucid circle, stopped with a jerk, and pointed to the same light foot-prints turned toward the house – the track of a woman in the snow. He stood still, his face working. "Bare feet…" he said.

The Deacon piped up in a quavering voice: "The feet of the dead."

Brand remained motionless. "The feet of the dead," he echoed.

Deacon Hibben laid a frightened hand on his arm. "Come away now, Brand; for the love of God come away."

The father hung there, gazing down at those light tracks on the snow – light as fox or squirrel trails they seemed, on the white immensity. Bosworth thought to himself "The living couldn't walk so light – not even Ora Brand couldn't have, when she lived…" The cold seemed to have entered into his very marrow. His teeth were chattering.

Brand swung about on them abruptly. "*Now!*" he said, moving on as if to an assault, his head bowed forward on his bull neck.

"Now – now? Not in there?" gasped the Deacon. "What's the use? It was tomorrow he said –." He shook like a leaf.

"It's now," said Brand. He went up to the door of the crazy house, pushed it inward, and meeting with an unexpected resistance, thrust his heavy shoulder against the panel. The door collapsed like a playing-card, and Brand stumbled after it into the darkness of the hut. The others, after a moment's hesitation, followed.

Bosworth was never quite sure in what order the events that succeeded took place. Coming in out of the snow-dazzle, he seemed to be plunging into total blackness. He groped his way across the threshold, caught a sharp splinter of the fallen door in his palm, seemed to see something white and wraithlike surge up out of the darkest corner of the hut, and then heard a revolver shot at his elbow, and a cry –

Brand had turned back, and was staggering past him out into the lingering daylight. The sunset, suddenly flushing through the trees, crimsoned his face like blood. He held a revolver in his hand and looked about him in his stupid way.

"They *do* walk, then," he said and began to laugh. He bent his head to examine his weapon. "Better here than in the churchyard. They shan't dig her up *now*," he shouted out. The two men caught him by the arms, and Bosworth got the revolver away from him.

IV

THE NEXT DAY Bosworth's sister Loretta, who kept house for him, asked him, when he came in for his midday dinner, if he had heard the news.

Bosworth had been sawing wood all the morning, and in spite of the cold and the driving snow, which had begun again in the night, he was covered with an icy sweat, like a man getting over a fever.

"What news?"

"Venny Brand's down sick with pneumonia. The Deacon's been there. I guess she's dying."

Bosworth looked at her with listless eyes. She seemed far off from him, miles away. "Venny Brand?" he echoed.

"You never liked her, Orrin."

"She's a child. I never knew much about her."

"Well," repeated his sister, with the guileless relish of the unimaginative for bad news, "I guess she's dying." After a pause she added: "It'll kill Sylvester Brand, all alone up there."

Bosworth got up and said: "I've got to see to poulticing the gray's fetlock." He walked out into the steadily falling snow.

Venny Brand was buried three days later. The Deacon read the service; Bosworth was one of the pall-bearers. The whole countryside turned out, for the snow had stopped falling, and at any season a funeral offered an opportunity for an outing that was not to be missed. Besides, Venny Brand was young and handsome – at least some people thought her handsome, though she was so swarthy – and her dying like that, so suddenly, had the fascination of tragedy.

"They say her lungs filled right up... Seems she'd had bronchial troubles before... I always said both them girls was frail... Look at Ora, how she took and wasted away! And it's colder'n all outdoors up there to Brand's... Their mother, too, *she* pined away just the same. They don't ever make old bones on the mother's side of the family... There's that young Bedlow over there; they say Venny was engaged to him... Oh, Mrs Rutledge, excuse *me*... Step right into the pew; there's a seat for you alongside of grandma..."

Mrs Rutledge was advancing with deliberate step down the narrow aisle of the bleak wooden church. She had on her best bonnet, a monumental structure which no one had seen out of her trunk since old Mrs Silsee's funeral, three years before. All the women remembered it. Under its perpendicular pile her narrow face, swaying on the long thin neck, seemed whiter than ever; but her air of fretfulness had been composed into a suitable expression of mournful immobility.

"Looks as if the stone-mason had carved her to put atop of Venny's grave," Bosworth thought as she glided past him; and then shivered at his own sepulchral fancy. When she bent over her hymn book her lowered lids reminded him again of marble eye-balls; the bony hands clasping the book were bloodless. Bosworth had never seen such hands since he had seen old Aunt Cressidora Cheney strangle the canary-bird because it fluttered.

The service was over, the coffin of Venny Brand had been lowered into her sister's grave, and the neighbours were slowly dispersing. Bosworth, as pall-bearer, felt obliged to linger and say a word to the stricken father. He waited till Brand had turned from the grave with the Deacon at his side. The three men stood together for a moment; but not one of them spoke. Brand's face was the closed door of a vault, barred with wrinkles like bands of iron.

Finally the Deacon took his hand and said: "The Lord gave –"

Brand nodded and turned away toward the shed where the horses were hitched. Bosworth followed him. "Let me drive along home with you," he suggested.

Brand did not so much as turn his head. "Home? What home?" he said; and the other fell back.

Loretta Bosworth was talking with the other women while the men unblanketed their horses and backed the cutters out into the heavy snow. As Bosworth waited for her, a few feet off, he saw Mrs Rutledge's tall bonnet lording it above the group. Andy Pond, the Rutledge farm-hand, was backing out the sleigh.

"Saul ain't here today, Mrs Rutledge, is he?" one of the village elders piped, turning a benevolent old tortoise-head about on a loose neck, and blinking up into Mrs Rutledge's marble face.

Bosworth heard her measure out her answer in slow incisive words. "No. Mr Rutledge he ain't here. He would'a' come for certain, but his aunt Minorca Cummins is being buried down to Stotesbury this very day and he had to go down there. Don't it sometimes seem zif we was all walking right in the Shadow of Death?"

As she walked toward the cutter, in which Andy Pond was already seated, the Deacon went up to her with visible hesitation. Involuntarily Bosworth also moved nearer. He heard the Deacon say: "I'm glad to hear that Saul is able to be up and around."

She turned her small head on her rigid neck, and lifted the lids of marble.

"Yes, I guess he'll sleep quieter now. And her too, maybe, now she don't lay there alone any longer," she added in a low voice, with a sudden twist of her chin toward the fresh black stain in the grave-yard snow. She got into the cutter, and said in a clear tone to Andy Pond: "'S long as we're down here I don't know but what I'll just call round and get a box of soap at Hiram Pringle's."

The Bolted Door

Edith Wharton

I

HUBERT GRANICE, pacing the length of his pleasant lamp-lit library, paused to compare his watch with the clock on the chimney-piece.

Three minutes to eight.

In exactly three minutes Mr Peter Ascham, of the eminent legal firm of Ascham and Pettilow, would have his punctual hand on the door-bell of the flat. It was a comfort to reflect that Ascham was so punctual – the suspense was beginning to make his host nervous. And the sound of the door-bell would be the beginning of the end – after that there'd be no going back, by God – no going back!

Granice resumed his pacing. Each time he reached the end of the room opposite the door he caught his reflection in the Florentine mirror above the fine old walnut *credence* he had picked up at Dijon – saw himself spare, quick-moving, carefully brushed and dressed, but furrowed, gray about the temples, with a stoop which he corrected by a spasmodic straightening of the shoulders whenever a glass confronted him: a tired middle-aged man, baffled, beaten, worn out.

As he summed himself up thus for the third or fourth time the door opened and he turned with a thrill of relief to greet his guest. But it was only the man-servant who entered, advancing silently over the mossy surface of the old Turkey rug.

"Mr Ascham telephones, sir, to say he's unexpectedly detained and can't be here till eight-thirty."

Granice made a curt gesture of annoyance. It was becoming harder and harder for him to control these reflexes. He turned on his heel, tossing to the servant over his shoulder: "Very good. Put off dinner."

Down his spine he felt the man's injured stare. Mr Granice had always been so mild-spoken to his people – no doubt the odd change in his manner had already been noticed and discussed below stairs. And very likely they suspected the cause. He stood drumming on the writing-table till he heard the servant go out; then he threw himself into a chair, propping his elbows on the table and resting his chin on his locked hands.

Another half hour alone with it!

He wondered irritably what could have detained his guest. Some professional matter, no doubt – the punctilious lawyer would have allowed nothing less to interfere with a dinner engagement, more especially since Granice, in his note, had said: "I shall want a little business chat afterward."

But what professional matter could have come up at that unprofessional hour? Perhaps some other soul in misery had called on the lawyer; and, after all, Granice's note had given no hint of his own need! No doubt Ascham thought he merely wanted to make another change in his will. Since he had come into his little property, ten years earlier, Granice had been perpetually tinkering with his will.

Suddenly another thought pulled him up, sending a flush to his sallow temples. He remembered a word he had tossed to the lawyer some six weeks earlier, at the Century Club. "Yes – my play's as good as taken. I shall be calling on you soon to go over the contract. Those theatrical chaps are so slippery – I won't trust anybody but you to tie the knot for me!" That, of course, was what Ascham would think he was wanted for. Granice, at the idea, broke into an audible laugh – a queer stage-laugh, like the cackle of a baffled villain in a melodrama. The absurdity, the unnaturalness of the sound abashed him, and he compressed his lips angrily. Would he take to soliloquy next?

He lowered his arms and pulled open the upper drawer of the writing-table. In the right-hand corner lay a thick manuscript, bound in paper folders, and tied with a string beneath which a letter had been slipped. Next to the manuscript was a small revolver. Granice stared a moment at these oddly associated objects; then he took the letter from under the string and slowly began to open it. He had known he should do so from the moment his hand touched the drawer. Whenever his eye fell on that letter some relentless force compelled him to re-read it.

It was dated about four weeks back, under the letter-head of "The Diversity Theatre."

"My Dear Mr Granice:

"I have given the matter my best consideration for the last month, and it's no use – the play won't do. I have talked it over with Miss Melrose – and you know there isn't a gamer artist on our stage – and I regret to tell you she feels just as I do about it. It isn't the poetry that scares her – or me either. We both want to do all we can to help along the poetic drama – we believe the public's ready for it, and we're willing to take a big financial risk in order to be the first to give them what they want. *But we don't believe they could be made to want this.* The fact is, there isn't enough drama in your play to the allowance of poetry – the thing drags all through. You've got a big idea, but it's not out of swaddling clothes.

"If this was your first play I'd say: *Try again*. But it has been just the same with all the others you've shown me. And you remember the result of 'The Lee Shore,' where you carried all the expenses of production yourself, and we couldn't fill the theatre for a week. Yet 'The Lee Shore' was a modern problem play – much easier to swing than blank verse. It isn't as if you hadn't tried all kinds –"

* * *

Granice folded the letter and put it carefully back into the envelope. Why on earth was he re-reading it, when he knew every phrase in it by heart, when for a month past he had seen it, night after night, stand out in letters of flame against the darkness of his sleepless lids?

"It has been just the same with all the others you've shown me."

That was the way they dismissed ten years of passionate unremitting work!

"You remember the result of 'The Lee Shore.'"

Good God – as if he were likely to forget it! He re-lived it all now in a drowning flash: the persistent rejection of the play, his sudden resolve to put it on at his own cost, to spend ten thousand dollars of his inheritance on testing his chance of success – the fever of preparation, the dry-mouthed agony of the "first night," the flat fall, the stupid press, his secret rush to Europe to escape the condolence of his friends!

"It isn't as if you hadn't tried all kinds."

No – he had tried all kinds: comedy, tragedy, prose and verse, the light curtain-raiser, the short sharp drama, the bourgeois-realistic and the lyrical-romantic – finally deciding that he would no longer "prostitute his talent" to win popularity, but would impose on the public his own theory of art in the form of five acts of blank verse. Yes, he had offered them everything – and always with the same result.

Ten years of it – ten years of dogged work and unrelieved failure. The ten years from forty to fifty – the best ten years of his life! And if one counted the years before, the silent years of dreams, assimilation, preparation – then call it half a man's life-time: half a man's life-time thrown away!

And what was he to do with the remaining half? Well, he had settled that, thank God! He turned and glanced anxiously at the clock. Ten minutes past eight – only ten minutes had been consumed in that stormy rush through his whole past! And he must wait another twenty minutes for Ascham. It was one of the worst symptoms of his case that, in proportion as he had grown to shrink from human company, he dreaded more and more to be alone... But why the devil was he waiting for Ascham? Why didn't he cut the knot himself? Since he was so unutterably sick of the whole business, why did he have to call in an outsider to rid him of this nightmare of living?

He opened the drawer again and laid his hand on the revolver. It was a small slim ivory toy – just the instrument for a tired sufferer to give himself a "hypodermic" with. Granice raised it slowly in one hand, while with the other he felt under the thin hair at the back of his head, between the ear and the nape. He knew just where to place the muzzle: he had once got a young surgeon to show him. And as he found the spot, and lifted the revolver to it, the inevitable phenomenon occurred. The hand that held the weapon began to shake, the tremor communicated itself to his arm, his heart gave a wild leap which sent up a wave of deadly nausea to his throat, he smelt the powder, he sickened at the crash of the bullet through his skull, and a sweat of fear broke out over his forehead and ran down his quivering face...

He laid away the revolver with an oath and, pulling out a cologne-scented handkerchief, passed it tremulously over his brow and temples. It was no use – he knew he could never do it in that way. His attempts at self-destruction were as futile as his snatches at fame! He couldn't make himself a real life, and he couldn't get rid of the life he had. And that was why he had sent for Ascham to help him...

The lawyer, over the Camembert and Burgundy, began to excuse himself for his delay.

"I didn't like to say anything while your man was about – but the fact is, I was sent for on a rather unusual matter –"

"Oh, it's all right," said Granice cheerfully. He was beginning to feel the usual reaction that food and company produced. It was not any recovered pleasure in life that he felt, but only a deeper withdrawal into himself. It was easier to go on automatically with the social gestures than to uncover to any human eye the abyss within him.

"My dear fellow, it's sacrilege to keep a dinner waiting – especially the production of an artist like yours." Mr Ascham sipped his Burgundy luxuriously. "But the fact is, Mrs Ashgrove sent for me."

Granice raised his head with a quick movement of surprise. For a moment he was shaken out of his self-absorption.

"Mrs Ashgrove?"

Ascham smiled. "I thought you'd be interested; I know your passion for *causes célèbres*. And this promises to be one. Of course it's out of our line entirely – we never touch criminal cases. But she wanted to consult me as a friend. Ashgrove was a distant connection of my wife's. And, by Jove, it *is* a queer case!" The servant re-entered, and Ascham snapped his lips shut.

Would the gentlemen have their coffee in the dining-room?

"No – serve it in the library," said Granice, rising. He led the way back to the curtained confidential room. He was really curious to hear what Ascham had to tell him.

While the coffee and cigars were being served he fidgeted about the library, glancing at his letters – the usual meaningless notes and bills – and picking up the evening paper. As he unfolded it a headline caught his eye.

"Rose Melrose Wants to Play Poetry.
Thinks She has Found Her Poet."

He read on with a thumping heart – found the name of a young author he had barely heard of, saw the title of a play, a "poetic drama," dance before his eyes, and dropped the paper, sick, disgusted. It was true, then – she *was* "game" – it was not the manner but the matter she mistrusted!

Granice turned to the servant, who seemed to be purposely lingering. "I shan't need you this evening, Flint. I'll lock up myself."

He fancied the man's acquiescence implied surprise. What was going on, Flint seemed to wonder, that Mr Granice should want him out of the way? Probably he would find a pretext for coming back to see. Granice suddenly felt himself enveloped in a network of espionage.

As the door closed he threw himself into an armchair and leaned forward to take a light from Ascham's cigar.

"Tell me about Mrs Ashgrove," he said, seeming to himself to speak stiffly, as if his lips were cracked.

"Mrs Ashgrove? Well, there's not much to *tell*."

"And you couldn't if there were?" Granice smiled.

"Probably not. As a matter of fact, she wanted my advice about her choice of counsel. There was nothing especially confidential in our talk."

"And what's your impression, now you've seen her?"

"My impression is, very distinctly, *that nothing will ever be known*."

"Ah –" Granice murmured, puffing at his cigar.

"I'm more and more convinced that whoever poisoned Ashgrove knew his business, and will consequently never be found out. That's a capital cigar you've given me."

"You like it? I get them over from Cuba." Granice examined his own reflectively. "Then you believe in the theory that the clever criminals never are caught?"

"Of course I do. Look about you – look back for the last dozen years – none of the big murder problems are ever solved." The lawyer ruminated behind his blue cloud. "Why, take the instance in your own family: I'd forgotten I had an illustration at hand! Take old Joseph Lenman's murder – do you suppose that will ever be explained?"

As the words dropped from Ascham's lips his host looked slowly about the library, and every object in it stared back at him with a stale unescapable familiarity. How sick he was of looking at that room! It was as dull as the face of a wife one has wearied of. He cleared his throat slowly; then he turned his head to the lawyer and said: "I could explain the Lenman murder myself."

Ascham's eye kindled: he shared Granice's interest in criminal cases.

"By Jove! You've had a theory all this time? It's odd you never mentioned it. Go ahead and tell me. There are certain features in the Lenman case not unlike this Ashgrove affair, and your idea may be a help."

Granice paused and his eye reverted instinctively to the table drawer in which the revolver and the manuscript lay side by side. What if he were to try another appeal to Rose Melrose? Then he looked at the notes and bills on the table, and the horror of taking up again the lifeless routine of life – of performing the same automatic gestures another day – displaced his fleeting vision.

"I haven't a theory. I *know* who murdered Joseph Lenman."

Ascham settled himself comfortably in his chair, prepared for enjoyment.

"You *know*? Well, who did?" he laughed.

"I did," said Granice, rising.

He stood before Ascham, and the lawyer lay back staring up at him. Then he broke into another laugh.

"Why, this is glorious! You murdered him, did you? To inherit his money, I suppose? Better and better! Go on, my boy! Unbosom yourself! Tell me all about it! Confession is good for the soul."

Granice waited till the lawyer had shaken the last peal of laughter from his throat; then he repeated doggedly: "I murdered him."

The two men looked at each other for a long moment, and this time Ascham did not laugh.

"Granice!"

"I murdered him – to get his money, as you say."

There was another pause, and Granice, with a vague underlying sense of amusement, saw his guest's look change from pleasantry to apprehension.

"What's the joke, my dear fellow? I fail to see."

"It's not a joke. It's the truth. I murdered him." He had spoken painfully at first, as if there were a knot in his throat; but each time he repeated the words he found they were easier to say.

Ascham laid down his extinct cigar.

"What's the matter? Aren't you well? What on earth are you driving at?"

"I'm perfectly well. But I murdered my cousin, Joseph Lenman, and I want it known that I murdered him."

"You want it known?"

"Yes. That's why I sent for you. I'm sick of living, and when I try to kill myself I funk it." He spoke quite naturally now, as if the knot in his throat had been untied.

"Good Lord – good Lord," the lawyer gasped.

"But I suppose," Granice continued, "there's no doubt this would be murder in the first degree? I'm sure of the chair if I own up?"

Ascham drew a long breath; then he said slowly: "Sit down, Granice. Let's talk."

II

GRANICE TOLD his story simply, connectedly.

He began by a quick survey of his early years – the years of drudgery and privation. His father, a charming man who could never say "no," had so signally failed to say it on certain essential occasions that when he died he left an illegitimate family and a mortgaged estate. His lawful kin found themselves hanging over a gulf of debt, and young Granice, to support his mother and sister, had to leave Harvard and bury himself at eighteen in a broker's office. He loathed his work, and he was always poor, always worried and in ill-health. A few years later his mother died, but his sister, an ineffectual neurasthenic, remained on his hands. His own health gave out, and he had to go away for six months, and work harder than ever when he came back. He had no knack for business, no head for figures, no dimmest insight into the mysteries of commerce. He wanted to travel and write – those were his inmost longings. And as the years dragged on, and he neared middle-age without making any more money, or acquiring any firmer health, a sick despair possessed him. He tried writing, but he always came home from the office so tired that his brain could not work. For half the year he did not reach his dim up-town flat till after dark, and could only "brush up" for dinner, and afterward lie on the lounge with his pipe, while his sister droned through the evening paper. Sometimes he spent an evening at the theatre; or he dined out, or, more rarely, strayed off with an acquaintance or two in quest of what is known as "pleasure." And in summer, when he and Kate went to the sea-side for a month, he dozed through the days in utter weariness. Once he fell in love with a charming girl – but what had he to offer her, in God's name? She seemed to like him, and in common decency he had to drop out of the running. Apparently no one replaced him, for she never married, but grew stoutish, grayish, philanthropic – yet how sweet she had been when he had first kissed her! One more wasted life, he reflected…

But the stage had always been his master-passion. He would have sold his soul for the time and freedom to write plays! It was *in him* – he could not remember when it had not been his deepest-seated instinct. As the years passed it became a morbid, a relentless obsession – yet with every year the material conditions were more and more against it. He felt himself growing middle-aged, and he watched the reflection of the process in his sister's wasted face. At eighteen she had been pretty, and as full of enthusiasm as he. Now she was sour, trivial, insignificant – she had missed her chance of life. And she had no resources, poor creature, was fashioned simply for the primitive functions she had been denied the chance to fulfil! It exasperated him to think of it – and to reflect that even now a little travel, a little health, a little money, might transform her, make her young and desirable… The chief fruit of his experience was that there is no such fixed state as age or youth – there is only health as against sickness, wealth as against poverty; and age or youth as the outcome of the lot one draws.

At this point in his narrative Granice stood up, and went to lean against the mantel-piece, looking down at Ascham, who had not moved from his seat, or changed his attitude of rigid fascinated attention.

"Then came the summer when we went to Wrenfield to be near old Lenman – my mother's cousin, as you know. Some of the family always mounted guard over him – generally a niece or so. But that year they were all scattered, and one of the nieces offered to lend us her cottage if we'd relieve her of duty for two months. It was a nuisance for me, of course, for Wrenfield is two hours from town; but my mother, who was a slave to family observances, had always been good to the old man, so it was natural we should be called on – and there was the saving of rent and the good air for Kate. So we went.

"You never knew Joseph Lenman? Well, picture to yourself an amoeba or some primitive organism of that sort, under a Titan's microscope. He was large, undifferentiated, inert – since I could remember him he had done nothing but take his temperature and read the *Churchman*. Oh, and cultivate melons – that was his hobby. Not vulgar, out-of-door melons – his were grown under glass. He had miles of it at Wrenfield – his big kitchen-garden was surrounded by blinking battalions of green-houses. And in nearly all of them melons were grown – early melons and late, French, English, domestic – dwarf melons and monsters: every shape, color and variety. They were petted and nursed like children – a staff of trained attendants waited on them. I'm not sure they didn't have a doctor to take their temperature – at any rate the place was full of thermometers. And they didn't sprawl on the ground like ordinary melons; they were trained against the glass like nectarines, and each melon hung in a net which sustained its weight and left it free on all sides to the sun and air...

"It used to strike me sometimes that old Lenman was just like one of his own melons – the pale-fleshed English kind. His life, apathetic and motionless, hung in a net of gold, in an equable warm ventilated atmosphere, high above sordid earthly worries. The cardinal rule of his existence was not to let himself be 'worried.' I remember his advising me to try it myself, one day when I spoke to him about Kate's bad health, and her need of a change. 'I never let myself worry,' he said complacently. 'It's the worst thing for the liver – and you look to me as if you had a liver. Take my advice and be cheerful. You'll make yourself happier and others too.' And all he had to do was to write a check, and send the poor girl off for a holiday!

"The hardest part of it was that the money half-belonged to us already. The old skin-flint only had it for life, in trust for us and the others. But his life was a good deal sounder than mine or Kate's – and one could picture him taking extra care of it for the joke of keeping us waiting. I always felt that the sight of our hungry eyes was a tonic to him.

"Well, I tried to see if I couldn't reach him through his vanity. I flattered him, feigned a passionate interest in his melons. And he was taken in, and used to discourse on them by the hour. On fine days he was driven to the green-houses in his pony-chair, and waddled through them, prodding and leering at the fruit, like a fat Turk in his seraglio. When he bragged to me of the expense of growing them I was reminded of a hideous old Lothario bragging of what his pleasures cost. And the resemblance was completed by the fact that he couldn't eat as much as a mouthful of his melons – had lived for years on buttermilk and toast. 'But, after all, it's my only hobby – why shouldn't I indulge it?' he said sentimentally. As if I'd ever been able to indulge any of mine! On the keep of those melons Kate and I could have lived like gods...

"One day toward the end of the summer, when Kate was too unwell to drag herself up to the big house, she asked me to go and spend the afternoon with cousin Joseph. It was a lovely soft September afternoon – a day to lie under a Roman stone-pine, with one's eyes on the sky, and let the cosmic harmonies rush through one. Perhaps the vision was suggested by the fact that, as I entered cousin Joseph's hideous black walnut library, I passed one of the under-gardeners, a handsome full-throated Italian, who dashed out in such a hurry that he nearly knocked me down. I remember thinking it queer that the fellow, whom I had often seen about the melon-houses, did not bow to me, or even seem to see me.

"Cousin Joseph sat in his usual seat, behind the darkened windows, his fat hands folded on his protuberant waistcoat, the last number of the *Churchman* at his elbow, and near it, on a huge dish, a fat melon – the fattest melon I'd ever seen. As I looked at it I pictured the ecstasy of contemplation from which I must have roused him, and congratulated myself on finding him in such a mood, since I had made up my mind to ask him a favor. Then I noticed that his face, instead of looking as calm as an egg-shell, was distorted and whimpering – and without stopping to greet me he pointed passionately to the melon.

"'Look at it, look at it – did you ever see such a beauty? Such firmness – roundness – such delicious smoothness to the touch?' It was as if he had said 'she' instead of 'it,' and when he put out his senile hand and touched the melon I positively had to look the other way.

"Then he told me what had happened. The Italian under-gardener, who had been specially recommended for the melon-houses – though it was against my cousin's principles to employ a Papist – had been assigned to the care of the monster: for it had revealed itself, early in its existence, as destined to become a monster, to surpass its plumpest, pulpiest sisters, carry off prizes at agricultural shows, and be photographed and celebrated in every gardening paper in the land. The Italian had done well – seemed to have a sense of responsibility. And that very morning he had been ordered to pick the melon, which was to be shown next day at the county fair, and to bring it in for Mr Lenman to gaze on its blonde virginity. But in picking it, what had the damned scoundrelly Jesuit done but drop it – drop it crash on the sharp spout of a watering-pot, so that it received a deep gash in its firm pale rotundity, and was henceforth but a bruised, ruined, fallen melon?

"The old man's rage was fearful in its impotence – he shook, spluttered and strangled with it. He had just had the Italian up and had sacked him on the spot, without wages or character – had threatened to have him arrested if he was ever caught prowling about Wrenfield. 'By God, and I'll do it – I'll write to Washington – I'll have the pauper scoundrel deported! I'll show him what money can do!' As likely as not there was some murderous Black-hand business under it – it would be found that the fellow was a member of a 'gang.' Those Italians would murder you for a quarter. He meant to have the police look into it… And then he grew frightened at his own excitement. 'But I must calm myself,' he said. He took his temperature, rang for his drops, and turned to the *Churchman*. He had been reading an article on Nestorianism when the melon was brought in. He asked me to go on with it, and I read to him for an hour, in the dim close room, with a fat fly buzzing stealthily about the fallen melon.

"All the while one phrase of the old man's buzzed in my brain like the fly about the melon. '*I'll show him what money can do!*' Good heaven! If *I* could but show the old man! If I could make him see his power of giving happiness as a new outlet for his monstrous egotism! I tried to tell him something about my situation and Kate's – spoke of my ill-health, my unsuccessful drudgery, my longing to write, to make myself a name – I stammered out an entreaty for a loan. 'I can guarantee to repay you, sir – I've a half-written play as security…'

"I shall never forget his glassy stare. His face had grown as smooth as an egg-shell again – his eyes peered over his fat cheeks like sentinels over a slippery rampart.

"'A half-written play – a play of *yours* as security?' He looked at me almost fearfully, as if detecting the first symptoms of insanity. 'Do you understand anything of business?' he enquired mildly. I laughed and answered: 'No, not much.'

"He leaned back with closed lids. 'All this excitement has been too much for me,' he said. 'If you'll excuse me, I'll prepare for my nap.' And I stumbled out of the room, blindly, like the Italian."

Granice moved away from the mantel-piece, and walked across to the tray set out with decanters and soda-water. He poured himself a tall glass of soda-water, emptied it, and glanced at Ascham's dead cigar.

"Better light another," he suggested.

The lawyer shook his head, and Granice went on with his tale. He told of his mounting obsession – how the murderous impulse had waked in him on the instant of his cousin's refusal, and he had muttered to himself: "By God, if you won't, I'll make you." He spoke more tranquilly as the narrative proceeded, as though his rage had died down once the resolve to act on it was taken. He applied his whole mind to the question of how the old man was to be "disposed of." Suddenly he remembered the outcry: "Those Italians will murder you for a quarter!" But no definite project presented itself: he simply waited for an inspiration.

Granice and his sister moved to town a day or two after the incident of the melon. But the cousins, who had returned, kept them informed of the old man's condition. One day, about three weeks later, Granice, on getting home, found Kate excited over a report from Wrenfield. The Italian had been there again – had somehow slipped into the house, made his way up to the library, and "used threatening language." The house-keeper found cousin Joseph gasping, the whites of his eyes showing "something awful." The doctor was sent for, and the attack warded off; and the police had ordered the Italian from the neighborhood.

But cousin Joseph, thereafter, languished, had "nerves," and lost his taste for toast and buttermilk. The doctor called in a colleague, and the consultation amused and excited the old man – he became once more an important figure. The medical men reassured the family – too completely! – and to the patient they recommended a more varied diet: advised him to take whatever "tempted him." And so one day, tremulously, prayerfully, he decided on a tiny bit of melon. It was brought up with ceremony, and consumed in the presence of the house-keeper and a hovering cousin; and twenty minutes later he was dead...

"But you remember the circumstances," Granice went on; "how suspicion turned at once on the Italian? In spite of the hint the police had given him he had been seen hanging about the house since 'the scene.' It was said that he had tender relations with the kitchen-maid, and the rest seemed easy to explain. But when they looked round to ask him for the explanation he was gone – gone clean out of sight. He had been 'warned' to leave Wrenfield, and he had taken the warning so to heart that no one ever laid eyes on him again."

Granice paused. He had dropped into a chair opposite the lawyer's, and he sat for a moment, his head thrown back, looking about the familiar room. Everything in it had grown grimacing and alien, and each strange insistent object seemed craning forward from its place to hear him.

"It was I who put the stuff in the melon," he said. "And I don't want you to think I'm sorry for it. This isn't 'remorse,' understand. I'm glad the old skin-flint is dead – I'm glad the others have their money. But mine's no use to me any more. My sister married miserably, and died. And I've never had what I wanted."

Ascham continued to stare; then he said: "What on earth was your object, then?"

"Why, to get what I wanted – what I fancied was in reach! I wanted change, rest, *life*, for both of us – wanted, above all, for myself, the chance to write! I traveled, got back my health, and came home to tie myself up to my work. And I've slaved at it steadily for ten years without reward – without the most distant hope of success! Nobody will look at my stuff. And now I'm fifty, and I'm beaten, and I know it." His chin dropped forward on his breast. "I want to chuck the whole business," he ended.

III

IT WAS AFTER MIDNIGHT when Ascham left.

His hand on Granice's shoulder, as he turned to go – "District Attorney be hanged; see a doctor, see a doctor!" he had cried; and so, with an exaggerated laugh, had pulled on his coat and departed.

Granice turned back into the library. It had never occurred to him that Ascham would not believe his story. For three hours he had explained, elucidated, patiently and painfully gone over every detail – but without once breaking down the iron incredulity of the lawyer's eye.

At first Ascham had feigned to be convinced – but that, as Granice now perceived, was simply to get him to expose himself, to entrap him into contradictions. And when the attempt failed, when Granice triumphantly met and refuted each disconcerting question, the lawyer dropped the mask suddenly, and said with a good-humored laugh: "By Jove, Granice, you'll write a successful play yet. The way you've worked this all out is a marvel."

Granice swung about furiously – that last sneer about the play inflamed him. Was all the world in a conspiracy to deride his failure?

"I did it, I did it," he muttered sullenly, his rage spending itself against the impenetrable surface of the other's mockery; and Ascham answered with a smile: "Ever read any of those books on hallucination? I've got a fairly good medico-legal library. I could send you one or two if you like..."

Left alone, Granice cowered down in the chair before his writing-table. He understood that Ascham thought him off his head.

"Good God – what if they all think me crazy?"

The horror of it broke out over him in a cold sweat – he sat there and shook, his eyes hidden in his icy hands. But gradually, as he began to rehearse his story for the thousandth time, he saw again how incontrovertible it was, and felt sure that any criminal lawyer would believe him.

"That's the trouble – Ascham's not a criminal lawyer. And then he's a friend. What a fool I was to talk to a friend! Even if he did believe me, he'd never let me see it – his instinct would be to cover the whole thing up... But in that case – if he *did* believe me – he might think it a kindness to get me shut up in an asylum..." Granice began to tremble again. "Good heaven! If he should bring in an expert – one of those damned alienists! Ascham and Pettilow can do anything – their word always goes. If Ascham drops a hint that I'd better be shut up, I'll be in a strait-jacket by tomorrow! And he'd do it from the kindest motives – be quite right to do it if he thinks I'm a murderer!"

The vision froze him to his chair. He pressed his fists to his bursting temples and tried to think. For the first time he hoped that Ascham had not believed his story.

"But he did – he did! I can see it now – I noticed what a queer eye he cocked at me. Good God, what shall I do – what shall I do?"

He started up and looked at the clock. Half-past one. What if Ascham should think the case urgent, rout out an alienist, and come back with him? Granice jumped to his feet, and his sudden gesture brushed the morning paper from the table. Mechanically he stooped to pick it up, and the movement started a new train of association.

He sat down again, and reached for the telephone book in the rack by his chair.

"Give me three-o-ten... yes."

The new idea in his mind had revived his flagging energy. He would act – act at once. It was only by thus planning ahead, committing himself to some unavoidable line of conduct, that he could pull himself through the meaningless days. Each time he reached a fresh decision it was like coming out of a foggy weltering sea into a calm harbor with lights. One of the queerest phases of his long agony was the intense relief produced by these momentary lulls.

"That the office of the *Investigator*? Yes? Give me Mr Denver, please… Hallo, Denver… Yes, Hubert Granice… Just caught you? Going straight home? Can I come and see you… yes, now… have a talk? It's rather urgent… yes, might give you some first-rate 'copy'… All right!" He hung up the receiver with a laugh. It had been a happy thought to call up the editor of the *Investigator* – Robert Denver was the very man he needed…

Granice put out the lights in the library – it was odd how the automatic gestures persisted! – went into the hall, put on his hat and overcoat, and let himself out of the flat. In the hall, a sleepy elevator boy blinked at him and then dropped his head on his folded arms. Granice passed out into the street. At the corner of Fifth Avenue he hailed a crawling cab, and called out an up-town address. The long thoroughfare stretched before him, dim and deserted, like an ancient avenue of tombs. But from Denver's house a friendly beam fell on the pavement; and as Granice sprang from his cab the editor's electric turned the corner.

The two men grasped hands, and Denver, feeling for his latch-key, ushered Granice into the brightly-lit hall.

"Disturb me? Not a bit. You might have, at ten tomorrow morning… but this is my liveliest hour… you know my habits of old."

Granice had known Robert Denver for fifteen years – watched his rise through all the stages of journalism to the Olympian pinnacle of the *Investigator*'s editorial office. In the thick-set man with grizzling hair there were few traces left of the hungry-eyed young reporter who, on his way home in the small hours, used to "bob in" on Granice, while the latter sat grinding at his plays. Denver had to pass Granice's flat on the way to his own, and it became a habit, if he saw a light in the window, and Granice's shadow against the blind, to go in, smoke a pipe, and discuss the universe.

"Well – this is like old times – a good old habit reversed." The editor smote his visitor genially on the shoulder. "Reminds me of the nights when I used to rout you out… How's the play, by the way? There is a play, I suppose? It's as safe to ask you that as to say to some men: 'How's the baby?'"

Denver laughed good-naturedly, and Granice thought how thick and heavy he had grown. It was evident, even to Granice's tortured nerves, that the words had not been uttered in malice – and the fact gave him a new measure of his insignificance. Denver did not even know that he had been a failure! The fact hurt more than Ascham's irony.

"Come in – come in." The editor led the way into a small cheerful room, where there were cigars and decanters. He pushed an arm-chair toward his visitor, and dropped into another with a comfortable groan.

"Now, then – help yourself. And let's hear all about it."

He beamed at Granice over his pipe-bowl, and the latter, lighting his cigar, said to himself: "Success makes men comfortable, but it makes them stupid."

Then he turned, and began: "Denver, I want to tell you –"

The clock ticked rhythmically on the mantel-piece. The room was gradually filled with drifting blue layers of smoke, and through them the editor's face came and went like the moon through a moving sky. Once the hour struck – then the rhythmical ticking began again. The atmosphere grew denser and heavier, and beads of perspiration began to roll from Granice's forehead.

"Do you mind if I open the window?"

"No. It is stuffy in here. Wait – I'll do it myself." Denver pushed down the upper sash, and returned to his chair. "Well – go on," he said, filling another pipe. His composure exasperated Granice.

"There's no use in my going on if you don't believe me."

The editor remained unmoved. "Who says I don't believe you? And how can I tell till you've finished?"

Granice went on, ashamed of his outburst. "It was simple enough, as you'll see. From the day the old man said to me, 'Those Italians would murder you for a quarter,' I dropped everything and just worked at my scheme. It struck me at once that I must find a way of getting to Wrenfield and back in a night – and that led to the idea of a motor. A motor – that never occurred to you? You wonder where I got the money, I suppose. Well, I had a thousand or so put by, and I nosed around till I found what I wanted – a second-hand racer. I knew how to drive a car, and I tried the thing and found it was all right. Times were bad, and I bought it for my price, and stored it away. Where? Why, in one of those no-questions-asked garages where they keep motors that are not for family use. I had a lively cousin who had put me up to that dodge, and I looked about till I found a queer hole where they took in my car like a baby in a foundling asylum... Then I practiced running to Wrenfield and back in a night. I knew the way pretty well, for I'd done it often with the same lively cousin – and in the small hours, too. The distance is over ninety miles, and on the third trial I did it under two hours. But my arms were so lame that I could hardly get dressed the next morning...

"Well, then came the report about the Italian's threats, and I saw I must act at once... I meant to break into the old man's room, shoot him, and get away again. It was a big risk, but I thought I could manage it. Then we heard that he was ill – that there'd been a consultation. Perhaps the fates were going to do it for me! Good Lord, if that could only be!..."

Granice stopped and wiped his forehead: the open window did not seem to have cooled the room.

"Then came word that he was better; and the day after, when I came up from my office, I found Kate laughing over the news that he was to try a bit of melon. The house-keeper had just telephoned her – all Wrenfield was in a flutter. The doctor himself had picked out the melon, one of the little French ones that are hardly bigger than a large tomato – and the patient was to eat it at his breakfast the next morning.

"In a flash I saw my chance. It was a bare chance, no more. But I knew the ways of the house – I was sure the melon would be brought in over night and put in the pantry ice-box. If there were only one melon in the ice-box I could be fairly sure it was the one I wanted. Melons didn't lie around loose in that house – every one was known, numbered, catalogued. The old man was beset by the dread that the servants would eat them, and he took a hundred mean precautions to prevent it. Yes, I felt pretty sure of my melon... and poisoning was much safer than shooting. It would have been the devil and all to get into the old man's bedroom without his rousing the house; but I ought to be able to break into the pantry without much trouble.

"It was a cloudy night, too – everything served me. I dined quietly, and sat down at my desk. Kate had one of her usual headaches, and went to bed early. As soon as she was gone I slipped out. I had got together a sort of disguise – red beard and queer-looking ulster. I shoved them into a bag, and went round to the garage. There was no one there but a half-drunken machinist whom I'd never seen before. That served me, too. They were always changing machinists, and this new fellow didn't even bother to ask if the car belonged to me. It was a very easy-going place...

"Well, I jumped in, ran up Broadway, and let the car go as soon as I was out of Harlem. Dark as it was, I could trust myself to strike a sharp pace. In the shadow of a wood I stopped a second and got into the beard and ulster. Then away again – it was just eleven-thirty when I got to Wrenfield.

"I left the car in a dark lane behind the Lenman place, and slipped through the kitchen-garden. The melon-houses winked at me through the dark – I remember thinking that they knew what I wanted to know... By the stable a dog came out growling – but he nosed me out, jumped on me, and went back... The house was as dark as the grave. I knew everybody went to bed by ten. But there might be a prowling servant – the kitchen-maid might have come down to let in her Italian. I had to risk that, of course. I crept around by the back door and hid in the shrubbery. Then I listened. It was all as silent as death. I crossed over to the house, pried open the pantry window and climbed in. I had a little electric lamp in my pocket, and shielding it with my cap I groped my way to the ice-box, opened it – and there was the little French melon... only one.

"I stopped to listen – I was quite cool. Then I pulled out my bottle of stuff and my syringe, and gave each section of the melon a hypodermic. It was all done inside of three minutes – at ten minutes to twelve I was back in the car. I got out of the lane as quietly as I could, struck a back road that skirted the village, and let the car out as soon as I was beyond the last houses. I only stopped once on the way in, to drop the beard and ulster into a pond. I had a big stone ready to weight them with and they went down plump, like a dead body – and at two o'clock I was back at my desk."

Granice stopped speaking and looked across the smoke-fumes at his listener; but Denver's face remained inscrutable.

At length he said: "Why did you want to tell me this?"

The question startled Granice. He was about to explain, as he had explained to Ascham; but suddenly it occurred to him that if his motive had not seemed convincing to the lawyer it would carry much less weight with Denver. Both were successful men, and success does not understand the subtle agony of failure. Granice cast about for another reason.

"Why, I – the thing haunts me... remorse, I suppose you'd call it..."

Denver struck the ashes from his empty pipe.

"Remorse? Bosh!" he said energetically.

Granice's heart sank. "You don't believe in – *remorse*?"

"Not an atom: in the man of action. The mere fact of your talking of remorse proves to me that you're not the man to have planned and put through such a job."

Granice groaned. "Well – I lied to you about remorse. I've never felt any."

Denver's lips tightened skeptically about his freshly-filled pipe. "What was your motive, then? You must have had one."

"I'll tell you –" And Granice began again to rehearse the story of his failure, of his loathing for life. "Don't say you don't believe me this time... that this isn't a real reason!" he stammered out piteously as he ended.

Denver meditated. "No, I won't say that. I've seen too many queer things. There's always a reason for wanting to get out of life – the wonder is that we find so many for staying in!"

Granice's heart grew light. "Then you *do* believe me?" he faltered.

"Believe that you're sick of the job? Yes. And that you haven't the nerve to pull the trigger? Oh, yes – that's easy enough, too. But all that doesn't make you a murderer – though I don't say it proves you could never have been one."

"I *have* been one, Denver – I swear to you."

"Perhaps." He meditated. "Just tell me one or two things."

"Oh, go ahead. You won't stump me!" Granice heard himself say with a laugh.

"Well – how did you make all those trial trips without exciting your sister's curiosity? I knew your night habits pretty well at that time, remember. You were very seldom out late. Didn't the change in your ways surprise her?"

"No; because she was away at the time. She went to pay several visits in the country soon after we came back from Wrenfield, and was only in town for a night or two before – before I did the job."

"And that night she went to bed early with a headache?"

"Yes – blinding. She didn't know anything when she had that kind. And her room was at the back of the flat."

Denver again meditated. "And when you got back – she didn't hear you? You got in without her knowing it?"

"Yes. I went straight to my work – took it up at the word where I'd left off – *why, Denver, don't you remember*?" Granice suddenly, passionately interjected.

"Remember –?"

"Yes; how you found me – when you looked in that morning, between two and three… your usual hour…?"

"Yes," the editor nodded.

Granice gave a short laugh. "In my old coat – with my pipe: looked as if I'd been working all night, didn't I? Well, I hadn't been in my chair ten minutes!"

Denver uncrossed his legs and then crossed them again. "I didn't know whether you remembered that."

"What?"

"My coming in that particular night – or morning."

Granice swung round in his chair. "Why, man alive! That's why I'm here now. Because it was you who spoke for me at the inquest, when they looked round to see what all the old man's heirs had been doing that night – you who testified to having dropped in and found me at my desk as usual… I thought *that* would appeal to your journalistic sense if nothing else would!"

Denver smiled. "Oh, my journalistic sense is still susceptible enough – and the idea's picturesque, I grant you: asking the man who proved your alibi to establish your guilt."

"That's it – that's it!" Granice's laugh had a ring of triumph.

"Well, but how about the other chap's testimony – I mean that young doctor: what was his name? Ned Ranney. Don't you remember my testifying that I'd met him at the elevated station, and told him I was on my way to smoke a pipe with you, and his saying: 'All right; you'll find him in. I passed the house two hours ago, and saw his shadow against the blind, as usual.' And the lady with the toothache in the flat across the way: she corroborated his statement, you remember."

"Yes; I remember."

"Well, then?"

"Simple enough. Before starting I rigged up a kind of mannikin with old coats and a cushion – something to cast a shadow on the blind. All you fellows were used to seeing my shadow there in the small hours – I counted on that, and knew you'd take any vague outline as mine."

"Simple enough, as you say. But the woman with the toothache saw the shadow move – you remember she said she saw you sink forward, as if you'd fallen asleep."

"Yes; and she was right. It *did* move. I suppose some extra-heavy dray must have jolted by the flimsy building – at any rate, something gave my mannikin a jar, and when I came back he had sunk forward, half over the table."

There was a long silence between the two men. Granice, with a throbbing heart, watched Denver refill his pipe. The editor, at any rate, did not sneer and flout him. After all, journalism gave a deeper insight than the law into the fantastic possibilities of life, prepared one better to allow for the incalculableness of human impulses.

"Well?" Granice faltered out.

Denver stood up with a shrug. "Look here, man – what's wrong with you? Make a clean breast of it! Nerves gone to smash? I'd like to take you to see a chap I know – an ex-prize-fighter – who's a wonder at pulling fellows in your state out of their hole –"

"Oh, oh –" Granice broke in. He stood up also, and the two men eyed each other. "You don't believe me, then?"

"This yarn – how can I? There wasn't a flaw in your alibi."

"But haven't I filled it full of them now?"

Denver shook his head. "I might think so if I hadn't happened to know that you *wanted* to. There's the hitch, don't you see?"

Granice groaned. "No, I didn't. You mean my wanting to be found guilty –?"

"Of course! If somebody else had accused you, the story might have been worth looking into. As it is, a child could have invented it. It doesn't do much credit to your ingenuity."

Granice turned sullenly toward the door. What was the use of arguing? But on the threshold a sudden impulse drew him back. "Look here, Denver – I daresay you're right. But will you do just one thing to prove it? Put my statement in the *Investigator*, just as I've made it. Ridicule it as much as you like. Only give the other fellows a chance at it – men who don't know anything about me. Set them talking and looking about. I don't care a damn whether *you* believe me – what I want is to convince the Grand Jury! I oughtn't to have come to a man who knows me – your cursed incredulity is infectious. I don't put my case well, because I know in advance it's discredited, and I almost end by not believing it myself. That's why I can't convince *you*. It's a vicious circle." He laid a hand on Denver's arm. "Send a stenographer, and put my statement in the paper."

But Denver did not warm to the idea. "My dear fellow, you seem to forget that all the evidence was pretty thoroughly sifted at the time, every possible clue followed up. The public would have been ready enough then to believe that you murdered old Lenman – you or anybody else. All they wanted was a murderer – the most improbable would have served. But your alibi was too confoundedly complete. And nothing you've told me has shaken it." Denver laid his cool hand over the other's burning fingers. "Look here, old fellow, go home and work up a better case – then come in and submit it to the *Investigator*."

IV

THE PERSPIRATION was rolling off Granice's forehead. Every few minutes he had to draw out his handkerchief and wipe the moisture from his haggard face.

For an hour and a half he had been talking steadily, putting his case to the District Attorney. Luckily he had a speaking acquaintance with Allonby, and had obtained, without much difficulty, a private audience on the very day after his talk with Robert Denver. In the interval between he had hurried home, got out of his evening clothes, and gone forth again at once into the dreary dawn. His fear of Ascham and the alienist made it impossible for him to remain in his rooms. And it seemed to him that the only way of averting that hideous peril was by establishing, in some sane impartial mind, the proof of his guilt. Even if he had not been so incurably sick of life, the electric chair seemed now the only alternative to the strait-jacket.

As he paused to wipe his forehead he saw the District Attorney glance at his watch. The gesture was significant, and Granice lifted an appealing hand. "I don't expect you to believe me now – but can't you put me under arrest, and have the thing looked into?"

Allonby smiled faintly under his heavy grayish mustache. He had a ruddy face, full and jovial, in which his keen professional eyes seemed to keep watch over impulses not strictly professional.

"Well, I don't know that we need lock you up just yet. But of course I'm bound to look into your statement –"

Granice rose with an exquisite sense of relief. Surely Allonby wouldn't have said that if he hadn't believed him!

"That's all right. Then I needn't detain you. I can be found at any time at my apartment." He gave the address.

The District Attorney smiled again, more openly. "What do you say to leaving it for an hour or two this evening? I'm giving a little supper at Rector's – quiet, little affair, you understand: just Miss Melrose – I think you know her – and a friend or two; and if you'll join us..."

Granice stumbled out of the office without knowing what reply he had made.

He waited for four days – four days of concentrated horror. During the first twenty-four hours the fear of Ascham's alienist dogged him; and as that subsided, it was replaced by the exasperating sense that his avowal had made no impression on the District Attorney. Evidently, if he had been going to look into the case, Allonby would have been heard from before now... And that mocking invitation to supper showed clearly enough how little the story had impressed him!

Granice was overcome by the futility of any farther attempt to inculpate himself. He was chained to life – a "prisoner of consciousness." Where was it he had read the phrase? Well, he was learning what it meant. In the glaring night-hours, when his brain seemed ablaze, he was visited by a sense of his fixed identity, of his irreducible, inexpugnable *selfness*, keener, more insidious, more unescapable, than any sensation he had ever known. He had not guessed that the mind was capable of such intricacies of self-realization, of penetrating so deep into its own dark windings. Often he woke from his brief snatches of sleep with the feeling that something material was clinging to him, was on his hands and face, and in his throat – and as his brain cleared he understood that it was the sense of his own loathed personality that stuck to him like some thick viscous substance.

Then, in the first morning hours, he would rise and look out of his window at the awakening activities of the street – at the street-cleaners, the ash-cart drivers, and the other dingy workers flitting hurriedly by through the sallow winter light. Oh, to be one of them – any of them – to take his chance in any of their skins! They were the toilers – the men whose lot was pitied – the victims wept over and ranted about by altruists and economists; and how gladly he would have taken up the load of any one of them, if only he might have shaken off his own! But, no – the iron circle of consciousness held them too: each one was hand-cuffed to his own hideous ego. Why wish to be any one man rather than another? The only absolute good was not to be... And Flint, coming in to draw his bath, would ask if he preferred his eggs scrambled or poached that morning?

On the fifth day he wrote a long urgent letter to Allonby; and for the succeeding two days he had the occupation of waiting for an answer. He hardly stirred from his rooms, in his fear of missing the letter by a moment; but would the District Attorney write, or send a representative: a policeman, a "secret agent," or some other mysterious emissary of the law?

On the third morning Flint, stepping softly – as if, confound it! his master were ill – entered the library where Granice sat behind an unread newspaper, and proferred a card on a tray.

Granice read the name – J. B. Hewson – and underneath, in pencil, "From the District Attorney's office." He started up with a thumping heart, and signed an assent to the servant.

Mr Hewson was a slight sallow nondescript man of about fifty – the kind of man of whom one is sure to see a specimen in any crowd. "Just the type of the successful detective," Granice reflected as he shook hands with his visitor.

And it was in that character that Mr Hewson briefly introduced himself. He had been sent by the District Attorney to have "a quiet talk" with Mr Granice – to ask him to repeat the statement he had made about the Lenman murder.

His manner was so quiet, so reasonable and receptive, that Granice's self-confidence returned. Here was a sensible man – a man who knew his business – it would be easy enough to make *him* see through that ridiculous alibi! Granice offered Mr Hewson a cigar, and lighting one himself – to prove his coolness – began again to tell his story.

He was conscious, as he proceeded, of telling it better than ever before. Practice helped, no doubt; and his listener's detached, impartial attitude helped still more. He could see that Hewson, at least, had not decided in advance to disbelieve him, and the sense of being trusted made him more lucid and more consecutive. Yes, this time his words would certainly carry conviction…

V

DESPAIRINGLY, Granice gazed up and down the shabby street. Beside him stood a young man with bright prominent eyes, a smooth but not too smoothly-shaven face, and an Irish smile. The young man's nimble glance followed Granice's.

"Sure of the number, are you?" he asked briskly.

"Oh, yes – it was 104."

"Well, then, the new building has swallowed it up – that's certain."

He tilted his head back and surveyed the half-finished front of a brick and limestone flat-house that reared its flimsy elegance above a row of tottering tenements and stables.

"Dead sure?" he repeated.

"Yes," said Granice, discouraged. "And even if I hadn't been, I know the garage was just opposite Leffler's over there." He pointed across the street to a tumble-down stable with a blotched sign on which the words "Livery and Boarding" were still faintly discernible.

The young man dashed across to the opposite pavement. "Well, that's something – may get a clue there. Leffler's – same name there, anyhow. You remember that name?"

"Yes – distinctly."

Granice had felt a return of confidence since he had enlisted the interest of the *Explorer*'s "smartest" reporter. If there were moments when he hardly believed his own story, there were others when it seemed impossible that everyone should not believe it; and young Peter McCarren, peering, listening, questioning, jotting down notes, inspired him with an exquisite sense of security. McCarren had fastened on the case at once, "like a leech," as he phrased it – jumped at it, thrilled to it, and settled down to "draw the last drop of fact from it, and had not let go till he had." No one else had treated Granice in that way – even Allonby's detective had not taken a single note. And though a week had elapsed since the visit of that authorized official, nothing had been heard from the District Attorney's office: Allonby had apparently dropped the matter again. But McCarren wasn't going to drop it – not he! He positively hung on Granice's footsteps. They had spent the greater part of the previous day together, and now they were off again, running down clues.

But at Leffler's they got none, after all. Leffler's was no longer a stable. It was condemned to demolition, and in the respite between sentence and execution it had become a vague place of storage, a hospital for broken-down carriages and carts, presided over by a blear-eyed old woman who knew nothing of Flood's garage across the way – did not even remember what had stood there before the new flat-house began to rise.

"Well – we may run Leffler down somewhere; I've seen harder jobs done," said McCarren, cheerfully noting down the name.

As they walked back toward Sixth Avenue he added, in a less sanguine tone: "I'd undertake now to put the thing through if you could only put me on the track of that cyanide."

Granice's heart sank. Yes – there was the weak spot; he had felt it from the first! But he still hoped to convince McCarren that his case was strong enough without it; and he urged the reporter to come back to his rooms and sum up the facts with him again.

"Sorry, Mr Granice, but I'm due at the office now. Besides, it'd be no use till I get some fresh stuff to work on. Suppose I call you up tomorrow or next day?"

He plunged into a trolley and left Granice gazing desolately after him.

Two days later he reappeared at the apartment, a shade less jaunty in demeanor.

"Well, Mr Granice, the stars in their courses are against you, as the bard says. Can't get a trace of Flood, or of Leffler either. And you say you bought the motor through Flood, and sold it through him, too?"

"Yes," said Granice wearily.

"Who bought it, do you know?"

Granice wrinkled his brows. "Why, Flood – yes, Flood himself. I sold it back to him three months later."

"Flood? The devil! And I've ransacked the town for Flood. That kind of business disappears as if the earth had swallowed it."

Granice, discouraged, kept silence.

"That brings us back to the poison," McCarren continued, his note-book out. "Just go over that again, will you?"

And Granice went over it again. It had all been so simple at the time – and he had been so clever in covering up his traces! As soon as he decided on poison he looked about for an acquaintance who manufactured chemicals; and there was Jim Dawes, a Harvard classmate, in the dyeing business – just the man. But at the last moment it occurred to him that suspicion might turn toward so obvious an opportunity, and he decided on a more tortuous course. Another friend, Carrick Venn, a student of medicine whom irremediable ill-health had kept from the practice of his profession, amused his leisure with experiments in physics, for the exercise of which he had set up a simple laboratory. Granice had the habit of dropping in to smoke a cigar with him on Sunday afternoons, and the friends generally sat in Venn's work-shop, at the back of the old family house in Stuyvesant Square. Off this work-shop was the cupboard of supplies, with its row of deadly bottles. Carrick Venn was an original, a man of restless curious tastes, and his place, on a Sunday, was often full of visitors: a cheerful crowd of journalists, scribblers, painters, experimenters in divers forms of expression. Coming and going among so many, it was easy enough to pass unperceived; and one afternoon Granice, arriving before Venn had returned home, found himself alone in the workshop, and quickly slipping into the cupboard, transferred the drug to his pocket.

But that had happened ten years ago; and Venn, poor fellow, was long since dead of his dragging ailment. His old father was dead, too, the house in Stuyvesant Square had been turned into a boarding-house, and the shifting life of New York had passed its rapid sponge over every trace of their obscure little history. Even the optimistic McCarren seemed to acknowledge the hopelessness of seeking for proof in that direction.

"And there's the third door slammed in our faces." He shut his note-book, and throwing back his head, rested his bright inquisitive eyes on Granice's furrowed face.

"Look here, Mr Granice – you see the weak spot, don't you?"

The other made a despairing motion. "I see so many!"

"Yes: but the one that weakens all the others. Why the deuce do you want this thing known? Why do you want to put your head into the noose?"

Granice looked at him hopelessly, trying to take the measure of his quick light irreverent mind. No one so full of a cheerful animal life would believe in the craving for death as a sufficient motive; and Granice racked his brain for one more convincing. But suddenly he saw the reporter's face soften, and melt to a naive sentimentalism.

"Mr Granice – has the memory of it always haunted you?"

Granice stared a moment, and then leapt at the opening. "That's it – the memory of it... always..."

McCarren nodded vehemently. "Dogged your steps, eh? Wouldn't let you sleep? The time came when you *had* to make a clean breast of it?"

"I had to. Can't you understand?"

The reporter struck his fist on the table. "God, sir! I don't suppose there's a human being with a drop of warm blood in him that can't picture the deadly horrors of remorse –"

The Celtic imagination was aflame, and Granice mutely thanked him for the word. What neither Ascham nor Denver would accept as a conceivable motive the Irish reporter seized on as the most adequate; and, as he said, once one could find a convincing motive, the difficulties of the case became so many incentives to effort.

"Remorse – *remorse*," he repeated, rolling the word under his tongue with an accent that was a clue to the psychology of the popular drama; and Granice, perversely, said to himself: "If I could only have struck that note I should have been running in six theatres at once."

He saw that from that moment McCarren's professional zeal would be fanned by emotional curiosity; and he profited by the fact to propose that they should dine together, and go on afterward to some music-hall or theatre. It was becoming necessary to Granice to feel himself an object of pre-occupation, to find himself in another mind. He took a kind of gray penumbral pleasure in riveting McCarren's attention on his case; and to feign the grimaces of moral anguish became a passionately engrossing game. He had not entered a theatre for months; but he sat out the meaningless performance in rigid tolerance, sustained by the sense of the reporter's observation.

Between the acts, McCarren amused him with anecdotes about the audience: he knew everyone by sight, and could lift the curtain from every physiognomy. Granice listened indulgently. He had lost all interest in his kind, but he knew that he was himself the real center of McCarren's attention, and that every word the latter spoke had an indirect bearing on his own problem.

"See that fellow over there – the little dried-up man in the third row, pulling his mustache? *His* memoirs would be worth publishing," McCarren said suddenly in the last *entr'acte*.

Granice, following his glance, recognized the detective from Allonby's office. For a moment he had the thrilling sense that he was being shadowed.

"Caesar, if *he* could talk –!" McCarren continued. "Know who he is, of course? Dr John B. Stell, the biggest alienist in the country –"

Granice, with a start, bent again between the heads in front of him. "*That* man – the fourth from the aisle? You're mistaken. That's not Dr Stell."

McCarren laughed. "Well, I guess I've been in court enough to know Stell when I see him. He testifies in nearly all the big cases where they plead insanity."

A cold shiver ran down Granice's spine, but he repeated obstinately: "That's not Dr Stell."

"Not Stell? Why, man, I *know* him. Look – here he comes. If it isn't Stell, he won't speak to me."

The little dried-up man was moving slowly up the aisle. As he neared McCarren he made a slight gesture of recognition.

"How'do, Doctor Stell? Pretty slim show, ain't it?" the reporter cheerfully flung out at him. And Mr J. B. Hewson, with a nod of amicable assent, passed on.

Granice sat benumbed. He knew he had not been mistaken – the man who had just passed was the same man whom Allonby had sent to see him: a physician disguised as a detective. Allonby, then, had thought him insane, like the others – had regarded his confession as the maundering of a maniac. The discovery froze Granice with horror – he seemed to see the mad-house gaping for him.

"Isn't there a man a good deal like him – a detective named J. B. Hewson?"

But he knew in advance what McCarren's answer would be. "Hewson? J. B. Hewson? Never heard of him. But that was J. B. Stell fast enough – I guess he can be trusted to know himself, and you saw he answered to his name."

VI

SOME DAYS PASSED before Granice could obtain a word with the District Attorney: he began to think that Allonby avoided him.

But when they were face to face Allonby's jovial countenance showed no sign of embarrassment. He waved his visitor to a chair, and leaned across his desk with the encouraging smile of a consulting physician.

Granice broke out at once: "That detective you sent me the other day –"

Allonby raised a deprecating hand.

"– I know: it was Stell the alienist. Why did you do that, Allonby?"

The other's face did not lose its composure. "Because I looked up your story first – and there's nothing in it."

"Nothing in it?" Granice furiously interposed.

"Absolutely nothing. If there is, why the deuce don't you bring me proofs? I know you've been talking to Peter Ascham, and to Denver, and to that little ferret McCarren of the *Explorer*. Have any of them been able to make out a case for you? No. Well, what am I to do?"

Granice's lips began to tremble. "Why did you play me that trick?"

"About Stell? I had to, my dear fellow: it's part of my business. Stell *is* a detective, if you come to that – every doctor is."

The trembling of Granice's lips increased, communicating itself in a long quiver to his facial muscles. He forced a laugh through his dry throat. "Well – and what did he detect?"

"In you? Oh, he thinks it's overwork – overwork and too much smoking. If you look in on him some day at his office he'll show you the record of hundreds of cases like yours, and advise you what treatment to follow. It's one of the commonest forms of hallucination. Have a cigar, all the same."

"But, Allonby, I killed that man!"

The District Attorney's large hand, outstretched on his desk, had an almost imperceptible gesture, and a moment later, as if an answer to the call of an electric bell, a clerk looked in from the outer office.

"Sorry, my dear fellow – lot of people waiting. Drop in on Stell some morning," Allonby said, shaking hands.

McCarren had to own himself beaten: there was absolutely no flaw in the alibi. And since his duty to his journal obviously forbade his wasting time on insoluble mysteries, he ceased to frequent Granice, who dropped back into a deeper isolation. For a day or two after his visit to Allonby he continued to live in dread of Dr Stell. Why might not Allonby have deceived him as to the alienist's diagnosis? What if he were really being shadowed, not by a police agent but by a mad-doctor? To have the truth out, he suddenly determined to call on Dr Stell.

The physician received him kindly, and reverted without embarrassment to the conditions of their previous meeting. "We have to do that occasionally, Mr Granice; it's one of our methods. And you had given Allonby a fright."

Granice was silent. He would have liked to reaffirm his guilt, to produce the fresh arguments which had occurred to him since his last talk with the physician; but he feared his eagerness might be taken for a symptom of derangement, and he affected to smile away Dr Stell's allusion.

"You think, then, it's a case of brain-fag – nothing more?"

"Nothing more. And I should advise you to knock off tobacco. You smoke a good deal, don't you?"

He developed his treatment, recommending massage, gymnastics, travel, or any form of diversion that did not – that in short –

Granice interrupted him impatiently. "Oh, I loathe all that – and I'm sick of travelling."

"H'm. Then some larger interest – politics, reform, philanthropy? Something to take you out of yourself."

"Yes. I understand," said Granice wearily.

"Above all, don't lose heart. I see hundreds of cases like yours," the doctor added cheerfully from the threshold.

On the doorstep Granice stood still and laughed. Hundreds of cases like his – the case of a man who had committed a murder, who confessed his guilt, and whom no one would believe! Why, there had never been a case like it in the world. What a good figure Stell would have made in a play: the great alienist who couldn't read a man's mind any better than that!

Granice saw huge comic opportunities in the type.

But as he walked away, his fears dispelled, the sense of listlessness returned on him. For the first time since his avowal to Peter Ascham he found himself without an occupation, and understood that he had been carried through the past weeks only by the necessity of constant action. Now his life had once more become a stagnant backwater, and as he stood on the street corner watching the tides of traffic sweep by, he asked himself despairingly how much longer he could endure to float about in the sluggish circle of his consciousness.

The thought of self-destruction recurred to him; but again his flesh recoiled. He yearned for death from other hands, but he could never take it from his own. And, aside from his insuperable physical reluctance, another motive restrained him. He was possessed by the dogged desire to establish the truth of his story. He refused to be swept aside as an irresponsible dreamer – even if he had to kill himself in the end, he would not do so before proving to society that he had deserved death from it.

He began to write long letters to the papers; but after the first had been published and commented on, public curiosity was quelled by a brief statement from the District Attorney's office, and the rest of his communications remained unprinted. Ascham came to see him, and begged him to travel. Robert Denver dropped in, and tried to joke him out of his delusion; till Granice, mistrustful of their motives, began to dread the reappearance of Dr Stell, and set a guard on his lips. But the words he kept back engendered others and still others in his brain. His inner self became a humming factory of arguments, and he spent long hours reciting and writing down elaborate statements of his crime, which he constantly retouched and developed. Then gradually his activity languished under the lack of an audience, the sense of being buried beneath deepening drifts of indifference. In a passion of resentment he swore that he would prove himself a murderer, even if he had to commit another crime to do it; and for a sleepless night or two the thought flamed red on his darkness. But daylight dispelled it. The determining impulse was lacking and he hated too promiscuously to choose his victim… So he was thrown back on the unavailing struggle to impose the truth of his story. As fast as one channel closed on him he tried to pierce another through the sliding sands of incredulity. But every issue seemed blocked, and the whole human race leagued together to cheat one man of the right to die.

Thus viewed, the situation became so monstrous that he lost his last shred of self-restraint in contemplating it. What if he were really the victim of some mocking experiment, the center of a ring of holiday-makers jeering at a poor creature in its blind dashes against the solid walls of consciousness? But, no – men were not so uniformly cruel: there were flaws in the close surface of their indifference, cracks of weakness and pity here and there…

Granice began to think that his mistake lay in having appealed to persons more or less familiar with his past, and to whom the visible conformities of his life seemed a final disproof of its one fierce secret deviation. The general tendency was to take for the whole of life the slit seen between the blinders of habit: and in his walk down that narrow vista Granice cut a correct enough figure. To a vision free to follow his whole orbit his story would be more intelligible: it would be easier to convince a chance idler in the street than the trained intelligence hampered by a sense of his antecedents. This idea shot up in him with the tropic luxuriance of each new seed of thought, and he began to walk the streets, and to frequent out-of-the-way chop-houses and bars in his search for the impartial stranger to whom he should disclose himself.

At first every face looked encouragement; but at the crucial moment he always held back. So much was at stake, and it was so essential that his first choice should be decisive. He dreaded stupidity, timidity, intolerance. The imaginative eye, the furrowed brow, were what he sought. He must reveal himself only to a heart versed in the tortuous motions of the human will; and he began to hate the dull benevolence of the average face.

Once or twice, obscurely, allusively, he made a beginning – once sitting down at a man's side in a basement chop-house, another day approaching a lounger on an east-side wharf. But in both cases the premonition of failure checked him on the brink of avowal. His dread of being taken for a man in the clutch of a fixed idea gave him an unnatural keenness in reading the expression of his interlocutors, and he had provided himself in advance with a series of verbal alternatives, trap-doors of evasion from the first dart of ridicule or suspicion.

He passed the greater part of the day in the streets, coming home at irregular hours, dreading the silence and orderliness of his apartment, and the critical scrutiny of Flint. His real life was spent in a world so remote from this familiar setting that he sometimes had the mysterious sense of a living metempsychosis, a furtive passage from one identity to another – yet the other as unescapably himself!

One humiliation he was spared: the desire to live never revived in him. Not for a moment was he tempted to a shabby pact with existing conditions. He wanted to die, wanted it with the fixed unwavering desire which alone attains its end. And still the end eluded him! It would not always, of course – he had full faith in the dark star of his destiny. And he could prove it best by repeating his story, persistently and indefatigably, pouring it into indifferent ears, hammering it into dull brains, till at last it kindled a spark, and some one of the careless millions paused, listened, believed…

It was a mild March day, and he had been loitering on the west-side docks, looking at faces. He was becoming an expert in physiognomies: his eagerness no longer made rash darts and awkward recoils. He knew now the face he needed, as clearly as if it had come to him in a vision; and not till he found it would he speak. As he walked eastward through the shabby reeking streets he had a premonition that he should find it that morning. Perhaps it was the promise of spring in the air – certainly he felt calmer than for many days…

He turned into Washington Square, struck across it obliquely, and walked up University Place. Its heterogeneous passers always allured him – they were less hurried than in Broadway, less enclosed and classified than in Fifth Avenue. He walked slowly, watching for his face.

At Union Square he felt a sudden relapse into discouragement, like a votary who has watched too long for a sign from the altar. Perhaps, after all, he should never find his face… The air was languid, and he felt tired. He walked between the bald grass-plots and the twisted trees, making for an empty seat. Presently he passed a bench on which a girl sat alone, and something as definite as the twitch of a cord made him stop before her. He had never dreamed of telling his story to a girl, had hardly looked at the women's faces as they passed. His case was man's work: how could a woman help him? But this girl's face was extraordinary – quiet and wide as a clear evening sky. It suggested a hundred images of space, distance, mystery, like ships he had seen, as a boy, quietly berthed by a familiar wharf, but with the breath of far seas and strange harbors in their shrouds… Certainly this girl would understand. He went up to her quietly, lifting his hat, observing the forms – wishing her to see at once that he was "a gentleman."

"I am a stranger to you," he began, sitting down beside her, "but your face is so extremely intelligent that I feel… I feel it is the face I've waited for… looked for everywhere; and I want to tell you –"

The girl's eyes widened: she rose to her feet. She was escaping him!

In his dismay he ran a few steps after her, and caught her roughly by the arm.

"Here – wait – listen! Oh, don't scream, you fool!" he shouted out.

He felt a hand on his own arm; turned and confronted a policeman. Instantly he understood that he was being arrested, and something hard within him was loosened and ran to tears.

"Ah, you know – you *know* I'm guilty!"

He was conscious that a crowd was forming, and that the girl's frightened face had disappeared. But what did he care about her face? It was the policeman who had really understood him. He turned and followed, the crowd at his heels…

VII

IN THE CHARMING PLACE in which he found himself there were so many sympathetic faces that he felt more than ever convinced of the certainty of making himself heard.

It was a bad blow, at first, to find that he had not been arrested for murder; but Ascham, who had come to him at once, explained that he needed rest, and the time to "review" his statements; it appeared that reiteration had made them a little confused and contradictory. To this end he had willingly acquiesced in his removal to a large quiet establishment, with an open space and trees about it, where he had found a number of intelligent companions, some, like himself, engaged in preparing or reviewing statements of their cases, and others ready to lend an interested ear to his own recital.

For a time he was content to let himself go on the tranquil current of this existence; but although his auditors gave him for the most part an encouraging attention, which, in some, went the length of really brilliant and helpful suggestion, he gradually felt a recurrence of his old doubts. Either his hearers were not sincere, or else they had less power to aid him than they boasted. His interminable conferences resulted in nothing, and as the benefit of the long rest made itself felt, it produced an increased mental lucidity which rendered inaction more and more unbearable. At length he discovered that on certain days visitors from the outer world were admitted to his retreat; and he wrote out long and logically constructed relations of his crime, and furtively slipped them into the hands of these messengers of hope.

This occupation gave him a fresh lease of patience, and he now lived only to watch for the visitors' days, and scan the faces that swept by him like stars seen and lost in the rifts of a hurrying sky.

Mostly, these faces were strange and less intelligent than those of his companions. But they represented his last means of access to the world, a kind of subterranean channel on which he could set his "statements" afloat, like paper boats which the mysterious current might sweep out into the open seas of life.

One day, however, his attention was arrested by a familiar contour, a pair of bright prominent eyes, and a chin insufficiently shaved. He sprang up and stood in the path of Peter McCarren.

The journalist looked at him doubtfully, then held out his hand with a startled deprecating, "*Why* –?"

"You didn't know me? I'm so changed?" Granice faltered, feeling the rebound of the other's wonder.

"Why, no; but you're looking quieter – smoothed out," McCarren smiled.

"Yes: that's what I'm here for – to rest. And I've taken the opportunity to write out a clearer statement –"

Granice's hand shook so that he could hardly draw the folded paper from his pocket. As he did so he noticed that the reporter was accompanied by a tall man with grave compassionate eyes. It came to Granice in a wild thrill of conviction that this was the face he had waited for...

"Perhaps your friend – he *is* your friend? – would glance over it – or I could put the case in a few words if you have time?" Granice's voice shook like his hand. If this chance escaped him he felt that his last hope was gone. McCarren and the stranger looked at each other, and the former glanced at his watch.

"I'm sorry we can't stay and talk it over now, Mr Granice; but my friend has an engagement, and we're rather pressed –"

Granice continued to proffer the paper. "I'm sorry – I think I could have explained. But you'll take this, at any rate?"

The stranger looked at him gently. "Certainly – I'll take it." He had his hand out. "Good-bye."

"Good-bye," Granice echoed.

He stood watching the two men move away from him through the long light hall; and as he watched them a tear ran down his face. But as soon as they were out of sight he turned and walked hastily toward his room, beginning to hope again, already planning a new statement.

Outside the building the two men stood still, and the journalist's companion looked up curiously at the long monotonous rows of barred windows.

"So that was Granice?"

"Yes – that was Granice, poor devil," said McCarren.

"Strange case! I suppose there's never been one just like it? He's still absolutely convinced that he committed that murder?"

"Absolutely. Yes."

The stranger reflected. "And there was no conceivable ground for the idea? No one could make out how it started? A quiet conventional sort of fellow like that – where do you suppose he got such a delusion? Did you ever get the least clue to it?"

McCarren stood still, his hands in his pockets, his head cocked up in contemplation of the barred windows. Then he turned his bright hard gaze on his companion.

"That was the queer part of it. I've never spoken of it – but I *did* get a clue."

"By Jove! That's interesting. What was it?"

McCarren formed his red lips into a whistle. "Why – that it wasn't a delusion."

He produced his effect – the other turned on him with a pallid stare.

"He murdered the man all right. I tumbled on the truth by the merest accident, when I'd pretty nearly chucked the whole job."

"He murdered him – murdered his cousin?"

"Sure as you live. Only don't split on me. It's about the queerest business I ever ran into... *Do about it*? Why, what was I to do? I couldn't hang the poor devil, could I? Lord, but I was glad when they collared him, and had him stowed away safe in there!"

The tall man listened with a grave face, grasping Granice's statement in his hand.

"Here – take this; it makes me sick," he said abruptly, thrusting the paper at the reporter; and the two men turned and walked in silence to the gates.

The Canterville Ghost

by Oscar Wilde

I

WHEN MR HIRAM B. OTIS, the American Minister, bought Canterville Chase, everyone told him he was doing a very foolish thing, as there was no doubt at all that the place was haunted. Indeed, Lord Canterville himself, who was a man of the most punctilious honour, had felt it his duty to mention the fact to Mr Otis when they came to discuss terms.

"We have not cared to live in the place ourselves," said Lord Canterville, "since my grandaunt, the Dowager Duchess of Bolton, was frightened into a fit, from which she never really recovered, by two skeleton hands being placed on her shoulders as she was dressing for dinner, and I feel bound to tell you, Mr Otis, that the ghost has been seen by several living members of my family, as well as by the rector of the parish, the Rev. Augustus Dampier, who is a Fellow of King's College, Cambridge. After the unfortunate accident to the Duchess, none of our younger servants would stay with us, and Lady Canterville often got very little sleep at night, in consequence of the mysterious noises that came from the corridor and the library."

"My Lord," answered the Minister, "I will take the furniture and the ghost at a valuation. I have come from a modern country, where we have everything that money can buy; and with all our spry young fellows painting the Old World red, and carrying off your best actors and prima-donnas, I reckon that if there were such a thing as a ghost in Europe, we'd have it at home in a very short time in one of our public museums, or on the road as a show."

"I fear that the ghost exists," said Lord Canterville, smiling, "though it may have resisted the overtures of your enterprising impresarios. It has been well known for three centuries, since 1584 in fact, and always makes its appearance before the death of any member of our family."

"Well, so does the family doctor for that matter, Lord Canterville. But there is no such thing, sir, as a ghost, and I guess the laws of Nature are not going to be suspended for the British aristocracy."

"You are certainly very natural in America," answered Lord Canterville, who did not quite understand Mr Otis's last observation, "and if you don't mind a ghost in the house, it is all right. Only you must remember I warned you."

A few weeks after this, the purchase was concluded, and at the close of the season the Minister and his family went down to Canterville Chase. Mrs Otis, who, as Miss Lucretia R. Tappan, of West 53d Street, had been a celebrated New York belle, was now a very handsome, middle-aged woman, with fine eyes, and a superb profile. Many American ladies on leaving their native land adopt an appearance of chronic ill-health, under the impression that it is a form of European refinement, but Mrs Otis had never fallen into this error. She had a magnificent constitution, and a really wonderful amount of animal spirits. Indeed, in many respects, she was quite English, and was an excellent example of the fact that we have really everything in common with America nowadays, except, of course, language. Her eldest son, christened Washington by his parents in a moment of patriotism, which he never ceased to regret, was a fair-haired, rather good-looking young man, who had qualified himself for American diplomacy by leading the German at the Newport Casino for three successive seasons, and even in London was well known as an excellent dancer. Gardenias and the peerage were his only weaknesses. Otherwise he was extremely sensible. Miss Virginia E. Otis was a little girl of fifteen, lithe and lovely as a fawn, and with a fine freedom in her large blue eyes. She was a wonderful Amazon, and had once raced old Lord Bilton on her pony twice round the park, winning by a length and a half, just in front of the Achilles statue, to the huge delight of the young Duke of Cheshire, who proposed for her on the spot, and was sent back to Eton that very night by his guardians, in floods of tears. After Virginia came the twins, who were usually called "The Star and Stripes," as they were always getting swished. They were delightful boys, and, with the exception of the worthy Minister, the only true republicans of the family.

As Canterville Chase is seven miles from Ascot, the nearest railway station, Mr Otis had telegraphed for a waggonette to meet them, and they started on their drive in high spirits. It was a lovely July evening, and the air was delicate with the scent of the pine-woods. Now and then they heard a wood-pigeon brooding over its own sweet voice, or saw, deep in the rustling fern, the burnished breast of the pheasant. Little squirrels peered at them from the beech-trees as they went by, and the rabbits scudded away through the brushwood and over the mossy knolls, with their white tails in the air. As they entered the avenue of Canterville Chase, however, the sky became suddenly overcast with clouds, a curious stillness seemed to hold the atmosphere, a great flight of rooks passed silently over their heads, and, before they reached the house, some big drops of rain had fallen.

Standing on the steps to receive them was an old woman, neatly dressed in black silk, with a white cap and apron. This was Mrs Umney, the housekeeper, whom Mrs Otis, at Lady Canterville's earnest request, had consented to keep in her former position. She made them each a low curtsey as they alighted, and said in a quaint, old-fashioned manner, "I bid you welcome to Canterville Chase." Following her, they passed through the fine Tudor hall into the library, a long, low room, panelled in black oak, at the end of which was a large stained glass window. Here they found tea laid out for them, and, after taking off their wraps, they sat down and began to look round, while Mrs Umney waited on them.

Suddenly Mrs Otis caught sight of a dull red stain on the floor just by the fireplace, and, quite unconscious of what it really signified, said to Mrs Umney, "I am afraid something has been spilt there."

"Yes, madam," replied the old housekeeper in a low voice, "blood has been spilt on that spot."

"How horrid!" cried Mrs Otis; "I don't at all care for blood-stains in a sitting-room. It must be removed at once."

The old woman smiled, and answered in the same low, mysterious voice, "It is the blood of Lady Eleanore de Canterville, who was murdered on that very spot by her own husband, Sir Simon de Canterville, in 1575. Sir Simon survived her nine years, and disappeared suddenly under very mysterious circumstances. His body has never been discovered, but his guilty spirit still haunts the Chase. The blood-stain has been much admired by tourists and others, and cannot be removed."

"That is all nonsense," cried Washington Otis; "Pinkerton's Champion Stain Remover and Paragon Detergent will clean it up in no time," and before the terrified housekeeper could interfere, he had fallen upon his knees, and was rapidly scouring the floor with a small stick of what looked like a black cosmetic. In a few moments no trace of the blood-stain could be seen.

"I knew Pinkerton would do it," he exclaimed, triumphantly, as he looked round at his admiring family; but no sooner had he said these words than a terrible flash of lightning lit up the sombre room, a fearful peal of thunder made them all start to their feet, and Mrs Umney fainted.

"What a monstrous climate!" said the American Minister, calmly, as he lit a long cheroot. "I guess the old country is so overpopulated that they have not enough decent weather for everybody. I have always been of opinion that emigration is the only thing for England."

"My dear Hiram," cried Mrs Otis, "what can we do with a woman who faints?"

"Charge it to her like breakages," answered the Minister; "she won't faint after that;" and in a few moments Mrs Umney certainly came to. There was no doubt, however, that she was extremely upset, and she sternly warned Mr Otis to beware of some trouble coming to the house.

"I have seen things with my own eyes, sir," she said, "that would make any Christian's hair stand on end, and many and many a night I have not closed my eyes in sleep for the awful things that are done here." Mr Otis, however, and his wife warmly assured the honest soul that they were not afraid of ghosts, and, after invoking the blessings of Providence on her new master and mistress, and making arrangements for an increase of salary, the old housekeeper tottered off to her own room.

II

THE STORM RAGED FIERCELY all that night, but nothing of particular note occurred. The next morning, however, when they came down to breakfast, they found the terrible stain of blood once again on the floor. "I don't think it can be the fault of the Paragon Detergent," said Washington, "for I have tried it with everything. It must be the ghost." He accordingly rubbed out the stain a second time, but the second morning it appeared again. The third morning also it was there, though the library had been locked up at night by Mr Otis himself, and the key carried upstairs. The whole family were now quite interested; Mr Otis began to suspect that he had been too dogmatic in his denial of the existence of ghosts, Mrs Otis expressed her intention of joining the Psychical Society, and Washington prepared a long letter to Messrs. Myers and Podmore on the subject of the Permanence of Sanguineous Stains when connected with Crime. That night all doubts about the objective existence of phantasmata were removed for ever.

The day had been warm and sunny; and, in the cool of the evening, the whole family went out to drive. They did not return home till nine o'clock, when they had a light supper. The conversation in no way turned upon ghosts, so there were not even those primary conditions of receptive expectations which so often precede the presentation of psychical phenomena. The subjects discussed, as I have since learned from Mr Otis, were merely such as form the ordinary conversation of cultured Americans of the better class, such as the immense superiority of Miss Fanny Devonport over Sarah Bernhardt as an actress; the difficulty of obtaining green corn, buckwheat cakes, and hominy, even in the best English houses; the importance of Boston in the development of the world-soul; the advantages of the baggage-check system in railway travelling; and the sweetness of the New York accent as compared to the London drawl. No mention at all was made of the supernatural, nor was Sir Simon de Canterville alluded to in any way. At eleven o'clock the family retired, and by half-past all the lights were out. Some time after, Mr Otis was awakened by a curious noise in the corridor, outside his room. It sounded like the clank of metal, and seemed to be coming nearer every moment. He got up at once, struck a match, and looked at the time. It was exactly one o'clock. He was quite calm, and felt his pulse, which was not at all feverish. The strange noise still continued, and with it he heard distinctly the sound of footsteps. He put on his slippers, took a small oblong phial out of his dressing-case, and opened the door. Right in front of him he saw, in the wan moonlight, an old man of terrible aspect. His eyes were as red burning coals; long grey hair fell over his shoulders in matted coils; his garments, which were of antique cut, were soiled and ragged, and from his wrists and ankles hung heavy manacles and rusty gyves.

"My dear sir," said Mr Otis, "I really must insist on your oiling those chains, and have brought you for that purpose a small bottle of the Tammany Rising Sun Lubricator. It is said to be completely efficacious upon one application, and there are several testimonials to that effect on the wrapper from some of our most eminent native divines. I shall leave it here for you by the bedroom candles, and will be happy to supply you with more, should you require it." With these words the United States Minister laid the bottle down on a marble table, and, closing his door, retired to rest.

For a moment the Canterville ghost stood quite motionless in natural indignation; then, dashing the bottle violently upon the polished floor, he fled down the corridor, uttering hollow groans, and emitting a ghastly green light. Just, however, as he reached the top of the great oak staircase, a door was flung open, two little white-robed figures appeared, and a large pillow whizzed past his head! There was evidently no time to be lost, so, hastily adopting the Fourth dimension of Space as a means of escape, he vanished through the wainscoting, and the house became quite quiet.

On reaching a small secret chamber in the left wing, he leaned up against a moonbeam to recover his breath, and began to try and realize his position. Never, in a brilliant and uninterrupted career of three hundred years, had he been so grossly insulted. He thought of the Dowager Duchess, whom he had frightened into a fit as she stood before the glass in her lace and diamonds; of the four housemaids, who had gone into hysterics when he merely grinned at them through the curtains on one of the spare bedrooms; of the rector of the parish, whose candle he had blown out as he was coming late one night from the library, and who had been under the care of Sir William Gull ever since, a perfect martyr to nervous disorders; and of old Madame de Tremouillac, who, having wakened up one morning early and seen a skeleton seated in an armchair by the fire reading her diary, had been confined to her bed for six weeks with an attack of brain fever, and, on her recovery, had become reconciled to the Church, and broken off her connection with that notorious sceptic, Monsieur de Voltaire. He remembered the terrible night when the wicked Lord Canterville was found choking in his dressing-room, with the knave of diamonds half-way down his throat, and confessed, just before he died, that he had cheated Charles James Fox out of £50,000 at Crockford's by means of that very card, and swore that the ghost had made him swallow it. All his great achievements came back to him again, from the butler who had shot himself in the pantry because he had seen a green hand tapping at the window-pane, to the beautiful Lady Stutfield, who was always obliged to wear a black velvet band round her throat to hide the mark of five fingers burnt upon her white skin, and who drowned herself at last in the carp-pond at the end of the King's Walk. With the enthusiastic egotism of the true artist, he went over his most celebrated performances, and smiled bitterly to himself as he recalled to mind his last appearance as "Red Reuben, or the Strangled Babe," his *début* as "Guant Gibeon, the Blood-sucker of Bexley Moor," and the *furore* he had excited one lovely June evening by merely playing ninepins with his own bones upon the lawn-tennis ground. And after all this some wretched modern Americans were to come and offer him the Rising Sun Lubricator, and throw pillows at his head! It was quite unbearable. Besides, no ghost in history had ever been treated in this manner. Accordingly, he determined to have vengeance, and remained till daylight in an attitude of deep thought.

III

THE NEXT MORNING, when the Otis family met at breakfast, they discussed the ghost at some length. The United States Minister was naturally a little annoyed to find that his present had not been accepted. "I have no wish," he said, "to do the ghost any personal injury, and I must say that, considering the length of time he has been in the house, I don't think it is at all polite to throw pillows at him" – a very just remark, at which, I am sorry to say, the twins burst into shouts of laughter. "Upon the other hand," he continued, "if he really declines to use the Rising Sun Lubricator, we shall have to take his chains from him. It would be quite impossible to sleep, with such a noise going on outside the bedrooms."

For the rest of the week, however, they were undisturbed, the only thing that excited any attention being the continual renewal of the blood-stain on the library floor. This certainly was very strange, as the door was always locked at night by Mr Otis, and the windows kept closely barred. The chameleon-like colour, also, of the stain excited a good deal of comment. Some mornings it was a dull (almost Indian) red, then it would be vermilion, then a rich purple, and once when they came down for family prayers, according to the simple rites of the Free American Reformed Episcopalian Church, they found it a bright emerald-green. These kaleidoscopic changes naturally amused the party very much, and bets on the subject were freely made every evening. The only person who did not enter into the joke was little Virginia, who, for some unexplained reason, was always a good deal distressed at the sight of the blood-stain, and very nearly cried the morning it was emerald-green.

The second appearance of the ghost was on Sunday night. Shortly after they had gone to bed they were suddenly alarmed by a fearful crash in the hall. Rushing downstairs, they found that a large suit of old armour had become detached from its stand, and had fallen on the stone floor, while seated in a high-backed chair was the Canterville ghost, rubbing his knees with an expression of acute agony on his face. The twins, having brought their pea-shooters with them, at once discharged two pellets on him, with that accuracy of aim which can only be attained by long and careful practice on a writing-master, while the United States Minister covered him with his revolver, and called upon him, in accordance with Californian etiquette, to hold up his hands! The ghost started up with a wild shriek of rage, and swept through them like a mist, extinguishing Washington Otis's candle as he passed, and so leaving them all in total darkness. On reaching the top of the staircase he recovered himself, and determined to give his celebrated peal of demoniac laughter. This he had on more than one occasion found extremely useful. It was said to have turned

Lord Raker's wig grey in a single night, and had certainly made three of Lady Canterville's French governesses give warning before their month was up. He accordingly laughed his most horrible laugh, till the old vaulted roof rang and rang again, but hardly had the fearful echo died away when a door opened, and Mrs Otis came out in a light blue dressing-gown. "I am afraid you are far from well," she said, "and have brought you a bottle of Doctor Dobell's tincture. If it is indigestion, you will find it a most excellent remedy." The ghost glared at her in fury, and began at once to make preparations for turning himself into a large black dog, an accomplishment for which he was justly renowned, and to which the family doctor always attributed the permanent idiocy of Lord Canterville's uncle, the Hon. Thomas Horton. The sound of approaching footsteps, however, made him hesitate in his fell purpose, so he contented himself with becoming faintly phosphorescent, and vanished with a deep churchyard groan, just as the twins had come up to him.

On reaching his room he entirely broke down, and became a prey to the most violent agitation. The vulgarity of the twins, and the gross materialism of Mrs Otis, were naturally extremely annoying, but what really distressed him most was that he had been unable to wear the suit of mail. He had hoped that even modern Americans would be thrilled by the sight of a Spectre in Armour, if for no more sensible reason, at least out of respect for their natural poet Longfellow, over whose graceful and attractive poetry he himself had whiled away many a weary hour when the Cantervilles were up in town. Besides, it was his own suit. He had worn it with great success at the Kenilworth tournament, and had been highly complimented on it by no less a person than the Virgin Queen herself. Yet when he had put it on, he had been completely overpowered by the weight of the huge breastplate and steel casque, and had fallen heavily on the stone pavement, barking both his knees severely, and bruising the knuckles of his right hand.

For some days after this he was extremely ill, and hardly stirred out of his room at all, except to keep the blood-stain in proper repair. However, by taking great care of himself, he recovered, and resolved to make a third attempt to frighten the United States Minister and his family. He selected Friday, August 17th, for his appearance, and spent most of that day in looking over his wardrobe, ultimately deciding in favour of a large slouched hat with a red feather, a winding-sheet frilled at the wrists and neck, and a rusty dagger. Towards evening a violent storm of rain came on, and the wind was so high that all the windows and doors in the old house shook and rattled. In fact, it was just such weather as he loved. His plan of action was this. He was to make his way quietly to Washington Otis's room, gibber at him from the foot of the bed, and stab himself three times in the throat to the sound of low music. He bore Washington a special grudge, being quite aware that it was he who was in the habit of removing the famous Canterville blood-stain by means of Pinkerton's Paragon Detergent. Having reduced the reckless and foolhardy youth to a condition of abject terror, he was then to proceed to the room occupied by the United States Minister and his wife, and there to place a clammy hand on Mrs Otis's forehead, while he hissed into her trembling husband's ear the awful secrets of the charnel-house. With regard to little Virginia, he had not quite made up his mind. She had never insulted him in any way, and was pretty and gentle. A few hollow groans from the wardrobe, he thought, would be more than sufficient, or, if that failed to wake her, he might grabble at the counterpane with palsy-twitching fingers. As for the twins, he was quite determined to teach them a lesson. The first thing to be done was, of course, to sit upon their chests, so as to produce the stifling sensation of nightmare. Then, as their beds were quite close to each other, to stand between them in the form of a green, icy-cold corpse, till they became paralyzed with fear, and finally, to throw off the winding-sheet, and crawl round the room, with white, bleached bones and one rolling eyeball, in the character of "Dumb Daniel, or the Suicide's Skeleton," a *rôle* in which he had on more than one occasion produced a great effect, and which he considered quite equal to his famous part of "Martin the Maniac, or the Masked Mystery."

At half-past ten he heard the family going to bed. For some time he was disturbed by wild shrieks of laughter from the twins, who, with the light-hearted gaiety of schoolboys, were evidently amusing themselves before they retired to rest, but at a quarter-past eleven all was still, and, as midnight sounded, he sallied forth. The owl beat against the window-panes, the raven croaked from the old yew-tree, and the wind wandered moaning round the house like a lost soul; but the Otis family slept unconscious of their doom, and high above the rain and storm he could hear the steady snoring of the Minister for the United States. He stepped stealthily out of the wainscoting, with an evil smile on his cruel, wrinkled mouth, and the moon hid her face in a cloud as he stole past the great oriel window, where his own arms and those of his murdered wife were blazoned in azure and gold. On and on he glided, like an evil shadow, the very darkness seeming to loathe him as he passed. Once he thought he heard something call, and stopped; but it was only the baying of a dog from the Red Farm, and he went on, muttering strange sixteenth-century curses, and ever and anon brandishing the rusty dagger in the midnight air. Finally he reached the corner of the passage that led to luckless Washington's room. For a moment he paused there, the wind blowing his long grey locks about his head, and twisting into grotesque and fantastic folds the nameless horror of the dead man's shroud. Then the clock struck the quarter, and he felt the time was come. He chuckled to himself, and turned the corner; but no sooner had he done so than, with a piteous wail of terror, he fell back, and hid his blanched face in his long, bony hands. Right in front of him was standing a horrible spectre, motionless as a carven image, and monstrous as a madman's dream! Its head was bald and burnished; its face round, and fat, and white; and hideous laughter seemed to have writhed its features into an eternal grin. From the eyes streamed rays of scarlet light, the mouth was a wide well of fire, and a hideous garment, like to his own, swathed with its silent snows the Titan form. On its breast was a placard with strange writing in antique characters, some scroll of shame it seemed, some record of wild sins, some awful calendar of crime, and, with its right hand, it bore aloft a falchion of gleaming steel.

Never having seen a ghost before, he naturally was terribly frightened, and, after a second hasty glance at the awful phantom, he fled back to his room, tripping up in his long winding-sheet as he sped down the corridor, and finally dropping the rusty dagger into the Minister's jack-boots, where it was found in the morning by the butler. Once in the privacy of his own apartment, he flung himself down on a small pallet-bed, and hid his face under the clothes. After a time, however, the brave old Canterville spirit asserted itself, and he determined to go and speak to the other ghost as soon as it was daylight. Accordingly, just as the dawn was touching the hills with silver, he returned towards the spot where he had first laid eyes on the grisly phantom, feeling that, after all, two ghosts were better than one, and that, by the aid of his new friend, he might safely grapple with the twins. On reaching the spot, however, a terrible sight met his gaze. Something had evidently happened to the spectre, for the light had entirely faded from its hollow eyes, the gleaming falchion had fallen from its hand, and it was leaning up against the wall in a strained and uncomfortable attitude. He rushed forward and seized it in his arms, when, to his horror, the head slipped off and rolled on the floor, the body assumed a recumbent posture, and he found himself clasping a white dimity bed-curtain, with a sweeping-brush, a kitchen cleaver, and a hollow turnip lying at his feet! Unable to understand this curious transformation, he clutched the placard with feverish haste, and there, in the grey morning light, he read these fearful words:

YE OTIS GHOSTE
Ye Onlie True and Originale Spook,
Beware of Ye Imitationes.
All others are Counterfeite.

The whole thing flashed across him. He had been tricked, foiled, and out-witted! The old Canterville look came into his eyes; he ground his toothless gums together; and, raising his withered hands high above his head, swore according to the picturesque phraseology of the antique school, that, when Chanticleer had sounded twice his merry horn, deeds of blood would be wrought, and murder walk abroad with silent feet.

Hardly had he finished this awful oath when, from the red-tiled roof of a distant homestead, a cock crew. He laughed a long, low, bitter laugh, and waited. Hour after hour he waited, but the cock, for some strange reason, did not crow again. Finally, at half-past seven, the arrival of the housemaids made him give up his fearful vigil, and he stalked back to his room, thinking of his vain oath and baffled purpose. There he consulted several books of ancient chivalry, of which he was exceedingly fond, and found that, on every occasion on which this oath had been used, Chanticleer had always crowed a second time. "Perdition seize the naughty fowl," he muttered, "I have seen the day when, with my stout spear, I would have run him through the gorge, and made him crow for me an 'twere in death!" He then retired to a comfortable lead coffin, and stayed there till evening.

IV

THE NEXT DAY THE GHOST was very weak and tired. The terrible excitement of the last four weeks was beginning to have its effect. His nerves were completely shattered, and he started at the slightest noise. For five days he kept his room, and at last made up his mind to give up the point of the blood-stain on the library floor. If the Otis family did not want it, they clearly did not deserve it. They were evidently people on a low, material plane of existence, and quite incapable of appreciating the symbolic value of sensuous phenomena. The question of phantasmic apparitions, and the development of astral bodies, was of course quite a different matter, and really not under his control. It was his solemn duty to appear in the corridor once a week, and to gibber from the large oriel window on the first and third Wednesdays in every month, and he did not see how he could honourably escape from his obligations. It is quite true that his life had been very evil, but, upon the other hand, he was most conscientious in all things connected with the supernatural. For the next three Saturdays, accordingly, he traversed the corridor as usual between midnight and three o'clock, taking every possible precaution against being either heard or seen. He removed his boots, trod as lightly as possible on the old worm-eaten boards, wore a large black velvet cloak, and was careful to use the Rising Sun Lubricator for oiling his chains. I am bound to acknowledge that it was with a good deal of difficulty that he brought himself to adopt this last mode of protection. However, one night, while the family were at dinner, he slipped into Mr Otis's bedroom and carried off the bottle. He felt a little humiliated at first, but afterwards was sensible enough to see that there was a great deal to be said for the invention, and, to a certain degree, it served his purpose. Still in spite of everything he was not left unmolested. Strings were continually being stretched across the corridor, over which he tripped in the dark, and on one occasion, while dressed for the part of "Black Isaac, or the Huntsman of Hogley Woods," he met with a severe fall, through treading on a butter-slide, which the twins had constructed from the entrance of the Tapestry Chamber to the top of the oak staircase. This last insult so enraged him, that he resolved to make one final effort to assert his dignity and social position, and determined to visit the insolent young Etonians the next night in his celebrated character of "Reckless Rupert, or the Headless Earl."

He had not appeared in this disguise for more than seventy years; in fact, not since he had so frightened pretty Lady Barbara Modish by means of it, that she suddenly broke off her engagement with the present Lord Canterville's grandfather, and ran away to Gretna Green with handsome Jack Castletown, declaring that nothing in the world would induce her to marry into a family that allowed such a horrible phantom to walk up and down the terrace at twilight. Poor Jack was afterwards shot in a duel by Lord Canterville on Wandsworth Common, and Lady Barbara died of a broken heart at Tunbridge Wells before the year was out, so, in every way, it had been a great success. It was, however an extremely difficult "make-up," if I may use such a theatrical expression in connection with one of the greatest mysteries of the supernatural, or, to employ a more scientific term, the higher-natural world, and it took him fully three hours to make his preparations. At last everything was ready, and he was very pleased with his appearance. The big leather riding-boots that went with the dress were just a little too large for him, and he could only find one of the two horse-pistols, but, on the whole, he was quite satisfied, and at a quarter-past one he glided out of the wainscoting and crept down the corridor. On reaching the room occupied by the twins, which I should mention was called the Blue Bed Chamber, on account of the colour of its hangings, he found the door just ajar. Wishing to make an effective entrance, he flung it wide open, when a heavy jug of water fell right down on him, wetting him to the skin, and just missing his left shoulder by a couple of inches. At the same moment he heard stifled shrieks of laughter proceeding from the four-post bed. The shock to his nervous system was so great that he fled back to his room as hard as he could go, and the next day he was laid up with a severe cold. The only thing that at all consoled him in the whole affair was the fact that he had not brought his head with him, for, had he done so, the consequences might have been very serious.

He now gave up all hope of ever frightening this rude American family, and contented himself, as a rule, with creeping about the passages in list slippers, with a thick red muffler round his throat for fear of draughts, and a small arquebuse, in case he should be attacked by the twins. The final blow he received occurred on the 19th of September. He had gone downstairs to the great entrance-hall, feeling sure that there, at any rate, he would be quite unmolested, and was amusing himself by making satirical remarks on the large Saroni photographs of the United States Minister and his wife which had now taken the place of the Canterville family pictures. He was simply but neatly clad in a long shroud, spotted with churchyard mould, had tied up his jaw with a strip of yellow linen, and carried a small lantern and a sexton's spade. In fact, he was dressed for the character of "Jonas the Graveless, or the Corpse-Snatcher of Chertsey Barn," one of his most remarkable impersonations, and one which the Cantervilles had every reason to remember, as it was the real origin of their quarrel with their neighbour, Lord Rufford. It was about a quarter-past two o'clock in the morning, and, as far as he could ascertain, no one was stirring. As he was strolling towards the library, however, to see if there were any traces left of the blood-stain, suddenly there leaped out on him from a dark corner two figures, who waved their arms wildly above their heads, and shrieked out "BOO!" in his ear.

Seized with a panic, which, under the circumstances, was only natural, he rushed for the staircase, but found Washington Otis waiting for him there with the big garden-syringe, and being thus hemmed in by his enemies on every side, and driven almost to bay, he vanished into the great iron stove, which, fortunately for him, was not lit, and had to make his way home through the flues and chimneys, arriving at his own room in a terrible state of dirt, disorder, and despair.

After this he was not seen again on any nocturnal expedition. The twins lay in wait for him on several occasions, and strewed the passages with nutshells every night to the great annoyance of their parents and the servants, but it was of no avail. It was quite evident that his feelings were so wounded that he would not appear. Mr Otis consequently resumed his great work on the history of the Democratic Party, on which he had been engaged for some years; Mrs Otis organized a wonderful clam-bake, which amazed the whole county; the boys took to lacrosse, euchre, poker, and other American national games, and Virginia rode about the lanes on her pony, accompanied by the young Duke of Cheshire, who had come to spend the last week of his holidays at Canterville Chase. It was generally assumed that the ghost had gone away, and, in fact, Mr Otis wrote a letter to that effect to Lord Canterville, who, in reply, expressed his great pleasure at the news, and sent his best congratulations to the Minister's worthy wife.

The Otises, however, were deceived, for the ghost was still in the house, and though now almost an invalid, was by no means ready to let matters rest, particularly as he heard that among the guests was the young Duke of Cheshire, whose grand-uncle, Lord Francis Stilton, had once bet a hundred guineas with Colonel Carbury that he would play dice with the Canterville ghost, and was found the next morning lying on the floor of the card-room in such a helpless paralytic state that, though he lived on to a great age, he was never able to say anything again but "Double Sixes." The story was well known at the time, though, of course, out of respect to the feelings of the two noble families, every attempt was made to hush it up, and a full account of all the circumstances connected with it will be found in the third volume of Lord Tattle's *Recollections of the Prince Regent and his Friends*. The ghost, then, was naturally very anxious to show that he had not lost his influence over the Stiltons, with whom, indeed, he was distantly connected, his own first cousin having been married *en secondes noces* to the Sieur de Bulkeley, from whom, as everyone knows, the Dukes of Cheshire are lineally descended. Accordingly, he made arrangements for appearing to Virginia's little lover in his celebrated impersonation of "The Vampire Monk, or the Bloodless Benedictine," a performance so horrible that when old Lady Startup saw it, which she did on one fatal New Year's Eve, in the year 1764, she went off into the most piercing shrieks, which culminated in violent apoplexy, and died in three days, after disinheriting the Cantervilles, who were her nearest relations, and leaving all her money to her London apothecary. At the last moment, however, his terror of the twins prevented his leaving his room, and the little Duke slept in peace under the great feathered canopy in the Royal Bedchamber, and dreamed of Virginia.

V

A FEW DAYS AFTER THIS, Virginia and her curly-haired cavalier went out riding on Brockley meadows, where she tore her habit so badly in getting through a hedge that, on their return home, she made up her mind to go up by the back staircase so as not to be seen. As she was running past the Tapestry Chamber, the door of which happened to be open, she fancied she saw someone inside, and thinking it was her mother's maid, who sometimes used to bring her work there, looked in to ask her to mend her habit. To her immense surprise, however, it was the Canterville Ghost himself! He was sitting by the window, watching the ruined gold of the yellowing trees fly through the air, and the red leaves dancing madly down the long avenue. His head was leaning on his hand, and his whole attitude was one of extreme depression. Indeed, so forlorn, and so much out of repair did he look, that little Virginia, whose first idea had been to run away and lock herself in her room, was filled with pity, and determined to try and comfort him. So light was her footfall, and so deep his melancholy, that he was not aware of her presence till she spoke to him.

"I am so sorry for you," she said, "but my brothers are going back to Eton tomorrow, and then, if you behave yourself, no one will annoy you."

"It is absurd asking me to behave myself," he answered, looking round in astonishment at the pretty little girl who had ventured to address him, "quite absurd. I must rattle my chains, and groan through keyholes, and walk about at night, if that is what you mean. It is my only reason for existing."

"It is no reason at all for existing, and you know you have been very wicked. Mrs Umney told us, the first day we arrived here, that you had killed your wife."

"Well, I quite admit it," said the Ghost, petulantly, "but it was a purely family matter, and concerned no one else."

"It is very wrong to kill anyone," said Virginia, who at times had a sweet puritan gravity, caught from some old New England ancestor.

"Oh, I hate the cheap severity of abstract ethics! My wife was very plain, never had my ruffs properly starched, and knew nothing about cookery. Why, there was a buck I had shot in Hogley Woods, a magnificent pricket, and do you know how she had it sent to table? However, it is no matter now, for it is all over, and I don't think it was very nice of her brothers to starve me to death, though I did kill her."

"Starve you to death? Oh, Mr Ghost – I mean Sir Simon, are you hungry? I have a sandwich in my case. Would you like it?"

"No, thank you, I never eat anything now; but it is very kind of you, all the same, and you are much nicer than the rest of your horrid, rude, vulgar, dishonest family."

"Stop!" cried Virginia, stamping her foot, "it is you who are rude, and horrid, and vulgar, and as for dishonesty, you know you stole the paints out of my box to try and furbish up that ridiculous blood-stain in the library. First you took all my reds, including the vermilion, and I couldn't do any more sunsets, then you took the emerald-green and the chrome-yellow, and finally I had nothing left but indigo and Chinese white, and could only do moonlight scenes, which are always depressing to look at, and not at all easy to paint. I never told on you, though I was very much annoyed, and it was most ridiculous, the whole thing; for who ever heard of emerald-green blood?"

"Well, really," said the Ghost, rather meekly, "what was I to do? It is a very difficult thing to get real blood nowadays, and, as your brother began it all with his Paragon Detergent, I certainly saw no reason why I should not have your paints. As for colour, that is always a matter of taste: the Cantervilles have blue blood, for instance, the very bluest in England; but I know you Americans don't care for things of this kind."

"You know nothing about it, and the best thing you can do is to emigrate and improve your mind. My father will be only too happy to give you a free passage, and though there is a heavy duty on spirits of every kind, there will be no difficulty about the Custom House, as the officers are all Democrats. Once in New York, you are sure to be a great success. I know lots of people there who would give a hundred thousand dollars to have a grandfather, and much more than that to have a family ghost."

"I don't think I should like America."

"I suppose because we have no ruins and no curiosities," said Virginia, satirically.

"No ruins! no curiosities!" answered the Ghost; "you have your navy and your manners."

"Good evening; I will go and ask papa to get the twins an extra week's holiday."

"Please don't go, Miss Virginia," he cried; "I am so lonely and so unhappy, and I really don't know what to do. I want to go to sleep and I cannot."

"That's quite absurd! You have merely to go to bed and blow out the candle. It is very difficult sometimes to keep awake, especially at church, but there is no difficulty at all about sleeping. Why, even babies know how to do that, and they are not very clever."

"I have not slept for three hundred years," he said sadly, and Virginia's beautiful blue eyes opened in wonder; "for three hundred years I have not slept, and I am so tired."

Virginia grew quite grave, and her little lips trembled like rose-leaves. She came towards him, and kneeling down at his side, looked up into his old withered face.

"Poor, poor Ghost," she murmured; "have you no place where you can sleep?"

"Far away beyond the pine-woods," he answered, in a low, dreamy voice, "there is a little garden. There the grass grows long and deep, there are the great white stars of the hemlock flower, there the nightingale sings all night long. All night long he sings, and the cold crystal moon looks down, and the yew-tree spreads out its giant arms over the sleepers."

Virginia's eyes grew dim with tears, and she hid her face in her hands.

"You mean the Garden of Death," she whispered.

"Yes, death. Death must be so beautiful. To lie in the soft brown earth, with the grasses waving above one's head, and listen to silence. To have no yesterday, and no tomorrow. To forget time, to forget life, to be at peace. You can help me. You can open for me the portals of death's house, for love is always with you, and love is stronger than death is."

Virginia trembled, a cold shudder ran through her, and for a few moments there was silence. She felt as if she was in a terrible dream.

Then the Ghost spoke again, and his voice sounded like the sighing of the wind.

"Have you ever read the old prophecy on the library window?"

"Oh, often," cried the little girl, looking up; "I know it quite well. It is painted in curious black letters, and is difficult to read. There are only six lines:

> "'*When a golden girl can win*
> *Prayer from out the lips of sin,*
> *When the barren almond bears,*
> *And a little child gives away its tears,*
> *Then shall all the house be still*
> *And peace come to Canterville.*'

But I don't know what they mean."

"They mean," he said, sadly, "that you must weep with me for my sins, because I have no tears, and pray with me for my soul, because I have no faith, and then, if you have always been sweet, and good, and gentle, the angel of death will have mercy on me. You will see fearful shapes in darkness, and wicked voices will whisper in your ear, but they will not harm you, for against the purity of a little child the powers of Hell cannot prevail."

Virginia made no answer, and the ghost wrung his hands in wild despair as he looked down at her bowed golden head. Suddenly she stood up, very pale, and with a strange light in her eyes. "I am not afraid," she said firmly, "and I will ask the angel to have mercy on you."

He rose from his seat with a faint cry of joy, and taking her hand bent over it with old-fashioned grace and kissed it. His fingers were as cold as ice, and his lips burned like fire, but Virginia did not falter, as he led her across the dusky room. On the faded green tapestry were broidered little huntsmen. They blew their tasselled horns and with their tiny hands waved to her to go back. "Go back! little Virginia," they cried, "go back!" but the ghost clutched her hand more tightly, and she shut her eyes against them. Horrible animals with lizard tails and goggle eyes blinked at her from the carven chimneypiece, and murmured, "Beware! little Virginia, beware! we may never see you again," but the Ghost glided on more swiftly, and Virginia did not listen. When they reached the end of the room he stopped, and muttered some words she could not understand. She opened her eyes, and saw the wall slowly fading away like a mist, and a great black cavern in front of her. A bitter cold wind swept round them, and she felt something pulling at her dress. "Quick, quick," cried the Ghost, "or it will be too late," and in a moment the wainscoting had closed behind them, and the Tapestry Chamber was empty.

VI

ABOUT TEN MINUTES LATER, the bell rang for tea, and, as Virginia did not come down, Mrs Otis sent up one of the footmen to tell her. After a little time he returned and said that he could not find Miss Virginia anywhere. As she was in the habit of going out to the garden every evening to get flowers for the dinner-table, Mrs Otis was not at all alarmed at first, but when six o'clock struck, and Virginia did not appear, she became really agitated, and sent the boys out to look for her, while she herself and Mr Otis searched every room in the house. At half-past six the boys came back and said that they could find no trace of their sister anywhere. They were all now in the greatest state of excitement, and did not know what to do, when Mr Otis suddenly remembered that, some few days before, he had given a band of gypsies permission to camp in the park. He accordingly at once set off for Blackfell Hollow, where he knew they were, accompanied by his eldest son and two of the farm-servants. The little Duke of Cheshire, who was perfectly frantic with anxiety, begged hard to be allowed to go too, but Mr Otis would not allow him, as he was afraid there might be a scuffle. On arriving at the spot, however, he found that the gypsies had gone, and it was evident that their departure had been rather sudden, as the fire was still burning, and some plates were lying on the grass. Having sent off Washington and the two men to scour the district, he ran home, and despatched telegrams to all the police inspectors in the county, telling them to look out for a little girl who had been kidnapped by tramps or gypsies. He then ordered his horse to be brought round, and, after insisting on his wife and the three boys sitting down to dinner, rode off down the Ascot road with a groom. He had hardly, however, gone a couple of miles, when he heard somebody galloping after him, and, looking round, saw the little Duke coming up on his pony, with his face very flushed, and no hat. "I'm awfully sorry, Mr Otis," gasped out the boy, "but I can't eat any dinner as long as Virginia is lost. Please don't be angry with me; if you had let us be engaged last year, there would never have been all this trouble. You won't send me back, will you? I can't go! I won't go!"

The Minister could not help smiling at the handsome young scapegrace, and was a good deal touched at his devotion to Virginia, so leaning down from his horse, he patted him kindly on the shoulders, and said, "Well, Cecil, if you won't go back, I suppose you must come with me, but I must get you a hat at Ascot."

"Oh, bother my hat! I want Virginia!" cried the little Duke, laughing, and they galloped on to the railway station. There Mr Otis inquired of the station-master if anyone answering to the description of Virginia had been seen on the platform, but could get no news of her. The station-master, however, wired up and down the line, and assured him that a strict watch would be kept for her, and, after having bought a hat for the little Duke from a linen-draper, who was just putting up his shutters, Mr Otis rode off to Bexley, a village about four miles away, which he was told was a well-known haunt of the gypsies, as there was a large common next to it. Here they roused up the rural policeman, but could get no information from him, and, after riding all over the common, they turned their horses' heads homewards, and reached the Chase about eleven o'clock, dead-tired and almost heart-broken. They found Washington and the twins waiting for them at the gate-house with lanterns, as the avenue was very dark. Not the slightest trace of Virginia had been discovered. The gypsies had been caught on Brockley meadows, but she was not with them, and they had explained their sudden departure by saying that they had mistaken the date of Chorton Fair, and had gone off in a hurry for fear they should be late. Indeed, they had been quite distressed at hearing of Virginia's disappearance, as they were very grateful to Mr Otis for having allowed them to camp in his park, and four of their number had stayed behind to help in the search. The carp-pond had been dragged, and the whole Chase thoroughly gone over, but without any result. It was evident that, for that night at any rate, Virginia was lost to them; and it was in a state of the deepest depression that Mr Otis and the boys walked up to the house, the groom following behind with the two horses and the pony. In the hall they found a group of frightened servants, and lying on a sofa in the library was poor Mrs Otis, almost out of her mind with terror and anxiety, and having her forehead bathed with eau de cologne by the old housekeeper. Mr Otis at once insisted on her having something to eat, and ordered up supper for the whole party. It was a melancholy meal, as hardly anyone spoke, and even the twins were awestruck and subdued, as they were very fond of their sister. When they had finished, Mr Otis, in spite of the entreaties of the little Duke, ordered them all to bed, saying that nothing more could be done that night, and that he would telegraph in the morning to Scotland Yard for some detectives to be sent down immediately. Just as they were passing out of the dining-room, midnight began to boom from the clock tower, and when the last stroke sounded they heard a crash and a sudden shrill cry; a dreadful peal of thunder shook the house, a strain of unearthly music floated through the air, a panel at the top of the staircase flew back with a loud noise, and out on the landing, looking very pale and white, with a little casket in her hand, stepped Virginia. In a moment they had all rushed up to her. Mrs Otis clasped her passionately in her arms, the Duke smothered her with violent kisses, and the twins executed a wild war-dance round the group.

"Good heavens! child, where have you been?" said Mr Otis, rather angrily, thinking that she had been playing some foolish trick on them. "Cecil and I have been riding all over the country looking for you, and your mother has been frightened to death. You must never play these practical jokes any more."

"Except on the Ghost! except on the Ghost!" shrieked the twins, as they capered about.

"My own darling, thank God you are found; you must never leave my side again," murmured Mrs Otis, as she kissed the trembling child, and smoothed the tangled gold of her hair.

"Papa," said Virginia, quietly, "I have been with the Ghost. He is dead, and you must come and see him. He had been very wicked, but he was really sorry for all that he had done, and he gave me this box of beautiful jewels before he died."

The whole family gazed at her in mute amazement, but she was quite grave and serious; and, turning round, she led them through the opening in the wainscoting down a narrow secret corridor, Washington following with a lighted candle, which he had caught up from the table. Finally, they came to a great oak door, studded with rusty nails. When Virginia touched it, it swung back on its heavy hinges, and they found themselves in a little low room, with a vaulted ceiling, and one tiny grated window. Imbedded in the wall was a huge iron ring, and chained to it was a gaunt skeleton, that was stretched out at full length on the stone floor, and seemed to be trying to grasp with its long fleshless fingers an old-fashioned trencher and ewer, that were placed just out of its reach. The jug had evidently been once filled with water, as it was covered inside with green mould. There was nothing on the trencher but a pile of dust. Virginia knelt down beside the skeleton, and, folding her little hands together, began to pray silently, while the rest of the party looked on in wonder at the terrible tragedy whose secret was now disclosed to them.

"Hallo!" suddenly exclaimed one of the twins, who had been looking out of the window to try and discover in what wing of the house the room was situated. "Hallo! the old withered almond-tree has blossomed. I can see the flowers quite plainly in the moonlight."

"God has forgiven him," said Virginia, gravely, as she rose to her feet, and a beautiful light seemed to illumine her face.

"What an angel you are!" cried the young Duke, and he put his arm round her neck, and kissed her.

VII

FOUR DAYS AFTER these curious incidents, a funeral started from Canterville Chase at about eleven o'clock at night. The hearse was drawn by eight black horses, each of which carried on its head a great tuft of nodding ostrich-plumes, and the leaden coffin was covered by a rich purple pall, on which was embroidered in gold the Canterville coat-of-arms. By the side of the hearse and the coaches walked the servants with lighted torches, and the whole procession was wonderfully impressive. Lord Canterville was the chief mourner, having come up specially from Wales to attend the funeral, and sat in the first carriage along with little Virginia. Then came the United States Minister and his wife, then Washington and the three boys, and in the last carriage was Mrs Umney. It was generally felt that, as she had been frightened by the ghost for more than fifty years of her life, she had a right to see the last of him. A deep grave had been dug in the corner of the churchyard, just under the old yew-tree, and the service was read in the most impressive manner by the Rev. Augustus Dampier. When the ceremony was over, the servants, according to an old custom observed in the Canterville family, extinguished their torches, and, as the coffin was being lowered into the grave, Virginia stepped forward, and laid on it a large cross made of white and pink almond-blossoms. As she did so, the moon came out from behind a cloud, and flooded with its silent silver the little churchyard, and from a distant copse a nightingale began to sing. She thought of the ghost's description of the Garden of Death, her eyes became dim with tears, and she hardly spoke a word during the drive home.

The next morning, before Lord Canterville went up to town, Mr Otis had an interview with him on the subject of the jewels the ghost had given to Virginia. They were perfectly magnificent, especially a certain ruby necklace with old Venetian setting, which was really a superb specimen of sixteenth-century work, and their value was so great that Mr Otis felt considerable scruples about allowing his daughter to accept them.

"My lord," he said, "I know that in this country mortmain is held to apply to trinkets as well as to land, and it is quite clear to me that these jewels are, or should be, heirlooms in your family. I must beg you, accordingly, to take them to London with you, and to regard them simply as a portion of your property which has been restored to you under certain strange conditions. As for my daughter, she is merely a child, and has as yet, I am glad to say, but little interest in such appurtenances of idle luxury. I am also informed by Mrs Otis, who, I may say, is no mean authority upon Art – having had the privilege of spending several winters in Boston when she was a girl – that these gems are of great monetary worth, and if offered for sale would fetch a tall price. Under these circumstances, Lord Canterville, I feel sure that you will recognize how impossible it would be for me to allow them to remain in the possession of any member of my family; and, indeed, all such vain gauds and toys, however suitable or necessary to the dignity of the British aristocracy, would be completely out of place among those who have been brought up on the severe, and I believe immortal, principles of Republican simplicity. Perhaps I should mention that Virginia is very anxious that you should allow her to retain the box, as a memento of your unfortunate but misguided ancestor. As it is extremely old, and consequently a good deal out of repair, you may perhaps think fit to comply with her request. For my own part, I confess I am a good deal surprised to find a child of mine expressing sympathy with mediævalism in any form, and can only account for it by the fact that Virginia was born in one of your London suburbs shortly after Mrs Otis had returned from a trip to Athens."

Lord Canterville listened very gravely to the worthy Minister's speech, pulling his grey moustache now and then to hide an involuntary smile, and when Mr Otis had ended, he shook him cordially by the hand, and said: "My dear sir, your charming little daughter rendered my unlucky ancestor, Sir Simon, a very important service, and I and my family are much indebted to her for her marvellous courage and pluck. The jewels are clearly hers, and, egad, I believe that if I were heartless enough to take them from her, the wicked old fellow would be out of his grave in a fortnight, leading me the devil of a life. As for their being heirlooms, nothing is an heirloom that is not so mentioned in a will or legal document, and the existence of these jewels has been quite unknown. I assure you I have no more claim on them than your butler, and when Miss Virginia grows up, I dare say she will be pleased to have pretty things to wear. Besides, you forget, Mr Otis, that you took the furniture and the ghost at a valuation, and anything that belonged to the ghost passed at once into your possession, as, whatever activity Sir Simon may have shown in the corridor at night, in point of law he was really dead, and you acquired his property by purchase."

Mr Otis was a good deal distressed at Lord Canterville's refusal, and begged him to reconsider his decision, but the good-natured peer was quite firm, and finally induced the Minister to allow his daughter to retain the present the ghost had given her, and when, in the spring of 1890, the young Duchess of Cheshire was presented at the Queen's first drawing-room on the occasion of her marriage, her jewels were the universal theme of admiration. For Virginia received the coronet, which is the reward of all good little American girls, and was married to her boy-lover as soon as he came of age. They were both so charming, and they loved each other so much, that everyone was delighted at the match, except the old Marchioness of Dumbleton, who had tried to catch the Duke for one of her seven unmarried daughters, and had given no less than three expensive dinner-parties for that purpose, and, strange to say, Mr Otis himself. Mr Otis was extremely fond of the young Duke personally, but, theoretically, he objected to titles, and, to use his own words, "was not without apprehension lest, amid the enervating influences of a pleasure-loving aristocracy, the true principles of Republican simplicity should be forgotten." His objections, however, were completely overruled, and I believe that when he walked up the aisle of St. George's, Hanover Square, with his daughter leaning on his arm, there was not a prouder man in the whole length and breadth of England.

The Duke and Duchess, after the honeymoon was over, went down to Canterville Chase, and on the day after their arrival they walked over in the afternoon to the lonely churchyard by the pine-woods. There had been a great deal of difficulty at first about the inscription on Sir Simon's tombstone, but finally it had been decided to engrave on it simply the initials of the old gentleman's name, and the verse from the library window. The Duchess had brought with her some lovely roses, which she strewed upon the grave, and after they had stood by it for some time they strolled into the ruined chancel of the old abbey. There the Duchess sat down on a fallen pillar, while her husband lay at her feet smoking a cigarette and looking up at her beautiful eyes. Suddenly he threw his cigarette away, took hold of her hand, and said to her, "Virginia, a wife should have no secrets from her husband."

"Dear Cecil! I have no secrets from you."

"Yes, you have," he answered, smiling, "you have never told me what happened to you when you were locked up with the ghost."

"I have never told anyone, Cecil," said Virginia, gravely.

"I know that, but you might tell me."

"Please don't ask me, Cecil, I cannot tell you. Poor Sir Simon! I owe him a great deal. Yes, don't laugh, Cecil, I really do. He made me see what Life is, and what Death signifies, and why Love is stronger than both."

The Duke rose and kissed his wife lovingly.

"You can have your secret as long as I have your heart," he murmured.

"You have always had that, Cecil."

"And you will tell our children some day, won't you?"

Virginia blushed.

Biographies & Sources

Kurt Bachard
Mourners
(Originally published in *Bards and Sages Quarterly*, 2012)
Kurt Bachard lives in South London, UK. A Pushcart Prize Nominee, his fiction and non-fiction have appeared in numerous publications, including the Black Quill Nominated *Shroud Magazine*, *Underground Voices*, *Suddenly Lost In Words*, and *Ryga: A Journal of Provocations*, and he has stories forthcoming in *Alfred Hitchcock Mystery Magazine*, among others. He's currently looking for an agent or publisher for his first novel, with more in the pipeline. He can be reached at bachard.wordpress.com.

Jonathan Balog
Stay Away from the Accordion Girl
(First Publication)
Jonathan Balog grew up in Maryland and graduated from Washington College in 2005 with a BA in English. His fiction and poetry have appeared in *Ares Magazine*, *Independent Ink Magazine*, *So It Goes: A Tribute to Kurt Vonnegut*, *Long Distance Drunks: A Tribute to Charles Bukowski*, *Chiral Mad 3*, *Ominous Realities* and the Stoker-nominated *Dark Visions vol 1.* He lives in Rome, Italy, with his girlfriend Heather and a pit bull named Kilo. He once met the Accordion Girl in a dream, but she was older, with eyes that burned with a fiery hunger, and she tore his throat out with razor-sharp teeth.

E.F. Benson
The Man Who Went Too Far
(Originally Published *The Room in the Tower and Other Stories*, Mills & Boon, 1912)
Edward Fredrick ('E.F.') Benson (1867–1940) was born at Wellington College in Berkshire, England, where his father, the future Archbishop of Canterbury Edward White Benson, was headmaster. Benson is widely known for being a writer of reminiscences, fiction, satirical novels, biographies and autobiographical studies. His first published novel, *Dodo*, initiated his success, followed by a series of comic novels such as *Queen Lucia* and *Trouble for Lucia.* Later in life, Benson moved to Rye where he was elected mayor. It was here that he was inspired to write several ghost story collections and novels including *Paying Guests* and *Mrs Ames.*

Trevor Boelter
Audio Tour
(First Publication)
Trevor Boelter has been published in *The Altar Collective*, *Indiana Crime Review 2014* and *Dark Fire Fiction*. Trevor is a Beatles expert and his one-act play *And Now It's All This!,* which dramatized John Lennon's infamous quote about being 'bigger than Jesus', premiered at the Ticket To Write Festival in Liverpool, England, in 2014. Every year during the month of October, Trevor challenges himself to 'write a creepy story a day', which he posts on his website www.octoberghosts.com. He lives in Los Angeles with his wife and daughter.

Robert W. Chambers
The Messenger
(Originally Published in *The Mystery of Choice*, D. Appleton & Co., 1897)
Robert W. Chambers (1865–1933) was born in Brooklyn, New York, with aspirations of a great American artist and fiction writer. His father was the famous lawyer William P. Chambers, and his mother Caroline Boughton was a direct descendent to the founder of Providence, Rhode Island. The great amount of success in his family perhaps contributed to him being a successful writer in so many genres: fantasy, horror, romance, science fiction, supernatural and historical fiction. His better-known works come from his short story collection *The King in Yellow*. Everett Franklin Bleiler, a respected scholar of science fiction and fantasy literature, described *The King in Yellow* as one of the most important works of American supernatural fiction.

Zach Chapman
Ghost Farm
(First Publication)
Zach Chapman grew up on a ranch just north of San Antonio, Texas, where he could see the cows grazing in the pasture from his bedroom window. His fiction has appeared on *Unsung Stories*, *Writers of the Future* and *Star Ship Sofa*. His literary influences span from Jack Vance to the latest Halo game and Batman comic. He currently lives in Austin, Texas, with his librarian wife Taylor, a cat, a rabbit and a lazy-eyed rescue dog named Dingo. Follow his future publication announcements on twitter: @chappyzach.

Wilkie Collins
Mrs Zant and the Ghost
(Originally Published in *The Ghost's Touch*, John W. Lovell, 1885)
William Wilkie Collins (1824–1889) was born in London's Marylebone and he lived there almost consistently for 65 years. Writing over 30 major books, 100 articles, short stories and essays and a dozen or more plays, he is best known for *The Moonstone* and *The Woman in White*. He was good friends with the novelist Charles Dickens, with whom he collaborated as well as took inspiration from to help write novels like *The Lighthouse* and *The Frozen Deep*. Finally becoming internationally reputable in the 1860s, Collins truly showed himself as the master of his craft as he wrote many profitable novels in less than a decade and earned himself the title of a successful English novelist, playwright and author of short stories.

Vonnie Winslow Crist
The Return of Gunnar Kettilson
(Originally Published in *Cemetery Moon*, 2010)
Vonnie Winslow Crist is a speculative author-illustrator from the USA. Her works include *The Enchanted Skean* (Compton Crook Award Finalist), *Owl Light*, *The Greener Forest*, *Leprechaun Cake & Other Tales*, *River of Stars*, *Essential Fables* and other books. Crist's writing has won awards from L. Ron Hubbard's Writers of the Future Contest, Maryland State Arts Council (USA), National League of American Pen Women and elsewhere. Published in magazines and anthologies across Australia, Canada, Italy, Spain, Finland, the UK and USA, her writing and art celebrate the power of myth.

Donna Cuttress
Flaming Fuses
(First Publication)
Donna Cuttress is a short story writer and reviewer from Liverpool in the UK. She has had previous work published by Crooked Cat, Sirens Call and in Firbolg Publishing's' *The Rogues Gallery*. Her piece for the *Latchkey Tales* journals came out in April 2015, and her work for Sirens Call and Kace Tripp Publishing's *Crooked Tales* is due for release. Donna writes reviews of classic horror films and TV programmes for *The Spooky Isles* website. She is currently working on her first novel.

Amanda C. Davis
The House, the Garden, and Occupants
(Originally Published in *Triangulation: Morning After*, Parsec Ink, 2012)
Amanda C. Davis lives, works and writes in semi-rural Pennsylvania. Her work has appeared in magazines and anthologies worldwide, including Crossed Genres, Andromeda Spaceways Inflight Magazine, Ténèbres 2015 and others. She is a member of SFWA and a proud local Municipal Liaison for National Novel Writing Month. She has an engineering degree and a fondness for baking, gardening and low-budget horror films, tweeting about them enthusiastically as @davisac1. You can find out more about her and read more of her work at www.amandacdavis.com.

Charles Dickens
The Signal-man
(Originally Published in *All the Year Round*, 1866)
The iconic and much-loved Charles Dickens (1812–1870) was born in Portsmouth, England, though he spent much of his life in Kent and London. At the age of 12 Charles was forced into working in a factory for a couple of months to support his family. He never forgot his harrowing experience there, and his novels always reflected the plight of the working class. A prolific writer, Dickens kept up a career in journalism as well as writing short stories and novels, with much of his work being serialized before being published as books. He gave a view of contemporary England with a strong sense of realism, yet incorporated the occasional ghost and horror elements. He continued to work hard until his death in 1870, leaving *The Mystery of Edwin Drood* unfinished.

Arthur Conan Doyle
The New Catacomb
(Originally Published in *Sunlight Year Book*, Lever Brothers Ltd., 1898)
Arthur Conan Doyle (1859–1930) was born in Edinburgh, Scotland, and became a well-known writer, poet and physician. As a medical student he was so impressed by his professor's powers of deduction that he was inspired to create the illustrious and much-loved figure Sherlock Holmes. In contrast to this scientific background, however, Doyle became increasingly interested in spiritualism, leaving him keen to explore fantastical elements in his stories. Paired with his talent for storytelling he wrote great tales of terror, such as 'The Horror of Heights' and 'The Leather Funnel'. Doyle's vibrant and remarkable characters have breathed life into all of his stories, engaging readers throughout the decades.

James Dorr

Victorians

(Originally Published in *Gothic Ghosts*, Tor Books, 1997)

Indiana (USA) writer James Dorr's *The Tears of Isis* was a 2014 Bram Stoker Award® nominee for Superior Achievement in a Fiction Collection. Other books include *Strange Mistresses: Tales of Wonder and Romance, Darker Loves: Takes of Mystery and Regret* and his all-poetry *Vamps (A Retrospective)*, soon to be out in a new edition from White Cat Publications. An Active Member of HWA and SFWA with nearly 400 individual appearances from *Alfred Hitchcock's Mystery Magazine* to *Yellow Bat Review*, James invites readers to visit his blog at jamesdorrwriter.wordpress.com.

Tim Foley

The Figure on the Sidewalk

(First Publication)

Tim Foley lives in Northern California in a house surrounded by ash trees. His dark fiction and critical essays have appeared in publications on both sides of the Atlantic, including All Hallows, Dark Hollow, Morpheus Tales, Supernatural Tales and Wormwood. His play *The Old Nurse's Tale* – an adaptation of Elizabeth Gaskell's 'The Old Nurse's Story' – was featured in the Wildclaw in the Wild festival in Chicago in 2014. He owns a number of ghost story collections, including a 1914 edition of Richard Middleton's 'The Ghost Ship'.

Mary Eleanor Wilkins Freeman

The Shadows on the Wall

(Originally Published in *Everybody's Magazine*, 1903)

The Wind in the Rose-Bush

(Originally Published in *Everybody's Magazine*, 1902)

The American author Mary Eleanor Wilkins Freeman (1852–1930) was born in Randolph, Massachusetts. Most of Freeman's works were influenced by her strict childhood, as her parents were orthodox Congregationalists and harboured strong religious views. While working as a secretary for the author Oliver Wendell Holmes, Sr., she was inspired to write herself. Supernatural topics kept catching her attention, and she began to write many short stories with a combination of supernatural and domestic realism, her most famous being 'A New England Nun'. She wrote a number of ghost tales, such as 'The Hall Bedroom' and 'Luella Miller', which were turned into famous ghost story collections after her death.

Nikolai Gogol

The Overcoat

(Originally Published in *Collected Works*, 1842)

Nikolai Gogol (1809–1852) was a famous Russian writer born in Sorochyntsi, Ukraine. Gogol is responsible for creating the foundation of the 19th century tradition of Russian Realism, a term used to describe, for example, his novel *Dead Souls* and his short story 'The Overcoat'. His later writings evolved from a fundamentally romantic sensibility to Surrealism and the Grotesque. Influenced by his Ukrainian childhood, his horror stories developed into great works such as his play *The Government Inspector*, which is now globally recognized.

Philip Brian Hall
The Waiting Room
(First Publication)
Born in Yorkshire, Oxford graduate Philip Brian Hall is a former diplomat, teacher, examiner and web designer. Sidelines have included standing for parliament, singing solos in amateur operettas, rowing at Henley and riding in over one hundred steeplechases. Writing mainly in speculative genres, he has had short stories published by *AE The Canadian Science Fiction Review*, *T Gene Davis's Speculative Blog* and *The Sockdolager*. His novel *The Prophets of Baal* is available as an e-book and in paperback. He lives on a very small farm in Scotland with his wife, a dog, a cat and some horses.

Washington Irving
The Legend of Sleepy Hollow
(Originally Published in *The Sketch Book of Geoffrey Crayon, Gent.*, 1820)
Washington Irving (1783–1859) was a famous American author, essayist, biographer and historian born in New York City. He was influenced by his private education and law school studies to begin writing essays for periodicals. Travelling and working all over the globe, Irving established a name for himself with his successful short stories 'Rip Van Winkle' and 'The Legend of Sleepy Hollow'. These works in particular reflected the mischievous and adventurous behaviour of his childhood. Years later, Irving lived in Spain as a US Ambassador. He returned to America towards the end of life, where he wrote several successful historical and biographical works including a five-volume biography of George Washington.

W.W. Jacobs
The Monkey's Paw
(Originally Published in *The Lady of the Barge*, Dodd, Mead & Co., 1902)
William Wymark ('W.W.') Jacobs (1863–1943) was born in Wapping, London, and he is known for his deeply humorous and horrifying works. Drawing upon his childhood experiences, Jacobs wrote many works reflecting on his father's profession as a dockhand and wharf manager. His first volume of stories, *Many Cargoes*, was a great success and gave Jacobs the courage to publish other stories such as 'The Monkey's Paw', which was at first formally called 'The Lady of the Barge'. Jacobs used realistic experiences as well as a combination of superstition, terror, exotic adventure and humour in each one of his famous tales.

Henry James
The Altar of the Dead
(Originally Published in *Terminations,* Harper & Brothers, 1895)
Henry James (1843–1916) was born in New York City, though spent a lot of time in England, with the dynamic between Europe and America playing a key role in his novels. Writing a massive amount of literary works throughout his lifetime, he published over 112 tales, 20 novels, 16 plays and various other autobiographies and literary criticisms. Each work is filled with characters of great social complexity as most of his works reflect his own complicated perspectives and satirical personality. James's works include *Daisy Miller*, *The Turn of the Screw*, *The Ambassadors*, *The Golden Bowl* and *The Portrait of a Lady*. James strongly believed novels had to be a recognizable representation of the realistic truth as well as filled with imaginative action.

M.R. James
Count Magnus
(Originally Published in *Ghost Stories of an Antiquary,* 1904)
The Five Jars
(Originally Published by Edward Arnold, 1922)
Lost Hearts
(Originally Published in *Ghost Stories of an Antiquary,* 1904)
Montague Rhodes ('M.R.') James (1862–1936), whose works are regarded as being at the forefront of the ghost story genre, was born in Kent, England. James dispensed with the traditional, predictable techniques of ghost story construction, instead using realistic contemporary settings for his works. He was also a British medieval scholar, so his stories often incorporated antiquarian elements. James wrote authoritatively in his essays about the best techniques for the genre, and his first collection of stories, *Ghost Stories of an Antiquary*, bred several sequels and remains popular today. His stories often reflect his childhood in Suffolk and talented acting career, which both seem to have assisted in the build-up of tension and horror in his works. The intention for many of his stories was that they be read aloud in the long custom of ghostly Christmas Eve tales.

Joseph Sheridan Le Fanu
An Authentic Narrative of a Haunted House
(Originally Published in the Dublin University Magazine, 1862)
The Spirit's Whisper
(Originally Published in *A Stable for Nightmares: or, Weird Tales*, New Amsterdam Book Company, 1896)
A prolific writer of Victorian ghost stories, Joseph Sheridan Le Fanu (1814–1873) was born in Dublin, Ireland. His gothic tales and mystery novels led to him becoming a leading ghost story writer in the nineteenth century. Three oft-cited works of his are *Uncle Silas*, *Carmilla* and *The House by the Churchyard,* which all are assumed to have influenced Bram Stoker's *Dracula.* Le Fanu wrote his most successful and productive works after his wife's tragic death and he remained a relatively strong writer until his death.

Raymond Little
An Englishman in St. Louis
(First Publication)
Ray was born in London and now lives in Kent, where he writes dark fiction. His short stories have appeared in anthologies in both the UK and the USA, and his first novel, *Doom*, will be released in 2016. Ray cites the ghost stories of Charles Dickens and M.R. James as childhood influences; he would often read them by torchlight in bed, which may explain quite a lot. He is currently working on a supernatural horror novel called *Thin Places*, and is selecting the best of his own stories for a proposed anthology, *Present Tense*. Discover more about Ray's work at www.raymondlittle.co.uk.

Luke Murphy
Death and Champagne
(First Publication)
Luke Murphy was born in West Berlin back when it was still called that, brought up in Ireland, and now lives in Toronto. His fiction writing has appeared in the *Tesseracts*

anthology, the *Growing Concerns* eco-horror collection and other speculative fiction outlets. He's loved horror, fantasy and ghost stories since, as a boy, he learned about Dame Alice Kyteler, the famous medieval witch in his Irish hometown of Kilkenny. He works as a freelance writer, animator, designer and filmmaker. See more at www.lukemurphy.com.

Edith Nesbit
The Mystery of the Semi-Detached
(Originally Published in *Grim Tales*, A.D. Innes & Co., 1893)
Edith Nesbit (1858–1924) was born in Kennington, England. Nesbit established herself as a successful author and poet, writing a variety of books ranging from children's books to adult horror stories. She co-founded the Fabian Society and was also a strong political activist. Marrying young and frequently moving home, Edith made many friendships including those with H.G. Wells and George Bernard Shaw. Although she gained most of her success from her children's books, including the ever-popular *The Railway Children*, she was also a well-known horror writer, with such collections as *Something Wrong* and *Grim Tales*. Her works are very well regarded and have often been cited by later authors as greatly influential.

Jeff Parsons
Lost Souls
(First Publication)
Jeff is a professional engineer enjoying life in sunny California, USA. He has a long history of technical writing, which oddly enough often reads like pure fiction. He was inspired to write by two wonderful teachers: William Forstchen and Gary Braver. Jeff got his first break with *SNM Horror Magazine*. SNM published his book of short stories titled *Algorithm of Nightmares* and also featured his stories in the *SNM Bonded by Blood IV* and *V* anthologies. He is also published in *The Horror Zine* and *Dark Gothic Resurrected Magazine*, and *The Moving Finger Writes* and *Golden Prose & Poetry* anthologies.

Michael Penkas
The Skeleton Crew
(First Publication)
Michael Penkas has lived in Chicago since 2004 and has worked as a librarian, a typesetter, an archivist, a proofreader and an editor. His work has appeared in a variety of publications that include *HWA Poetry Showcase* (volumes I and II), *Dark Moon Digest*, *DarkFuse 1*, *Lady Churchill's Rosebud Wristlet*, *Shock Totem*, *One Buck Horror*, *Midnight Echo* and *Black Gate*. His first novel, *Mistress Bunny and the Cancelled Client*, was published in November 2014. He maintains a website at www.michaelpenkas.com.

Edgar Allan Poe
Ligeia
Originally Published in *The Baltimore American Museum*, 1838)
The Black Cat
(Originally Published in *The Saturday Evening Post,* 1843)
The versatile writer Edgar Allan Poe (1809–1849) was born in Boston, Massachusetts. Poe is extremely well known as an influential author, poet, editor and literary critic

that wrote during the American Romantic Movement. Poe is generally considered the inventor of the detective fiction genre, and his works are famously filled with terror, mystery, death and hauntings. Some of his better-known works include his poems 'The Raven' and 'Annabel Lee', and the short stories 'The Tell Tale Heart' and 'The Fall of the House of Usher'. The dark, mystifying characters of his tales have captured the public's imagination and reflect the struggling, poverty-stricken lifestyle he lived his whole life.

Brian Rappatta
Songs for the Lost
(Originally Published in *To Sift the Sacred, and Other Fantasy Stories*, Infinite Jester Publications, 2012)
Brian Rappatta is an American expat who currently lives and works in South Korea. His short fiction has appeared in *Shock Totem*, *Writers of the Future*, *Zencore: Scriptus Innominatus* (the 7th volume of the Nemonymous anthology series, which was shortlisted for a British Fantasy Society Award for Best Anthology), and in various other anthologies and publications. He is a graduate of the Odyssey Fantasy Writers Workshop, where he studied with Writer in Residence George R.R. Martin.

Rhiannon Rasmussen
An Unquiet Slumber
(Originally Published in *Arcane: Thirty Weird and Unsettling Stories*, 2011)
Rhiannon Rasmussen graduated with a B.F.A., emphasis on Printmaking, from Portland State University in 2012. An illustrator, writer, printmaker and graphic designer, Rhiannon's work has appeared in galleries & magazines including *Lightspeed Magazine*, *Grand Science Fiction*, *Shimmer*, *Kobold Quarterly*, *ARCANE*, *Innsmouth Free Press*, *The Sockdolager*, several volumes of the *Tankadere* comics anthology, *Weird Tales*, *Autzen Gallery* (Portland, OR) and *STORE Gallery* (Portland, OR). Further work can be found at www.rhiannonrs.com or on Twitter @charibdys.

M. Regan
Almost
(Originally Published in the Gustavus Journal *Firethorne*, 2011)
M. Regan has been writing in various capacities for over a decade, with credits ranging from localization work to scholarly reviews, advice columns to short stories. Particularly fascinated by those fears and maladies personified by monsters, she enjoys composing dark fiction and studying supernatural creatures. She currently lives and works in Kyoto, Japan, where she draws inspiration from the country's rich history of *youkai*, as well as the more modern influences of its popular culture.

Annette Siketa
The Bulge in the Wall
(First Publication)
Annette Siketa was diagnosed with breast cancer on September 11th, 2001 (THE September 11th), and was told she would not live beyond Christmas. Seven years later, a routine eye operation tragically rendered her blind. Her life changed dramatically, and it was her penchant for creating imaginative stories that 'saved' her, though at the time, she

knew nothing about professional writing. From a literary standpoint, her first novel, *The Dolls House*, was an unmitigated disaster. However, she persevered and learned the craft, and has now written a wide variety of award-winning short stories and novels, including 'The Ghosts of Camals College'.

Cathy Smith
The Psychic Fair
(First Publication)
Cathy Smith is an aboriginal writer who lives on an Indian Reservation within Canada. Her stories 'Pretty White Snake' and 'Where is Shingibiss' were podcasted on *Anthropomorphic Dreams*, and 'Gifts from a Grim Godfather' was published in Burial Day Books' *Gothic Blue Book IV: The Folklore Edition*. 'Jubilee' will be published in *Game Fiction: Volume One*. She has also won an honorable mention from the L. Ron Hubbard's Writers of the Future contest. You can follow her latest projects at khiatons.wordpress.com and via the page 'Khiatons, Cathy Smith, I write' on Facebook.

Lesa Pascavis Smith
Unclaimed
(First Publication)
Lesa Pascavis Smith lives in West Virginia and often draws inspiration for her stories from the Appalachian hills and hollows rich with mystery and intrigue. Lesa wrote her first ghost story at the tender age of seven and now gravitates toward the darker side of writing, often weaving spiritual and supernatural elements throughout the pages. Lesa's works have been featured in *The Were-Traveler* e-zine and *Bones I, II and III*, edited by James Ward Kirk. Her short story 'The Revenge of the Combine Killer' will also be appearing in the upcoming *Redneck Zombies of Outer Space*, edited by Jonathan Maberry.

Robert Louis Stevenson
The Bottle Imp
(Originally Published in *New York Herald,* 1891)
Robert Louis Stevenson (1850–1894) was born in Edinburgh, Scotland. He became a well-known novelist, poet and travel writer, publishing the famous works *Treasure Island, Kidnapped* and *The Strange Case of Dr Jekyll and Mr Hyde*. All of his works were highly admired by many other artists, as he was a literary celebrity during his lifetime. Travelling a lot for health reasons and because of his family's business, Stevenson ended up writing a lot of his journeys into his works and wrote works mainly related to children's literature and the horror genre.

Dr Dale Townshend
Foreword: Chilling Ghost Stories
Senior Lecturer in Gothic and Romantic Literature at the University of Stirling, Scotland, and Director of the MLitt in The Gothic Imagination. In the field of Gothic studies, his most recent publications include *The Gothic World* ; *Ann Radcliffe, Romanticism and the Gothic;* and *Terror and Wonder: The Gothic Imagination*.

Edith Wharton
Bewitched
(Originally Published in *Pictorial Review*, 1925)
The Bolted Door
(Originally Published in *Scribner's Magazine*, 1909)
Edith Wharton (1862–1937), the Pulitzer Prize-winning writer of *The Age of Innocence,* was born in New York. As well as her talent as an American novelist, Wharton was also known for her short stories and designer career. Wharton was born into a controlled New York society where women were discouraged from achieving anything beyond a proper marriage. Defeating the norms, Wharton not only grew to become one of America's greatest writers, she grew to become a very self-rewarding woman. Writing numerous ghost stories and murderous tales such as 'The Lady's Maid's Bell', 'The Eyes' and 'Afterward', Wharton is widely known for the ghost tours that now take place at her old home, The Mount.

Oscar Wilde
The Canterville Ghost
(Originally Published in *Court and Society Review*, 1887)
Oscar Wilde (1854–1900) was born in Dublin, Ireland, and was a successful author, poet, philosopher and playwright with an impressive gift for language. With several acclaimed works including his novel *The Picture of Dorian Gray* and the play *The Importance of Being Earnest,* Wilde was known for his biting wit and flamboyant personality in the Victorian era. He was famously imprisoned on homosexual charges, an imprisonment that proved disastrous to his health. He continued to write while in prison, and following his release he left for France and spent his remaining days in exile, essentially in poverty. 'The Canterville Ghost' was the first of Wilde's stories to be published, and has remained an ever-popular story that has since been adapted to many mediums.

GOTHIC FANTASY